D1716876

Greytar's Dangerous Denizens of Tellene

The tome you hold in your hands is a copy of the highly sought after 'Dangerous Denizens of Tellene' — a traveler's field guide of sorts to the various animals and monstrosities known to inhabit the world. It is often referred to as the Takavil Kamelikar, or 'Slayer's Guide', though some refer to it as the Hacklopedia of Beasts. Greytar the Gentle (formerly the Chief of Scribes at the Royal Library in P'Bapar but now on extended sabbatical at Frandor's Keep far on the borderlands of the realm) originally penned the work.

He spent endless years compiling this manual. Initially conceived as little more than a useful reference catalog to facilitate his dilettantish magical research and a means of assembling his disordered collection of notes on the subject, once amalgamated into the initial bound journal he realized both what he held and what it could become. This framework was admirably suited for recording much more than esoteric uses for various creature parts.

As fate would have it, Greytar's work was interrupted by the call of adventure. Former associates had located the reclusive mage and, after several bottles of Orlurian brandy, convinced him to accompany them on a quixotic trek through the Legasa Peaks in search of a fabled treasure. Though the quest would prove a disappointment to most of the troupe, Greytar's knack for observation served him well as he dutifully recorded the unique tactics employed by each creature they encountered, annotated notes as to perceived strengths and weaknesses as well as remarking on the location and terrain in which they had encountered the beasts. After returning to civilization, he struck upon enlisting the talents of an artist to illustrate the savage monsters he had witnessed. The addition of these sketches to his growing treatise added a welcome visual element to the book and would prove to be valuable in popularizing it outside of academic circles.

As time worn on, it became clear that one man alone was incapable of compiling the breadth of information Greytar envisioned this work containing. He thus settled upon enlisting the aid of contributors. The mage sought those whose experience was dissimilar from his own so as to provide as broad a perspective as possible. He was fortunate to have the acquaintance of an experienced bounty hunter who, though semi-literate, provided a verbal account of many creatures Greytar would scarcely have dared to approach. Much of this supplemental data though was gleaned from the journals and diaries of adventurous souls he never met in person. Where possible he exercised due diligence seeking to corroborate these observations but sadly the old sage candidly admitted that this could not always be done.

Although originally written for an academic audience, copies of Greytar's Dangerous Denizens eventually made their way into the hands of military commanders, caravan masters, hunters, adventurers and others who all recognized the value of this work. In so doing, it has become an object in high demand by those who crave the knowledge it contains.

Over the years various authors have added to the work; some improving upon its offering - others introducing factual errors and blurring the lines with common folklore and unsubstantiated claims. As such, there are dozens of variations of the book in circulation. Many copies, which undoubtedly served as field guides, have hand written notes in the margins.

The Bestiary

Appendicies

The Field Researchers

Greytar the Gentle

In his own words, Greytar's sole intent when compiling Dangerous Denizens was "to catalogue all the strange and deadly creatures of Tellene. Those rustlers of the night that creep about, the stalkers in shadows, the vile predators intent on killing men."

As an academic and a scholar, he initially devoted himself to such details as a creature's diet, habitat, and useful parts that could further his own study of magic and the arcane.

However, as he threw himself into his research he became more thorough. He began seeking answers to nagging questions that constantly kept popping up. How best to fight a creature if one found himself facing one? How do various creatures respond when encountered? Do they flee? Stand and fight? Pursue? What tactics do they favor in combat? For that matter, what tactics are effective against them? What parts, if any, could be shorn from a slain creature and have value in the marketplace, for research purposes or as raw material for manufacture?

As the years passed, Greytar's focus (and the book) slowly broadened. No more was it a simple work of a naturalist inspired by scientific curiosity, but an all-encompassing field guide of use to readers from all backgrounds and professions. Soon he was going back and jotting down tips on tracking such creatures (as well as evading those that may be following you) in the margins and noting such things as how to detect the signs of a creature in the area and how to defend against one if encountered (or, better yet, how to avoid encountering one in the first place).

Unable to study or witness most of the creatures first-hand, and usually dealing with dead specimens, Greytar sought out others with the knowledge he required. Early on he gravitated to the bounty master's stall at Frandor's Keep where hunters and soldiers brought their kills to collect the bounties. Over drinks and meals at the local tavern, he gleaned as much information as such individuals were willing to offer. He even employed the talents of a local artist to sketch the various creatures; some based on dead specimens brought to the Keep, others based on descriptions provided by those who had encountered them in the wild.

Greytar has often been criticized for including many factual errors in his work but most concur that his book of denizens is one of the most important and most complete guides on the subject to-date. Even so, rumor has it that Greytar is working on future volumes.

Greytar's personal observations and commentary are indicated by the following symbol: ⟜

Dealaan Daarmae

Dealaan Daarmae is a canny Reanaarian who has applied himself to many endeavors over the years, but prides himself for being a "master thief unequaled in the arts of stealth, cunning and eluding justice." Born a street urchin in Geanavue, he has since traveled the known world having won and lost both fortunes, fame, and many a lord's lady.

He has dedicated his life to lifting the property of others and making them his own without losing his head in the process.

This is not to say that he doesn't have ambition. Several times during his life he attempted to turn over a new leaf and apply his skills toward more legitimate pursuits. Once as the Captain of the Guard at Bet Kasel, he was entrusted with defending the crown jewels. Eventually, temptation (prompted by a staggering gambling debt) proved too great and he made off with the goods – but not before detailing the building of traps, locks and other measures in a commissioned work for his master.

Written from a thief's point of view, Dealaan couldn't resist including notes on how to thwart such measures, making it a popular book indeed in the underworld when it was eventually stolen.

Dealaan eventually became a teacher for the Dark Omen, the infamous thieves' guild of Zenshahn. There he continued his writing, primarily focusing on various creatures of Tellene and how stealth and cunning could most effectively be used to get at their guarded hoards. Of course, as is typical for a thief, it has since been determined that many portions of his works were lifted from other sources and embellished to brand them as bits of knowledge gleaned from personal experience.

Greytar has graciously opted not to follow Dealaan's plagiaristic lead and has annotated the rogue's personal observations and contributions to this work with the following symbol: ⋈ He cannot, though, certify the originality of said observations.

Helena Vitira, Cleric of the Eternal Lantern

Helena Vitira was reared in the faith of The Eternal Lantern. Dedicated to the Shining One when she was only 10, the temple would be her home for the next thirteen years as she threw herself into her lessons and training. Mokira, her mentor, was so impressed that he urged her to take the unusual step of beginning her mission directly after her investiture. It was his hope she would return to the temple once her fieldwork was complete to mentor and inspire others, but it was not to be. Once outside the confines of the temple, Helena was enthralled with a world she had never seen. "At morn I await the rapturous arrival of He that doth shimmer for each daye presentest a new bounty!" she wrote in her journal. Helena embraced the life of a wandering missionary in spite of its hardships and took an open-ended sabbatical, extending her evangelical mission indefinitely.

Filled with naïve wonder, each new day was one of discovery, though she would quickly learn first-hand that the world outside the chapel was a dark place filled with many evils. Rather than being discouraged, this only buttressed her faith. "The world doth cry out in wont for the Light of the Lanthorne Eternal..." she wrote, "And I shallst bear it to every dark hollow and smitest all who wouldst seek such cover dark from whence to contrive yon villainy."

Helena has a particular interest in unnatural creatures of the night — especially agents of evil and the undead. Like a physician seeking a cure for disease, she threw herself into the impossible task of ridding the world of such terrors. Toward that end she engaged in countless harrowing missions, battling many nefarious powers of dread. In her heart she knows that she has more than a touch of the vigilante, and to console the occasional guilt over neglecting her cloistered brethren, she diligently inscribed memoirs of her adventures - taking care to provide any observations on the creatures she fought so that the Assembly of Light may disperse this knowledge. She dutifully sends these journals back to her mentor before setting out on a new quest, knowing always that this may be her last.

Mokira has admonished her in prose many times, asking her to devote more energy towards converting people to the faith and less time in the endless pursuit of nefarious creatures. Helena's return correspondence always beats a subtly combative tone, confirming perhaps that she has become a true scintillant warrior forever lost to the mundane. "Pathfinder be I for the Luminous Laird. For doth not demonstrative evidence of his righteous brilliance inspire downetrodden wretches for to call upon his exalted name? Willst they not but seek the succor of He Who Shineth Bright when it is He that deliverest them from darkest peril. Nay, I doth admonish thee good Mokira that thou mightst pave mine path with thine acolytes aplenty."

Greytar stumbled upon her letters while residing in Bet Rogala. He was both impressed with her keen observations and frightened by her tales. He made a very generous contribution to the Pekalese Assembly of Light in recognition of their granting him permission to copy this correspondence. He considered gaining this valuable information - without having to experience it first hand - a price well worth paying.

He has indicated her contributions to his work with the following symbol: ◔

"The Ravager"

The Ravager was a *nom de guerre* of a famous sword-for-hire and adventurer who wandered throughout the Sovereign Lands some fifty to sixty years ago. The historian Glandree, in his book, 'The Death Merchants', chronicled the exploits of the Ravager. Although a historical figure whose true identity remains shrouded in mystery, many of the deeds attributed to him are more folklore than fact. Adding to the myth surrounding the man is the fact that he disappeared without a trace, never to be heard from again. For years, the legends claimed he had departed the Sovereign Lands and crossed the oceans to find new realms to explore.

Sadly, those legends were shattered when the mummified husk of the warrior's remains were found at the bottom of a spider pit near the Mines of Chaos a few years ago. His journal was found laying nearby in a satchel - a treasure for which Greytar laid out a handsome sum to secure.

The journal was packed with detailed accounts of his encounters with all things dark and dangerous. He wrote about how various creatures behaved in toe-to-toe fights, their fighting tactics, effective strategies to counter them, as well as details on tracks, scat and other signs. This wealth of information Greytar pulled into his own work.

As a warrior and a mercenary, the Ravager was obsessed with humanoids in all forms, especially orcs, bugbears and kobolds, whom he considered challenging opponents. Much of his journal concerned itself with tactics on fighting such creatures in large numbers.

Although the Ravager loved the thrill of the hunt, he was also a self-professed opportunist who engaged in a fight whenever and wherever one could be found. He took everything of value from a kill that he thought could be sold in the bazaars back in the big cities. His journal reflects that mind set.

Greytar was apparently enthralled with the Ravager, for he included several excerpts and anecdotes from the warrior's journal detailing memorable encounters with various creatures.

Greytar has indicated the Ravager's personal observations and contributions to his work by the following symbol: ꝼ

Dorran Randril

Dorran is a Brandobian born to a wealthy merchant family in Dalen. From an early age he was a disappointment to his father, who naturally wished the bright boy to follow in his footsteps. Commerce held no interest for Dorran, however. Instead, he was fascinated with the family pets – many of which were exotic species his father brought back from Svimohzia to delight and amuse his daughters. These creatures, mostly birds and small lizards, did not thrive so far removed from their natural habitat, but Dorran cared for them, becoming obsessed with every nuance of their habits and personalities. He kept meticulous records of their diet, learning what they preferred to eat, and developed an artistic talent by sketching these animals.

As he matured, Dorran yearned to learn more about the natural world that was so different from the crowded city streets. He began to visit the rustic hamlets that surrounded Dalen and there made friends with a number of farmers, who were all too happy to gain the confidence of the son of a wealthy merchant. He began to spend more and more time away from home and, in the company of these rustics, embraced the Conventical of the Great Tree.

Dorran's father had tolerated his son's eccentricities, but to him this was far enough. He demanded that the boy cease his "lowborn" religious practices and accept his role in the family. Rather than conform, Dorran fled to become an acolyte of the Old Oak. Dorran excelled in this service and eventually became a missionary, travelling far and wide to extoll the virtues of a bucolic lifestyle in harmony with nature. During these journeys he has had the pleasure (and sometimes misfortune) of cataloging many of nature's most intriguing creatures.

Dorran, now being an esteemed master of herbology, is routinely sought out by mages for consultation. In time, this brought him to Greytar's attention, and the old wizard and he have corresponded for years. One evening, when Dorran's work brought him to P'Bapar, the two spent a long evening over herbal tea discussing various matters of common interest. The subject of Greytar's "little book" came up, prompting Dorran to share his travel journal. The mage was stunned at the scope of knowledge contained therein, offering to buy the travelogue there and then, knowing it would fill a known and gaping void in his manuscript. To his complete surprise, Dorran said it was his pleasure to assist the magician in his important work, and that he could keep the book if doing so would help educate learned people on matters dear to his heart.

Greytar has indicated Dorran's personal observations and contributions to his work by the following symbol:

Larzon Bayz

Larzon Bayz is all about finding man-killers. Tracking them. Slaying them. Bagging them. As far as he's concerned, no challenge is too great – as long as there's money or treasure involved.

An experienced bounty hunter, Larzon has worked the border region of the Legasa Peaks for years and has a well-earned reputation for being one of the best in his field. This is perhaps why Greytar went to such lengths to include his commentary in his works.

Moving from town to town, he pitches himself as something of a 'problem solver.' He deals with meddlesome pests, be they man or beast, and moves on once his work is finished. Recently, however, he's taken a prolonged hiatus at Frandor's Keep on the borderlands where he's found more than enough work (and coin) to keep him busy.

He's become something of a minor celebrity at the Keep after hauling in countless bounties (including a half-dozen bugbears he claims to have taken single handedly). He quickly caught the attention of fellow Keep resident Greytar, who went to great lengths to befriend the giant of a man. Since both men enjoy pulling a cork, they spent many nights in an upstairs room at the Tilted Keg with Greytar hunched over his pen and parchment, asking Larzon questions and then faithfully transcribing his answers. Larzon was more than willing to share his wealth of experience as long as the mead kept flowing.

The information Greytar gleaned proved invaluable. Larzon knew first-hand that lizard man flesh makes "good eating when in a pinch – so long as you boil it and are careful to drain the fat." He related that a wounded owlbeast will "play dead if outnumbered only to rise back up and attack again at the most inopportune moment" and that kobolds sometimes "intentionally lay down tracks hoping to lure the unwary into a kill zone or elaborate trap." Greytar couldn't write fast enough. "Worth every copper piece I laid out for mead!" he later wrote.

Unfortunately, Larzon is also prone to exaggeration as well as being greatly superstitious. Many readers have raised an eyebrow at his claim that "sprinkling salt around a campfire will keep the undead at bay" or his belief that "keeping the thumb of a known thief in a coin pouch will improve the bearer's luck and increase his profits." Sometimes one has to take Larzon with a grain of salt.

Greytar has indicated Larzon's personal observations by the following symbol:

Monster Descriptions & Data

Our crack team of dedicated scholars and field agents has fully researched every creature detailed in this encyclopedic offering. We know from first-hand accounts that no such creature should be taken lightly. Even the most (seemingly) innocuous can be an effective challenge for even hardened heroes, if utilized by a GameMaster of clever and cunning mind – as I'm sure you are (or will be) or you wouldn't be reading this book.

If you're a player, well, let's just say that you're on your way to arming yourself with potent knowledge – forcing your GM to become clever and cunning or run the risk of you running roughshod over his precious campaign.

The following introduction explains how to interpret the monster listings contained within each entry.

Explanatory Notes

Monster Name:

Each creature is listed alphabetically, compiled in order by the name to which it is most commonly referred by sages, scholars, hunters and those in-the-know. Names less-oft used, but still relatively common, are listed as "aka" or "Also Known As...." immediately thereafter.

Expert Commentary:

Each Hacklopedia entry includes a first-hand account in the form of an excerpt from the memoirs, field notes, scholarly works or penned books of one of the foremost authorities on the creature in question (see the appropriate biographical entry on pages 6 through 8 for each such expert). Each commentary includes tidbits of useful information written by a professional with direct, personal experience with the creature. Common annotations range from useful items that may be taken from such a kill or how to evade (or fight) the beast to tips on tracking it. Of course, the type and extent of (and even quality) of the records varies depending on the source. While the editors of this exalted tome have taken every effort and spared no expense on verifying the accounts presented, we cannot guarantee that the field details related herein are completely universal or conclusive. For the intrepid player relying on this encyclopedia, that means be wary and forewarned.

Monster Description:

The information immediately subsequent to the authoritative commentary is more detailed and contains certain rule-specific data that falls largely in the realm of the GM, although, in a break from the traditions of previous HackMaster editions, it is not outside the purview of players to read these sections. That said, players should be wary of all entries in this book as their GM may receive clarifications and further information to which they are not privy, making complete reliance on this tome a dangerous thing, indeed. Accordingly, if you are a player, you should refrain from studying these beasts until completing at least your first encounter, and then make your own notes in the margin as your experience under your particular GameMaster could vary somewhat or even depart dramatically from that of the experts referenced and cited in this Hacklopedia of Beasts.

Each monster description is broken into the following categories (as appropriate for each creature):

Combat/Tactics:

This entry describes how the monster fights, whether singly or as part of a group (or both). Does the beast attempt to avoid encounters or does it boldly or recklessly rush in, taking on all challengers? Will it fiercely protect its young and/or home? Does the thing know no fear? Is it a toe-to-toe fighter or does it prefer to pick off enemies at range? Creatures intelligent enough to employ weapons, armor and other tools may also have lists of these and other such favored instruments of war frequently used.

Habitat/Society:

The monster's natural habitat, its social organization, mating habits, gestation period, life span, description of lairs and so forth as well as any other factoids that might be useful to the GameMaster find their way here.

Ecology:

This section describes how the monster integrates with its environment, such as the manner in which the monster fits into the world and environment it occupies. What niche does it fill? What other creatures is it related to on the evolutionary tree? Where does it fall in the food chain? How does it fit in the grand scheme of things?

On Tellene:

Although HackMaster can be played using any campaign setting, play is maximized on the default world of Tellene (the Kingdoms of Kalamar campaign world). This short entry briefly describes where the creature fits into that setting (soon to join the superior ranks of the HackMaster product line).

Animal Signs: This area displays the monster's tracks to help your character recognize when he's entered a creature's range or to otherwise track a specimen. Additional information may also include other 'signs' of the beast's activity in the area, such as scat, territorial markings and nesting/sleeping areas.

These tracks and markings reveal the presence of skitter rats.

Relative Size: Shown here is a representation of the relative size of an average, mature creature of the indicated type compared to a typical 6-foot tall human. Note that specimens may vary in size somewhat, so, depending on species, be prepared for smaller (whether adolescent, pygmy or simply undersized adults) or larger creatures than shown.

A fearsome drake dwarfs an average human.

Tellene Range: This chart shows a small map of Tellene displaying the monster's typical range or territories. These are the areas where the species is most common but note well that this does not mean that the creatures will never be encountered outside of their typical range as pockets of creatures may appear in unlikely locations. However, outside of the listed ranges, the probability of encountering the creature in question drops dramatically.

QUICK REFERENCE DATA BLOCKS

The right-hand margin of each entry contains three quick-reference data blocks. Here the GM can quickly find a summary of game information for that particular monster entry. To further increase efficacy and speed of use in-game, three categories further subdivide the data blocks:

Combat Rose

The Combat Rose is a standard icon containing all pertinent monster combat data elements in one convenient box. It yields the following information:

Speed: This statistic describes how much time (in seconds) passes before the creature can attempt to make another attack after its previous strike. For creatures with varied attack routines (*e.g.* the griffyn has a Speed 3 and lists two claw rakes (2d4p+4) and a bite (4d8p) as its attack routine), the attacks occur in sequence as listed.

For instance, a griffyn makes its first attack for 2d4p+4 potential damage upon closing within Reach distance of its opponent. Three seconds later it again attacks for 2d4p+4 potential damage and three more seconds later (7 total) it attacks again, this time with a bite for 4d8p potential damage. Three seconds after that, it again attacks for 2d4p+4, and so on.

Initiative: This number is added to any Initiative die roll. Quick and nimble monsters receive a bonus (negative numbers improve their reaction time) while slow or ponderous creatures are usually saddled with a penalty.

Attack: Monsters add this value to their d20p attack roll when striking an opponent.

Defense: Monsters add this value to their d20p Defense roll when defending against an opponent. Note that monsters listed with "Shield Use" as a special defense receive a d20p-4 Defense die when not employing a shield, but other monsters use a standard d20p at all times (the -4 penalty is already factored into their natural attack ability).

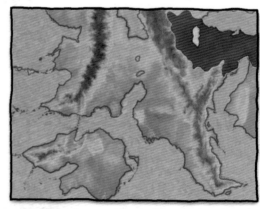

Sturm-wolves are most commonly found on the cold northern plains of the Drhokker horse lords.

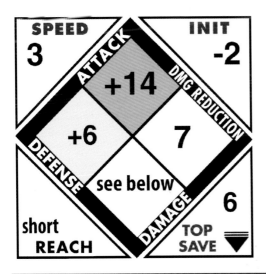

SPEED
3

INIT
-2

ATTACK
+14

DMG REDUCTION
7

DEFENSE
+6

see below

DAMAGE
6

short
REACH

TOP
SAVE

ATTACK:
Griffyns attack with two individual rakes of their avian foreclaws (doing 2d4p+4 points of damage each) and a vicious bite of their hooked bill (the latter inflicting 4d8p damage)

SPECIAL DEFENSES:
Flight

The griffyn's combat rose.

Damage Reduction (DR): Whether gained through body armor, an exoskeleton, bulk, the supernatural or sheer orneriness, this is the number by which the GM should reduce the damage of any successful hit inflicted upon a monster (a hit may be reduced to zero effective damage). Creatures that normally wear armor are listed with their most commonly worn armor incorporated into this figure, but natural hide (if any) will also be listed so that the GM can easily remove or modify armor type.

Damage: This value lists the damage a creature inflicts when it successfully lands a blow. For humanoid, human or demi-human creatures, this figure corresponds to the most likely weapon they may employ. The creature's Strength score has been incorporated into this value, but appear so that the GM can employ different weapons with ease.

Reach: This indicates at what distance the creature can strike. Reach is important because the unsurprised indi-

vidual or monster with superior reach gains the opportunity to strike first.

As a GM, if you need to quickly calculate reach in feet, you can generally treat short as 2 feet, medium as 3 feet and long as 5 feet (or if the monster carries a weapon, use its Reach instead). If the latter is applicable, this information is annotated in the monster's statistics.

Threshold of Pain (ToP) Save: When struck by a single blow exceeding 40% of its maximum Hit Points, a creature must roll this figure or below on a d20 to avoid the debilitating effects of a grievous wound. Creatures with a value of "n/a" need never make a Threshold of Pain save as they either cannot feel or are immune to pain.

For example, an orc with 28 Hit Points needs to make a Threshold of Pain save whenever it suffers 12 points of damage from a single hit (28 x 40% = 11.2, round up because 11 is insufficient to force a ToP save). Because orcs have a Damage Reduction value of 3, the actual blow must be for 15 or more points of damage. Thus if this orc is struck by a longsword for 15 points of damage (suffering 12 points of damage), it must then attempt a ToP save. The orc must roll 6 or below on a d20 or be rendered temporarily incapacitated for 5 seconds times the difference in the save rolled and the required ToP save number (in this case, 6).

Special Attack: Certain creatures have attacks that have ancillary effects other than Hit Point damage. These are listed here. If a creature has any skills useful in attacking they will be listed here as well, space permitting.

Supplemental Poison Rules: Many creatures possessing a toxic bite or sting may deliver this venom via an attack form insufficient to penetrate its target's damage reduction [DR] rating. This does not mean that said attack failed, merely that it was insufficient to inflict a measureable wound. It may well have broken the skin and disgorged its poison despite the innocuous wound.

In order to simulate this very likely possibility, the following rule applies:

When successfully attacked by a creature with a poisonous bite that caused insufficient damage to penetrate one's armor, the difference between the armor's DR and the bite damage is applied as a bonus to the resultant saving throw.

For example, a very large spider bites a character in chainmail. The bite causes only 2 points of damage, insufficient to penetrate the mail. The character thus sustains no Hit Point damage. However, the bite may still have bypassed his armor to deliver a very minor laceration or puncture sufficient to allow the venom to enter his system. The difference between his armor's DR [5] and the bite damage [2] is 3. He thus must attempt a saving throw versus poison but adds +3 to his check.

Special Defense: Certain creatures have defenses that have ancillary benefits other than a defense bonus. These are listed here. If a creature has any skills useful in defense (such as Hiding or Sneaking) they will be listed here as well, space permitting.

Data Blocks

Herein lies everything the GM needs to conduct combat using the monster. Relevant statistics include everything from Hit Points to combat statistics to movement rates. We've presented this information so that GameMasters have all the salient data right at their fingertips.

General Info: This block contains a summary of information pertaining to the creature. This box proves most useful to the GM when planning encounters and placing monsters, but is not cluttered with in-combat-related values.

Yield Box: While including some information relevant to encounter planning on a macro-level (such as EPV), this block can really be described as the 'post encounter' section. Here one can find details on anything useful that might be taken from a fallen monster (including experience points) once successfully defeated.

The three data blocks and their subentries are described in detail, below.

COMBAT DATA BLOCK

Hit Points: Each creature possesses a range of Hit Points for the monster. To determine the exact total, simply roll the indicated dice and add the resulting sum to any base HP number listed for each individual creature encountered.

Regeneration: Some monsters (trolls for example) have a superlative capability to recover from any injuries they've sustained. In the description, it will be said to regenerate wounds at a rate of 1 hit point per X seconds. This means that the creature will recover one hit point per time interval regardless of the number of individual wounds it has sustained. This point will be subtracted from the most severe wound.

Size/Weight: This category summarizes the creature's physical mass and height (or length) as well as the typical weight. Smaller creatures are far more susceptible to knock-backs resulting from massive blows (regardless of whether or not the blow bypasses the monster's 'damage reduction' statistic to cause actual damage).

Tenacity: Tenacity (Morale) is an indication of just how willing a monster is to engage in combat and stay in the fray once suffering injury, losing a comrade, etc. Creatures with animal intelligence or that act on instincts have Tenacity listed. Intelligent creatures typically have Morale. Some monsters have a tenacity entry of 'none'. Such a rating indicates that the creature will never retreat due to fear or injury no matter how dire the situation is or seems.

Tenacity/ [Morale level]	Tenacity [Morale] Roll modifier	Trigger event
None	n/a	n/a
Fearless	+2	50%+ in one hit.
Brave	+1	Suffer enough for ToP check; attacked from rear, front and flank; battle appears hopeless.
Steady	0	Suffer 25% dmg in one blow; flanked on 2 sides; character and allies unable to significantly damage foes in 30 seconds; outnumbered.
Nervous	-4	Suffer 20% damage in one blow; flanked; unable to significantly damage foe in thirty seconds; even numbers or worse.
Cowardly	-8	Any wound; double-teamed; unable to damage foe after two attempts; do not outnumber opponent 2:1

Size Category	Description
T (tiny)	1'-2' in height or length (examples: giant rat, weasel)
S (small)	3'-4' in height/length (examples: halfling, kobold)
M (medium)	5'-7' in height/length and without significant girth (example: human)
L (large)	7'-9' in height or length [or shorter with appropriate bulk or girth] (examples: bugbear, gnole)
H (huge)	9'-15' in height or length (examples: griffyn, ogre)
G (gigantic)	15'-25' in height or length (example: hoar frost giant)
E (enormous)	26'-40' in height or length (example: Arakian Queen, Tetzylwyrm)
C (Colossal)	over 40' in height or length (example: Worm, Titanic)

Movement Type	Very Fast	Fast	Quick	Standard (human)	Sluggish	Slow	Very Slow
Crawl	15	10	5	2.5 feet/sec	1.25	0.625	0.3125
Walk	20	15	10	5 ft/sec	2.5 sec	1.25	0.625
Jog	25	20	15	10 ft/sec	5 ft/sec	2.5	1.25
Run	30	25	20	15 ft/sec	7.5sec	3.75	2.5
Sprint	35	30	25	20 ft/sec	10 ft/sec	5 ft/sec	3.75

Checking Morale: Individuals check morale any time they suffer a hit in combat (or other event) that results in a trigger event for their Tenacity level. Thus, a Nervous creature must make a tenacity check any time one of the following events occurs: it suffers 20% damage in one blow, becomes flanked, is unable to significantly damage its foe in thirty seconds, its allies have even numbers or worse.

Tenacity checks are handled by a competing d20p roll. The subject of a check modifies his roll by the Morale Modifier for his Tenacity Level while the counter-die is modified by the Charisma Morale Modifier of the attacker (if a character) or the Tenacity Modifier as indicated in the HoB entry (if a creature). If the subject's roll is lower, it has failed its check.

A failure means creatures with Intelligence of 6/01 or more immediately begin executing a fighting withdrawal and move to leave combat – they can return if the triggering event is no longer in play (e.g., healed or no longer surrounded) or they are rallied by a leader. Creatures with lower intelligence immediately flee with a failed result.

Intelligence: This entry shows the relative level of a monster's intelligence/cunning compared to humans.

Fatigue Factor: After every 30 seconds of combat, monsters must attempt a competing d20p save (modified by its Fatigue Factor score) against a straight d20p. Failure indicates the creature is winded and suffers a -2 penalty to its Attack and Defense, a +1 penalty to Speed and -1 to damage. Successive failures double these penalties each time (i.e. -4 Attack *et al.* after the second failure, -8 *et al.* after the third). A listing of n/a indicates that the creature can never become fatigued.

Movement: This section shows the creature's speed for various types of locomotion as shown in the chart at the top of the page.

In addition to standard movement, any special movement types will be listed here, for example, flight, brachiation, swimming, burrowing and so forth.

Saves: During combat monsters may be required to make various saving rolls. This section lists the base saving throw including any inherent modifiers based on any special mental acuity or physical advantage.

Intelligence Value	Comparable Intelligence Score
Non	nil
Semi	0/01 to 1/100
Animal, Low	2/01 to 4/100
Animal, High	3/01 to 5/100
Obtuse	4/01 to 7/100
Slow	7/01 to 9/100
Average	10/01 to 12/100
Bright	12/01 to 14/100
Smart	15/01 to 16/100
Brilliant	17/01 to 18/100
Genius	19/01 to 20/100
Supra-genius	21/01 to 22/100
God-like	23+

WILL FACTOR

Know that the sight of a black-cloaked figure in brightest day may well be a wraith on some villainous errand. They fear not the light and may challenge ye with the sun directly overhead. Thou must beware but make this encounter known to those who mayest gauge if it be a harbinger of events most foul.

WILL FACTOR 18

This statistic is only listed for undead creatures. It is both a measure of their ability to resist the will of cleric turn attempts and an indication of the fortitude of their special attacks.

To Turn one of these unnatural beasts, the cleric must be within sight of the creature or otherwise have its attention, boldly present his holy symbol and speak (in any language) a prayer or command of his religion. The player then rolls a d20p and adds both his character's level and his Turning Modifier (based on Charisma) to the roll. The GM also rolls a d20p, adding the monster's Will Factor to the result. If the priest's roll exceeds the monster's, it is turned back and must immediately flee from the cleric at its maximum rate for 3d4p minutes. If the results indicate a tie, the monster is held at bay for 5 seconds and then may re-engage.

Turning takes 5 seconds to complete and may be performed any number of times, as long as the priest is successful or ties. Once a priest fails, he may try again, but the undead receives a +4 bonus to its roll. Each successive failure results in a further cumulative +4 bonus. Attacking in melee or otherwise forcing oneself or allies onto the creature negates the repelling effects (though missile attacks do not), but does not otherwise affect future attempts or provide a bonus to the undead's Will check.

GENERAL INFO DATA BOX

Activity Cycle: The Activity Cycle entry indicates which times of day/night the creature is typically active. Of course, there are always exceptions to the rule, e.g., goblin guards are active during the day even though goblins are nocturnal.

No. Appearing: Average number of creatures of the indicated type that might be encountered in a wilderness area in the creatures' home range. Certain entries will contain details about lairs, hunting parties and other ways of encountering different numbers from the main entry. The GM should adjust these numbers up or down depending on the situation.

% Chance in Lair: This is the chance a monster is actually at home, important for determining whether the female human thief gets mauled by a family of intelligent grizzlies or finds unguarded valuables, like comfy furniture and porridge.

Frequency: The Frequency entry represents the relative likelihood of the creature inhabiting an area. The occurrence chances are based on areas likely to be traversed by human and demi-human heroes and the like and general population density of the creature in question.

Frequency	Liklihood of Encounter
Ubiquitous	~50% (5040 per 10,000)
Commonplace	~ 25% (2520 per 10,000)
Frequent	~ 12.6% (1260 per 10,000)
Infrequent	~ 6.3% (630 per 10,000)
Sporadic	~ 3.1% (314 per 10,000)
Unusual	~ 1.6% (157 per 10,000)
Scarce	~ 0.8% (78 per 10,000)
Exotic	~ 0% (1 per 10,000)

For example, a bugbear might be encountered infrequently in human lands, its frequency might become commonplace in a goblinoid Netherdeep kingdom. Further, while a bugbear might be encountered infrequently near a human village, its ability to hide or slay any witnesses might mean that no living local has ever seen one.

Alignment: This is the typical alignment for the creature. Unintelligent monsters have no alignment at all; they behave purely on instinct.

Vision Type: This entry is an indication of a monster's eyesight. Normal, low light vision, hindrance by sunlight, sight in complete darkness, and more are covered.

Low Light Vision: Creatures with low light vision may operate without penalty in the region of dim, shadowy light created by any light source.

Such is the visual acuity of these individuals that they can still make out objects if within 120 feet of a torch or lantern. They are, however, subject to both -4 Attack and -2 Defense penalties in this extended range.

Extreme Low Light Vision: Creatures with extreme low-light vision are supremely adapted to conditions of darkness requiring only the barest measure of illumination.

If within 120 feet of a torch or lantern they may function without penalty. Even in conditions perceived by those with eyes less sensitive to be complete darkness (e.g., up to 200 feet from a light source), they can see well enough to differentiate between objects and so can target opponents with projectiles and move about without fear of crashing into objects. In these incredibly dim conditions, even their superlative vision is challenged, causing them to suffer both -4 Attack and -2 Defense penalties.

Farsight: Creatures with this vision type, primarily aerial hunters, have extremely acute long distance vision being able to perceive details at up to tenfold the range of an average human. While extremely beneficial at the extended distances flight permits, its utility is not statistically significant within the abbreviated confines in which combat takes place.

Undead Sight: The undead have a visual perception totally unlike that of the living. To these creatures, everything appears slightly surreal as if in a monochromatic dream. Ambient light is not required nor does its absence detract from their ability to 'see' the world around them. These evil phantoms can thus never be rendered sightless – at least in the traditional sense. Though some may flee the sun's rays, they do so for it pierces the shroud of dark energies fueling their aberrant existence rather than because it blinds them.

Awareness/Senses: Some creatures have unique or situational weaknesses/advantages that may affect an encounter. For example a black bear might smell an approaching party from a mile or more away. These other senses are summarized in this block.

Habitat: This entry indicates the creature's preferred habitat. Some burrow underground while others live in trees, underwater, in nests, hives, lodges and so on.

Diet: A basic summary of the animal's diet or eating habits has been included. Knowing whether the creature eats man-flesh or is a herbivore certainly helps with its motivations. Obviously, a herbivore won't attack a dwarf for food .

Organization: The general social structure of the creature is described here. Knowing whether the monsters have a hive mentality, or are solitary, tribal, etc., is of great use when designing encounters and lairs alike.

Climate/Terrain: This entry indicates where the creature tends to be found. Climate includes the full spectrum ranging from arctic, subarctic, temperate and tropical. Terrain includes plains, scrub, forest, hills, rough, mountains, swamps and deserts. Sometimes a simple range will be given, (i.e., "Cold" indicates both artic, subarctic and cold temperate climes).

YIELD DATA BOX

Every adventurer who drops a monster hopes to gain something from the experience. Slaying a monster invariably leaves the conqueror with a pile of meat, fur, bones and/or feathers. If he is really lucky, there may even be treasure in the form of carried items or hoarded items in a nearby lair.

Real treasure is usually obvious, while other yield items, perhaps not so much. GameMasters should never volunteer yield information to players. Such knowledge should be gleaned during game play. For example a character notices Owlbeast claws are fetching 1 gold coin each at a local market and slaps himself in the forehead when he realizes he left a fortune lying in a gut heap along a mountain trail not two days prior. Of course, players that have invested in this tome likely have a leg up on their buddies.

Note that some yield items may require certain skills in order to be successfully harvested.

Once collected or harvested, yield items must be safely stored. Don't forget that meat rots and uncured hides draw flies, not to mention the stench of a kill is sure to draw scavengers.

Medicinal: Yield listed under this category are parts of an animal that have curative or medicinal powers. Dust from the ground-up horn of a minotaur sprinkled over a wound might stop the wound from bleeding, for example.

Spell Components: Of interest to any practitioner of magic — animals and monsters are a valuable source of spell components.

Hide/Trophy: This entry indicates the street value of any fur, teeth, claws, etc. that such items taken from the indicated creature will fetch in the city markets. Note that such trophies must be carefully taken using any appropriate skills. Prices should be adjusted accordingly for creatures with maximum Hit Points (upward) or who were maimed or took unusual damage when felled (fireballed, for example).

Treasure: Treasure items that the monster is likely carrying or has squirreled away in its lair will be indicated here. Treasure can be anything from hard coin to gemstones to armor and weaponry.

Edible: Sometimes the greatest immediate yield taken from a fallen monster is much needed sustenance. This category indicates whether or not a monster's flesh can be eaten (note that some monsters are poisonous). Edible meat may also fetch a good price at the town/city markets, exotic meats considered a delicacy especially so.

Other: Yield items that do not fall in any of the other categories will be listed here.

EPV: This is the base number of Experience Points that should be awarded for defeating a monster of that type. Note that monsters encountered singly should offer only half the EPV listed. Monsters encountered in groups double the size of the party such that their superior numbers can come into play should be awarded 150% of the EPV of the group. Even larger numbers should be adjusted as warranted based on the monsters' ability to use numbers to their benefit.

AARNZ HOUND

Also Known As: Gorund, Ape Wolf
Shadow Hound, Stalking Hound

There's an old saying among Ahznom merchants venturing west into Zazahni that goes "Walk fast, stay alert and pray to the gods that you sprout eyes in the back of your head."

These terrifying creatures are notorious for following their prey for days, selectively attacking and pulling lone victims into the underbrush as the opportunity presents itself, then continuing the hunt.

Aarnz hounds prefer to attack from behind, typically raking their victim with powerful claws then sinking their fangs into any exposed flesh and ripping away. I've seen three to four of these beasts take down a grown man and drag him off kicking and screaming into the undergrowth as his comrades look on dumb with astonishment. Often one or two large aarnz bitches will take an aggressive posture after an attack, daring any would-be rescuers to follow, before disappearing into the shadows.

Packing two hundred pounds of fang, claw, spit and fury these savage brutes are best avoided.

Attacks can also come from above, for the large beasts can climb trees, leaping from branch to branch with amazing agility. In fact, they seem to travel faster in this manner than they do on the ground.

Anyone traveling in aarnz hound territory would be well advised to assign eyes to watch the treetops. Branches suddenly bowing as if under weight and then springing upward is a sure sign that you're being stalked. But don't neglect the undergrowth along the trail's edge or those low hanging branches that create dark shadows. Aarnz hounds often use distraction in the form of rustling leaves, claw strikes against bark and low guttural barks to turn a group's attention in one direction while the real attack comes from another. — S

Aarnz hounds are a massive, hairy cross between a breed of large, savage apes and wild dogs. Their thick fur ranges from slate gray to dark brown and black, and their crazed eyes glow with amber luminescence whether encountered in the dark or in the light. Their jaws gape in terrifying ferocity, lined with long, sharp fangs that protrude forth and ooze with saliva, ready to deliver a devastating bite. Their claws, too, are frightening to behold, for they are large and culminate in thick, dagger-sharp nails. Indeed, they too are capable of inflicting tremendous damage to creatures of softer flesh.

Because of their mixed breeding, aarnz hounds can not only run, but also climb trees and swing (albeit clumsily) along any branches strong enough to support their weight.

The average aarnz hound has a total body length of roughly 6 feet and an average weight of 200 pounds, standing about 3 feet tall at the shoulder. Nocturnal hunters, these beasts are equipped with low light vision.

Combat/Tactics:

Aarnz hounds hunt and attack in packs, choosing creatures that happen to be alone, fall behind the main group or that appear weak or ill. After silencing any stragglers, aarnz hounds track the remaining prey and repeat the process, eventually slaughtering the whole group until each hound has its own kill to consume.

When confronting heavily armored or obviously stronger

SIGN/TRACKS

claw strikes will always be prominent.

Fore

Hind

RANGE ON TELLENE

SIZE COMPARISON

6 ft

3 ft

opponents, aarnz hounds quietly surround their prey. They then charge from their hidden location, attack viciously, then quickly dart out of striking range before circling back to attack again.

They take great delight in running down prey; when prey flees, it sends their hunting instincts into overdrive. If a character tries to flee, any hounds within 20 feet of him break off the attack and chase the sorry fool down. Thus, fleeing from an aarnz hound is a really bad idea.

Habitat/Society:

These bloodthirsty mongrels are not as adaptable to their environment as other pureblooded canines, and inhabit a breeding range of warm and tropical woodlands exclusively. Aarnz hounds keep dens like their canine cousins, but they make these in trees 50% of the time. In such a case, their den will be located high in the canopy, near the trunk.

Aarnz hounds live in packs of 11 to 20 individuals, including several large males, twice as many breeding-aged females, and young equal to 50% of the adult population. Hunting packs are generally composed of four or more hounds including one alpha male.

The alpha male gains first access to the breeding-aged females, once per year in the late fall months. Lesser males are then allowed to mate with the remaining females, but only after the alpha male has made his choice. Gestation is usually 95 days, with each female bearing a litter of one to four pups. Pups mature to adolescence in about a year, with about half-hit points and damage at that point. By eighteen months they are sexually mature and at full-strength.

Ecology:

They feed primarily on deer, goats, sheep, boar, water buffalo and other such creatures, with no qualms about running down a human, demi-human or any other tasty prey. They particularly hate gnoles, hyenas and jackals, but they seem to leave kobolds alone. Likewise, they have no interest in halflings and instinctually do not hunt them. Conversely, they love the taste of gnome.

On Tellene:

Legend has it that a Svimohz man named Aarnz was the first known casualty of this savage beast, thus lending it his name for all time. His sons, ready to avenge their father's death, studied the beasts, tracked them, and killed the hound responsible before barely escaping the rest of the pack. It is from their studies, so the story goes, that today's hunters learned to track aarnz hounds from their defecation markers (keeping the pack from navigating the same terrain too often and also allowing the pack to know the whereabouts of its members).

Despite this tale, aarnz hound dens are far more numerous in the Obakasek Jungle than in the Vohven Jungle, while these beasts are more likely to build burrows in central Svimohzia than in Tarisato, where they are hunted by organized militia.

[1]*Aarnz hound saliva is often used as a salve for burns, permitting them to heal at an accelerated rate (as if tended to by a Master of First Aid) as long as the saliva is applied daily.*

[2]*One ounce of muscular tissue from an aarnz hound can be used as an alternate material component for the Journeyman spell Tireless Run.*

[3]*Meat is stringy and tough and not generally eaten but it is edible in emergency survival situations. It has a strong gamy taste and may cause nausea in sensitive stomachs.*

[4]*Primitive warriors fashion the long forearm bone (ulna) as clubs. In proficient hands, these clubs add 1 point to damage.*

AARNZ HOUND

HIT POINTS:	26+2d8
SIZE/WEIGHT:	M/200 lbs
TENACITY:	Steady
INTELLIGENCE:	Slow
FATIGUE FACTOR:	-2

SPEED 4 — INIT -1 — ATTACK +6 — DMG REDUCTION — DEFENSE +4 — 3 — see below — short REACH — DAMAGE 8 — TOP SAVE

MOVEMENT

CRAWL:	5
WALK:	10
JOG:	15
RUN:	20
SPRINT:	25
BRACHIATE:	10

SAVES

PHYSICAL:	+7
MENTAL:	+5
DODGE:	+6

ATTACK:
Aarnz hounds attack with alternative swipes of their sharply clawed fore paws (doing 2d4p+2 damage) followed by a bite for 2d8p

SPECIAL ABILITIES:
Tracking skill mastery 50%

GENERAL INFO

ACTIVITY CYCLE:	Nocturnal (primarily but not exclusively)
NO. APPEARING:	4-12
% CHANCE IN LAIR:	n/a
FREQUENCY:	Sporadic
ALIGNMENT:	Neutral Evil
VISION TYPE:	Low Light Vision
AWARENESS/SENSES:	Keen sense of smell
HABITAT:	Jungle and vicinity
DIET:	Carnivorous
ORGANIZATION:	Pack
CLIMATE/TERRAIN:	Tropical jungle

YIELD

MEDICINAL:	saliva, used as a salve for burns[1]
SPELL COMPONENTS:	tissue, for the Tireless Run spell[2]
HIDE/TROPHY:	pelts are worth 20 sp
TREASURE:	none
EDIBLE:	yes, if necessary[3]
OTHER:	forearm bones serve as clubs[4]
EXPERIENCE POINT VALUE:	300

Amoeba, Giant

Also Known As: Gelatinous Slime, The Blob

Once I was traveling with a group of linen merchants in the Sotai Gagalia Headlands when a squall approached from Reanaaria Bay, and it began to rain so hard we feared we would be swept downriver along with our mounts and goods. After scouting out the area for cover, one of the servant boys announced he had found a cave — high and dry with room enough for us all as well as our horses and mules.

It was here that I had my first encounter with a gelatinous slime — something whose existence I had been blissfully unaware of for sixty-four years of my well traveled and informed life.

We had just built a fire and I was settling down to scrawl in my journal when one of the mules brayed unexpectedly. Looking to the back of the cavern, where the animals had been tethered, it was quickly surmised that one of them had gone missing and that the others were in a state of sheer panic.

The caravan master grabbed a torch and was just about to investigate when something amazing happened. A gelatinous appendage — looking like a handless arm — shot out from the darkness and grabbed another mule, dragging it into the shadows. With the torch now held up high, we witnessed the poor creature's demise as it was absorbed into a large quivering mass I can only describe as looking like tetranberry jam. Swallowed alive before our very eyes.

Needless to say we spent the rest of the night fending for ourselves under the open sky — soaked to the bones but alive. — ⌘

While common amoebae are generally microscopic, giant amoebae can grow to 10 feet in diameter. These giant, translucent blobs are active scavengers that feed on carrion, refuse, mosses and other filth, but will eat living creatures if they can catch them. Their sheer size and instinctual drive to feed makes them feared opponents.

Under the right conditions, a giant amoeba can appear completely transparent. In dimly lit or dark conditions, when spread across gray stone, in water and so on, the amoeba has a Hiding skill of 90%. This chance drops to 50% if moving, but still in the same conditions. In bright light, when covering a contrasting stone or earth (such as very dark or very light colors), their Hiding mastery drops to 25%.

The amoeba has a solid outer shell that supports its inner cytoplasm. The cytoplasm inside the cell is capable of shifting states from solid to liquid and vice-versa. The fluid state of the cytoplasm is called plasmasol; the more solid state is called plasmashell. When the amoeba locomotes, the plasmasol flows toward the direction of movement and the foremost portion becomes plasmashell. When the plasmashell moves internally, it becomes solid again. This way the creature can propel itself as a whole but can also send pseudopodia in any direction. It can move faster than 5 feet per second, but only if traveling downhill.

Besides locomotion, the flexibility of the cytoplasmic structure allows the giant amoeba to conform to its surrounds. Thus, the amoeba can assume any shape necessary, from laying flat on the ceiling to avoid detection, to sliding under a door, to oozing through a tiny sinkhole or crevasse; no shape is too small or too irregular.

Sign/Tracks

Scattered metal items, coins and debris littering a slime trail are a sure sign of a giant amoeba. Take heed and do not rush into danger. Darkness is an especial friend to the creature, for its jelly-like mass is so bereft of solidity that light flows through it like water. Keep well back from the walls where it lurks, especially if ye be underground, for the Netherdeep is a well-fashioned spawning ground for the strange beasts.

Size Comparison

12 ft

6 ft

A mature amoeba can be as large as 10 feet in diameter.

Combat/Tactics:

A giant amoeba is constantly searching for food and does not hesitate to attack anything smaller than itself. Though slow moving, it can lash out with a pseudopod at remarkable speed. Anyone stuck suffers from both the concussive force of the blow as well as digestive enzymes. These enzymes incorporate a strong anesthetic such that anyone failing a saving throw is incapacitated for 4d4p x10 seconds. Unless driven off, the amoeba engulfs its prey and proceeds to digest it.

Creatures enveloped by a giant amoeba suffer 4d4p damage per 10 seconds — use a fractional result if somehow removed prior to a complete 10 seconds. *For example, if a character is saved after 4 seconds, he suffers 4d4p times 4/10 damage (round to the nearest integer).*

Because the amoeba's nervous system is floating in cytoplasm and the plasmashell can self-heal readily, certain attacks affect it differently. The giant amoeba has Damage Reduction 10 versus crushing weapons, DR 8 against piercing weapons and DR 2 against hacking weapons.

Habitat/Society:

Giant amoebae are very sensitive to ultraviolet radiation and rapidly desiccate in low humidity. These weaknesses severely limit their range. As such, they are rarely encountered outside of damp caves or other environs sheltered from the burning rays of the sun.

Giant amoebae reproduce through cellular fission. Once they reach approximately 10 feet or larger, the amoeba halts all activity, expels any retained items stuck within its cell and begin duplicating all of its organs. Before it reproduces, it rounds up into a 10-foot diameter ball with tiny pseudopodia extensions. While it appears very imposing at this time, in actuality the amoeba is very vulnerable as the pseudopods are incapable of striking out while in this state.

Consequently, amoebae look for dark caves and holes in which to hide during this time. Over the next three hours, the amoeba splits into two smaller, identical amoebae. The new amoebae are independent creatures and immediately begin moving in a random direction in search of food.

Ecology:

Within their ecosystem, they perform a valuable role by ingurgitating waste. They are unable to digest metallic or ceramic objects and thus may have objects of value within their cytoplasm encased in phagosomes.

On Tellene:

Giant amoebae are generally only found in the Netherdeep. Although it is theoretically possible to meet one in a dank cellar or similar locale, no known specimen has ever been found outside of a deep tunnel complex, large dungeon or dark, dismal swamp.

[1]*Used sparingly, fresh Giant Amoeba cytoplasm can numb the pain of severe wounds.*

GIANT AMOEBA

HIT POINTS:	35+4d8
SIZE/WEIGHT:	H/several tons
TENACITY:	Steady
INTELLIGENCE:	Non
FATIGUE FACTOR:	n/a

SPEED	INIT
6	0

ATTACK +7
DMG REDUCTION
DEFENSE 0
varies
DAMAGE 4d4p
medium REACH
TOP SAVE n/a

MOVEMENT

CRAWL:	1¼
WALK:	2½
JOG:	5
RUN:	7½ (downhill only)
SPRINT:	10 (downhill only)

SAVES

PHYSICAL:	+9
MENTAL:	n/a
DODGE:	+4

ATTACK:
Strikes with pseudopod for 4d4p points of damage - those hit must save versus VF 11 poison or be incapacitated for 4d4p x10 seconds

SPECIAL:
DR 10 (vs crushing), DR 8 vs piercing, and DR 2 (vs hacking).
Hiding skill mastery of 90% in dim light (50% if moving, 25% in bright light).

GENERAL INFO

ACTIVITY CYCLE:	Always active
NO. APPEARING:	1 (rarely 2)
% CHANCE IN LAIR:	n/a
FREQUENCY:	Infrequent
ALIGNMENT:	Non
VISION TYPE:	n/a
AWARENESS/SENSES:	Standard
HABITAT:	Any sheltered from sunlight
DIET:	Omnivorous
ORGANIZATION:	Individuals
CLIMATE/TERRAIN:	Humid Subterranean

YIELD

MEDICINAL:	cytoplasm is a topical analgesic[1]
SPELL COMPONENTS:	nil
HIDE/TROPHY:	no
TREASURE:	incidental, contained within cell
EDIBLE:	nil
OTHER:	no
EXPERIENCE POINT VALUE:	250

ANAXAR

Also Known As: Giant Mantis, Gint'mur, Anax

Strike at the antennae if given the opportunity.

Long considered the scourge of the common farmer, the anaxar has the unfortunate habit of seeking out tilled ground where crops are planted. Not that I'm sorry for it — many times I have fattened my coin pouch hunting down and ridding rural communities of this pest at the behest of farmers willing to pay money they can't afford to be rid of them. As such I've learned a thing or two about these killers.

Anaxar hate fire. If you suspect you've got an infestation be sure to have torches on hand. A jabbing motion with a hot flame to the abdomen, striking limbs or head usually forces them back. If the infestation is heavy — setting the fields ablaze is the surest way to flush them out.

Attacking with polearms is preferred, for these bastards have considerable reach. Those who try fighting toe-to-toe with a sword are certain to regret it. I've seen them grasp and rip the shield off a man's arm with one claw while impaling him in the chest with the other.

Anaxar are burrowers. They love to lie just below the surface and pop up on unsuspecting victims passing over them. If you see freshly worked earth that seems out of place in a field, in the middle of a trail or along a path leading to a spring — take care. As a habit I always step around such spots. Investigating by prodding with a polearm might save you some grief as well. One other tip — if you're getting the worst of it go for the antennae. A good blow will sometimes sending them running. — ⚲

These man-killers have an aversion to fire and smoke.

Anaxar are a gigantic (a typical specimen being 15 feet long) species of aggressive predatory insect resembling a praying mantis. The creature's chitinous exoskeleton is usually leafy green or brown in color with a softer, lighter underside, though various shades and patterns of two or more colors have been noted. Some anaxar have the coloration and/or texture of sticks, tree bark, withered leaves, blades of grass, flowers or even rocks, making them nearly undetectable (Hiding mastery of 40%) when concealed amongst similar objects.

Combat/Tactics:

Anaxar prefer to attack from ambush, whether this be striking out of dense foliage or erupting from the ground when they sense vibrations above. These burrowing creatures can rapidly dig through loamy soil and will do so if they detect surface vibrations. This latter form of initiating an attack allows them to employ an initiative die three lower than that of their prey.

If the anaxar successfully strikes an opponent with its forelegs (a single attack), it has securely grasped the victim and will subsequently attack with its fearsome mandibles every 10 seconds thereafter. An anaxar's grip loosens with a successful knock-back attack or a Feat of Strength check (*vs. d20p+16*). The latter can be attempted every 10 seconds; if successful, freedom comes with an additional d4p damage as the character slides (or is pulled) through the anaxar's serrated limbs (DR does not apply here). While so-held, a victim can only attack with a Small sized weapon. The victim also serves as a shield for the anaxar. Halflings and elves provide Defense and DR appropriate for a small shield, while dwarves and

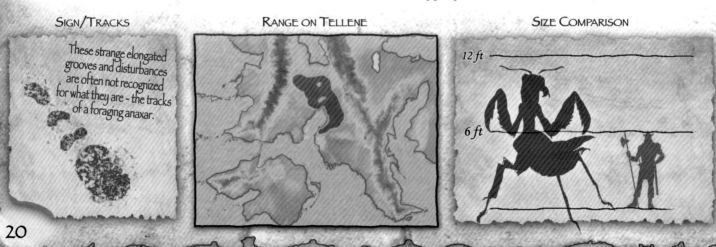

SIGN/TRACKS	RANGE ON TELLENE	SIZE COMPARISON
These strange elongated grooves and disturbances are often not recognized for what they are - the tracks of a foraging anaxar.		12 ft — 6 ft —

humans act as medium shields.

When surprised, anaxar stand tall and spread their forelegs in an attempt to seem even larger and more threatening than they already are. If the harassment persists, the anaxar strikes with its forelegs and attempts to slash or bite its foe.

The undersides of an Anaxar are not solidly armored with a resultant DR of 4. Generally this vulnerability is only presented to individuals directly in front of it.

Habitat/Society:

Anaxar are drawn to farmland and other rich soils that house giant beetles and other large insects, their favorite meals. They do not live in alpine, arctic or sub-arctic conditions, preferring tropical and subtropical environments where food is plentiful. They can also be found in temperate zones, but generally then, only near farmlands with rich soil.

Due to competition for resources, most anaxar are solitary, though hordes of three to four related females may be encountered in high crop yield areas. Males and females are rarely seen together except when mating (and never thereafter, as the female bites off the male's head upon consummation of the act).

The mating season in temperate climates typically begins in autumn, but can occur at any time in sub-tropical and tropical regions. The female lays between 20 to 40 eggs, depositing them in a frothy mass that hardens, creating a protective capsule with a further protective coat. During this time, the eggs also gain a solid shell, much like a bird egg. The mass can be attached to a flat surface, wrapped around a plant or even deposited in the ground. The mother stays to guard her eggs, leaving only to hunt. Despite her protection and the durability of the eggs, they are often preyed on, especially by giant wasps. After hatching, the mother leaves the hatchlings to fend for themselves. As the anaxar grows, it molts away its exoskeleton, leaving behind sure evidence to any hunter.

The natural lifespan of an anaxar in the wild is about six years, but males do not live through a breeding season. In colder areas, females will die during the winter (as well as any surviving males) if a hard frost occurs. Given this susceptibility, Anaxar receive no saving throw for reduced damage versus spells that have a cold or frost effect.

Ecology:

Farmers on Tellene suffer from the depredation of common pests, but those in particularly fecund regions also draw the ravenous attentions of giant beetles and other insects that feast upon the crops and lay eggs in the soft, rich soil. Anaxar feed upon these beetle grubs and routinely burrow underground searching for such larvae. Though this is their preferred diet, anaxar are flexible carnivores. They have learned to hunt many terrestrial mammals but seem to target domesticated animals as easier quarry. When they sense tremors on the surface, anaxar burst through the soil to ambush the presumed meal above.

On Tellene:

In temperate zones, the anaxar will generally only be found in fertile farm areas. In sub-tropical to tropical regions the anaxar is just as likely to be found hunting in rainforests or other areas where prey is plentiful.

ANAXAR

HIT POINTS:	36+5d8
SIZE/WEIGHT:	H/1 ton
TENACITY:	Brave
INTELLIGENCE:	Animal, Low
FATIGUE FACTOR:	n/a

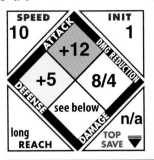

SPEED 10 — INIT 1 — ATTACK +12 — DICE REDUCTION — DEFENSE +5 — 8/4 — see below — long REACH — DAMAGE — n/a — TOP SAVE ▼

MOVEMENT

CRAWL:	2½
WALK:	5
JOG:	15
RUN:	20
SPRINT:	25

SAVES

PHYSICAL:	+9
MENTAL:	n/a
DODGE:	+4

ATTACK: Can burrow through soil to gain surprise (3 initiative dice lower); Grabs prey with forearms doing 4d4p+2 and grasping securely (Feat of Strength vs. d20p+16 to break), then proceeds to eat character alive (mandible attack doing 6d6p damage)

DEFENSES: Can use grabbed PC as shield; Underside only has DR 4; Hiding 40% in dim light; no save permitted vs. frost spells

GENERAL INFO

ACTIVITY CYCLE:	Diurnal
NO. APPEARING:	1 or 2-4
% CHANCE IN LAIR:	n/a (or 50% while guarding eggs)
FREQUENCY:	Infrequent
ALIGNMENT:	Non
VISION TYPE:	Standard
AWARENESS/SENSES:	Detect surface vibrations within 60 feet
HABITAT:	Lowlands (farmland in colder climates)
DIET:	Omnivorous
ORGANIZATION:	Solitary or Group of Siblings
CLIMATE/TERRAIN:	Temperate to Tropical

YIELD

MEDICINAL:	nil
SPELL COMPONENTS:	nil
HIDE/TROPHY:	nil
TREASURE:	nil
EDIBLE:	yes
OTHER:	eggs may be worth up to 15 silver each to the right buyer
EXPERIENCE POINT VALUE:	925

ANIMATING SPIRIT

Also Known As: Blesdar, Fabric Phantom

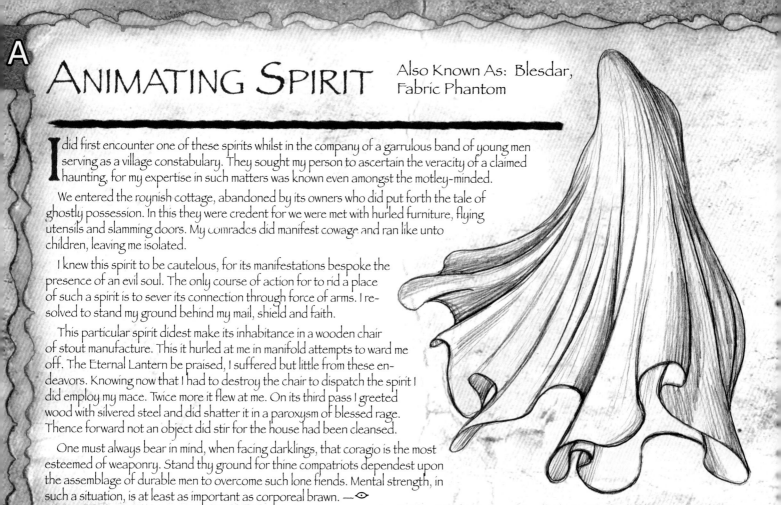

I did first encounter one of these spirits whilst in the company of a garrulous band of young men serving as a village constabulary. They sought my person to ascertain the veracity of a claimed haunting, for my expertise in such matters was known even amongst the motley-minded.

We entered the roynish cottage, abandoned by its owners who did put forth the tale of ghostly possession. In this they were credent for we were met with hurled furniture, flying utensils and slamming doors. My comrades did manifest cowage and ran like unto children, leaving me isolated.

I knew this spirit to be cautelous, for its manifestations bespoke the presence of an evil soul. The only course of action for to rid a place of such a spirit is to sever its connection through force of arms. I resolved to stand my ground behind my mail, shield and faith.

This particular spirit didest make its inhabitance in a wooden chair of stout manufacture. This it hurled at me in manifold attempts to ward me off. The Eternal Lantern be praised, I suffered but little from these endeavors. Knowing now that I had to destroy the chair to dispatch the spirit I did employ my mace. Twice more it flew at me. On its third pass I greeted wood with silvered steel and did shatter it in a paroxysm of blessed rage. Thence forward not an object did stir for the house had been cleansed.

One must always bear in mind, when facing darklings, that coragio is the most esteemed of weaponry. Stand thy ground for thine compatriots dependest upon the assemblage of durable men to overcome such lone fiends. Mental strength, in such a situation, is at least as important as corporeal brawn. —👁

Animating spirits are evil maligned spirits returned from beyond the grave. In life they were betrayed by friends and family members and now most often inhabit an item related to their betrayal and death. Driven solely by revenge, the animating spirit attacks anyone who betrayed it in life. Those standing in its way or inhibiting its vengeful desires will likewise find themselves a victim of its wrath.

A spirit, the creature is invisible and intangible. It may be harmed normally when dwelling inside an inanimate object, but when without, it can only be struck by true magic weapons or silvered ones blessed by a cleric. Persons nearing such a spirit may notice a slight dip in temperature and catch a whiff of the scent of lavender.

Combat/Tactics:

The spirit can propel an object that it abides within to hack, crush or pierce its foe in a manner appropriate to said object's form. Any physical injury this causes is based not on the object's material or statistics, but on the animating spirit's ability to attack with that object. The animating spirit can only control objects weighing up to 50 pounds. *Note that since the spirit's essence is contained within this object, it is considered a melee attack not ranged.*

On some occasions, the spirit animates a sheet (typically the sheet of a violated marital bed) or garment of a decent size (e.g., a cloak or gown but not a shoe or hat) and waits for its victim to don or use it. If this tactic fails, the animated object flies forward and attempts to wrap itself around the target. If this attack is successful, the spirit has wrapped the fabric around its target, inflicting automatic constriction damage thereafter every 10 seconds. Constriction can be broken with a successful knock-back attack from an ally or a Feat of Strength (vs. d20p+18), which can be attempted every 10 seconds. While constricted, the target can attack only with a dagger or smaller weapon.

Note that physical attacks on a spirit enveloping a character also damage the character. The enveloped victim suffers 75% of puncturing damage, 50% of crushing damage or 25% of hacking damage, with the

SIGN/TRACKS

SIZE COMPARISON

If you are traveling after dusk near a crypt, cemetery, battlefield or ground where it is known blood has been spilled — be on guard. Keep holy icons at the ready. Mutter a prayer of protection. If the birds suddenly grow silent, you feel a chilled wind on the back of your neck or suddenly the hairs on your arm stand on end — these are all signs of an animated spirit gathering form nearby.

WILL FACTOR 8

6 ft

3 ft

remainder damaging the spirit. Magical effects that cause physical damage divide the hit point loss equally between the animating spirit and its enveloped prey exept in the case of area effect spells. In the latter case, both suffer full effects (if a saving throw is permitted for reduced damage, this is attempted by the spirit and, if successful, both it and the entrapped victim suffer the lesser damage amount).

The spirit imbues the animated object with its own undead energies; with the result that otherwise weak or seemingly fragile objects can withstand blows they normally could not. Any damage to the object beyond the spirit's Hit Point total destroys both the object and the animating spirit.

An animating spirit may also be encountered in non-corporeal form. This may either be when it exits an object to avoid destruction or simply in its natural state. In this form it has no means of attack. Locating a non-corporeal spirit can be very difficult as it is not merely invisible but intangible. The *Sense Invisible Beings* spell may work but the spirit is entitled to a saving throw that, if successful, renders it immune to this sensory enchantment.

Physically attacking the incorporeal spirit presents a number of challenges. It first must be located (see above). Blindly swinging at it is always ineffective as it will simply avoid such individuals and can easily pass through any solid object effectively interposing another person or a wall or even the solid ground between it and danger. Secondly, even if its presence is known, only true magic weapons or silvered ones enchanted with a *Bless Weapon* spell may do it harm. If these preconditions are met by someone wishing to strike an incorporeal spirit, the creature's standard combat statistics apply (excepting any attack).

Note that it requires 10 seconds for an animating spirit to either take on or release itself from material form via an object. During this period it is vulnerable to attack as normal.

Ecology:

Animating spirits are undead entities without a corporeal form. By possessing an inanimate object, they gain the ability to wreak vengeance upon the living but also risk destruction if said object is destroyed while they are inhabiting it.

These creatures are immune to spells that mentally afflict living creatures, such as *Charm* and *Panic*.

On Tellene:

No one knows where the animating spirit originates, for the first documented case has been corrupted by urban legend. Coincidentally (or not), this 'fabric phantom' was the spirit of an expert Mendarn tailor, Blesdar Forband, a man with the reputation of making the most magnificent clothing in the kingdom. However, one customer (a noble by the name of Granden) refused payment until he saw perfection. Blesdar locked himself in his shop and worked his hardest, though Granden proved unsatisfied with the first five attempts. Finishing his sixth effort with an unexpected speed, Blesdar presented himself at the noble's home to show off his latest creation.

It was there, stumbling into Granden's bedroom, that he accidentally learned the truth — Granden had cruelly kept Blesdar working so he could seduce the tailor's wife. Collapsing from exhaustion and shock, Blesdar died.

The following week, Granden took the tailor's last creation from his wardrobe, intending to wear the exquisite ensemble at his next ball. There, he was the talk of the party. When asked where he had commissioned such wonderful clothing, Granden claimed that his consort (Blesdar's widow) had made them for him. Moments later, Granden fell dead to the floor. The noble's chest had been crushed inward.

Supposedly, since that event, animating spirits have appeared across the Sovereign Lands. Some say Blesdar's fabric had been resold and his vengeful spirit cursed any object that touched it. Others say that the story is no more than myth and that some type of unseen demon stalks the land. The Brandobians call this creature a 'blesdar,' with no other understanding of what it might be.

ANIMATING SPIRIT

HIT POINTS:	20+4d8
SIZE/WEIGHT:	Insubstantial
TENACITY:	Fearless
INTELLIGENCE:	Average
FATIGUE FACTOR:	n/a

SPEED	3	INIT	-4
ATTACK	+8	DMG REDUCTION	
DEFENSE	+6		9
		DAMAGE	2d4p
short REACH		TOP SAVE	n/a

MOVEMENT

CRAWL:	1¼
WALK:	2½
JOG:	5
RUN:	7½
SPRINT:	10

SAVES

PHYSICAL:	+8
MENTAL:	immune
DODGE:	+8

ATTACK:
The animating spirit can propel small objects inflicting 2d4p damage upon successful impact; it may alternatively attempt to wrap itself around a foe and once affixed automatically inflict 3d4p constriction damage every 10 seconds (DR does not apply)

SPECIAL DEFENSES:
Enveloped victims may absorb damage

GENERAL INFO

ACTIVITY CYCLE:	Always Active
NO. APPEARING:	1
% CHANCE IN LAIR:	n/a
FREQUENCY:	Sporadic
ALIGNMENT:	Neutral Evil
VISION TYPE:	Undead Sight
AWARENESS/SENSES:	Standard
HABITAT:	Any
DIET:	n/a
ORGANIZATION:	Solitary
CLIMATE/TERRAIN:	Any

YIELD

MEDICINAL:	nil
SPELL COMPONENTS:	nil
HIDE/TROPHY:	nil
TREASURE:	possible; dependent upon status prior to death
EDIBLE:	no
OTHER:	nil
EXPERIENCE POINT VALUE:	492

ANT, GIANT

GIANT ANT
GIANT WARRIOR ANT

Also Known As:
Ankur, Sulum

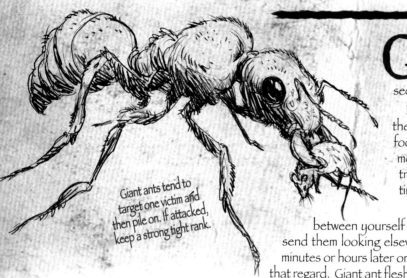

Giant ants tend to target one victim and then pile on. If attacked, keep a strong tight rank.

Giant ants can be found almost anywhere. I've run across them in the limestone caves near Miclenon, the Vohven Jungle and even in the bitter cold Rytarr Woods. They seem to thrive where other creatures do not.

Being scavengers and foragers, they are constantly on the hunt to supply food for the colony, and they will take food in most any form; grains and fruits from farmers' field, meat curing over a smoking fire or the food stores of traveling caravans. They will also attack creatures many times their own size to acquire food.

Keep in mind that giant ants fear fire. Tossing torches between yourself and any foraging ants will often keep them at bay and send them looking elsewhere for a meal. But beware — giant ants may return minutes or hours later once they've gotten a scent, and can be quite persistent in that regard. Giant ant flesh makes excellent bait for bear traps. It also makes a good repellant to keep wild boars, beetles and other foraging pests away from a campsite. —

These foraging insects grow up to 2 feet long, but otherwise are similar to their tiny kin, with six legs, elbowed antennae, and a distinctive node-like structure with a slender waist. Colors vary; most are red or black. Green is less common, though some tropical species have a metallic luster.

Warriors (sterile females) have larger heads and mandibles than workers, and are usually only encountered within an anthill (there being one giant warrior ant for every five workers) or when their nest attacks a rival nest.

Combat/Tactics:

They defend by biting and (for warrior ants) stinging. Should intruders threaten the queen, warriors swarm the attacking force and fight to the death. If a giant warrior ant scores a hit with its powerful mandibles, it receives a free secondary attack with its venomous stinger. If successful, its adversary must save vs. poison (VF 10) or suffer 3d4p points of damage (a successful save reduces damage to a mere d4p).

Giant ants are able to climb sheer walls and are excellent burrowers. Few passive defense works are able to keep them out. Giant ants are also highly resistant to falling damage having a base -50 feet adjustment.

Ecology:

Giant ants exist on almost every landmass on Tellene, save for certain remote or inhospitable islands and the frozen lands far to the north. Thanks to a generally pleasant climate, giant ants are active all year long, with a state of reduced activity or dormancy only in the coldest winters.

Predators and scavengers, they feed on other insects or mammals, fruits, vegetables and grains, and are very partial to sugary substances. Giant ants have a proportionally larger appetite and may scavenge food crops or tunnel into buildings. When foraging, giant ants may travel many miles from their nest, using scent trails to find their way back.

A giant ant's natural enemies primarily include the brown bear and giant toad, both of whom feed on common and giant ants.

While not intelligent, they are sufficiently intuitive to solve simple problems (such as forming chains of individuals to bridge gaps over water and the like). Fortunately, giant ant colonies usually contain only a few dozen individuals, instead of the thousands comprising a colony of normal ants.

SIGN/TRACKS

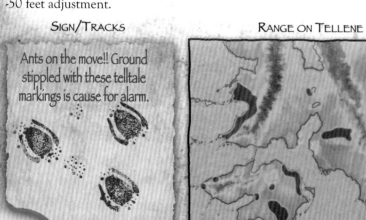

Ants on the move!! Ground stippled with these telltale markings is cause for alarm.

RANGE ON TELLENE

SIZE COMPARISON

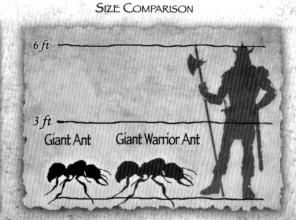

6 ft

3 ft

Giant Ant   Giant Warrior Ant

GIANT WORKER ANT

HIT POINTS:	5+2d8
SIZE/WEIGHT:	T/7 lbs.
TENACITY:	Brave
INTELLIGENCE:	Semi
FATIGUE FACTOR:	n/a

SPEED 8 INIT 0

ATTACK +3

DMG REDUCTION 3

DEFENSE +2

DAMAGE 2d6p

short REACH TOP SAVE n/a

MOVEMENT

CRAWL:	1¼
WALK:	2½
JOG:	5
RUN:	7½
SPRINT:	10

ATTACK:
Worker ants boldly attack any creature seeing them as both competitors and potential meals; their mandible attack inflicts 2d6p points of damage

SAVES

PHYSICAL:	+3
MENTAL:	+3
DODGE:	+3

WEAKNESSES:
Worker ants may be kept at bay with an aggressively presented open flame

GIANT SOLDIER ANT

HIT POINTS:	10+3d8
SIZE/WEIGHT:	T/10 lbs.
TENACITY:	Brave
INTELLIGENCE:	Semi
FATIGUE FACTOR:	n/a

SPEED 5 INIT 0

ATTACK +5

DMG REDUCTION 4

DEFENSE +2

DAMAGE 2d8p

short REACH TOP SAVE n/a

MOVEMENT

CRAWL:	1¼
WALK:	2½
JOG:	5
RUN:	7½
SPRINT:	10

ATTACK:
Soldier ants attack with mandibles doing 2d8p damage and a poisonous stinger; the latter requires a CON check versus VF 10, a save results in only 1d4p damage while failure indicates 3d4p damage

SAVES

PHYSICAL:	+3
MENTAL:	+4
DODGE:	+3

WEAKNESSES:
Soldier ants may be kept at bay with an aggressively presented open flame

Ants often appear in fables and children's stories to represent industriousness and cooperative effort, and are even mentioned in religious texts of The Holy Mother and The Raiser.

In the jungles of Tarisato, giant ants are considered to be the messengers of the gods, and their bites are often said to have curative properties by bringing relief from fever.

Where their territories overlap, goblinoids have been known to use ant bites in initiation ceremonies as tests of endurance.

[1] Giant ant saliva can be used with mud to create a strong poultice that will help lacerations to heal faster than normal (comparable to a character with Novice mastery in First Aid tending the wound). This treatment is not cumulative with any First Aid skills, merely an alternative.

[2] Giant ant legs may be used as an alternative material component in the mage's Wall Walk spell. Doing so increases movement rate by 25%.

[3] The pincers of the giant soldier ant are prized in warrior cultures and may bring as much as 10-30 sp depending upon size and condition.

[4] Giant ant eggs are delicacies in many locales, especially with nobility and other wealthy individuals. They sell for 80 sp per pound.

[5] Giant ant poison can be gathered and used by nefarious types, and is worth, in certain circles, 100 sp per dose.

GENERAL INFO

ACTIVITY CYCLE:	Diurnal
NO. APPEARING:	1 scout, 2d4 foragers, 20+4d12 colony
% CHANCE IN LAIR:	25%
FREQUENCY:	Commonplace (workers), Frequent (soldiers)
ALIGNMENT:	Non
VISION TYPE:	Standard
AWARENESS/SENSES:	Pheromone communication
HABITAT:	Any
DIET:	Omnivorous
ORGANIZATION:	Colony
CLIMATE/TERRAIN:	Any

YIELD

MEDICINAL:	saliva, as poultice[1]
SPELL COMPONENTS:	legs, in the Wall Walk spell[2]
HIDE/TROPHY:	pincers[3]
TREASURE:	incidental
EDIBLE:	yes[4]
OTHER:	corpses contain one dose of poison[5]
EXPERIENCE POINT VALUE:	40 (workers), 100 (soldiers)

APE

GORILLA
KILLER APE

Also Known As:
Angry Man of the Jungle

According to Svimohzish legend, the "Angry Men of the Jungle" were slavers in a previous life — cursed by the gods to "return in the skins of beasts and be set upon by men, hunted and sold as they themselves had done." It's a interesting tale but I don't hold to it.

I've seen the great apes both in captivity at the great arenas and in the wild. I've detected nothing human about them — no divine spark, no hint of a soul or intellect. On the other hand, I can't say they are evil.

They are wild beasts to my eye and, like any other wild animal, they will fight fiercely when cornered, protecting themselves or their young. Otherwise, they seem shy by nature and are more prone to avoid a fight than to seek one.

When traveling in the Vohven Jungle years ago, a band of gorillas followed our party for the better part of a day. Though initially unsure of their intent, we ascribed it to curiosity than any ill purpose. By nightfall we had grown accustomed to catching glances of them from afar and were no more concerned about their presence than if we had seen a field of cattle.

This genial tale should not presuppose one to believe that they're not to be feared or respected. As with most legends, there is some kernel of truth behind the Svimohzish view of the ape. They can be aggressive during times of famine or drought when food is scarce. They are territorial by nature. Stories abound of unfortunates who ventured too near a nest of young, or passed some imaginary line in the forest and paid dearly for their boldness.— ᛟ

These primates have long, dark hair and powerful arms longer than their legs. They live in tropical or subtropical forests over a wide range of elevations from mountaintops to valleys as low as sea level. They are highly intelligent when compared to most animals, and can be quite dangerous when provoked.

A mature male gorilla stands 5½ to 5¾ feet tall and can weight as much as 450 pounds. Their unusually long arm span (7 to 8½ feet) provides them greater reach than a human. These slump-shouldered creatures move quadrupedally using a gait called knuckle-walking. They can climb trees sturdy enough to support their weight but apes are ground dwellers and climb only to reach succulent fruits. Gorillas are not swimmers.

The killer ape male is slightly larger than the gorilla, being over 6 feet tall when upright and weighing over 500 pounds. Killer apes have even darker hair, long canines that protrude from the mouth even when closed, and pronounced bony crests on the top and back of their skulls. These crests give their heads a more conical shape and help anchor their powerful jaw muscles.

The females of both species stand about a foot shorter and weight half as much as males.

SIGN/TRACKS

Knuckle Strike

Hind

RANGE ON TELLENE

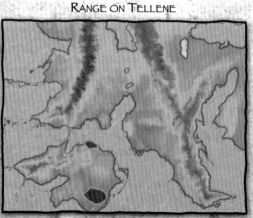

SIZE COMPARISON

8 ft

4 ft

Killer Ape

Gorilla

GORILLA

HIT POINTS:	30+4d8
SIZE/WEIGHT:	L / 325-450 lbs
TENACITY:	Steady
INTELLIGENCE:	Obtuse
FATIGUE FACTOR:	-2

SPEED: 4 INIT: -1
ATTACK: +8
DEFENSE: +3
DMG REDUCTION: 6
DAMAGE: see below
medium REACH
TOP SAVE: 8

MOVEMENT

CRAWL:	5
WALK:	10
JOG:	15
RUN:	20
SPRINT:	25

SAVES

PHYSICAL:	+10
MENTAL:	+7
DODGE:	+8

ATTACK:
If provoked, gorillas attack by mauling an opponent, using their tremendous strength to inflict 2d4p+6 with their fists.
Bite attacks deal 2d3p damage.

SPECIAL ABILITIES:
Hiding and Sneaking 50% each

KILLER APE

HIT POINTS:	30+5d10
SIZE/WEIGHT:	L / ≥ 500 lbs
TENACITY:	Steady
INTELLIGENCE:	Slow
FATIGUE FACTOR:	-2

SPEED: 3 INIT: -2
ATTACK: +12
DEFENSE: +6
DMG REDUCTION: 8
DAMAGE: see below
medium REACH
TOP SAVE: 8

MOVEMENT

CRAWL:	5
WALK:	10
JOG:	15
RUN:	20
SPRINT:	25

SAVES

PHYSICAL:	+13
MENTAL:	+8
DODGE:	+8

ATTACK:
Can maul as gorillas for 2d4p+7; they may alternatively use clubs (attacking with Speed 5 for 2d6p+7 points of damage).
Bite attacks deal 2d3p+3 damage.

SPECIAL ABILITIES:
Hiding and Sneaking 60% each

GENERAL INFO

ACTIVITY CYCLE:	Diurnal
NO. APPEARING:	3-12
% CHANCE IN LAIR:	20%
FREQUENCY:	Frequent
ALIGNMENT:	Non
VISION TYPE:	Standard
AWARENESS/SENSES:	Standard
HABITAT:	Rainforest
DIET:	Herbivorous
ORGANIZATION:	Troop
CLIMATE/TERRAIN:	Tropical woodlands

GENERAL INFO

ACTIVITY CYCLE:	Nocturnal
NO. APPEARING:	2-8
% CHANCE IN LAIR:	65%
FREQUENCY:	Sporadic
ALIGNMENT:	Neutral Evil
VISION TYPE:	Low Light Vision
AWARENESS/SENSES:	Standard
HABITAT:	Rainforest
DIET:	Omnivorous, but prefers meat
ORGANIZATION:	Troop
CLIMATE/TERRAIN:	Tropical woodlands

[1] A pinch of gorilla fur can be used as a component for the ninth level Polymorph to Primate spell, and can be sold for 1 sp per pinch. There is, of course, a limited market for this specialty item and bulk purchasers will opt to buy an entire pelt (see below).

[2] Gorilla pelts go for about 15 sp on the open market. Gorilla fangs are worth 1 sp per fang.

[3] 'Bush meat' is a prized meal when available and some inhabitants of Svimohzia consider gorilla brains to be extremely fine delicacies. A butcher will buy a fresh gorilla carcass for 60 sp.

[4] The consumption of gorilla blood and flesh is considered unclean in Ozhvinmish. Those who ignore this taboo will be shunned.

Notes and figures quoted apply to killer apes as well. Most individuals are unaware of the difference.

YIELD

MEDICINAL:	nil
SPELL COMPONENTS:	fur, in the Polymorph to Primate spell[1]
HIDE/TROPHY:	pelts and fangs[2]
TREASURE:	none of their own (killer apes may act as guards)
EDIBLE:	yes[3]
OTHER:	blood and flesh unclean in some areas[4]
EXPERIENCE POINT VALUE:	450 (gorilla), 925 (killer ape)

Combat/Tactics:

Gorillas are usually not aggressive unless threatened, though merely looking directly into the ape's eyes may be enough to provoke it into attacking. Killer apes are much more temperamental, especially when hungry (and since they need to eat about 20 pounds of food each day, hunger is rarely far away).

If challenged, an ape screams, beats his chest and/or breaks branches, bares his teeth and then charges forward. Apes attack first with their fists to grasp their opponent or knock him to the ground. Once an ape successfully grabs an opponent with its massive fist, it automatically inflicts a bite attack with its sharp canines every 5 seconds thereafter. An ape's grip can be broken with a successful knock-back or Feat of Strength (vs. d20p+13). The latter can be attempted after each bite attack. While caught, a victim can only attack with a Small-sized melee weapon.

Gorillas and killer apes are highly intelligent animals and able to use simple tools and even weapons in the case of killer apes (such as improvising a club from a fallen tree branch). The latter may be taught to use more effective weapons.

Habitat/Society:

Gorillas live in jungles or on the tree-covered slopes of mountains, in groups of 5 to 10 individuals led by at least one dominant male. Humans often refer to this leader as a silverback because of the distinctive silver hair that appears as the male matures. Younger males without silvery hair are simply called blackbacks.

Killer apes are born into gorilla troops, leaving when they are about 11 years old and silver hair starts to appear on their backs. After departing, they travel alone or with a group of blackback killer apes until they can attract females to form a new group and start breeding. As with the less bloodthirsty gorillas, the silverback is the most powerful killer ape and leads the troop, making all the decisions, mediating conflicts (often by simply killing the ape that annoys him most), determining the movements of the troop, leading the others to food and taking responsibility for their safety and well being.

In both species, gestation lasts about nine months, with single births being most common and twins being quite rare. The young stay with their mother for several years, and reach maturity between the ages of eight to 13 years old.

A typical ape's lifespan is roughly 30 years in the wild, though a well cared for pack ape might live to be as much as 50 years old.

Ecology:

The typical gorilla is a mostly herbivorous creatures, feeding on hundreds of different kinds of plants, including fruits, leaves and shoots, though it occasionally enjoys the pulpy crunch of small insects. Because they live in regions containing highly nutritious, locally abundant vegetation, they travel much shorter distances; they also have smaller home ranges and larger group sizes than their meat-eating kin.

The killer ape is technically an omnivore, able to subsist upon the same plants as the common gorilla, but it has strong carnivorous tendencies. When hunting, killer apes stalk with a silence that seems incredible for such a large beast, waiting until the last moment to pounce. Killer apes are jealous creatures and often hide their kills in dense vegetation or carry them up trees. Because they prefer to hunt for prey, killer apes have larger home ranges and daily travel distances than the herbivorous gorillas. Their diet consists mostly of monkeys and various ungulates, but they will eat almost any living creature from dung beetles to large humanoids.

Despite their size and strength, both species of primates are naturally afraid of crocodiles and alligators and cross water only if they can do so without getting wet. They occasionally compete for resources with leopards, lions and other big hunting cats.

On Tellene:

Some talented animal trainers are able to train gorillas for use as beasts of burden. They can be trained to carry equipment and provisions, can negotiate tunnels and underground passages in ways that mules cannot and also have the advantage of being able to hand the owner what he needs. Other than these special abilities, pack apes are identical in appearance and statistics to the standard gorilla; a killer ape cannot be trained as a pack ape.

Of course, of particular concern to the owner of a pack ape is their dangerous nature if not well treated. A mistreated or overloaded pack ape sheds its training more quickly than any other beast of burden, and when it does, it can be extremely dangerous. Such a pack ape attacks its master with great ferocity, doing double damage due to extreme rage.

The largest populations of gorillas and killer apes can be found in the Miznoh Forest and the barely accessible regions of the dense Vohven Jungle, the latter being a foreboding stretch of tropical rain forest occupying much of southern Svimohzia. The monarchs of the isle are mostly content to leave it as it is, to let sleeping terrors lie undisturbed, or to pretend it does not exist at all.

RED DIAMONDS, RED BLOOD

My chilling encounter with killer apes

Venture into the Vohven Jungle and you'll find a massive and largely uncharted wilderness occupied by great numbers of wild beasts and tribesmen of many races. There seems to be no end to the strange creatures that live in that green emerald sea, and among them are the apes that I'll speak of now. Pay careful attention to my tale and perhaps you won't make the same mistakes I did.

I was in Emosvom, the largest settlement on the jungle edge, when a powerful member of the Golden Alliance approached my band of treasure hunters. He wanted us to seek out a lost city deep within the rain forest, which legends said stood upon the only known ground where one could find the rare red diamonds. We agreed to his terms, and began our journey into the jungle only two days later.

Although I could tell it pained him to do so, our new employer sent his best hunter, a half-dozen fighting men and a couple of porters with us. I suspect he was more worried by the possibility we might take the diamonds and run, rather than being concerned for our welfare. The hunter, Zhuvar of the Vezdor family, boasted that he had slain with his own hand over 100 gorillas. In hindsight, I believe this conversation was what lowered my defenses; if a crude man like this could easily kill the hulking beasts, we probably had little to fear from them or the other jungle creatures that awaited us.

I do not know how many miles our journey covered, though I'm sure the Izhoven River voyage alone carried us over 200 miles. Finally, we left the shallow boats and found ourselves deep in the rain forest. Even the fallen leaves were soggy under my boots, and the damp made the earth and standing waters somewhat odorous.

After nearly a week of cautious walking, and a few minor encounters with native humans and humanoids, Zhuvar pointed out certain gorilla signs. Thick tree boughs were scattered upon the ground with the husks of wild plants, and a large nest showing that an ape had spent the night there. Further on, Zhuvar studied the ground and proclaimed that two gorillas had been fighting or mating there. I was surprised to see that the prints were so large; they were certainly 8 inches long and 6 inches across the huge round toes.

I questioned Zhuvar then about why, in our entire journey, we hadn't seen any apes. There were many of the smaller primates – so many that even our breakfast consisted of tea, hard biscuit and cold monkey – but I had still hoped to see a gorilla. Zhuvar merely shrugged and said he was sure I would see a gorilla before I reached Emosvom again. How right he was…

Some three days later, we came upon a grassy clearing near a bright stream, with half-buried pottery fragments and worked stone ruins clearly showing that a building of some sort once stood here. We became excited then, and picked up our pace as best we could, accompanying the stream and the littered trail of ruins into a small, secluded valley.

Following a sharp bend in the stream, we suddenly saw a massive five-terraced stone pyramid, so unexpectedly close that it seemed to have appeared out of the air. Beyond the pyramid stood numerous irregular buildings, smaller and more greatly dominated by the vegetation that grew on and around them, but still showing us clearly that the lost city we had been searching for was here.

Excited, we all let out unthinking whoops of excitement and congratulations, but even before the echoes had died down we heard an answering call. I had already heard the roar of the lion and the panther, plus other hideous sounds, but nothing approached this new sound. If you can imagine the primitive yell of a hill giant mixed with a lion's roar, you may get some approximate notion of what I heard then. To make matters worse, it wasn't just one cry or two. It was the roar of dozens, perhaps hundreds of creatures, pouring out their voices in an unrestrained fervor of emotion. It seemed like the entire jungle was trembling, and my ears felt like they were going to burst from the noise. Then, out of each of the ruined doorways, windows and holes in the walls sprang many gorillas, grinning horribly and beating their chests with their fists to produce a loud hollow sound like a drum.

I had expected a large, burly monkey but nothing had prepared me for creatures like these. Their great hairy bodies seemed too large for their legs and their muscular arms too long for their bodies. Each had a bristled crest that rose and fell with the working of their wrinkled foreheads, and the expressions of rage and fury on their jet-black faces was almost demonic. Worse, the sharp teeth and fangs bore strong evidence that these were not the simple plant-eating gorillas that Zhuvar so cavalierly dispatched. No, these were carnivores – and we were their prey.

However, this was no time to contemplate this nightmare. We were clearly outnumbered. We retreated hurriedly, attempting to maintain some order of discipline, when the creatures rushed us. They approached with amazing rapidity, shuffling hastily on all fours in a strange rocking motion, all the while displaying those fearful teeth and tusks. Our orderly procession quickly fell to shreds and we fled without thought of honor or dignity.

The horrors I saw that day still cause me restless nights. The image of a carnivorous ape seizing Zhuvar's wrist and dragging the hand into its maw, chomping greedily on it like a piece of ripe fruit, will haunt me until the day I die. All around me, friends old and new fell like wheat before the scythe, and the rich coppery scent of blood filled the air as rapidly as the horrific screams of the dying.

Fortunately, I was a fine runner in those days, and managed to keep a fast enough pace that I stayed barely ahead of my pursuers. Only the lucky chance of a nearby tributary into the Izhoven saved me, as I dived in and let the current sweep me away. — ᚠ

ARAKIAN

Also Known As: Burrowers, Tunnel Terrors, Barakans, Death Beetles. Krumurs

Brood guards are fierce combatants and will fight to the death to protect both their queen and the hive's brood.

I have long been both fascinated and terrified by these mysterious tunnel dwelling creatures. In Paru'Bor I was laying over in the town of Vurinido waiting for a courier to deliver a message when a large building and a portion of the town's wall collapsed into a huge sink hole.

Further investigation soon revealed a complex of arakian tunnels had collapsed bringing down the structures above it. The mystery of why dozens of townspeople had gone missing in the previous months had been solved.

Arakian workers had honeycombed the earth under the entire town and warriors had been snatching victims under the cover of darkness — food for the brood chambers.

A fierce campaign to eradicate the menace was mounted and a bounty in silver was paid to mercenaries who would join in on the effort. In the end it was a clan of dwarves from the Byth Mountain, their battle skills honed by decades of driving goblins from similar warrens, that succeeded in killing the queen and saving the town. To this day I'm told an annual festival is held celebrating the unity cemented between the Byth dwarves and their Paruvian neighbors.

I still have the mandible of an arakian warrior on my bookshelf — hollowed out to hold lamp oil with several wick holes drilled into it. Many a night I've written by its light and been reminded of my adventures in Vurinido. — ᚠ

The surest way of identifying a fearsome arakian warrior is the lack of a vertical mandible (note the arakian brood watcher above) and a pair of large antennae.

These insectoid creatures resemble giant beetles with large, distinctive mandibles, four long, jointed legs and two jointed arms. Their exoskeletons are usually a shiny black or dull green in color. Other physical characteristics of a single arakian, however, depend on its physical caste. In an arakian colony, there are workers, warriors, brood watchers and queens, each with a distinct role and morphology.

Workers have a single small mandible opposite a much larger, scimitar-like one, which they use in combination to carry food, manipulate objects, cut vegetation and to tunnel through the earth to construct nests. Their ridged exoskeleton is roughly $4\frac{1}{2}$ to 5 feet long and weighs around 100 pounds. Warriors are slightly larger, with a smooth exoskeleton about 6 feet long, weighing around 200 pounds, and with a pair of sharp, poisonous mandibles. Workers and warriors also sport long antennae atop their heads, which they use to detect air currents and vibrations as well as transmit and receive signals by touch.

Brood watchers lack these antennae, but instead have a large beak-like hood that serves in that function, as well as being sturdy enough to provide additional protection for its head. Brood watchers have a body with a ridged, spiked upper area and smooth lower back that can reach 8 feet in length and weigh over 400 pounds.

SIGN/TRACKS

Tracks of an arakian warrior.

RANGE ON TELLENE

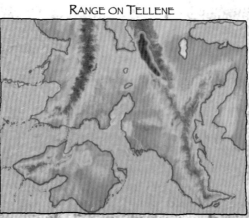

SIZE COMPARISON (BROOD WATCHER)

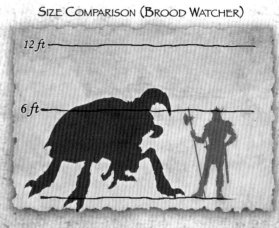

12 ft

6 ft

A typical colony has only a single queen, though larger nests may have multiple queens. These giant females resemble a massive grub with the legs and antennae of a worker or warrior, and a huge head with two razor-sharp mandibles. An arakian queen can grow to be nearly 27 feet long and weigh as much as three tons. The giant body and small legs makes them roughly immobile. For every season a queen lives, her bulk increases, making it necessary for workers to enlarge her chambers on a regular basis.

Arakians are also sensitive to the pheromones of their species; all arakians leave a trail of these pheromones as they travel along the ground. The scent provides a path for other arakians to follow, though the pheromones eventually dissipate unless reinforced by frequent travel.

Combat/Tactics:

Unless interrupted or attacked, workers ignore other creatures, concentrating only on the instructions their leaders provide. Warriors, on the other hand, assault any non-arakian that approaches too closely. Warriors attack with their sharp mandibles (inflicting 2d10p damage and subjecting the victim to an enzymatic toxin) but will likely initiate combat by spitting sticky goo at a single enemy up to 10 feet away. Any Medium or smaller creature struck is helplessly immobilized for 20+2d20p minutes, unless he succeeds at a Feat of Strength check (vs. d20p+8) to break free from the goo. Large creatures are less covered by the goo and need only check vs. d20p+4, while Huge and larger creatures are not impeded at all.

Brood watchers are even more terrifying, with razor-sharp mandibles, more adhesive spittle (Medium vs. d20p+10, or Large vs. d20p+6) and a poisonous bite. Fortunately, the brood watchers rarely leave the confines of the hive. Their primary concern is the protection of the queen and her eggs. Brood watchers prepare for possible disaster by cocooning no less than 2 to 12 warriors and 3 to 4 workers, as well as several sources of food (which usually includes some human or demi-human victims). If a battle appears to be going against the hive, a brood watcher transmits the signal to the workers to collapse the tunnels, thus cutting off the enemy from the queen.

When threatened, brood watchers produce a loud and fearsome hissing noise by squeezing air out from under their exoskeleton.

Because of her immensely bloated body, the queen cannot physically attack. However, she can exert a form of psychic mind control. Those failing an opposed Wisdom check (vs. d20p+12) become automatons under her control. This power is limited to a 30' radius. Those under her control will perform any action she desires short of self-destruction.

The queen coordinates all hive activity including defense. If attacked and brought below 25% of her total Hit Points, she sends a pheromone alert to the entire nest, instructing them to gather as many eggs as they can and flee to safety. With these eggs, they will start a new hive. If the surviving arakians include two brood watchers, the hive splits, each following a watcher, and creating two hives. Warriors protecting the queen stay and fight to the death.

ARAKIAN WARRIOR

HIT POINTS:	25+3d8
SIZE/WEIGHT:	M/200 lbs
TENACITY:	Brave
INTELLIGENCE:	Animal, Low
FATIGUE FACTOR:	n/a

SPEED 8 / INIT 0 / ATTACK +7 / +4 / DMG REDUCTION 6 / DEFENSE / see below / short REACH / DAMAGE / TOP SAVE n/a

ATTACK:
Warriors attack every 8 seconds with their mandibles doing 2d10p damage. Additionally, any wound subjects the recipient to an enzymatic toxin. This causes an additional 2d8p points of damage unless a save versus a VF 7 poison is made.

SPECIAL DEFENSES:
not subject to Threshold of Pain checks

MOVEMENT

CRAWL:	5
WALK:	10
JOG:	15
RUN:	20
SPRINT:	25

SAVES

PHYSICAL:	+8
MENTAL:	+5
DODGE:	+6

GENERAL INFO

ACTIVITY CYCLE:	Nocturnal
NO. APPEARING:	2-5 (1 per 8-12 workers in hive)
% CHANCE IN LAIR:	75%
FREQUENCY:	Sporadic
ALIGNMENT:	Non
VISION TYPE:	Standard
AWARENESS/SENSES:	Pheromone communication
HABITAT:	Subterranean tunnels
DIET:	Omnivorous
ORGANIZATION:	Hive
CLIMATE/TERRAIN:	Subterranean

YIELD

MEDICINAL:	poison glands may be used for anti-venom
SPELL COMPONENTS:	yes, in the Viscous Webbing spell[2]
HIDE/TROPHY:	mandibles, for unique curios worth up to 50 sp
TREASURE:	nil
EDIBLE:	yes[3]
OTHER:	nil
EXPERIENCE POINT VALUE:	300

Habitat/Society:

Arakians live in warm and temperate climes, beneath the surface of mountains and hills, in complex hive constructions. Here, it is the workers' job to burrow the miles of tunnels necessary for a thriving arakian hive. The warriors' duty is to protect the hive and its populace at all costs, while the brood watchers coordinate the queen's orders. While they do not carry eggs, they direct the workers that do. In well-populated hives, one brood watcher may be assigned to guard the mid-way point of one of the important tunnels to the queen.

Although the queen is the only member of the hive to collect treasure, her main function is to lay eggs (which she does on a frequent basis). In spite of her great fertility, 50% of the eggs do not develop to maturity and are consumed by the queen, whose egg production requires her to eat almost constantly.

An arakian queen can live for decades, though her servants live no more than a handful of years at most.

Ecology:

Arakians are predator, herbivore and scavenger all in a single package, and so are able to exploit a wide diversity of foodstuffs, including farm crops, livestock, dung, carrion, giant insects, spiders and other arthropods, plus human, demi-human and monster flesh. While they are not common, they do pose a deadly threat to anything that comes too near their nest. The arakians' most common sapient foes include the dwarves, goblins and other races dwelling beneath the earth.

On Tellene:

Among the Dejy of Shynabyth, there is some speculation that the Byth Mountain arakians are more prolific than anyone knows. One tale speaks of an underground dwarven outpost where more than a dozen guards slowly went missing over a period of months.

The mystery was suddenly and unexpectedly solved when nearly half of the outpost collapsed into a huge sinkhole. Supposedly, further investigation revealed a complex of arakian tunnels beneath. The monstrous workers had honey-combed the earth under the outpost and warriors had been grabbing victims under the cover of the constant darkness — as food for the brood chambers. When asked, most dwarves of Draska scoff at this rumor, though a few have been said to act shiftily or stomp away in anger.

[1] *Saliva has natural healing properties and may stave off infection.*

[2] *Arakian webbing can be used in the mage's sixth level Viscous Webbing spell. One strand of arakian webbing is worth 2 cp.*

[3] *Meat from an arakian thorax is thought to be extremely healthy, but not unless thoroughly cleaned and boiled in water for at least half an hour (the latter only for warriors and brood watchers. If this step is not performed, there may be remnants of poison that could make any-one who eats it sick enough to need bed rest for two days.) The meat is worth about 1 sp per pound on the open market.*

[4] *Smearing fluid from an arakian worker's scent gland on one's skin or clothing can fool warriors into accepting the individual as a 'friendly' and thus not targeted for attack.*

ARAKIAN WORKER

HIT POINTS:	18+2d8
SIZE/WEIGHT:	M/100 lbs
TENACITY:	Cowardly (or fearless)
INTELLIGENCE:	Semi
FATIGUE FACTOR:	n/a

SPEED 10 — INIT 5 — ATTACK +4 — DEF REDUCTION 4 — DEFENSE 0 — DAMAGE see below — REACH short — TOP SAVE n/a

MOVEMENT

CRAWL:	2½
WALK:	5
JOG:	10
RUN:	15
SPRINT:	20

SAVES

PHYSICAL:	+4
MENTAL:	0
DODGE:	+2

ATTACK:
Workers will not initiate attacks unless signaled to do so in a last ditch attempt to overwhelm attackers. In this latter case, they simply swarm at the nearest opponent biting for 2d6p while sacrificing their lives for the safety of the queen.

SPECIAL DEFENSES:
not subject to Threshold of Pain checks

GENERAL INFO

ACTIVITY CYCLE:	Nocturnal
NO. APPEARING:	20-200
% CHANCE IN LAIR:	100
FREQUENCY:	Infrequent
ALIGNMENT:	Non
VISION TYPE:	Poor
AWARENESS/SENSES:	Pheremone communication
HABITAT:	Subterranean tunnels
DIET:	Herbivorous
ORGANIZATION:	Hive
CLIMATE/TERRAIN:	Subterranean

YIELD

MEDICINAL:	saliva used to stave off infection[1]
SPELL COMPONENTS:	nil
HIDE/TROPHY:	nil
TREASURE:	nil
EDIBLE:	yes[3]
OTHER:	scent gland fluid[4]
EXPERIENCE POINT VALUE:	10 (or 48 if attacking)

ARAKIAN BROOD WATCHER

HIT POINTS:	30+5d8
SIZE/WEIGHT:	L/400 lbs
TENACITY:	Fearless
INTELLIGENCE:	Animal, High
FATIGUE FACTOR:	n/a

SPEED 7 — INIT -1
ATTACK +9
DMG REDUCTION 9
DEFENSE +5
see below
DAMAGE n/a
medium REACH
TOP SAVE ▼

MOVEMENT

CRAWL:	5
WALK:	10
JOG:	15
RUN:	20
SPRINT:	25

SAVES

PHYSICAL:	+10
MENTAL:	+8
DODGE:	+9

ATTACK: Watchers attack every 7 seconds with their powerful mandibles (both lateral and horizontal) doing 2d12p+2 damage. Additionally, any wound caused subjects the recipient to an enzymatic toxin. This causes an additional 2d8p damage unless a save vs. VF 9 poison is made.

SPECIAL DEFENSES: not subject to Threshold of Pain checks

ARAKIAN QUEEN

HIT POINTS:	40+12d8
SIZE/WEIGHT:	E/6000+ lbs
TENACITY:	Cowardly
INTELLIGENCE:	Smart
FATIGUE FACTOR:	n/a

SPEED n/a — INIT 0
ATTACK n/a
DMG REDUCTION 8
DEFENSE +2
none
DAMAGE n/a
short REACH
TOP SAVE ▼

MOVEMENT

CRAWL:	0
WALK:	0
JOG:	0
RUN:	0
SPRINT:	0

SAVES

PHYSICAL:	+10
MENTAL:	+16
DODGE:	+4

ATTACK: The queen is unable to physically attack. However, she can exert a form of mind control. Those failing an opposed Wisdom check (vs. d20p+12) become automatons under her control. This power is limited to a 30' radius.

SPECIAL DEFENSES: not subject to Threshold of Pain checks

GENERAL INFO

ACTIVITY CYCLE:	Nocturnal
NO. APPEARING:	3-12
% CHANCE IN LAIR:	100%
FREQUENCY:	Scarce
ALIGNMENT:	Non
VISION TYPE:	Extreme Low Light Vision
AWARENESS/SENSES:	Pheromone communication
HABITAT:	Tunnels
DIET:	Carnivorous
ORGANIZATION:	Hive
CLIMATE/TERRAIN:	Subterranean

GENERAL INFO

ACTIVITY CYCLE:	Nocturnal
NO. APPEARING:	1
% CHANCE IN LAIR:	100%
FREQUENCY:	Exotic
ALIGNMENT:	Neutral
VISION TYPE:	Extreme Low Light Vision
AWARENESS/SENSES:	Pheromone communication
HABITAT:	Special brood chamber
DIET:	Carnivorous
ORGANIZATION:	Solitary (hive mother)
CLIMATE/TERRAIN:	Subterranean

YIELD

MEDICINAL:	poison glands may be used for anti-venom
SPELL COMPONENTS:	yes, for the Viscous Webbing spell[2]
HIDE/TROPHY:	mandibles, for unique curios worth up to 100 sp
TREASURE:	none
EDIBLE:	yes[3]
OTHER:	none
EXPERIENCE POINT VALUE:	700

YIELD

MEDICINAL:	none
SPELL COMPONENTS:	unknown; scholarly research is needed
HIDE/TROPHY:	none
TREASURE:	incidental belongings of creatures eaten
EDIBLE:	toxic
OTHER:	none
EXPERIENCE POINT VALUE:	1000

BARROW-WIGHT

Also Known As: Cairn Creature, Witch-corpse Vostarr

If amongst the cairns or barrows of the dead, heedest to the crickets and other chirruping insects of the night, for when they do fall silent knowest thou danger looms. Shouldest thou feel a chill so cold that it doth threaten to freeze the marrow in your bones and the sickly scent of death wafts nigh, know well that the barrow-wight is near.

Often the power of the witch-corpse is such that he doth wield dominion over other undead horrors. He willst employ these minions to distract and weaken those whom deign to disturb his eternal rest before striking himself with his life draining touch. Fight him you must for nay but eternal oblivion awaits those who succumb. Be forewarned though that thy steel blades will but prick the wight. Only truest silver hath the power to surely wound.

The bond betwixt the witch-corpse and his cairn is strong and doth require the strongest admonition from the blessed powers to compel him to retreat. Acolytes must know that their faith may often prove insufficient for this task. Even my own resolute convictions have been tested by these creatures.

Lest ye be mortally feared, be comforted that the wight doth have vulnerabilities. For as a creature of the night, it is without power in the full light of the sun and must escape the luminating rays lest it perish. Such is its hatred of the sun that even the dimmest illumination, such as one might encounter at dawn or dusk, markedly weakens the creature.

Shouldest thou be blessed with fortune and slay the witch-corpse, open its barrow to the sunlight and expose its treasures to the light above. Thus will the creature be forever gone. ◓

This dreadful creature is an animated corpse whose spirit was so evil in life that it continues its existence to wreak vengeance and terror upon the living. A typical barrow-wight retains most of its now withered and petrified flesh, though it may have limbs or even large areas of its torso where muscles and tendons are so sparse that it seems impossible the bones still hold together. The state of the corpse may, however, be difficult to ascertain at first as the barrow-wight is usually clad in rich gowns or shrouds appropriate to funeral custom for a person of high status.

Though its organs no longer function, the dark energies sustaining the barrow-wight permit it speech. However, they prefer to communicate in an eerie voice that echoes softly in the heads of nearby living creatures. Barrow-wights do not require nourishment, rather they sustain their unlife by tapping the élan vital of the living. It is said that the mere touch of the creature's cold flesh may cause a hero's stamina to fail when he needs it most.

Combat/Tactics:

A barrow-wight's chilling touch drains Constitution equal to the damage rolled (armor or other damage reduction not withstanding). These cairn creatures are incredibly resistant to blows from ordinary steel weapons necessitating the use of silvered blades by heroes wishing to inflict telling blows upon the witch-corpse.

Unlike automatonic lesser undead, the barrow-wight is a cunning and patient foe, willing to (seemingly) retreat before

These evil undead are the bane of the living and are often smelled long before they are seen or make themselves known. Not the stench of rotting flesh, but rather damp musty smell of the tombs and subterranean vaults they tend to dwell in.

WILL FACTOR
12

SIZE COMPARISON

6 ft

3 ft

his enemies and return when they are less guarded. He may even gather other, less powerful, undead under his command and send them forth to weaken his victims before he arrives.

Barrow-wights cannot tolerate the direct light of the sun, for it incapacitates them, forcing them to immediately withdraw to a dark or shadowed locale. Even dim and shadowy sunlight (such as occurs at dusk, dawn, or possibly even extremely overcast or stormy days) confers a -4 penalty to the creature's Attack and Defense.

Habitat/Society/Ecology:

Many barrow-wights sullenly haunt their burial mound, deriving grim pleasure by killing despoilers of their tomb. Other wights, having a more restless or purposeful spirit, dwell in a variety of dark and desolate abodes, at times serving evil masters even more powerful than themselves.

In life, barrow-wights were often of noble birth or held some position of power over others (*e.g.*, a knight, duke or even a wealthy merchant). It is unheard of for a serf, squire or other menial person's corpse to spawn the evil of a barrow-wight, perhaps because they lacked any feeling of power in life and so their spirit does not strive to hold onto it after death.

It is thought that a barrow-wight cannot arise from a consecrated corpse or a body lacking any limb or digit thereof, though this may be merely an old wives' tale.

A wight's barrow is not only his tomb but, in large measure, his eternal prison as well. Those immutably bound to this sepulcher have but one one hope of escape, that being the ensnarement of a surrogate guardian. Any sapient human, demi-human or humanoid slain by the wight may serve this purpose. Of course, wights were doubtless haughty and proud in life and carried this trait through to their current existence. It wouldn't suit their legacy to have some orkin graverobber ensconced in their tomb. Thus they are choosy about whom they may grant unlife to even at the cost of their own freedom. Those deemed acceptable will be clad in their funereal garb and likely other objects denoting the wight's former status. The corpse will be laid upon the very same funeral slab once occupied by the current master and permitted to rise from death as a barrow-wight.

On Tellene:

The Fhokki people have a long tradition of burying their dead in cairns or barrows. Many of the oldest of these tombs are located in O'Par or Dodera and predate Kalamaran occupation of these lands. Given their age, they are frequently mistaken for hillocks or other terrain features as the burial customs of the Fhokki who once dwelled here are long forgotten – indeed if they were ever known at all.

That these long-dead corpses might, in fact, be restless spirits with vengence in their hearts is not unknown to Fhokki legend. In fact, the subject is common enough in the sagas such that these beings have a name: the *vostarr*. Tradition holds that the cairns of individuals who, in life, manifested such evil strength of will that those burying them feared their return were marked with runestones to warn visitors of the possible threat.

B

BARROW-WIGHT

HIT POINTS:	27+4d8
SIZE/WEIGHT:	M/insubstantial
TENACITY:	Brave
INTELLIGENCE:	Bright
FATIGUE FACTOR:	n/a

SPEED	INIT
10	-1

ATTACK: +11

DAMAGE REDUCTION

DEFENSE: +3

19

see below

medium REACH

n/a

TOP SAVE ▼

MOVEMENT

CRAWL:	2½
WALK:	5
JOG:	10
RUN:	15
SPRINT:	20

SAVES

PHYSICAL:	+11
MENTAL:	immune
DODGE:	+11

ATTACK:
Chilling touch inflicts 2d4p points of damage and CON drain equal to damage (save for half).

SPECIAL:
Can only be damaged fully by silvered weapons (reduces DR to 10). Weakened by sunlight.

GENERAL INFO

ACTIVITY CYCLE:	Nocturnal
NO. APPEARING:	1-4
% CHANCE IN LAIR:	95%
FREQUENCY:	Sporadic
ALIGNMENT:	Neutral Evil
VISION TYPE:	Undead Sight
AWARENESS/SENSES:	Standard
HABITAT:	Barrows
DIET:	n/a
ORGANIZATION:	Individuals
CLIMATE/TERRAIN:	Any

YIELD

MEDICINAL:	nil
SPELL COMPONENTS:	nil
HIDE/TROPHY:	nil
TREASURE:	wights are buried with many valuable grave goods
EDIBLE:	no
OTHER:	nil
EXPERIENCE POINT VALUE:	792

BASILISK

Also Known As: Great Mar'un, Stone Kregalus

I've long been fascinated with these creatures and was convinced they existed in legend only until first hand study convinced me otherwise.

Years ago a merchant arrived at the keep with an unusual item for sale - a statue of a woman with a wagging finger. The detail was amazing. The pores of the skin on her forehead. The mole on her right nostril. But most interesting of all — that wagging finger. At some point during that statue's travels it had been broken off.

Revealed inside? Intricate details in stone of bone, veins and sinew. The merchant claimed the woman had encountered a basilisk that had wandered onto her farm and was rummaging in the barn — no doubt after the livestock.

Thinking it was her drunken husband back from a night of carousing at the local tavern she burst in to scold him. She was found in her stance of cold stone the next morning. The statue (and the story) had been passed along numerous times over the years. It now stands in the corner of the Broken Hilt Tavern at Frandor's Keep and is fondly known as the "Nagging Wife". A reminder of what might be waiting for you when you return home.

It used to be a general belief that if a man on horseback killed one of these beasts with a spear, the poison would run up the weapon and kill, not only the rider, but the horse as well. Seems like poppycock to me.

Still, perhaps it is no less strange than the fact that this dreadful lizard can be killed with the effluvium of the weasel. It is a thing I can tell you I've tried with success, when I once served a king who desired to see its body when killed but feared to risk its gaze. I simply threw the animal into the hole of the basilisk, which I spotted from the soil around it being infected. The weasel destroyed the basilisk by its odor, but died in this struggle of nature against its own self. Good for me, bad for it. — ᚠ

It is widely believed the basilisk cannot turn its head or look up. Don't you believe it. They are swift-acting and alert creatures always darting their heads about.

A basilisk has the power to turn flesh to salt with a single glance, making it a creature to be avoided. These creatures resemble certain smaller lizards, with a bulbous forehead and a large finned crest, but much larger and with four additional legs (for a total of eight). A typical adult stretches to 9 feet in length, including the tail, and weighs nearly 250 pounds. Most basilisks have tan-colored hides and dwell in arid deserts, where they simply bury themselves under sand dunes or occupy ruins or other desolate areas. Others have greenish-yellow hides, and make their homes in dense woodlands where they lair in hidden caves and burrows.

When a basilisk hisses, all other serpents and reptiles flee from it in fear (no saving throw). The tan-colored variety can destroy shrubs, not only by its contact, but those even that it has breathed upon; it scorches grasses, and even breaks stones, so tremendous is its noxious influence. Many believe that the basilisk creates deserts from once plentiful lands.

SIGN/TRACKS

Fore

Hind

RANGE ON TELLENE

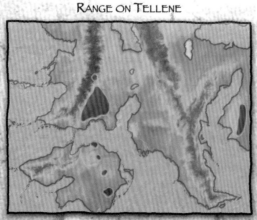

SIZE COMPARISON

6 ft

3 ft

Combat/Tactics:

A basilisk's flesh-to-salt power (Dexterity save vs. d20p+10) is only effective when an opponent meets its gaze. However, as these lizard-like creatures have a 300° field of view, any that approach within 30 feet of the basilisk (unless from the rear) are presumed to have met its gaze unless they take countermeasures (see below). Basilisks are immune to the petrifying gaze of other *great mar'un* but not to their own.

Characters covering their eyes, wearing blind-folds, and so-on suffer a -8 penalty on attacks. Characters that simply avert their gaze may be able to detect the creature through kicked-up dust, seeing its tail or feet, through peripheral vision and so on. These characters suffer a -4 to their Attack, but are still susceptible to the creature purposefully gazing at their eyes. Fortunately, in the latter case, the character gains a +4 bonus to his save. Unfortunately, those that avert their gaze or use a similar method that causes their body to contort unnaturally in combat (in contrast to simply wearing a blind-fold), suffer a -3 to all Damage rolls as well.

Basilisks have other, horrific natural weapons as well. Their fanged bite causes damage as well as a fatal poison[1] (save indicates mere weakness and loss of strength). Further, their blood causes paralysis on contact[2]. Those employing hacking weapons that score a successful hit cause all those within a 5-foot radius to save versus poison or fall victim to paralysis. Due to their nature, puncturing weapons only cause a save for the wielder, and with a +4 bonus, but the poison runs up the blade and will inflict any mount ridden or others that may come in contact with the shaft (such as those in the front rank if wielded from a back rank). Crushing weapons, of course, require no save as blood is not actually spilt.

Strangely, basilisk powers are completely ineffective against weasels, their natural enemies. Weasel urine even acts as a VF 12 poison that slays a basilisk on contact, should it fail its saving throw (vs. d20p+12).

Those converted to salt must be handled carefully and avoid water as the salt pillar will dissolve. The basilisks use their victims as salt licks, so if left in the lair, creatures converted to salt will be ingested over time (and unrecoverable by spell).

Habitat/Society/Ecology:

A basilisk burrow typically consists of a shallow ditch or tunnel with a central chamber and several exits. The central chamber often measures up to 12 feet in diameter and lies 5 to 15 feet deep in the soil, with the entrance covered by dirt or sand when the basilisk is at home.

Females tolerate the presence of males only long enough to mate, lay and hatch their eggs, which they do several times within their century-long lifespan. Male and female basilisks eat all but one of each young basilisk that hatches from their eggs.

On Tellene:

Basilisks can be found in the Elos desert and eastern Elenon slopes with frightening regularity. They can also be found in various jungles and desolate woodlands as well as the Khydoban desert.

[1] *Basilisk venom is a Virulence Factor 9 poison. Failing a saving throw results in physical incapacitation within 2d6 minutes followed by death 4d6 hours thereafter (clerical remediation prior to death is, of course, possible). If the save is made, the victim suffers weakness and nausea resulting in a -2 penalty to Attack, Defense and Damage rolls for 2d12 hours. These effects are cumulative for multiple bites.*

[2] *Basilisk blood is a paralytic toxin resulting in incapacitation for 4d6 hours if a saving throw is failed. Onset time is a mere 3d10 seconds.*

BASILISK

HIT POINTS:	24+5d8
SIZE/WEIGHT:	M/250 lbs.
TENACITY:	Steady
INTELLIGENCE:	Animal, low
FATIGUE FACTOR:	3

SPEED		INIT
10	ATTACK +9	4
DEFENSE +3	DMG REDUCTION 5	
2d10p		8
short REACH	DAMAGE	TOP SAVE ▼

MOVEMENT

CRAWL:	1¼
WALK:	2½
JOG:	5
RUN:	7½
SPRINT:	10

SAVES

PHYSICAL:	+9
MENTAL:	+7
DODGE:	+8

ATTACK: Gaze turns flesh to salt (DEX save vs d20p+10, with +4 bonus for averting eyes but -3 Damage). Bite deals 2d10p plus VF 9 poison (failed saves incapacitates for 4d6 hours and death; success only -2 to Attack, Defense and Damage for 2d12 hours).

SPECIAL: Blood causes paralysis on contact (within 3d10 seconds).[2]

GENERAL INFO

ACTIVITY CYCLE:	Diurnal
NO. APPEARING:	1
% CHANCE IN LAIR:	33%
FREQUENCY:	Sporadic
ALIGNMENT:	Non
VISION TYPE:	Standard
AWARENESS/SENSES:	Standard
HABITAT:	Burrows in deserts and woodlands
DIET:	Carnivorous
ORGANIZATION:	Solitary
CLIMATE/TERRAIN:	Sub-Tropical to Temperate lowlands

YIELD

MEDICINAL:	bile, for Stone to Flesh (not Salt to Flesh!) antidote
SPELL COMPONENTS:	eyes, for a potent Flesh to Salt or Stone to Flesh spell
HIDE/TROPHY:	frill can fetch a decent price (100-200 sp)
TREASURE:	incidental in lair
EDIBLE:	yes, but poisonous blood infuses all meat[2]
OTHER:	nil
EXPERIENCE POINT VALUE:	850

BEARS
BLACK BEAR   GRIZZLY BEAR
BROWN BEAR   CAVE BEAR

While somewhat common, bears are, nevertheless, quite breathtaking to behold in their natural habitat. Their magnificent muscle tone, great bulk and regal heads always fill me with great respect.

If proper precautions are taken one has little to fear from bears. They spend their time hunting for food, sleeping and caring for their young. They can even be quite playful at times, and often, when they do attack, it is only because they have been searching for food.

Bears do not normally go looking for fights in my experience. Trouble often comes when one finds himself between a bear and some food source or when the animal feels it (or its young) are threatened.

When traveling in bear country, I find it best to make some sort of sound as I walk. That way, I don't suddenly come upon a bear and surprise it. The last thing you want to do is surprise a bear. Trust me on this.

Always beware when entering caves for these amazing beasts use caves for shelter. They rarely enjoy having unexpected visitors within their lairs. That is cause for an unbridled attack in their minds. — ⚡

These bulky, robust animals are mostly found in the northern continent forests or scrub. Four particular subspecies dominante, as listed below.

Black Bear

The smallest of the bear family, the black-furred omnivores stand about 2½ to 3 feet tall at the shoulder and weigh around 400 pounds. When rearing up on its hind legs, a black bear stands about 5 feet tall. Its fur is soft and can range from blonde to light brown to jet black, though the lighter color variations are rare.

Brown Bear

A typical brown bear weighs in the vicinity of 600 pounds, is 3½ feet tall at the shoulder when on all fours and stands roughly 6½ feet tall on its hind legs. Despite the name, the actual shade of its thick, shaggy fur can vary from light sand to reddish to dark brown. Brown bears also have a large hump of muscle on the upper back, which gives them increased digging power with their foreclaws.

SIGN/TRACKS

RANGE ON TELLENE

SIZE COMPARISON

Fore

Hind

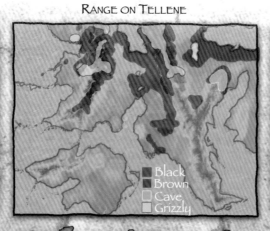

Black
Brown
Cave
Grizzly

10 ft

5 ft

Cave Bear

Grizzly Bear

Black Bear

Brown Bear

BLACK BEAR

HIT POINTS:	29+4d8
SIZE/WEIGHT:	L/400 lbs.
TENACITY:	Steady
INTELLIGENCE:	Animal, High
FATIGUE FACTOR:	-4

SPEED 4 · INIT -1 · ATTACK +8 · DMG REDUCTION · DEFENSE -1 · 9 · 2d6p+4 · 11 · short REACH · DAMAGE · TOP SAVE

MOVEMENT

CRAWL:	10
WALK:	15
JOG:	20
RUN:	25
SPRINT:	30

SAVES

PHYSICAL:	+9
MENTAL:	+8
DODGE:	+7

ATTACK:
Black bears generally attack only if provoked; when doing so they bat opponent with their paws

SPECIAL DEFENSES:
none

GENERAL INFO

ACTIVITY CYCLE:	Any (primarily Diurnal)
NO. APPEARING:	1-3
% CHANCE IN LAIR:	n/a
FREQUENCY:	Ubiquitous
ALIGNMENT:	Non
VISION TYPE:	Standard
AWARENESS/SENSES:	Keen sense of smell (Tracking 90%)
HABITAT:	Dens near water
DIET:	Omnivorous
ORGANIZATION:	Individuals
CLIMATE/TERRAIN:	Temperate forest

YIELD

MEDICINAL:	gall bladder used as antidote to poison
SPELL COMPONENTS:	nil
HIDE/TROPHY:	hides used for clothing and rugs
TREASURE:	incidental
EDIBLE:	yes
OTHER:	none

EXPERIENCE POINT VALUE: 417

BROWN BEAR

HIT POINTS:	36+6d8
SIZE/WEIGHT:	L/600 lbs.
TENACITY:	Steady
INTELLIGENCE:	Animal, High
FATIGUE FACTOR:	-3

SPEED 4 · INIT 0 · ATTACK +12 · DMG REDUCTION · DEFENSE +3 · 11 · 2d6p+7 · 12 · medium REACH · DAMAGE · TOP SAVE

MOVEMENT

CRAWL:	10
WALK:	15
JOG:	20
RUN:	25
SPRINT:	30

SAVES

PHYSICAL:	+14
MENTAL:	+10
DODGE:	+11

ATTACK:
Brown bears attack by swatting foes with their paws; if this bear scores two consecutive hits, it has grabbed its foe in a bear hug and every 4 seconds thereafter inflicts damage automatically (do not roll to attack); the hug can be broken by a successful Feat of Strength

GENERAL INFO

ACTIVITY CYCLE:	Nocturnal
NO. APPEARING:	1-6
% CHANCE IN LAIR:	n/a
FREQUENCY:	Commonplace
ALIGNMENT:	Non
VISION TYPE:	Standard
AWARENESS/SENSES:	Keen sense of smell (Tracking 90%)
HABITAT:	Dens near water
DIET:	Omnivorous
ORGANIZATION:	Individuals
CLIMATE/TERRAIN:	Temperate forest

YIELD

MEDICINAL:	bile is said to cure hemorrhoids
SPELL COMPONENTS:	nil
HIDE/TROPHY:	hides used for clothing and rugs
TREASURE:	incidental
EDIBLE:	yes
OTHER:	none

EXPERIENCE POINT VALUE: 792

GRIZZLY BEAR

HIT POINTS:	41+8d8
SIZE/WEIGHT:	H/1000 lbs.
TENACITY:	Brave
INTELLIGENCE:	Animal, High
FATIGUE FACTOR:	-2

SPEED 4 — **INIT** 0
ATTACK +16
DMG REDUCTION 13
DEFENSE +6
2d8p+9
medium **REACH** — **DAMAGE** — **TOP SAVE** 12

MOVEMENT

CRAWL:	10
WALK:	15
JOG:	20
RUN:	25
SPRINT:	30

SAVES

PHYSICAL:	+18
MENTAL:	+13
DODGE:	+15

ATTACK:
Grizzlies attack by swatting foes with their paws; if this bear scores two consecutive hits, it has grabbed its foe in a bear hug and every 4 seconds thereafter inflicts damage automatically (do not roll to attack); the hug can be broken by a successful Feat of Strength

GENERAL INFO

ACTIVITY CYCLE:	Nocturnal
NO. APPEARING:	1-4
% CHANCE IN LAIR:	n/a
FREQUENCY:	Frequent
ALIGNMENT:	Non
VISION TYPE:	Standard
AWARENESS/SENSES:	Good hearing/smell (Listening, Tracking 80%)
HABITAT:	Dens near rivers or coasts
DIET:	Omnivorous
ORGANIZATION:	Individuals
CLIMATE/TERRAIN:	Sub-arctic to Temperate forest

YIELD

MEDICINAL:	consuming genitals said to cure impotence
SPELL COMPONENTS:	nil
HIDE/TROPHY:	hides used for clothing and rugs
TREASURE:	incidental
EDIBLE:	yes
OTHER:	none

EXPERIENCE POINT VALUE: 1,425

CAVE BEAR

HIT POINTS:	42+9d8
SIZE/WEIGHT:	H/1250 lbs.
TENACITY:	Fearless
INTELLIGENCE:	Animal, High
FATIGUE FACTOR:	-2

SPEED 3 — **INIT** -2
ATTACK +18
DMG REDUCTION 12
DEFENSE +9
3d6p+10
long **REACH** — **DAMAGE** — **TOP SAVE** 13

MOVEMENT

CRAWL:	10
WALK:	15
JOG:	20
RUN:	25
SPRINT:	30

SAVES

PHYSICAL:	+20
MENTAL:	+14
DODGE:	+15

ATTACK:
Cave bears attack by swatting foes with their paws; if this bear scores two consecutive hits, it has grabbed its foe in a bear hug and every 3 seconds thereafter inflicts damage automatically (do not roll to attack); the hug can be broken by a successful Feat of Strength

GENERAL INFO

ACTIVITY CYCLE:	Nocturnal
NO. APPEARING:	1-2
% CHANCE IN LAIR:	50%
FREQUENCY:	Infrequent
ALIGNMENT:	Non
VISION TYPE:	Standard
AWARENESS/SENSES:	Good hearing/smell (Listening, Tracking 80%)
HABITAT:	Caves near water
DIET:	Carnivorous
ORGANIZATION:	Individuals
CLIMATE/TERRAIN:	Sub-arctic to Temperate forest

YIELD

MEDICINAL:	bile is said to cure hemorrhoids
SPELL COMPONENTS:	nil
HIDE/TROPHY:	hides used for clothing and rugs
TREASURE:	incidental
EDIBLE:	yes
OTHER:	none

EXPERIENCE POINT VALUE: 1,842

Grizzly Bear

The grizzly bear is a subspecies of brown bear, only much larger and with elongated canine teeth. It stands over 5 feet tall at the shoulder (or more than 10 feet tall when rearing upright) and easily weighs half a ton or more. Young grizzlies can be mistaken for adult brown bears if seen at a distance, but when viewing the maw up close and personal there can be no doubt what it truly is.

Cave Bear

Cave bears have a very broad, domed skull with a steep forehead, long thighs, massive shins and in-turning feet, making it similar in skeletal structure to the brown bear. This is the largest bear known to exist, standing over 7 feet tall at the shoulders and more than 12 feet tall when standing on its hind legs. The body is covered in thick fur of various shades of brown, but most commonly dark, chestnut brown. Thanks to its size and musculature, the cave bear (also known as the bulldog bear, because of its short muzzle) weighs well over a half-ton.

Combat/Tactics:

Most bears habitually avoid humans and their dwellings, as well as those of demi-humans and other similar creatures, but such a temperament is not predictable enough to rely on. Any bear may attack if it is surprised or feels that it, its territory or its offspring are somehow threatened. The larger the bear, the greater also is the chance that it stands and confronts opponents rather than fleeing. Regardless of size, however, only a fool believes he faces no danger where a bear is concerned.

If a brown, grizzly or cave bear successfully attacks with two consecutive claw attacks, it traps its opponent in a crushing hug, inflicting automatic damage thereafter every 4 seconds. The hug can be broken with a successful knock-back or Feat of Strength (the check varying depending on the bear; brown vs. d20p+16, grizzly vs. d20p+18, cave vs. d20p+20). A Feat of Strength can be attempted every 4 seconds after the victim is enveloped in the hug attack. While trapped in a crushing hug, a victim can only attack with a dagger or knife.

Habitat/Society:

The black bear feeds principally on plants, nuts, berries, tree bark and insects, while the brown bear supplements its similar diet with fish, caribou, bison and similar prey. The grizzly and cave bears can also subsist on vegetation and insects if necessary, but they have a distinct taste for meat and marrow. The cave bear feeds on bone even more so than the grizzly, making a cave layered with bone fragments a likely sign of cave bear habitation.

The black and brown bears dwell in open lands as well as dense woodlands, even along the coasts, though grizzlies and cave bears are only found further inland. A typical bear's den may be a small cave, or merely a hollowed-out area under a tree or rocks, inside a large tree cavity, a culvert or a shallow depression in the ground that is hidden by foliage. The cave bear prefers large caves exclusively, often ones connecting to great underground tunnel systems, in which it can feed on other underground denizens.

Bears are diurnal creatures, with black bear being most active during the day and the brown and grizzly bears preferring dawn, dusk and nighttime instead. The cave bear rarely ventures outside its lair except after dusk has fallen, though it may be active within its lair during the day. Hibernation, when a bear remains in its den for anywhere from three to seven months (shorter times in warmer climates), begins in late fall.

Whatever the species, bears also tend to be solitary, except during the summer mating season, when they remain with their new mate for several days. Any cubs from this mating (usually two) arrive about eight months later and remain with their mother for about two to four years.

The average lifespan of a bear is about 18 years.

Ecology:

Because of the black bear's tendency to hunt during the day, black bear pelts are more prevalent among hunters and trappers; the larger, more nocturnal, bears have coarser fur and their greater size and ferocity makes any increased value (due to rarity) hardly worth the effort.

Black and brown bear territories are often segregated, though the larger bears have no qualms about entering a smaller species' territory when in search of food. Smaller bears almost always flee from larger ones, only fighting when there is no other choice.

Other than men and other bear species, a bear's most common foe is the wolf pack, with which it often quarrels over a kill. Other, smaller scavengers are merely pests to the larger bear.

On Tellene:

Bears have a great range, and can be seen throughout much of the main continent, though they are least common in the southernmost lands and quite rare in the deserts.

The black bear is the most common type of bear found throughout Tellene, with a range from north of Lake Jorakk all the way down to the southern coast of Kalamar, though sightings seem to be fewer the further south one goes.

Brown and grizzly bears favor Brandobia, in particular the western slopes of the great Elenon Mountain range, while the Rokk Woods and Vrykarr Mountains are said to be the favorite haunts of cave bears.

It is rumored that, far to the north of Shadesh Bay, white-furred bears are more common, though this has not been confirmed with any degree of reliability.

BEETLE, GIANT

GIANT BEETLE
GIANT BOMBARDIER BEETLE
GIANT BORING BEETLE
GIANT FIRE BEETLE

Bastards have no necks! Find a blind spot and exploit it!

Also Known As: Armored Crawlers, Kravans

Giant beetles are a nuisance and can be real danger to those who are weak of body or lack the mettle to fight. They can deliver a painful bite usually after a rotting log is turned over or a pile of dead leaves is stepped on. Often they'll quickly scurry away to avoid a fight. Most farmers I know make little distinction between the the breeds, killing them all on sight.

The giant fire beetle and the giant bombadier beetle, however, are the ones with a well-earned reputation for fight. Avoid them at all costs.

They are much more dangerous and oft times aggressive. That hot beetle juice, as I call it, of the bombadier is quite painful and injurious if it gets on your skin. It can even cause blindness if you take you take a hit from it in the eyes.

Many a careless wanderer through the Whiven Marsh can show you the scars received from this burning liquid.

How to avoid them? If you hear a clicking sound while in the wood stop in your tracks and study the shadows around you. It may be a giant bombadier clacking it's mandibles or rubbing is hind legs as it goes into a striking stance.

Giant fire beetles are easy to spot at night or in darkened places when their glowing bodies light up. If you must fight one be sure to use the proper weapons; hacking and piercing weapons are the most effective. — ⚔

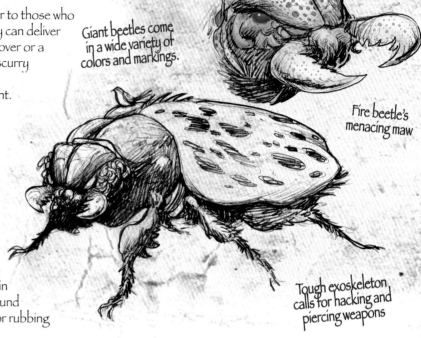

Giant beetles come in a wide variety of colors and markings.

Fire beetle's menacing maw

Tough exoskeleton calls for hacking and piercing weapons

Like their much smaller relatives, giant beetles have six multi-segmented legs and bodies divided into three parts (a head, thorax and abdomen). They also possess hard exoskeletons that are mostly shiny black or metallic in color. A pair of antennae give the giant beetle a strong olfactory sense, while two large, pincer-like mandibles enable it to hack and slash at food or foes, using small finger-like mouthparts to pull the food inside. Female giant beetles appear identical to the males. The average giant beetle is 3 feet long and weighs between 6 and 10 pounds.

The giant fire beetle is identifiable by its larger mandibles and the fact that it exhibits bioluminescence, emanating from two steadily glowing orange-yellow glands on its back and an additional one on the abdomen. The giant fire beetle also has the ability to flex its body segments. If trapped on its back, this flexing propels it off the ground with an audible click, enabling it to right itself.

Most giant bombardier beetles have a black abdomen and large black wings, with thorax, legs and head of a deep red color. However, one subspecies of giant bombardier beetle has a thorax, legs and head of deep orange, with dark brown stripes on its head an thorax and two orange spots on its large black wings. In the daylight hours, this latter beetle is sometimes mistaken for a large fire beetle (which causes quite a surprise

---

SIGN/TRACKS

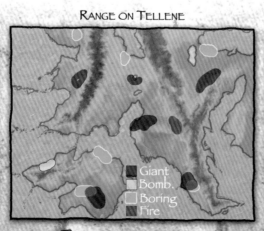

Tracks have three distinct holes

direction of travel

RANGE ON TELLENE

Giant
Bomb.
Boring
Fire

SIZE COMPARISON

6 ft

3 ft

Giant Bombardier Beetle

Giant, Fire and Boring Beetles

GIANT BEETLE

HIT POINTS:	10+1d8
SIZE/WEIGHT:	S/6 to 10 lbs.
TENACITY:	Cowardly
INTELLIGENCE:	Non
FATIGUE FACTOR:	n/a

SPEED		INIT
10	ATTACK	0
	+1	DMG REDUCTION
-1		3
DEFENSE	2d4p	
short REACH	DAMAGE	n/a TOP SAVE ▼

MOVEMENT

CRAWL:	1¼
WALK:	2½
JOG:	5
RUN:	7½
SPRINT:	10

SAVES

PHYSICAL:	+1
MENTAL:	0
DODGE:	+1

ATTACK:
Mandibles deal 2d4p points of damage.

SPECIAL DEFENSES:
none

GENERAL INFO

ACTIVITY CYCLE:	Crepuscular
NO. APPEARING:	1-20
% CHANCE IN LAIR:	n/a
FREQUENCY:	Commonplace
ALIGNMENT:	Non
VISION TYPE:	Standard
AWARENESS/SENSES:	Can sense vibrations within 30 feet
HABITAT:	Forests and fields
DIET:	Omnivorous
ORGANIZATION:	Nest
CLIMATE/TERRAIN:	Any Temperate to Tropical lands

YIELD

MEDICINAL:	said to cure skin lesions (when powdered)
SPELL COMPONENTS:	nil
HIDE/TROPHY:	nil
TREASURE:	incidental
EDIBLE:	yes
OTHER:	nil
EXPERIENCE POINT VALUE:	11

GIANT BOMBARDIER BEETLE

HIT POINTS:	14+1d8
SIZE/WEIGHT:	S/10 to 20 lbs.
TENACITY:	Cowardly
INTELLIGENCE:	Non
FATIGUE FACTOR:	n/a

SPEED		INIT
11	ATTACK	1
	+2	DMG REDUCTION
-1		2
DEFENSE	see below	
short REACH	DAMAGE	n/a TOP SAVE ▼

MOVEMENT

CRAWL:	1¼
WALK:	2½
JOG:	5
RUN:	7½
FLY:	20

SAVES

PHYSICAL:	+2
MENTAL:	0
DODGE:	+2

ATTACK:
Mandibles deal 2d4p points of damage. Three times per day, against targets within 10 feet, can attack with VF 8 poison (2d6p tissue damage at 1 point per 10 seconds; saves reduce damage to 2d4p)

SPECIAL DEFENSES:
none

GENERAL INFO

ACTIVITY CYCLE:	Crepuscular
NO. APPEARING:	3-12
% CHANCE IN LAIR:	n/a
FREQUENCY:	Infrequent
ALIGNMENT:	Non
VISION TYPE:	Standard
AWARENESS/SENSES:	Can sense vibrations within 40 feet
HABITAT:	Forests, fields, wetlands
DIET:	Omnivorous
ORGANIZATION:	Nest
CLIMATE/TERRAIN:	Any Temperate to Tropical lands

YIELD

MEDICINAL:	said to cure rashes (when applied as paste)
SPELL COMPONENTS:	none yet known though promising
HIDE/TROPHY:	nil
TREASURE:	incidental
EDIBLE:	no
OTHER:	alchemists use acid sacs in experiments
EXPERIENCE POINT VALUE:	40

GIANT BORING BEETLE

HIT POINTS:	12+1d8
SIZE/WEIGHT:	S/6 to 10 lbs.
TENACITY:	Cowardly
INTELLIGENCE:	Non
FATIGUE FACTOR:	n/a

MOVEMENT

CRAWL:	1¼
WALK:	2½
JOG:	5
RUN:	7½
SPRINT:	10

SAVES

PHYSICAL:	+1
MENTAL:	0
DODGE:	+1

SPEED 10   **INIT** 2
ATTACK 0
DMG REDUCTION
DEFENSE -1   3
DAMAGE 2d4p
short REACH   n/a
TOP SAVE ▼

ATTACK: Mandibles deal 2d4p points of damage. Roll full damage on any shield hit to reflect capacity to chew through wood.

SPECIAL DEFENSES: none

GENERAL INFO

ACTIVITY CYCLE:	Crepuscular
NO. APPEARING:	3-18
% CHANCE IN LAIR:	45%
FREQUENCY:	Commonplace
ALIGNMENT:	Non
VISION TYPE:	Standard
AWARENESS/SENSES:	Can sense vibrations within 30 feet
HABITAT:	Forests, fields, urban
DIET:	Omnivorous
ORGANIZATION:	Nest
CLIMATE/TERRAIN:	Any Temperate to Tropical lands

YIELD

MEDICINAL:	said to cure skin lesions (when applied as paste)
SPELL COMPONENTS:	useful in anti-lignin applications
HIDE/TROPHY:	nil
TREASURE:	incidental
EDIBLE:	yes
OTHER:	nil
EXPERIENCE POINT VALUE:	11

GIANT FIRE BEETLE

HIT POINTS:	17+1d8
SIZE/WEIGHT:	S/6 to 10 lbs.
TENACITY:	Cowardly
INTELLIGENCE:	Non
FATIGUE FACTOR:	n/a

MOVEMENT

CRAWL:	1¼
WALK:	2½
JOG:	5
RUN:	7½
SPRINT:	10

SAVES

PHYSICAL:	+2
MENTAL:	0
DODGE:	+1

SPEED 12   **INIT** 2
ATTACK +1
DMG REDUCTION
DEFENSE -2   3
DAMAGE 4d4p
short REACH   n/a
TOP SAVE ▼

ATTACK: Mandibles deal 4d4p points of damage.

SPECIAL DEFENSES: none

GENERAL INFO

ACTIVITY CYCLE:	Crepuscular
NO. APPEARING:	1-12
% CHANCE IN LAIR:	n/a
FREQUENCY:	Frequent
ALIGNMENT:	Non
VISION TYPE:	Standard
AWARENESS/SENSES:	Can sense vibrations within 30 feet
HABITAT:	Forests, fields, wetlands
DIET:	Omnivorous
ORGANIZATION:	Nest
CLIMATE/TERRAIN:	Any Temperate to Tropical lands

YIELD

MEDICINAL:	said to cure stomach cramps (when powdered)
SPELL COMPONENTS:	can substitute as component in Infravision spell
HIDE/TROPHY:	nil
TREASURE:	incidental
EDIBLE:	yes
OTHER:	organ glows for 2d4 days (10-foot-radius)
EXPERIENCE POINT VALUE:	25

B

when its victim gets a faceful of acid). They weigh between 10 and 20 pounds.

The destructive boring beetle (also known as the deathwatch, or woodboring, beetle) has a cylindrical body that is normally rusty brown in color but can range from reddish brown to black, sometimes with areas of pale hairs. To attract a mate, boring beetles create an audible ticking sound as they tap their heads or jaws on the sides of their wooden tunnels.

Combat/Tactics:

Giant beetles and giant fire beetles prefer to flee unless cornered or protecting their homes or young. When forced into combat, they use their sharp mandibles, slicing at an attacking enemy. They continue to attack this same foe, fleeing only when severely damaged and rarely choosing to change opponents.

As well as its own mandibles, the bombardier beetle has an additional method of attack against a single creature within 10 feet. When threatened, it combines two liquids in an internal chamber and then discharges the compound from twin tubes in the rear of its abdomen. When this now hot, acidic vapor spews forth, an audible popping sound can be heard. These tubes can swivel in almost any direction and thus enable the beetle to more easily aim at its opponent's face. This VF 8 poison causes 2d6p points of tissue damage at a rate of 1 HP per 10 seconds (if failed; saves reduce damage to 2d4p). The giant bombardier beetle can use this attack up to three times each day.

Boring beetles are voracious eaters, particularly of wooden objects. Thus, characters carrying such items (e.g., shields) may find themselves subject to some unwelcome attention. Boring beetles have even been known to collapse mines onto unsuspecting characters, though this is not through any malicious intent. Rather, the boring beetle simply consumes enough of the wooden beams to weaken the overall structure and cause the collapse.

Habitat/Society:

Giant beetles can easily be found throughout Tellene, though none have been yet reported in the seas or the frozen north. These giant insects dwell primarily in the large trees or rotting logs of marshes, but can also be found in forests, caves, abandoned wooden structures, or by the edges of ponds and rivers. Giant beetles are crepuscular and mostly solitary by nature, though anecdotal evidence hints at both daylight activity and the existence of sizeable nests.

Most female giant beetles lay between three to eight white eggs in or near the same foodstuffs they eat, with the eggs hatching into white larvae just nine days later. Larvae are generally about 6 inches long, and appear as a white grub with six legs, a reddish to brown head and a rear end that may be of any brown or black color (depending on what nourishment the grub has been ingesting). Most grubs mature over a period of 9 to 12 months, then set off to fend for themselves. Several small spines (resembling hairs or bristles) on the underside of the grub's tail are all that provide a clue to its species. The standard giant beetle larvae, for instance, has two rows of spines that diverge the further they get from the tail tip, while the fire beetle larvae has two rows of parallel spines and the bombardier larvae bears spines arranged into a 'V' shape. At the tip of its abdomen, the boring beetle larvae sports a single large spine of greater size and thickness than the other beetles; it uses this to push itself through its wooden tunnels.

Female woodboring beetles lay a few more eggs than most (some 10 to 20) in the holes and cracks of large wooden objects (usually trees). These larvae take a full year to develop from egg to adult, constantly widening their holes and tunnels as they grow and further weakening the strength of the wood. Once the larvae reaches maturity, it bores to the surface of the wood and immediately seeks a mate, ready to begin the whole cycle over again with a new generation.

Ecology:

Giant beetles feed primarily on fungi, plants (including all sorts of agricultural crops), offal and carrion. However, they also enjoy devouring giant ant larvae, making the presence of the giant beetle somewhat of a mixed blessing for farmers. Boring beetles, while they do consume such organic matter, favor rotting wood over all else.

Beetles may also serve unwitting instigators for cultures of various molds, slimes and other such fungal substances, as they gather various forms of decaying matter and waste (both magical and nonmagical) for their larvae to consume.

On Tellene:

Varieties of the giant beetle can be found throughout Tellene, but giant bombardier beetles seem most common in the Whiven Marsh – a brackish coastal swamp bordering the Brandobian Ocean on the northwest side of the Dashahn Mountains. Likewise, giant fire beetles are common to the Erasar'Kol Marsh – one of Kalamar's desolate, uninhabited eastern territories bordering the Katagas Rise just south of the Doreba River. Giant boring beetles are found in the densest forests in both the Svimohzish Isle and the northern continent.

The superstitious folk of Tellene associate the clicking of a woodboring beetle with quiet, sleepless nights (when it can be heard clearly) and believe the sound to be an omen of impending death.

Giant beetles are even mentioned in the Kabataroth, an ancient tome written by a mad prophet. In one bit of rambling text, entitled 'The Beetle and the Eagle', a giant eagle kills a family of hares despite a giant woodboring beetle's appeals. The beetle takes revenge by twice destroying the eagle's eggs. A deity (opinions on which one vary wildly) then learns of the beetle's earlier plea that the eagle had ignored. The god scolds the eagle and urges the beetle to stay away from the bird, but its effort to persuade the beetle fails; instead, the god changes the breeding season of the eagles to take place at a time when the boring beetles are not above ground. Because several of the Kabataroth's prophecies seem to have come true, scholars have spent their lifetimes studying it, hoping to make sense of this scribbled tale (among many others), but to no avail.

BOAR

GIANT BOAR
WILD BOAR

Also Known As: Razorback, Tusker, Warthog, Hogzilla

Some signs that you are entering wild boar territory are tusk slashes on tree trunks, tracks and offal. You may see a lot of trampled grasses as well. These creatures love to bed down in such material and lie in hiding.

The presence of razorbacks will be most obvious during mating season (usually in the last months before the winter snows begin to fall). This is also when their presence poses the greatest threat to you.

You see, tuskers behave oddly during mating season. They are meaner then, too, as they seem crazed-bent on a fight and proving their mettle to any prospective mates that might happen along.

Even when not mating, boars see humans as threats. Try not to let them get your scent if you can help it. Where you know that a female is raising her young, for instance, you are best to cut a wide berth around her territory if you can. Even then they oft times charge. I like to use tiger urine to hide my scent when I know I'm in wild boar territory, but you can use scat if you don't mind the smell. Some of my comrades say that the scent of any big hunting cat works, but I still have enough tiger scent left from my last trip into the Obakasek jungle. Don't ask. Anyway, wild boars don't seem to like that smell and will avoid you more than they won't.

Boars can bring you a few silver from their tusks and hides, but I don't know that the danger is worth the potential profit, myself. These creatures are quick — quick on their feet, quick with a tusk slash and quick tempered to boot. And again, unpredictable. Best avoided unless you're in boar territory and desperate for some coin but can't find any easier ways to get it.

The wild boars I've encountered seem to have some sort of inbred animosity toward dogs of any sort. I've seen them run past a pack bearer to get at a canine companion and continue pressing the attack against the poor animals even while they are speared and slashed at by masters coming to their aid. So, don't take your favorite hound with you if you want to bring it back home.

When you do fight, remember that the best shot is in the neck. If you can get an arrow or a blade in that area between the shoulder and ear you might be able to drop it in its tracks. The tough hides and the fatty tissue, plus the massive bones and rib cage, make it hard to kill. Try to find a wallow that the boars frequent and wait there for one to show itself. They move fast at night, though, so you've got to be quick. Oh, and don't try to track a wounded boar at night unless you have a death wish.

If you succeed, you will find boar meat is quite tasty if prepared properly, although some claim it to be tough and stringy. Myself, I didn't like the strong smell at first but I soon got used to it. Plus, if you're not wasteful, one giant wild boar animal can easily feed a party of several men for multiple meals. That can be real handy out in the woods when you're low on provisions. —

SIGN/TRACKS

Fore

Hind

RANGE ON TELLENE

■ Boar
■ Giant Boar

SIZE COMPARISON

6 ft

3 ft

Wild Boar

Giant Boar

These wild pigs have thick, bristled coats ranging in color from gray to brown to black. A prominent ridge of hair runs down the back, earning it its nickname of razorback. It is also known as a tusker, due to the two sharp tusks (some 3 to 12 inches long) that extend from its lower jaw. These tusks serve as both weapons and tools; wild boars often grind their lower tusks against their upper ones to produce sharpened edges. As well as their other obvious differences, wild boars have longer legs and a longer, straighter snout than domesticated pigs.

Adult boars usually stand about 3 feet tall at the shoulder and weigh roughly 275 pounds, while the giant variety grow as much as 5 feet tall and weigh about 1,000 pounds or more. Female boars, both giant and regular, have smaller tusks than the males.

Combat/Tactics:

Boars guard their hunting territory, their young and their meals with a savage ferocity. Upon scenting their prey, boars charge into combat and use their tusks to slash their target. Boars are most aggressive during the fall mating season. Wolves are a boar's natural enemy, and a boar will attack a lone wolf or dog on sight. Boars are very unpredictable, especially if they become startled or cornered, or they are encountered in mating season. During these times a boar's natural response in these situations is usually to attack. Giant boars act no differently than their smaller kin, though they can cause considerably more damage.

Habitat/Society:

Boars live in groups called sounders, which typically number around 20 animals. Typically there are only two to three sows in each sounder, with one being the dominant female. The remainder are males that come and go, usually when they reach sexual maturity at around four years of age. Boars will forage for food throughout the night, resting several times, as needed. Boars are unique among hoofed animals in that they dig burrows.

A boar's sexual activity changes with the seasons and they become more interested in mating as the days become shorter, most often in the autumn. Solitary males will seek out groups of females for mating. Fights with rival males for dominance are a common occurrence in the fall. During mating season boars are highly aggressive, with the most dominate and largest males mating most often.

During pregnancy a female boar will leave its sounder to form a mound-like nest a few days prior to delivery. Boars bear litters of four to six piglets but smaller groups are fairly common. Piglets are typically evenly split between males and females and the mother and piglets will remain in the nest for several days after birth. Upon returning to the sounder piglets will cross feed from other sows, if needed.

BOAR

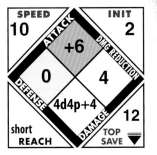

HIT POINTS:	25+3d8
SIZE/WEIGHT:	M/275 lbs.
TENACITY:	Steady
INTELLIGENCE:	Animal, High
FATIGUE FACTOR:	1

SPEED	INIT
10	2

ATTACK +6
DMG REDUCTION
DEFENSE 0 / 4
DAMAGE 4d4p+4
short REACH
TOP SAVE ▼ 12

ATTACK:
Slashes with tusks for 4d4p+4 points of damage.

SPECIAL ABILITIES:
Listening 65%, Tracking 85% mastery

MOVEMENT

CRAWL:	5
WALK:	10
JOG:	15
RUN:	20
SPRINT:	25

SAVES

PHYSICAL:	+6
MENTAL:	+6
DODGE:	+6

GENERAL INFO

ACTIVITY CYCLE:	Nocturnal
NO. APPEARING:	1-6
% CHANCE IN LAIR:	n/a
FREQUENCY:	Ubiquitous
ALIGNMENT:	Non
VISION TYPE:	Poor eyesight
AWARENESS/SENSES:	Good hearing and sense of smell
HABITAT:	Burrows
DIET:	Omnivorous
ORGANIZATION:	Individuals
CLIMATE/TERRAIN:	Temperate to Tropical woodlands

YIELD

MEDICINAL:	nil
SPELL COMPONENTS:	nil
HIDE/TROPHY:	various[1]
TREASURE:	incidental
EDIBLE:	yes
OTHER:	Vicelords use wild boar parts in their religion[2]

EXPERIENCE POINT VALUE: 242

GIANT BOAR

HIT POINTS:	34+5d8
SIZE/WEIGHT:	L/1000 lbs.
TENACITY:	Fearless
INTELLIGENCE:	Animal, High
FATIGUE FACTOR:	4

SPEED 9 — INIT 2
ATTACK +8
DMG REDUCTION
DEFENSE 0 — 5
6d4p+7
short REACH — DAMAGE — TOP SAVE 14

MOVEMENT

CRAWL:	10
WALK:	15
JOG:	20
RUN:	25
SPRINT:	30

SAVES

PHYSICAL:	+12
MENTAL:	+12
DODGE:	+12

ATTACK:
Slashes with tusks for 6d4p+7 points of damage.

SPECIAL ABILITIES:
Listening 70%, Tracking 80% mastery

GENERAL INFO

ACTIVITY CYCLE:	Nocturnal
NO. APPEARING:	1-8
% CHANCE IN LAIR:	n/a
FREQUENCY:	Frequent
ALIGNMENT:	Non
VISION TYPE:	Poor eyesight
AWARENESS/SENSES:	Good hearing and sense of smell
HABITAT:	Burrows
DIET:	Omnivorous
ORGANIZATION:	Individuals
CLIMATE/TERRAIN:	Temperate to Tropical woodlands

YIELD

MEDICINAL:	nil
SPELL COMPONENTS:	nil
HIDE/TROPHY:	various[1]
TREASURE:	incidental
EDIBLE:	yes
OTHER:	Vicelords use wild boar parts in their religion[2]
EXPERIENCE POINT VALUE:	500

Ecology:

Wild boars can be found in almost any region except for deserts and high mountain ranges, though they prefer forests that offer plenty of foraging opportunities. They are omnivores, and may destroy crops, kill livestock, and even dig up the dead in their search for food. In fact, boars will eat just about anything, and boars have been known to attack humans when particularly hungry. This is most true for the giant wild boars.

On Tellene:

Though wild boars range throughout the temperate lands of Tellene, the giant wild boar is found primarily in remote areas of Cosdol and northern Eldor. Boar hunts are not only a way of providing meat and preventing crop damage, but also serve as a test of bravery. Only the bravest men dare to finish off a boar with a dagger; the wisest stand back and use a spear.

Many cultures revere boars as symbols of strength and power. They are often sacrificed during times of religious significance.

[1]*Hunters may mount the head as a trophy or wear necklaces of wild boar teeth. Boar hairs are used in brushes, their hides are tanned for boots and clothes, and their tusks are carved into knives, tools and jewelry in a fashion similar to ivory.*

[2]*The boar is a significant animal in the church of the Vicelord. Priests of the Vicelord hold the animal sacred; boar genitals, tusks and hair are often used as religious icons and in ceremonies.*

TERROR AT DUSK
A deadly chance encounter with boars

One of the first lessons I beat into any new blade or recruit taken under my wing is that of respect. You must have respect for tooth, nail and claw both big and small! In other words, keep your eyes open for the beasts of the field, not only evil monsters.

It has been my experience over the years that over-confidence and complacency are the fighting man's two worst enemies. Once you dismiss a beast, even a simple wild pig, as being of no threat or consequence you are simply asking for trouble.

I think it was several years ago when I was slinging swords with a dwarf named Durnlee and a couple of imperial deserters we had joined up with. They didn't talk much, but that wasn't a surprise when we learned that one of them had been tortured by having his tongue cut out. The other was simply morose. We were working our way over the mountains somewhere in northern Brandobia. I believe it was in the Krond Hights, though it might have been the Legasa Peaks. In any case, we were taking in coin where we could or selling our sword arms in exchange for an occasional hot meal of the local variety — bread, ale, cheese, and soup or stew.

We had just slaughtered a savage lesser ettin that had been extorting regular tributes of meat and grain from one of the local villages, and had set up camp on a rocky craig on the forests's edge. We had silver in our pouches and bellies full of mead. We were a happy bunch.

While setting up camp and pitching our tents we had noticed fresh tracks and the rooting furrows of large foraging wild boar.

I though perhaps it was a giant boar, because of the great size of the hoof mark, and my gut instinct was to post a guard watch for the night. Unfortunately I was ignored and I did not press the issue further like I should have. We were celebrating a good fight and sore and stiff from sewn wounds, scrapes and bruises. The entire company was bone tired and myself not the least of them.

So, I let it go without much argument. Somewhere in my addled head, I figured we'd pile the firewood up high and get a good blaze going and I would sleep with one eye open with my sword at the ready should trouble arise.

Yes, it was definitely poor judgement on my part. We had just taken on an extremely challenging foe and wild boars didn't seem all that much of a concern in comparison.

The trouble started just after dark. We were still raising toasts and gambling — by throwing daggers at the ettin heads impaled on stakes nearby — when there was a disturbance from the forest's edge.

Four wide-eyed wild boar piglets emerged from the brush, and apparently were just as surprised to see us as we were to see them. They began to squeal wildly in alarm and disappeared back into the woods.

I barely had time to digest what had just transpired when suddenly the entire foliage wall at camp's edge exploded.

A giant wild boar sow, her tusks dripping with drool, had burst into the clearing. Her dark wicked eyes danced in the light of of our campfire, her sides heaving as she grunted her displeasure and pawed at the ground. Mother boar had arrived.

I saw the dwarf drop his mug and roll toward his bedroll seeking his battle axe. The two deserters, true to form, bolted for some rocks nearby without a second glance back at the rest of us. I cursed them loudly but got no answer.

My fingers had barely found their way to the hilt of my sword when she charged. The dwarf had drawn her attention, it seemed, for she was upon him in a flash. She caught him in the chest with her snout, and I could see the dwarf desperately trying to push her away. Of course, she was too heavy and had too much momentum. The big sow bowled him over with ease, savagely thrusting her sharp tusks with great ripping motions as she trampled him beneath her cloven hoofs.

With one of the threats to her piglets — as she thought we were — lying motionless in a broken heap, she continued her charge toward the rocks where our two cowardly comrades-in-arms lay in hiding.

After grunting her disapproval for not being able to get at them, she quickly turned her attention toward me. In the flickering flame light I could see her entire snout and face, crimsoned with dripping dwarven blood. Several dangling bits of my poor comrade's entrails were hanging from one tusk, and I felt my simple dinner churning inside my stomach.

As she turned and bobbed her head and readied for the charge I raised my sword and stood alone, cursing myself for my complacency. Were it not for a convenient rock formation where I could take the higher ground and use the reach of my bastard sword to do her injury without much harm to myself, I'm sure I would not be writing this today. My bones would be on the ground with the dwarf and my possessions in the hands of two cowards instead of the other way around. — $\mathcal{S}$

BROWNIE

Also Known As: Browney, Kafla, Wee'un, Forest Folk

Brownies are a curious breed. They're one I am fond of and with whom I've had many positive encounters. I say that, however, having never seen one with my own eyes. They are shy about their ways and mysterious. It takes great patience to to spot one — the sort of patience I apparently lack.

I once lived in the ruins of an abandoned manor house just south of Bet Rogala with a group of fellow mercs between jobs. Wounded, broke and low on provisions, we huddled among the ruins cursing our misfortune. I well remember how we coughed and hacked from the winter chill as we licked the wounds from a recent fight. We had been camping there for the better part of nine days when we discovered we were not alone.

More than once I awoke to find my dirty clothing laundered and neatly folded. Often we awoke to find a skinned and gutted hare roasting over a fire and dripping grease, or a growing pile of freshly gathered fire wood stacked nearby. On another particular day we found a wooden bowl of healing salve that had been left on the toe of a pair of boots drying by the fire. Who was our mysterious benefactor?

Apparently a group of brownies lived in the trunk of a large hollow tree nearby. They had observed our plight and decided to intervene on our behalf. They quite possibly saved our lives, and they most certainly eased our suffering. Yet nary a glance of them were we ever offered. The only evidence of their comings and goings were their small tracks.

Since that time, when traveling through woods known to be occupied by brownies, I often leave small items as a show of thanks. Nothing much, just little things like a ball of twine (something I hear they are quite fond of), an urn of good stout ale, or a bit of salted fish.

There are folks who don't think so kindly of the wee'uns. Some think them petty thieves and blame every missing tent peg, glove or boot on them. It's true, they can be mischievous at times, and a handful in combat if provoked or angered. — ⚲

Although small, do not dismiss these wee-folk as being of no account. You may well regret it.

A brownie lives a simple life among its own kind. Often, a brownie secretly observes passing travelers and offers them help - but only if they are in dire need.

Brownies stand about 20 inches tall and weigh around 13 pounds, resembling tiny humans with long noses and pointed ears. They have brown skin and wrinkled faces, so even the youngest brownies appear older than they really are. Most brownies live in forested areas, caves, hollow trees, or underground warrens.

Brownies are fast, have tough skin and are said to be the hairiest of the small fey. It is rumored that the first brownies were the offspring of halflings and pixies, and that they live for up to 1,000 years.

Combat/Tactics:

Brownies enter combat as a last resort when protecting themselves, their families, or their territory. Otherwise, they prefer to avoid combat, and use their many abilities to avoid capture.

When forced into combat, brownies compensate for their small size by gathering en masse. Although a pack of less than a dozen may be easily abused, a brownie tribe of nearly 100 individuals can be overwhelming for any foe. In most circumstances, when brownies are faced with inevitable

SIGN/TRACKS

Brownie tracks can be extremely difficult to detect.

They'll often leave them however if they want their prescence known.

RANGE ON TELLENE

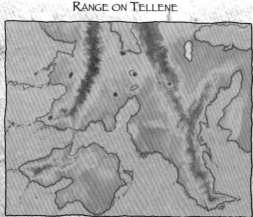

SIZE COMPARISON

6 ft

3 ft

combat, they prefer to charge forward in a screaming, disorganized mass, hoping to hide their numbers and overbear their opponents through appearance alone.

When offended, a brownie may simply disappear or, worse, perform a curse (depending on the severity of the offense). Anyone cursed by a brownie (no saving throw) suffers -1 to all die rolls for 1d6 days and loses a point of Honor. A brownie can perform this curse once per day.

In addition, brownies have mage abilities of at least 3rd level.

Habitat/Society/Ecology:

Most brownies live in forested areas, caves, hollow trees, or underground warrens. Some brownies wear no clothes, while others wear tattered rags and still others travel to cities and dress themselves at the height of fashion. These latter 'urban brownies' are generally considered part of the property owner's family, for they perform arduous tasks in the kitchen, barn, or workshop and expect no payment but that of kindness. Payments or gifts offered for their services, except for the lending of a private room (usually an attic or cellar) are offensive to them. Most brownies speak the regional human language as well as the languages of common animals.

On Tellene:

Brownie clans are most commonly found in the Lendelwood and Kalalali Forests, where they can live quietly, assured that the forest is under the protection of the elves.

Most civilized races have always ignored the brownies, and the elves actually classified them as vermin for a good portion of their history. Zachani Bojhardi, a halfling herbalist, was the first to actually accept the brownies. He utilized their zeal and massive numbers to help protect his grove and later introduced the tribes to other herbalists in and around the Kalalali Forest.

In the years following Bojhardi's acceptance of the 'brownie,' as he named them, the brownies spread through the Kalokopeli Forest, the Brindonwood and the Ryakk Woods. Many of the locals came to accept them as a permanent part of their woodland homes and the brownies were quick to accept their self-appointed roles as forest guardians.

However, brownies can also be found in other areas, such as the Crondor or Narond Woods of southern Mendarn. Adventurers passing through the Narond woods have been heard to encounter two kindly old brownies named Lema and Voldor who live in a well-camouflaged warren beneath a copse of trees. Supposedly, this old married couple has dwelt there together for over 400 years and consider the area within a league or two to be their backyard.

They are intimately familiar with the area and even know most of the animals by name. Voldor, the male, is a frequent visitor to the port city of Dayolen where he trades for goods that he cannot get in either the forest or in the nearby village of Yelden.

[1] Eating a brownie is thought to cause permanent gastroesophageal reflux disease.

BROWNIE

HIT POINTS:	8+1d8
SIZE/WEIGHT:	T/13 lbs.
TENACITY:	Nervous
INTELLIGENCE:	Bright
FATIGUE FACTOR:	-2

SPEED	4	INIT	-2
ATTACK	+3	DMG REDUCTION	
DEFENSE	+11		0/1
	see below		
short REACH		DAMAGE	n/a TOP SAVE ▼

MOVEMENT

CRAWL:	2½
WALK:	5
JOG:	10
RUN:	15
SPRINT:	20

SAVES

PHYSICAL:	+17
MENTAL:	+19
DODGE:	+20

ATTACK:
Brownies use small weapons that can inflict 1d4p damage on a hit. Mage abilities of at least 3rd level. Can curse once per day (no saving throw) causes -1 to all rolls for 1d6 days.

SPECIAL DEFENSES:
Hiding mastery 90%.
Turn invisible at will.

GENERAL INFO

ACTIVITY CYCLE:	Diurnal
NO. APPEARING:	2-10
% CHANCE IN LAIR:	10%
FREQUENCY:	Sporadic
ALIGNMENT:	Neutral Good
VISION TYPE:	Standard
AWARENESS/SENSES:	Standard
HABITAT:	Forest homes
DIET:	Omnivorous
ORGANIZATION:	Family or Clan
CLIMATE/TERRAIN:	Temperate to Semi-Tropical woodlands

YIELD

MEDICINAL:	nil
SPELL COMPONENTS:	bones make cursed magic items
HIDE/TROPHY:	nil
TREASURE:	trinkets only; brownies do not hoard wealth
EDIBLE:	yes[1]
OTHER:	nil
EXPERIENCE POINT VALUE:	100

BUGBEAR
Also Known As: Giant Goblin, Bogeyman, Goblibear, Great Goblin

Bugbears are huge brutes with bone crushing weapons and the temperament and bloodlust of a rutting grizzly sow. They're mean-spirited bastards who fight with no regard towards honor or cause. I've never seen a bugbear who didn't see (or smell) me first and attempt to do me in. In fact, by the time you detect one in the bush, lying low behind some rocks or creeping in the underbrush by the edge of your camp, you can be sure he has sized you up, and that he and his comrades have already decided how they are going to divvy up your goods. Once you've seen one it's too late. You're in for a bad time and a fight's about to be on.

Now there are those folk who will tell you they are slow-thinkers. Don't you believe it. Their minds are constantly being honed for one thing — battle.

When they aren't fighting at any given moment they are thinking, planning or looking for the next fight. Not to mention these voracious carnivores are known man-eaters. One of the reasons they are so feared is because they are constantly looking to feed their appetites.

They love the ambush and sneak attack, and are expert at setting bait traps. Back during my days as a village provider in the Masau Hills, a pair of bugbears snatched a small lad when he wandered too close to the forest's edge. One blink and he was gone without a sound.

We tracked those goblibears for the better part of two days before we realized the tables had turned and we ourselves had become the prey. After leading us to a ravine where over a dozen of their brethren lay waiting, we found ourselves fighting for our lives.

In the end, the child (along with four of my comrades-in-arm) were lost. The monsters took their bodies from the field of battle and later butchered and ate them. — ⅀

Bugbears prefer large, battering, bone crushing weapons they can put their large muscular frames and weight behind.

Members of this evil race resemble large versions of their smaller goblin cousins. Massive shoulders, large animalistic ears and a nose with a prominent bridge give them a different silhouette and facial features vaguely reminiscent of those of a black bear.

Such a visage, when taken together with their large size and lumbering ursine gait, makes the origins of their namesake quite obvious. Their long arms extend almost to their knees and dangle just off the ground when they shuffle along. These frighteningly powerful arms end in massive, thick hands with long, sausage-thick fingers, which in turn end in jagged filthy nails. These nails are long enough to damage foes if a bugbear had a mind to claw (which they seldom do purposely excepting for a near-perfect defense in which case they can inflict 2d4p+4 damage).

Bugbears are massively built. While their 6- to 7-foot height makes them shorter than gnoles and only slightly taller than most humans, their burly frame carries a beefy 350 pounds or so of bulk. Females are slightly shorter (3 to 4 inches) and about 50 pounds lighter on average. Dark fur covers their body and ranges in color from various browns and dark reds to black.

Despite their prodigious size and lumbering gait, bugbears are not slow by any means; in fact, they are quite nimble and

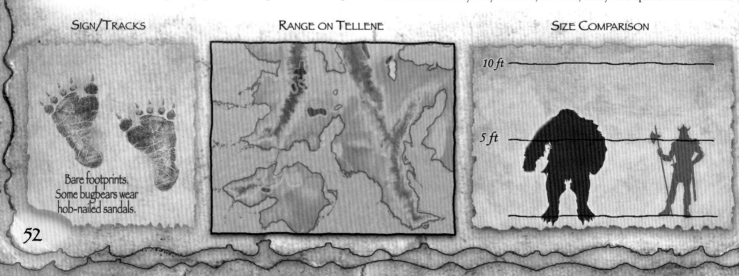

SIGN/TRACKS

Bare footprints. Some bugbears wear hob-nailed sandals.

RANGE ON TELLENE

SIZE COMPARISON

10 ft

5 ft

just as fast as humans. Their thick hide gives them an impressive Damage Reduction 3 even without armor.

These large, sturdy, solid monsters make formidable opponents. Their stocky build and large size makes them tough to knock-back. Despite their size, they are stealthy hunters (possessing a mastery of 50 in both Hiding and Sneaking) and have excellent senses of hearing and olfaction, making them tough to surprise (Listening 40% and an Observation of 50%, with a 1-point bonus to Initiative and one initiative die lower than called for in any situation).

Further, their lanky appendages provide plenty of reach to strike ahead of most foes (+1 foot reach added to weapon length). They are a stout and hearty race, with plenty of Hit Points to withstand even mighty blows, and a very solid threshold of pain and resulting save, should an adversary manage to land a powerful hit.

Ferocious in battle, the bugbear weapon of choice tends to be large crushing and physically imposing weapons, like the morningstar, mace, halberd, great axe and maul. That said they do employ the breadth of available weaponry.

Their weapons are taken from fallen foes as bugbears do not inconvenience themselves with designing or making their own tools; why do so when there are ample quantities available for the taking amongst the other, smaller races?

Bugbears are large enough to wield most two-handed weapons in one massive paw, allowing shield use with all weaponry save pole-arms, bows and crossbows. They like to utilize ranged weapons to soften up their foes, especially from ambush. Their favorites are hurled weapons like axes, clubs, javelins, hammers and so on, which they can lob for full Strength effect without the need to jog, or with an additional +2 Damage with the benefit of momentum gained from a jog. They can even hurl larger pole arms such as spears if balanced appropriately, but must jog forward while throwing for the full effect.

As to shields, bugbears can deploy any size from Medium to Body with ease (smaller shields can be strapped to their arm and used as a buckler and bucklers are too tiny and produce little effect). They do not wear armor of the standard variety. Sometimes they adorn themselves with thick hides and furs, or have their slaves fashion leather or studded leather armors for them, but most often they tie together bits and pieces from various armors to provide protection.

For example, a bugbear might bear a suit of human-sized chainmail over their chest and torso, tied in the back, in order to gain chainmail protection for the front. They may tie two large shields 'sandwich style' on their front and back, gaining protection equivalent to plate on both sides. They supplement other bits and pieces of things to cover the knees or other exposed areas. While it looks disheveled, years of experience has created a rather effective methodology behind this odd practice. On average, bugbears have a Damage Reduction increase from 3 to 6 thanks to these protections. Note also that some of the smaller females can actually wear larger human-sized armors as they were designed to be used.

BUGBEAR

HIT POINTS:	32+3d8
SIZE/WEIGHT:	L/350 lbs.
TENACITY:	Steady
INTELLIGENCE:	Average
FATIGUE FACTOR:	-5/-4

MOVEMENT

CRAWL:	2½
WALK:	5
JOG:	10
RUN:	15
SPRINT:	20

SAVES

PHYSICAL:	+7
MENTAL:	+7
DODGE:	+7

ATTACK: Damage by weapon with +4 bonus (*e.g.* 2d8p+4 morning stars); Often harass foes with fusilade of hurled weapons prior to melee.

SPECIAL: Utilize one initiative die lower & -1 to that roll; Shield use (*e.g.*, medium shields increase Defense from 0 to +6); Body armor provides 6 DR (unarmored bugbears have 3 DR); Hiding 50%, Listening 40%, Observation 50%, Sneaking 50%.

GENERAL INFO

ACTIVITY CYCLE:	Nocturnal
NO. APPEARING:	1-4 (hunters); 3d4p (warband); 4d12p (clan)
% CHANCE IN LAIR:	25%
FREQUENCY:	Infrequent
ALIGNMENT:	Chaotic Evil
VISION TYPE:	Low Light Vision
AWARENESS/SENSES:	Keen sight, smell, and hearing[1]
HABITAT:	Any, but common to forest caves[2]
DIET:	Carnivorous
ORGANIZATION:	Clan[3]
CLIMATE/TERRAIN:	Any[4]

YIELD

MEDICINAL:	nil
SPELL COMPONENTS:	nil
HIDE/TROPHY:	other humanoids sometimes carry bugbear thumbs as trophies to demonstrate their battle prowess.
TREASURE:	varies[5]
EDIBLE:	yes, but you'd have to be desperate (or a troll) to eat it.
OTHER:	bugbears are trophy takers, and lairs are often filled with kills and loot taken from their victims.
EXPERIENCE POINT VALUE:	175

Every warband has a leader with at least 49 Hit Points and an extra +1 to Attack, Defense and Damage along with better armor affording a +1 to Damage Reduction.

Overall numbers include one such leader for every 10 bugbears. If 25 or more are encountered, there is also a chief with 56+d8 Hit Points, and an extra +2 to Attack, Defense and Damage along with better armor affording a +2 to Damage Reduction. Besides the chief, there will also be two sub-chiefs with leader stats and an additional +1 (for a total of +2 in one of the four mentioned statistics).

Clerics and shamans are fairly rare, generally only serving in a cloistered capacity and never leaving the lair on raids. Each tribe has but a 35% chance of having a shaman of this type and 25% of shamans also have some mage ability. Their levels of spellcasting ability are not substantial, only d10p-4 for clerical and d10p-6 in mage (negative and zero rounding to 1st).

While not extremely intelligent, they are not dumb, and are perhaps best characterized as cunning and clever. They put these traits to use tormenting those weaker than themselves – a category into which most sapient races fall. Like their smaller goblin cousins, they revel in torture, doing so for the mere enjoyment and rarely to extract information or confession, but rather just to hear the agonizing cries of another. Bugbears eat any type of meat, but vastly prefer to eat sentient races over say, venison.

Sages disagree as to whether it is the taste of the meat itself or the notion of eating a self-aware being that bugbears find most appealing. Although, the bugbear penchant for taking trophies from victims and their obvious delight associated with this act as well as the pride in which they display them indicates that the latter may well be the case. Prizes include very personal items like skulls, scalps, ears, fingers, hands and so on, as well as other items such as clothing, weapons, armors and additional treasures. Larger items taken from pillaging raids are also cherished, for example, whole pieces of furniture or mantles and so on, even a front door (and associated frame) yanked from a plundered house.

Although reasonably intelligent, bugbears are not industrious and are content to live in caves, abandoned areas and ruins. If not readily available, these creatures have no qualms about finding a nice location and then murdering the current owners and moving in. Sometimes, a bugbear tribe will simply move into a goblin warren, for instance, proclaim it theirs and lord over the little deviants. While intolerable for the goblins, this is a great solution for the bugbears who not only gain a nice lair, but also a large cadre of slaves. Most other potential slave-races seek to avoid this situation and mount a defense against the bugbears for as long as possible.

Home taking such as this seldom lasts in civilized lands, as overrunning a human settlement (for example) generally invites the ire of a larger military than the bugbears are equipped to handle. In these latter instances, the bugbears sneak away in the night, carrying whatever loot they can manage.

While energetic and enthusiastic in battle, bugbears are indolent when it comes to things like mining, chores and constructive efforts. They are a raider society living off the fruits of the races that they bully or conquer. They are strong and can mine reasonably well, but do not unless forced by a powerful leader or the promise of some great end in short sight. That said, they are adaptable and survive well within the Netherdeep, in surface caves or living in the open lands. Bugbears can survive and indeed thrive in any climate, including both sultry and wintry conditions.

Bugbears care little for beauty or personal hygiene. They dress in flea-ridden and lice infested hides as long as the clothing is warm or can turn a blade. They never willingly bathe, but are good swimmers and have no fear of the water (and, in fact, greatly enjoy salmon and trout, which they are adept at catching with their clawed hands).

Bugbears tend to bully other humanoids unless their victims have sufficient numbers to make it dangerous, or at least thorny enough to make the attempt not worth the effort. Bugbears do show some friendliness toward goblins (and hobgoblins to a lesser extent) over the other races and sometimes cooperate with them. They dislike gnoles and consider them their nearest natural competitors. Bugbears view halflings and gnomes as little more than food and hardly even notice the various fairie-kin. They hate elves of all types (including grel) and attack them on sight. Bugbears have a fondness for elf-flesh and rarely capture them, preferring to eat them raw just after the battle.

Combat/Tactics:

Bugbears use their great stealth to lay in wait and ambush their prey or to sneak into an enemy camp, home, lair, etc, and attack with surprise. They prefer to begin an assault with a surprise ranged attack, typically using hurled weapons, although they can also use bows and crossbows to dangerous effect. After the initial barrage, they will savagely charge in, seeking to scatter their opponents with massive blows and sheer ferocity, eliminating the possibility of organized resistance.

Bugbears will seek to isolate opponents so that two of them can pulverize a victim and then quickly move to the next. The idea is to quickly neutralize enemies with grievous wounds and then overwhelm any more powerful survivors with sheer numbers. If forced to flee, bugbears always scatter in different directions, meeting up later at a designated rendezvous point, far from their lair. From here they either mount a counter-assault or head back to their domicile.

Habitat/Society:

Bugbears can be found in any climate and are equally at home above or below ground. Their favorite dwellings are natural caves in forested areas not far from human populations (especially large populations with plenty of infants available). Otherwise, they inhabit homes (above or below ground) previously created by other races.

Bugbears live in a disorganized society where the strongest rule the weak. The chieftain will always be the strongest, wiliest and most underhanded. The chieftain's position is under constant threat from rivals seeking to murder him and seize control for themselves. These rivals may be sub-chiefs or younger, foolish bugbears. As chief, his challenge is to supplicate his sub-chiefs and make life easy enough for them to enjoy the status quo, but not so easy as to appear weak. Further, the chief's power only extends to his immediate presence as bugbears are generally an unruly, chaotic lot.

Females make up a solid 50% of the population of the tribe. They fight with -2 to Damage and only d8 (instead of 3d8) for Hit Points relative to the larger males. While they are not liberated by any means, females can exercise great control over the males through sexual relations (or rather, lack thereof) and manipulation of rival males.

Bugbears have an average lifespan of about 60 years, but replenishing numbers is a difficult task as they reproduce slowly. While females comprise a solid 50% of their population, they have a difficult time reproducing. Females refuse relations when not in heat and only enter heat under odd circumstances. Females become fertile only after consuming an infant or small child (of any race) and then only for three days. Thus, males interested in copulation, will enter villages or farmhouses and whisk away small children from basinets. Because of this, in human lands, bugbears are sometimes known as bogeymen and many a children's tale centers around these stealthy fiends.

A bugbearess' gestation period is 7 months, although the infant mortality rate is around 40%, factoring thefts from rival male specimens. Those surviving infancy have a 70% chance of surviving to adulthood with sexual maturity arriving around 12 years of age. Young comprise only 20% of a tribe's numbers. Half the young fight only if cornered (using goblin statistics), while the other half fight as bugbear adults but with only 20+d8 Hit Points and a 3-point penalty to Attack, Damage and Defense.

Bugbears speak their own guttural language as well as Goblin and Hobgoblin. Some 50% percent of them can speak Orcish and 10% might speak a language of another nearby tribe, be it human, humanoid or demi-human.

A bugbear lair typically has slaves equal to 10% to 30% of the adult bugbear population. These slaves provide a source of labor as well as fresh food.

Ecology:

Bugbears sit at the apex of the food chain. While ogres and giants are larger and stronger, they lack the numbers to affect more than individual tribes in specific locations. Only humans, hobgoblins and grevans have strength and numbers sufficient to challenge and drive them from an area, and the former two lack the physical prowess to defeat bugbears in an even fight. And given the bugbear capabilities for stealth and guerilla warfare, they can seldom be driven away by a large determined force. A band of bugbears considers every living thing to be a possible food source with larger creatures taken individually by a group working in concert and smaller creatures slaughtered on a whim.

Luckily, bugbears are incapable of raising large numbers due to their slow birth rate and odd mating requirements and even when many bands have come together, after any major, pitched battle, any sorts of serious losses set them back for generations. Thus, even where very active, they are merely a nuisance and not a threat to the more populous races such as humans, demi-humans and the larger humanoids.

Religion:

Bugbears are quite superstitious and almost without exception pay homage to one god or another depending on the circumstances in which the bugbear needs or desires aid. Shamans tend to favor the Creator of Strife or the Confuser of Ways, but occasionally worship the Prince of Terror or Seller of Souls. Bugbears often pay homage to the Battle Rager before an impending battle. That said, the average bugbear is not very religious and while he may mumble off a prayer in the hopes of gaining some benefit on whatever endeavor on which he is about to embark, he freely ignores shamans and would openly revolt if forced to perform any sort of formal services (or even attend).

On Tellene:

Bugbears live in all climes and can be found raiding in numbers in almost any sparsely-populated area. They live on the outskirts of human society, but also on the fringe of dwarven, elven or humanoid societies. Many tribes live near Ul-Karg and Norga-Krangrel, preying on the hobgoblins for loot and gear. Several large clans roam the Wild Lands, the deserts and wastes and so on. Even Slen has a bugbear nuisance with which it must deal. Grevans love to fight bugbears, considering them worthy opponents, but call their tactics cowardly, especially when they steal from their camps and refuse to engage directly.

[1] **Awareness/Senses:** *Bugbears see well in dimly lit conditions, but cannot see in the dark. They have a well-developed sense of smell and excellent hearing.*

[2] **Habitat:** *Direct sunlight does not bother them and they are well-suited to living conditions both above and below ground.*

[3] **Organization:** *Bugbears are organized by clans, each with a chieftain and several sub-chiefs. Leadership goes to the most powerful, but their exercisable power extends only to the end of their weapon (or the speed at which they can catch another). Sometimes clans will band together into larger groups for the purpose of warring on other races, but they generally stick to their own area.*

[4] **Climate/Terrain:** *Highly adaptable, bugbears live in every climate from tropical to arctic, above ground, in caves and in the Netherdeep as well.*

[5] **Treasure:** *Bugbears carry 3d12p trade coins, 3d8 cp, 2d6p sp and d4p-3 gp each (treat negatives as zero). Bugbear lairs can contain vast amounts of wealth in the form of precious metals, gems, jewelry, arms and armors, works of art, furnishings, livestock and anything that can be pillaged from the surrounding lands and neighboring communities.*

CAMEL
Also Known As: Baktaar, Sand Mules, Grints, Ships of the Desert

Camels have always held a special fascination with me. They are so uniquely equipped to deal with harsh desert climates, so strong and durable, and yet so damn ugly, annoying and cantankerous.

In spite of their flaws, they are popular as beasts of burden and mounts, being even more affordable than horses in some locations. They can travel further on little food and water and are capable of bearing greater loads.

I've heard they can even be trained to ride into battle, but their natural inclination to run from danger can show itself at the most inopportune moments. As such, they can be unreliable in combat.

For use in caravans or when traveling great distances over arid, sandy terrain, they cannot be surpassed. They're called the 'ships of the desert' for good reason. Trade, the life's blood of empires, moves to and fro on their backs.

I've passed endless lines of them on my travels. Traversing the sand dunes one beast after the other. Their long necks arching proudly, heads swaying gently, moving faithfully and steadily as their handlers prod them on with a tap of their staves on their haunches.

There are wild camels living in Tellene, in the Elos and Khydoban deserts. They too are magnificent animals. I'm told once captured they are, for the most part, easy to train and domesticate — provided one has the patience and skill. Handling such a creature improperly can ruin them for any useful purpose resulting in a mean, easily agitated and dangerous beast.

Make no mistake about it, camels are quick to anger and hold a grudge. They will buck, kick or spit if offended and their wicked jagged teeth can rend flesh in an instant.

Be sure you have the gentle — yet firm — temperament needed to handle such an animal or the foresight to hire someone who does. I've found it's always worth the silver to hire one or two drovers when traveling by camel. — ⚶

Be sure to hobble or tether your camels securely at night. Even during short rests and stops on your journey. Some will bolt and run without warning.

Whether single-humped or two-humped, the typical adult camel stands about 6 feet tall at the shoulder and 7 feet tall at the hump. This hump of fatty tissue provides the beast with needed fat reserves while reducing the amount of heat-trapping fat elsewhere.

This hump, as well as several other physiological trappings, helps the camel thrive in desert areas where other mounts would suffer. For instance, the camel's thick blonde to reddish fur serves as insulation from the heat of the sun, while its long ear hair and eyelashes help protect these organs from blowing sand. Its insides retain water most efficiently, and it can masticate thorny desert plants that would pierce the flesh of many other creatures. Its long legs and wide feet also give it better traction over the desert sand.

Single-humped and most wild camels weigh a little over 1,000 pounds. Two-humped and domesticated draft camels may weigh up to 1,500 pounds, the latter having been bred to carry more weight. Females are nearly identical to the males, but weigh slightly less (about 10%).

Combat/Tactics:
If annoyed, a camel often shows its temperament by stamping its feet. Those who miss this sign might find themselves bucked off, bitten, kicked or even suffering the indignity of a globule of spittle in the face.

SIGN/TRACKS

RANGE ON TELLENE

SIZE COMPARISON

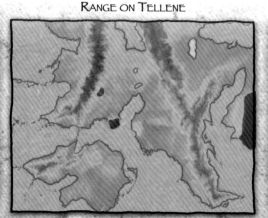

Some desert tribes notch their camels' hooves to show ownership

10 ft

5 ft

Fighting while mounted on a camel requires a minimum of Average mastery of the Riding skill (melee penalties apply to both attacks and defense). A rider fighting on camelback is thrown off if he suffers a knock-back or the camel succumbs to a Threshold of Pain check. Should this occur, the rider suffers 1d4p points of damage and is delayed 10 seconds while he regains his bearings.

If a camel encounters danger, its natural reaction is to flee. This requires a rider (if any) to succeed at a Riding skill check (Average difficulty) to rein it in. Likewise, a wounded camel will also attempt to flee, requiring a Riding check (Very Difficult) to restrain it each time the animal is wounded.

Camels can be trained for specific feats, such as biting, tripping another mount, throwing it to the ground by putting its head between the other mount's legs or using its powerful head and neck to push its opponent to its knees.

Habitat/Society:

Camels have been domesticated for perhaps longer than any other animal on the main continent. Thus, although wild camels do still live in the deserts of Tellene, most camels encountered are domesticated ones raised as beasts of burden (as well as for their flesh and milk, which are staples of desert cuisine).

After mating, a camel's gestation period lasts for roughly 400 days with an offspring of a single calf. A calf reaches maturity between three and five years old, and has an average lifespan of about 45 years.

Ecology:

Camels are not discriminating diners, feeding on more than 80% of the available tree leaves, shrubs and bushes, as well as any available crops. Camels have few natural enemies except for wolves, and encounters between the two are rare, except at watering holes. Otherwise, a wild camel's main enemies are overgrazing, poisoned water sources and drought.

On Tellene:

Cantankerous, single-humped dromedaries are most common in the Khydoban Desert, as well as in the southern Elos Desert near the city of Miclenon. Two-humped camels, on the other hand, are more likely to be found in the northern Elos along the Norga Tors foothills of the Elenon Mountains. Camels are occasionally transported to the Kalamaran Empire for use in circuses, so an escapee from an ambushed or careless merchant caravan might be encountered wandering the Kalamaran wilderness, but predators ensure these loners rarely survive for long.

[1] A pinch of camel hair, used as an additional Material Component in the cleric's second level Endure Temperature spell (Endure Heat only), increases the spell duration by 10% (round down).

Never turn your back on one of these beasts. They're biters and can leave a nasty wound.

CAMEL

HIT POINTS:	22+5d8
SIZE/WEIGHT:	L/1000-1500 lbs.
TENACITY:	Nervous
INTELLIGENCE:	Animal, Low
FATIGUE FACTOR:	-7

SPEED	10	ATTACK +2	DMG REDUCTION	INIT 0
DEFENSE +3			2	
short REACH		d6p-2	DAMAGE	TOP SAVE 7

MOVEMENT

CRAWL:	15
WALK:	25
JOG:	30
RUN:	35
SPRINT:	40

SAVES

PHYSICAL:	+2
MENTAL:	+2
DODGE:	+2

ATTACK:
Camel bites or kicks deal d6p-2 points of damage. A successful spit attack (once per encounter, against creatures within 5 feet) blinds the victim for 10+2d10 seconds.

SPECIAL DEFENSES:
none

GENERAL INFO

ACTIVITY CYCLE:	Diurnal
NO. APPEARING:	1-12 (wild), or as dictated by owner
% CHANCE IN LAIR:	n/a
FREQUENCY:	Frequent
ALIGNMENT:	Non
VISION TYPE:	Standard
AWARENESS/SENSES:	Standard
HABITAT:	Hills and plains
DIET:	Herbivorous
ORGANIZATION:	Herd
CLIMATE/TERRAIN:	Arid semi-desert to desert

YIELD

MEDICINAL:	camel hair can be used to sew stiches
SPELL COMPONENTS:	hair, for Endure Temperate (Endure Heat only)[1]
HIDE/TROPHY:	hides can be used in place of leather
TREASURE:	nil
EDIBLE:	yes
OTHER:	nil
EXPERIENCE POINT VALUE:	30

CATOBLEPAS

Also Known As: Gru, Katopa

I pray the gods will forgive my impertinence but oft times I question the "why" when it comes to the seemingly endless number of evil and horrid creatures that roam Tellene. Take the catobelpas for example. A solitary creature that can kill with but a glance and breathes poison? Its existence alone is proof positive the gods are either insane or have the sense of humor of an executioner. What possible purpose can they serve? A guardian monster created by some mage of old that escaped into the wild? I often wonder.

The armored scales on the backs of females turn turquoise blue during rutting season.

A Tarisatan lord, in his infinite wisdom, issued a bounty for the capture of a live catoblepas for festival time a few years ago. The crowds drawn to his new arena had grown tired of watching men have at it with swords or being pitted against half-starved hobgoblins or bugbears. His glorious new arena stood half empty. He hoped a catoblepas would provide some entertainment and fill the seats once again. Unfortunately, he got more than he bargained for. After months going by and the bounty remaining unclaimed, a live specimen finally arrived at the palace — the gift of a Ahznomahn merchant prince.

The four soldiers charged with uncovering the crate died within minutes from breathing in the foul breath of the creature. Later, during feeding time in the stables, two more handlers were killed when they couldn't take their eyes off the mysterious creature. Six horses in the stables also succumbed to the deadly gaze.

Beware the gaze of the katopa. There is death in that stare.

By the time festival day came around it is rumored two dozen men had been killed by the beast. Mind you, without ever being let out of its cage or touching a single person. The arena fight itself was anticlimactic. Grun, the arena champion, didn't fancy going up against such a creature unprepared. After studying up on the matter he emerged from the pits with a mirrored shield. Seeing its own gaze the beast immediately dropped dead, leaving the noble red-faced with anger and the crowd demanding its money back. —

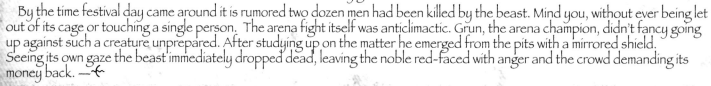

This sluggish creature has the body of a horse and a porcine head, complete with small tusks, with a heavy mane. It also has round bloodshot eyes, shaggy eyebrows, and a back protected by tough gray scales. Its horse-like body is mounted on short, stocky legs befitting a hippopotamus complete with stumpy, clawed feet, like one might find on an elephant. Altogether, the catoblepas appears as a strange combination of creatures, and is unsightly to behold. Fortunately for those it encounters, its head droops toward the ground; otherwise it would be a greater danger, for most any creature it sees may die.

The average catoblepas grows to about 4½ feet tall at the shoulder and weighs about 600 pounds.

Combat/Tactics:

When frightened or angered, this creature can attempt to kill with a look (one target within 10 feet; save vs. d20p+5). A catoblepas is vulnerable to its own power (though not to others of its species) should it happen to see its own magical gaze in a reflective surface. It can also breathe poisonous gas against one target within 5 feet (VF 7; failures suffer a 2-point penalty to Attack, Defense and Damage for 2d12 hours).

| SIGN/TRACKS | RANGE ON TELLENE | SIZE COMPARISON |

6 ft

3 ft

Catoblepas are very strong and can inflict considerable injury with a kick. During combat they often rise up on their hind legs to strike those in front, or kick backwards with their rear legs, attacking those enemies to the rear. Despite their size, the creatures are fairly agile. Catoblepas also bite in self-defense.

Habitat/Society:

Catoblepas are solitary creatures that gather only when mating, and for up to a year afterwards, as the young mature. Gestation is extremely fast and the process of mating to birth is typically only eight to 10 weeks. During the growth process the adults live together to protect their young from predators. At night, the adult catoblepas take turns sleeping and standing guard over their young against night attacks. The primary defense is herding, where the young catoblepas are protected by the older, larger adults of the group. Upon maturation of the young, adult catoblepas separate until the need to mate arises again.

Typically these creatures live in isolated above ground lairs, or naturally sheltered areas. Poisonous plants are almost always found in any area where a catoblepas may lair. Particularly dense concentrations of poisonous plants often draw the attention of catoblepas at some point. They are most active in the evening and early morning, sleeping for hours during midday.

Because they are vulnerable to their own gaze, they possess autonomic responses that cause their eyes to close upon taking certain actions such as bending down to drink. Lying in wait at a watering hole is an excellent opportunity to ambush these creatures.

Catoblepas can live for up to 30 years.

Ecology:

Catoblepas are herbivores, consuming mostly poisonous plants. Their blood is rumored to be strongly magical, offering resistance to the harmful effects of poison, which is why they can eat plants no other beast would be able to tolerate. This gives them little to no competition for their food.

Its natural enemies (lions, tigers, and other great hunting cats, who are immune to its gaze but not to its poisonous breath), attempt to cut out a young, or ill, catoblepas and attack so as not to deal with more than one creature at a time.

Catoblepas are often hunted by wizards for their body parts, many of which are useful in crafting items of power, or spells.

On Tellene:

Catoblepas are native to Svimohzia, grazing in the Miznoh Forest and the briars and thickets of the Svomawhom Forest near the Imomena Hills. They may be found elsewhere on the ancient isle, but are unheard of outside of its shores.

[1]Drinking a pint of fresh catoblepas blood adds +3 to all poison saves for d4+1 hours

[1]A pair of catoblepas eyeballs can be used as an additional material component when casting the eighth level Paralysis spell, doubling its area of effect so that the mage can affect two creatures instead of one. The spell's efficacy is unchanged (total Hit Points to be affected cannot be more than twice the HP of the mage).

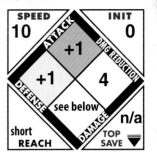

CATOBLEPAS

HIT POINTS:	18+3d8
SIZE/WEIGHT:	L/600 lbs.
TENACITY:	Nervous
INTELLIGENCE:	Semi
FATIGUE FACTOR:	2

SPEED 10 — ATTACK +1 — INIT 0 — DMG REDUCTION — +1 — 4 — DEFENSE — see below — DAMAGE — short REACH — TOP SAVE — n/a

MOVEMENT

CRAWL:	1¼
WALK:	2½
JOG:	5
RUN:	7½
SPRINT:	10

SAVES

PHYSICAL:	+1
MENTAL:	+1
DODGE:	+1

ATTACK:
Hooves deal 4d4p points of damage, bite deals d6p-4 points.
Poison breath (save vs. VF 7) causes -2 to Attack, Defense, and Damage for 2d12 hours. The death glance kills a target within 10 feet (save vs d20p+5). No effects on a successful save.

SPECIAL ABILITIES:
Listening 55% skill mastery

GENERAL INFO

ACTIVITY CYCLE:	Crepuscular
NO. APPEARING:	1 (solitary), 2-4 (family), 3-24 (herd)
% CHANCE IN LAIR:	55%
FREQUENCY:	Unusual
ALIGNMENT:	Non
VISION TYPE:	Standard
AWARENESS/SENSES:	Good hearing
HABITAT:	Caves and wooded groves
DIET:	Herbivorous
ORGANIZATION:	Herd
CLIMATE/TERRAIN:	Any, save arctic

YIELD

MEDICINAL:	blood heightens resistance to toxins[1]
SPELL COMPONENTS:	eyeballs, for Paralysis spell[2]
HIDE/TROPHY:	scales decorate leather armor made from its hide
TREASURE:	incidental
EDIBLE:	no
OTHER:	nil
EXPERIENCE POINT VALUE:	388

CENTAUR

Also Known As: Kentauroi, Horse Men

Cenataurs love to posture and intimidate as a way of sizing up strangers. Stay calm but alert and ready, for fear is seen as a sign of weakness.

Centaurs are swift on open ground, but uneven terrain, dense scrub and woodlands are usually avoided.

My first encounter with centaurs is something I'll never forget, such was the impression they made upon me. Half man. Half beast. And the eyes... those menacing eyes...

I vividly remember their eyes upon me. Gazing with no hint of the thoughts behind them. Centaurs — the dark, determined, denizens of the forest.

Though they blended in with their surroundings and were near invisible as we passed through their territory, we could feel their eyes. Watching, only watching. As we struggled to escape the cruel forest, lost and starving, we knew they were watching. Not protecting, but not attacking.

For that, at least, I was thankful. Clearly, they could have dispatched us with ease if they wished. This was their home.

At the last, just before our rescue, I finally had a good look at our observers. Among humans, they would be the most graceful. Among horse-kind, they would be kings. They moved not through the trees but somehow with them, and I instinctively sensed they could fight the same way (and secretly prayed we wouldn't learn if my hunch was right).

One of several, I will never know exactly how many, caught my eyes in those last moments. Clear, intelligent and beautiful, her eyes were like leafs come to life, her hair strands of soft bark. The land itself become aware... sentient. I would tell myself her gaze lingered longer than it should.

Satisfied that we no longer threatened their home, they left us. But ever after I would follow the way of The Bear. And I hoped someday to return to that land, to thank those silent observers, to someday be allowed to share in their celebration, and connection to the forest around them. For through them I came to see the natural world as it is: neither caring nor uncaring, but in perfect balance. Exquisite... —

A centaur has the upper torso of a human and the body of a large horse. The human waist blends into where a normal horse's neck would be. They are muscular in both human and horse parts; if there are out-of-shape centaurs they are kept well-hidden. Human features are generally matched to the equine section, most often fur and hair are brown. Eye color varies as much as human eyes, though blue irises are believed to be extremely rare. Markings fit into the same categories as those of normal horses.

Though they wear little or no clothing, centaurs often mark rank with increasingly complex decorations and jewelry, usually head-dresses involving horns, feathers, and teeth of hunted beasts. Male centaurs can grow beards. A few tribes are known to make extensive use of tattoos. Many use war paint when expecting battle.

Centaurs can sleep standing up, legs locked into position. Their human heads usually lean back slightly when doing this, their torso also locked in a way true bipeds cannot accomplish. From this position, they can awake very quickly and ready for action.

SIGN/TRACKS

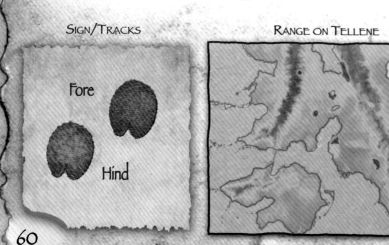

Fore

Hind

RANGE ON TELLENE

SIZE COMPARISON

6 ft

3 ft

Combat/Tactics:

Centaur bands never travel outside their homes unarmed. Despite their chaotic nature, they fight very well in small groups, quickly readying themselves for battle whenever they encounter outsiders. Centaurs fight fiercely and intelligently, and have mastered skirmish tactics. They know their terrain very well and use it to their advantage. They begin with ranged attacks and often target spellcasters before closing in for melee. Centaurs understand the relative strengths and weaknesses of the major races and their weapons.

Many centaurs consider themselves expert archers. While most centaurs can use longbows, half of centaur warriors will be specialized. When traveling, at least a quarter of centaurs will have longbows in hand, and centaurs almost always carry 10-20 arrows each. Centaurs can also use light lances, and leaders can use medium lances.

In melee, centaurs usually wield clubs (50%), staves (30%) or spears (20%). Because of their strength, training, and determination, centaurs inflict +3 damage when wielding weapons. They can attack with either a weapon or with two hooves. Some centaurs like to disarm opponents before pummeling them.

If expecting battle, centaurs sometimes don armor for both their horse and human parts, typically with leather[1] but sometimes chain[2]. Plate is virtually unknown. In most cases, though, they rely on speed and skill. Warriors and leaders will often wear a plumed helmet as a sign of prowess and to intimidate foes.

Most adult male centaurs are fighters, about 25% of those rangers. Scout leaders are typically 2nd to 5th level, while chieftains generally range from 4th to 10th level. Some 10% percent of centaurs encountered are clerics, and each lair includes at least one cleric. They will not hesitate to use entangle spells and any enchantment to best advantage. They can also heal their warrior allies in battle. There are no centaur mages as they do not have the patience, temperament or inclination to study musty old tomes.

They have no qualms about ambushing those seen as threats. Despite a culture that despises fear, they will also retreat if necessary. They rarely seek to fight to the death, but they have long memories and deep passions. Just as they will not forget a foe, pursuing enemies until they pose no further threat, they are staunch allies for those who earn their hard-won friendship.

Habitat/Society:

Intelligent creatures who shun the company of other races, centaurs dwell in their remote glades deep in the woodlands. Their initial reaction to others is almost always one of distrust, if not outright hostility. Centaurs have little use for most of the other sentient races, though they are known to speak and trade with elves for food and wine. They will also sometimes tolerate gnomes and individual humans, though these are never more than guests. Despite their joy in life, their unique styles of music, tales of dancing and copious drinking at celebrations, they remain aloof to strangers.

CENTAUR

HIT POINTS:	28+4d8
SIZE/WEIGHT:	L/750 lbs.
TENACITY:	Brave
INTELLIGENCE:	Average
FATIGUE FACTOR:	-5/-4

MOVEMENT	
CRAWL:	20
WALK:	25
JOG:	30
RUN:	35
SPRINT:	40

SAVES	
PHYSICAL:	+8
MENTAL:	+8
DODGE:	+8

ATTACK: Centaurs gain a +3 bonus to damage with melee weapons (*e.g.,* clubs at d6p+d4p+3; staves at 2d4p+3; or spears at 2d6p+3 - speed listed is for spear use); They may also attack with hooves to deal 4d4p points of damage (@ Speed 10).

SPECIAL DEFENSES: Shield use (*e.g.,* medium shields increase Defense to +11); may wear leather or chainmail armor

GENERAL INFO

ACTIVITY CYCLE:	Any
NO. APPEARING:	6-65
% CHANCE IN LAIR:	10%
FREQUENCY:	Sporadic
ALIGNMENT:	Chaotic Good
VISION TYPE:	Standard
AWARENESS/SENSES:	Standard
HABITAT:	Hidden groves and glens near water
DIET:	Omnivorous
ORGANIZATION:	Loosely organized tribes and clans
CLIMATE/TERRAIN:	Temperate woodlands

YIELD

MEDICINAL:	nil
SPELL COMPONENTS:	nil
HIDE/TROPHY:	centaur heads may easily appear to be human
TREASURE:	they have little use for treasure but may trade it
EDIBLE:	yes, but considered cannibalism by most folk
OTHER:	nil
EXPERIENCE POINT VALUE: 325	

Centaurs live in temperate forests, organized into tribes and clans, with each establishing a territory for itself. Their homes include natural sources of fresh, running water and pastures. In areas that know cold, they may also construct lean-to shelters and small huts. Experts at horticulture, a centaur lair will be well defended with traps, snares, and natural overgrowth that intruders can only pass with great difficulty and much noise.

Centaur lairs typically include from 5 to 20 families. Centaurs mate for life, usually in their teen years. The formation of these unions are occasions of great celebration in a centaur community, but then most anything is a cause for celebration in a centaur community. Single births are the norm after about 5 months, and a family usually consists of two parents and one to four young. Education of the young is shared by the entire community. Centaurs reach adolescence at 7 years and maturity at age 12. At the ripe old age of 35, their hair begins to turn gray or silver, at which point they are considered elders and rarely leave the homestead.

Clans are tight knit groups, with each member well aware of both their own status and that of those around them. Chieftains are almost always the most skilled warriors, though they are always superlative in some sense. Sometimes they will be simply the fastest or the best archer.

Archery contests are common entertainment, both within and between tribes. They begin practice with the bow as soon as they can hold one, often before learning to use other weapons.

Only in desperate situations will a centaur allow a being to ride it. They are not known to wear saddles unless strongly compelled in some way, and when free of the compulsion they will be extremely resentful of such treatment.

Ecology:

Centaurs are a sentient race, fully aware that they are top predators. They seek a harmonious balance with the forest that sustains them. They never over-fish or over-hunt a species and take (often extreme) umbrage with those who do. Centaurs are omnivorous, though some very rare tribes exist that do not eat meat at all. Though sentient, centaurs are not known to domesticate other animals. However, they relate well to most wild species and in dire situations may ask these animals to assist their efforts.

Centaurs make their livings by hunting, foraging, fishing, and trading. They have little use for individual treasure, but they are well aware of its value to other races and will take advantage of this knowledge when they do trade. Wealth captured from monsters (or unfortunate treasure hunters) that cannot be used by a member of the tribe is kept collectively until it can be traded. Some elder centaurs develop minor skill with whitesmithy (silver or gold). Centaur wine is reputed to be excellent, and centaur tolerance for alcohol is legendary.

Centaurs take threats to their land very personally. In times of great threat, tribes ally with each other or even other races. This requires a uniquely charismatic leader, however, one who will likely become the subject of centaur tales and songs for many generations.

On Tellene:

Though centaurs can be found almost anywhere in the northern continent, they are extremely rare on Svimohzia. There are also no known tribes in the Elos Desert or the Khydoban. In Norga-Krangel, centaurs are extremely reclusive and sometimes use guerilla tactic against hostile forces. Given their loose social organization, they have no official relations with any political union formed by other races, but very occasionally a centaur does contract wanderlust and may even be seen in a city. Centaur clerics almost always follow The Bear, and tend to look on fellow followers and allies less unfavorably than they view the general population.

Though they do interact with other tribes for trade and occasionally individuals will follow a mate to a new tribe, some scholars say that centaur tribes interact with each other only slightly more often than with other races. Centaurs will sometimes help "friends of the forest", elves or rangers, but mostly prefer to remain aloof. Centaur territories sometimes overlap with elves, but they do not involve themselves in each others affairs unnecessarily. About 20% of centaurs speak Low Elven. About 10% can truly speak the local human language, though most know a few rudimentary words.

[1] *Statistics in Leather: Speed 10, Defense +4, Init -1, DR 9*
[2] *Statistics in Chainmail: Speed 11, Defense +1, Init 0, DR 12*

Despite inebriated deliberations one might absorb in a tavern, there are no recognized instances of centaurs mating with horses; indeed most respected scholars agree that such mating would not result in offspring of any kind. While their resemblance to two very distinct species is obvious, it is generally accepted that the centaur race is of magical origin rather than natural breeding.

The fact that there is no evidence of any general changes in centaur appearance over many generations, and that historical records suggest that their culture has been stagnant for centuries, also supports this conclusion. Discussion continues concerning whether centaurs can truly be considered quadrupeds, as they technically possess six limbs, a matter to which I shall focus as I discuss my examinations of the few physical specimens available for research over the previous half-century…

MY JOURNEY TO
THE VALLEY OF THE CENTAURS

As I settle down with my quill to pen this memoir, I recall the writings of an elder druid who wrote that centaurs are the ideal of human skill and wisdom blended with all that is best and noblest of animal instinct, strength and swiftness. I could hardly have described them better myself, though perhaps these ramblings of mine will help to convey a bit more to you.

At the time of which I speak, it was spring. My companions and I had spent the night in a small cave on the hilly edge of a tree-dappled valley, having been forced there by foul weather the night before. It made my heart merry to see the sunlight breaking through the clouds, casting such brilliant reflections off the dew-covered plain that the land seemed to sparkle with diamonds. Yet, that was not the greatest sight. Barely a few dozen yards ahead, between a little stream and a nearby stand of oaks, stood nineteen or twenty centaurs.

Roughly half of them were male; these stood silently, keeping a watchful eye on the female and the young. The females stood about in quiet conversation, while their youngsters played up and down the hilly slopes in happy pursuit of each other, the cool breeze drying the sweat from their naked flanks. The male nearest us, quickly spotting our presence, raised his head and called some unintelligible word to the others. His tone, whatever the words he spoke, was too full of meaning to be disregarded. Immediately, the females and the young ceased their talk and play, moving to stand between the males with such rapidity and lack of fuss that it reminded me of some military maneuver. That done, five of the males approached. Though none of them wore armor and each bore only a single blade, their bulk and apparently unwavering confidence lent to their persons an aura of invulnerability.

I had not heard the words their leader spoke, but had the advantage of knowing certain words of sylvan origin. Thus, taking advantage of the moments before battle might be joined, I quickly bent one knee (to the astonishment of my companions) and greeted them in halting forest-speak. Though my tongue stumbled over the words, seeing this simple act won some of their confidence. They too knew the local language of man, and though they looked askance at the tack and harness of our horses, it was not that long before we had entered into a temporary peace.

Then, one by one, both centaurs and men began to relax and converse amongst one another. We were in search of a certain object said to have been secreted behind a crack in one of the nearby crags, and much of the talk centered on questions of the local landscape. I do not propose to give further details of that valley, for those who were my companions know its location already, and those rivals in my trade might cause harm to fall upon those noble beasts, while casual readers of my words would fail to appreciate the knowledge regardless. For my own part, I left such details to those of my companions who are learned in such things, and instead sought out the centaur with the greatest knowledge of botany and of the forest creatures.

I was surprised to find him one of the largest centaurs, the horse form being thick-legged, with a muscular body and a handsome blue roan shade marked with four black stockings and a saddle-stripe across his back. Too, I was amused to note that his odor, sweet and slightly pungent in my nostrils, was also like that of the horse. The aspect of man was also as well muscled as that of our fighter, if not more so, and he twirled his blade dexterously, before idly slipping it into its sheath with a flourish.

At first, he was peevish and irascible, mistrusting our strange and urban ways, but our common love of nature soon brought us together. He knew nothing of book learning and his thought processes hardly followed what I would consider a rational manner, but he 'felt' the world around him as if it was no less an extension of his body than were his arms or legs. Though I visited with him nearly the day entire, minutes seemed to pass like seconds, and it grieved me greatly when it came time to depart from the valley of the centaurs. — ⚑

CENTIPEDE

GIANT CENTIPEDE
MASSIVE CENTIPEDE

Also Known As:
Slink-Bug, Slaas

I must confess to having something of a morbid fear of giant centipedes, especially the larger tyranno-centipede — from whose poison I almost died back in my days among the halfings.

These unintelligent predators always tend to show up when not expected. Lunging with amazing speed for the eyes, chest or groin, they attack on sight — usually springing out of pile of rotting leaves or some dark hole among the rocks or briars. I can scarce describe how painful their sting can be.

Massive centipede head

Use a torch to keep these creatures at bay.

I was dipping a waterskin into a stream to fill it when suddenly the log I had rested my hand on to stoop down moved. It was not a log at all I discovered but a giant centipede!! I took a bite on the shoulder before I could blink. My arm was searing in pain almost immediately as my chest tightened and I fought to breathe. It was just about to drag me away into the weeds when a group of halfling fishermen saw my predicament and came to my rescue. That's how close I came to being larvae food! It took a week of feverish nights under the watchful eye of my diminutive rescuers to fight off the poison and regain my strength. —⨍

Despite the name, these predatory arthropods may have anywhere from 20 to over 300 legs, with each pair on an individual segment. The giant centipede has 15 leg-bearing segments (30 legs) and a body length of between 1 to 2 feet. Giant centipedes have a greenish copper-colored body with yellow spotting and weigh about 2 pounds.

The massive centipede has a dull green body between 6 and 8 feet long, dark green and brown striped legs, and large forcipules that it uses to inject venom and hold onto its prey. Despite its size, its flat body means that a typical specimen still weighs no more than 10 pounds. This light weight also helps it to move quickly.

Combat/Tactics:

Giant and massive centipedes are aggressive creatures, but may attack creatures far larger than themselves only when disturbed or hungry. Their poisonous glands cause necrotic tissue damage.

Habitat/Society:

Both varieties are nocturnal creatures, preferring to spend their days hidden in cool, damp underground nests. For the typical giant centipede, this nest is usually composed of moist soil and leaf litter,

underneath stones and deadwood or inside rotting logs. The massive centipede, however, requires a much larger living area and dwells in deep caves with access to an underground water source. It particularly favors caves characterized by sinkholes, stalactites and stalagmites, as it uses these and other similar rock formations to leap from and surprise its prey.

Female giant centipedes lay their larvae (about a dozen) in the warmer months, keeping a close watch over them for the six weeks it takes for them to hatch. Juveniles are sometimes thought to be a different kind of giant centipede, due to their slightly smaller size, black coloration, thinner bodies and spherical red heads. It takes several stages of molting before a juvenile becomes an adult.

Ecology:

The typical giant centipede preys mostly on large earthworms, supplemented by small reptiles, spiders, rodents and amphibians, though it has been seen leaping from the ground to catch birds and bats in mid-flight. The massive centipede also feeds on such prey, along with larger creatures (including humans and demi-humans) that wander haplessly into its den.

SIGN/TRACKS

Centipede tracks can be difficult to detect even to the trained eye.

RANGE ON TELLENE

SIZE COMPARISON

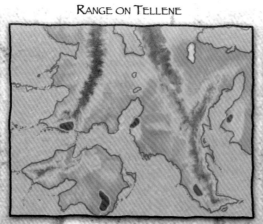

6 ft

3 ft

Giant Centipede

Massive Centipede

GIANT CENTIPEDE

HIT POINTS:	1d4
SIZE/WEIGHT:	T/2 lbs.
TENACITY:	Cowardly
INTELLIGENCE:	Non
FATIGUE FACTOR:	n/a

SPEED 5 — INIT -1 — ATTACK 0 — DMG REDUCTION 0 — DEFENSE +1 — poison — DAMAGE — short REACH — TOP SAVE — n/a

MOVEMENT

CRAWL:	1¼
WALK:	2½
JOG:	5
RUN:	7½
SPRINT:	10

SAVES

PHYSICAL:	+0
MENTAL:	+0
DODGE:	+0

ATTACK:
Bite inflicts no initial damage, but injects VF 5 poison (save or suffer d6p points of damage at a rate of 1 point per 10 seconds until damage is reached). Size H and larger creatures are unaffected.

SPECIAL DEFENSES:
immune to Threshold of Pain checks

GENERAL INFO

ACTIVITY CYCLE:	Any
NO. APPEARING:	1
% CHANCE IN LAIR:	n/a
FREQUENCY:	Commonplace
ALIGNMENT:	Non
VISION TYPE:	Low Light Vision
AWARENESS/SENSES:	Sensitive to vibrations within 15 feet
HABITAT:	Damp, dark places under rubble or litter
DIET:	Carnivorous
ORGANIZATION:	Solitary
CLIMATE/TERRAIN:	Any, save arctic

YIELD

MEDICINAL:	diluted poison used to treat mild cough
SPELL COMPONENTS:	nil
HIDE/TROPHY:	corpses sometimes used to play practical jokes
TREASURE:	nil
EDIBLE:	yes, but the head is poisonous
OTHER:	nil

EXPERIENCE POINT VALUE: 14

MASSIVE CENTIPEDE

HIT POINTS:	13+3d8
SIZE/WEIGHT:	S/10 lbs.
TENACITY:	Nervous
INTELLIGENCE:	Non
FATIGUE FACTOR:	n/a

SPEED 8 — INIT -2 — ATTACK +4 — DMG REDUCTION 3 — DEFENSE +1 — 1d6p + poison — DAMAGE — short REACH — TOP SAVE — n/a

MOVEMENT

CRAWL:	2½
WALK:	5
JOG:	10
RUN:	15
SPRINT:	20

SAVES

PHYSICAL:	+4
MENTAL:	+4
DODGE:	+4

ATTACK:
Bite inflicts 1d6p points of damage, and injects corrosive VF 8 poison (suffer 2d8p points of damage at a rate of 1 point per 10 seconds until damage is reached). Successful saves suffer only half damage from the poison.

SPECIAL DEFENSES:
immune to Threshold of Pain checks

GENERAL INFO

ACTIVITY CYCLE:	Any
NO. APPEARING:	1
% CHANCE IN LAIR:	n/a
FREQUENCY:	Infrequent
ALIGNMENT:	Non
VISION TYPE:	Low Light Vision
AWARENESS/SENSES:	Sensitive to vibrations within 30 feet
HABITAT:	Subterranean
DIET:	Carnivorous
ORGANIZATION:	Solitary
CLIMATE/TERRAIN:	Any, save arctic

YIELD

MEDICINAL:	diluted poison used to treat severe cough
SPELL COMPONENTS:	nil
HIDE/TROPHY:	nil
TREASURE:	nil
EDIBLE:	yes, but the head is poisonous
OTHER:	nil

EXPERIENCE POINT VALUE: 200

CHANGELING

Also Known As:
Doppelgänger, Kamaloi

Changelings! How I despise these creatures of deceit. Make no mistake — they do exist. This is a truth I know only too well from personal experience. Forever be on guard against them.

I once had a friend named, Kahli — an old sword from the city of Thygasha. He hired on with our party after our numbers fell short crawling the Vrykarr mountain peaks. He was a trustworthy mate who always had my back and never expected more than he deserved. Best of all he was handy with a blade and not afraid of a good fight. All in all a rare breed. It didn't take long for us to become fast friends.

Well one day we were approaching the town of Hiakk when a courier dispatched by the mayor who ran the town halted us. Apparently our reputation had preceded us and we were told we would not be allowed to enter the town.

After requesting permission to send a man forth to buy provisions, the answer came back that our request was granted. Drawing straws, Kahli won the privilege to head up the task. Being a man fond of women and drink, we knew we'd be in for a bit of a wait. So we weren't concerned the next morning when he was overdue. "Sleeping it off in the arms of some whore" I explained.

I didn't know it then but I would never see the friend I knew as Khali again for the person that eventually rode into camp, who looked and talked like him, was a doppelgänger. It took weeks for us to realize the truth. At first it was just an odd feeling that something was out of place. He was a bit distant, of less cheer and became prone to keeping to himself. We assumed he was in a queer mood and that it would pass. I thought perhaps his thoughts were on the home fires, the son he had not seen in years, or his widowed mother. Such melancholy is no stranger on the trail.

Our suspicions were not aroused until silver and other items began disappearing from the party's treasury, and always taken while Kahli had been on watch. His inability to answer certain questions bolstered our conjecture that he was an impostor. Sensing he'd been found out, the changeling struck first by leaving in the middle of the night with most of our hard coin and all our horses. Six weeks he rode with us and we hadn't known. And for six weeks the man I called friend lay dead — only the gods know where — his life as well as his identity stolen. — ℈

A changeling taking on a new form.

In its true form, this creature resembles a hairless human with a toothless mouth cavity and a long lizard-like tongue, two small nostril slits instead of a nose, and two large stereoscopic eyes on the sides of its head. Its hands and feet resemble tongs, as if a human's five toes and fingers had been fused into a group of two and three. Furthermore, its skin appears slightly translucent, though not enough to enable sight of its internal organs.

However, changelings are rarely seen in their true form, since they can physically alter the shape of their bodies, shifting, stretching, compressing or expanding any part. This allows them to imitate any Small or Medium animal, human, demi-human or humanoid, provided they first touch the body of the creature to be duplicated.

Changelings need not be in their natural form when they touch a victim, nor is there any known time limit between touching and transformation. Merely walking through a crowded marketplace can provide a changeling with dozens of potential aliases for the future, with not only form, but also copies of recent memories.

SIGN/TRACKS

These creatures are nearly impossible to track as they can change their prints at will.

RANGE ON TELLENE

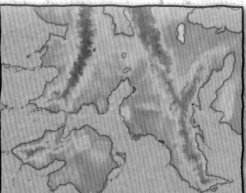

SIZE COMPARISON

6 ft

3 ft

An average changeling stands about 5 feet tall and weighs around 175 pounds.

Combat/Tactics:

A changeling typically attacks when threatened, or when it wants to eliminate a creature it copied. Being a creature of deceit and confusion, a changeling prefers to attack when its victim is alone and, preferably, sleeping. It relies on swords, daggers and the like when imitating a creature but in its natural form can bludgeon opponents with its arms.

Habitat/Society:

Changelings spawn asexually once in their lifetime, with the new organism being genetically identical to its parent. However, the offspring automatically assumes the shape of the first non-changeling it touches and cannot shift its shape further until it reaches six years of age. This inconvenience led the changeling species to adapt into brood-parasites, manipulating and using host individuals from other species to raise their young. To ensure maximum survival of its offspring and to relieve itself from the investment of rearing, newly spawned changelings are often swapped with a human child. The kidnapped child is then eliminated, sold into slavery or left to die of exposure.

A changeling spawn's natural cunning keeps its true nature a secret, though signs of a changeling child include malicious temper, paleness, and a vast vocabulary that betrays its intelligence. Changeling children often leave home when their shape-shifting abilities manifest, sometimes to the relief of the host parent.

A changeling has an average lifespan of 50 years.

Ecology:

Changelings have senses similar to those of humans, and can feed on any food source edible by that prolific race. Animals often avoid changelings, even when transformed to resemble such a beast, for the animal's natural odor is not duplicated.

On Tellene:

Invisible Lives, the canon of the Imposters (clerics of The Confuser of Ways), includes an origin myth about the changeling. According to this unholy tome, The Confuser of Ways created the changeling race when the world was younger, using them to sow confusion among the demi-human worshippers of other gods.

However, when the human population began to increase beyond that of the demi-humans (and certainly beyond that of the changelings), the deity turned his attentions to this new race, favoring them beyond his own creation. Thus, the book says, the jealous changelings take great delight in causing pain and suffering to humans. Though their powers are to be envied, they are never to be trusted.

[1]Chameleon organs can be used in the fourth level Transmogrify spell (and similar body changing spells) in order to double the duration.

CHANGELING

HIT POINTS:	25+4d8
SIZE/WEIGHT:	M/175 lbs.
TENACITY:	Nervous
INTELLIGENCE:	Smart
FATIGUE FACTOR:	0

MOVEMENT

CRAWL:	2½
WALK:	5
JOG:	10
RUN:	15
SPRINT:	20

SAVES

PHYSICAL:	+20
MENTAL:	immune
DODGE:	+20

SPEED 6 | **INIT** -4
ATTACK +10
DMG REDUCTION
DEFENSE +4 | 8
medium REACH | by weapon +6
DAMAGE | TOP SAVE ▼ 7

ATTACK: Changelings attack with various weapons suitable to their imitated form (though doing +6); in natural form bludgeons for 1d12p+6

SPECIAL DEFENSES: Shapechanger, immune to mind-affecting spells, Mind Reading ability

GENERAL INFO

ACTIVITY CYCLE:	Any
NO. APPEARING:	1-3
% CHANCE IN LAIR:	15%
FREQUENCY:	Unusual
ALIGNMENT:	Neutral Evil
VISION TYPE:	Standard
AWARENESS/SENSES:	Standard
HABITAT:	Any
DIET:	Omnivorous
ORGANIZATION:	Individuals
CLIMATE/TERRAIN:	Any

YIELD

MEDICINAL:	nil
SPELL COMPONENTS:	organs, for the Transmogrify spell[1]
HIDE/TROPHY:	nil
TREASURE:	coins, rings & jewelry worth 500-750 sp
EDIBLE:	no
OTHER:	nil
EXPERIENCE POINT VALUE:	1000

CHEETAH, WOOLY   Also Known As: Morgg, Miracinonyx, Hurjara

My one and only glimpse of this beast occurred when my companions and I had bartered our talents to a horselord waging some little war of territory in Skarrna. For many turnings of the moons, we were fighting somewhere, and the days and nights were little different one from another. Each held occasional keen clashes of sword and axe mingled with shouts of victory (though I knew not whether it be our own or the enemy's) attesting some temporary advantage. Then, one morning at daybreak, the enemy was gone. We moved forward over the abandoned field of battle, through the debris of empty camps, and among the bodies of the fallen.

These skilled predators are terrifyingly fast. It is best to stand your ground and take your chances.

From the edge of the field leading down the declivity were the tracks of men and horses, the yellow grass beaten down by their numbers. Clearly, our fighter said as he examined the tracks, they passed this way rather than withdraw by the country roads.

It was as I looked down the hill towards the next gentle crest that the cries of several men rose up from my right. Peering in the direction of their pointing fingers, I saw it. Loping rapidly along the edge of the nearby copse came a large and powerfully built spotted cat, moving at such a speed I have never seen before. I had but barely spotted the hare flying in panic before it, when its pursuer snatched up its prey in its mouth and disappeared into the distance, never once faltering its stride.

Our mage scoffed at our wonder, boasting of a spell that can imbue such speed. I kept silent, but knew that no magic could also provide the graceful, savage movements of this truly magnificent beast. - ᚺ

This powerful feline is a northern cousin to the cheetah, but with a wooly coat and a large, muscular body roughly 8 feet long (nose to tail). It has a short head with high-set eyes and large mouths filled with sharp teeth. A wooly cheetah is also armed with massive paws bearing retractable claws that it uses for hunting and defense. A wooly cheetah can swim or climb to escape danger, though it is not particularly adept at either. Wooly cheetah fur is coarse and short, and predominantly dull yellow spotted with black. Its underside tends more towards light yellow or even white, and is unspotted.

A typical adult wooly cheetah stands about 3 feet tall at the shoulder and weighs roughly 150 pounds, though even larger specimens have been reported in the northern steppes above Lake Jorakk.

Combat/Tactics:

The wooly cheetah is a stalk-and-chase predator. Its mode of capturing its prey is to creep up to within a moderate distance of between 100 to 200 yards, taking advantage of inequalities of the ground, bushes or other cover, and then rush in to leap onto the back of its prey and attack. Wooly cheetahs prefer to use a claw/claw/bite routine. If it lands two successive claw attacks, it has grabbed its opponent and automatically inflicts a

SIGN/TRACKS

Note the front paw is larger than the back.

Fore

Hind

RANGE ON TELLENE

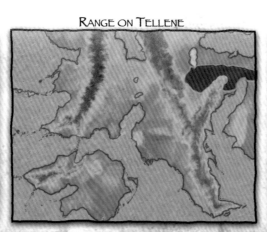

SIZE COMPARISON

6 ft

3 ft

bite attack dealing 4d4p points of damage every 5 seconds thereafter. A wooly cheetah's grip can be broken with a successful knock-back or Feat of Strength (*vs. d20p+12*). The latter can be attempted after each bite attack. While caught, a victim can only attack with a dagger or knife.

Wooly cheetahs seem to have a strong dislike of fire, and the waving of torches is often effective in causing an attacking wooly cheetah to disengage.

Habitat/Society:

Though prairies and plains adjacent to dense woodlands are its natural habitat, the wooly cheetah ranges across a variety of terrain and elevations. It keeps mostly to the northern climes and rarely travels very far south except in times of famine when the availability of game becomes scarce.

Except for mother-cub groups, wooly cheetahs are mostly solitary creatures that only meet to court, mate or fight for territory. These instances are often punctuated with the wooly cheetah's powerful roar as it seeks to drive away competitors; intensive bouts of counter-roarings are not uncommon. The male wooly cheetah has a territory of around 20 miles in size, with the female's range being about half of that; a male's range usually overlaps with the range of one or more females. Packs are rare, but when they do occur they are always composed of siblings of the same sex.

Wooly cheetahs reproduce year-round, with an average gestation time of three months and a litter of three to five cubs. Cubs are born blind and gain sight after about two weeks. They are weaned at three months old but remain with their mother for at least three more months before being taught how to hunt. Cubs remain with their mother for another year before she leaves them, after which they form a sibling pack for another year or two. After this time, they leave to establish their own territories.

The average lifespan for a wooly cheetah is roughly 12 years in the wild, though some elder Fhokki horselords claim to have played with wooly cheetah cubs in their childhood, keeping them for as long as 20 years of age and training them to hunt elk. So far as is known, these stories are merely tall tales designed to inflate the speaker's life story.

Ecology:

These felines hunt deer, elk, boars and other ungulates primarily, but will eat any smaller mammals they can catch, as well as reptiles and fish. They also seem to have a taste for geese. When farms and villages lie within a wooly cheetah's territory, almost every livestock holding is at risk of predation. This can be particularly damaging unless the farmer can somehow take preventative action when the depredation occurs.

On Tellene:

The wooly cheetah lives primarily on the prairies and plains surrounding the Rokk Woods, but also dens in the Vrykarr Mountains, the Narrajy Forest and the Rytarr Woods. However, it is rarely encountered deep within, preferring to use the brush and boulders only for sleeping and cover.

WOOLY CHEETAH

HIT POINTS:	20+3d8
SIZE/WEIGHT:	M/150 lbs.
TENACITY:	Steady
INTELLIGENCE:	Animal, Low
FATIGUE FACTOR:	3

SPEED	INIT
5	-3
ATTACK +7	DMG REDUCTION
DEFENSE +5	4
	see below
short REACH	DAMAGE 6
	TOP SAVE ▼

MOVEMENT

CRAWL:	20
WALK:	30
JOG:	35
RUN:	40
SPRINT:	45

SAVES

PHYSICAL:	+4
MENTAL:	+4
DODGE:	+10

ATTACK: Wooly Cheetahs attack with their forepaws (2d6p+1 damage) and attempt to bring down their prey (two successive hits indicating this); thereafter they automatically inflict a bite (4d4p) every 5 seconds; breaking their grasp requires a Feat of Strength vs. d20p+12

SPECIAL DEFENSES: none

GENERAL INFO

ACTIVITY CYCLE:	Crepuscular
NO. APPEARING:	1-5
% CHANCE IN LAIR:	15%
FREQUENCY:	Frequent
ALIGNMENT:	Non
VISION TYPE:	Low Light Vision
AWARENESS/SENSES:	Standard
HABITAT:	Wooded prairies and plains
DIET:	Carnivorous
ORGANIZATION:	Solitary or sibling pack
CLIMATE/TERRAIN:	Cold to temperate lowlands

YIELD

MEDICINAL:	powdered snorted feces are said to cure migraines
SPELL COMPONENTS:	fur may be used as Cheetah Speed component
HIDE/TROPHY:	pelt worth 50+ sp
TREASURE:	nil
EDIBLE:	yes
OTHER:	nil
EXPERIENCE POINT VALUE:	375

CHIMERA

Also Known As: Chimaera, Rabela's Spawn

I caught a glimpse of a chimera once, on the plains of Svimohzia one hot afternoon, as I took shade beneath the branches of an old canopied tree.

A band of warriors had accidentally flushed the beast from its hiding place in the thicket it had apparently been hiding in. No doubt the men thought they'd been tracking a lion.

Realizing their mistake too late they tried to break off and disengage, but the angered chimera was having none of it.

It attacked with a ferocity I've seldom seen in any other beast. Visibility was limited from my vantage point but I saw men flung through the air as though they were discarded rags. At one point I saw the beast pin one soldier to the ground and hold him with a great paw while simultaneously mauling another in its powerful jaws even as its serpent tail struck at yet another victim. It was a horrific sight.

I say I only caught a 'glimpse' because I was so concerned by the shouts of pain and panic that I quickly gathered up my satchel and walking stick and began running in the opposite direction. Purely to get aid for these poor men, of course. — ⚶

The female chimera is smaller than its male counterpart and lacks the regal looking mane.

The serpent tail has a venomous bite that is deadly.

This grotesque monster combines lion, goat and snake all in one dangerous composite. Some chimeras have the body of a lion with a great serpent for a tail and a goat's head stretching out of its back or side, while others have all three heads branching out from a single neck in the manner of a hydra, and still others place the heads in even more bizarre locations.

In terms of appearance and coloration, the leonine body parts appear identical to those of a male or female lion, so much so that female chimeras lack the male's thick mane (which varies from blond to black). The reptilian parts likewise resemble those of a snake with dark olive, olive green, grey brown or metal-colored scales and an inky black mouth. The goatlike head is brown, with long, pendulous ears, a convex nose and short curving horns that stay close to its head. A chimera's mane and scales generally becomes darker as the chimera ages.

A typical male chimera stands over 4 feet tall at the shoulder and is quite heavy (the calculated weight being 500 to 600 pounds), with an 8-foot long body plus an additional 4 feet of lion tail or serpent. Female chimeras stand less than 4 feet tall and weigh about 30% less than the males. Females are also smaller, being only about 5 feet long with 3-foot long tails.

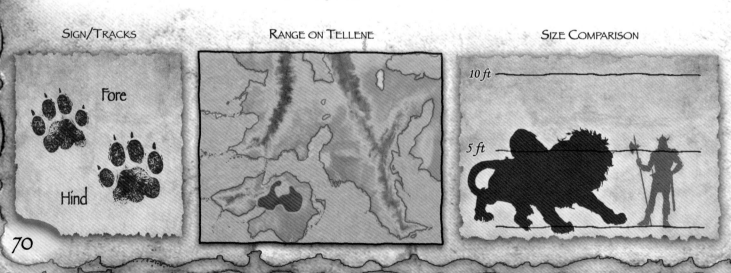

SIGN/TRACKS	RANGE ON TELLENE	SIZE COMPARISON
Fore / Hind		10 ft / 5 ft

Combat/Tactics:

Chimeras attack smaller prey with their claws, while larger prey are grasped then bitten. If the chimera has successfully attacked a target with both claws, it has grabbed its prey and can automatically inflict any bite attack every 5 counts thereafter. Once a victim makes a successful saving throw against the serpent head's venom (Virulence Factor 8; -2 to Attack, Defense and Damage for 2d12 hours on a failed saving throw with '1 or 2' indicating death; otherwise no effect), he need not make another save against that chimera's venom during this encounter.

A chimera's grip can be broken with a successful knock-back or Feat of Strength (vs. d20p+14). The latter can be attempted after each bite attack. While caught, a chimera's prey can only attack with a dagger, knife or claws of its own.

Alternatively, with a successful attack, a chimera's goat head can breathe fire at a single target up to 15 feet away for 3d8p points of damage (half damage on a successful Dexterity save vs. d20p+12).

Chimeras take advantage of factors that reduce visibility; many kills take place near some form of cover or at night. They sneak up to the victim until they come within 100 feet. When in a pair, the chimeras work together and flank their prey from different points. The attack is short and powerful; they attempt to catch the victim with a fast rush and final leap. Smaller prey may simply be killed by a swipe of a chimera's paw, while larger prey receives a savage bite. Only when facing intelligent prey or in fear for their life do chimeras usually resort to a fire breathing attack (as they prefer their meat raw).

Ecology:

Female chimeras do the majority of the hunting, being more agile than the males and unencumbered by the heavy and conspicuous mane. However, if near the hunt, males have a tendency to dominate the kill once the female has succeeded and eaten. Males rarely share food they have killed by themselves. When game is scarce, a chimera can survive by using its goatlike head to consume a wide range of vegetation.

On Tellene:

Chimeras primarily inhabit the grasslands, brush and forests of Svimohzia, where they range widely and sporadically, either singularly or in pairs.

A line in Mezo Hilam's long *"Poem of the Dark"* calls the chimera *"a thing of immortal make, not human nor demi-human nor of any humanoid known, lion-fronted and snake behind, a goat but one winter's young in the middle, and snorting out a terrible breath of bright flame."* He also attributes the rearing of the first chimera to a mythical creature named Rabela, who he calls *"half a nymph with glancing eyes and fair cheeks, and half again a huge snake, great and awful, with speckled skin, eating raw flesh beneath the secret parts of the Netherdeep. There, then, did the gods appoint her a glorious house to dwell in: and she keeps guard beneath the earth, grim Rabela, a nymph who dies not nor grows old all her days."*

[1] A Chimera heart, if eaten as a supplemental material component by the recipient of a Feat of Strength spell, performs this feat as if possessed of 25/51 Strength. A tooth from a Chimera's goat head may be used as a supplemental material component in the Fire Finger spell. Doing so permits the caster the option of expending up to 50 additional spell points on the enchantment over and above the maximum. A Chimera goat's head has 32 teeth.

HIT POINTS:	40+7d8
SIZE/WEIGHT:	L/350-600 lbs.
TENACITY:	Brave
INTELLIGENCE:	Animal, High
FATIGUE FACTOR:	2

MOVEMENT

CRAWL:	10
WALK:	15
JOG:	20
RUN:	25
SPRINT:	30

SAVES

PHYSICAL:	+12
MENTAL:	+12
DODGE:	+12

ATTACK: Claws deal two 2d4p+4, with 2d8p+6 from lion head bites or 2d4p+4 from snake or goat head. Grip broken with FoS (vs d20p+14). Snake head also injects poison (VF 8; save or suffer -2 to Attack, Defense, and Damage for 2d12 hours; a 'nat 1 or 2' save equals death). Alternatively, goat head can breathe fire for 2d8p points (save vs d20p+12 for half).

GENERAL INFO

ACTIVITY CYCLE:	Crepuscular
NO. APPEARING:	1-2
% CHANCE IN LAIR:	40%
FREQUENCY:	Unusual
ALIGNMENT:	Non
VISION TYPE:	Low light vision
AWARENESS/SENSES:	Excellent hearing (Listening 85%), smell (Tracking 70%)
HABITAT:	Savannas, brush, forests
DIET:	Omnivorous
ORGANIZATION:	Individuals
CLIMATE/TERRAIN:	Semi-tropical to tropical grasslands

YIELD

MEDICINAL:	none
SPELL COMPONENTS:	yes[1]
HIDE/TROPHY:	hide worth 200-400 sp as rug or wall hanging
TREASURE:	incidental
EDIBLE:	yes (except tail)
OTHER:	nil
EXPERIENCE POINT VALUE:	1100

COCKATRICE   Also Known As: Zazahni Cock, Vohven Terror

If you ever find yourself in the south of the Awhom Forest there's a hill known as 'the Giwhani' just off the trail where some peculiar white statues stand arranged in haphazard fashion around the large stump of an ancient tree. Word to the wise — just keep walking and don't let your curiosity get the better of you.

'Giwhani' literally means 'Hill of the Unwary', I believe, and the unwary forever posed in stone on it's hilltop are not statues but all that remains of those who foolishly ipaused on their journey to investigate further.

At last report there are 26 statues on that hill. All victims of the ancient cockatrice cock rumored to live in the stump.

I have never seen a living cockatrice first hand and I'm thankful for it. I did have an opportunity to examine a rotting cockatrice corpse once. The creature had been found flattened by cart and wagon wheels near a busy byway in Ahznomahn. If not for its bizarre bat-like wings and scaly tail one would think it a common cock. Someone had already removed its poison sack (which can fetch a nice sum of silver) but I did manage to take a feather. It's a prized possesion which I use as a quill to this day. — ⚜

A cockatrice will use its wings to appear larger than it actually is when threatened.

When a cockatrice's comb stands erect it is in attack posture. Beware!

The cockatrice resembles a large chicken covered in feathers varying from iridescent green to chartreuse, possessing dark red eyes, a scaly tail and diminutive reptilian wings. A typical adult cockatrice stands roughly 3 feet tall and weighs about 50 pounds. Males can be differentiated from females by their rooster-like comb and wattle. Cockatrices are not capable of long distance flight, although they are generally capable of flying for short distances, such as over fences or into trees (where they roost). They sometimes fly to explore their surroundings, but usually do so only to flee perceived danger.

Combat/Tactics:

The cockatrice is a fearsome creature, for its merest touch can turn flesh to stone. Any living creature touching or touched by a cockatrice* must attempt a saving throw (vs. d20p+10) or be instantly turned to stone. Cockatrices are immune to the stone touch of other cockatrices. A cockatrice can also breathe poison (one target within 5 feet; VF 7 poison; failed saves suffer -2 to Attack, Defense and Damage for 2d12 hours).

A cockatrice's malevolent powers are completely ineffective against both weasels and chickens (including hens, roosters and chicks). Weasel urine is a Virulence Factor 12 poison to a cockatrice that kills on contact if it fails its saving throw (vs. d20p+12). The cry of a rooster will cause a cockatrice to flee in terror if it fails a saving throw (vs. d20p+10).

*A character has been 'touched' by a cockatrice if it lands a successful hit in melee. Shield hits are ignored.

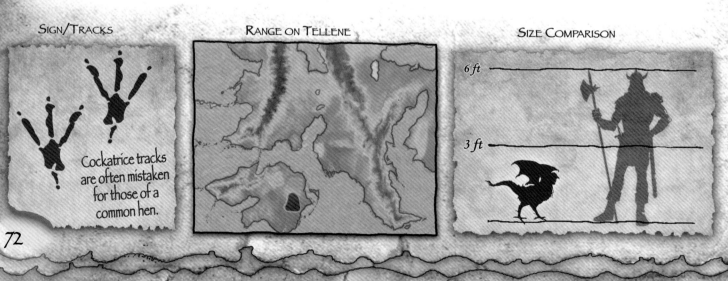

SIGN/TRACKS

Cockatrice tracks are often mistaken for those of a common hen.

RANGE ON TELLENE

SIZE COMPARISON

6 ft

3 ft

Habitat/Society:

Cockatrices are gregarious creatures, living in small flocks of up to six individuals with a communal approach to the incubation of eggs and raising of young. Individual cockatrices in a flock dominate others, establishing a 'pecking order' with dominate individuals having priority for access to food and nesting locations. Killing the dominate cockatrice causes a temporary disruption to this social order until a new pecking order is established.

Flocks of cockatrices nest in sheltered trees, with ample coverage and low hanging branches. Nests can be found in one tree, or several, depending on the layout of the area. They prefer areas where there is thick, natural cover. Nests are firmly established, depending on the pecking order, and every cockatrice in the flock knows its place. Some birds have been known to collect shiny objects and coins. These are always found in the nest of the dominate male.

A cockatrice may live for up to 11 years.

Ecology:

There is much debate among sages on how to properly classify a cockatrice. Some claim the creature is a bird, where others state it is some sort of aberration or supernatural creature. Still others say the creature is more of a reptile. Thus far any attempts to identify the creature with one species have been met with failure.

This debate has led to many misconceptions about the creature. Unfortunately, cockatrices are difficult to track and even harder to capture, leading many to believe the debate will never be properly solved. One legend states that cockatrice are born when a chicken egg is fertilized by a serpent, though this is no more true than the fable that a basilisk is spawned from a serpent or toad egg raised by a hen. Despite all the confusion surrounding cockatrices one thing is for sure, cockatrices do lay eggs. These eggs are highly prized and can often be sold to interested scholars.

Cockatrices subsist primarily on grass, bugs, and bugs that eat grass, which includes mostly grubs and worms. When food is scarce they eat small mammals such as rodents, whether hunted or found already dead. A starving cockatrice will eat just about anything, even attacking larger creatures to feed itself, if necessary.

On Tellene:

Cockatrices are native to Svimohzia, though mostly encountered in the lands of Zazahni, in and around the Awhom Forest and the Vohven Jungle. In the village of Sarmish, a local legend is that a cockatrice terrorized the village until it was imprisoned in a cellar. A prize of land was offered to anyone who could kill the creature, but none was successful, until a man named Volzar lowered a polished bronze mirror into the cellar. The cockatrice battled against its own reflection until exhausted, at which point Volzar was able to kill it. Today there is still an area of land near Sarmish called Volzar's Acres.

COCKATRICE

HIT POINTS:	10+2d8
SIZE/WEIGHT:	S/50 lbs.
TENACITY:	Nervous
INTELLIGENCE:	Animal, Low
FATIGUE FACTOR:	-1

SPEED		INIT
10	ATTACK +5 DMG REDUCTION	2
	DEFENSE +7 0	
	see below	3
short REACH	DAMAGE	TOP SAVE

MOVEMENT

CRAWL:	1¼
WALK:	2½
JOG:	5
RUN:	7½
SPRINT:	10

SAVES

PHYSICAL:	+5
MENTAL:	+5
DODGE:	+5

ATTACK: Poison breath (VF 7; save or suffer -2 to Attack, Defense and Damage for 2d12 hours).
Stone touch (save vs. d20p+10 or turn to stone)

WEAKNESSES: Weasel urine (VF 12) kills on contact with a failed save. Rooster crows cause a cockatrice to flee in terror on a failed save (vs. d20p+10).

GENERAL INFO

ACTIVITY CYCLE:	Diurnal
NO. APPEARING:	1-6
% CHANCE IN LAIR:	35%
FREQUENCY:	Sporadic
ALIGNMENT:	Non
VISION TYPE:	Standard (plus gaze attack)
AWARENESS/SENSES:	Standard
HABITAT:	Savannas and woodlands
DIET:	Omnivorous
ORGANIZATION:	Individuals or flock
CLIMATE/TERRAIN:	Warm temperate to tropical lowlands

YIELD

MEDICINAL:	nil
SPELL COMPONENTS:	unknown
HIDE/TROPHY:	nil
TREASURE:	incidental
EDIBLE:	no
OTHER:	eggs can be sold for up to 60 sp
EXPERIENCE POINT VALUE:	500

C

CROCODILE

GREATER CROCODILE
LESSER CROCODILE

Crocodiles are extremely dangerous animals. It is almost impossible to break free of the powerful jaws of these ambush predators once they've gotten hold of you and start to execute their 'death roll.'

The best way to keep from becoming the dinner of a crocodile is to avoid the edge of any river, stream or brackish water until you've taken precautions — for that is where they love to lie in wait. If you get within a body length of the water where they are, it is too late. It's good practice to prod the water with a long pole before crossing or drawing nearer. Observe other animals in the area. If they are taking to the water it may be safe. If they are keeping their distance, be leery.

Crocodile bellies are vulnerable and soft, so, if you need to attack one, try to get at its underside with a sharp blade. If that's not possible, attack the soft parts of the mouth or the eyes.

They are pure eating machines, built to strike. The last thing many crocodile victims have seen has been an explosion of water and foam followed by the flash of teeth. I thoroughly believe that the disappearance of several fellow wanderers is the direct result of them being eaten by crocodiles. You never want to meet one if you are by yourself. That is almost certainly the end of your existence. —

Crocodiles are large aquatic reptiles, with size varying by species (lesser and greater). Both species have brown to dark green leathery hides that, when partially submerged, give them the appearance of a floating log. Lesser crocodiles have an average length of 12 feet and weigh about 800 pounds, while greater ones stand roughly 18 feet long and weigh over 2 tons.

Combat/Tactics:

The most common tactic for a crocodile is to wait, submerged and camouflaged until its prey comes close. It then lunges from the water, biting with its powerful jaws. A successful attack means the crocodile grabs its prey in its mouth, dealing damage appropriate for its size (4d4p+4 lesser, 4d4p+10 greater). Once its jaws are clamped down, only a successful Feat of Strength (*vs. d20p+12* lesser or *vs. d20p+18* greater) can open them. The crocodile then moves towards the water (if not already there), taking its prey under until it drowns.

If somehow prevented from retreating underwater, the crocodile's movements and grinding of teeth inflict automatic half damage every few seconds (based on its Speed) as it attempts to retreat with its meal. Crocodiles have no interest in fighting. Rather, their only desire is to grab a meal and escape.

Cold spells deal double damage against crocodiles.

Habitat/Society/Ecology:

Lesser crocodiles live in freshwater habitats like rivers, lakes and wetlands where they feed mostly on vertebrates like fish, reptiles and mammals, or sometimes on invertebrates like mollusks and crustaceans. Greater crocodiles are found in brackish or saltwater areas, and eat similar (if larger) foods.

Crocodiles have even been encountered in moats, large caverns and dungeon pools, having been captured young and placed there by nefarious or forward-thinking individuals.

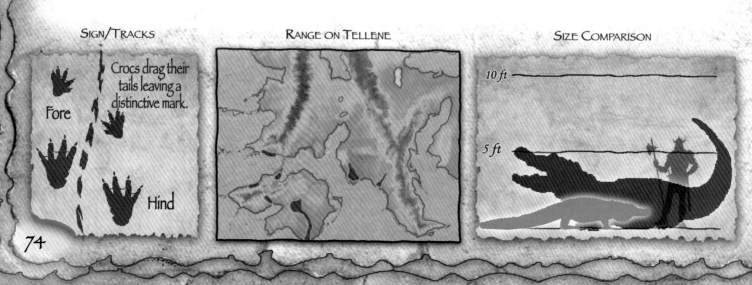

SIGN/TRACKS	RANGE ON TELLENE	SIZE COMPARISON

Crocs drag their tails leaving a distinctive mark.

Fore

Hind

10 ft

5 ft

LESSER CROCODILE

HIT POINTS: 30+5d8
SIZE/WEIGHT: L/800 lbs.
TENACITY: Steady
INTELLIGENCE: Animal, Low
FATIGUE FACTOR: 3

MOVEMENT

CRAWL: 2½
WALK: 5
JOG: 10
RUN: 12½
SWIM: 15

SAVES

PHYSICAL: +9
MENTAL: +9
DODGE: +9

SPEED 7 | INIT -1
ATTACK +9
DEFENSE +4 | DMG REDUCTION 5/3
DAMAGE 4d4p+4
short REACH | TOP SAVE 7

ATTACK: Lesser crocodile bites deal 4d4p+4 points of damage (break free with FoS vs. d20p+12). Automatic half damage every 7 seconds grasped (DR from armor and body applies).

WEAKNESSES: The creature's underbelly is less well protected (DR 3). Cold spells deal double damage against lesser crocodiles.

GREATER CROCODILE

HIT POINTS: 40+10d8
SIZE/WEIGHT: H/2 tons
TENACITY: Brave
INTELLIGENCE: Animal, High
FATIGUE FACTOR: 3

MOVEMENT

CRAWL: 2½
WALK: 5
JOG: 10
RUN: 15
SWIM: 20

SAVES

PHYSICAL: +14
MENTAL: +14
DODGE: +14

SPEED 6 | INIT -1
ATTACK +14
DEFENSE +4 | DMG REDUCTION 8/4
DAMAGE 4d4p+10
short REACH | TOP SAVE 8

ATTACK: Powerful jaws deal 4d4p+10 points of damage (break free with FoS vs. d20p+18). Automatic half damage every 6 seconds grasped (DR from armor and body applies).

WEAKNESSES: The creature's underbelly is less well protected (DR 4). Cold spells deal double damage against greater crocodiles.

GENERAL INFO

ACTIVITY CYCLE:	Diurnal
NO. APPEARING:	3-24
% CHANCE IN LAIR:	n/a
FREQUENCY:	Frequent
ALIGNMENT:	Non
VISION TYPE:	Keen eyesight
AWARENESS/SENSES:	Excellent hearing (Listening 80%) and smell (Tracking 50%)
HABITAT:	Freshwater lakes and rivers
DIET:	Carnivorous
ORGANIZATION:	Float
CLIMATE/TERRAIN:	Semi-tropical to tropical wetlands

GENERAL INFO

ACTIVITY CYCLE:	Diurnal
NO. APPEARING:	1 or 2-12
% CHANCE IN LAIR:	n/a
FREQUENCY:	Infrequent
ALIGNMENT:	Non
VISION TYPE:	Keen eyesight
AWARENESS/SENSES:	Excellent hearing (Listening 80%) and smell (Tracking 50%)
HABITAT:	Brackish water and coastal areas
DIET:	Carnivorous
ORGANIZATION:	Solitary to bask
CLIMATE/TERRAIN:	Semi-tropical to tropical wetlands

On Tellene:

Crocodiles are common throughout the warm lands of the Svimohzish Isle, southern Brandobia, and the southern Kalamaran Empire.

The most deaths in a single crocodile attack may have occurred during the time of Fortnight's Battle, when 900 hobgoblin soldiers (in an attempt to ambush the Zazahni legions) crossed the swamps at the mouth of the Durbattum River. Over 400 hobgoblins were said to have been eaten by the local crocodiles, although the Zazahni claimed that their swordplay was undoubtedly the largest contributory factor.

YIELD

MEDICINAL:	nil
SPELL COMPONENTS:	nil
HIDE/TROPHY:	yes, hides for clothing and teeth for jewelry
TREASURE:	incidental
EDIBLE:	yes
OTHER:	eggs, worth up to 10 sp
EXPERIENCE POINT VALUE:	400 (lesser); 1150 (greater)

CYCLOPS

Also Known As: Chycosh, Great Eye, Skarran Giant

The eye makes a tempting target.

Cyclops prefer to use crude smashing weapons such as wooden clubs.

The Skarran giant can always be counted on for a good fight. Nasty brutes they are undisciplined fighters usually attacking out of blind rage and often as the result of some perceived offense such as trespassing what it regards as its territory.

Determining if you are in 'marked' cyclops territory can be as challenging as solving a sphinx's riddle. A stick leaning on a rock. A boulder tilted just so. This lunacy is supposed to mean something to the cyclops.

They're dumb as rocks in my opinion. I've seen them wantonly take on superior, well-armed parties without hesitation, even those with mages. If they are capable of negotiation or barter I've not witnessed it first hand. They seem to be motivated by one purpose — keeping others out.

Once while traveling through a mountain pass known to enter cyclops territory, our fighting man came up with the bright idea to load down a mule with meat and ale. "Let's send a pack bearer up ahead to negotiate safe passage!" Try as the rest of us might we could not persuade him of the folly of his idea. The poor packbearer selected to carry out the mission wasn't too keen on it either and demanded a bribe in silver to buy his compliance — money he would never have a chance to spend.

To make a long story short, the fighter received four broken ribs after being clubbed with that very packbearer's body. A lesson on cyclops nature hard learned. — 𝔖

This brutish one-eyed giant is often confused with the hill giant from a distance, for both dress in skins and furs and carry massive clubs as weapons. When approached, however, the creature's single eye easily identifies it as one of the cyclopes race. Standing nearly 20 feet tall and weighing over 3 tons, a cyclops has gray flesh often caked with dust, for it never bathes. Its greasy hair is black and its large single eye is yellow with a dark brown iris.

Combat/Tactics:

With only one eye, the cyclops lacks proper depth perception, and thus is unable to use ranged or hurled weapons with much accuracy. If the cyclops attacks with such a weapon, it suffers a –6 penalty to its attack roll. The cyclops suffers no depth perception penalties to melee combat.

Habitat/Society:

The cyclopes are extremely territorial creatures with a foul disposition, defining their borders through simple marks or

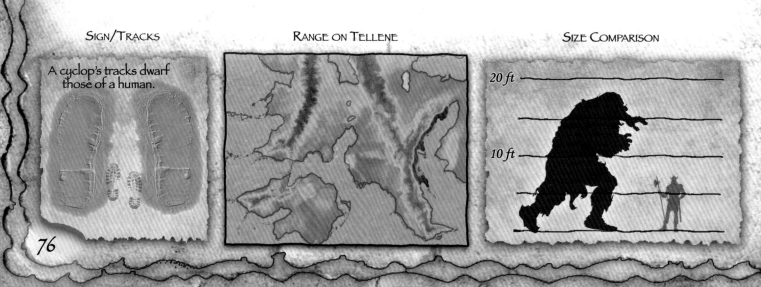

SIGN/TRACKS

A cyclop's tracks dwarf those of a human.

RANGE ON TELLENE

SIZE COMPARISON

20 ft

10 ft

paintings on large rocks. Once a cyclops has marked its territory, it does not allow other humanoid or giant races within its borders. It has no qualms with simple, unintelligent beasts and allows them to roam freely across its territory (provided they do not become a nuisance or attack its sheep), but races even as diminutive as kobolds are considered a threat to the cyclops' solitude.

Although otherwise crude, cyclops are deft hands at stonecarving, and their mountain caves are no mere holes in the ground. Instead, the ceilings and floors are flat or appropriately stepped, and the walls are smooth and curve outwards as if designed for a race much rounder and fatter than the cyclopes. These walls are colorfully painted in white, blue, red and black, and often enhanced with figural decorations such as reliefs and friezes.

Most cyclopes live for 800 years, reaching maturity after 120 years. A female can give birth every 50 years, but a family with more than three children is unusual. Cyclopes can communicate (if only in pidgin) with most other giants, and worship the Battle Rager, whom they call Ugarik.

Ecology:

A cyclops' diet consists mainly of meat (usually from the sheep or giant goats it herds), fish (when rivers and lakes are nearby), vegetables, fruit, roots, and nuts. Most cyclopes seem to have an instinctive dislike of grains, beans, milks, sugary desserts, cheeses and salt.

As noted above, a cyclops rarely has a single natural enemy; rather, it has several (or dozens) of sapient foes that have banded together in order to resist its predations or even eliminate its presence from the region.

On Tellene:

It is said that the cyclops originally came from a land to the north, migrating south through Torakk and then through Drhokker, to the somewhat warmer climates of Skarra and northern Reanaaria Bay. In fact, it was the Ridijo Dejy who gave the giant its name, calling it the 'chycosh' (now mutated into the word 'cyclops'). The hardy giants have continued to populate the area since, spreading south on both sides of the bay, raiding small villages and stealing livestock all the while.

Sightings of these creatures are rare, but Reanaarian sailors have occasionally claimed to see cyclops walking the coastline as far south as Zoa and as far north as Shyff.

[1] A cyclops eye can be used as an material component in the ninth level Clairoptikos spell, enabling the mage to double the spell's duration.

[2] Traveling showmen that charge for viewing collections of oddities and preserved monsters will certainly be interested in adding a cyclops' head to their exhibit.

CYCLOPS

HIT POINTS:	52+14d8
SIZE/WEIGHT:	G/over 3 tons
TENACITY:	Brave
INTELLIGENCE:	Slow
FATIGUE FACTOR:	-4

SPEED		INIT
11	ATTACK +22*	5
	+8	DICE REDUCTION 8
	4d10p+16	
long REACH	DEFENSE / DAMAGE	TOP SAVE ▼ 12

MOVEMENT

CRAWL:	10
WALK:	15
JOG:	20
RUN:	25
SPRINT:	30

SAVES

PHYSICAL:	+28
MENTAL:	+16
DODGE:	+19

ATTACK:
Cyclops favor giant clubs with which to smash their foes.

WEAKNESSES:
*A cyclops' poor vision imposes a -6 penalty on Attack rolls with ranged or hurled weapons.

GENERAL INFO

ACTIVITY CYCLE:	Any
NO. APPEARING:	1-8
% CHANCE IN LAIR:	40%
FREQUENCY:	Unusual
ALIGNMENT:	Chaotic Evil
VISION TYPE:	Poor depth perception
AWARENESS/SENSES:	Standard
HABITAT:	Caves
DIET:	Omnivorous
ORGANIZATION:	Gang
CLIMATE/TERRAIN:	Temperate mountains

YIELD

MEDICINAL:	nil
SPELL COMPONENTS:	eye, for Clairoptikos spell[1]
HIDE/TROPHY:	heads, for trophies or traveling shows[2]
TREASURE:	mass of coins and misc. goods worth ≥ 2500 sp
EDIBLE:	yes, but may be considered cannibalism
OTHER:	nil
EXPERIENCE POINT VALUE:	2300

DEVIL

Also Known As: Azagon, Horned Fiend, Scrann

Beware any man that doth proffer thee that which seemest grossly in thine favor. Shouldest he be of kindly heart, ye be like unto a robber for surely in taking so advantage of his ignorance you do steal his labor or goods. Having ministered my day's moral lesson, thinkest upon the alternative. Let the buyer beware, for the bauble you purchase may not be what thou believest.

A greater villain than the cheat does exist. He too doth offer what you desire. This may be rare items but may also be intangible desires of the heat such as fame, power, or the heart of a maiden. For these treasures he asks no coin. Rather he requests a minor service which in thine heart ye knowest to be iniquitous. Thou mightest think that such a venal sin is small price to pay for such a reward.

If thou havest good fortune, thine newfound patron may be but a ruthless criminal or scheming noble. All ye risk losing is thine life. Shouldest he be a devil, thou hast made the first footfall upon the road to eternal damnation.

Having become indebted to the fiend, he will leverage this influence to corrupt thine heart. Always he will offer the easy and effortless route. He will grow to know thine foibles and will ask from ye all that ye are willing to do but never more. In time, as ye bcome accustomed to these commodious gifts, the price will escalate but few then possess the will to resist. It is then that ye will comprehend that ye have volunteered to become its slave. What awaits is a fiery afterlife of torment. -◉

In its natural form, a devil appears to be a muscular 7-foot tall humanoid with cloven-hoofed goat's legs and a sinuous barbed tail. Its skin tone is a deep reddish hue with auburn body hair. Their heads are not unlike those of humans – albeit with two vestigial horns and pointy ears. Devils are uniformly bald but may have bearded chins.

It is unlikely that devils will be encountered in their true form, for they possess the ability to take on the physical form of a human or humanoid. They are limited to one body for the duration of their mission on the Terraverse, so this is not to be confused with the far more mutable capabilities of a creature such as the changeling (*q.v.*).

Though powerful combatants, devils are far more than supernatural enforcers. Indeed, resorting to combat (especially in their true form) is only a last resort and generally indicative of the fact that their mission has been fatally compromised.

Combat/Tactics:

In their human or humanoid guise, devils assume a role that supports their wider aim. Clothing, gear and armaments will be selected to support this ruse. As such, it is difficult to precisely define the combat skills of any specific devil's humanoid form. In general, they utilize a standard weapon with a +13 Attack and +6 Damage bonus. Armor worn, if any, does not contribute to the devil's DR rating. Devils may feign injuries if necessary to support their cover story (perhaps creating an illusion of a gaping wound to bolster the ruse).

Devils are all magicians capable of producing a variety of magical effects.[1] The mere effect of engaging a devil in

---

Be not foolish in thinking you can reveal the presence of a devil by attempting to force any of whom you suspect duplicitousness to retreat before your divine icon. Even should they prove to be a devil in guise, such attempts will prove an utter failure until it has revealed its true nature. Worse yet, you will have revealed yourself to the beast and conceded to it the opportunity to react accordingly.

WILL FACTOR 24

SIZE COMPARISON

6 ft

3 ft

conversation carries the weight of a Charm spell, while their orders may carry the weight of the Command spell any time they desire. They may also cause anyone within 15 feet to *Panic* and can Teleport, read minds[2] (as with the *Mind Reading* spell) and create illusions at will. As denizens of Hell, they are immune to fire of all sorts regardless of intensity. Toxins and diseases have no effect as well. Only silvered and greater magical weapons may seriously injure them. They regenerate wounds at a rate of 1 hp/10 seconds unless holy water has been applied to the injury.

In their natural form, devils are formidable adversaries frequently wielding a wickedly barbed fork that inflicts 5d4p+6 damage. They may also sting with their venomous tail. This causes 2d4p damage but injects a paralytic toxin that persists for 2d12p hours unless a successful poison save (*vs. d20p+13*) is made.

Habitat/Society:

Devils originate in Hell where they are but lesser servitors of extraordinarily powerful beings. In this setting they are most typically subalterns in the legions of evil, taskmasters or petty bureaucrats. They report to and execute the orders of more powerful and ruthless nefarious beings in the tightly controlled hierarchy.

On Tellene:

With few important responsibilities on their home plane yet possessed of intelligence, guile and determination to better their position, devils are often sent forth to Tellene to further the cause of subjugating all beings under the yoke of eternal tyranny. Infrequently, this takes the form of direct action wherein they assume command or act as advisors to evil armies (either human or humanoid) poised to conquer the lands of goodly folk.

More often, however, they insinuate themselves into society in order to corrupt the hearts and minds of these same people. They work assiduously to tempt people into wickedness by catering to their weaknesses — be it sloth, vice, greed or other.

Most devils have a miscellaneous skill or two at which they have Expert mastery or better. They employ these skills to tempt, goad or shame others into engaging in a contest, frequently offering a fantastic prize as an incentive. There's but one catch, and that's the forfeiture of one's immortal soul if defeated. Such skills may include Riddling, Oratory, Musician or other.

Folktales honor brash individuals who've beaten a devil at his own game. However, they are rare and fortunate persons. Devils rarely lose and their contracts are iron-clad.

Devils may also be summoned to Tellene by very powerful mages and bound by writ of magical law to perform some service. Devils despise such servitude and seek to abide only by the strictest literal interpretation of any commands in order to pervert their intent. At times, this may even involve a temporary alliance with morally opposed parties as a means to gain vengeance upon the mage.

[1] *Devils are considered to be 13th level casters for saving throw purposes*
[2] *Devils must focus their attention to employ this power*

DEVIL

HIT POINTS:	27+7d8
SIZE/WEIGHT:	M/200 lbs.
TENACITY:	Fearless
INTELLIGENCE:	Smart
FATIGUE FACTOR:	n/a

SPEED 5 · INIT -3 · ATTACK +13 · MAGIC REDUCTION · +8 · 18* · DEFENSE · by weapon +6 · DAMAGE · n/a · medium REACH · TOP SAVE ▼

ATTACK: Devils prefer deception and magic to physical combat; if forced into the latter, they attack with a barbed fork (5d4p+6 damage, 5' reach) plus a poisonous tail (2d4p damage plus save vs. d20p+13 or paralyzed)

SPECIAL DEFENSES: immune to fire and poison.; regeneration
*Silvered/magic weapons reduce DR to 10

MOVEMENT

CRAWL:	2½
WALK:	5
JOG:	10
RUN:	15
SPRINT:	25

SAVES

PHYSICAL:	+14
MENTAL:	+18
DODGE:	+12

GENERAL INFO

ACTIVITY CYCLE:	Any (always active)
NO. APPEARING:	1
% CHANCE IN LAIR:	nil
FREQUENCY:	Exotic
ALIGNMENT:	Lawful Evil
VISION TYPE:	Undead Sight
AWARENESS/SENSES:	Mind readers
HABITAT:	Any
DIET:	nil
ORGANIZATION:	Individuals (in the Terraverse), or brigade
CLIMATE/TERRAIN:	Any

YIELD

MEDICINAL:	nil
SPELL COMPONENTS:	skin may be used to enscribe a Protection from Devils scroll
HIDE/TROPHY:	nil
TREASURE:	jewelry (esp. relevant to special skill) ≥1000 sp
EDIBLE:	no
OTHER:	nil

EXPERIENCE POINT VALUE: 1313

DINOSAUR MEGALOSAURUS

There are no shortage of man-eaters on the face of Tellene — this is a fact. There are those who believe it was never the gods' intention for such creatures to roam the world. Me? I believe it was their way of keeping our numbers in check or perhaps even a cruel trick for their own amusement.

Of all these man-eaters, one of the most fearsome I've ever seen is the sugok. You'll find them in Tarisato within the reaches of the Obakasek Jungle and in the western foothills of the Lopoliri Mountains. I've even heard rumors they've even been spotted in southern Svimohzia.

Most often they are solitary hunters, though sometimes they hunt in small packs but without the cooperation evidenced by wolves or hyenas. When they hunt in groups it tends to be a free-for-all with sugok piling on the slowest victim and tearing it apart before moving on to the next.

I don't fancy fighting one of them, I can tell you that. They are quick and agile with a jaw and set of teeth that can make quick work of flesh — armored or not. Their powerful tails can topple horse and rider and lash out so swiftly as it spins and turns in battle that it's near impossible to attack them from all directions — a tactic that often works so well against other larger monsters. If you must fight one, arm yourself with knowledge.

Reflecting the sun off of polished metal and into the eyes of the sugok distracts them. Loud shouting, banging on shields and blowing whistles or horns also confuses them. Head shots are not all that effective against their thick skulls and small brains. Go for the belly and throat! — §

Watch the teeth on the sugok — these beasts are quick and love to bite the heads off their victims.

These creatures love to rush at their opponents and seem almost pleased when they have to chase down prey.

This large, powerful dinosaur stands about 30 feet long and 10 feet tall and weighs around 4 tons. The megalosaurus is a biped and a fast runner despite its large size. It is also a carnivore, using its sharp teeth to rip apart the flesh of its prey. It has a large reptilian head with serrated teeth, a long tail, three-toed feet and short three-clawed hands and arms, though these are not as short nor as vestigial as the arms of the tyrannosaurus rex. Its scaled hide varies in color, with grays, greens and browns being most common.

Combat/Tactics:

The megalosaurus' great muscle power and speed help it to bring down even the largest opponents with its ferocious biting attacks. Furthermore, it is an efficient predator with a high intelligence for its kind; this makes it difficult to fool or lead astray with simple distractions.

Against smaller prey (size M or less), it will attempt to pin the creature underfoot. If successful, the attack does 3d6p damage and traps its opponent (requiring a Feat of Strength *vs.* d20p+15 to escape). Subsequent biting attacks on a pinned individual are made with a +18 bonus instead of +12 (Attack speed remains the same). Larger opponents and smaller ones too nimble to pin are subject to the creature's powerful bite.

Although it has a long, powerful tail, it uses this primarily as a means of balancing its body, and rarely uses it to ward off enemies.

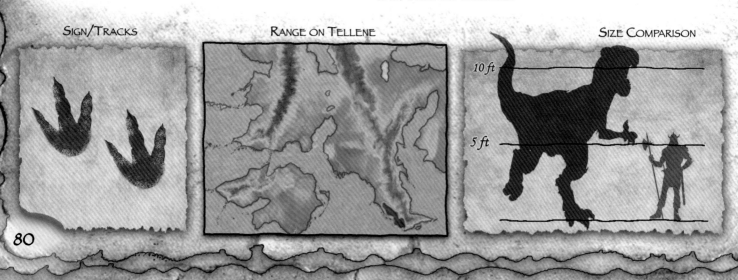

SIGN/TRACKS	RANGE ON TELLENE	SIZE COMPARISON
		10 ft 5 ft

Habitat/Society:

The megalosaurus is a regular hunter, consuming the flesh of other large lizards and mammals, such as sauropods, elephants, deer and great hunting cats, as well as any other living creatures that can slake its hunger and provide enough food to keep its massive frame alive. However, it will also scavenge kills from other predators if given a chance; except with predators larger than itself, its mere presence is often enough to cause the original hunter to flee. A megalosaurus also swallows small stones, though not for sustenance; these gizzard stones aid digestion by breaking down food once it enters the stomach.

Megalosauri are mostly solitary creatures, coming together only for mating. When it comes time to lay the eggs, the female digs a nest in the ground, then lays a clusters of two to twelve eggs (each over 6 inches long and weighing over 3 pounds), two at a time, all in one sitting. The nest is then covered with sand or vegetation to keep it warm. The parents remain in the area for the incubation period (an average of 2 months long) and keep close watch over the eggs. After the eggs hatch, they feed them with masticated flesh and guide the hatchlings for a few months before leaving them to their fates. Despite this surprising amount of early care from such a dangerous carnivore, the survival rate is low, with an average of one megalosaurus per nest surviving to adulthood.

If its lifespan is not cut short, a megalosaurus on Tellene might live to be about 30 years old.

Ecology:

Because the megalosaurus is both a predator and a scavenger, it sometimes comes into conflict with other carnivores over a meal. Typically, these competitors are other dinosaurs such as the tyrannosaurus rex, for most smaller creatures instinctively flee at the sight of this massive lizard approaching. However, large flying creatures (such as the pterosaur or the giant eagle) may be able to drive off a megalosaurus from their kill by swooping in and slashing at its eyes, though only the most hungry and starving fliers dare such an attack.

On Tellene:

The megalosaurus, like other dinosaurs, is a rare sight in the Sovereign Lands. Rumors of giant lizards come from many areas, though the most likely areas for the megalosaurus are the Obakasek and Vohven Jungles, with their vast unexplored areas and large animal populations to serve as a food source.

[1]*Megalosaurus skin makes boots, armor and other leather items of good, durable quality. When sold as a hide to a leatherworker, it can fetch 20-40 sp per hide.*

A megalosaurus head is desirable for display purposes, usually to show prowess. Vain or insecure people of means may pay up to 500 sp for such a trophy.

MEGALOSAURUS

HIT POINTS:	30+12d8
SIZE/WEIGHT:	G/8000 lbs.
TENACITY:	Brave
INTELLIGENCE:	Animal, Low
FATIGUE FACTOR:	-4

SPEED		INIT
10	+12	2
	+6	6
	6d6p	
medium REACH		TOP SAVE 9

MOVEMENT

CRAWL:	15
WALK:	20
JOG:	25
RUN:	30
SPRINT:	35

SAVES

PHYSICAL:	+15
MENTAL:	+9
DODGE:	+12

ATTACK: Megalosauri are aggressive predators that rush opponents and savage them with a massive bite (6d6p). It may attempt to pin size M and smaller prey (requiring a Feat of Strength *vs. d20p+15* to escape) inflicting 3d6p in so doing. Bite attacks occur at the same speed as standard attacks. Victims cannot attack while pinned.

GENERAL INFO

ACTIVITY CYCLE:	Diurnal
NO. APPEARING:	1
% CHANCE IN LAIR:	0
FREQUENCY:	Unusual
ALIGNMENT:	Non
VISION TYPE:	Standard
AWARENESS/SENSES:	Standard
HABITAT:	Savanna
DIET:	Carnivorous
ORGANIZATION:	Individuals
CLIMATE/TERRAIN:	Subtropical to tropical wilderness

YIELD

MEDICINAL:	nil
SPELL COMPONENTS:	nil
HIDE/TROPHY:	various[1]
TREASURE:	incidental
EDIBLE:	yes
OTHER:	nil
EXPERIENCE POINT VALUE:	1067

DINOSAUR   PTEROSAUR   Also Known As: Yardrans, Warshandii

Warshandii are intimidating creatures and greatly feared. However, their reputations are not well deserved, at least in my opinion.

They are awkward flyers and nearly helpless if they ever find themselves on the ground, for they are treetop perchers and cliff clingers. They are more a threat to children, small humanoids and livestock than to men. Of course, there are those who disagree with this statement.

I saw one flying over the plains of Tarisato many years ago and while the great beast startled the horses and sent men scrambling for cover beneath the canopy of nearby trees, it made no attempt to attack or molest and continued on its way.

In a market in Pagalido I came upon a curious saddle and bit — the owner claimed it was of goblin make and was a warshandii saddle. I didn't know what to make of it and wasn't sure if he was jesting with me or if it was real. Although I've heard the legends of the "flying goblins", I've neither heard nor seen anything that convinces me they are real. This same merchant also had some strange arrows with broad four-pronged sharpened blades — he claimed they were for firing at warshandii and were designed to shred their leathery wings and bring them down. — ᚠ

Look for these strange creatures on cliff faces and high branches where they love to drop and swoop on unsuspecting prey.

This flying reptile has a body about 5 to 6 feet tall and weighing between 30 to 50 pounds, with leathery, membranous tissue stretching between its four skinny legs. When in flight, with legs outstretched, this tissue forms a total wingspan of around 25 feet. Despite this connective tissue, the pterosaur can also walk in a semi-upright stance (albeit slowly). Pterosaurs primarily fly by using their wings to soar with the wind currents, but can also flap them and fly by means of muscle power.

Its head is distinguished by a prominent crest, which varies somewhat in size and shape depending on the creature's age, sex and species. Males, for instance, tend to have large backwards-pointing crests with severe corners, while females often have smaller, rounded crests.

Both sexes, however, have an elongated, bony beak filled with needle-sharp teeth able to bite through even hardened crustacean shells. Female pterosaurs are little over half the size of the males, and outnumber them by two to one.

Some pterosaurs have light, furry coats similar to those of bats, though most have hairless bodies of a mottled green or light brown. Their crests, however, are usually solid yellow, green, blue or red, or a pattern of two such colors together.

Combat/Tactics:

Pterosaurs hunt by perching on trees and cliff faces with their necks stretched out, looking for potential prey. When a pterosaur spots its prey, it lifts its head up high

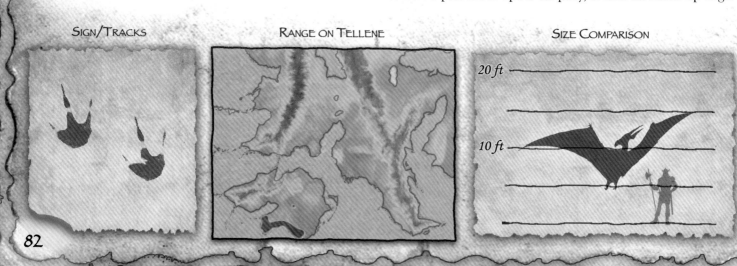

SIGN/TRACKS	RANGE ON TELLENE	SIZE COMPARISON

20 ft

10 ft

and screeches loudly, then lowers its head and swoops down towards its intended meal, using its horrid, serrated beak to pierce the flesh.

Habitat/Society:

Pterosaurs may nest together in small flocks, though they usually hunt alone or in pairs. They favor fish and small vertebrates, although a starving pterosaur may attempt to feast on any creature smaller than itself. They are also scavengers, feeding off of carcasses slain by other creatures or having expired by less grizzly means.

To attract the female, the male pterosaur relies heavily on the condition, size, shape and color of his crest, displaying it proudly in combination with a mating dance or cry. Thus, the strongest pterosaur males with the most brightly colored crests have a better chance of being chosen by the female. The female has a gestation period of about 2 to 3 months, after which she lays nearly three dozen leathery eggs in an isolated cliffside nest. The female rears the hatchlings alone, though they grow quickly, able to fly and set off on their own after only a few days.

The average pterosaur matures within 24 months after hatching and has a lifespan of about 20 to 40 years.

Ecology:

When it comes to competing for fish and other small vertebrates, pterosaurs have few natural rivals besides giant eagles and other such fliers. Their principal rivals on land are the megalosaurus and other scavengers, with whom they compete for the meaty carcasses of freshly dead animals. Of course, the pterosaurs' flight advantage requires the megalosaurus to gain the advantage of surprise while the pterosaurs feed. Pterosaurs rarely attack humans or similar creatures, since they seldom share the same territory (though such an incident might certainly occur if a good opportunity presents itself).

On Tellene:

The pterosaur is restricted largely to the coastal areas of the Obakasek and the Vohven Jungles, where they rarely come into contact with humans or demi-humans. Recently, however, some pterosaurs have been spotted in southern Zazahni, perhaps having slowly migrated outside the Vohven by following the Izhoven River to the Mewhi Marsh. The village of Zhinsahn, in particular, finds the creatures more than a nuisance as they prey on small livestock and even children.

[1] *Pterosaur blood can alleviate symptoms of the Fear of Heights quirk for two hours (this is a placebo effect dependent on the unerring belief of the patient in its efficacy).*

[2] *A square foot flap of pterosaur wing can be used as an alternate material component for the fifth level Levitation spell to add 1d6p minutes to the duration.*

PTEROSAUR

HIT POINTS:	12+3d8 (males)
	10+1d8 (females)
SIZE/WEIGHT:	M/30-50 lbs.
TENACITY:	Cowardly
INTELLIGENCE:	Semi-
FATIGUE FACTOR:	0

SPEED		INIT
10	ATTACK +4	1
DEFENSE +3	DMG REDUCTION 2	
	DAMAGE 3d4p	TOP SAVE 5
short REACH		

MOVEMENT

CRAWL:	¾
WALK:	1¼
JOG:	2½
FLY:	30

SAVES

PHYSICAL:	+4
MENTAL:	+2
DODGE:	+6

ATTACK: Pterosaurs glide through the sky on thermal gradients scanning the land or sea below for food; it attacks by diving down at prey (treat as a charge); if its meal is contested, it will make a perfunctory attempt to guard the kill but readily flies off in the face of a determined competitor

GENERAL INFO

ACTIVITY CYCLE:	Diurnal
NO. APPEARING:	1-2, or 3-10 in nesting areas
% CHANCE IN LAIR:	20
FREQUENCY:	Unusual
ALIGNMENT:	Non
VISION TYPE:	Farsight
AWARENESS/SENSES:	Standard
HABITAT:	Coastal regions (nest in cliff faces near saltwater)
DIET:	Carnivorous
ORGANIZATION:	Individuals or flock
CLIMATE/TERRAIN:	Subtropical to tropical wilderness

YIELD

MEDICINAL:	blood alleviates Fear of Heights[1]
SPELL COMPONENTS:	wing[2]
HIDE/TROPHY:	preserved bodies can be prized trophies
TREASURE:	incidental
EDIBLE:	yes, meat is stringy but edible
OTHER:	nil
EXPERIENCE POINT VALUE:	100

DINOSAUR

TYRANNOSAURUS REX

Also Known As: Ghanozhi, King Lizard

During my sojourn amongst the Zazahnii, I was the guest of a minor noble house at their villa south of Noszhahni. In the midst of the celebration of the warlord's daughter's betrothal, a most extraordinary (and terrifying) thing occurred.

A king lizard (or ghanozhi, as they are locally known) broke out of the jungle, rammed its great skull against the dried-mud wall of the compound and broke through in an instant. Those of us on the rooftop court of the warlord's home all sat in a state of shock with motionless goblets of wine and meat in hand.

As the guards were summoned and the alarm sounded, the great beast moved toward the stable and from among the terrified horses swirling about reached down and grabbed one by the back snapping it with one bite of its powerful jaws. It then began moving back toward the jungle with the carcass still wriggling in its enormous maw.

A dozen men with spears unwisely attempted to give pursuit. Six of them survived the ordeal and only because they chose to run after the first few bloody seconds of battle. Men were flung like dead chickens, stomped and bitten in half as we watched in horror.

As the creature withdrew into the foliage, the warlord turned to me and said, "A dozen horses to choose from and it grabs my favorite! Why do the gods hate me?" —

This large jungle predator often waits in hiding among the shadows only to explode from the foliage and charge its victim. It can charge with surprising speed — holding its seeking maw lined with razor-sharp teeth low to the ground.

The wrath of this savage carnivore is frightening to behold, should one be so foolish as to venture near. With a bulky bipedal body over 40 feet long and over 12 feet tall at the hips, with a weight of about 7 tons, it is one of the most frightening creatures on Tellene - and thus one of the most dangerous to provoke.

Its two clawed forelimbs are relatively small (about 3 feet long) and used primarily to grasp already wounded prey rather than to attack, though this is of little comfort to the victim that fell prey to the dinosaur's many sharp, blade-like teeth or its long, heavy bludgeoning tail. Tyrannosaur eyes (each about the size of a grapefruit) also face predominantly forward, giving them excellent binocular vision with which to spot prey. Its hearing is average, but it does also have a keen sense of smell.

The tyrannosaurus' thick hide tends towards shades of brown between dun and chestnut, often dappled with pale yellows or greens, though other configurations of colors are possible. The underbelly is usually of a lighter shade of the same or a complementary color. Males are usually lighter colored

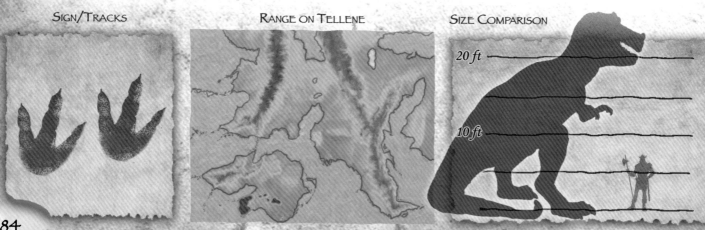

SIGN/TRACKS

RANGE ON TELLENE

SIZE COMPARISON

20 ft

10 ft

than are the females.

The female tyrannosaurus is also the most robust and dangerous of the species, being slightly bulkier and more easily provoked than the male.

Combat/Tactics:

A tyrannosaurus rex typically rushes at its opponent, with its body approximately parallel to the ground and tail extended behind, then opens its mouth wide for a powerful bite. When forced to fight at a standstill, it can swing its large tail to batter an opponent at its rear and use its mighty bite against a facing foe.

However, its large, horizontally-oriented body takes longer to turn, requiring 2 seconds to change its facing to the side or 3 seconds to change its facing to the rear. Unlike vertically-oriented creatures like humans and demi-humans, this movement is not free when combined with another movement or action.

Habitat/Society:

This jungle predator mostly feeds on other dinosaurs and large mammals. However, because of its large size, this great lizard requires a good deal of nourishment; thus, it will easily resort to scavenging another predator's kill should it come upon one.

The tyrannosaur rex's life is a solitary one. Except when mating or fighting, it does not keep the company of its own kind.

To mate, a male tyrannosaur must first be in the vicinity of the female's mournful mating call, then approach with an appearance of strength and a colorful hide that appeals to the female, as well as being able to present her with a fresh carcass. After multiple couplings over a period of several days spent with her new mate, the female drives the male away.

After a few months, when the female is ready to lay her eggs, she constructs a nest of moss, lichen and other vegetation. Once laid, the female remains with the eggs until they hatch, the lack of food and nervous expectation of egg predators making her even more dangerous than usual.

A brood of tyrannosaurus hatchlings remain with their mother for a few months, until they are able to strike out on their own, are killed by their siblings or the mother consumes them as food.

If its lifespan is not cut short, a tyrannosaurus rex can live to be about 30 years old.

Ecology:

The tyrannosaurus rex is with extremely rare exception the largest carnivore in its territory, and rarely confronted. Its principal rival is the megalosaurus, whose greater speed and agility make it a competent foe despite its smaller size. It also faces some minor competition from birds and other small meat-eating mammals that are easily able to land or slip through the underground and steal portions a kill.

[1] If a tooth is used as an optional material component in the 5th level Panic spell, the caster gains +3 on his d20 roll for saving throws.

[2] Tyrannosaurus Rex hide is supple, extremely durable and unusual making it very valuable. Its leather can be used in many capacities, from clothing and armor to drum heads, shelters, ship sails or hulls and treasure chests. It sells for 200 sp per hide. The head is one of the most prized trophies known to man.

TYRANNOSAURUS REX

HIT POINTS:	35+18d8
SIZE/WEIGHT:	G/7 tons
TENACITY:	Fearless
INTELLIGENCE:	Animal, Low
FATIGUE FACTOR:	-4

SPEED 5 — INIT -2
ATTACK +18
DMG REDUCTION
DEFENSE +5 — 9
see below
long REACH — DAMAGE 13
TOP SAVE

MOVEMENT

CRAWL:	10
WALK:	15
JOG:	20
RUN:	25
SPRINT:	30

SAVES

PHYSICAL:	+10
MENTAL:	+6
DODGE:	+9

ATTACK:
A t-rex prefers to strike from ambush if possible, though its sheer size may often preclude this; it attacks every 5 seconds alternating between a devastating bite (10d8p) and battering with its tail (4d6p); the tail swipe is forfeited if no creature lies within a 90° arc behind the dinosaur; incapacitated foes are left to expire of their wounds rather than being repeatedly attacked.

GENERAL INFO

ACTIVITY CYCLE:	Diurnal
NO. APPEARING:	1
% CHANCE IN LAIR:	0
FREQUENCY:	Scarce
ALIGNMENT:	Non
VISION TYPE:	Standard
AWARENESS/SENSES:	Standard
HABITAT:	Forests, swamps
DIET:	Carnivorous
ORGANIZATION:	Individuals
CLIMATE/TERRAIN:	Subtropical to tropical wilderness

YIELD

MEDICINAL:	nil
SPELL COMPONENTS:	teeth[1]
HIDE/TROPHY:	hide has many uses[2]
TREASURE:	incidental
EDIBLE:	yes
OTHER:	nil
EXPERIENCE POINT VALUE:	2000

D

DOGS

ogs? Don't get me started on dogs. When it comes to the art of redistributing men's worldly possessions, which some folk deign to call thievery, dogs have caused me more trouble than all the monstrous aberrations and walking dead I've ever had the misfortune to encounter. The fact is, they simply can't be trusted. Listen to my tale and see if you don't agree.

I'd been accepted into a certain noble family's circle for well over a year, never giving any cause for suspicion even while I figured all the easy ins and exits of the manor. Now, this family had but a single guard dog, Kay by name, let loose inside the house at night. I'd never met a dog that barked or bit so little; even an accidental trodding upon his tail aroused no more from Kay than a disgruntled look. Furthermore, I was forever bringing him treats, and he adored me no less than the family he served.

Well, then came the night I just happened to stay late in the hall, drinking with the lord while his family and most of the servants were absent. The addition of a bit of powder into his wine did wonders for his wakefulness, and he slumped into a deep sleep right there at the table. Light on my feet as always, I slipped quickly and quietly into the library and towards the desk with the hidden compartments, not knowing that Kay slept beneath it.

Man's best friend can also be a formidable foe.

With a killing instinct and savage tenacity many dogs fight to the death.

I tell you truth, I had barely slipped open the first drawer when those sharp teeth locked into my leg like an iron bear trap. Though I managed to hold my tongue and use my club to loose his jaws from my leg, the beast started barking like his life depended on it. I cursed vilely then, and more when in between Kay's staccato I heard the sound of at least a pair of guards running footsteps. Perhaps they were no more than a couple of servants that I could have slugged into dreamland, but I was through the window shutters as quick as I could manage and didn't stay to find out. -✠

V alued by humans and halflings, dogs are known for their keen sense of smell, speed and consequent ability to aid in hunting. Both races breed domesticated dogs for a variety of purposes including herding livestock, hunting, rodent control, guarding, helping fishermen with nets, pulling loads and mounts (the latter reserved for halflings and perhaps human children). Such husbandry activities have created a wide variety of shapes and sizes. Wild dogs resemble wolves, but can be distinguished by their curled tails and smaller paws, as well as their relatively shorter legs and snouts.

Hunting dogs come in several shapes and exhibit varying characteristics depending on purpose. Some have heightened vision and hearing and are used for game retrieval and pointing, while others have a heightened olfactory sense for use in tracking game (or other targets).

Watch dogs are generally smaller dogs, often employed by merchants and the like on board ships or wagon trains. Their keen hearing and fondness for barking alerts their owners to trespassers in the vicinity. Guard dogs, on the other hand, are used to ward off foes through acting aggressively and biting. Their natural disposition to punish trespassers makes them perfect for warehouse usage and the like. Guard dogs have a slightly better tenacity than other dogs.

Like the guard dog, war dogs have been bred and trained for aggression and battle. The average war dog is solidly built, with a short coat and forelegs set wide apart. Largest of the breeds, they stand over 3 feet tall at the withers and weigh between 100 to 200 pounds. Their tenacity is even higher than that of a guard dog as all but very grievous wounds leave them undeterred.

Working dogs herd other animals, carry loads (including halflings at times), keep predators at bay and so on. Some (particularly in cities) are used for rodent control – hunting rats, mice, cats, snakes, rodents and worse.

Humans (and halflings) use dogs to supplement their own senses. While sapient races have better visual acuity

WILD/HUNTING/WORKING DOG

HIT POINTS: 16+1d8

SIZE/WEIGHT: M/ ~70 lbs.

TENACITY: Nervous

INTELLIGENCE: Animal. High

FATIGUE FACTOR: -1

SPEED	INIT
10	-2
ATTACK +2	DMG REDUCTION
DEFENSE +4	2
1d4p+1	
short REACH	DAMAGE	TOP SAVE 7

MOVEMENT

CRAWL: 5

WALK: 15

JOG: 20

RUN: 25

SPRINT: 25

SAVES

PHYSICAL: +2

MENTAL: +2

DODGE: +3

ATTACK:
These breeds of dogs have similiar combat statistics but vary in training; Wild dogs are feral and most wolf-like; hunting and working dogs attack if trained to do so

SPECIAL ABILITIES:
Listening 90%; Tracking 75% to 90% for tracking (working) scent dog breeds

GENERAL INFO

ACTIVITY CYCLE:	Diurnal
NO. APPEARING:	Varies (3-12 for wild)
% CHANCE IN LAIR:	20
FREQUENCY:	Ubiquitous
ALIGNMENT:	Non
VISION TYPE:	Extreme Low Light Vision
AWARENESS/SENSES:	Keen hearing and sense of smell
HABITAT:	Dictated by owner, or in forests or plains
DIET:	Omnivorous
ORGANIZATION:	Pack
CLIMATE/TERRAIN:	Any, save arctic

GUARD/SENTRY DOG

HIT POINTS: 21+2d8

SIZE/WEIGHT: M/100+ lbs.

TENACITY: Steady

INTELLIGENCE: Animal, High

FATIGUE FACTOR: 0

SPEED	INIT
10	-2
ATTACK +3	DMG REDUCTION
DEFENSE +3	2
2d4p+2	
short REACH	DAMAGE	TOP SAVE 9

MOVEMENT

CRAWL: 5

WALK: 10

JOG: 15

RUN: 20

SPRINT: 25

SAVES

PHYSICAL: +4

MENTAL: +2

DODGE: +2

ATTACK:
Sentry dogs are trained to discover and attack intruders; war dogs go for the neck, head and shoulders; the dog's master may cease an attack with a successful Animal Training check (Easy)

SPECIAL ABILITIES:
Listening 90%; Tracking 75% to 90% for scent dog breeds

GENERAL INFO

ACTIVITY CYCLE:	Diurnal
NO. APPEARING:	Dictated by owner
% CHANCE IN LAIR:	100
FREQUENCY:	Ubiquitous
ALIGNMENT:	Non
VISION TYPE:	Extreme Low Light Vision
AWARENESS/SENSES:	Keen hearing and sense of smell
HABITAT:	Dictated by owner
DIET:	Omnivorous
ORGANIZATION:	Individuals or pack
CLIMATE/TERRAIN:	Dictated by owner

YIELD

MEDICINAL:	hair used in hangover cures[1]
SPELL COMPONENTS:	nose[2]
HIDE/TROPHY:	none
TREASURE:	none
EDIBLE:	yes[3]
OTHER:	none

EXPERIENCE POINT VALUE: 22 (dog); 84 (guard dog)

[1] Dog hair is reported to cure hangovers and to instantly sober up an intoxicated person if added to ale or mead.

[2] The seventh level Clairnosmia spell's area of effect can be boosted to 100 feet using a dog's nose as an optional material component.

[3] Dog meat is edible, though many people consider eating dog to be demeaning. This is most common in cultures where other protein sources are readily available, and dogs are trained as pets and protectors instead of as food.

in daylight, dogs have low light vision and extremely high visual discrimination for movement, even at very long distances (double normal low light vision). They can detect sounds far beyond the upper auditory limit of all sapient races (even elves and humanoids), hear them at quadruple the distance and can rotate their ears so as to pinpoint a sound's origin (Listening mastery of 90%) making watch dogs the bane of even skillful thieves.

Combat/Tactics:

Sight dogs hunt like wolves, spotting prey from a distance, then stalking, pursuing and attacking it ("coursing"), while scent dogs specialize in following a smell even for long distances over rough terrain. Scent dogs can track using their impressive sense of smell (75% Tracking mastery for most breeds, 90% for 'bloodhounds' bred for tracking).

Sight dogs tend to hunt individually, while scent dogs hunt in packs. When attacking, dogs typically go for the head, neck and shoulders of the target (unlike wolves, that attack their victim's extremities). Some dogs may locate the target's den and then bolt in and kill it, while still other dogs (like hunting dogs and war dogs) may simply wait to follow their owner's commands.

Dog Pack Mauling Rules:

Any attack by a dog that exceeds the defender's roll by 5 or more indicates that the dog has not only injured its victim for standard damage, but that it also grabbed one of the defender's limbs. Roll randomly to determine which arm or leg the dog latched onto. However, the following caveat applies: if the shield arm is indicated, re-roll the result. A second consecutive result of this limb indicates that the shield arm has indeed been grabbed and it is, along with and defensive benefits provided by the shield, useless until freed.

Once having grabbed on to an opponent, the canine will pull and tug inflicting d4p damage every 10 seconds (no Defense roll allowed nor Attack roll required though armor DR applies). Further, the defender suffers a 2-point penalty to all rolls and cannot use the ensnared limb for any action other than spending 5 seconds attempting to free it of the canine's hold (requiring a Feat of Strength vs. d20p+8). If a leg has been grabbed, the victim cannot move at more than a crawling pace while he drags the dog behind him. If the dog's jaws hold a weapon arm, attack is impossible and any defensive bonuses gained from weapon skill are forfeited. (Note though that the weapon is rarely dropped – a successful

CARPENTER 2010

Feat of Strength *vs.* *d20p+3* retains control of any held weapon). A dog that has grabbed a character may also be compelled to loosen its grip via a successful knock-back or by inflicting sufficient damage to cause a Threshold of Pain check.

A single dog provides little more than a nuisance, particularly to armored characters, either slowing down an intruder (when the leg is grabbed) or hindering his attacks or defense (an arm grab). Far more frightening, however, is when a pack of dogs works in concert to pull down a victim. A second dog that successfully grabs the same defender saddles the victim with a 6-point penalty to all rolls and two limbs are now incapacitated. Thereafter, any successful attack by an additional dog will knock Small creatures prone, an attack of 5 or more in excess of that required to hit will knock a Medium creature prone and 10 or more will knock a Large creature prone. Even if its quarry is not knocked prone, a successful attack by a third dog will automatically grab hold. When held by three dogs, an attack by a fourth reduces the defender's effective size by one category if a fourth dog attacks, and so on.

Any prey knocked prone will be viciously mauled by all nearby dogs, who bite with bonuses of +2 to Speed and +6 to Attack, although it is 50% likely that each limb will be freed as the dogs will be more concerned with mauling than tugging.

Ecology:

Large carnivores such as big cats, dire wolves or alligators are natural predators of dogs and regard them as a food source. That said, they recognize the natural weaponry of dogs and particularly respect them in packs or when supported by their master. The dog itself is primarily a carnivore, though it can healthily digest a variety of foods, including vegetables and grains (wild dogs are primarily scavengers, often eating available plants and fruits).

Dogs reach sexual maturity in under a year (and as early as six months). At this time, the female, or bitch, will reach estrus, a semiannual event for dogs. Litters of six to 12 pups arrive about eight to 10 weeks after fertilization. Pups are born live and wean in about six to eight weeks. The average dog lives 10 to 12 years.

On Tellene:

The best war dogs are said to come from the kennels of Major Baenar, cleric of the Temple of Armed Conflict in the city of Saaniema, where they are highly esteemed.

WAR DOG

HIT POINTS:	26+2d8
SIZE/WEIGHT:	M/150+ lbs.
TENACITY:	Brave
INTELLIGENCE:	Animal, High
FATIGUE FACTOR:	0

MOVEMENT

CRAWL:	5
WALK:	10
JOG:	15
RUN:	20
SPRINT:	25

SAVES

PHYSICAL:	+5
MENTAL:	+2
DODGE:	+2

ATTACK:
These dogs are trained to attack bipedal creatures acting in tandem to overwhelm and then maul opponents (see Dog Pack mauling rules); the dog's master may cease an attack with a successful Animal Training skill check (of Easy difficulty)

SPECIAL ABILITIES:
Listening 90%; Tracking 75% for scent dog breeds

GENERAL INFO

ACTIVITY CYCLE:	Diurnal
NO. APPEARING:	Dictated by owner
% CHANCE IN LAIR:	100
FREQUENCY:	Ubiquitous
ALIGNMENT:	Non
VISION TYPE:	Extreme Low Light Vision
AWARENESS/SENSES:	Keen hearing and sense of smell
HABITAT:	Dictated by owner
DIET:	Omnivorous
ORGANIZATION:	Individuals or pack
CLIMATE/TERRAIN:	Dictated by owner

YIELD

MEDICINAL:	hair used in hangover cures[1]
SPELL COMPONENTS:	nose[2]
HIDE/TROPHY:	none
TREASURE:	none
EDIBLE:	yes[3]
OTHER:	none
EXPERIENCE POINT VALUE:	100

DRAKE

Also Known As: Kanfrum, Mynraax

My favorite story concerning drakes is of the hamlet of Imurish in the Imomena Hills. Don't bother looking for it on a map — you won't find it.

The settlement was founded in the year 304 C.M. by group of retired soldiers who brought their families and belongings to the area to carve out their own small sanctuary far from their countrymen. The veterans hoped the mental scars of the battles they had experienced in the Miznoh Forest would fade as they took up the hoe and plow.

Sadly they chose to build near caves where several hibernating drakes had lain dormant for nearly twenty years — one of the reasons the area had remained fallow. As chance would have it, the drakes awoke just about a year to the day of the hamlet's founding. Famished, they didn't have to go far to find a meal for one had been laid out before them on their door stoop.

Of the five score inhabitants, only two survived to tell the tale — these being a woman and her daughter who had sought refuge in a cellar and went unnoticed.

I'm reminded of an old Svímohzish proverb when I think of Imurish. "Sometimes fate comes looking for you. Sometimes you unknowingly go looking for it." —

Don't be caught off guard by bone-battering tail attacks.

Often confused with dragons, these creatures are quickly roused to anger and are prone to fighting to the bitter end.

The drake appears as an enormous wide-bodied lizard possessing a bony frill down its spine. Its tail is long and muscular with a bony spur at the end from which homy growths emerge giving it the visage of a spiked club. Its legs are of a disproportionate size as is the crocodiline head.

Unlike reptiles, drakes exhibit bradymetabolism – meaning that while normally quite active regardless of ambient temperature, they may enter a hibernation state. Drakes may hibernate for decades.

Combat/Tactics:

Drakes are active hunters capable of surprising speed and agility. When aroused, they are voracious and are seemingly incapable of being sated. They are not particularly clever and usually rely on sheer brawn to overwhelm their prey.

Drakes tend to attack aggressively with their powerful maw while batting lesser foes aside with their forelegs. They also flail their spiked tail about to prevent anyone else approaching too closely so as to take it from the rear. This may be autonomic behavior as they exhibit the same defensive mannerism while feeding.

SIGN/TRACKS

Fore

Hind

RANGE ON TELLENE

SIZE COMPARISON

20 ft

10 ft

Were these formidable powers insufficiently impressive, drakes additionally possess the capacity to breath fire. It is a power they employ with reluctance and never more than thrice daily for it irritates their esophagus for days thereafter. This fiery expulsion take the form of a cone 60 feet long and 20 feet wide at its base. Those scorched by these flames sustain 10d8p points of damage (though a successful Dexterity check reduces this to half damage). The drake's enemies, if aware of this endowment, may be forewarned as it will cease attacks and begin insufflating for 10 seconds prior to spewing this firestorm.

After expelling this maelstrom, it will have a coughing fit for 5 seconds (lowering its Defense to +5 and precluding attacks). A second use of fire breath increases this fit to 10 seconds and the third use to 20 seconds.

Drakes are naturally immune to fire regardless of intensity.

Habitat/Society:

After a prolonged bout of gorging itself, a drake will seek out an isolated location to sleep. Often these are deep caves sheltered from the elements and located in remote and inaccessible sites.

Mating occurs during these gorge fests — an ample belly signaling the female to enter estrus. The female has the ability to wait weeks, until she feels climatic conditions are right, before she lays her eggs. Once lain, these eggs hatch in about two months. Other than when joining together for procreating, drakes are solitary creatures.

Ecology:

A drake seems to be in tune with the ebb and flow of the regional ecosystem perhaps picking up on subtle environmental cues. Its emergence is invariably during times of plenty when quarry is bountiful.

Drakes may live for centuries or more, only awakening periodically to rampage in search of food.

On Tellene:

Drakes are found in the foothills of fertile areas such as the Imomena Hills and in Mendarn and Pel Brolenon.

[1]Drakes hibernate for years followed by brief intervals of wholesale destruction.

[2]Blood prepared as a soup is said to cure colds.

[3]Drake saliva is a useful additional component in many fire-based spells, boosting efficacy by 1d10p points. It sells for 30 sp per ounce.

[4]Drakes are hoarders. Their hibernating caves are usually filled with an enormous quantity of pillaged treasures - most of which is junk as the hoarding impulse overrides discrimination. However, given the sheer quantity of loot present, a mere portion of coins, jewelry and other valuables still comprises a veritable king's ransom.

[5]Flesh is edible and spicy. It sells for 30 sp per pound, as it is so rare.

DRAKE

HIT POINTS:	36+11d8
SIZE/WEIGHT:	E/5-6 tons.
TENACITY:	Brave
INTELLIGENCE:	Slow
FATIGUE FACTOR:	-5

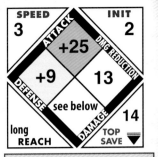

SPEED		INIT
3	ATTACK +25	2
DEFENSE +9		DMG REDUCTION 13
long REACH	see below	DAMAGE TOP SAVE 14

MOVEMENT

CRAWL:	5
WALK:	10
JOG:	15
RUN:	20
SPRINT:	25

SAVES

PHYSICAL:	+24
MENTAL:	+16
DODGE:	+18

ATTACK: Drakes attack by battering away lesser foes (two claw attacks each doing 2d12p damage) reserving their bite (4d12p) for dangerous foes that have done them harm; in addition they sweep their posterior with a tail (an attack of opportunity against anyone approching their rear - damage is 3d10p); may also breathe fire (10d8p) but must halt other attacks to do so

SPECIAL DEFENSES: immune to fire

GENERAL INFO

ACTIVITY CYCLE:	Crepuscular[1]
NO. APPEARING:	1
% CHANCE IN LAIR:	100 (if hibernating); 5 (otherwise)
FREQUENCY:	Scarce
ALIGNMENT:	Chaotic Evil
VISION TYPE:	Low Light Vision
AWARENESS/SENSES:	Standard
HABITAT:	Hills and mountains
DIET:	Carnivorous
ORGANIZATION:	Individuals
CLIMATE/TERRAIN:	Temperate to tropical wilderness

YIELD

MEDICINAL:	blood is said to cure colds[2]
SPELL COMPONENTS:	saliva[3]
HIDE/TROPHY:	many uses for hide
TREASURE:	various[4]
EDIBLE:	yes[5]
OTHER:	nil
EXPERIENCE POINT VALUE:	3300

DRYAD

Also Known As:
Tree Sprite, Vila

These shy and beautiful creatures avoid encountering others not of their race.

As a devoted follower of The Bear and a lover of trees and the creatures of the forest, I cannot sing enough the praises of the dryad. These guardians of the forests are as lovely a creature as ever breathed air on Tellene. Their delicate frames, their pleasant expression, their flowing hair and shimmering, diaphanous gowns make them one of the most enjoyable beings to spy. That is, unless, you are of the uncouth breed of men who despoil the forests and pillage its beauty for your own gain.

If so, the dryad's expression may change to one of fury. She will become a formidable foe, and rightly so. Her faithful watching of the woods is a blessing, and I must encourage wanderers through these woodlands to respect the surroundings and the spirit of the trees that live there. These beings can be a true blessing to those in harmony with the natural world. Keep that in mind.

Each time I step within the forest boundary, I sense the presence of the dryad. Sometimes, I catch a glimpse of her out of the corner of my eye. Sometimes, I can hear the sound of her tinkling laughter blending with the wind blowing through the leaves.

I have studied her more fully in moments when I have been very still, patiently awaiting her appearance. Then, I have been delighted at the appearance of several of these creatures, as they flit about joyfully. They sing with the birds very early in the mornings, when they think no one will know. But I know. I have heard the music of the trees.

I have also seen a dryad defending her sacred tree. Her animals fight for her, the ones who love her and are charmed by her smile. They can battle quite fiercely.

I have also, to my sorrow, witnessed the death of a dryad whose arboreal home has been destroyed. In my view, there is nothing more tragic than the death of a dryad. —

Dryads appear as incredibly beautiful fey women with long curly hair whose color changes with the seasons, and skin like white, pure moonlight. They are usually clothed in leaves or diaphanous white material gathered from cobwebs, and decked with garlands of flowers. Dryads grow with their trees, so that the largest and most ancient trees may have dryads that resemble giants! The average dryad, however, stands about 5 feet tall and weighs around 100 pounds.

Combat/Tactics:

Most dryads are shy and non-violent, but should a human settlement (or that of any other race) start to encroach upon their territory with fire or axe, a dryad may take action. When confronted, a vila attempts to charm lesser foes, then commands animal allies (such as bears, boars and wolves) to attack any enemies that remain unaffected. If overwhelmed, a dryad flees — only to return later with reinforcements (such as fey creatures, additional animal cohorts, ents or more of her kind).

SIGN/TRACKS

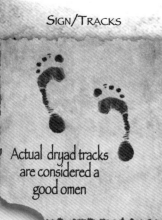

Actual dryad tracks are considered a good omen

RANGE ON TELLENE

SIZE COMPARISON

6 ft

3 ft

A dryad's beguiling beauty can ensnare anyone viewing her with effects comparable to the Charm spell. Those gazing upon her must attempt an opposed Wisdom check immediately upon seeing a vila (the tree sprite rolling d20p+12 against males or d20p+8 against females). Only one save is needed per encounter.

These creatures may freely enter any large tree and conceal themselves within its very trunk. If of an identical species to her tree, she may utilize it as a conduit and teleport unerringly back to her home.

Ecology:

Dryads live in temperate woodlands and consider themselves the guardians of their chosen territory, which usually ranges over 10 to 20 square miles. A dryad's life is bound to the tree that birthed it, though not to any particular area. If a dryad feels that her tree is safe, she may not visit it for many years. This is rare, however, for a dryad will die when her tree does.

Dryads are most often born of oak trees, followed by ash, apple and walnut trees. The older and larger the tree, the more powerful and larger the dryad; the dryad of the ancient trees in the deep forests are said to be a force to be reckoned with. A dryad's tree does not radiate magic.

Some dryads are extremely vain and do not like to see beauty in females of other races, going so far as to ignore them or lead them astray. However, dryads always protect lost children in their territory, as well as the natural animals and plants that reside therein. They may even guide travelers lost in the woods. Dryads react to magically spawned plants and animals depending on the creature's actions.

Dryads may converse empathetically with natural animals and typically are fluent in the most common human or demi-human language of the area.

On Tellene:

So far, dryads have only been found in Brandobia, the Young Kingdoms and the Wild Lands and never in Svimohzia. Fhokki woodcutters fear the dryads, for they lose many men to them in the Rytarr Woods. An old wives' tale from Ek'Gakel states that those who are born on either Pelsday or Veshday can sense the trees inhabited by dryads, and that the tree sprites are more likely to be sympathetic to such persons.

---

[1] Sap from a dryad's tree restores the appearance of youth, reducing fine lines around the eyes and mouth while rejuvenating and strengthening the skin. This miracle crème can be very valuable.

[2] Dryad hair can be used in Charm spells, increasing their potency (the caster gains +2 on his opposed d20 roll). A dryad may chose to gift a hair or two to a particularly handsome suitor.

[3] A dryad's collection of jewlery is never less than 200 sp in value.

DRYAD

HIT POINTS:	19+3d8
SIZE/WEIGHT:	M/100 lbs.
TENACITY:	Nervous
INTELLIGENCE:	Bright
FATIGUE FACTOR:	1

SPEED 7 · **INIT** -2 · **ATTACK** +8 · **DMG REDUCTION** · **DEFENSE** +3 · 0 · by weapon -2 · **DAMAGE** · **short REACH** · **TOP SAVE** 4

MOVEMENT

CRAWL:	2½
WALK:	5
JOG:	10
RUN:	15
SPRINT:	20

SAVES

PHYSICAL:	+17
MENTAL:	+23
DODGE:	+19

ATTACK:
Dryads rarely engage in melee combat, instead they rely upon woodland allies to drive off attackers; in extremis they may employ a dagger (2d4p-2) for personal defense

SPECIAL DEFENSES: Opponents are subject to ensnarement by Charm merely by viewing her; may conceal herself within tree; teleportation

GENERAL INFO

ACTIVITY CYCLE:	Diurnal
NO. APPEARING:	1
% CHANCE IN LAIR:	15
FREQUENCY:	Sporadic
ALIGNMENT:	Neutral
VISION TYPE:	Standard
AWARENESS/SENSES:	Standard
HABITAT:	Old growth forests
DIET:	Herbivorous
ORGANIZATION:	Individuals
CLIMATE/TERRAIN:	Temperate

YIELD

MEDICINAL:	sap restores youthful appearance[1]
SPELL COMPONENTS:	hair, in Charm spell[2]
HIDE/TROPHY:	nil
TREASURE:	dryads may wear attractive woven items/jewelry[3]
EDIBLE:	no
OTHER:	nil
EXPERIENCE POINT VALUE:	250

DWARF   Also Known As: The Deep Folk, Karastan

Dwarves have a reputation for being greedy, untrusting, reclusive and of serious demeanor. They are also ascribed the attitude that anything and everything that lies beneath the surface belongs to them by birthright.

As with most things in life, there is some truth behind these notions. It's also true that dwarves are among the most misunderstood and little known of the intelligent races. This is a shame for there is much to be admired and worthy of emulation among this hearty breed. No strangers to hard work, they rarely shy away from it and despise others who shirk a task or avoid a duty.

Friendship with a dwarf is something that's hard earned and takes months if not years to nurture. But once that bond is made only death can break it. A dwarf will defend friend or ally as he would his own whelps expecting no favor, save an unquestioned willingness to do the same in return should the need arise. This is perhaps why dwarves and men don't always get along for, in my experience, there is a sad shortage of men having such qualities.

Perhaps it is our brief lifespan, compared to that of the dwarven race, that causes them to see us as short sighted with our word, bonds and commitments often changing on a whim and fleeting as our years.

There's an old dwarven proverb that goes, "It is not a new sun that rises each morn. It is the same sun that set last night." - connoting that a person's word one day should be the same as the next and that an ally made yesterday is an ally today. In dwarven eyes, men change their allegiances as frequently as they would their shirts. — ᚠ

These sturdy warriors are respected by friend and enemy alike for their battle prowess.

Dwarves are a hearty race, preferring the alpine beauty of rugged mountains but may be found in all climes. They are excellent miners and seem built for the task with their short but powerfully built frames. These sturdy, compact creatures make tough warriors, but poor skirmish troops against faster creatures, owing to their short legs. A dwarf's stocky build, weighing roughly 160 pounds with a height of only 4 ½ feet on average, makes them tough to move by force, so despite their stature, a dwarf suffers knock-backs like a size Large creature.

Fierce in battle, the dwarven weapon of choice tends to be axe and shield, but they employ a great variety of weapons, including the great axe, sword, crossbow, short bow, mattock, warhammer, great hammer, maul or pick. Dwarven war parties generally equip themselves with well-made chainmail and medium shields. It is not uncommon for leaders to wear plate armor or superior-quality chainmail.

Dwarves tend to be martial by nature with the standard dwarven warrior a level one fighter. Dwarven thievery is uncommon (and thieves are generally despised and driven out from the clan or community) but most warbands do have a scout (thief) of level one as well. For every 10 dwarves encountered, one will be a second level fighter and for every

SIGN/TRACKS	RANGE ON TELLENE	SIZE COMPARISON

Dwarves wear heavy boots & make little effort to conceal their tracks

6 ft

3 ft

twenty there will be an additional 3rd level fighter. If 40 dwarves are encountered, there will be one lead fighter of 4th to 11th level (d8+3) with a scout thief of ⅔rds the leader's level. For every 100 clan members, there will be a mighty chieftain of 12th to 17th level or higher (d6p+11 plus another d4p levels for every additional 100 dwarves).

Clerics are fairly rare, generally only serving in a cloistered capacity, but large warbands of 200 or more will have a cleric of 2d4p+4 level. Dwarven mages are very rare, with only a 10% chance for one to accompany a band of 300 or more. Those few dwarven mages on Tellene have risen to great fame, particularly those that specialize in armor or weaponsmithing as these masters alone can create the most powerful magical arms and armor available.

Though they typically dwell underground, it is not in dank warrens. Rather they construct magnificent vaulted caverns that are both engineering marvels and possessed of unparalleled aesthetic beauty. They are serious, hard-working folk whose interest lies in precious metals and gems. No obstacle is too overwhelming to deter dwarves from delving far beneath the earth in search of these treasures. This frequently brings them into conflict with goblins and other humanoid races that inhabit the Netherdeep.

In the areas of smithing, metalwork and stonework, dwarves excel. What is average for a dwarf is expert for most other races, and the most talented dwarves far surpass the capabilities of any other race. They delight in finely crafted items, especially those crafted from precious metals and jewels, perhaps giving dwarves the not-entirely unearned reputation for being avaricious and greedy. Dwarves also make excellent, if unimaginative, engineers. They are superior at everything from defense works and plumbing to road construction and, of course, mining.

Stern and taciturn, these rugged creatures make hardy and reliable, if somewhat grumpy, traveling companions. Often pejoratively dismissed as dour and grumpy, this perception stems from a typical dwarf's disinterest in gossip and small talk. While generally viewed as surly and brusque by most right-minded folk, dwarves generally do have a sense of humor and can even be jovial when with their own kind, but also with those whose friendships have been forged through the fire of trying times, such as battle against a common foe. Most tend to be reserved and brooding, responding to queries with one-word or very short answers, however, dwarves can also be very argumentative when they feel they've been slighted or have differing ideas on a matter of importance.

Utilitarian to the core, dwarves tend to dress in the most functional attire for the circumstances. They bathe only when required for health considerations or some other functional reason (e.g., diplomatic or ceremonial). Dwarves do, however, take special care of their beards, often braiding them neatly with fine interlaced strands of silver, silk or the like. While they disdain finery and fashion of most kinds (particularly those of the elvish sort and anything involving fine

DWARF

HIT POINTS:	33+1d10
SIZE/WEIGHT:	M/150 lbs.
TENACITY:	Brave
INTELLIGENCE:	Average
FATIGUE FACTOR:	-3/-4

ATTACK: Most wield battle axes; attacks are well coordinated utilizing supporting missile fire; dwarves do not usually ambush.

SPECIAL DEFENSES: Shield use (e.g., medium shields increase Defense to +3). Additional +6 Defense vs. giants, ogres and trolls. Most are clad in chainmail (unarmored dwarves have DR 0).

MOVEMENT

CRAWL:	1¼
WALK:	2½
JOG:	5
RUN:	7½
SPRINT:	10

SAVES

PHYSICAL:	+10
MENTAL:	+9
DODGE:	+8

GENERAL INFO

ACTIVITY CYCLE:	Diurnal[1]
NO. APPEARING:	1-8, or 3d4p+8 (warband) or 20d20p (clan)
% CHANCE IN LAIR:	75%
FREQUENCY:	Frequent
ALIGNMENT:	Lawful Good
VISION TYPE:	Low Light Vision
AWARENESS/SENSES:	poor smell/hearing, sensitive hands[2]
HABITAT:	Usually underground lairs[3]
DIET:	Omnivorous
ORGANIZATION:	Individuals or clan[4]
CLIMATE/TERRAIN:	Typically subterranean[5]

YIELD

MEDICINAL:	ground genitalia used to neutralize poisons[6]
SPELL COMPONENTS:	bone marrow and eyelashes[7]
HIDE/TROPHY:	braided beards[8]
TREASURE:	10d4p sp each[9]
EDIBLE:	yes[10]
OTHER:	nil
EXPERIENCE POINT VALUE:	84

hosiery), most dwarves do have a weakness for oversized, foppish hats.

Dwarves get along well with gnomes, humans and halflings (in that order), but don't trust elves, a mistrust arisen from suffering on the losing end of several struggles when Tellene was young and humans were not part of recorded history. Today elves and dwarves no longer take up arms against one another and have in fact come to each other's aid against common foes (generally orcs, hobgoblins, goblins and other evil humanoids) as needed over the last dozen centuries.

After millennia of living in confined conditions, dwarves have developed a robust constitution, seldom taking ill or succumbing to fatigue or the like. Accordingly, dwarves receive a +4 bonus to their Constitution score and are considered size Medium for initial Hit Point determination. Further, dwarves are naturally resistant to poisons and magic, gaining a +1 on saving throws versus poison for every 3 points of Constitution.

Unfortunately, their dour and introspective nature makes them lesser leaders than others (-2 to starting Charisma) and their personal appearance isn't what most species would consider pleasing to the eye (-2 to Looks).

Combat/Tactics:

Dwarves like a fair fight and seldom ambush their foes, preferring to call out to them, perhaps insulting their race, lineage or calling into question their foes' personal bravery. They are not stupid, however, and use ranged weapons when it makes sense, bows in the out-of-doors and crossbows when underground or in confined areas. Their stout build helps them stand their ground even against the largest and strongest of foes. Dwarves seldom flee an encounter, at least partially due to their slow movement rate, especially when heavily armored, but also due to their powerful pride and personal honor. Centuries of refusing to yield to giants, ogres and trolls has given dwarves the ability to better fight these foes; dwarves receive a +6 to Defense rolls against such creatures. Unfortunately, dwarves have short arms, leading to poor Reach (effective weapon Reach is -1 foot).

Dwarves often tame and train animals to serve them. Mules and donkeys are most common, but dwarves are also 25% likely to have 5d4p war dogs in their lair, and/or 2d4p brown bears (35% chance).

Habitat/Society:

Dwarves prefer to dwell in great mountainous cities, mines or nearby rocky terrain. Equipped with low-light vision and less affected by uncomfortable heat or cold than humans or other demi-humans, dwarves are well-suited to the subterranean environment, whether working in the mines or at the fiery anvil. Due to the unfortunate losses of several dwarven underground citadels and mines (Krimppatus, Elenons, Legasas, Kronds, Byth and most recently Ka'Asas), many dwarves can be found dispersed throughout civilized lands in all climes and terrains, or prospecting individually in hilly or mountainous terrain.

Dwarves organize themselves into large familial clans where the names of their ancestors are handed down for generations, with each name included again in the names of their children. It is not uncommon for a dwarf to trace his lineage back a millennia or more based on his name alone.

Each clan pays homage to the king of their domain, but since so many dwarven cities have fallen to invaders or have been abandoned, a majority of dwarves are either refugees or are now living in foreign (human) lands. In the former case, they reside in one of the remaining dwarven strongholds or mines (where they are welcomed and given their fair share of work). In the latter, they find work as armorers, smiths, traders, engineers and the like. Regardless of background, all dwarves learn to mine at a tender age, thus, each dwarf has some training in the Mining skill (one free mastery roll, although more can certainly be learned).

Dwarves speak Dwarven amongst their own, but prefer not to utter their own tongue when in the company of non-dwarves, choosing instead to use the local language (human or otherwise), which they inevitably speak with an accent. Dwarves take great pride in their heritage and clan, and reveal their true Dwarven names to few outsiders, instead using a name chosen from earth, metals or alchemical substances in the local language.

Dwarves have an average lifespan of 225 years, but replenishing numbers is a difficult task as they reproduce slowly. Females comprise a mere 25% of the population and dwarven gestation is a three-year process (young make up no more than 5% of the total population). Further, she-dwarves are completely liberated, being equal partners to the males in all respects and many eschew nuptials completely. They appear exactly as males (although, on average, they are an inch or two shorter), including beards, attire and accouterments, and cannot even be distinguished by voice. Male dwarves can, of course, tell them apart, but other races cannot without examination of the genitalia. This has led to the mistaken belief that the Founder forged from iron or chiseled the dwarves from the living rock of the mountain's roots.

Dwarves are a proud race, quick to defend their personal or clan honor. Slights are not easily forgotten or forgiven, with the memory of major ones ensured by an inscription in the clan's Book of Grudges, a massive tome, or series of such, kept by each family. Of course, with remuneration and apology suitable to the slight, a dwarf will appropriately absolve... but perhaps not forget.

Ecology:

Since they live in mines, caves and in the Netherdeep, dwarves tend not to grow their own food (they dislike moss and lichens and grow tired of a steady diet of mushrooms). Accordingly, they trade tools, metals, worked goods and even engineering works to local human and demi-human communities for foodstuffs and game. The dwarven choice of underground settlement often places them in direct conflict with other races that choose to (or are forced to) live in the

Netherdeep.

Among the myriad of natural foes, dwarves hate goblins, orcs and hobgoblins above all other races, gaining a +2 Attack bonus when battling such creatures.

Subraces:

All dwarves belong to the same species, having originated from the same racial stock. Dwarves have never been capable of breeding with other races, thus, half-dwarves exist in no form. Due to the many disparate dwarven clans and nations, living deep underground hundreds and thousands of miles apart, several sub-races of dwarves exist.

Hill Dwarves

The most common dwarves found on Tellene are the hill dwarves, named so by humans because they seem to have chosen hills as their home. This is actually inaccurate, as the vast majority of hill dwarves are simply diaspora from one of the many lost, destroyed or abandoned kingdoms. Sometimes called lowland dwarves, hill dwarves are actually a racial mixture of the many clans now inhabiting the human lands (or nearby hills).

Mountain Dwarves

More isolated than their hill dwarf cousins, mountain dwarves consider themselves the only true clans. This is actually false, as they have had their fair share of interbreeding, and even the oldest of today's kingdoms are young in comparison to several of the ancient, fallen cities and mines, making these dwarves the most settled of a refugee and explorer race. Also called highland dwarves, the mountain dwarves tend to be slightly smaller than their lowland cousins, perhaps due to lack of sunlight or the efficacy gained by reduced stature underground.

Stone Dwarves

Stone dwarves inhabit the deepest areas of the Netherdeep. Their greed knows few bounds, and few wise creatures trust them. Stone dwarves ally with foul underground races. They appear very different than the other dwarves, with gray skin and white hair. In fact, both hill and mountain dwarves refuse to acknowledge that stone dwarves are in fact dwarves, referring to them instead as goblins or orcs, the worst insult a dwarf can use against another. Notwithstanding these claims, genetically, stone dwarves are clearly the same species as the other dwarves.

Religion:

Dwarves prefer to worship the Founder, the Speaker of the Word, The True, The Mule and the Holy Mother. Dwarven societies seldom accept any other religions, although The Peacemaker, the Pure One and the Lord of Silver linings are tolerated in some areas.

On Tellene:

The largest dwarven kingdom on Tellene is Karasta, also known as the First Kingdom of the Seven Clans. Located in the Ka'Asa mountains and rich with jewels and precious metals, the mountain fortress and mines were recently taken by force by a combined army of human (Kalamaran), hobgoblin and giantish troops. Unlike all previous dwarven losses (all at the hands of humanoids), the dwarves were not simply slaughtered or driven out, but are being retained as miners and craftsmen by an occupying force. Dwarves across the continent consider this a great affront to their kind and hope to free the place as soon as possible (although, frankly, not so soon as to take a break from their own mines).

The other major kingdom lies in the Byth Mountains and is known as Draska, the Hidden City. Ruled by King Norbaren, the city is obscured beneath the Byth range. The only evidence of its existence is an occasional stream of smoke from the forges deep below the surface. Other free dwarven settlements exist in the Dashahn and Tanehz Ranges. The Faunee Rise has a large refugee population from Karasta, as do the Kakidelas.

Dwarves also dwell in the Elenon Mountains, though they have no known cities there.

[1] **Activity Cycle:** *Dwarves have a standard daytime activity cycle, but are careful to post guards during off hours and during the night.*

[2] **Awareness/Senses:** *Dwarves see well in dimly lit conditions, but cannot see in the dark. They have a sub-par sense of smell, but have sensitive hands able to detect tiny fractures in stone and metal. Dwarven hearing tends to be sub-par and grows steadily worse as they age due to the noisy conditions in which they live.*

[3] **Habitat:** *Dwarves prefer underground lairs cut from solid rock, but sometimes are also surface dwellers.*

[4] **Organization:** *Dwarves are organized by clans, each with a chieftain. In their massive cities or complexes, one chieftain will rule as king with all of the clans swearing fealty. Individual clans are competitive with one another on virtually every level, but never to the point of harmful physical hostility (although brawling is not out of the question) and all band together readily against outsiders.*

[5] **Climate/Terrain:** *Dwarves prefer subterranean kingdoms and mines, but can live and thrive in any climate.*

[6] **Medicinal:** *Dust from the ground genitalia of a male dwarf when mixed with a certain concoction can neutralize even the most dangerous of poisons.*

[7] **Spell Components:** *Dwarven bone marrow is said to improve the effectiveness of any protection spells. Eyelashes are the standard material component in a Low Light Vision spell.*

[8] **Hide/Trophy:** *Carrying the braided beard of a dwarf indicates having defeated one in combat but also marks the bearer as a target for attacks from other dwarves.*

[9] **Treasure:** *Dwarves carry 10d4p sp each. Dwarven lairs can contain vast amounts of wealth in the form of precious metals, gems, finished and worked metals and jewels of all types as well as superior quality arms and armors.*

[10] **Edible:** *According to ogres, dwarves taste just like chicken.*

EAGLE, GIANT

Also Known As: Akurr, Eshji, Ogatala

Though my companions know nothing (and care less) about the diverse giant eagle family, I feel it my duty to set down these scribblings for the benefit of others. My research into the creature's taxonomy and habitat indicates that there are perhaps as many species of giant eagle as there are of its smaller kin, and surely such learning should be documented. I myself have seen several, and gained reports of many more, all of them sharing the powerful build, broad wings, large head and hooked beak, and being of a similar size. However, they vary in certain distinguishing features, such as color and leg length (relative to the body size, of course).

For instance, the giant eagles that soar over the forests of the P'Tikor Hills have all-black plumage with a yellow bill and splayed yellow feet. The fliers of southern Zazahni are also heavily black in plumage but with purple highlights about the head, throat and back, a black bill and brown legs, and a forward-swooping crest of feathers atop its head. In Pekal, along the Elos Bay and about the great Lake Eb'Sobet, one may spy a species of giant eagle quite distinguished in appearance, with yellow legs and beak, an evenly brown body, and a white-feathered head and tail. Such white markings give these eagles an appearance of wisdom and command greater than their fellows, and caused my companions to seek one of its eggs as a trophy. Considering what happened when the great bird came upon us in its eyrie, however, I doubt they desire to make a second attempt. - ☙

A male giant eagle carrying off a wolf pup that caught its attention.

These large birds of prey have powerful hooked beaks, strong muscular legs and powerful talons, as well as incredible eyesight that allows them to spot prey in open terrain from up to 1 mile away. The male giant eagle is roughly 12 feet long with a wingspan of around 25 feet and weighing about 400 pounds. Females are about 25% larger than males.

There are various sub-classifications of giant eagles, as defined by their choice of food or habitat, though these differences are of more interest to scholars than the average fighting man. All types of giant eagles share similar physical features with coloration being the major difference between them. For example, many tropical giant eagles have a brown body and black wings with white head, breast and tail, while those in colder regions may have mostly white bodies with brown wings.

Combat/Tactics:

Eshji hunt by swooping down on prey making a single attack with their talons for 2d12p damage. A successful strike results in quarry weighing up to 100 pounds being grasped in their claws. An immediate Feat of Strength may be attempted to break free of this grip (vs. d20p+4). Failing this, the giant eagle carries it aloft and back to its nest. Captured prey may continue to struggle but risk plummeting to their death once the akurr is airborne.

Should its prey break free, a giant eagle may attempt to finish it off by attacking with its beak (inflicting 2d8p with such attacks) but will not engage in a protracted struggle on the ground. Determined resistance will encourage it to take flight and seek easier prey (though if particularly hungry it may sim-

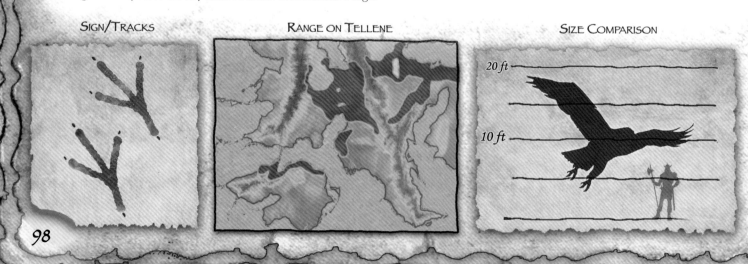

SIGN/TRACKS

RANGE ON TELLENE

SIZE COMPARISON

20 ft

10 ft

ply circle about and seek another opportunity to strike from above). Ogatala are intelligent hunters and a mated pair may utilize tactics to panic and drive creatures away from their herds so as to facilitate easier hunting for the other.

Habitat/Society:

Giant eagles can be found in any climate from sub-artic to tropical and can be found nearly anywhere in Tellene. They build their huge nests (eyries; up to 20 feet in diameter) on tall cliffs or in high trees. When not solitary, they live in mated pairs. Giant eagles take a mate for life. Eyries will contain d4 eggs or young.

Giant Eagles are intelligent, capable of language and generally well disposed towards fey creatures and others who have made a conscious choice to venerate nature. Elderly sages and woodland priests have been known to associate with these beings and may even call upon them as allies in times of great need.

The Eshji are sworn foes of most evil humanoids for the latter are wanton destroyers of both game and habitat. Though it is rare for giant eagles to directly attack such humanoids (especially when found in numbers), they are generally aware of the locations and movements of these evil creatures for hundreds of miles surrounding their nests. Such information, when shared with individuals friendly to the ogatala, may prove far more valuable than sporadic harassing.

Giant eagles can serve as flying mounts for creatures as large as humans. Such service may never be compelled only freely volunteered. In general, it is only offered to those with whom they have a long and cordial relationship.

Ecology:

The giant eagle feeds mostly on deer, moose, and herd animals such as sheep and cattle. Should larger food be scarce, it may also dine on smaller prey such as rabbits, squirrels, reptiles, birds, fish, and giant insects.

Giant eagles often compete for food with other large fliers, such as griffyns, hippogriffs, rocs and perytons.

In the wild, giant eagles live roughly 20 to 30 years, though it isn't entirely uncommon for the rare bird to reach 40.

On Tellene:

Giant eagles are revered by many cultures as symbols of power and dignity. The image of the giant eagle means many different things, but it is commonly used in heraldry and spoken of in legends that teach about wisdom and nobility.

Some Fhokki clans revere the giant eagle as sacred religious objects and one of the great teachers of the world. Eagle feathers are highly sought after so that they may be used in important religious ceremonies. Some Fhokki grant eagle feathers as gifts to outsiders for important acts; such gifts are rare and meaningful.

[1]*Adding a giant eagle feather as a material component in the casting of the fourth level cleric spell Know North provides a spell duration of 5 minutes.*

GIANT EAGLE

HIT POINTS:	30+3d8
SIZE/WEIGHT:	L/400 lbs.
TENACITY:	Steady
INTELLIGENCE:	Obtuse
FATIGUE FACTOR:	1

MOVEMENT

CRAWL:	1¼
WALK:	2½
JOG:	5
RUN:	7½
FLY:	60

SAVES

PHYSICAL:	+9
MENTAL:	+8
DODGE:	+10

ATTACK:
Giant eagles make a unified attack with their talons for 2d12p and may bite for 2d8p.

SPECIAL DEFENSES:
none, other than their great size and ability to fly

GENERAL INFO

ACTIVITY CYCLE:	Diurnal
NO. APPEARING:	1-2
% CHANCE IN LAIR:	15%
FREQUENCY:	Infrequent
ALIGNMENT:	Neutral (good tendencies)
VISION TYPE:	Excellent; can spot prey up to 1 mile
AWARENESS/SENSES:	Standard
HABITAT:	Cliffs and giant trees near water
DIET:	Carnivorous
ORGANIZATION:	Individuals or mated Pair
CLIMATE/TERRAIN:	Sub-arctic to tropical woodlands

YIELD

MEDICINAL:	eating eyes is thought to cure blindness
SPELL COMPONENTS:	feather, to improve Know North spell duration[1]
HIDE/TROPHY:	feathers may be used in religious ceremonies
TREASURE:	incidental
EDIBLE:	yes
OTHER:	nil
EXPERIENCE POINT VALUE:	400

ELEMENTAL, AIR

From our library of religious texts we know the gods inhabit other worlds far from our own. These are often referred to as the planes of existence, and are no doubt very different places from our own mundane world. Many scholars even talk of planes of existence that contain the elements upon which Tellene is built - but to a much larger degree.

The Elemental Plane of Air, for instance, would be a vast expanse of never-ending sky and clouds where the four chief winds and their kin could dwell. Likewise, are there places composed primarily of earth, fire and water, and in these elemental planes dwell sentient incarnations of the building blocks of matter. Indeed, there are more than a few accounts of these matter corpuses dwelling in our own lands at times. The high priests of The Mother of the Elements oft claim they know of certain portals that lead to these other realms, though they share such words only in their worship services and never reveal their locations to outsiders, even if such they know.

The first air elemental I myself saw was in the village of Taulegun. I had been walking the beach, idly passing the day, when ahead came a whirl of sand in a distinctly human shape. I stepped back in alarm, even as the grit fell to the ground, indistinguishable from the particles already present. I exhaled loudly in relief, but in shock felt as if my breath began to be pull from my body, rather than expelled through my own will. I shut my mouth instantly, and fled. I did not seem to be pursued, but how could I tell?

Interestingly, this village also suffered frequent pirate attacks. Each time, the people gathered to pray that the Madame of the Wind would send an elemental to aid them. Supposedly, the wind would blow and the approaching ships would sail off into the distance. Other times, nothing happened; this fact they attributed to some lack of faith on their part. Even if this were true, I do not know why coastal folk would not instead pray to Wave Crusher. At the time, I thought it neither civil nor wise to ask. - ⚶

An air elemental is composed exclusively of gases and thus is invisible. However, when present in the material world, the Marut's form may become contaminated with miniscule solid particles of dust, smoke or water vapor. At this stage, most air elementals are of a gray, white or bluish color. During freezing weather, however, the sunlight scattering through the elemental is often tinted green. An air elemental near an ongoing or recently extinguished forest fire may have a yellowish tint due to pollutants in the smoke, while red, orange or pink colorations may occur at sunrise and sunset.

The natural shape of its body is formless, though it often retains a central core of a body, a head with tempest-filled eyes and a menacing mouth, and two to four appendages. After having encountered sapient creatures, it attempts to mimic their appearance as a means of adjusting to this alien world. Thereafter, the most common shape for it to take is a nude maiden composed of swirling fog or dust.

Combat/Tactics:

To detect the faint shimmer of a hidden air elemental's presence requires the character to cast a *Sense Invisible Beings* spell or make a successful Observation check (Difficult in bright light, Very Difficult in dim light, and impossible in darkness). Only one check is needed per encounter, unless the character intentionally or otherwise turns his attention away from the air elemental.

When an air elemental takes form in the immediate area, it sometimes feels as though your breath is being pulled from you as the pressure drops. Should you feel your hair suddenly being swept or tousled on an otherwise windless day, or birds suddenly and inexplicably taking flight, you may be seeing harbingers of the approach of an air elemental.

SIZE COMPARISON

20 ft

10 ft

When an air elemental attacks in melee, it is becomes visible as a 10-foot-diameter cyclone with small stones, debris and dust swirling within it. All creatures within this area suffer an automatic 2d12p points of damage/10 s as their bodies are abraded by the debris. The air elemental can also attempt to hurl creatures within it (resist with a Feat of Strength vs. d20p+7) to a distance of 15 feet, dealing 2d6p upon impact.

Pavan cannot be damaged by physical force. However, as elemental air is responsible for imparting motion to objects, it is vulnerable to magic that counteracts this force and receives no saving throw. Spells that inflict cold damage rob it of kinetic energy and thus weaken it. Less commonly known is that spells such as *Retard Reaction* and *Induce Fatigue* (which also serve to impede motion) are effective countermeasures. These two spells inflict 4d4p and 4d6p respectively when directed at an air elemental.

Air elementals can easily transform their shape while retaining the same volume. Any barrier that is not airtight can by bypassed with ease. For example, if a person was running from an air elemental and closed and locked a door to escape the creature, it could seep through any gap in the door or frame. Once it emerged on the other side, it would return to its preferred form and resume combat.

Air and Earth Elementals, as diametrically opposing forces of nature, annihilate each other on contact. The consequent release of pure energy inflicts 12d8p damage to any creature within 20 feet, 8d6p to those within 50 feet and 3d4p as far as 100 feet from the explosion. Natural and armor damage reduction will temper this force.

Habitat/Society:

An air elemental's native habitat is its own dimension of reality – another plane commonly referred to as the Elemental Plane of Air. Some sages theorize that this plane is composed of endless sky, containing little more substantial than clouds and strong winds. However, an air elemental can travel from this plane to Tellene through specific elemental points of contact. These points of contact are certain geographical locations rumored to dimensionally overlap the Elemental Plane of Air, such as the highest peak of the Elenon Mountains.

Air elementals are usually solitary when encountered. On their own plane, however, they are not sentient beings as we mortals would consider the term. Rather, they are pure turbulent air whose will is responsible for the currents that buffet this plane. It is only in the mortal world that they can assume a form as the presence of all four elements is required. Such existence is unstable for the Marut cannot long tolerate the influence of the other three elements.

On Tellene:

The city of Bet Dodera is the home of Gabilano, the most famous sage of all things avian. In addition to birds, Gabilano claims to know many things about air elementals, djinni and other elemental creatures. Rumors persist that the vanishing maiden seen sometimes at his isolated home is a sylphid; she certainly is not known to any of the locals.

AIR ELEMENTAL

HIT POINTS:	25+10d8
SIZE/WEIGHT:	H/insubstantial
TENACITY:	Brave
INTELLIGENCE:	Slow
FATIGUE FACTOR:	n/a

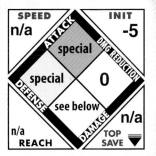

SPEED	n/a	INIT	-5
ATTACK	special	DMG REDUCTION	
DEFENSE	special		0
	see below		
REACH	n/a	DAMAGE	n/a
		TOP SAVE	▼

MOVEMENT

CRAWL:	n/a
WALK:	n/a
JOG:	n/a
RUN:	n/a
FLY:	up to 75

SAVES

PHYSICAL:	see text
MENTAL:	n/a
DODGE:	see text

ATTACK:
Air elementals deal automatic abrading damage of 2d12p to all within their 10-ft diameter winds. Can hurl victims 15 ft for 2d6p damage.

SPECIAL DEFENSES:
Man only be damaged by magical cold and other spells that impede motion.

GENERAL INFO

ACTIVITY CYCLE:	Any
NO. APPEARING:	1
% CHANCE IN LAIR:	0
FREQUENCY:	Scarce
ALIGNMENT:	Non
VISION TYPE:	Standard
AWARENESS/SENSES:	Standard
HABITAT:	Any
DIET:	Special
ORGANIZATION:	Individuals
CLIMATE/TERRAIN:	Any

YIELD

MEDICINAL:	nil
SPELL COMPONENTS:	nil
HIDE/TROPHY:	nil
TREASURE:	nil
EDIBLE:	no
OTHER:	nil
EXPERIENCE POINT VALUE:	1500

Elemental, Earth

Also Known As: Bhümi, Kshiti

The sun had begun its descent when we finally reached the mine. The hidden valley was behind us, and now there was only tunnel to follow. Forming our line of advance, we stepped confidently into the mountain, through the worked dwarven tunnels that oft contracted to a narrow space and then again grew into giant caverns sometimes a hundred yards in breadth. The light from our torches sent insects scurrying home into the cracks and crevices, lightening the glistening walls and floor ahead.

It was when our light first struck the body that I realized the stories had not been exaggerated for our benefit. The corpse had been crushed as if by a heavy weight. A shapeless head distinguishable only by its thick dwarven braids gave mute evidence of a hopeless fight. It was then that the thudding of heavy feet approached.

We had barely formed our pattern of attack when its shape wavered in the darkness of the tunnel ahead. As it stepped into the light we saw it: a single living rock creature nearly twice the height of a man. Though it was of greater stature, we readied ourselves for a quick battle. We outnumbered it, and could easily flank it in this cavern. Surely it would not be too difficult a foe to overwhelm.

It was not until the third of us fell in battle that I realized our efforts were futile; we might chip away at the thing for hours before making any serious headway, and our poor armors provided little resistance against its stony fists. I had just about said this aloud when the elemental (for so I guessed it to be) missed our agile thief and crashed its fist against the wall, making kindling of the ceiling's wooden support.

In some way, my remaining companions and I escaped the collapse of that tunnel, though all I remember is but staring helplessly at the rubble filling the tunnel mouth. A fortune in gems might lie beyond, but it would take days if not weeks to clear the earth and stone, and there was still the little matter of living rock... - ⸙

The overall shape of an earth elemental's body is changeable, though it tends to retain a central core of a body and two to four appendages. In color, its body usually ranges from obsidian to any shade of brown, but other colors are possible depending upon the body's primary mineral or combination of minerals. For instance, an earth elemental mostly composed of clay could appear in any color from a dull gray to a deep orange-red.

Perhaps the most common shape is a 10 to 12-foot-tall humanoid composed of stone and earth (and thus weighing about 3,500 pounds). Although this shape often lacks any obvious facial features, it has no difficulty sensing other creatures through the vibrations that they make. When earth elementals do have features, these may be gems or pebbles, where a human would have eyes or simply scattered about the head in no particular design.

Combat/Tactics:

An earth elemental fights its battles by pummeling targets into immobile bloody pulps. Above all else, it seeks to halt movement of any sort and killing an opponent certainly accomplishes this end. In line with this objective and precluding other overriding directives (such as the commands of a summoner), Bhümi will preferentially attack creatures exhibiting the greatest degree of mobility (expressed in terms of movement rate).

Elemental earth provides solidity to material objects. As such, it is vulnerable to to forces that disrupt this solidity. Unique among elemental-kind, Bhümi can be damaged by

Composed of rock, dirt and even sand, the monolith is exceedingly difficult to track. Any record of it passing through an area simply looks like nothing more than overturned rocks and disturbed soil. They rarely appear on the surface and are usually encountered in caves deep below ground in the lands of the Netherdeep.

SIZE COMPARISON

12 ft

6 ft

physical weaponry with crushing implements being vastly more effective at this task that those which merely slice.

Note that because of its mass and density, it counts as size G for purposes of knock-backs during combat.

Kshiti are largely immune to magic save that which inflicts pure concussive damage (such as *Magic Projectile*) or otherwise acts to disrupt structural integrity (as an example of the latter, *Fracture Object* inflicts 4d4p damage to this entity). Lightning is also an effective attack form in that acts directly upon the creature's inherent electromagnetic bonds whereas impotent attacks by fire merely roast the elemental as a whole – something its ample specific heat capacity can readily accommodate.

Earth elementals can freely pass through any solid non-living object at their normal speed. They cannot traverse solid bodies of water and must either walk around or under any such obstacle.

Earth and Air Elementals, as diametrically opposing forces of nature, annihilate each other on contact. The consequent release of pure energy inflicts 12d8p damage to any creature within 20 feet, 8d6p to those within 50 feet and 3d4p as far as 100 feet from the explosion. Natural and armor damage reduction will temper this force.

Habitat/Society:

Earth elementals are natives of the Elemental Plane of Earth and form its very architecture. Linked arm in arm, they form the quintessential immovable object possessing infinite inertia. Locked forever in this cubic closest-packed structure, Bhümi do not 'exist' in the mortal sense. Rather, their collective (or covalent) will serves to influence the material plane of existence and provides objects with physical form.

Most sages believe the Elemental Plane of Earth is an infinitely cold solid mass of rock striated by metals of all varieties. Portals to the Elemental Plane of Earth are said to exist in various caves on Tellene, a speculation strengthened by the fact that earth elementals favor deep subterranean realms dominated by large caverns and many winding tunnels.

Kshiti may be unseated from their positions when acted upon by magic or by other elemental forces (primarily air and fire). The latter occurs at a so-called planar portal.

Though unquestionably solid (in point of fact, the very definition of said), the influence of air and fire infuses an earth elemental with warmth and mobility permitting it to be animate in the material world. Kshiti are uncomfortable with both of these sensations are desire nothing more than to return to the void they left in the great metastructure.

On Tellene:

Nivler Nund is a controversial sage who studies geology, meteorology and the Elemental Plane of Earth. He claims that he once visited the Plane of Earth by falling into a hole. Since then he claims that Svimohzia and the main continent are moving apart, and that extensive mining by the dwarves will cause all of Brandobia to fall into the Brandobian Ocean. The Purgers (clerics of the House of Scorn) love this kind of propaganda and spread his writings wherever they go.

EARTH ELEMENTAL

HIT POINTS:	35+13d8
SIZE/WEIGHT:	H/3500 lbs.
TENACITY:	Brave
INTELLIGENCE:	Obtuse
FATIGUE FACTOR:	n/a

MOVEMENT

CRAWL:	1¼
WALK:	2½
JOG:	5
RUN:	7½
SPRINT:	10

SAVES

PHYSICAL:	+24
MENTAL:	n/a
DODGE:	+12

SPEED 7 | INIT 6
ATTACK +24 | DMG REDUCTION
DEFENSE +8 | see below
6d8p DAMAGE
medium REACH | TOP SAVE n/a

ATTACK:
Bludgeons with a powerful fist for 6d8p points of damage.

SPECIAL DEFENSES:
DR varies by weapon type (18 hacking or piercing; 6 crushing); Counts as size G for knock-backs; Immune to most spells

GENERAL INFO

ACTIVITY CYCLE:	Any
NO. APPEARING:	1
% CHANCE IN LAIR:	0
FREQUENCY:	Scarce
ALIGNMENT:	Non
VISION TYPE:	Standard
AWARENESS/SENSES:	Can sense vibrations through the earth
HABITAT:	Any
DIET:	Special
ORGANIZATION:	Individuals
CLIMATE/TERRAIN:	Any

YIELD

MEDICINAL:	nil
SPELL COMPONENTS:	nil
HIDE/TROPHY:	nil
TREASURE:	nil
EDIBLE:	no
OTHER:	nil
EXPERIENCE POINT VALUE:	1900

E

ELEMENTAL, FIRE

At the time of which I now speak, my companions and I had ventured into the Ka'Asa Mountains. You no doubt know, or have heard tell, that these peaks are the scourge of eastern Kalamar. In addition to the noxious fumes lingering for miles beyond their central fires, they are home to all sorts of giants and monsters. Yet, this range of fiery peaks is also rich in diamonds and other jewels, and the reward may be well worth the risk.

On the morning of the second day, we came upon several small patches of burned earth. Though some looked oddly like the mixed tracks of man and giant lizard, others were mere trails of scorched ground that put me in mind of a snake's locomotion. I knelt down cautiously to examine them, when an audible hissing sound came faintly through the air. Looking about, we saw a luminous shape like a globe of fire that skimmed over the rocks with that same soft hiss. Though it was less than a few dozen yards away, it ignored us, and made its way up towards a nearby crater, of which we could see no more than the rim. Curious, we slowly clambered upwards with weapons drawn and peered cautiously over the edge.

The globe had vanished. Instead, standing by an exposed pool of molten rock, was a creature made entirely of flame, though its proportions resembled a lanky human with the legs and tail of a giant lizard. It seemed to glory in the heat, like a reptile basking in the sun.

Suddenly, a blast of hot air hit our faces, causing me to drop my staff, which clattered and rolled down the slope behind us. It may have been that noise that caused the creature to depart, or it may have been coincidence; I know not. Regardless, it was then that the creature stepped into the lava pool and vanished from sight. - ᚽ

A fire elemental is a being of living fire and may appear as a seemingly normal (though exceedingly tempestuous) conflagration. Alternatively, it may assume a vaguely humanoid form some ten feet in height and frequently exhibiting a tail of flame. The latter form is more likely once it has encountered living creatures and attempts to adapt to this entirely unfamiliar world.

Fire elementals are all of a roughly constant temperature (around 2000 Kelvin) and as such emit a uniform reddish-yellow luminescence. A Tejas burns brightly seemingly to glow even in the midday sun. If encountered underground or at night, they passively illuminate the largest of caverns or acres of open ground. Fire Spirits leave a trail of scorched earth in their wake.

Combat/Tactics:

Fire elementals cannot comprehend an existence polluted by the influence of earth, air and especially water. Living beings, so it seems, are decidedly tainted by the influence of the latter element and must be purified by the flame.

They strike with fiery appendages causing severe burns. This damage cannot be ameliorated by armor and has the ancillary effect of igniting any combustible material worn or carried by the individual. Linens, wool and leather will burst into flame necessitating that 3d4p seconds be allocated to extinguishing

Fire elementals that have made their way to the Terraverse should not be difficult for you to detect. They leave a trail of scorched earth and burning debris wherever they pass.
An unexpected warming blast of air is oft a sign that an elemental point of contact to the realm of Fire is nearby - particularly should you be near a volcano or other such natural fire source.

SIZE COMPARISON

said or suffer 1d6p points of additional damage every 10 seconds as the character is scorched by his own clothing.[1]

Agni will not focus their incineration on a single individual. Rather, once a target has been set aflame, they will proceed to the next nearest creature. These elementals are satiated only when they have thoroughly freed the fire essence from all sentient beings by reducing them to ashes.

Combatting this elemental may be problematic for they cannot be damaged by weaponry. They are, however, diminished (i.e. injured) by contact with water suffering 1d6p damage per quart. Dweomers that generate cold or frost are particularly efficacious in that the fire elemental suffers full damage and receives no saving throw. Similarly, the *Extinguish* spell automatically inflicts 4d4p damage upon the Tejas.

Fire elementals prefer to retain their chosen form, but may freely and instantaneously alter their form to fit virtually any shape while retaining the same volume.

Habitat/Society:

Fire elementals are native to the Elemental Plane of Fire, a different dimension of reality. Some scholars speculate that it is a land of coal-black earth with rivers of magma and acid rain, where fires burn constantly without needing air or kindling to fuel them. This notion is entirely fanciful and demonstrates a "matter bias" on the part of said scholars unable to fathom that all matter is comprised of differing proportions of elemental earth, fire air and water conjoined to form the tangible objects we are familiar with. Stripped of the tempering influence exerted by the other three elements, the elemental plane of fire is naught but a great conflagration.

Within their own plane of existence, fire elementals do not manifest themselves as individuals. Rather, they are constituent components of the great roiling sea of flame that constitutes this alternate dimension. As with other elementals, fire spirits are immortal though that term requires contextualization for they are not truly alive in our mortal sense. They are fundamental forces of nature only given form when in a unified field produced by the interaction of all four elements such as exists within the material world.

Though Agni rarely depart their home plane, they can reach the material world through elemental points of contact. These nodes (certain geographical locations rumored to dimensionally overlap the Elemental Plane of Fire) are said to exist in various volcanoes on Tellene.

When entering the Terraverse, the presence and influence of the other three divergent elements of matter permits them to take on a material form. For these travelers, this is a wholly alien experience and one that that cannot endure indefinitely.

On Tellene:

A volcano high in the Ka'Asa Mountains is rumored to be an elemental node where one can enter the Elemental Plane of Fire. Supposedly, the node is actually located at the head of a continuous river of magma. This boiling molten stone river has flowed down each of the nearby valleys and is known to change direction with little warning.

[1] *A maximum of 10 points of damage can be sustained before clothing & gear is thoroughly consumed.*

FIRE ELEMENTAL

HIT POINTS:	30+11d8
SIZE/WEIGHT:	H/negligible
TENACITY:	Brave
INTELLIGENCE:	Slow
FATIGUE FACTOR:	n/a

SPEED	7	INIT	-2
ATTACK	+21	DMG REDUCTION	0
DEFENSE	special		
	4d8p		
medium REACH		TOP SAVE	n/a

MOVEMENT

CRAWL:	5
WALK:	10
JOG:	15
RUN:	20
SPRINT:	25

SAVES

PHYSICAL:	see text
MENTAL:	n/a
DODGE:	see text

ATTACK:
Emits tongues of flame that burn for 4d8p points of damage.

SPECIAL:
Cannot be damaged by weapons.
Cold spells deal standard damage (no saving throw), while water deals d6p points per quart.
The Extinguish spell deals 4d4p damage.

GENERAL INFO

ACTIVITY CYCLE.	Any
NO. APPEARING:	1
% CHANCE IN LAIR:	0
FREQUENCY:	Scarce
ALIGNMENT:	Non
VISION TYPE:	Standard
AWARENESS/SENSES:	Standard
HABITAT:	Any
DIET:	Special
ORGANIZATION:	Individuals
CLIMATE/TERRAIN:	Any

YIELD

MEDICINAL:	nil
SPELL COMPONENTS:	nil
HIDE/TROPHY:	nil
TREASURE:	nil
EDIBLE:	no
OTHER:	nil
EXPERIENCE POINT VALUE:	1750

E

ELEMENTAL, WATER

Also Known As: Jala, Undine

My first encounter with elemental incarnations was during a sea voyage through the Straights of Svimohzhia. As we sailed past the Dragon's Teeth, the straits became suddenly violent and all hands were called on deck to quickly batten down the hatches. When I emerged from the hold I saw jagged peaks of rock rising from the sea nearby. But what caught my eye was a very rare sight indeed. On a lower promontory I saw what at first seemed to be some form of a volcanic eruption occurring and shedding its fiery load into the steaming sea. But as I watched I saw the large bodies of moving creatures formed from the very elements at play. The rock heaved upward with mighty fists and flailed against a human torch that was itself locked in a violent grapple with what seemed to be an impossible shape of a person formed of the seawater. All the while steam and fierce winds buffeted their contest and the very air itself seemed to take shape and join the fray. I conjectured later that we had passed some sort of magical doorway to another world where perhaps these matter-formed brutes live and roam freely. Later, after my long years of study, I learned more about what I had seen as a young man — a great battle between elemental beings.

From our long history of religious texts we know that the gods inhabit other worlds far from our own. These are often referred to as the planes of existence. And some of these planes are very different places from the normal world that we live in. There are planes that contain the basic building blocks upon which our world is built but to a much larger degree.

The plane of earth is a vast expanse of various types of rock and soil. Likewise are there places composed primarily of air, fire and water. And in these elemental planes, dwell sentient incarnations of the building blocks of matter. Indeed, there are numerous accounts of these matter corpus dwelling in our abode at times, though little is known about how they come and go. - ᚠ

Water elementals are composed of a tasteless, odorless liquid that resembles normal water with trace amounts of mesoglea. They are naturally formless, lacking any internal skeleton or structural support, but can create surface tension at will to take a desired form.

These ectothermic beings can allow their body temperature to vary with ambient temperatures, though most remain between 60 to 80 degrees Fahrenheit. Water elementals are not colorless, but have a slight blue tint that becomes a deeper blue with an elemental's increasing thickness. As translucent creatures, their apparent coloration can also be affected by the color of any ambient light or background, though their actual color does not change.

When appearing before sapient creatures, a water elemental often attempts to accomodate their form biases by assuming a shape resembling that of a nubile elven female or a male with rippling muscles. This form may be nude or even clad in seaweed. However, as this simulacrum is made of living water that constantly shifts and ripples as it moves, it often proves just as disconcerting (if not more so) than addressing a pool of water.

Combat/Tactics:

Jali are the embodiment of fluidity. Infinitely malleable, their material form cannot be harmed by physical force. They readily

The elemental points of contact that give rise to the appearance of such watery beings are perhaps better known to creatures of the deep than to dwellers of the air such as you or I.
Still, keep your eyes alert for signs. Water boiling where it has no right to do so, or swirling in a funnel where no such current should exist, are the most obvious clues to a water elemental's appearance.

SIZE COMPARISON

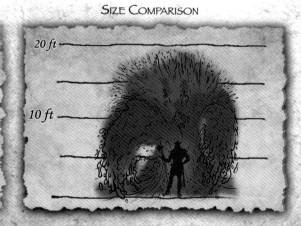

20 ft

10 ft

deform when struck by weaponry and concussive spells such as *Magic Projectile* simply pass right through them leaving a small hole in their wake that is rapidly filled.

A water elemental 'attacks' by extending a pseudopod to touch its opponent (defenders employing a shield are automatically hit). Upon contact, it flows around the creature forming a thin watery film that fills the victim's lungs and nasal cavities with water. They immediately begin to drown suffering 1d3p points of damage every 10 seconds. Short of receiving the benefit of a *Cutaneous Respiration* spell, he will eventually succumb to asphyxiation unless the Undine is slain.

A jala is only susceptible to magic that alters its physical state to gaseous (via fire) or solid (via cold). Saves are not permitted vesus these attack forms.

Water elementals may alter their shape at will and can pass though any barrier that is not watertight.

Water and Fire Elementals, as diametrically opposing forces of nature, annihilate each other on contact. The consequent release of pure energy inflicts 12d8p damage to any creature within 20 feet, 8d6p to those within 50 feet and 3d4p as far as 100 feet from the explosion. Natural and armor damage reduction will temper this force.

Habitat/Society:

Like their complementary elementals, jali are native to their own extraplanar realm. Theories among certain scholars speculate that the Elemental Plane of Water is a vast fluidic realm in perpetual motion, with no air or solid substances.

Although this Elemental Plane of Water exists on a different dimension of reality, water elementals can travel to Tellene through elemental nodes or via powerful magic forces. The former points of contact are certain geographical locations rumored to dimensionally overlap the Elemental Plane of Water. On Tellene, certain spots in the seas have been reported to coexist with the Elemental Plane of Water (though these connections are tenuous and last only weeks).

Within their own plane of existence, water elementals do not manifest themselves as individuals. Rather, they are integral components of the limitless ocean that constitutes this alternate dimension. Their influence upon the material world is to provide fluidity (in the case of liquids) and malleability (for solids).

As with other elementals, jali are immortal though that term requires contextualization for they are not truly alive in our mortal sense. They are fundamental forces of nature only given form when exposed to the interaction of all four elements such as exists within the material world. When entering the Terraverse and taking on a mortal form, Jali are perplexed by the constrains imposed upon them by this very strange place. Within the depths of the sea, this is tolerable but upon dry land with the immovable earth beneath and surrounded by air seeking always to evaporate its form the Undine cannot long remain.

On Tellene:

A swarthy Svimohz named Vanamir claims to have personally saved the coastal city of Sobeteta from a slew of water elementals, when they streamed from a mystical gate that opened a quarter mile off the island.

WATER ELEMENTAL

HIT POINTS:	32+12d8
SIZE/WEIGHT:	M to H/varies
TENACITY:	Brave
INTELLIGENCE:	Slow
FATIGUE FACTOR:	n/a

MOVEMENT

CRAWL:	5
WALK:	10
JOG:	15
RUN:	20
SWIM:	25

SAVES

PHYSICAL:	see text
MENTAL:	n/a
DODGE:	see text

SPEED: 8 INIT: -1
ATTACK: +12
DMG REDUCTION: 0
DEFENSE: special
DAMAGE: special
REACH: long
TOP SAVE: ▼
n/a

ATTACK:
Upon contact, surrounds defender in a thin film of water that induces drowning.

SPECIAL DEFENSES:
May only be damaged by magic that alters its physical form to gas (via fire) or solid (via cold).

E

GENERAL INFO

ACTIVITY CYCLE:	Any
NO. APPEARING:	1
% CHANCE IN LAIR:	0
FREQUENCY:	Scarce
ALIGNMENT:	Non
VISION TYPE:	Standard
AWARENESS/SENSES:	Standard
HABITAT:	Any
DIET:	Special
ORGANIZATION:	Individuals
CLIMATE/TERRAIN:	Any

YIELD

MEDICINAL:	nil
SPELL COMPONENTS:	nil
HIDE/TROPHY:	nil
TREASURE:	nil
EDIBLE:	no
OTHER:	nil
EXPERIENCE POINT VALUE:	1425

ELEPHANT
Also Known As: Loxodon, Oliphant

A bull oliphant preparing to charge.

The tales of the oliphant are many, and for years it was my fondest desire to see one of these strange beasts and record my observations on it. At first, I knew not what to expect, for the only secondhand information I could gather made no sense at all. My initial knowledge of the creature came from an obscure bit of northern lore scribbled in a halfling scholar's bestiary, which described only it as "a moving hill" and "as big as a house." To find one, it said, I would have to go south. Unfortunately, it was to be some time before my companions and I made our way from P'Bapar and our misadventures at a certain mountainous keep, and traveled to warmer climes.

Eventually, our travels took us to Svimohzia, where oliphants were said to be the most numerous. Shortly after landing upon the ancient isle, I entered a dark beggars' enclave where I had heard I could learn more. Several of the wretches claimed to have laid hands upon an oliphant, but their stories were little better than jumbled ramblings. One man would say that the oliphant was like a wall, while another would assert it resembled a husking basket, and still another claimed it to be like a spear. In the midst of my conversation, still three more beggars joined us and each asserted three more differing perspectives, saying that the oliphant was actually like a snake, a tree and a rope. In the end, they came to blows over the question and I stumbled from the lightless hut with no greater knowledge than when I had entered. My chagrin was complete when I found that each of the men was blind, and thus totally unreliable. - ⚶

There are two known species of elephant on Tellene, both having the traditional thick skin, sturdy legs, long distinctive trunk and large floppy ears. However, the elephants of the Obakasek peninsula are slightly hairier as well as being physically smaller, with a pink-speckled gray hide, a mostly flat back, less prominent ears and only the males having tusks. Those of the Svimohzish Isle are the largest elephants, being less hairy and having rounded backs, larger ears and tusks for both males and females. Female elephants are slightly smaller than the males.

The Obakasek elephant stands about 7 to 12 feet tall and weighs roughly 7,000 to 11,000 pounds. The Svimohzish elephant stands from 10 to 13 feet tall, weighing between 8,000 and 13,000 pounds, with elephants living in the island's Vohven Jungle being on the smaller size and those dwelling in the savannas favoring the larger measurements.

Combat/Tactics:
Any elephant attacks if it feels that it or its calf is threatened, though adult bull elephants are particularly aggressive during musth (a periodic rise of testosterone levels that can last for

SIGN/TRACKS

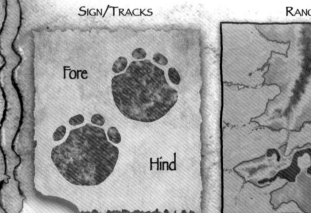

Fore

Hind

RANGE ON TELLENE

SIZE COMPARISON

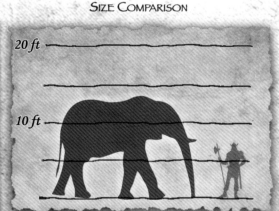

20 ft

10 ft

several weeks) and may attack for seemingly no reason at all. In most cases this is a "mock charge" meant to scare creatures off (usually signaled by the ears being extended outwards). If the ears are back, the loxodon intends more than bluff.

An Oliphant moving to contact will head-butt the first creature in its path inflicting a 4d8p+12 point wound if it hits. Every six seconds thereafter it may take one of the following actions: *a)* gore an opponent with its tusks for 4d8p+4 *b)* grab a size M or smaller creature with its trunk and hurl them 8d4p feet away[1] (using a shield for defense against this attack ensures success for the elephant as can envelop the shield and user together!) or *c)* advance by trampling[2] whomever is in front of it (giving ground is ineffective as the elephant's movement is double a human's). The choice of attack method is contingent on the battle.

Loxodon are not malicious creatures and do not fight to kill their opponents. Driving them off is its goal. As such, it will not pursue an enemy in full retreat.

[1] *creatures thrown suffer 3d6p damage; armor DR does not apply*
[2] *trampling causes 5d6p damage; armor DR does not apply*

Habitat/Society:

Elephants spend much of their days in warm savannas or forests, grazing on vegetation such as grass, leaves, fruits, herbs and bark, using the trunk to pick up the food and transfer it to the mouth. They also drink a considerable amount of water, sucking it up into the trunk and then spraying it into the mouth.

Female elephants live in herds consisting of about a dozen adult females and a variable number of younger males and females. The male elephant lives a mostly solitary life except when fighting other males for dominance or approaching females for mating. The female elephant has a gestation period of about 22 months, bearing a single calf weighing around 250 pounds. A calf typically reaches maturity at the age of 14 and has a lifespan of about 60 years.

Ecology:

Because of their size, elephants have few natural predators other than dinosaurs, lions and giant birds, though the latter two usually restrict themselves to lone calves or weak and wounded members of the herd. Svimohz humans occasionally band together and attempt to capture an elephant calf to be trained and used as a beast of burden (often at docks or timber yards).

On Tellene:

Elephants are native to the Svimohzish Isle and the Obakasek peninsula, though they have been transplanted to other regions (such as the Kalamaran Empire, for their circuses) with limited success.

[3]*Tusks are used as a source of ivory for carvings, ornamental items, knife handles, jewelry, musical instruments, inlays and various other uses. Each tusk has a value of 200+10d20p silver pieces.*

ELEPHANT

HIT POINTS:	40+10d8
SIZE/WEIGHT:	E/to 13,000 lbs.
TENACITY:	Steady
INTELLIGENCE:	Animal, High
FATIGUE FACTOR:	-8

SPEED 6 — INIT 0
ATTACK +8
DEFENSE 0 — DMG REDUCTION 8
see below
long REACH — DAMAGE — TOP SAVE ▼ — n/a

MOVEMENT

CRAWL:	10
WALK:	15
JOG:	20
RUN:	25
SPRINT:	30

SAVES

PHYSICAL:	+11
MENTAL:	+8
DODGE:	+6

ATTACK:
Initiates battle by head-butting closest opponent for 4d8p+12; every 6s thereafter may gore with tusks (4d8p+4); grab and hurl an opponent ~25' (doing 3d6p) or trample for 5d6p

SPECIAL DEFENSES:
none, other than their intimidating presence

GENERAL INFO

ACTIVITY CYCLE:	Diurnal, or as dictated by owner
NO. APPEARING:	1-20 (wild), or as dictated by owner
% CHANCE IN LAIR:	n/a
FREQUENCY:	Frequent
ALIGNMENT:	Non
VISION TYPE:	Standard
AWARENESS/SENSES:	Standard
HABITAT:	Savannas and forests
DIET:	Herbivorous
ORGANIZATION:	Individuals or herd
CLIMATE/TERRAIN:	Semi-Tropical to tropical grasslands

YIELD

MEDICINAL:	brains are said to cure senility
SPELL COMPONENTS:	unknown; more scholarly research is needed
HIDE/TROPHY:	yes; head, tusks and feet are common trophies
TREASURE:	incidental
EDIBLE:	yes
OTHER:	tusks are used as a source of ivory[3]

EXPERIENCE POINT VALUE: 1000

ELF

Also Known As: Lathlani, Doulathan, Aralarai, Kyndri

Elves often seem as elusive to the affairs of men and their ways as the dwarves are — yet the reality is they are quite fascinated by us and take a keen interest in our doings.

To most people, the elven race is perceived as haughty and aloof (though, in fact, these same folk are readily taken in by the charm of any individual elf they may encounter). In truth, elves do tend to keep to their own kind and rarely actively engage with other civilized races. In large part this is a curse of their immortality. A human lifespan is but a fleeting moment and even a dwarf's hardly less so. It saddens elves to watch a dear friend grow old and die in the wink of an eye. Many young and gregarious elves learn this hard lesson early in life and progressively become less and less willing to form such temporary and ultimately melancholy relationships. Given these facts, elves tend to live deep within old growth forests far removed from the civilization and infrastructure of other races.

There are exceptions however. Some elves, known as 'kyndri' or 'wandering souls,' overcome the tendency to shun immortals and set off to learn more. The reasons for this are not fully known to us but I've encountered several over the years. We even have an elvish fletcher working here at the Keep.

Although charming, there's always the feeling that elves look down on humans. Not in a disparaging way but rather in the manner an adult regards a child. Superior in intellect and in possession of more knowledge and wisdom than we could gain in a lifetime, one senses a wishful desire they could impart the same upon us. It's as though they see potential in our kind but the notion is tempered by the fact we all too willingly squander it. — ⨍

An elven warrior preparing to go into battle.

Kyndri or 'wandering souls' are usually the only elves most humans will ever encounter.

Elves are the largest and most human-like of the fey races. Though nearly as tall as a man (males being 5½ feet in height and women just over 5 feet tall), they are of slight build with narrow shoulders, thin limbs and long graceful fingers. Their faces are long and narrow with high cheekbones, while their ears have an elongated helix that gives them their distinctive "pointy" shape. Skin tones tend to be very pale and their hair is usually blonde. While it might seem intuitive that such alien features would be off-putting, quite the contrary is true. Inexplicably, most humans find these pale skinny waifs irresistibly alluring. Go figure.

Elves tend to live deep within old growth forests far removed from the civilization and infrastructure of other races. Here they live in harmony with their surroundings frequently incorporating natural features into their homes. The notion that elves live in treehouses is a ridiculous bedtime tale told to children. Elven structures are built from stone and masterfully constructed to last for centuries. They typically feature an open floor plan, vaulted ceilings, copper or slate gabled roofs and plenty of large glass windows drawing in as much natural light as possible. Cellars are atypical as most elves are uncomfortable being underground. Homes are invariably surrounded by

SIGN/TRACKS

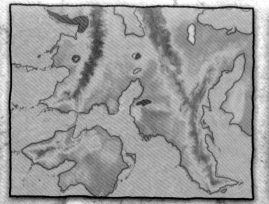

Tracking an elf is like boiling water with a candle. Extremely difficult!

RANGE ON TELLENE

SIZE COMPARISON

6 ft

3 ft

tasteful landscaping favoring indigenous plant species.

An elven community can be confusing to navigate for an outsider as there is no apparent rhyme or reason to building placement. There are no neat broad thoroughfares or even proscribed districts. It is not the elven way to mandate order and this is certainly reflected in their villages. Buildings are placed where the topography, tree growth, lighting and other subtleties best blend to accept the structure. (Were an accomplished mathematician to analyze the cooperative, he would be surprised to learn that it conforms closely to fractal geometry.)

Visitors unfamiliar with elven customs may be surprised to find their communities devoid of inns, taverns and boarding houses. Those rare visitors are always the guest of an elf and housed and fed in his or her home.

Elves are fantastic craftmen exceeding the skill of any mortal race. That being said, their design philosophy differs markedly from other master artisans. At all times they seek a blended whole in which fitness for use is balanced against weight, extreme durability and aesthetic beauty. While a skilled dwarven smith may be able to craft technically superior blades and armor, they are most unlikely to be as maintenance-free, as lightweight and as visually pleasing.

In all facets of craftwork, elven goods have a reputation for being magical. From clothing and tools all the way through jewelry, they exhibit great forethought and incredible attention to detail. All such items are highly desired by humans and their ilk and those few baubles acquired by outsiders are frequently passed along for generations as heirlooms.

Elves design objects to function as desired for a very, very long time. Frequent in usage is 'elven steel' (a corrosion-resistant alloy) as well as the seemingly wasteful – if not extravagant – use of gold, platinum and mithril for common tools and utensils. However, elves have a different perspective. Why expend the effort to craft an implement that requires periodic maintenance and will wear out in a mere decade or two, when a quality analogue can be fabricated that will last a century or more (if not longer)?

The elves have had dealings with virtually every civilized and not so civilized race on Tellene. Dealings have not always been peaceful, though it must be said that the elves rarely believe this stems from any fault of their own.

For the most part, elves are content to remain in their own lands and let the short-lived races lead their own lives. War is for the younger races; the high elves are tired of endless posturing and threats over land. However, any race encroaching on elven lands receives a swift reminder of how elves survived on Tellene for so long.

Elves have little understanding of how short-lived races experience time, for their own immortal existences compel them to ponder actions on the timescale of centuries. In particular, the short-term motivations humans are often inscrutable to elves, seeing as how they frequently mortgage their futures for what seems to be the merest pittance of im-

ELF

HIT POINTS:	21+2d10
SIZE/WEIGHT:	M/100 lbs.
TENACITY:	Brave
INTELLIGENCE:	Average
FATIGUE FACTOR:	-3/-4

SPEED 9 / INIT 1 / ATTACK +5 / DICE REDUCTION / DEFENSE +4 by weapon / by weapon 5 / REACH by weapon / DAMAGE / TOP SAVE 4

MOVEMENT

CRAWL:	2 ½
WALK:	5
JOG:	10
RUN:	15
SPRINT:	20

SAVES

PHYSICAL:	+3
MENTAL:	+6
DODGE:	+5

ATTACK:
Elf warriors are typically armed with longswords and longbows while wearing lightweight elfin mail. Elves utilize one Initiative die lower.

SPECIAL DEFENSES:
Shield use (e.g., medium shields increase Defense to +10). 75% mastery in Hiding and Sneaking when in natural terrain; unarmored DR is 0

GENERAL INFO

ACTIVITY CYCLE:	Diurnal
NO. APPEARING:	2-5 (traveling); 12-17 (warder band)
% CHANCE IN LAIR:	10
FREQUENCY:	Infrequent
ALIGNMENT:	Chaotic Good
VISION TYPE:	Standard
AWARENESS/SENSES:	Standard (Initiative die type is one better)
HABITAT:	Isolated woodland cities
DIET:	Omnivorous
ORGANIZATION:	Any
CLIMATE/TERRAIN:	Any, save arctic (temperate woodlands preferred)

YIELD

MEDICINAL:	nil
SPELL COMPONENTS:	nil
HIDE/TROPHY:	ears can be mistaken for those of other monsters
TREASURE:	possessions[1]
EDIBLE:	yes
OTHER:	nil
EXPERIENCE POINT VALUE:	100

mediate gain. If elves seem slow to react to a specific provocation, it is because they see the forest for the trees and do not readily pursue ephemeral goals.

Combat/Tactics

Elves abhor war, for they have living memories (going back millennia) of countless battles and the horror of butchery. Humans tend to romanticize these battles when the memories of the warriors fade in old age, inspiring a new and naïve generation with saccharine tales of high adventure and glory. Elves, however, know the truth and don't sugarcoat the young with exaggerations of their exploits. In part, this is because they do not have the luxury of passing the mantle of responsibility to a brash young generation and one day may end their (or one of their dear friends') otherwise timeless life on an orc's blade.

Hating war is not synonymous with burying one's head in the sand and hoping it will go away. Elves accept it for what it is and go to great lengths to mitigate its consequence. Nearly every elf, both male and female, is a trained warrior and quite adept in both the blade and bow.

Elves are rarely the aggressor in any conflict preferring to monitor political developments within their regional area and intervening very early on when they sense a situation brewing that could have long-term consequences. Rarely will the elves' hands be seen in these machinations as they work through trusted third parties of 'elf friends' to influence and shape events through bribery, propaganda and, if the situation warrants, assassination. This approach is far less effective with respect to those humanoids like orcs and hobgoblins with a vehement hatred of elvenkind.

Elves maintain an active defense of their homeland through small teams that function as spies, scouts or commandos as the situation warrants. It is this role that elves are eminently suited for given their skills in Sneaking, Hiding, Observation and the ability to both camouflage themselves in natural surroundings and little need for sleep. These bands number a dozen or so individuals and are commanded by an experienced leader (typically a 3rd to 6th level ranger, though a multiclassed fighter/mage is not uncommon). They armor themselves in lightweight chainmail, swords and longbows.

When outside their immediate homeland, these groups make every effort to remain hidden so as not to alert their quarry that they're being observed. It is likely that one or more of the group has an aptitude for thievery, which he may use to appropriate an enemy's gear or weaponry for later use in misleading the elves' foes. Scouts frequently make use of orkin or hobgoblin missiles when conducting raids in order to deceive their target as to the true identity of their assailant.

Even when faced with an aggressive enemy intent on hostile action, elves rarely seek to fight a 'set piece' battle. Rather, they harry the foe by luring him into prepared ambushes or deadfalls, sniping at sentries or stragglers, and sneaking into camps and cutting throats. While no single action can hope to destroy the aggressor, multiple attacks serve to attrite the enemy numbers, frustrating them with stinging blows against which they cannot retaliate.

Habitat/Society:

Elven society is not governed by a formal set of laws. Individuals are free to pursue their own aspirations unfettered by an inimical hierarchy. In most cases, said goals further the good of the community. In the rare instance of a malevolent elf, most often they leave of their own accord without formal sanction.

Elves do not marry in the formal and often legally binding manner of other races. Instead, they enter into romantic relationships by mutual love, ending them when one or both partners ceases to love their consort. While some couples may stay together for millennia, serial monogamy is more the norm. It is not unknown for younger elves to become involved with humans, even marrying them and siring half-elven children. Though this may seem outwardly to break with elven convention, it is actually directly in line with said as a 50 or 60-year marriage is but a brief dalliance for an elf.

Though physically capable of bearing children for their entire adult lives, elven women do so rarely. Women are accorded equal status in elven society and are both free and encouraged to participate in all important roles. It is the duties and responsibilities of these other positions that discourage motherhood rather than any dislike of children. Indeed, children are treasured within elven society more so than in any other race. Parenting is a responsibility taken on with the utmost seriousness demanding the fullest attention for decades and precludes the distractions of a secondary profession.

Elves are fascinated by magic and it forms one of their few vices. Elven communities nearly always have an accomplished mage of 17th-20th level with a 11th-14th level mage for every 30 inhabitants. Fully one-eighth of elves have some proficiency in magic whether solely as mages or as an adjunct to another class. Even warrior leaders are as likely to be fighter/mages as they are pure fighters.

Ecology:

Elven communities are self-sufficient and see little reason to trade for purely economic reasons (other than for refined metals). What commerce they engage in often has ulterior motives such as fostering relationships with their neighbors and insinuating their influence and reputation with persons of influence.

Unlike human pastoral communities, one does not encounter fields of cereal crops surrounding an elven village. Food crops are integrated into the landscape often serving a dual purpose as décor. Roadsides, rooftops and public spaces are invariably beautified with a variety of plants that also bear nutritive fruits or vegetables.

The elven diet can be characterized by quality over quantity for elves are frugal in their meals eating only enough to support life and never gorging. A meal is a social event to be enjoyed with companions and spiced with both herbs and conversation. They do eat meat, such as can be hunted within their realms, but this is not a daily occurrence. A significant minority of elvenkind practice vegetarianism.

Of the wild grains in their diet, many are ground to make flour, which is in turn baked to form bread. Although elves know of the properties of yeast, they rarely use it in their cooking. Elven bread is flat, surprisingly light and flaky, and is baked on hot stones until crisp. Many varieties exist, depending on what other ingredients are added. Honey is added for sweet bread (*colinleff*), which is eaten as a snack; fruit and nuts are added to form meal bread (*hosilvleff*), so named because it is considered a meal in itself; and special herbs fortify wayfarer bread (*starierleff*), a bread commonly found among the wanderers of the race.

Subraces:

Much of what has come before applies to all elves in general. The most commonly encountered – and hence *de facto* standard – elf is the high elf, or *lathlani*. Members of this races are often given to wanderlust in their youth and it is not uncommon to find them associating with humans, halflings and even the occasional dwarf as they explorer the stretches of Tellene in search of adventure.

There are some subraces of elves – some distinctive more for their cultural differences than their physical ones. For the most part, high elves get on very well with their surface kin, though many gray elves are too haughty and introverted even for high elves, who dislike being treated like wayward children by their cousins. Wood elves and high elves often share the same areas of forest, and trade between the two subraces is frequent (often exchanging high elf goods for wood elf musical instruments, bows or carved wooden objects).

Gray Elves

Once the preeminent mentors of the lesser races (to wit, dwarves, humans and gnomes), gray elves were horribly dispirited by the hubris and racism their erstwhile pupils the Brandobians developed after centuries of careful and patient counsel. Most of their kind has withdrawn from any contact with humankind and settled in the wooded uplands east of Voldor Bay.

No one can say with certainty why they are called the gray elves (it is not a term they themselves employ instead referring on the Low Elven name *doulathan* when referenced by non-elves). Some claim it is a reference to their ancient culture and wisdom – others to their coloring for their hair is most often silver. None of these is true but they serve as common explanations for an etymological mystery.

Gray elves are exemplary seamen and shipwrights having long ago mastered blue water navigation and capable of building sleek cliper ships able to weather the roughest seas.

In appearance they are none too different from their high elven kin. If anything, they are slightly larger and even more palely complected.

Wood Elves

Also called sylvan elves, they have eschewed societal conventions and opted to live an austere life in the forest more in keeping with the fey side of elvishness. They do, in fact, often live in arboreal houses and in many respects conform to more traditional human concepts of what an elf is. The Low Elven word for this race, *aralarai*, translates best as "earth children."

In appearance, they are slightly shorter but somewhat broader in the chest and shoulders. Their coloration is also darker than high elves with auburn or brown hair fairly common. Wood elves are not renowned artisans (save for their proficiency in woodworking at which they excel) but are adroit trackers, hunters and woodsmen.

The wood elves are far less concerned with the common weal than their kin and tend to favor the narrow self-interests of their own communities over that of others. They are natural allies of other forest creatures such as dryads, centaurs and the fey races but their interest in and hence desire to become entwined with politics external to their forest home is minimal. Woe to the interloper that would seek to disrupt their arboreal realm for they are vigorous in the defense of their homeland.

Religion:

For a race unconcerned with a precipitously short lifespan, elves are remarkably spiritual. The Raconteur and the Shimmering One are particularly favored as elves seem to seek inspiration and beauty from religion, rather than salvation or power. They are, however, olerant of differing viewpoints and religious dogma has never been a source of strife for the elves.

On Tellene:

The largest elven communities – and certainly the ones most welcoming to outsiders –are located in the northern Brandobian kingdom of Cosdol. This may be viewed (and is by many) as a *de facto* elven country, for elves and half-elves outnumber humans within the realm. In point of fact, it is a human kingdom governed by a Brandobian descendant of Veseln who sided with the elves some three-and-a-half centuries past, during the Brandobian civil wars. While elven influence is certainly widespread, it really is more of a blended community.

True elven lands are typified by Lendelwood, a fey realm and sanctuary meandering outward from the western foothills of the Legasa Peaks. The ancient elven city of Lathlanian lies within the heart of this wood. Reputedly, the city spreads a faint magical aura over the whole domain. Its residents are not welcoming to strangers because, for centuries, the Kingdom of Eldor has been in passive conflict with the elves of this forest.

Other elven communities of note for their renewed vigor in opposing the evil machinations of the Kalamaran throne are those within the Kalalali Forest (having instigated the revolt of Pekal and actively supporting Paru'Bor), as well as the Edosi Forest and its gray elven city of Doulathanorian.

---

[1] *Nearly everything an elf possess is considered treasure; simple tools or furnishings are highly valued in wider society while actual objets d'art can command exhorbitant prices. Traveling elves may carry 3d20 silver coins with which to engage in commerce, if need be, with humans. In their own communities, elves employ a byzantine system of barter and favor trading that substitutes for a monetary economy.*

ENT

Also Known As: Tree Giant, Treant, Tree Shepherd

We had made camp early that evening, in a forest clearing of the kind so popularized in fanciful tales. In the center lay a dark-eyed pool, while yellow waves of flowers decorated the brush and the melancholy cry of the daws in the high trees echoed through the stillness.

While my companions chattered away, I sat quietly, forcing stale rations down my gullet and pondering the trees ringing the space. I knew trees well – their families, the shapes of their leaves, those that are good for carving, those whose drooping branches are best for basket weaving, and the others that are barely remarkable at all. The trees here seemed to be of the latter variety, with nothing particular to interest me.

Then, amongst the shadows, I saw it. Not a tree, but a tree-thing. One of the trees-that-were-not. The story of the first such creature goes back nearly 1,000 years, with the oldest Brandobian texts simply calling it an 'ent' (their word for 'giant'). Scholars still argue about whether this first giant encountered by the Brandobians was a godly avatar or mortal monster. Myself, I prefer to think each ent is a collective individual, with a single mind manifested from a thousand individual trees so that the plants might better understand man by being like him. However, I digress.

It was not a rapid movement, merely a vague, faint alteration that grew steadily, though still obscurely, outwards. The creature had not the mere prettiness of single trees, but instead seemed massed and mountainous. The limbs, I now saw, were arms and legs; the knots and hollows were a face staring at me expressionlessly.

Suddenly, the campfire flamed up splendidly under the large brewing copper, the crackling wood so startling that I leapt up and turned towards the fire, blade in hand. When I looked back, the ent was gone and only the laughter of my unknowing companions remained. ~

Ents are expert in the art of surprise attacks. Many victims meet their swift end having no clue what happened.

A typical ent has a green-gray hide with a rough bark-like texture and a brawny, somewhat cylindrical body. Its arms and legs are thick and knobby like the branches and the trunk of a tree, while fingers and toes resemble branches and roots. Where a human has hair follicles, an ent has trichome-like outgrowths, though the function of these is relatively similar to the hairs of man. Head growths are thick, like twigs with sprouting leaves, with mossy face or body growths.

Their eyes are of a deep brown color and well adapted to seeing shades of green and yellow, though they have difficulty distinguishing other colors and have poor long-distance vision except in twilight and the darker hours. Ent mouths are toothless,

but can easily crush any item more fragile than the ent itself.

Like humans, ents may vary in appearance depending on the individual and place of origin. Ents that dwell in primarily coniferous forests tend to have ancestors who resembled the local pines, cypresses or similar softwoods. Ents that live where broadleaf or hardwoods (e.g., chestnut, oak, hickory) dominate are more likely to resemble those species.

A typical adult ent stands over 15 feet tall with a thick frame nearly 5 feet wide and weighing around 2½ tons.

Combat/Tactics:

When initiating a surprise attack, an ent waits until its foe's back

---

SIGN/TRACKS

Ents are territorial and tend to move about the same area of the forest their entire lives, migrating from one root-hole to the next where they settle to draw nourishment from the soil. Older ents occasionally remain motionless long enough to 're-root.'

RANGE ON TELLENE

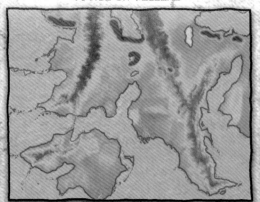

SIZE COMPARISON

20 ft

10 ft

114

is turned or its attention is diverted, and then bludgeons the enemy into pulp with its massive branch-like arms.

Every 10 seconds, instead of attacking, an ent can animate an otherwise normal Gigantic or Enormous sized tree within 20 feet and direct it to attack. Each ent can command up to three animated trees simultaneously while attacking or performing other actions. Gigantic animated trees have 40+7d8 Hit Points and deal 4d8p points of damage with a successful attack, while Enormous trees have 45+9d8 Hit Points and deal 6d6p points of damage per attack. Otherwise, their combat statistics are as those of normal ents.

An ent's bark-like hide is quite resistant to damage having a DR of 16 versus crushing and piercing weapons and 10 versus hacking weapons.

Habitat/Society:

Ents are mostly crepuscular creatures that dwell in temperate or tropical forests. They are active year round except in the northern parts of their range. When winter snows cover the ground, ents in these regions go into a resting state, drastically reducing their activity.

Ents are mostly solitary, though female ents often share territory and occasionally meet in resting groves. Males rarely form groups except when uniting to maintain their position against foreign males or other potential invaders. Exactly when an ent can be described as male or female, however, depends upon its current stage of growth.

A single ent contains both sexes and slowly alternates between them as it ages. Once in each ent's life, during a female stage, it may intentionally cause a fist-sized leathery seed to sprout from its body. After 18 months, the seed is attached only by a slender stalk, at which time the ent detaches and buries it. The seedling then consumes nutrients from the soil, growing 12 inches annually for the first 9 to 10 years. At this stage, it frees itself from the soil and sets off on its own, growing slowly to maturity over the next 40 years.

Most ents maintain their sapience for approximately 1,000 years. However, such a long lifespan leads to listlessness and inertia. Older ents rarely move, essentially "taking root" in one spot, with the result that the resemblance to a normal tree becomes stronger. Eventually, ents lose their sapience permanently and are indistinguishable from normal trees.

Ecology:

Ents take much of their nourishment from the rain, soil and the light of the sun. However, ents are not true plants, even though they appear as such, and may also consume plant material (such as fungus, fruits and nuts), invertebrates (insects and worms) and vertebrates (birds and rodents) in order to build up an intake of calories needed for winter.

On Tellene:

The ancient Kalalai forest is under the patronage of the local elves, whose purpose is to frighten away such intruders rather than to harm them. However, in times of great trouble they can call upon ent allies (among others). As the would-be foresters of Ek'Kasel can attest, seeing the trees marching towards you is a frightful sight indeed.

[1]A severed bit of ent doubles a spell's duration and volume of effect (if any) when replacing a similar (leaf, twig) component.

ENT

HIT POINTS:	35+10d8
SIZE/WEIGHT:	G/2½ tons
TENACITY:	Fearless
INTELLIGENCE:	Bright
FATIGUE FACTOR:	2

SPEED 4 · INIT -3 · ATTACK +20 · DICE REDUCTION · +9 · 16 · DEFENSE · 3d6p+8 · DAMAGE · long REACH · n/a TOP SAVE

MOVEMENT

CRAWL:	5
WALK:	10
JOG:	15
RUN:	20
SPRINT:	25

SAVES

PHYSICAL:	+20
MENTAL:	+20
DODGE:	+20

ATTACK:
Limb attacks deal 3d6p+8 damage; Animates G trees (40+7d8 HP, 4d8p damage). Animates E trees (45+9d8 HP, 6d6p damage).

DEFENSES:
DR only 10 when attacked with hacking weapons

GENERAL INFO

ACTIVITY CYCLE:	Crepuscular
NO. APPEARING:	1-20
% CHANCE IN LAIR:	15
FREQUENCY:	Unusual
ALIGNMENT:	Neutral Good
VISION TYPE:	Standard
AWARENESS/SENSES:	Standard
HABITAT:	Deep inside old forests
DIET:	Omnivorous
ORGANIZATION:	Individuals
CLIMATE/TERRAIN:	Temperate to tropical woodlands

YIELD

MEDICINAL:	nil
SPELL COMPONENTS:	severed bits replace common leaves, twigs, etc.[1]
HIDE/TROPHY:	nil
TREASURE:	incidental
EDIBLE:	no
OTHER:	nil
EXPERIENCE POINT VALUE:	1800

ETTIN, LESSER

Also Known As: Gronk

These nocturnal cave dwellers love to hunt at night — one of the reasons they are frequent camp-raiders. Spotting a campfire or catching a whiff of venison roasting over an open fire often lures them in.

Nearly twice the height of a man, they brandish crude weapons that they use with amazing agility. We once had an Ettin come crashing through our camp with arms swinging like a farmer threshing wheat. Splitting heads. Bowling men. Kicking down tents. Six piercing eyes on three snouted heads seeking out all comers. We had our hands full.

In my experience they usually go for the horses or mules and then move on once they've slung one over their broad shoulders to leave you licking your wounds.

If you've got no horseflesh in camp may the gods help you for man-flesh is a suitable substitute and they're not shy about taking it where they can get it.

Oft times, however, they'll attack just for the sport of it when their bellies are full. They can be cruel in that regard. I've seen them snap the legs of men leaving them writhing in pain while they dispatch other combatants only to return later to torment them further before finishing them off.

I once passed the body of three men tied to a tree who had been used for hurled-rock targeting practice. — ⚲

Tabor — the infamous lesser ettin that terrorized the village of Dirocden before being vanquished by Larzon and his band.

Lesser ettins resemble their more massive kin, with a reddish hide and three heads marked by pig-like snouts and lower jaw tusks. One head always remains awake, making the ettin quite difficult to surprise. Its six eyes glint red and its hair is coarse and black. Furthermore, an ettin's hand has only three fingers and a thumb (the latter sprouting from the base of its palm rather than the side), and its elbows are not hinged but move freely on ball-and-socket joints.

There have also been rumors of similar creatures with either two or four heads (depending on the teller of the tale). Whether these are true relatives of the lesser ettin, or merely stories based on misconceptions, is unknown.

A typical adult male lesser ettin stands about 11 feet tall and weighs around 1250 pounds. The female greatly resembles the male, only slightly smaller and with three larger breasts.

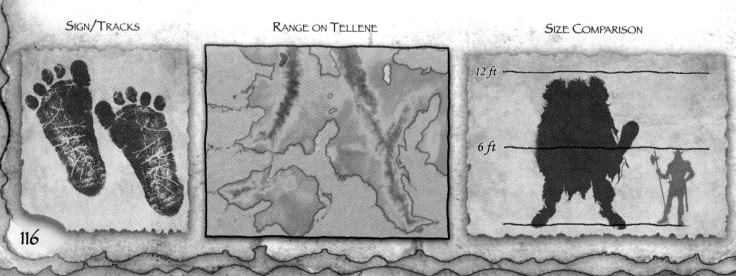

SIGN/TRACKS	RANGE ON TELLENE	SIZE COMPARISON
		12 ft — / 6 ft —

Combat/Tactics:

The creature's special physiognomy (*i.e.*, the three heads, ball-and-socket elbows and thumb placement) help make the ettin an even more fearsome giant. Because one of its three heads is always awake, its Initiative dice are improved by three. *For example, if the circumstances would normally call for the GM to roll a d12, the ettin instead gets a d6.* This racial bonus cannot improve an ettin's Initiative below a d4.

In addition, an ettin uses a d20p-4 Defense die (plus Defense Bonus and other modifiers) for attackers to the rear, rather than the standard d8p.

A lesser ettin carries two clubs, one in each hand. When attacking, it swings one club first and then the other club on the following second. Because its three brains allow it to focus on more than one thing at a time, these attacks may be against the same target or two different targets.

Habitat/Society:

Lesser ettins are nocturnal cave-dwelling creatures that hunt only at nighttime, dawn or dusk. They spend their daylight hours resting. Lesser ettins hunt singly or in pairs, and live in a family unit that includes a mated pair and young from prior seasons. Female lesser ettins can bear one youngling per year. They nurture this offspring primarily on ettin milk and the crushed and pulped hearts, lungs and livers of other intelligent beings.

Ecology:

Lesser ettins feed primarily on large ungulates such as horses, donkeys, pigs and sheep raided from farms, but they have no qualms about eating the flesh of sapient creatures. They consider elf meat to be a fine treat and attack them on sight, devouring their prey immediately after a successful battle.

The lesser ettin hates all other creatures, though it may ally with more powerful beings in order to achieve some greater aim (such as in exchange for expanded hunting territory). It may even aid lesser creatures such as orcs (in exchange for treasure or food tributes) when faced with an enemy the orcs cannot defeat on their own.

They enjoy destruction, and when bored often swing their clubs to bash half-heartedly at trees and other nearby objects in a haphazard fashion. Such destruction helps skilled trackers by providing them with an obvious trail of the creature's movements.

On Tellene:

Wanderers speak of the lesser ettin presence wherever orcs are prominent, though they seem to be particularly numerous in the Krond Heights and the Odril Hills.

[1]*Ettins favor quantity over quality in their hoards. There is likely to be large quantities of coins, armor and plundered foodstuffs but all of low to middling individual value.*

LESSER ETTIN

HIT POINTS:	36+6d8
SIZE/WEIGHT:	H/1250 lbs.
TENACITY:	Steady
INTELLIGENCE:	Obtuse
FATIGUE FACTOR:	-7

MOVEMENT

CRAWL:	5
WALK:	10
JOG:	15
RUN:	20
SPRINT:	25

SAVES

PHYSICAL:	+12
MENTAL:	+7
DODGE:	+9

ATTACK:
Club wielded in right hand deals 6d6p+5 while the weaker southpaw only inflicts 4d8p+5. Ettins always lead with the right and then alternate.

SPECIAL DEFENSES:
No penalty to Defense against attackers to the rear; Initiative die three better

---

GENERAL INFO

ACTIVITY CYCLE:	Nocturnal
NO. APPEARING:	1-4
% CHANCE IN LAIR:	15
FREQUENCY:	Sporadic
ALIGNMENT:	Chaotic Evil
VISION TYPE:	Standard
AWARENESS/SENSES:	Standard (Initiative die type is three better)
HABITAT:	Caves
DIET:	Carnivorous
ORGANIZATION:	Individuals or gang
CLIMATE/TERRAIN:	Temperate mountains and forests

YIELD

MEDICINAL:	kidneys are thought to cure allergies
SPELL COMPONENTS:	nil
HIDE/TROPHY:	nil
TREASURE:	quantity over quality[1]
EDIBLE:	yes, but very tough
OTHER:	nil

EXPERIENCE POINT VALUE: 1242

FANTOM DOG

Also Known As: Adjule, Devil Dog, Moor Hound

I counsel thee for to trust to providence shouldest ye be pursued by these shadow hounds betwixt eve and morn. Yet divine grace is best tempered by sagacity for the circumspect traveler needst sup little from the former. I myself do risk opprobrium in relating this cautionary tale for scant lore had I ere I met these fantoms.

'Twas a score of years past when I yet basked in the naivety of heedless youth that I was upon a tarriance with a fair gentleman who in Brehden dwellst. One eve, as we did traipse along the edge of the moorlands far from the inquisitory oversight of our elders, his gaze did fix over my shoulder and his pulchritudinous complexion did pale with fear. Turning, I saw naught but shadows formed by the convolutions of the land, and so queried him as to his fright. He didst claim to have sighted but a steely grey wolf, of which he was ashamedly sore afraid. Though I didst suspect a fabrication, I inquired no further.

Do not gaze into souless black eye sockets of the fantom dog!

It is nearly impossible to outrun these creatures -- they seem to defy gravity.

On the night that followed, my leofman was absent and of his whereabouts none couldst affirm. Afeared for his safety, venture did I upon the lonesome moor. Sickened was I to chance upon his spiritless corpse. Though for some space I stood agape, my wits I did steel and sought to make an examination of his body. I was sore puzzled, for the wounds he bore were like unto those of a wolf's prey yet not so grave as to prove lethal for in this matter I was assured through ministering to fallen warriors.

Quell did I the urge to mourn for my pragmatic nature did assert. I started away to where I didst gauge his fearsome gaze had the eve prior fallen. I had traversed little distance when, from the darkness, there emerged such a hound as Radiance forbid should ever be at my heels again. Having the advantage of me, it tore into my flesh afore I couldst react. I was overcome with a strange sensation - not only mortal pain but accompanied by an eerie sense of my soul being wrenched away. Instinctively, I held forth my icon and commanded the foul beast to flee. My faith in the Lanthorne was rewarded for it did bound away forthwith. - 👁

These undead spectral dogs are malevolent spirits that take the guise of canines. In appearance, they resemble enormous coal-black hounds with long, whip-like tails, but are like no beast that mortal eyes should ever see. Should a character gain the opportunity to stare at such a waiting beast, he could see that the creature is not truly opaque, but translucent. They have incredible leaping ability and run along the ground or just above it.

Their eye sockets are cavernous black wastes devoid of any sight-generating orbs, yet somehow glow with an unearthly red light. Their mouths are large and drooling, snarling or snapping with great ferocity. These maws are packed with a seemingly inordinate quantity of razor-sharp teeth.

Fantom dogs stand about 3 feet tall at the shoulder.

Combat/Tactics:

Those who have survived a fantom dog attack say that the pack appears as a far off wavy shadow or a sickly green mist. This is followed by the howl, which sounds like the cry of a million souls in torment. The howl of a single fantom dog resembles that of a wolf, only with an unearthly vibrato. It can be unnerving but has no special effect. When three or more

The unearthly baleful howling of these beasts doth chill the spine. Shouldest the spectral hounds in unison bay, know thee well that the terror may overwhelm those who bear not the resolute heart forged by years of acclimation to manifestations most eerie.

WILL FACTOR 7

SIZE COMPARISON

6 ft

3 ft

fantom dogs howl in unison, however, it has the effect of a Panic spell on all creatures (with less than 50 HP[1]) within a furlong[2] of the undead dogs. Fantom dogs cannot perform this howl during combat.

The slavering mouth and sharp teeth of a fantom dog are deceptive, for its bite deals only d4p points of damage. However, this bite also drains the victim's Constitution for a like amount of damage (armor provides no protection; other Damage Reduction not withstanding). Fantom dogs hunt their prey by stalking in packs, striking at the legs. Once the prey has been felled, the undead canines rip away at the character's Constitution until he has been completely drained.

Fleeing from a fantom dog is difficult for they seem seem unaffected by the pull of gravity and are able to run over gorges and pits as if over solid ground. They can leap effortlessly over obstacles up to 10 feet tall but cannot pass through solid matter. Thus, while not even the widest canyon can stop them, a barred portal will.

Fantom dogs are incredibly resistant to ordinary weapons, though silvered ones often succeed in wounding these undead beasts. Direct sunlight incapacitates them unless they can immediately withdraw to the shadows. They suffer a -4 penalty to Attack and Defense in dim sunlight (such as twilight or even heavily overcast days).

Habitat/Society:

Fantom dog packs are most common near heaths and moorlands, roaming through the fog and picking off isolated herdsmen and travelers on the lonely roads. They can also be found allied with other undead, accompanying shadows, wraiths and other such spirits. Powerful barrow-wights, vampires and other such undead beings may command fantom dogs like any human master with his own hounds.

Ecology:

Fantom dogs can feed off the life energy of the living, though doing so is not a requirement for survival. They care nothing for animals and nonsapient creatures, perhaps hinting at some base enjoyment of the taste of fear generated by intelligent beings. Fantom dogs interact and coexist well with other undead creatures, and may be found in their company.

On Tellene:

Most tales of the fantom dog come from the more northerly lands of Cosdol, P'Bapar, Ek'Gakel, Shynabyth and Drhokker, possibly hinting at some innate preference of latitude.

Parents often tell tales of 'the awful fantom dog with vacant black eyes' to frighten children from going outdoors at night. These stories provide a variety of origins for the creature, such as the death of a hanged baliff, the spirit of a huntsman falsely executed for murder, the incarnation of a shape-changing sorcerer, and even the spirit of a funeral bier.

[1] All characters with fewer than 7 experience levels are subject to the effects of a Fantom Dog's howling regardless of their hit point total. Higher leveled characters are immune.

[2] i.e. 660 feet

FANTOM DOG

HIT POINTS:	25+3d8
SIZE/WEIGHT:	M/insubstatial
TENACITY:	Fearless
INTELLIGENCE:	Animal, High
FATIGUE FACTOR:	n/a

SPEED	INIT
9	-2
ATTACK +7	DMG REDUCTION
DEFENSE +5	18
see below	
short REACH	DAMAGE n/a
	TOP SAVE ▼

MOVEMENT

CRAWL:	10
WALK:	15
JOG:	20
RUN:	25
SPRINT:	30

SAVES

PHYSICAL:	+6
MENTAL:	immune
DODGE:	+8

ATTACK: Bites deal d4p and drain equivalent CON (no DR from armor). Three simultaneous howls cause Panic to all within eyesight and less than 50 HP. -4 to Attack and Defense in dim sunlight.

SPECIAL DEFENSES: Listening mastery of 65%. Jump easily over 10-ft-tall obstacles, can run over air (chasms, pits) as if it were solid ground. Silvered weapons reduce DR to 9.

GENERAL INFO

ACTIVITY CYCLE:	Nocturnal
NO. APPEARING:	1-12, or as dictated by master
% CHANCE IN LAIR:	n/a
FREQUENCY:	Sporadic
ALIGNMENT:	Neutral Evil
VISION TYPE:	Undead Sight
AWARENESS/SENSES:	Good hearing and sense of smell
HABITAT:	Heaths and moorlands, or as dictated
DIET:	n/a
ORGANIZATION:	Individuals, pack or as dictated by master
CLIMATE/TERRAIN:	Any

YIELD

MEDICINAL:	nil
SPELL COMPONENTS:	nil
HIDE/TROPHY:	nil
TREASURE:	nil
EDIBLE:	no
OTHER:	nil
EXPERIENCE POINT VALUE:	350

GARGOYLE

Also Known As: Goji, Stone Demon

The gargoyle is a shrewd creature capable of disguising its form amongst ordinary stone or even man-made construction. Hunting the beast can often prove to be a vexing task, for their ability to fly from one perch to another affords scant chance to track their movements. Often the most forthright method for killing these creatures is to lie in ambush and draw them into the open. It is then that the time-tested implements of butchery can be employed to maximum effect.

Goji are not completely stupid beasts, and some measure of trickery is called for if one is to successfully lead them into a killing zone. They are most unlikely to swoop down upon an armored warrior with silvered weapons held aloft. Practical experience has shown time and again that this will not work. The craven monster simply lacks the honor necessary to accept such a challenge.

The surest method of enticing a gargoyle is to present it with attractive prey that is gullible, defenseless and slow. Fortunately these are qualities quite often found in porters and linkboys. Coaxing one of these serviles into flushing out an evasive monster is often remarkably effective. – ᛋ

You will need the fates on your side before facing the gargoyle.

These grotesque creatures have a generalized form not overly dissimilar from that of a human or humanoid. However this template is grossly misshapen with an additional pair of arms, hands which terminate in clawed digits, large bat-like wings and a pointed tail. Its cranium hints at some monstrous aberration for it is wholly unlike that of any known race having swept back horns and ears, small feline eyes, a flattened nose and a frightening fanged maw.

Gargoyles uniformly have a powerful musculature that permits them to inflict serious wounds using only their claws. Most have a very pale skin tone but being feral creatures they are usually covered in dirt or soot and are often misidentified as being grayish in color.

Combat/Tactics:

Gargoyles are pugnacious brutes that delight in inflicting pain and misery. That said, they have no virtue and will always seek to ambush or otherwise engage in tactics that place their quarry at a disadvantage. Their powers of flight and their skill at remaining unseen until attacking [Hiding mastery 40%] are often used to facilitate this strategy. Gargoyles preferentially seek out the weakest of their opponents for they are natural bullies.

Their demonic heritage offers them unique advantage as combatants. Only silvered weapons may harm them to full effect – mere steel blades are far less efficacious at inflicting mortal wounds. In addition, they are resistant to fire, being able to tolerate exposures that would ordinarily cause burns of up to 12 points in any 10 second interval. Gargoyles cannot be poisoned nor are they susceptible to disease.

Habitat/Society:

Gargoyles originated as the spawn of demon molestation of sapient races – humans surely, but likely orcs and goblinoids as well. In truth it matters little for the demonic characteristics overwhelm those of the maternal lineage.

SIGN/TRACKS	RANGE ON TELLENE	SIZE COMPARISON

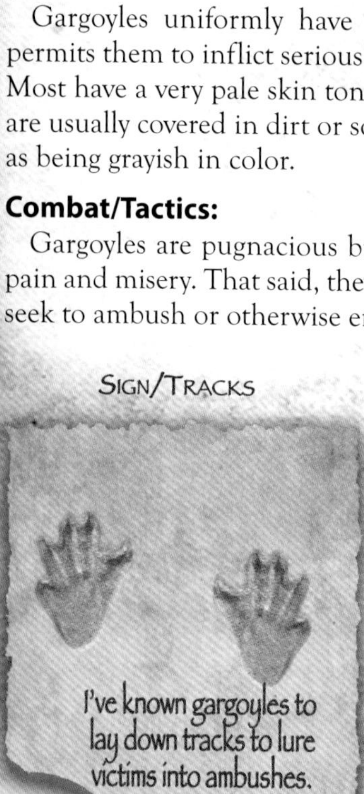

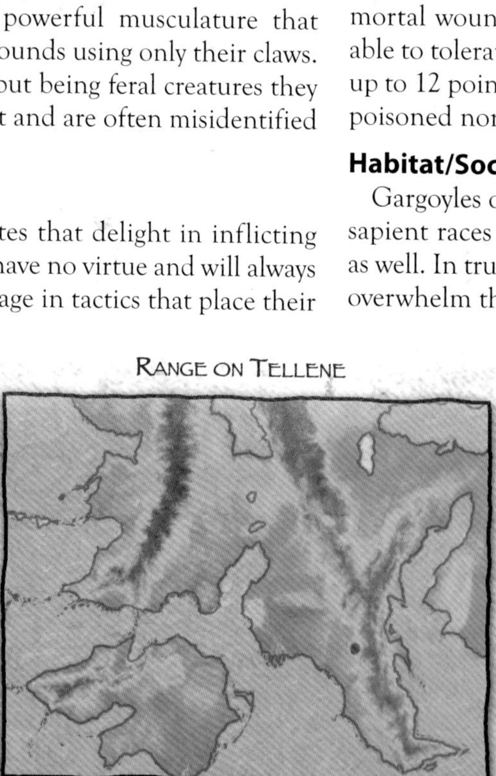

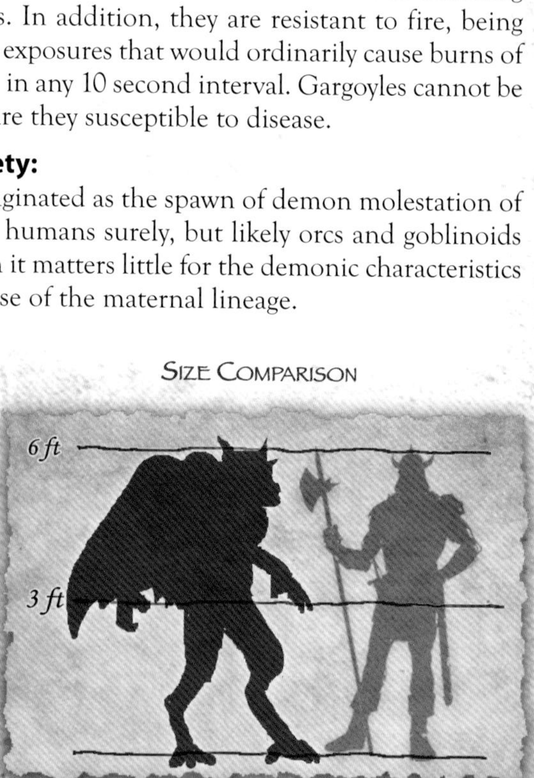

I've known gargoyles to lay down tracks to lure victims into ambushes.

6 ft

3 ft

These horrific encounters are not the sole source of gargoyles, merely the genesis. Mature specimens can interbreed and produce offspring. Subsequent procreation from the very rare instances of first order gargoyles is responsible for most of these creatures inhabiting the world.

Gargoyles are truculent and hence mostly solitary by nature, living in groups (known as 'wakes') only when a sustainable food source can support the entire wake. In a gargoyle wake, sexuality plays no role in terms of leadership or relationship dominance, both sexes being roughly equivalent in size and ferocity. Both wakes and solitary gargoyles live in high mountains and large forests, nesting in trees or occasionally on cliff ledges. Occasionally they are ensnared by more powerful creatures and employed as brigands and ruffians.

Most female gargoyles breed no more than once a decade and generally have a litter of two to five offspring at a time, caring for them for 3 to 4 years until they have become such rotten nuisances that the mother abandons them.

The average gargoyle has a lifespan of about 200 years.

Ecology:

Gargoyles are nocturnal, and particularly active at twilight, their favorite feeding time. In urban areas, gargoyles prefer to feast upon the flesh of sapient creatures relishing in the anguished cries of their victims as they are eaten alive. If forced to scavenge by an overly wary population, they may subsist on food scraps (mostly meat from butchers and tanners).

In the wild, they continue to favor sapient creatures often opportunistically waylaying travelers or preying upon humanoid tribes. They are capable hunters though and if denied intelligent prey they can bring down large herd animals, feast on birds and their eggs or even scavenge carrion.

On Tellene:

A legend concerns Saint Romanar, later in life to become a exemplar High Priest of the True. It is said that as a young curate ministering to the faithful in eastern Kalamar, he was called upon to deliver the country around Tuhido from the deprivations of a winged demon. With only the aid of a shepherd boy (for all others were sore afraid), he did track the beast and in mortal combat slew the creature. When he returned to town with the carcass of the gargoyle in tow, the people did rejoice and held a celebration in his honor. The centerpiece of these festivities was a bonfire upon which they laid the corpse of the demon spawn. To the townsfolks' horror, the body did not burn. Assured by Romanar that it was most certainly vanquished, they left it to char upon the embers. The following day, all that remained of the monster was its head – apparently fused to rock by the hot coals.

The head was retained as a trophy and mounted upon the Temple of the True. Subsequent enchantments were laid upon it to act as a ward against similar demonic beings. In time it became fashionable to copy this relic and mount this statuary on all manner of building so as to impart a measure of its protective power.

[1] A gargoyle tooth or claw improves the Withstand Fire spell to DR 8.
[2] A fired gargoyle head may be enchanted to serve as a ward against evil.

GARGOYLE

HIT POINTS:	24+4d8
SIZE/WEIGHT:	M/800 lbs.
TENACITY:	Steady
INTELLIGENCE:	Obtuse
FATIGUE FACTOR:	n/a

SPEED 2 | INIT -2
ATTACK +8
DEFENSE +1 | DR/DAMAGE REDUCTION 15*
DAMAGE 2d4p+4
short REACH | TOP SAVE n/a

MOVEMENT

CRAWL:	2½
WALK:	5
JOG:	10
RUN:	15
FLY:	25

SAVES

PHYSICAL:	+10
MENTAL:	+6
DODGE:	+9

ATTACK: Gargoyles prefer to waylay lone targets or stragglers often swooping down from elevation; they attack with a fury of quick blows (every 2 sec)

SPECIAL DEFENSES: Gargoyles are skilled at concealment [Hiding mastery 40%]; only silvered weapons are truly effective in harming gargoyles reducing their DR to 5; resistant to fire

G

GENERAL INFO

ACTIVITY CYCLE:	Nocturnal
NO. APPEARING:	1-14
% CHANCE IN LAIR:	25%
FREQUENCY:	Sporadic
ALIGNMENT:	Chaotic Evil
VISION TYPE:	Low Light Vision
AWARENESS/SENSES:	Standard
HABITAT:	Rocky terrain, may be drawn to settled areas
DIET:	Carnivorous
ORGANIZATION:	Individuals
CLIMATE/TERRAIN:	Any, save Arctic

YIELD

MEDICINAL:	nil
SPELL COMPONENTS:	tooth or claw, for Withstand Fire[1]
HIDE/TROPHY:	head may ward against evil[2]
TREASURE:	Gargoyles prize religious artifacts stolen from good temples; will hoard rings and other small jewelry
EDIBLE:	no
OTHER:	nil
EXPERIENCE POINT VALUE:	417

GHAST

Also Known As: Crypt Lurker

Vile creatures, the ghast. Their evil is matched only by the pungent odor they emit.

The ghast is one of the most abhorrent creatures thou mayst deal with. Their stench is foule, spreading a cloud of death to those who art infirm, young or eld of years. Truly these amort are of the darkest, most foule undead to ever beshrew the living.

I wast called to battle several such monstrosities when the coil of their unholiness in a local cemetery came to mine attention. The gentles of the town hadst been unable to visit the resting places of their dead and so entreated mine help. Twas fortune true that several members of mine faith conducted me. As strong and confident as were we, our propagate onto the burial ground wast assaulted by waves of decaying evil and appalling stench. I feel shamed to say my faith wast at first lacking and I felt the urge to retire on first sight. Yet, the gentles were serving as our beadsmen while safe apace, and their prayers for my renewed strength were surely heard.

Though we hadst been prepared for the stench by placing pouncet cloths about our noses and mouths, the smell of rotten chaudron overpowered — we gagged and foined the overwhelming urge to void our bowels. Though forwearied, we continued.

Highing our resistance to the evil inhabiting that place, hefting up our lanterns and our icons of divinity, we were able to forfend the creatures of their desires. As our hardiment helmed them inch-meal from the cemetery, their limbs took dribbling, or so it seemed to mine eyes.

In a last attempt to halt their destruction, a ging of the creatures rallied unexpectedly and frushed us badly. To our credit, we were valiant a-foin. At the last, with prayer and the blessed aid of the Shining One, the ghasts lost their heels at the cliff-edge and fell, dashed to pieces by the rocks below. The gentles of the town stood happy, and we were able to consecrate the grounds, recuring the evil presence and winning several converts by our deeds. — 👁

Ghasts share many of the predilections of ghouls, as they are eager to disinter graves. Unlike human tomb robbers, their interest is not in the grave goods or treasures buried with the departed but rather in the molding flesh of the remains themselves for they are corpse eaters that feast upon the dead.

Their appearance bears some relation to zombies, ghouls and other animated remains. Their cadaverous flesh is milky white broken up by large patches of festering rot. The latter does little to detract from their intimidating appearance though for unlike lesser undead that present a ragged appearance of an emaciated human corpse, ghasts resemble a very strong and heavily muscled humanoid with broad shoulders and thick arms. Like ghouls, they have inordinately long and dirty fingernails and long, forked tongues.

These creatures are readily distinguishable from other undead for they emit an unmistakable and extremely pungent odor of death and decay. Perhaps it is due to their diet or perhaps for some other reason. Either way, there is no mistaking their presence.

Ghasts are a particularly dangerous threat for they combine the macabre powers of the undead with a cunning intelligence. Unlike lesser undead, they possess the ability to strategize and to adapt to conditions their desired prey may employ to thwart their goals.

Combat/Tactics:

Ghasts are aggressive combatants eager to take on nearly anyone in the hope of gathering a supply of new corpses. They are not, however, foolhardy and will utilize any ghouls in their thrall to feel out the capabilities of their opponents and assess where

---

SIGN/TRACKS

Should you come upon unburied dead, think not first upon the fallen. Rather think on your own mortality for there may be undead fiends afoot. Smell the air! There is no mistaking the presence of a ghast for their vile odor betrays their presence. Take great care when confronting these unliving beasts for unlike zombies and ghouls, they possess cunning. Be not hasty in pursuit for scattering ghasts may lead you into an ambush.

WILL FACTOR 9

SIZE COMPARISON

6 ft

3 ft

to attack (preferring to savage weak or disabled opponents).

Their presence will be felt long before they enter combat for it will be readily apparent that ghasts are present. These creatures emit an overpowering charnel house reek so vile as to cause any living creature within 20 feet to lose 2d4p points of Strength should they fail to withstand the noxious odor (requiring a Con check *vs.* d20p+9). Characters removed from the reeking area regain lost Strength at a rate of one point per minute.

In melee, they attack by raking with their iron-hard nails and by biting. While these attacks are dangerous enough to foes on their own, each carries the possibility of inducing incapacitating nausea. Any time a ghast successfully strikes an opponent (excepting hits upon a shield), the victim must make a Constitution check (*vs.* d20p+9) or succumb to a bout of vomiting, retching and/or severe nausea lasting 2d4p minutes. During this time, the sickened individual is unable to defend himself (as if he failed a Threshold of Pain check).

As with all undead, ghasts exist by the invigorating power of dark energy and so are immune to magic that requires a living being to act upon, to wit spells that induce a mental state such as fear or a biological one such as Sleep.

Habitat/Society:

Ghasts are frequently encountered leading packs of ghouls, as the creatures share similar predilections for disinterring corpses and feasting on the dead. Ghasts are far bolder than ghouls, and packs led by one or more ghasts tend to be considerably more disruptive than ghouls alone. Rather than eke out a secretive existence at the fringes of human (or humanoid) society, ghasts frequently take proactive measures to ensure a steady supply of corpses. Raiding (even in daylight) is one such tactic. Ghasts are very clever, though, and these may only be probing attacks designed to lure pursuers into a trap.

Ghast deviousness can manifest itself in other ways for they are more than capable of hatching a complicated scheme. It is not beyond them to poison wells, kill livestock or undertake other actions to ensure a high morbidity of the settlement they choose to prey upon.

Ecology:

Unlike ghouls, ghasts derive some existential benefit from devouring corpses – particularly ones in which putrification has set in but not so old as to be withered husks. Perhaps this is the driving force behind their aggressiveness. This need can result in some horrific scenes as latecomers to a ghast kill may bear witness to rows of bloated and rotting corpses lying in the midday sun, awaiting just the right amount of decomposition to suit their ghastly tastes.

On Tellene:

Ghasts are rumored to be agents of the Harvester of Souls – sapient beings so wicked in life that they now sustain themselves by literally feasting on death.

[1] *Ghasts have an exceptionally keen olfactory sense for putrification and can smell a corpse a mile away*

[2] *A ghast finger may be used as a material component of the Stink Bomb spell, increasing its nausea effect by 20 seconds.*

GHAST

HIT POINTS:	25+4d8
SIZE/WEIGHT:	M/250 lbs.
TENACITY:	Brave
INTELLIGENCE:	Bright
FATIGUE FACTOR:	n/a

SPEED	INIT
3	1

ATTACK +7
DMG REDUCTION
DEFENSE +1
see below
3
short REACH
DAMAGE
n/a
TOP SAVE

MOVEMENT

CRAWL:	5
WALK:	10
JOG:	15
RUN:	20
SPRINT:	25

SAVES

PHYSICAL:	+9
MENTAL:	immune
DODGE:	+9

ATTACK: Anyone approaching within 20' must first contend with a ghast's debilitating odor (Con check vs. d20p+9 or lose 2d4p points of Strength); in melee attacks with two rakes and a bite for 2d4p+2 / 2d4p+2 / 2d8p; any hit mandates a CON check (vs. d20p+9) or victim debilitated with nausea for 2d4p minutes (treat as a Threshold of Pain failure for effect)

SPECIAL DEFENSES: Immune to magically induced fear and sleep

GENERAL INFO

ACTIVITY CYCLE:	Nocturnal
NO. APPEARING:	1-6
% CHANCE IN LAIR:	15%
FREQUENCY:	Sporadic
ALIGNMENT:	Neutral Evil
VISION TYPE:	Undead Sight
AWARENESS/SENSES:	Standard, keen carrion detection[1]
HABITAT:	Fringes of civilization
DIET:	Scavengers of rotting corpses
ORGANIZATION:	Individuals or pack
CLIMATE/TERRAIN:	Any, save arctic

YIELD

MEDICINAL:	nil
SPELL COMPONENTS:	finger, to improve Stink Bomb spell duration[2]
HIDE/TROPHY:	nil
TREASURE:	jewelry and trinkets from victims
EDIBLE:	no
OTHER:	nil
EXPERIENCE POINT VALUE:	425

G

GHOUL

Also Known As: Dead Riser, Apse Horror

Spawned by dark forces, these creatures are immune to many forms of magic.

Ihast striven against the scathful ghouls during my mission, oft confronting but one or two, and aided by comrades strong of arm to help mine hand in the fight and take the vantage quickly. This, I admit, led to rashness on mine part, and twas not long before I wast in receipt of a primer in humility.

Once, anight, I and my pew-fellows took arms against a pack of ghouls quite twice our number. A foule bout, true, but worse stood behind them in three priests of the Rotlord, directing the attacks of their feodaries — and loffing as ones horn-mad with each blow the foule creatures laid upon us.

The Shining One, our beloved Lord of Luminosity, wast at our backs even anight, yet there were too many for our few number. We could turn but a handful, and some of our persons suffered the gnaws of their awful mouths. One of our lief missionaries, Kelkate Jaclad by name, had his throat torn out and wast quelled as readily as one struck down by a thunderbolt. Twas even worse that we could not reach him before those devotees of the Malignant One propertied him as one of their undead minions. To seest the unliving flesh of a man once so pure, so dedicated to the worship of light and the destruction of darkness, now compeled against us wast like a stab to my breast.

With vengeance blazing in our hearts like the light of Radiance, we strove still harder. Mine own weapon crushed the head of one wicked man, whilst my fellowes followed suit. As the last priest of evil fell, their mastery over the ghouls breaked, and we wert able to refute the dead risers with somewhat greater ease. Kelkate, too, we returned to his rightful solace.

It wast some comfort that we could perform cleansing rituals and final shrifts upon his body, settling him properly for the translation of his soul unto Radiance. Kelkate's soul, awash in the Shining One's light, wouldst suffer no tinct from the Prince of Carrion. — ◉

The dead riser is a corpse eater. A mere touch by one of these creatures can cause you to freeze with fright!

Ghouls are macabre undead with a predilection for human or demi-human corpses. Both cannibals and necrophiliacs, they are universally reviled, feared and despised.

Their appearance at first glance may be confused with zombies for they too are pale corpses. However, one quickly realizes that these are very dissimilar fiends for the ghoul is exceptionally quick and nimble. Their flesh is taut and their faces are grotesquely misshapen.

Most ghouls have inordinately long, dirty fingernails and forked tongues. Their tongues apparently provide a sense of smell similar to snakes, so they often flick their tongues while holding their nose aloft and turning their head to and fro in order to better catch a scent. They masterfully track prey if the need arises.

Ghouls are also self-aware and capable of independent action though possess no knowledge of their former life, except in the rarest of circumstances such as their state being granted by a deity or other supernatural being. They are intelligent, although not very bright, and will take action for self-preservation, to increase their chances of remaining undetected or to better their odds in a fight.

Ghouls take pains to remain concealed from public scrutiny so they can feast on corpses without being disturbed. If accosted or their lair is discovered, they attack with great ferocity.

SIGN/TRACKS

Beware the touch of a ghoul for it can paralyze a man with fright. If hunting a ghoul pack, one is best advised to seek the aid of a knight for these fearless warriors are trained to deal with such horrors.

WILL FACTOR

6

SIZE COMPARISON

6 ft

3 ft

Combat/Tactics:

In combat, ghouls attack with their claw-like hands and a vicious bite. Any creature struck by a ghoul must make an opposed Wisdom check versus the ghoul's Will Factor or be paralyzed with fear for 2d4p minutes. Immobilized victims may be immediately torn to shreds if the ghoul is not otherwise engaged in combat. Alternatively, the victim might be retained for subsequent torture if the ghoul feels secure and not rushed.

While attacking or chasing prey, a ghoul may emit a guttural growling sound to frighten its quarry. It is, however, capable of intelligible speech if the need arises (although that is the rarest of circumstances).

As with all undead, ghouls exist by the invigorating power of dark energy and so are immune to magic that requires a living being to act upon, to wit spells that induce a mental state such as fear or a biological one such as Sleep.

Habitat/Society:

Ghouls are considered by most sentient beings to be the vilest of the undead. Though there are other such creatures far more wrathful and terrifying, only the ghasts share their revolting habit of disinterring and feasting upon (or otherwise defiling) the remains of loved ones. Even if not the target of their predation, one can feel deeply violated witnessing a cemetery with its gravestones knocked aside, plots dug up and the gnawed remains of one's forefathers scattered about as so many chicken bones.

These creatures are most commonly found skulking on the fringes of human society. Large towns and cities are notorious for their ghoul haunts as these crowded conditions foster disease and resultant morbidity. Some ghouls have been known to burrow under cemeteries, taking graves from below in order to remain unnoticed.

Ecology:

Ghouls are undead and so do not strictly need to feed on corpses. They do so for the pure wicked pleasure of it and, apparently, the taste. The only thing they cherish more is to kill or steal the bodies of young women and children, then defile the corpses in an abhorrent manner – even leaving the remains for the family to discover. While a distant third, ghouls do sometimes enjoy killing sentient beings and feasting on their remains. Packs of ghouls have been known to terrorize whole villages.

On Tellene:

The sprawling city of Bet Kalamar is rumored to be plagued by unknown numbers of ghouls living in some wretched corner of that metropolis. The truth is unknown though the indigent do seem to disappear with alarming regularity.

Many Fhokki are notoriously adamant in their hatred of these creatures, for such wicked beasts violate some of their most ancient taboos. Some young men, upon reaching manhood, take a blood oath to destroy these villains no matter what the danger. It is said that the hated Slen harbor ghouls in their midst.

[1]Ground ghoul bone can be used to replace the usual spell components for the fifth level spell Disembodied Floating Hand and/or the tenth level Ghostform spell and will increase the duration of these spells by d10 seconds. One quarter-ounce of ghoul bone is worth 3 sp on the black market. It is dangerous to attempt to sell such items in most societies openly, as many consider the act evil and some communities have made such activity illegal.

GHOUL

HIT POINTS:	24+2d8
SIZE/WEIGHT:	M/165 lbs.
TENACITY:	Steady
INTELLIGENCE:	Obtuse
FATIGUE FACTOR:	n/a

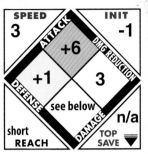

MOVEMENT

CRAWL:	5
WALK:	10
JOG:	15
RUN:	20
SPRINT:	25

SAVES

PHYSICAL:	+6
MENTAL:	immune
DODGE:	+6

ATTACK:
Attacks with two claws and a bite for 2d4p / 2d4p / 2d6p; any hit mandates a WIS check (vs. d20p+6) or victim becomes rigid with fear for 2d4p minutes

SPECIAL DEFENSES:
Immune to magically induced fear and sleep

GENERAL INFO

ACTIVITY CYCLE:	Nocturnal
NO. APPEARING:	3-12
% CHANCE IN LAIR:	30%
FREQUENCY:	Infrequent
ALIGNMENT:	Neutral Evil
VISION TYPE:	Undead Sight
AWARENESS/SENSES:	Keen sense of smell
HABITAT:	Fringes of civilization
DIET:	Scavengers of corpses
ORGANIZATION:	Pack
CLIMATE/TERRAIN:	Any, save arctic/sub-arctic

YIELD

MEDICINAL:	nil
SPELL COMPONENTS:	ground ghoul bone[1]
HIDE/TROPHY:	nil
TREASURE:	jewelry and trinkets from victims, plunder from tombs
EDIBLE:	no
OTHER:	nil
EXPERIENCE POINT VALUE:	290

Giant, Hill

Also Known As: Hurler, Hill Lumberer, Narumph

The hill giant Adaar defending a mountain pass.

It is widely considered that hill giants are primitive, dumb brutes. This reputation is well-earned; hill giants place no value on mental acuity. They prefer to smash what they do not understand, and they do not understand much. Hill giants are extremely superstitious, and displays of magical talent never fail to agitate them. However, rather than being cowed, they always seek to slay the offender. Forewarned is forearmed...

Of course, the pleasure they take in squashing wielders of magic is not greater than that of smashing powerful foes, which also brings honor amongst their kind. They take trophies for the same reasons as others might, in remembrance of glory or conquest, but they are unable to comprehend that they sometimes do this in a gruesome way. Were they employing forethought, at least it might be considered purposeful intimidation, but such would be giving too much credit. They live utterly without pretense, and such limited guile as they might possess is used only to gain advantage over their kin.

Great care must be exercised when doing battle with hill giants. These are no mere gnoles or ogres. Though employing predictable tactics, these are usually sufficient to match any opponent seeking to match strength against strength. Choosing this route is an invitation for disaster as these foes can quickly batter the life from even the most formidable swordsman.

Rather than a frontal assault, employ stealth. Take them on as individuals or pairs but ensure no alarm is raised. Use decoys to lure away the guards. Distract them and have them focus their attention elsewhere. Use illusions to good effect.

Proper infiltration tactics are absolutely mandatory. For those unwilling or unable to employ them, I suggest you simply walk away. - ⌽

Hill giants look like muscular, 12-foot tall human savages. They typically weigh about three-quarters of a ton. Hair and eye color ranges only from brown to black. They often have wild beards and thick matted hair. Hill giants wear hides and leather from virtually any animal, and usually from many different animals at once due to their size.

Combat/Tactics:

Hill giants do not think or act quickly but what they lack in agility and grace they make up for in brute strength. They prefer simple weapons that smash or squash, the most common being the club. In their hands it delivers 4d6p+8 points of damage. Without a weapon, a hill giant can use fist, foot or even forehead to deliver 2d4p+6 points of damage.

These giants are also capable of hurling large stones (weighing around 10 pounds) as missile weapons. When throwing these rocks, they have an effective range comparable to a short bow. As these attacks rely more on finesse and technique rather than brute force, they receive only a +5 Attack bonus. Anyone hit by one of these missiles suffers 3d4p+8 points of crushing damage.

Hill giants exhibit little tactical organization in battle preferring

Sign/Tracks

Hill giants may often go barefooted.

Their huge footprints are twice the size of a human's.

Range on Tellene

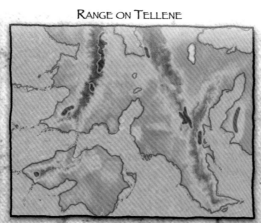

Size Comparison

20 ft

10 ft

to simply wade in as a mob and slug it out with the nearest opponent. Their size and strength engenders a fearless attitude in battle for they are confident that few if any creatures can withstand their onslaught.

While most hill giants wear hides as armor, some (about 10%) include metal pieces, not really recognizable as 'armor' or fitted in any particularly meaningful way, but does increase their Damage Reduction to 8. Sans any armor, their DR is 4.

Hill giant chieftains have in excess of 100 Hit Points, while adolescent giants have statistics comparable to ogres.

Habitat/Society:

Hill giants generally live in small or extended family groups. They expect to be bullied by the more powerful, and in turn pick on those weaker than themselves. If something bigger and stronger is nearby and they are unable to destroy it, hill giants move to another location where they are the biggest, meanest things around.

They respect only strength and prowess in battle, though leaders are often those with the closest to average intelligence. A normal hill giant lair includes a chief with one to three mates, several males each with one mate (no more) and half a dozen young, for a total of 20 or so. Occasionally, a very strong chief can gather a few dozen hill giants in one area. If he is not slain by a rival, this situation usually results in widespread raids against any target the giants can find.

Females gestate for 16 months and single births are the norm. Weak or deformed young are left to die and quickly forgotten. Healthy hill giants can live 200 years if not slain in battle. They reach adolescence at 20 and full maturity at 35.

Hill giants speak the tongue of giants and may also converse freely with ogres. They have no written language.

Giants are fond of keeping wolves as hunting animals and pets. They also employ ogres as lackeys. Accordingly, any lair may include 2-8 ogres (50% of the time) or 2-8 dire wolves (50%). Said lair is a usually a chaotic mess. There is no discernible form of organization, piles of hides, refuse, broken items, and treasure will be strewn about haphazardly.

Ecology:

Hill giants can live in any climate, but their lairs are only found in lands that are temperate with rolling hillsides or low mountain ranges. Though technically omnivores, they vastly prefer to eat meat and make no distinctions between types of creatures when considering the source. If they run low on animals to hunt, they will grudgingly expand their territory. Typical game includes most large herbivorous mammals.

On Tellene:

Hill giants live in areas sparsely populated by the major races. Large concentrations of people with armies are too much for them to handle, but some clans prefer to stay at the outskirts of civilization where they lead a comfortable existence exploiting the local runts. Hill giant populations are evenly distributed from the Brandobian Ocean to the Arajyd Hills and from Shadesh Bay to the southern reaches of Svimohzia. The only places they have not been spotted are the remotest reaches of the Elos and Khydoban Deserts, and the extreme frozen wastes of the north.

---

[1] *If hill giant sweat is employed as an optional material component when casting Feat of Strength, the Feat is performed as if possessing 20/51 Strength rather than 18/00.*

[2] *No one in polite society would eat a hill giant, but in emergency situations their flesh is edible.*

HILL GIANT

HIT POINTS:	47+8d8
SIZE/WEIGHT:	H / ¾ ton
TENACITY:	Fearless
INTELLIGENCE:	Slow
FATIGUE FACTOR:	-6

SPEED 10 — INIT 3
ATTACK +16
DEFENSE +7
DMG REDUCTION 6
DAMAGE 4d6p+8
long REACH
TOP SAVE 10

MOVEMENT

CRAWL:	5
WALK:	10
JOG:	15
RUN:	20
SPRINT:	25

SAVES

PHYSICAL:	+20
MENTAL:	+12
DODGE:	+14

ATTACK:
Attacks with huge clubs for 4d6p+8 or fist/foot for 2d4p+6 crushing damage; may also hurl rocks with a +5 Attack bonus for 3d4p+8 crushing damage

GENERAL INFO

ACTIVITY CYCLE:	Diurnal
NO. APPEARING:	1-3 (hunting party) or 20+ (lair)
% CHANCE IN LAIR:	30%
FREQUENCY:	Infrequent
ALIGNMENT:	Chaotic Evil
VISION TYPE:	Standard
AWARENESS/SENSES:	Standard
HABITAT:	Hills and low mountains
DIET:	Omnivorous (but prefers meat)
ORGANIZATION:	Individuals or clan
CLIMATE/TERRAIN:	Sub-tropical to tropical highlands

YIELD

MEDICINAL:	nil
SPELL COMPONENTS:	sweat[1]
HIDE/TROPHY:	giant-sized objects always attract interest
TREASURE:	hill giants are known to have vast quantities of loot
EDIBLE:	yes[2]
OTHER:	nil
EXPERIENCE POINT VALUE:	1425

GIANT, HOAR FROST

Nothing in this world is colder than the heart of a hoar frost giant, or so my mentor spoke to me in hushed tones when we first turned to the topic of the giant races. In truth, to battle these fearsome foes you must lose your own compassion. These hoar frost giants remain cold, but they fight as if their blood is afire with rage. One of the best ways to recognize their territory is the near complete lack of edible animals and very large bootprints. Of course, if there are hoar frost giants close enough you'll likely see more than a few raids which few other creatures could easily imitate (smashed buildings, and again those huge footprints).

When fighting these oversized barbarians, you need to make sure you're protected. They don't need a lot of time to finish you off, so you're best off if you can take them one at a time. Of course, knowing this they will try to avoid giving you the opportunity to do so. I still say concentrate on attacking one at a time. If at all possible, go after a leader type or a particularly brave-seeming warrior. If you can take one hoar frost giant down fast enough, the others may retreat. Don't ask me what you're doing hunting giants, though; odds are they will regroup with allies and come back with tactics adapted for whatever you threw at them in the previous fight. Giants are like elephants – they never forget.

There's another plan, too. You can run. Gotta run fast, and gotta decide on that course of action fast, but not everyone can face a hoar frost giant or three. Most who say they have are lying. Just leaves more for me.

Be sure and finish them off — they never forget a face. - ☥

Hoar frost giants bear more than a passing resemblance to fantastically oversized Fhokki humans. Full grown male hoar frost giants are over 15 feet tall and can weigh over 2,600 pounds with giantesses being somewhat smaller. They dress in pelts and skins of alpine creatures and adorn these with jewelry of all types, particularly silver.

They move over tundra and cold plains at a quick pace, and can jog and run for long stretches at high speeds. As masters of their terrain, little escapes them (they possess skill masteries of 60% in Listening and 70% in Observation). Their thick skin and sheer size affords them a Damage Reduction of 5 sans armor, though warriors typically do wear armor, most often a light mail shirt forged by their own smiths. While immune to the most severe natural chilling, if subject to supernatural cold they have a DR rating of 20 versus any effect.

Combat/Tactics:

Once a decision to fight has been made, the giants waste no time in closing the distance to their opponents. Though their fighting is fierce and may appear to be a kind of battle rage, they are in fact always aware and in control. Chieftains adjust tactics according to the flow of battle. Hoar frost giants usually fight until opponents surrender. When the battle is over, they loot the vanquished and take survivors as captives, though they aren't too concerned if some survivors die by accident. They are very thorough when looting corpses, and sometimes hack up a body to make sure they can shake out every last copper piece.

In battle, hoar frost giants wield giant battle axes. These giants are also capable of hurling large stones weighing around a dozen or more pounds as missile weapons. When throwing these rocks, they have an effective range comparable to a light crossbow. As these attacks rely more on finesse and technique rather than brute force, they receive only a +6 Attack bonus. Anyone hit by one of these missiles suffers 3d4p+10 points of crushing damage.

SIGN/TRACKS

Hoar Frost Giants are easy to track in the snow as their boot prints are large and deep.

RANGE ON TELLENE

SIZE COMPARISON

20 ft

10 ft

Hoar frost giants fight fiercely in defense of their lair. Infants and extremely young giants are non-combatants, but adolescents can fight (use bugbear combat statistics) as can young adults (use hill giant combat statistics). A typical lair houses 18 to 24 giants, with half of those being young (25% infants or very young, 25% adolescents and 50% young adults).

Very powerful chiefs can command tribes of over 50 hoar frost giants. Most chieftains have at least 110 Hit Points and 50% have superior weapons (+1 to +3). In the rare case of defeat in combat, hoar frost giants retreat quickly to regroup and rearm.

Habitat/Society:

These giants live in frigid wastelands, arctic tundra, cold mountains, and areas with long winters and heavy snowfall. They often make their homes in huge caverns or giant log homes.

Tribes live by raid and conquest, though occasionally they trade with neighbors whom they respect for their battle prowess. Chiefs choose up to three mates from among all the females in the tribe when they take power, even from among those currently mated to others. Young giants remain with their fathers, though the entire tribe participates in the upbringing and training of the young.

Hoar frost giants gestate for nearly 20 months and single births are the norm. Weak or deformed young are left in the cold, usually on mountaintops. If they survive, they are claimed and raised by shamans. Healthy hoar frost giants can live to 250 years if not slain in battle. They reach adolescence at 21 and full maturity at 36. Though tribes appear very patriarchal in traditional structure, females fight as well as males and may accompany them on raids.

Each tribe also has its own spiritual leader. Often an elder giant, 25% of the time this leader has the powers of a 5th to 10th level cleric of the Emperor of Scorn. They have their own version of music, largely based on percussion and chanting.

Hoar frost giants enjoy keeping prisoners for sport, ransom, sacrifice and slave labor. There is a 50% chance that a lair includes prisoners (1-2 prisoners per adult hoar frost giant). These prisoners can be of almost any bipedal race.

Hoar frost giant lairs almost always include other creatures. There is an 80% likelihood that a pack of 1-6 sturm wolves is kept as hunting beasts and a 50% chance that 2-12 ogres are present as thralls. Hoar frost giants speak Giantish and most can communicate with the ogres. It is also not uncommon for a hoar frost giant to have some rudimentary knowledge of the dominant local human or demi-human language.

Ecology:

Hoar frost giants consider themselves the fiercest hunters around and are therefore entitled to anything they can take by force of arms. Though omnivores, their diet consists almost exclusively of meat. Though they prefer traditional prey (such as bears and seals), they do not hesitate to consume the flesh of intelligent creatures.

On Tellene:

Most hoar frost giants dwell in or near the Jorakk, Deshada, and Byth Mountains though they have also been confronted in Tharggy. A handful of tribes are known to inhabit the area of the Krond Heights and explorers claim to have also encountered them among the Legasa Peaks.

[1] Hoar frost giants carry large bags that hold throwing rocks and various mundane items. They also typically contain 6d100p sp and 2d20p gp. Hoar frost giant lairs can contain vast amounts of wealth accumulated over decades, in the form of precious metals, gems, jewelry, arms and armors too small for them to employ, works of art (rarely destroyed but never really appreciated) and anything that can be pillaged from surrounding lands and neighboring communities.

HOAR FROST GIANT

HIT POINTS:	47+10d8
SIZE/WEIGHT:	G / 1¼ tons
TENACITY:	Brave
INTELLIGENCE:	Average
FATIGUE FACTOR:	-7

SPEED 12   **INIT** 2

ATTACK +18   DMG REDUCTION

DEFENSE +8   9

4d8p+10

long REACH   DAMAGE   11   TOP SAVE

MOVEMENT

CRAWL:	5
WALK:	10
JOG:	15
RUN:	20
SPRINT:	25

SAVES

PHYSICAL:	+18
MENTAL:	+18
DODGE:	+18

ATTACK:
Attacks with huge battle axes for 4d8p+10 hacking damage; may also hurl rocks (see text)

SPECIAL:
DR 20 vs. magical cold; Listening 60%, Observation 70%

GENERAL INFO

ACTIVITY CYCLE:	Diurnal
NO. APPEARING:	1-4 (patrol), 2-8 (raiders), 18-24 (lair)
% CHANCE IN LAIR:	25%
FREQUENCY:	Sporadic
ALIGNMENT:	Neutral Evil
VISION TYPE:	Standard
AWARENESS/SENSES:	Good hearing and eyesight
HABITAT:	Ice caves
DIET:	Omnivorous (though primarily meat)
ORGANIZATION:	Tribal
CLIMATE/TERRAIN:	Arctic wilderness

YIELD

MEDICINAL:	The blood can cure a fever if taken internally. Hoar frost giant blood is worth 5 sp per ounce.
SPELL COMPONENTS:	nil
HIDE/TROPHY:	nil
TREASURE:	yes[1]
EDIBLE:	yes, but subject to cultural taboos regarding eating sapient beings
OTHER:	nil
EXPERIENCE POINT VALUE:	1750

G

GNOLE

Also Known As: Raagh'gum (in Orcish) or Noll

It is said a gnole can smell fear in an opponent and is quick to exploit such weakness.

When a naïve youth, I thought the appearance of gnoles comical. Surely these hyena-headed beasts could not afford the likes of me a serious challenge! One slap of my sword and these miserable curs would scamper away like cowardly mutts that begged for table scraps. In this I was proved terribly wrong.

I learned a valuable lesson in my first encounter with a gnole pack. Never rely on spurious anecdotes and the boasting of old men! Rather than fleeing, the hyena-men battered me like a rag doll. My trusty shield — which served me quite adequately when confronting goblins and orcs — proved a more dubious defense as blow upon blow hammered upon its oaken face and frequently drove me back.

What frightened me most of all was the barking and endless baying. I thought it a cacophony designed to drive me mad! Though I was later to learn that it was no more than their speech, at the time I thought it primordial howling, for the notion that these creatures could possess a language eclipsed the insular and ignorant lessons I was taught as a child.

I lost a good friend that day — my shieldmate Balan felled by a great spiked morning star. Many more would have lain beside him had we not fled for our mounts fortuitously secreted behind a nearby hillock. The dwarven brothers that accompanied us to the gnole encampment — whose names I have long forgotten — were not so fleet of foot. I never did see them again... - §

Unmistakably unique in appearance, the bipedal gnole stands a full 6½ to 7½ feet tall and has hyenine features, especially the hindquarters and the short tail.

These mangy beasts have short, matted patchwork fur covering their jet-black skin. Their hide ranges in color from tan to medium brown, with mottled spotting on the rump and rear legs (complete body-spotting having been lost in adolescence). A gnole's thin and wiry limbs belie their massive strength, supported by their thick, muscled torso and a long, powerful neck. Their lean frames weigh in at about 250 pounds.

Their hind legs have large padded canid feet, while their forepaws are similar, but have an odd thumb-like opposable pad they use to grip weapons and tools. Their hyena-like mouths have powerful teeth and, although they rarely use these in battle (other than in a near-perfect defense situation), they make rapacious use of them when feeding on their prey. Their teeth are designed for both tearing of flesh and grinding down bones, as well as for consumption.

Gnoles have thick hides, affording them some limited damage reduction, but they also wear armor (DR 2 unarmored or, more commonly, DR 6 with armor). Since they do not design or make their own armor, it is generally ill-fitting. However, even when assembled piecemeal or inappropriately-sized, their armors still add protection from blows, which is the most important thing to a gnole. On occasion, gnoles may be found wearing superior quality human-sized items.

SIGN/TRACKS

Fore

Hind

RANGE ON TELLENE

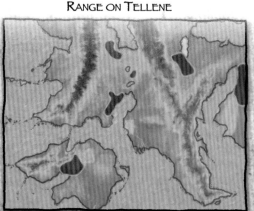

SIZE COMPARISON

10 ft

5 ft

Gnoles recognize the benefits of shields and tend to employ their usage, again, always pilfered from fallen foes or taken forcefully from weaker comrades. They utilize shields of all shapes and sizes, but the medium shields predominate (with smaller versions cast-aside as bigger ones become available).

Gnoles arm themselves with a variety of weapons, making use of whatever is available, their lanky build affording them a +1 foot Reach that typically gives them an advantage over many opponents. Their favorites are larger, more damaging weapons, which they can wield with great effect, their great strength and size allowing them to brandish large two-handed weapons with but one paw. They sometimes carry polearms and other long weapons with two hands, setting them for charge or attacking from the back rank if unable to reach their foes. Gnoles prefer to fight up-close, rather than from the second-rank and regardless of numbers, will always fight in skirmish formations, or rather mob formation, and never in a rank and file orderly manner, even if bullied by more powerful creatures.

While they like to get in close and mix it up, gnoles do recognize the value of ranged weapons. They like to hurl weapons prior to engaging enemies, if possible, but also delight in shooting their victims with mechanical ranged weapons of all sorts. Their great strength allows them to handle longbows with ease. Favorite weapons include flails, morning stars, swords (preferring two-handed or bastard but also using other types), great axes, great mauls, spears, polearms, crossbows, and hurled axes and javelins (these latter receive strength bonuses to damage even when a gnole doesn't jog due to its strength and body proportions).

Gnoles are voracious predators and marauders. Any creatures weaker or smaller than themselves are fair game. Organized into matriarchal clans, they maraud other nearby communities rather than actually produce or trade goods of their own. They can work if required, but must be forced with constant threat of physical pain. Gnoles prefer to laze about, hunting only when hungry, plundering villages when opportunity arises or when the urge strikes. Because they hate work and love to bully others, gnoles frequently keep slaves of various races to perform any labor they require, be it mining, menial or otherwise.

For every two dozen gnoles encountered, there will be a powerful leader with maximum Hit Points and an additional 1 point bonus beyond standard to Attack, Damage and Defense and a 2 point bonus to Initiative.

For every gross encountered, there will be not only a half-dozen leader types, but also a matriarch or clan chief with chainmail and an extra Hit Die, also with maximum Hit Points. Further, the matriarch has a 2 point bonus beyond standard to Attack, Damage and Defense and a zero (0) Initiative rating. Surrounding her will be a retinue of 2d4p warriors with the same statistics as the lead female, but only with maximum Hit Points for the first two Hit Dice.

Gnoles are the scourge of every clime, although only certain subraces are equipped to inhabit arid deserts and the

GNOLE

HIT POINTS:	30+2d8
SIZE/WEIGHT:	L/250 lbs.
TENACITY:	Brave
INTELLIGENCE:	Slow
FATIGUE FACTOR:	-2/-1

MOVEMENT

CRAWL:	5
WALK:	10
JOG:	15
RUN:	20
SPRINT:	25

SAVES

PHYSICAL:	+6
MENTAL:	+2
DODGE:	+5

ATTACK: Gnoles can hurl axes and javelins to gain +3 damage while they advance on a foe; In melee they prefer large weapons (flails being favorites - stats above reflect its use) so as to inflict maximum carnage; improved Initiative (one die)

DEFENSES:
*Shield use (e.g., medium shields improve Defense from -4 to +2). Unarmored gnoles have a DR of 2.

GENERAL INFO

ACTIVITY CYCLE:	Nocturnal
NO. APPEARING:	1-12 (hunting); 3d6p+8 (war party); 20d10p (band)
% CHANCE IN LAIR:	25%
FREQUENCY:	Infrequent
ALIGNMENT:	Chaotic Evil
VISION TYPE:	Low Light Vision
AWARENESS/SENSES:	Keen scent/hearing (improved Initiative one die)
HABITAT:	Caves and ruins
DIET:	Carnivorous
ORGANIZATION:	Pack
CLIMATE/TERRAIN:	Any (see subraces for arctic and desert)

YIELD

MEDICINAL:	female external genitalia, ground and mixed with a proper infusion can help to make a barren woman fruitful
SPELL COMPONENTS:	gnole hearts can be used for spells that cause rage
HIDE/TROPHY:	while mangy, gnole hide is thick and provides warmth
TREASURE:	3d4p silver pieces or equivalent[1]
EDIBLE:	no; inedible to all but trolls, ogres, orcs and the like
OTHER:	nil

EXPERIENCE POINT VALUE: 122

frigid arctic landscapes. As nocturnal hunters, gnoles can see well in daylight and also in near darkness. At night, their haunting glowing eyes, reflecting torchlight or campfire-light might reveal their presence.

Gnoles dens are equally likely to be found in subterranean lairs as surface caves or burrows or in the open (33% chance of each). In the latter case, they likely occupy a former dwelling of human or similar origins, such as a ruined village, destroyed castle or other abandoned construction. There are no recorded instances of gnoles erecting a building, shelter or monument of any sort; although, if compelled due to inclement weather, some clans have felled trees or built lean-tos to survive a particularly terrible storm. In most cases where they have no cave or construction for protection, they seek natural shelter under trees and the like. If encountered in their lair, gnoles have an additional 4d4p female warriors serving as attendants to the matriarch.

Gnole packs sometimes compete with one another for food and hunting grounds, but generally are on as amicable terms as such creatures can be. Differing clans never recognize the leadership of matriarchs from other clans, but, unlike orcs, they somehow avoid major confrontations when encountering one another. Such unions are brief, typically only to further an assault on a larger or more formidable target or series of targets, or to counter a common threat. The matriarchs orchestrate these bandings, with the others following in kind.

Gnoles also cooperate with other humanoid races. Being natural bullies, they subjugate kobolds, goblins, grel, orcs and even hobgoblins if given the opportunity, enslaving them if possible. Gnoles have a deep-seated, irrational hatred of lions of all types, probably originating from competition for food sources at some point in pre-history. Lions share this mutual hatred and kill gnoles if given the opportunity. In areas where they share domains, gnoles hate grel and grevans, attacking the former and fleeing from the latter unless they have far superior numbers.

Gnoles may band together with bugbears, ogres and trolls, but only if they have sufficient numbers to avoid bringing oppression of any sort upon themselves. In subterranean lairs, they may have a handful of trolls living amongst them symbiotically – the trolls help guard the lair, while the gnoles provide a portion of their kills. When living in the open, especially on the savannah, gnoles train hyena to serve as guards and hunting companions. Each terrestrial den will likely (75%) have about 3d6p hyenas or sometimes (10%) have 2d4p massive hyenas (also known as hyaenodons).

Gnoles wear mangy cloaks or garments, generally torn and oft-caked in dried blood from the previous owner and matted fur from the gnole. They stink with their own distinct odor as they never bathe, but also have two anal scent glands, which open into the rectum just inside the anal opening. These glands produce a gray paste that the gnole deposits on belongings, near their den, around a kill or to mark territory.

Gnoles are aggressive creatures, not only when attacking enemies, but also in their daily routine. A relative newcomer, indeed most probably the youngest and least evolved of all the sentient races, gnoles are one short evolutionary step away from beasts. Consequently, the balance between rational thought and emotional reaction leans far closer to the latter than any other humanoid race. Because of this, a gnole is quick to temper and will regularly fly into violent rage at the slightest problem or difficulty. A gnole might destroy a valuable piece of furniture taken in a raid simply because it stubbed its toe, or perhaps scatter the brains of an otherwise useful, loyal and competent slave simply because the servant looked at it wrong. While it later might regret its actions, the gnole mental structure ensures repeated offenses. Smarter leader types are better able to control these urges, but not completely by any means.

Gnole communities are stinking, jumbled messes consisting of former kills strewn randomly about the place and layered across piles of reeking bedding, as well as piles of plunder taken from past victims, destroyed tools, equipment, furnishings and past loot of all types. Intermixed amongst all of this is the reek of glandular paste, gnole feces, troll or hyena droppings, the flaky brown-stained blood of infighting and, more often, felled slaves and the charred remains of fires, some gone awry. All gnole lairs contain several slaves, typically 10% to 30% or more of the total quantity of gnoles. Periodic revolts and killing sprees lessen these numbers, while recent raids swell them.

Combat/Tactics:

Gnoles are big and strong and they know it. While they sometimes hurl or shoot ranged weapons prior to engaging their foes, they genuinely enjoy the adrenalin-charged thrill of hand-to-hand combat and never hesitate to engage (unless afraid of their foe, as getting maimed or killed is a lot less fun). They attack seemingly weaker or known enemies remorselessly, with little regard to self preservation until injured significantly. Gnoles will attack in a pack, ferociously attempting to surround their quarry, each in an effort to get in on the action; even weaker gnoles tend not to hang back from the action. These beasts will flee if a combat turns against them, running in a disorderly, every-gnole-for-himself manner.

Gnoles use their superior reach to clobber foes prior to their enemies even executing an attack. With blows powerful enough to shatter shields, gnoles may even attack them directly and purposely* gaining a 2-point Damage bonus on such an attack. With plenty of hit points and a solid Damage Reduction due to hide and armor, gnoles are tough and hard to bring down.

*Such attacks are made with a +10 Attack bonus as the defender is actively using it to block blows. Damage to the shield is half weapon damage plus all bonuses.

Habitat/Society:

Quite adaptable, gnoles are equally comfortable above or below ground. Their favorite habitat is a subtropical savannah with plentiful game, including human tribal populations ripe for the taking.

Females stand 6 to 12 inches taller than males and are larger even at birth. Their size and aggressive disposition naturally dictate a matriarchal society; gnoles always have an alpha female in charge of the clan. Below her, a pecking order is established based on size, personal power and ferocity, but this hierarchy is not cast in stone and is only recognizable when within reach of a the more powerful superior. Surprisingly, though, gnoles tend not to battle one another, even in fights for dominance, making them perhaps a bit more civilized than orcs. Those at the bottom of the pecking order tend to pull guard duty, while the bigger, stronger gnoles laze about.

Beyond size, females and males are very difficult to distinguish. She-gnoles nurse their young and thus have mammaries, but these are flat when not producing milk, and only the presence of nipples (two, generally, but sometimes four) betray their existence. Even female external genitalia appear similar to those of the male. Females number about 60% of the adult tribe, likely due to their superior survival rate as young and larger size and strength as adults. Whatever the number of able-bodied adults in a community, cubs will be found at a full 100% of that quantity. Half of these are grown enough to pose a danger (use hobgoblin combat statistics), another 25% have lesser fighting ability (use kobold combat statistics), and the remaining 25% are non-combatants.

She-gnoles choose their mate, with the strongest females gaining first choice. They only mate when in heat and only for purposes of reproduction. Gnoles can have one litter per year (live birth), but it can provide anywhere from two to six pups. Gnole pups have a high mortality rate, newborns die at an alarming rate, suffering at the hands of their siblings and sometimes pets and guests (trolls). Runts and defective pups are eaten by the mother as soon as their disability is discernable. After about 8 weeks, young fend for themselves, feasting on scraps or dying in the process of acquiring them.

Gnoles reach adolescence at 4 to 5 years and attack as full-strength adults shortly after. Those in the 2 to 3 year range are almost full-grown, but spindly and susceptible to attack by adults, pets, slaves and trolls. Only the biggest, fastest and strongest actually make it to adulthood. Gnoles live fast and hard, with adults feeling the inevitable degradation of aging around 20 to 25 years, inevitably perishing around this timeframe (although, gnoles kept in captivity and fed a healthy diet of flesh can live to their mid-30s).

Gnoles speak their own language and can communicate directly with hyenas, jackals, wild dogs, lions and hyaenodons. They also have little difficulty conversing with their smaller kin, the kobolds. Certain smarter members of a clan have learned to speak with other humanoid tribes or even human language, depending on who occupies the neighboring communities.

Ecology:

Gnoles occupy the top of the food chain and they know it. While more organized humans, elves, grevans and other races can prove superior due to numbers and superior strategy, gnoles rarely understand this and tend to view their place relative to the here-and-now. In their view, no race is stronger, not even ogres, trolls and bugbears, all of whom they can overrun with numbers. Of course, determined opposition can drive gnoles from an area, but they simply move into a new hunting ground and raid there.

Subraces:

Gnoles have several subraces exhibiting a wide-range of coloration, presumably adapted to their chosen habitat through natural selection. The various subraces can, in fact, breed with one another, but given the disparity of their territories, such an event is highly unlikely.

Savanna Gnole

The most common, or standard gnole, is the savannah gnole, so-named because the first recorded evidence of them came from the savannahs of Svimohzia. The majority of this entry describes them, so there is no need to further elaborate here.

Arctic Gnole

Found in the northernmost reaches and sometimes on mountain peaks, the rare arctic gnole has thick, white fur with black skin and other features. Slightly smaller than the other gnole races, they are also more productive, actually hunting natural prey for a goodly portion of their sustenance. They live in ice caves and will not hesitate to savagely attack any being within their territory.

Sand Gnole

Found in numbers in both the Khydoban and Elos deserts, the sand gnole has adapted to thrive in low moisture environments. Also known as the brown gnole or striped gnole, these creatures have brown skin and sandy fur that blends in to the desert landscape. Its striped appendages further help the beast to blend in and surprise its quarry.

Religion:

Gnoles do not generally practice organized religion, but they do recognize the Creator of Strife (whom they believe to be a great gnole demon residing in the Abyss) as their patron, believing him to be their own racial deity. All recorded gnole shamans have been clerics of the Creator of Strife.

On Tellene:

Gnole bands can be found marauding in just about every land and nation. Areas with a strong central authority and a powerful military, such as in Central Kalamar, are unhealthy for gnoles, so they will be rare in these areas having been driven out or long-since hunted to extinction. While they can be found in the most remote regions, gnoles prefer to raid and scavenge from intelligent races rather than hunt their own food or mine their own riches, so, likewise, they are found very infrequently in isolated areas. Generally, they can be found on the fringes of human society, or openly and boldly attacking and pillaging where counter-measures and opposing military is weak or chaos reigns. They are most numerous in the Wild Lands, many areas of the Young Kingdoms and especially central Svimohzia.

[1]Gnoles carry 3d4p silver pieces or the equivalent. Their lairs can hold hundreds or even thousands of each type of coin, a large quantity of gems and jewelry and possibly even some well-crafted arms and armors or magical items.

G

GNOME
Also Known As: Dalgul, Mythar, Fulmaran

It was my dear halfling friend that introduced me to the gnomes. Indeed, without his introduction the cautious folk may well have remained hidden from sight despite my congenial grandfatherly appearance.

Our initial talks had great sport with me, the gnomes sparing no effort to 'cut me down to size' (or so they expressed 'having a good belly laugh at my expense'). When it became clear I was a tolerant fellow and not so pompous as to take serious offense, the gnomish clan welcomed me as a friend.

Gracious hosts were they, plying me with sweet wines and delicious pastries. Someday I must return to that wooded glen and avail myself of the recipe for no bakery I have subsequently visited has matched the flavor of these desserts.

When the sun had long set and conversation turned to matters personal, I — perhaps feeling a bit giddy from the quantity of wine consumed — let slip my interest in windmills and other such mechanical contrivances. I unwittingly had stumbled upon a shared interest with one grizzled old gnome who immediately bade me to tour his workshop. While reluctant to depart such pleasant company, such was the gleam in the venerable gnome's eye that refusal of his offer was nigh impossible.

Upon entering his shop I marveled at the sheer industriousness of this tinkerer. All manner of devices lay strewn about his worktables. Most I could scarce identify but was nonetheless fascinated with the bronze gears that seemed to be a consistent theme in his work. His latest invention, one that he was most eager to demonstrate, was a strange crossbow he said could reload itself! Alas, it failed to work as promised much to his disappointment. Muttering under his breath he mentioned having to shake the gremlins out. This I did not comprehend, for how such a mischievous creature figured into the device's operation was beyond me. - ⚜

Gnomic features are similar to dwarves, but with much larger noses and (generally milk-white) beards that fall nearly to their feet, albeit sans moustache, which most gnomes cannot grow at all.

They have much smaller frames than dwarves, lacking the heartiness of that race and, although about the same height, have slighter frames than halflings, probably because they don't eat six meals a day. They are good miners, but dislike the dark and dank of the subterranean setting, preferring instead secluded grassy hills and quiet, rocky deciduous woodlands.

Among the sentient races, gnomes prefer the company of other gnomes and gnomish subraces, dwarves and halflings, in that order. While they generally get along with most other creatures, they approach bigger folk with caution, preferring to hide in the garden or woods and observe for quite a while before revealing themselves (if ever). Gnomes enjoy the company of the smaller woodland mammals such as chipmunks, badgers and the like and have actually learned to communicate with such animals. Their favorites are the burrowing types (moles, voles, mice, gophers and so forth).

Gnomes are very durable for their size, making them fair warriors, but they prefer not to engage in frontal combat, since gnomes weigh-in only at about 3½ feet and about 60 pounds. Instead, gnomes prefer the work of skirmishers, peppering opponents with crossbow bolts and then blending back into the woods. Since they can't run very quickly, they prefer to wear leather or studded leather armors that don't exacerbate their poor movement rates much more, although leaders tend to wear chainmail or even heavier armors.

Gnomes prefer to carry small shields in order to dissuade opposing missile fire. For weaponry, gnomes use short swords,

SIGN/TRACKS

RANGE ON TELLENE

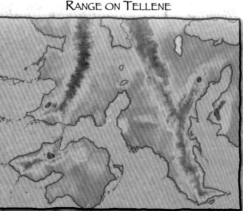

SIZE COMPARISON

6 ft

3 ft

clubs, daggers, spears and especially crossbows.

Fighters are obviously the most common class of gnomish war parties, but they have far more than their fair share of thiefly classes among them for use as spies, scouts, saboteurs and infiltrators. For every 10 gnomes encountered, d4p will be thieves and sub-classes of the same. For every 40 gnomes there will be a warrior of 2nd to 8th level (2d4) to lead the group, as well as d6p thieves of levels d4p each (in additional to the other d4p per 10 gnomes). If 150 or more are encountered there will be those numbers plus a major leader (fighter) of level 9th to 12th level (d4+8). If 200 or more are encountered, they will have a cleric of d12 level with them to handle spiritual matters. If 300 are encountered, one will be a mighty chieftain of 12th to 15th level fighter or higher (d4p+11 plus another d4p levels for every additional 100 dwarves). For every 50 gnomes, there is a 10% cumulative chance of a mage, with 90% of those being illusionists.

Gnomes prefer to dwell among their own kind, but frequently visit with halflings and dwarves, with whom they prefer to trade because the size of most items other than garments is most appropriate. The standard gnomic abode is a great earthen burrow, but they also occupy larger, hollowed-out trees and sometimes build small cottages. In any case, gnomes share their dwellings with many woodland pets, so they generally stink of animal, a disgusting smell to those not accustomed to it. Gnomic homesteads tend to be sparsely furnished, except for the workshop, which is generally a clutter of workbenches, tools, parts, sawdust, tailings, empty or half-filled containers of hardware, paint or trash and heaps of leftover scrap. Gnomes aren't terribly appreciative of paintings and the like and their walls tend to be barren save for displays of favorite contraptions or toys or an occasional jutting, wayward tree-root that needs trimming.

Gnomes are very solid in the areas of smithing, metalwork and gem-cutting, although not as talented as dwarves, except in the latter discipline. Gnomes love gems of all types and spend countless hours cutting, polishing, setting and re-polishing them. They delight in finely crafted items, especially those crafted from precious metals and jewels, giving gnomes a dwarf-like reputation for greed. Solid engineers, although not as accomplished as dwarves, gnomes tend to be very creative, often working on frivolous pursuits (something a dwarf would never consider). Very patient and undeterred by abject failure, gnomes have a willingness to attempt inventions others would never imagine. Gnomes are particularly adept at making tiny items with many working parts, such as elaborate timepieces, music boxes and toys. They also excel at woodworking, delighting in building toys, devices, tools and contraptions entirely out of wood. Gnomes also enjoy baking, especially cookies and deserts.

Not as serious as dwarves or as complacent as halflings, gnomes make pretty decent traveling companions. They love a good joke, but tend to have a dark sense of humor. In fact, most gnomes are oddly pessimistic and sarcastic in nature, generally suggesting (repeatedly and annoyingly) how any venture is likely to fail. Gnomes love to trick others, especially

GNOME

HIT POINTS:	20+1d8
SIZE/WEIGHT:	S/60 lbs.
TENACITY:	Steady
INTELLIGENCE:	Bright
FATIGUE FACTOR:	-3/-2

MOVEMENT

CRAWL:	1¼
WALK:	2½
JOG:	5
RUN:	10
SPRINT:	15

SAVES

PHYSICAL:	+1
MENTAL:	+2
DODGE:	+3

ATTACK: When making war, gnomes typically wear studded leather armor and carry small shields. They carry a variety of weapons but short swords are most common. Many of their number will bear light crossbows.

SPECIAL DEFENSES: Gnomes receive a 50% Hiding and Sneaking bonus when in woodland terrain. They make good use of these skills to avoid pitched battles; likely use of small shields (increase Defense to +8)

GENERAL INFO

ACTIVITY CYCLE:	Diurnal[1]
NO. APPEARING:	1-8 (traveling, hunting); 3d4p+8 (warband); 20d20p (clan)
% CHANCE IN LAIR:	85%
FREQUENCY:	Frequent
ALIGNMENT:	Neutral, CG, NG or CN (equal chance of each)
VISION TYPE:	Low-light vision
AWARENESS/SENSES:	Nearsighted, Excellent hearing/smell[2]
HABITAT:	Burrows; occasionally mines or caves.[3]
DIET:	Vegetarian
ORGANIZATION:	Individuals, family, or clan[4]
CLIMATE/TERRAIN:	Temperate[5]

YIELD

MEDICINAL:	nil
SPELL COMPONENTS:	gnomish scalp draped over the eyes is said to provide true sight against any illusionary spell or effect
HIDE/TROPHY:	gnome noses are trophies for both goblins & kobolds, Skin can be used for book bindings[6]
TREASURE:	gnomes carry 5d4 sp each; more in lairs[7]
EDIBLE:	kobolds claim that gnomes taste like lamb and are a highly nutritious part of their diet
OTHER:	nil
EXPERIENCE POINT VALUE:	42

big folk. These tricks frequently include playing pranks or practical jokes, often physically painful for the recipient.

Gnomes fancy themselves snappy dressers, although their idea of fashion differs from the other sentient races. They prefer earth tones, plus bright greens and bright reds. They love intricately-carved horn buttons and polished brass or bright jewels. Tall, brimless conical hats seem to be in fashion, with bright colors being the most sought-after, while their footwear tends to be colorful slippers or stockings with up-turned pointy-toes. Gnomes exhibit decent personal hygiene, but have far less regard for their beards than dwarves. They never trim; hastily stuffing their abundant whiskers into a belt is about the most a gnome can muster.

Gnomes are nimble little buggers, enjoying a +2 bonus to starting Dexterity (relative to humans). They also tell a great story and are fun to be around (especially to companions not the brunt of scathing ribbings or painful practical jokes) and generally have solid social skills, netting them a +2 bonus to starting Charisma. Their diminutive stature makes them weaker than most (a 2-point penalty to Strength) characters but it also makes them better at Sneaking and Hiding (gaining a free mastery roll in each skill). A gnome's personal appearance, especially the massive 'schnoz,' isn't what most species consider pleasing to the eye (a 2-point penalty to Looks).

Combat/Tactics:

Gnomes are small and quick like a rabbit (a +4 Defense bonus), but not very fast in straight-line running or distance travel. Their stature also tends to limit their Hit Points and ability to take a blow without getting knocked about, so they're not much use going toe-to-toe against bigger folk. Thus, these little bastards prefer to ambush foes rather than engage in melee. If given enough time, they set up traps using natural materials available (e.g., swinging logs, covered pits, pointy sticks, rocks, hard clumps of dirt, or mud) – anything that might result in painful and humorous (to them) results. After the initial trap(s) activate (or if they lack the chance to set one), gnomes pepper their opponents with crossbow bolts.

Gnomic crossbow bolts are easily identified by the inscriptions inevitably carved into the shaft. They vary dramatically in actual text, but are always intended to insult, belittle or mock the mark. If their ranged assault can't finish their foes, they'll try to taunt them into an ill-advised attack giving the gnomes some sort of advantage, whether higher ground or yet another humiliating trap. Finally, they engage in melee, fighting fiercely, but always willing to flee into the undergrowth, brambles or other natural barrier to the enemy if the situation proves too dire. Centuries of refusing to yield to giants, ogres and trolls has given gnomes the ability to better fight these foes; gnomes receive a bonus to Defense rolls (+6) against such creatures. Unfortunately, gnomes have short arms, leading to poor reach (effective Weapon Reach is -1 foot).

Gnomes have plenty of animal friends bred and trained to thwart their enemies and to serve as pets and beasts of burden. They develop such strong bonds with these animals that they can sense one another's emotions when within 20 feet. Most of these animal friends are harmless rodents, such as ground squirrels, rabbits, voles and the like; while useful spies, they provide little resistance in the form of defense. A few can, however, contribute in this area, namely badgers and wolverines of vicious temperament with a 50% and 25% chance in numbers of 4d6p and 2d4p, respectively. Further, Gnome clans have a 25% chance of 1d4p wolverines and 2d6p giant badgers.

Habitat/Society:

Gnomes prefer to dwell in rolling hillsides or nestled in the cozy dales below. Their preferred home is one burrowed into the side of a hillock, but some gnomes, particularly when all the best burrowing locations have been taken, reside in houses or in the trunks of large, hollowed (but still living) trees. Gnomic homes have small windows that allow just enough light to make effective use of their low light vision, but can be considered dark and stuffy to humans and elves. Halflings find gnomish abodes to be a mite filthy and not nearly cozy enough for their tastes, although the size suits them well.

Communities are structured around extended families or clans that enjoy healthy rivalry in the form of competitions of any type or disagreements on virtually any topic one can imagine. While distinct in name, these clans are inter-related with the gnomic tradition being one of intermarriage between clans (and the husband becoming part of the wife's clan after the wedding is consummated). Each clan has a leader, chosen in a dizzying variety of ways and in large communities; these leaders form a sort of counsel of elders and nominally have authority over the populous.

Gnomes speak Gnomish and prefer others to use their language, but are not as rude about it as elves if the outsider in question struggles with Gnomish or doesn't know it at all. Gnomes also pick up on any regional languages nearby, generally, Low Elven, Dwarven and the dominant human tongue (primarily to trade with the local halflings). Gnomes can communicate with burrowing mammals, although these aren't languages as such. Still, they can communicate emotions and ideas about food, water, danger and so on, including information about interlopers and 'big folk' in general.

Gnomes have a long lifespan, living close to half a millennium, but reproduce slowly. Females comprise 50% of the population, but remain fertile (and interested in relations) only for the first 30 years of adulthood (from 100 to 130 years, roughly). Females, while feminine and beardless, prefer to garden, knit and the like and seem to have no 'biological clock', taking less interest in males than most other races. Males seem to prefer work and freedom to marriage, further slowing down the reproductive rate. Gestation is just under 18 months, and communities have few children (5% to 10% of the total) for these reasons. The ones that exist are greatly cherished by the collective whole as community treasures.

Ecology:

Gnomes aren't fond of farming, but love to harvest fruit, nuts and other foods of nature's bounty. They're also not above gathering produce from human farms and gardens. When neither of those situations satisfies dietary requirements, gnomes trade worked goods, metals and jewels to halfling farmers for a share of their excellent produce. Gnomes are vegetarians and become annoyed with others that eat meat, and visibly upset if the meat is a small rodent of some type.

Gnomes live in areas that are also favorable to kobolds, and have been harried since anyone can remember by the little dog-like creatures. Further, any digging for precious jewels is likely to bring gnomes into conflict with dwarves (with whom they compete in a friendly manner) and goblins (with whom they war). While generally easy-going and able to keep their cool in most situations, gnomes hate goblins and kobolds with a fiery passion, gaining a bonus (+2) to Attacks against such creatures. Gnomes always attack them on sight and with great prejudice.

Subraces:

While the majority of this entry covers the standard gnome, there are three subraces of gnome that bear mentioning. The first, gnome titans, are the same race as standard gnomes, but their clans have remained isolated so long that they appear to be a distinct species (this is, in fact, not the case).

Gnomelings are actually a gnome-halfling crossbreed, included here because halflings staunchly refuse to recognize any part in their bloodlines. The gnomes grudgingly accepted them, if for no other reason than to boast about a gnome's ability to attract a halfling female (the flip side is that such a boast presumes no halfling male in his right mind would bed a gnome female, and this author is not willing to comment on that presupposition one way or another).

Finally, we have the mythical deep gnomes that have shunned the light of day for a dwarvenesque lifestyle.

Gnome Titans

Gnome titans are tough little devils, scrappy in a fight and never surrendering, whatever the odds. They lack the charm of their gnomish cousins (-1 Cha), but are a tad stronger (-1 Str relative to humans) and tougher (+2 Con). Some say they can't grow beards as well as the standard gnome, but this is untrue. They actually trim them short to a goatee (they can, indeed, grow mustaches 75% of the time) so that foes cannot grab their beards during a scuffle. As one might imagine, gnome titans have the mental attitude it takes to be a decent fighter, despite their diminutive size.

Gnomelings

These annoying little twerps represent what both gnomes and halflings consider the worst of their parentage. Unable to grow a proper beard, these characters have large, shaggy sideburns and thick, matted hair. While larger than gnomes, they've not gained any gnomic strength, making them physically weak (-3 Str). They don't suffer in the looks department, having gained some of the halfling (relatively-speaking) comeliness. They also have some nimbleness despite their rotund nature (+2 Dex) and have retained some of the resistance of the halfling blood (+1 Con). Gnomelings are great at skulking and sneaking around and consequently are chiefly thieves and vagabonds. Luckily, gnomelings are infertile and cannot reproduce.

Deep Gnomes

Deep gnomes are creatures of lore, existing (so far) only in folktales amongst the wee-folk. They supposedly live deep underground, delving the depths for precious gemstones and metals. The legends vary as to whether they support weal or woe, or if they are in league with orcs and dark elves or helping the dwarves battle the goblins, but they are generally cast in an annoying and decidedly unheroic light. All accounts agree they are skilled tunnelers, love mushrooms and moss (which gives their erstwhile grey skin a blue sheen) and have white hair. Little else is known about these creatures, although their nature and existence is surrounded by copious speculation.

Religion:

Gnomes worship various deities, including all of the chaotic good deities, a smattering of neutral good ones and a few neutral and chaotic neutral. The Old Oak is very popular in certain communities, while others prefer the Shimmering One, Lord of Silver Linings and the Laugher. Truth-be-told, each community and clan has favorites, and each household from within those.

On Tellene:

Gnomes have many small communities dispersed throughout the known lands, generally living in the hills on the fringes of human society. The largest concentrations lie the gnomish Confederacy of Nissen (including the nearby town of Baethel), the Mizhor Woodlands, the slopes of the gentle Dashahn Mountains, the Dopromond Downs and in and around the Vrykarr Mountains (the last being gnome titans).

[1] **Activity Cycle:** *Gnomes have a standard diurnal cycle. They have many nocturnal animal friends that keep guard while foraging around a gnomic burrow (which they generally share).*

[2] **Awareness/Senses:** *Gnomes can see well in dimly lit conditions, even when Veshemo is new, but they cannot see in complete darkness. That said, they tend to become near-sighted when young and require bifocals as they age. Their other senses are excellent, especially their sense of smell, which appears to be aided by their enormous noses and their sense of hearing, likewise aided by largish ears. Gnomes have nimble little fingers that can detect the smallest of bumps on a surface in need of polishing.*

[3] **Habitat:** *Gnomes make their homes in small burrows on the hillside, but occasionally use large hollowed-out (but still living) trees integrated into a greater community of burrows. Some prefer rustic little miniature cottages, also incorporated with a natural blend into their little burrow community. Occasionally, they live in mines and caves, but only for a few years before returning to surface life, vastly preferring the warmth and brightness of the sun.*

[4] **Organization:** *Gnomes are organized by competing family clans, each with a chief or leader of some type. In larger communities, they tend to have a council of sorts, comprised of the heads of the various families. The decisions of the council are final, but followed (or ignored) on a needs-be basis. Individual clans compete with one another for everything but survival, for which they are quick to aid as needed, banding together against physical threats from others. Aside from that, the antagonism between families can rise to the level of injurious, but seldom lethal, practical jokes.*

[5] **Climate/Terrain:** *Gnomes prefer a temperate climate and are rarely found in areas without plentiful foliage and many deciduous trees.*

[6] **Hide/Trophy:** *Kobolds and goblins carry strings of defeated gnome snouts as a show of bravery. Such a trophy marks the individual for death for any gnome that sees it. Gnome skin can be used for scrolls and book coverings and is especially prized by evil illusionists.*

[7] **Treasure:** *Gnomes carry 5d4p sp each. Gnomish lairs can contain vast amounts of wealth in the form of precious metals and especially polished gems. While they treasure their garb, it's pretty worthless.*

G

GOAT, GIANT
Also Known As: Cabra, Capara

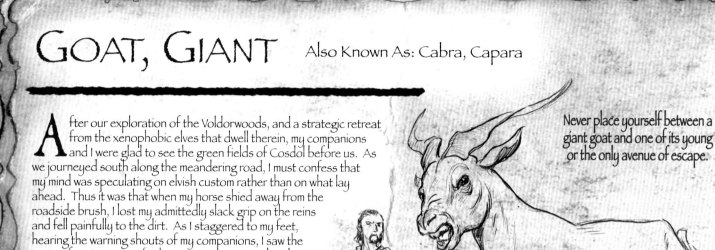

After our exploration of the Voldorwoods, and a strategic retreat from the xenophobic elves that dwell therein, my companions and I were glad to see the green fields of Cosdol before us. As we journeyed south along the meandering road, I must confess that my mind was speculating on elvish custom rather than on what lay ahead. Thus it was that when my horse shied away from the roadside brush, I lost my admittedly slack grip on the reins and fell painfully to the dirt. As I staggered to my feet, hearing the warning shouts of my companions, I saw the reason for my mount's fright. Two great eyes with pale irises and black, slit-shaped pupils glared at me from a massive head and neck stretching over the brush. I felt its hot breath on my face, and its lips moved in what I dazedly took to be an odd attempt at speech.

I stood as a man hypnotized, until the opening of the beast's impressive jaws caused me to recall myself and move away. It returned to its feeding, paying little heed to us, and I was able to make some observations on its anatomy. Like most goats, it has two horns, though these appear sharper and more menacing than those of the smaller breeds. However, it did not have a beard or wattle, and its tail hung down rather than pointing up.

Any further observations I hoped to make were cut short as our thief, who is native to this region, spotted an approaching herd of more giant goats watched over by two figures with the size and gait of ogres. Still weary from our forest battles, we continued our journey at once, and I have not yet had the opportunity to study the giant goats further. – ℜ

Never place yourself between a giant goat and one of its young or the only avenue of escape.

Fighting these creatures on rocky or uneven ground will put you at a disadvantage.

These nimble-footed quadrupeds have rough coats of brown, black, dirty white or a combination of these. Male giant goats also have a prominent beard of scruffy fur. Both male and female giant goats have curving, pointed horns. A typical adult giant goat stands an impressive 6 feet tall at the shoulder and weighs around 900 pounds.

Giant goats are quite clever, and once a weakness (in a wall or in combat) has been discovered, they exploit it repeatedly. Giant goats are also very coordinated and can climb and hold their balance in the most precarious places.

Males are known as bucks or billy goats, females as does or nanny goats and immature goats as kids. There is little sexual dimorphism among giant goats except for the female's horns, which are roughly half the size of the male's.

Combat/Tactics:

Giant goats are most prone to attack when cornered, provoked or in rut (the latter for male giant goats only). In a fight, a giant goat rears up on its hind legs and strikes down with a powerful horned head butt. Among their herd, they do this to establish their social dominance, but it works well enough against other creatures too. They can also deal an unpleasant bite to the unsuspecting.

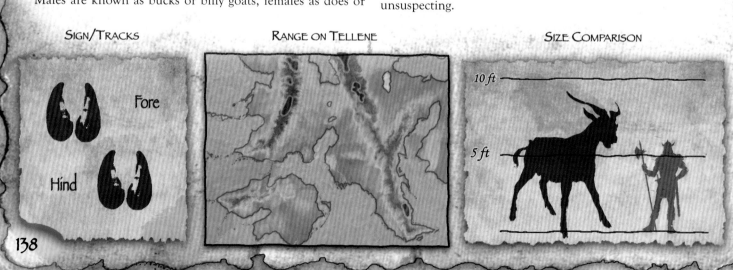

SIGN/TRACKS   Fore   Hind

RANGE ON TELLENE

SIZE COMPARISON   10 ft   5 ft

In the wild, giant goats are smart enough to lure their pursuers to an area where firm footing is difficult to find (*e.g.*, mountainsides, rocky hills) then readily turn on them.

Habitat/Society:

In the wild, giant goats live in maternal herds of up to a dozen individuals (adult males are solitary). Male goats enter a period called a rut, where they are both ready to mate and easily annoyed. During the rut, more mature and larger males drive younger males from the maternal herds.

Domestic giant goat herding is rare except among such large sapients as giants and ogres, who can handle such beasts. These herdsman occasionally conflict with other races when they bring their herds into pastures normally occupied by the smaller cattle, sheep and common goats of human or demi-human herdsmen.

As with their smaller kin, giant goats are typically bred as dairy producers (for cheese, milk and goat butter) or shorn for wool. However, they also give dung for fuel and can be trained to pull carts (requires a successful Animal Training: Goats skill check of Easy difficulty). Longhair breeds also produce fiber for clothing. Even a dead goat can be useful, providing meat for food, bone for tools and sinew for stringed musical instruments or surgical sutures. Their hides can be fashioned into vellum or simple water and wine bottles.

A nanny goat has a gestation period of around five months, and generally produces two or three kids each spring. Kids reach maturity at around three years of age.

A typical goat has a lifespan of nearly 18 years.

Ecology:

Giant goats love to feast on scrub, trees and other vegetation, making them quite a hazard when a herd wanders into cultivated farmland. After all, a single giant goat devours an average of 50 pounds of food each day! Should a giant goat gobble up some solid object not normally part of its diet (*e.g.*, a coin, parchment, bit of clothing), the item passes out of the creature within 12+3d4p hours. Only gems, coins, metal buttons or similarly hard objects pass out intact.

On Tellene:

Giant goats dwell throughout the rocky hills and mountains of Tellene, with sightings having been reported in the eastern P'Rorul Peaks, the Legasa Peaks and the northern Elenon Mountain Range, to name only a few. In Korak's low lying Adiv Hills (as in many other lands), goat herding is a primary occupation, and more than a few locals have dreams of someday taming and raising a herd of giant goats.

A popular superstition in the Sovereign Lands is that goats whisper malign words in the ears of the saints, a superstition which is not lessened by the fact that the goat is the holy animal of the Covetous Ones (the clergy of the deity known commonly as The Corrupter). A common depiction of the faith is a tipped scale resting on a goat's skull; thus, celebrations of the faith typically call for the skull of a giant goat in order to present a more impressive spectacle for both faithful and unbelievers.

[1] Goat hide can be tanned and used to make clothing or boots. Giant goat hide sells for 30 sp per hide. The horn from a giant ram sells for 10 sp each and is used for carving and fashioning into various durable and artistic items such as sword hilts, musical instruments, household items and containers.

[2] Goat meat is highly nutritious and delicious. It sells for 4 cp per pound. Goat milk is also nutritious and often used to feed infants. It sells for 4 cp per pint.

GIANT GOAT

HIT POINTS:	29+4d8
SIZE/WEIGHT:	L/900 lbs.
TENACITY:	Nervous
INTELLIGENCE:	Animal, High
FATIGUE FACTOR:	0

SPEED 8 — INIT 2
ATTACK +6
DMG REDUCTION 5
DEFENSE +3
DAMAGE 5d4p
short REACH
TOP SAVE 12

MOVEMENT

CRAWL:	10
WALK:	15
JOG:	20
RUN:	25
SPRINT:	30

SAVES

PHYSICAL:	+7
MENTAL:	+4
DODGE:	+7

ATTACK:
Initial attack will be a charge with normal damage and double-knock-back; headbutts for 5d4p damage; may also bite for 1d6p

GENERAL INFO

ACTIVITY CYCLE:	Diurnal
NO. APPEARING:	1 (male) or 9-12 (nannies and kids)
% CHANCE IN LAIR:	n/a
FREQUENCY:	Frequent
ALIGNMENT:	Non
VISION TYPE:	Standard
AWARENESS/SENSES:	Standard
HABITAT:	Grasslands, hills
DIET:	Herbivorous
ORGANIZATION:	Individuals or herd
CLIMATE/TERRAIN:	Temperate to sub-arctic highlands

YIELD

MEDICINAL:	nil
SPELL COMPONENTS:	giant goat hide makes excellent vellum for scrolls or spell books
HIDE/TROPHY:	hide and horns[1]
TREASURE:	nil
EDIBLE:	yes[2]
OTHER:	nil

EXPERIENCE POINT VALUE: 175

GOBLIN

Also Known As: Ga'uk (in Orcish), Goter, Ashugg

Death is preferable to being taken alive by one of these cruel malicious creatures.

As individuals, goblins are weak foes easily bested by the most junior of swordsmen. While this may engender disdain for the race as less than worthy opponents, one must always bear in mind that goblins function as a collective. As Master Hukek so eloquently wrote, "A lone twig may snap easily but a bundle resists the axe more effectively than the stoutest oak."

In battle these little fiends can quickly overwhelm a theoretically superior opponent. Unless careful tactics are employed, they will surround you. So many will simultaneously attack that you cannot employ your shields against all of them. And when one falls, two are ready to stick their blades into your exposed flank. Their archers will also fire directly into combat caring little for the welfare of their comrades.

Should you survive the onslaught and drive them back, do not believe for a moment you have succeeded. It is then that goblins become most dangerous. Their miserable holes are filled with traps. Some are quite ingenious for the creatures have a cunning aptitude for crude but effective mechanical devices. Pursue with great care and a watchful eye.

One important word of advice is this – always ensure your escape route. Overly zealous crusaders have penetrated a goblin warren only to suffer some unexpected critical injury (most often at the hands of the aforementioned traps) that necessitated evacuation of the injured party only to learn that the exit had been blocked. Trapped as they were, they faced the unenviable choice between leaving a man behind and making a bull rush for the door or dragging along an injured companion while fighting a pitched battle with goblins emboldened by the scent of blood.

If you face this dilemma, Honor demands a mercy killing. Better your friend die swiftly by your hand than fall into goblin clutches. Trust me on this. ~ J

These small, savage humanoids have narrow snouts, largish ears and sharp, jagged teeth, ideal for tearing flesh, cooked or not. Their skin ranges form a deep brownish color to various greens, purples and even jet black. They have knotty, greasy unkempt black and dark brown hair growing on their scalps, although receding hairlines and male-pattern baldness is very common in adult males. Their bodies are generally not hirsute, except for their backs and arms (both sexes). Open sores, boils and skin lesions are plentiful under their armor and sometimes on their faces. Scars from past grievous wounds and torture stints are quite common. These wretched creatures stand about 3½ to 4½ feet tall, but they stoop and often appear shorter. They walk erect, but have poor posture, older ones hunching so low as to bend at the waist and drag their elbows. They weigh anywhere from 70 to 100 pounds.

Goblins hate life and beauty of all types. They gleefully destroy flowers, fell trees and set alight bush and grass simply for sport. They hate hunting, but love the kill, reveling in the suffering of a wounded fawn or, better yet, pixie-fairy. Even fine, delicate and valuable jewelry will be smashed then melted down to gain the base metals and gems.

Conversely, goblins approach the prospect of torture and

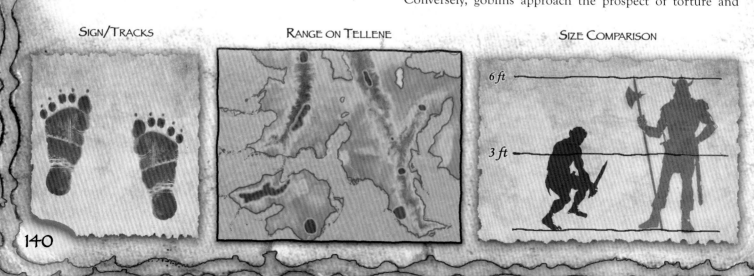

SIGN/TRACKS	RANGE ON TELLENE	SIZE COMPARISON

suffering with such enthusiastic giddiness, one would think they had discovered buried treasure. They are actually quite creative, but use their energies to invent new weapons, siege engines, torture equipment, horrific traps and other items of destruction. They like to build and create new things and make arms and armor prolifically. The shoddy quality of their manufactured items is evident in the high failure rate; their arms and armors only survive a battle or two before becoming damaged, outright broken or visibly inferior, dull or marred (-1 penalty cumulative for all purposes after each d4p-1 uses). If a goblin owns a broken or inferior item, he simply tosses it aside as new ones become available, which is often. Damaged goods are collected and the materials re-used or burned for fuel.

Goblins are sneaky little scum, as well as naturally lazy, and like to steal and backstab their way to the easy life. Rarely successful, they generally find themselves working as a cog in the machine, toiling away for the faceless goblin king. Cowards to the core, a goblin will certainly work hard enough if he believes the punishment for slacking off is both severe and forthcoming. Consequently, most goblin work groups have overly-zealous, whip- and scourge-wielding taskmasters.

Goblins love battle when they have numbers on their side or a clear advantage. A goblin's weapons of choice tend to be short sword and shield, but they also like to use hammers, morning stars, clubs, daggers, spears, crossbows and slings. They use shields whenever possible since goblins prefer to avoid injury and hope their peers can maim the foe (but are quick to provide the killing thrust if the opponent is wounded or helpless). They typically wear leather armor, which they construct from cured animal hides, although leaders are often much better armored.

They are not particularly strong in battle (-1 to Damage for weapons) and have weak Hit Points and a low tolerance for pain, although they make up for the latter with decent resistance, no doubt from practicing the art of torture on one another throughout their formative years. Their small stature causes a reach suffrage of -1 foot, and further, makes it tough for them to stand their ground in the face of strong opposing blows. What they lack in combat prowess, however, they make up for with numbers and enthusiasm.

Goblins fight well in the darkness, having twice the range of low light vision than other races, but have great difficulty fighting in very bright light. Sunlight causes them to suffer a 2-point penalty to Attack and Defense rolls, while dark, cloudy conditions or sunlight just after dawn or before dusk force a 1-point penalty on Attack rolls (but no penalty for defense). Goblins suffer no penalties under storm clouds and see perfectly well in starlight, even if all moons are new and the sky is overcast.

For every 20 goblins encountered, one will be a sergeant with 23 Hit Points and a 1-point improvement to Attack, Defense and Damage over the others. He wears studded leather armor.

If 40 are encountered, there will be four sergeants and one captain who has combat statistics similar to a hobgoblin and wears ringmail.

If 100 or more, one will be a chainmail clad sub-chief with hobgoblin-like statistics, but with an additional hit die and a further +1 point improvement to Attack, Defense and Damage. He has 2d4p bodyguards with captain statistics. The goblin chieftain, or king, lives in their lair. The king has combat statistics similiar to a bugbear and somewhat resembles these fearsome creatures -

GOBLIN

Hit Points:	17+1d6
Size/Weight:	S/85 lbs.
Tenacity:	Nervous
Intelligence:	Slow
Fatigue Factor:	-2/-1

ATTACK: Typical goblin armament consists of a crude short sword (2d6p-1), leather armor and small shield.

DEFENSES: None explicitly, but most goblins are ingenious trap makers. *Shield use (e.g., small shields increases Defense from +2 to +6). These creatures possess no natural DR but often wear leather armor (improving DR from 0 to 2).

MOVEMENT

Crawl:	1¼
Walk:	2½
Jog:	5
Run:	10
Sprint:	15

SAVES

Physical:	+3
Mental:	+2
Dodge:	+4

GENERAL INFO

Activity Cycle:	Nocturnal
No. Appearing:	varies[1]
% Chance in Lair:	50%
Frequency:	Frequent
Alignment:	Lawful Evil
Vision Type:	Extreme Low Light Vision
Awareness/Senses:	+10% Listening and Observation[2]
Habitat:	Caves and other[3]
Diet:	Omnivorous[4]
Organization:	Solitary to tribal[5]
Climate/Terrain:	Any[6]

YIELD

Medicinal:	nil
Spell Components:	nil
Hide/Trophy:	none worth boasting about
Treasure:	2d12p cp each[7]
Edible:	yes, but may be diseased[8]
Other:	nil

Experience Point Value: 22

G

particularly in his girth. He wears platemail if heading to war. Another 2d4p sub-chiefs protect him.

Note: Detailed combat statistics for goblin leader types appears on page 366.

Clerics and shamans are far more common among goblins than other humanoids, serving an active role in the community and often participating on raids. Typically, there is one cleric for every three captains and bodyguards and one witch doctor for every three sub-chiefs. Their levels of spellcasting ability are 2d6p for the highest level cleric and 2d4p-1 for the greatest mage. The others are dispersed evenly in decreasing levels below each respective highest-level caster.

Aside from spellcasters, sometimes dire wolves and/or wargs accompany goblin warbands. There is a 30% (1-5% wargs, 6-10% 50-50 mix of both and 11-30% dire wolves) chance that 10% of the goblin troops are mounted on such beasts and another 3d12p riderless dire wolves and/or wargs will accompany them.

Together with orcs, goblins are without question the most numerous humanoids. Their resourcefulness, tenacity and ability to breed in numbers allows them to recover from any heavy losses sustained at the hands of their many enemies – and they have many enemies. Goblins war with every known race.

Goblins' preferred underground habitation frequently brings them into conflict with the dwarves with whom they compete for territory. Goblin contingents assigned hunting duties or mining closer to the surface can run afoul of gnomish clans, so war with that race is not uncommon, either. Over the millennia, goblins developed a deep-seated jealousy and hatred for these two races and attack them on sight (their hatred for dwarves runs a bit deeper, so given the choice, they attack dwarves first and foremost).

They loathe all other creatures and seek to conquer and enslave them, especially fairy-kin, demi-humans and humans. They avoid fighting with hobgoblins and bugbears because they generally suffer losses in such battles; they also feel a bit of a kindship to their cousin races. Consequently, they may join forces with their cousins in order to battle a common foe or to raid a larger target. Goblins have been known to ally with kobolds, sometimes forcing the small dog-men to serve them. Goblins also share a symbiotic relationship with wolves, dire wolves and wargs, hunting and warring in teams. Their lupine partners gain fire and food in winter and other lean times, while the goblins gain mounts and spies.

Combat/Tactics:

These spineless little twerps only like to fight when they have the upper hand, such as when their foe is unarmed, asleep, unaware, vastly outnumbered or outclassed. They love to fire ranged weapons from hidden locations and then cut and run, hoping to lead pursuers through dangerous traps while they hide and shoot again from cover. They engage in hand-to-hand combat only when they have superior numbers or some clear advantage. If forced into combat, they use delaying tactics in order to increase their odds for survival and to hang on until reinforcements can arrive to overpower their enemies. Failing that, they scatter, hoping to escape by running in different directions, a method of overcoming their slow movement rate. They are not above hamstringing an ally to slow him down, while making good on an escape.

Habitat/Society:

Goblins prefer to live deep within the earth, mining and carving great halls from the living rock. Blessed with magnificent low-light vision and less affected by uncomfortable heat or cold than other races (much like dwarves), goblins are well-suited to the subterranean environment, whether working deep within the mines or at a blistering foundry. While adept miners and smiths, goblins cannot compete with their natural enemies, the dwarves in these areas. Generally lazy, goblins prefer to force dwarves from their homes and live in expertly built dwarven cities, chock full of plunder that's just the right size. Each goblin lair has several ingenious and deadly traps designed to injure, maim, fool, delay and outright slay intruders.

Goblins organize themselves into work groups and warbands, each led by a taskmaster or sergeant, as the case may be, who pays fealty to a higher authority (usually a captain or other leader-type). When groups meet, they do not fight like orcs, Instead, the leaders engage in ritualistic combat (sometimes fatal, but more often simply resulting in a maiming). After a winner is determined, the entire group supports the new leader. Ultimately, the whole tribe pays homage to a single leader or chieftain. When no other leader is present but one, that chieftain is known as the king. It is rumored that all of the goblin kings pay homage to one Great Goblin King.

Goblins speak their own language, which is closely related to Hobgoblin and Dwarven (allowing them to effectively communicate with either race). Goblins sometimes learn the languages of their neighbors, especially if involved in trade or spying. Any goblin has a 10% chance of knowing one of the following languages: Orcish, Kobold, Gnomish, or a local human tongue if located near the surface. Clerics have a 50% (and mages 80%) chance of knowing an additional language with a further 10% for every other language listed.

Goblins have an average lifespan of only 40 to 50 years, but those living outside of goblin kingdoms (for example, a well-cared-for slave or a captive in human lands) have lived up to nearly 70 years. Females comprise a full 50% of the population. They appear very similar to males, but have mammaries and wider hips. Little more than a slave class, females enjoy no rights or privileges. They wear rags or nothing at all, huddling together for warmth in completely unlit caverns. The she-goblin bitches are kept in restricted areas and relegated to producing food supplies (and preparing the same), breeding programs and rearing the pups. If food supplies run low, elderly females are butchered and consumed by the warriors and workers.

The goblin gestation is 6 months, with bitches capable of conception just four weeks after giving birth. Consequently, there are an equal number of young as there are adults. Infant mortality and violent ends keep the numbers from becoming even higher. Goblins reach sexual maturity at the age of eight, but by the age of four, males are already separated out to work in the mines; thus, each has at least Novice mastery in the Mining skill. By adolescence, the most promising and largest join the warrior class. Those showing initiative or unusual intelligence are trained in a trade or to become spies or scouts. The remaining youths are left to toil in the mines. If the population becomes too much to sustain, goblins aggressively expand their territories or make war on their neighbors.

Most goblin lairs have wolf dens near the surface. There is a 50% chance that a goblin warren contains 3d12p wolves, a 40% chance of 2d12p dire wolves and a 20% chance of wargs (roll for each independently). These companions, even those used as mounts, are on a more-or-less equal footing to the goblins and rank as equals working for the same ends rather than as any type of servant.

Some (25%) goblin lairs have 2d4p bugbears as guests. Such bugbears will work cooperatively with their smaller cousins, sharing in raids and spoils. However, if given the opportunity, the bugbears subjugate the little runts and establish themselves as rulers.

Ecology:

Since they live in mines, caves and in the Netherdeep and have an aversion to work not related to butchery, maiming, torture or mass-destruction, goblins are not much interested in farming or animal husbandry. Instead, they hunt animals (and will hunt any available food from rodent to deer or larger to extinction), other humanoids and demi-humans, and raid farms and villages. Occasionally, by order of a leader-type, they force their bitches to grow mushrooms, fungus and the like to support their deeper mines.

Goblins have been known to trade metals, ores, gems and finished and manufactured goods to other races, even humans (typically through an intermediary) for foodstuffs and other goods. The goblin choice of underground settlement inevitably places them in direct conflict with other races that choose to live in the Netherdeep, especially dwarves and dark elves. Among the myriad of natural foes, goblins hate dwarves and gnomes the most and attack them on sight, capturing and enslaving them if at all possible.

Subraces:

Goblins come in all shapes and sizes. At one time there may have been subraces, but they have clearly interbred. It is certain that there are differing racial features between the various tribes that live far from one another, perhaps even enough to create a different species for the goblins inhabiting deep, dark rain forests versus those deep within arctic mountains, but, frankly, no sage cares enough to classify their variances.

Religion:

Goblins are an unexpectedly religious lot, likely arising from their extremely superstitious nature, blaming everything from catastrophe to minor gambling victory on unseen supernatural forces and luck (or ill-luck). They fear magic of all types and consequently their priests and shamans wield great power amongst the masses and even the leaders. Because goblins worship a wide array of deities, their clergies can never really manage to usurp control (although it has happened at various points in the past) as competing religious orders always find a way to weaken the power base of the greater ones.

The most popular religions are the House of Shackles, Order of Agony, the Church of Endless Night, the House of Scorn, the House of Knives and the Fraternal Order of Aptitude. Lesser followings are held by the Founder's Creation, the Courts of Inequity, the Temple of Strife, the Temple of Armed Conflict, and the Congregation of the Dead.

On Tellene:

Goblins can be found in numbers near any dwarven or gnomish mine as they follow the same ores and have similar interests in mining. Thus, goblins can be found on the outskirts of the kingdoms of Karasta and Draska as well as in the Dashahn and Tanehz ranges. Goblins fight a war of attrition, willing to suffer heavy losses at the hands of the dwarves, knowing that over the centuries or even millennia if need be, they will eventually overrun the dwarves and take control of their massive underground kingdoms and mines. The largest goblin kingdom lies deep under the Krond Heights (believed to be the first and greatest of the dwarven kingdoms). It is there that most sages believe the Great Goblin King holds court, plotting the demise of the demi-human (and eventually the humanoid) races. Goblins from this kingdom played a key role in helping Kruk-ma-Kali rise to power and enjoyed a place in his terrestrial kingdom. Goblins, unhappy with their share of the spoils and place in the new order, are also believed to be his assassins.

Savage goblins in large numbers can also be found in the dark reaches of the Vohven jungle and in the Obakasek jungle, de facto ruling the latter with their massive population and ability to tame certain of the beasts therein. Goblins frequently raid outside of the deep forests and jungles into the surrounding human lands.

[1] **No. Appearing:** 1-8 (traveling, hunting); 3d4p+8 (warband); 20d20p (tribe)

[2] **Awareness/Senses:** Goblins see extremely well in the near-dark, even in very dimly lit conditions. Their low light vision has twice the range of normal low-light vision, but they cannot see in complete darkness. Closer to their animalistic roots than most demi-human races, they have a +10% to Listening and another +10% to Observation, the latter due to a heightened sense of smell and only affecting Observation checks where smell is relevant. Like dwarves, they have sensitive hands able to detect tiny fractures in stone, ceramic and metal, but also making them susceptible to torture techniques that take advantage of the heightened nerves.

[3] **Habitat:** Goblins prefer underground lairs cut from solid rock. They may come to the surface at night to raid, but greatly prefer life in the Netherdeep. That said, some live and thrive above ground in dismal forests, ruins and other places.

[4] **Diet:** Although technically omnivorous, some wealthier goblins live their whole lives eating only flesh, while others may eat nothing but mushrooms from first solid food to last. They are prone to cannibalism in times of famine.

[5] **Organization:** Goblins are organized into tribes, each with a chieftain. In their massive underground complexes, one chieftain rules as king with all of the tribes swearing loyalty. Goblins are rumored to have one massive, powerful ruler known only as the Great Goblin King.

[6] **Climate/Terrain:** Goblins prefer dank, dark subterranean mines, but their ingenuity allows them to survive in any climate and any terrain.

[7] **Treasure:** Goblins carry 2d12p cp each. Goblin lairs can contain wealth in the form of uncut gems, ores, worked precious metals, jewels, finished and worked goods of poor quality and manufacture (especially arms and armor, torture implements and horrible inventions for inflicting pain or annoyance). A lair that has been successful in raids will contain all types of items, even of human or demi-human manufacture as well as superior quality arms and armors (surely in use by the leaders). Goblins keep many animal pelts, especially those of wolves.

[8] **Edible:** Goblin blood or meat has a 75% chance of transmitting disease (usually 'The Shakes'). Most people are wise enough to avoid it. Orcs and ogres are immune to these effects and are reputed to enjoy the taste well enough, partaking when no better food is available.

G

GOLEM, CLAY

Also Known As: Brinu, Ajja-Vonan

During my incautious youth, I frequently accompanied a band of young heroes of the noblest intent. If they possessed a fatal flaw, it was a desire to aid the poor and downtrodden regardless of the implications for their own safety.

One notable adventure occurred in the bleak hinterlands of the Byth Mountains. We received a surreptitious plea for assistance via an agent of the Brotherhood of Industry. Slennish raiding had steadily progressed to a calamitous zenith and frontier settlements were in dire peril of complete eradication.

Rightfully sensing a unique and malevolent purpose to this renewed evil vigor, we trekked north and encountered an unusual ardor in the wicked Dejy tribesmen. Interrogation of our sole live captive revealed the stimulus. The Order of Agony were now possessed of a formidable evil power and charged with the subjugation of all lands north of the upper Byth river.

When we did raid the Slennish temple, the barbarous disciples did battle our company with unnatural intensity, as is their wont. They could not though bar our passage to the unholy sanctum. It was there we did encounter the horrible creature.

Half again as tall as a man and appearing much as a sculptor's unfinished statue, the humanoid mass advanced upon us in defense of its masters. Alas, my dweomers proved feckless and dispatchment of the thing became a task for our veteran swordsmen. They too were impotent – failing in many attempts to harm the construct despite landing blows that would have hewn an orc in half.

As fate would have it, the creature itself proved our salvation. After crushing the skull of our impetuous knight, the monster seemed to slacken for a moment and now apparently imbued with a berserk fury did attack all within its reach be they friend or foe. Gravely weakened by our exploits, we sought an expeditious retreat from the ensuing carnage. We returned some days later to bear witness to the devastated temple in which no living creature stirred. ~

A brinu who was summoned to tear down and carry away the gates of Burlven.

These creations appear as large animated, amorphous, anthropomorphic creatures with an opening at the mouth. These monsters are comprised of reddish-brown or gray colored clay often etched with religious symbols and runes integral to the creation of the creature. Other golems may have these important symbols written on tablets or scrolls that are stored inside the monster itself. No matter what form it takes, there is always a scroll that is used to control the brinu stored inside its body. Clay golems range in height from 7 to 10 feet and may weigh several hundred pounds. Some creators have been known to honor their deity by crafting golems in their likeness.

Combat/Tactics:

In combat, a clay golem follows the orders it is given literally with no interpretation. If told to guard an area or bring a bucket of water from a well sans other superseding instructions, it does so. Only the creator or the current owner of the commanding scroll has the power to redirect the golem once an order has been issued. Given the ease for misinterpretation, orders are usually simple and unambiguous such as "defend me" or "attack those heathens!" Passive golems defend themselves if attacked as they have an innate defense mechanism to prevent them from being destroyed when their creator or controller is absent. In such cases, the golem attacks anyone within

Many decades ago, a brinu appeared outside the town gates of Burlven. After a fierce battle in which a dozen men were killed, the creature tore down the gates and carried them off. It was a mystery as to why the creature appeared and who had sent it. After the accidental death of a wealthy merchant several years later the stolen gates were discovered in the gardens of his hillside manor.
Apparently he had commissioned the golem as retribution for the town seizing properties within its walls, after the guild ruled against him in a legal matter. ~

SIZE COMPARISON

10 ft

5 ft

sight at the time it is assaulted, relentlessly pursuing its attackers until death or commanded to stop, and returning to its resting spot when it completes its task.

On rare occasions, Ajja-Vonan have been known to tear free from their creator's control and embark upon a rampaging frenzy. For every 25 seconds that a clay golem is engaged in melee combat, there is a 1% cumulative chance that it goes berserk, severing the bond of control and commencing a violent rampage. In such cases the golem is motivated solely by a monomaniacal drive to kill all living beings, smashing into, or through, any obstruction in its relentless pursuit of anything that moves. Unlike other golems, control can never be reasserted and the only way to halt the creature's frenzied spree of destruction is to destroy it.

Clay golems are virtually immune to hacking and piercing weapons – only damage in excess of 30 points from these weapons causes any harm to the construct. Bludgeoning weapons are far more effective. These golems are also immune to nearly all magical dweomers, save a few rare incantations that act directly upon raw earth.

Habitat/Society:

Clay golems have no explicit habitat or society, as they are animated constructs created through a complex religious ritual. These creatures are most often created to serve as temple guardians, specifically to protect temple treasuries. As such, they may be viewed as a facet of the host temple and their actions – such as they are – being manifestations of the congregation's societal viewpoint.

Ecology:

Most sages believe the clay golem was first created by clerics of the Landlord in order to serve as guardians for vaults and places that held great wealth. Others speculate that golems were first created by priests of the Guardian as mighty sentinels to protect their towns against invasion. Whatever the truth may be, patriarchs of every religious persuasion have access to the rituals necessary to create an Ajja-Vonan.

That said, the cost involved in constructing and animating a Clay Golem is so steep that only the wealthiest of temples may contemplate creating one. Golems built to guard important areas are often given instructions that will last the test of time, such as "guard this area against all who refuse to display our divine icon".

In order to animate a clay golem, the form must first be built. A master potter is required to build the creature prior to bringing it to life. While the monster need not be a work of art, it must be built in such a way that it can be assembled without shattering or cracking, even though its strength and integrity are a result of the magic used to create it.

Once built and imbued with vitality, the owner inserts the control scroll into the golem's mouth, thus gaining control of it. Prior to his death, the master of the golem can arrange to pass control to another through the use of a divinely enchanted will. This will must be freely written and blessed in a religious ceremony in order to have the proper effect. Prudent elders prepare this document ahead of time and store it in a secure location should the unthinkable happen.

It is believed that destroying the runes on a clay golem, or the tablets and scrolls inside, deactivates or destroys the creature. Unfortunately, it is virtually impossible to do so without animating the monster.

On Tellene:

Clay golems are typically found in temples, or in the vicinity of their creator priests. They usually serve as guardians of important religious sites.

CLAY GOLEM

HIT POINTS:	80
SIZE/WEIGHT:	L/600+ lbs
TENACITY:	n/a
INTELLIGENCE:	none
FATIGUE FACTOR:	n/a

SPEED			INIT
10			6
	ATTACK +21	DMG REDUCTION	
	+6	special	
	5d10p		
short REACH		DAMAGE	n/a TOP SAVE

MOVEMENT

CRAWL:	1¼
WALK:	2½
JOG:	5
RUN:	7½
SPRINT:	10

SAVES

PHYSICAL:	+21*
MENTAL:	+21*
DODGE:	+21*

ATTACK: A clay golem attacks every 10 seconds with a devastatingly powerful smashing blow of its arm(s).

SPECIAL DEFENSES: These creatures are virtually immune to hacking & piercing weapons having a DR of 30 versus such attacks. They are more susceptible to crushing weapons having a mere DR 12 versus that attack form.
* also immune to nearly all magic spells save those that affect raw earth.

GENERAL INFO

ACTIVITY CYCLE:	Always active
NO. APPEARING:	1
% CHANCE IN LAIR:	100%
FREQUENCY:	Exotic
ALIGNMENT:	Non
VISION TYPE:	Standard
AWARENESS/SENSES:	Can detect movement within 40 feet
HABITAT:	Special (typically temples)
DIET:	Non-living
ORGANIZATION:	Solitary (singular creation)
CLIMATE/TERRAIN:	Any

YIELD

MEDICINAL:	wounds treated with mud (ground up remains from golem) heal at twice the normal rate
SPELL COMPONENTS:	nil
HIDE/TROPHY:	nil
TREASURE:	none of its own (though it may act as guardian)
EDIBLE:	no
OTHER:	nil
EXPERIENCE POINT VALUE:	3000

G

Golem, Flesh

Also Known As: [Creator Name]'s Monster

Little did I or my comrades dream of what strange sight we were destined to see tonight. I still shudder when I think of it, but I must put quill to parchment before it fades from my mind. The shortness of the candle tells me it nears midnight, but it seems as if many nights have come and gone since that grisly event. It was some hours ago now, when we exited the squalid pub on the waterfront, no more sober than we ought to be, and saw the fog hanging heavy over all.

Passing the hospitalers, the stench of death and meat long gone bad wafted over us. Still, we made light sport of it, claiming that such and such man we disliked had died in a sickbed for not paying us the coin he owed, and proclaiming loudly and drunkenly that we would die in battle and not on our backs in some healer's bed.

It was then that we saw it, and we could not have mistook it, for the thing stepped fully from the shadows into a patch of candlelight shining from a nearby window. It was a man of sorts, but a man of many men. He stood well over a head taller than the tallest among us, with yellowish skin so tautly pulled that it barely disguised the workings of the vessels and muscles underneath. All about his body, he bore the tailor's mark on him, with great patchings and stitches as if he were a patchwork doll crudely formed on his maker's worktable.

As we stood frozen in surprise, the patchwork man wheeled about and rushed into an unlit alley, which custom had dignified with the title of thoroughfare. We recovered from our surprise, but too late, for the creature was gone, and all that remained were high-piled bales, boxes and casks casting dense shadow that our drunken souls cared little for exploring. Perhaps we shall feel differently in the morn. - ᚠ

Flesh golems are sometimes mistaken for ghouls.

A flesh golem appears as a 7 to 8 foot tall corpse-like creature, stitched together from the body parts of several cadavers. These creatures are usually somewhat disproportionate and barely preserved with watery, glowing eyes. Embalming fluid leaks from their seams, creating a glistening mucus that is ever present on the creature's skin. Since it takes several different cadavers to create a flesh golem, each one is unique is size, shape and appearance.

During the process of creation, large, muscled corpses are most highly sought, as those who would create flesh golems typically covet brute strength and resilient bodies. Most of its flesh is pallid, with newer and better preserved body parts retaining a semblance of their previous color. Most flesh golems (90%) cannot speak, though they can moan or grunt in response to a question. Since they do possess a brain (or what is left of a brain) they can follow orders with some degree of success. However, some (10%) can be taught speech and even some reading and writing, provided the brain was literate in life.

Flesh golems wear whatever their creators dress them in, though often this is tattered and discarded clothing stitched together to accommodate their overly-large frames.

Sign/Tracks

The bare footprints of a flesh golem are much like those of a man, only larger. Should you not take care in examing such prints, you might easily mistake such sign for the feet of a youthful giant. Yet, there are indications of its true nature, though these are rare indeed.
A golem master unable to procure two feet from the same corpes may show this lack in the two different foot sizes, while flesh golems with damaged feet may exhibit such sign in a line of stitching that disturbs the dust of its print with some unusual line or indentation. - ᚠ

Size Comparison

10 ft

5 ft

Combat/Tactics:

Most flesh golems retain only enough intellect to use some reasoning in combat (though on rare occasion one may have better or even genius intelligence). While they can be duped or tricked they rarely fall for the same ploy twice. Against overwhelming numbers a flesh golem is smart enough to halt an attack or wait for better opportunities at a later date. When pursuing prey they are tireless and have been known to bash through walls and doors to get at those in hiding.

Flesh golems do not possess a functional nervous system and don't feel pain in the way people do; however, they instinctively know that fire is "bad" and do what they can to avoid it. Those naïve enough to think they can drive the creature away by swinging a torch may be in for a shock, as flesh golems often first attack people who wield fire in such a dangerous manner.

Flesh golems are loyal to their creators and follow orders to the best of their ability. In the event that the creator dies, the creature can do as it pleases, though typically its first act is to avenge the death of its master.

Despite its loyalty, flesh golems do sometimes go insane. For every 25 seconds the golem is engaged in melee, there is a 1% cumulative chance that it goes berserk, breaking free of its master to engage in a semi-coherent, murderous rampage. These fits often confuse the golem to the point that it wanders the countryside trying to recall some guidance from its muddled brain. The creator (if present) may attempt to regain control with a 10% chance of success for every 10 seconds expended in the effort. Golems are easily soothed by music (though the tune and instrument varies by creator), increasing the cumulative chance to 20% per every 5 seconds that the golem's tune is played.

Habitat/Society:

Flesh golems have no habitat or society, as they are created through a complex magical process. In the rare event a golem is freed it will wander the world in a confused state, eventually drawing enough attention to itself to be hunted down by those that view the creature as a danger to their way of life, and rightfully so.

Ecology:

The act of creation is a messy affair and sages speculate that certain body parts impact the golems ability to successfully perform a task. These theories usually involve the heart and brain. Other internal organs are not vital to the operation of the golem but are usually included. No one knows for sure if one creature's brain makes for a better golem than another.

Crafting a golem can be a lengthy process, as body parts must be harvested in one manner or another, be it through freshly killed corpses or by grave robbing.

On Tellene:

Golems can be found anywhere on Tellene where there is a mage with the abilities and the will to create one.

[1] If under control of its creator, a golem will perform as ordered regardless of circumstances. If its creator is absent, treat as Brave.

[2] Flesh Golems may be programmed to react to certain events that may supersede conventional awareness.

[3] If a bit of brain matter from a flesh golem is used as an alternate material spell component for Immunity to Apprentice Magic, the spell duration is doubled.

FLESH GOLEM

HIT POINTS:	70
SIZE/WEIGHT:	L/500 lbs.
TENACITY:	Brave[1]
INTELLIGENCE:	Usually Slow
FATIGUE FACTOR:	n/a

SPEED 5 — INIT 3
ATTACK +13
DMG REDUCTION
DEFENSE +2 — DAMAGE 18
3d12p
medium REACH — TOP SAVE — n/a

MOVEMENT

CRAWL:	5
WALK:	10
JOG:	15
RUN:	20
SPRINT:	25

SAVES

PHYSICAL:	+13
MENTAL:	+13
DODGE:	+13

ATTACK:
A flesh golem attacks every 5 seconds with alternative body blows from its incredibly powerful arms and fists.

SPECIAL DEFENSES:
Flesh golems are immune to nearly all magic spells save cold attacks (which halves the golem's speed for 10 seconds per 6 points of damage delivered). Electrical attacks restore Hit Points to the golem on a 1:4 basis (every 4 points dealt restores 1 HP).

GENERAL INFO

ACTIVITY CYCLE:	Always active
NO. APPEARING:	1
% CHANCE IN LAIR:	100%
FREQUENCY:	Scarce
ALIGNMENT:	Non
VISION TYPE:	Standard
AWARENESS/SENSES:	Special[2]
HABITAT:	Any
DIET:	None
ORGANIZATION:	Solitary (singular creation)
CLIMATE/TERRAIN:	Any

YIELD

MEDICINAL:	nil
SPELL COMPONENTS:	brain matter[3]
HIDE/TROPHY:	nil
TREASURE:	none of its own (though it may act as guardian)
EDIBLE:	no
OTHER:	nil
EXPERIENCE POINT VALUE:	1425

G

GORGON

Also Known As: Burakog, Khalkotaur

The thunderous beats of a gorgon's wings sounds like the beating of a drum.

A most unnatural creature, the gorgon. Whether it is related to the common aurox is unknown, though the habits of the beast bespeak a connection.

Gorgons are aggressive, unpredictable beasts given to foul moods. It is fortunate that they often advertise their irritation with a ritualistic display of wings and stamping hooves meant to warn off attackers. It is best to take heed for there is little to gain and much to lose in tangling with such a monster. Do not infuriate the gorgon with pinpricks delivered from afar. These will likely inflict little damage and serve to goad the creature into making a dangerous charge.

Should a confrontation prove unavoidable, it is best to act the part of the wolf pack. Attack from all sides at once. Hold nothing in reserve. A prolonged battle surely spells disaster for it allows the gorgon to utilize its deadly breath.

If you find yourselves overwhelmed by a gorgon's ferocity, it is best to scatter. Do not flee as a group for that but attracts the attention of the beast and invites a final charge. As the gorgon is capable of flight, you have little chance to outpace it. By scampering in several directions you will confound the beast. As a territorial creature, it will likely be satisfied with having driven off its attackers and stood its ground. - ♀

Gorgons often posture, stamp the ground and present their broad sides in an attempt to scare off challengers.

A gorgon is a large, feral beast that greatly resembles a bat-winged bovine. All gorgons have an incredibly dense, nearly hairless hide of predominantly dark colors. Adult males (bulls) are black while the females and young (cows and calves) are dark brown, though the latter also have a reddish-brown tinge that progresses to black as they age. Gorgon hooves also have a faint bronze sheen.

Gorgons have dichromatic vision and have trouble distinguishing certain colors (*e.g.*, they cannot distinguish green from red, but can easily differentiate between yellow and blue).

Gorgons are light sleepers, napping for less than 10 minute stretches and rarely getting more than an hour's worth of sleep in a single day. This unusual trait, combined with their good sense of smell, makes them quite difficult to surprise.

A typical male gorgon stands just over 7 feet tall at the shoulder, with a bulky body some 9 to 10 feet long, weighing roughly 3,000 pounds and with a wingspan of around 20 feet. Female gorgons stand over 5 feet tall at the shoulder, have a length of 8 to 9 feet, weight of about 1 ton and a roughly 18 foot wingspan.

Both male and female gorgons have horns, though the bulls have larger and thicker horns than the cows.

Combat/Tactics:

Gorgons are temperamental beasts and may charge unprovoked, particularly in the summer months when the heat and buzzing insects cause them to be even more irritable than normal. However, a gorgon often warns off the attacker in advance; this threat involves turning its body broadside to show off how big and powerful it is.

A gorgon attacks by charging, using its head to butt and then slashing with its horns or trampling on any opponent knocked

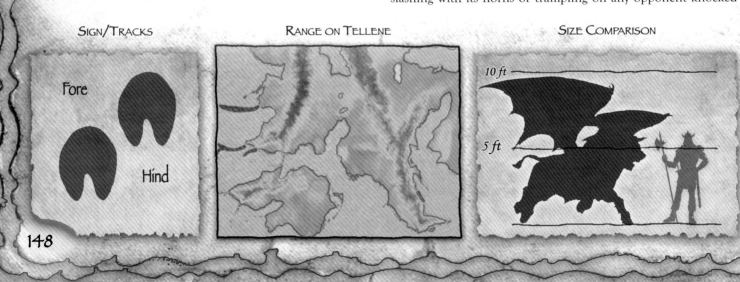

SIGN/TRACKS — Fore, Hind

RANGE ON TELLENE

SIZE COMPARISON — 10 ft, 5 ft

to the ground. If frustrated by attackers wounding it, but seemingly too adroit to slash with its long horns, a gorgon will utilize its most fearsome weapon – to wit, a cloud of petrifying vapor.

After no less than 30 seconds of combat, a gorgon will produce a noxious fluid in its lungs which it can expel in a 10-foot diameter cloud directly in front of it. All living beings (save gorgons) contacted by this aerosol must succeed at a CON saving throw (*vs. d20p+10*) or be immediately transformed to stone. Once used, it requires another 30 seconds for additional fluid to build up before the gorgon may employ this attack mode again.

When alarmed, a gorgon lets out a high, resonant whistle to warn other gorgons of approaching danger; this sound can carry up to 1 mile. Should gorgons be encountered with calves and thus unwilling to take flight, the adults shield the young as best they can with their bodies, even forming a circle around the calves if there are enough adults to do so.

Habitat/Society:

Gorgons dwell primarily in dense forest groves, often on small islands within easy flight of the mainland. They prefer to live alone or in pairs, and are rarely encountered in herds due to the grazing limitations of their natural habitat. When they do form herds, it is usually during the late winter and early spring, for the purpose of mating. These herds are typically composed of eight to 10 individuals, mostly cows. After a gestation period of about nine months, a pregnant cow bears a single calf. Gorgon calves can walk and then run shortly after they are born, and can even take to the skies within six months, though they are not fully weaned until after seven to 10 months. Gorgons grow quickly, becoming sexually mature at age two or three.

A typical gorgon has an average lifespan of 20 years.

Ecology:

Gorgons are herbivores that feed primarily upon leaves and grasses, as well as herbs, shrubs and trees. Gorgons also have a fifth stomach (the toxicum) that connects to the rumen and reticulum and represents the same functional space, but allows a gorgon to process saltwater and poisonous vegetation with no ill effects. After swallowing its food, a gorgon can return the cud (i.e., the partly digested material) back to its mouth for more chewing. A gorgon rarely chews cud except during its resting periods. Gorgons are voracious eaters, spending more than half the day grazing. As they are diurnal creatures, their primary grazing hours are at dawn and dusk.

Gorgons have few natural enemies, due in part to their formidable size and dangerous breath, but big hunting cats and saltwater crocodiles do occasionally attack gorgons, perhaps instinctively mistaking them for common bovines.

On Tellene:

Gorgons seem to be most common on the uninhabited islands of the Brandobian Ocean. However, they have also been reported throughout Reanaaria Bay, mostly along the coastline to the east of the P'Rorul Peaks.

[1] *Gorgon lungs can be used as a powerful material component in the eighth level Paralysis spell. There is a 50% chance that the use of lung tissue in this spell will make the effects of the spell permanent unless a Dismiss Enchantment is used. Gorgon lungs sell for 600 sp. Note that the lungs must be handled with leather gloves to avoid contact with residual petrifying fluid contained within.*

[2] *A Cooking/Baking check (Very Difficult) is required to properly prepare gorgon lungs. Failure results in food poisoning that causes -2 to Attack, Defense and Damge for 2d12 hours, beginning after an onset of 20+3d20 minutes.*

GORGON

HIT POINTS:	30+8d8
SIZE/WEIGHT:	L/1 ton
TENACITY:	Brave (bulls only)
INTELLIGENCE:	Animal High
FATIGUE FACTOR:	-5

MOVEMENT

CRAWL:	5
WALK:	10
JOG:	15
RUN:	20
FLY:	30

SAVES

PHYSICAL:	+10
MENTAL:	+8
DODGE:	+8

ATTACK: Bull gorgons will initially charge an opponent gaining +4 Attack and doing 4d6p+8 damage (and doubly effective knock-back due to momentum), anyone knocked prone will be trampled (a normal attack doing 4d6p damage - can be initiated directly after the charge if free of active opponents); in melee they attempt to gore with their horns for 3d12p; 30 seconds after initiating combat they may release a 10' diameter cloud of petrifying vapor (save vs. d20p+10 or turned to stone) - they may utilize this breath every 30 seconds thereafter

GENERAL INFO

ACTIVITY CYCLE:	Diurnal
NO. APPEARING:	1-2 or 8-10
% CHANCE IN LAIR:	n/a
FREQUENCY:	Sporadic
ALIGNMENT:	Non
VISION TYPE:	Standard
AWARENESS/SENSES:	Standard
HABITAT:	Open grasslands
DIET:	Herbivorous
ORGANIZATION:	Individuals or herd
CLIMATE/TERRAIN:	Temperate to sub-tropical wilderness

YIELD

MEDICINAL:	nil
SPELL COMPONENTS:	lungs[1]
HIDE/TROPHY:	head is a valuable trophy (up to 250 sp)
TREASURE:	nil
EDIBLE:	yes, although the internal organs should be avoided, particularly the lungs which are poisonous[2]
OTHER:	nil
EXPERIENCE POINT VALUE:	1400

GOUGER

Also Known As: Bloody Biter, Marabok, Vipago

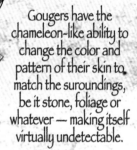

We call 'em gougers, for the ravenous beasts are well equipped to gouge a man's flesh. Seen it happen many a time. Ya have to be careful when explorin' territory known to harbor these creatures for they live up in the trees and are difficult to spot. Very good at blendin' in with the foliage. Personally, I encountered 'em down in the swamps south of Bet Kalamar. We was trackin' down some bandits and out a nowhere this snake lookin' thing darts outta a tree and grabs a hold a of one a my fellow vigilantes. Wrapped its claws tight around 'im and wouldn't let go. The poor feller couldn't do nuthin' but scream fer help, seein' as his arms were bound tight by the thing's coils. Durned if the thing didn't lift him right off the ground and begin gnawing at him straightaway without battin' one of its creepy eyes.

Now we was at quite a disadvantage comin' to his aid as he was just danglin' outta that tree. I was of no use at all seein' as my blade was too short to be any good. Lucky one a us had a halberd and was able ta poke at the gouger even though he was a squirmin' way up high. One good hit tore out its belly and it dropped outta that tree along with our buddy afore he got all ate up. Shook us up good though, and we were a right bit more careful 'bout wanderin' too close to any more big trees fer the rest of the day. - ⚨

Gougers have the chameleon-like ability to change the color and pattern of their skin to match the suroundings, be it stone, foliage or whatever — making itself virtually undetectable.

Gougers are ambush predators of reptilian origin. They have frog-like heads, a thick serpentine torso and a barbed tail. This prehensile tail is adapted so the gouger can anchor itself to a tree or other vertical surface and lower itself onto enemies. Its forearms have unusually long, sharp talons used to grasp and dismember prey. The gouger's hide is scaly and dry, usually dark and the same color as the surrounding environment.

Its large eyes are a brilliant fluorescent green, yellow or orange. The gouger's main sensory device, however, is the thermosensory pits that remsemble two small nostrils. These allow the gouger to sense radiant heat (or the lack of it) in warm- or cold-blooded creatures. These pits have such an incredible degree of accuracy that even a blind gouger can target an enemy's vulnerable body parts.

Most adult gougers have a body length ranging from 12 to 17 feet and weigh more than 200 pounds.

Combat/Tactics:

Gougers lower themselves from large trees or dark overhangs, then attack. If a gouger successfully attacks with its talons, it has grabbed its quarry and immobilized it. Breaking this hold requires a Feat of Strength (*vs. d20+14*). Once it has secured its prey, the gouger begins to viciously bite it, gaining an additional +6 Attack bonus due to the inability of its captured victim to defend itself. While doing so, it hoists the tasty morsel back into its tree in order to feast undisturbed.

Gougers can change their coloring after being in contact with a surface for 10 to 15 minutes; when complete, this gives them an excellent Hiding skill mastery (90%). Males are particularly bad-tempered during and after mating season, and are 90% likely to attack any creature nearby.

SIGN/TRACKS

The gouger leaves a trail like a giant serpent

Human boot prints

RANGE ON TELLENE

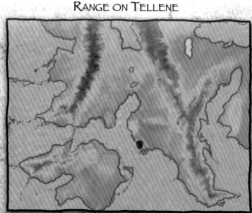

SIZE COMPARISION

6 ft

3 ft

Habitat/Society:

Gougers are carnivores that hunt wherever they nest (e.g., tree branches, cave systems and mineshafts). They prefer tropical climates with little seasonal temperature variations, but can occasionally be found in temperate zones where the winters are mild.

They are mostly solitary, but have been observed to cooperate in pairs while hunting. Typically, one gouger makes itself visible in order to distract or lure the target away, while the second gouger moves to attack from behind or raid the creature's nest or temporarily abandoned provisions.

The rainy season is the gouger's mating season. Female gougers clack their talons together loudly to attract the males, often attracting more than one simultaneously. When this occurs, the males fight until one is victorious. The male then arouses the female by slowly and continuously scratching her with his talons, inducing her to mate. Females are oviparous and lay three to six oblong eggs with a leathery shell, which they carry inside a flesh pouch until they hatch. During this time (two to three weeks), male gougers bring their mates food, while the female hides and incubates the eggs. Gouger hatchlings stay with their mothers for at least a full season, then disperse to find their own territories. If they do not fall to other predators, the young grow rapidly. They reach sexual maturity in their first few years, after which their rate of growth continues at a slower pace.

A typical gouger has a lifespan of 15 to 20 years.

Ecology:

Gougers eat a wide variety of prey, including fish, birds, bats, ungulates and other mammals, reptiles and almost anything they can manage to overpower. Except for mating and the time immediately following it, gougers have little interaction with creatures they do not eat. Gougers forage primarily in the twilight and nighttime hours and sleep during the day.

Their natural enemies include any fleshy creature that dares to wander into (or under) their territory, or with whom they compete for food. Of the latter, these typically include such predators as crocodiles, killer apes and big hunting cats. When threatened by these competitors, gougers often wave their distinctive talons in an intimidating manner.

On Tellene:

Legends and fireside stories abound which feature the vicious gouger as a clever and sneaky villain. In areas where gougers have frequently threatened the local population, such as the swamp camps and villages on the western Alubelok Coast, the recounting of a gouger-inspired legend can win the storyteller many new friends (especially if it features the defeat and destruction of the beast).

---

[1] Gouger skin may be used as an alternate material component in the Springing spell. Doing so permits jumps to be 5 feet longer.

[2] A Cooking/Baking check (Difficult) is required to properly prepare gouger liver and other organs. Failure results in mild food poisoning that causes -1 to Attack, Defense and Damge for 2d12 hours, beginning after an onset time of 1d3 hours.

GOUGER

HIT POINTS:	24+2d8
SIZE/WEIGHT:	M/230 lbs.
TENACITY:	Steady
INTELLIGENCE:	Animal, Low
FATIGUE FACTOR:	0

SPEED 10* · ATTACK +6* · INIT -1 · DMG REDUCTION · DEFENSE +4 · see below · 2 · long REACH · DAMAGE · TOP SAVE 6

MOVEMENT

CRAWL:	1¼
WALK:	2½
JOG:	5
RUN:	10
SPRINT:	15

SAVES

PHYSICAL:	+4
MENTAL:	+3
DODGE:	+6

ATTACK: Gougers make an initial attack from a concealed position in order to grab prey with their talons (4d6p); once they capture a person, they hold him fast (requiring a Feat of Strength vs. d20+14 to break free) and gnaws away (with an additional +6 bonus [total 12] every 6 seconds and inflicts 2d6p damage); victims held fast may only roll d8p for defense

SPECIAL ABILITIES:
Hiding skill mastery 90%

GENERAL INFO

ACTIVITY CYCLE:	Nocturnal
NO. APPEARING:	1
% CHANCE IN LAIR:	100%
FREQUENCY:	Infrequent
ALIGNMENT:	Non
VISION TYPE:	Standard and Heat-Detecting
AWARENESS/SENSES:	Standard
HABITAT:	Rainforest, subterranean
DIET:	Carnivorous
ORGANIZATION:	Individuals
CLIMATE/TERRAIN:	Tropical to temperate wilderness

YIELD

MEDICINAL:	nil
SPELL COMPONENTS:	skin, for the Springing spell[1]
HIDE/TROPHY:	gouger talons are popular for fashioning into knives
TREASURE:	incidental
EDIBLE:	yes, although the internal organs should be avoided, particularly the liver which is poisonous[2]
OTHER:	nil

EXPERIENCE POINT VALUE: 240

GREL

Also Known As: Sarlangans, Grunge Elf

A worthy opponent are these Sarlangans. For they are a race that truly embodies the warrior ethos. Unlike the dumb and savage races of orcs and goblins that are no more than vicious bullies gathering strength and courage from sheer numbers, the grel deserve to sit in the hallowed halls of the battle gods.

A race that I hold in such esteem demands the utmost in care, preparation and experience before engaging in battle for such a contest is a true test. You cannot rely solely on sheer brawn to best these opponents for they will not fight on your terms. While an ogre or even a giant can be a fell adversary, they will invariably match strength with strength. Not so the grel.

Combatting the grunge elves is a test of skill. It is, in some ways, like the difference between using a mattock and a rapier. The mattock, when it strikes true, can deliver a devastating blow. But once committed to a course of action, it is nigh impossible to react to a changing situation. The rapier however may, in the hands of a skilled swordsman, be employed to execute feints within feints so as to deceive an adversary into employing seemingly prudent but ultimately disastrous tactics.

Beware your initial encounter with these crafty foes for it is likely you are being probed to learn of your likely course of action. It is a game of bluff and revealing your hand may prove most costly in the long run. In these initial gambits, alter your strategy. Hold back your strength and let less seasoned warriors take the lead. Above all, do not permit yourself to be angered or fall prey to impetuous responses for in so doing you foreshadow your doom. ~ S

The Sarlangans, more colloquially known as Grel (or derogatorily, Grunge Elves), forever lurk in the minds of those who live within their reach. They are the antithesis of civilization — they are destroyers. They are a warrior race instilled with a deep sense of wanderlust that constantly brings them into contact with new enemies and new conflicts. The grel were born to fight, yet refuse to fight *en masse* or adopt the military disciplines in which their elven cousins have proven so adept. The grel prefer the elements of fear, surprise and evil cunning rather than careful planning and steadfastness when it comes to the art of war. It comes naturally to them and great armies dread any prospect that involves fighting these proud warriors.

Long before recorded human history, when the great elven commonwealths presided over the civilized areas of Tellene (although the dwarven and gnomish clans disagree on this last point as certainly do the orcs, goblins and hobgoblins), a great elvish civil war took place. The dispute centered upon the type of governance they sought with regard to other intelligent races. On one side stood those advocating shepherding the other races so that all might live in peace and harmony with

SIGN/TRACKS	RANGE ON TELLENE	SIZE COMPARISON

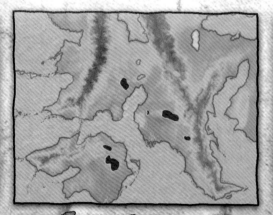

Grel are difficult to track as they often obscure signs of their passage.

6 ft

3 ft

one another, each in time perfecting the arts and studying the cosmos as they saw fit. The opposing side desired to dominate and enslave all other races; 'the elves are superior in all ways, so the others should rightfully serve us' was the logic. No one knows how long the conflict raged for specific details have blurred into legend. That even the elves have forgotten bespeaks of an era at the dawn of the world (although this obscurity may be a feigned affectation, as such a divisive fraternal conflict runs contrary to the carefully managed image that elves portray to outsiders).

The conflict itself was exceedingly bloody with terrible casualties sustained on both sides. Unmentionable atrocities were indiscriminately perpetrated on all participants, including the other races frequently used as proxies. Legend tells that the Creator made man in her image and elevated him as the heir to Tellene as punishment to the elves, Her formerly cherished race. In any event, the end result was the severance of supreme elvish power for their numbers were too denuded to control more than deep sylvan areas of the world. The evil elves were defeated in this epic conflict and the victors mercilessly hunted down the survivors.

At this point a schism tore apart the once united evil elves. One faction fled into caves and hid far below Tellene's surface, never to see the light of day. These evolved into the dark elves or drow. Those that chose to continue the fight by other means remained on the surface but scattered to the deepest wilderness, eventually becoming the grunge elves of today. The grel never forgave the drow for accepting defeat and to this very day a bitter enmity exists between these two rival elven strains.

Banished from their tranquil homelands and deprived of numbers and resources, the grel developed their own peculiar brand of warfare. As the years passed their battle skills were honed and their character and bodies toughened. Master Tunik El Thek once wrote, "... in a fair fight, a hundred grel against a legion of well trained, well armed human warriors would probably be an even match. But," he adds, "if I were betting on such a match my coin would be on the grel because they NEVER fight fair."

Grel put the dark elves to shame, and many consider them one of the greatest threats to the civilized world. The elves have gone to war with them on numerous occasions with an eye toward eradicating this painful legacy. The grel have always bounced back, even in the face of such determined opposition. They seem to revel in the fact that the entire world is against them. Perhaps this explains why they admire bravery in their enemies, especially when faced with overwhelming odds. Indeed, Grel warriors have been known to spare the lives of such audacious individuals. They are a fearsome warlike race that derives great pleasure from preying upon the weak. They follow the Way of the Berserk most often due in no small part to the warlike teachings of the Brothers in Blood. The Thunderer's temple also has a large following amongst warbands as does the House of Knives. The latter

GREL

HIT POINTS:	28+2d10
SIZE/WEIGHT:	M/120 lbs.
TENACITY:	Fearless
INTELLIGENCE:	Average
FATIGUE FACTOR:	-2/-1

MOVEMENT

CRAWL:	2 ½
WALK:	5
JOG:	10
RUN:	15
SPRINT:	20

SAVES

PHYSICAL:	+5
MENTAL:	+3
DODGE:	+5

ATTACK: Grel usually attack from ambush often employing traps or snares to initiate combat. They employ standard weaponry gaining a +2 bonus to speed and damage. Grel use missile liberally throwing hand axes as they approach and having dedicated bowmen. Though fearless, they will disengage from battles they clearly cannot win preferring to regroup and attacking again in more favorable circumstances.

SPECIAL DEFENSES: Shield use (small: +4 Defense); +65% bonus to Sneaking and Hiding skill checks; unarmored DR 0

G

GENERAL INFO

ACTIVITY CYCLE:	Diurnal
NO. APPEARING:	d8p (traveling); 3d4p+8 (band); 30d12p (clan)[1]
% CHANCE IN LAIR:	25%
FREQUENCY:	Sporadic
ALIGNMENT:	Chaotic Evil
VISION TYPE:	Standard
AWARENESS/SENSES:	Observation & Listening +25%
HABITAT:	Woodlands[2]
DIET:	Omnivorous
ORGANIZATION:	Tribal, the strongest rule the weaker
CLIMATE/TERRAIN:	Temperate to tropical[3]

YIELD

MEDICINAL:	nil
SPELL COMPONENTS:	brain matter, to brew a Potion of Courage
HIDE/TROPHY:	nil
TREASURE:	2d4p sp each[4]
EDIBLE:	grel flesh is edible, but gamey
OTHER:	nil
EXPERIENCE POINT VALUE:	140

may account for so much of grel religious activity tending toward darkness and focused upon vengeance. Purger shamans teach of the potential destruction of the grel race at the hands of their enemies and therefore fight other races for "preemptive vengence." Most other religions with a neutral, chaotic or evil bent also have minor adherents amongst the grel.

A prominent danger when encountering the grel is their penchant for enslaving those who possess the skills or knowledge they need. It is estimated that most grel war bands are comprised of 30% slaves. Surprisingly, grel treat their slaves well — as long as they contribute to the livelihood of the band. Orc slave-fighters are highly prized by the grel because the brutes are such spirited combatants as long as food is plentiful and they receive a share of any war booty.

Sarlangans value warriors above all other professions and even not fighter-class grel will master a combat talent or two. A hunter-driven society, all grel excel in the arts associated with hunting game of all types, including sentient (one free mastery roll in each Observation, Listening, Sneaking and Tracking as well as an improved initiative die of one type). Further, brush, thickets and undergrowth in the natural hunting grounds (or any lands in which a grel has hunted for a season) do not slow a Sarlangan (count such terrain as simply open terrain for movement purposes).

When preparing for war, hunting or a skirmish of some sort, grel prefer non-metal armors, with studded leather about as heavy as they might employ, although leader-types can be armored even to the point of chainmail, especially if the clan has recently raided enemies rich in arms and armor. Even so, armors heavier than studded are often stowed, used only when the situation dictates certain battle at a set position (such as when raiding a town or community or other static target). The standard grel hit-and-run tactic obviously requires mobility and stealth not afforded by heavy suits of chain or plate. Grel often carry small shields as part of their force, first hurling javelins or hand axes, then later engaging up-close, however, a portion of every fighting force will be shield-less experts in the short-bow. For personal weaponry, Sarlangans prefer spear, short swords, hand-axes and daggers. Leaders, of course, will always have the choicest, best-made weaponry (always picked from the corpse of the defeated enemy or pilfered from overrun enemy locations as grel don't generally bother to waste time smithing).

Grel war parties tend to be a 50/50 split of lightly-armored fighters and hunter-thieves, making the entire band a group of scouts, assassins and infiltrators, especially given their various advantages to initiative, tracking and sneaking. For every 8 grel encountered, one will be a leader with maximum hit points. For every 20 grel encountered, there will be one fifth to eighth level (d4+4) fighter plus 0-2 thieves or assassins (d3-1, 50% of each). For every 100 grel there will be an additional warrior of 8th-11th level (d4+7) to lead the group. If 150 or more are encountered there will be those numbers plus a major leader (fighter) of level 12th to 17th level (d6+11) and an extra 2d4p fighter/thieves of 2d6p levels each. Very superstitious, every grunge elf community will have d4 clerics of levels 1-10 (d10). Mages are quite rare with only a 1% chance of per clan, with their levels being anywhere from 1st to 11th or higher (2d6p-1).

Most scholars believe that the reason the grel are now a distinct race with a far shorter life expectancy than elves (in the rare instance that one survives to geriatricy) is due to interbreeding with their slaves. To replenish their numbers and improve their robustness, the grel have bred with any favorable specimen. Unlike elves and drow, they can even breed with orcs, a fact that supports the scientific assertion that they interbred with humans and hobgoblins, sufficiently diluting their elven blood to eventually facilitate these unions. The result has been hardier and taller race (although Sarlangans claim their greater stature compared to the other elven races is a measure of their greater honor), but one less attuned to nature and magic.

Owing to their interbreeding, the typical Sarlangan specimen commands a more imposing physical musculature than his elvish cousins. More on-par with humans in this regard, grel suffer no penalty to their Strength. While still nimble, they have lost some of their cousin's natural agility gaining a +1 to Dexterity (rather than a +2). Further, they lack some the native elven defensive bonus, instead gaining a greater heartiness, also on par with humans both in hit points and Constitution. Grel are also generally stouter in battle, suffering knock-backs as humans. All combined, this makes the athletic grel great natural combatants. The trade-off to this physical prowess has been a corresponding loss of mental acuity. Likely, the societal lack of emphasis on intellectual pursuits coupled with mating with cerebrally inferior races created this permanent loss of intelligence (-1 Intelligence and a -1 mastery die modifier for all skills involving intelligence). Due to a lack of a formal educational program, all grel suffer a -2 mastery die modifier for all skills where int is the only attribute. Finally, a combination of living like animals in the wilds, a disdain for all things of beauty and said breeding practices have not only diminished the natural elvish attractiveness, but make for a fairly ugly creature (-1 Looks).

Society:

The grel are a nomadic race that follows the migratory patterns of various game animals. They are despised by settled races for their penchant of over-hunting and depleting food and resources before moving on but are truly feared for their raider culture. The grel routinely assail and loot settlements as they range over Tellene. Grel revel in completely overrunning a small village, killing or enslaving its inhabitants and then spending several weeks (or even months) living off any resources and food stores the town can provide. Once the grel have depleted a town of its resources, they will torch the community and move on.

This predatory lifestyle is contingent on a weak and docile populace upon which to prey. Accordingly, they are almost never found in civilized human or demi-human lands where a central authority can mount an active counter to their depredations. Grel have no interest in holding territory and would rather move on in search of easier victims than waste their resources battling a determined foe.

To a grel, Honor is paramount and most of their life revolves around assiduously improving one's Honor (or at least maintaining it). They are supremely egotistical and always desirous of making an impression on others. This explains much of otherwise enigmatic grel behavior. Warriors have been known to turn their back on a capable, armed enemy as a show of disrespect as well as to demonstrate in the boldest manner their own fearlessness. Tunik El Thek advises, "If a grel turns his back to you, strike the bastard down where he stands or you'll soon regret not taking advantage of the situation."

Despite their hardiness, Grel despise the cold and can't abide it, though they will steadfastly insist that the paucity of game is the true reason behind their avoidance of colder climates. Either way, their warbands are only encountered in temperate to tropical zones and lowlands, although in summer they can sometimes be found as far north as northern Cosdol, Shadesh Bay or Lake Jorakk.

Grel have their own language, Sarlangan, a derivative of elvish that has morphed over the centuries as it absorbed taints from enslaved groups and nearby cultures and also suffered at the hands of multiple generations (unlike elven which enjoys the stewardship that the elvish lifespan provides). Many grunge elves also learn to speak orcish, the language of their most common slaves and natural competitors. Shamans or other more educated grel may also take the time to master a local human language, low elvish or a smattering of drow.

Grel have an average lifespan probably twice as long as humans, perhaps even longer. Their way of living and constant exposure to violence, however, makes any guess as to lifespan difficult; any grel with honor will die with it before succumbing to age and frailty. Females, comprise only about 35% of the population, although the birth rate is 51% in their favor over males due to the prevalent abandonment of the weaker race at birth or shortly thereafter due to social stigma related to siring the weaker sex. In any event, females surviving to sexual maturity and procreating, gestate in about 14 months. Those not with child or rearing young (once weaned to solid food, they're generally left to their own devices and survival), make weapons or assist the hunt. Those gifted enough to compete with the men physically (about 20%), join the tribe as full warriors and are only subjected to bigotry to the extent they cannot defend themselves violently, thus gaining respect of the braves. Males are larger than females, but not overly so, roughly 3-inches taller and 20-30 pounds heavier.

Grel cherish children only as a means to increase their numbers for warfare and hunting. Their offspring learn to fight and track at an early age, fending for themselves far before puberty and both sexes undergoing brutal coming-of-age rituals when reaching maturity. Roughly 25% of any Grel tribe will be helpless runts, another 25% adolescents (fight as goblins).

The non-combatants run freely throughout the community, fighting (sometimes lethally) for scraps while the older ones make weaponry, cook food, build fortifications and train to become warriors and hunters.

Tactics:

Grel wear disruptive camouflage over their armor and shields that allows them to blend into wooded environments even better than their elven kin (65% bonus to Hiding and Sneaking skills in woodlands). They carry throwing axes and spears for hunting, and knives for skinning and cleaning animals. While clearly elven in feature, they adopt a fearsome visage, often sporting mohawks and displaying many horrific tattoos.

Grel are masters of irregular warfare and, given sufficient time, can prepare elaborate ambushes. They use covered pit traps and punji stakes to impede an enemy's forward or flanking movement, while hurling axes into their enemies' midst from concealed locations. A swinging log trap is often the harbinger of such an ambush. When the grel reveal themselves, it is with their fierce Angawa Battle Cry that forces anyone hearing it to make an immediate morale check.

Tattoo Magic:

Grel love the flesh of pixie fairies. Although they consider it a delicacy in its own right, the fact that it's brimming with magical energies is the underlying reason for their avaricious pursuit of this meat. The consumption of pixie fairies allows grel to assimilate faerikin tattoo magic. Any grel who consumes a pixie fairy can add one pixie fairy tattoo type (see pixie fairies) and reap the magical benefits of that tattoo. Only one tattoo from any particular pixie fairy devoured may be incorporated into the host grel's corporeal being. The penalties and drawbacks of such a tattoo are the same as those imposed on the pixie fairy.

[1] **No. Appearing:** d8p (traveling, hunting); 3d4p+8 (warband); 30d12p (clan)

[2] **Habitat:** Grel live in woodlands or temporarily in villages of the conquered

[3] **Climate/Terrain:** Grel despise the cold and suffer the following penalties in chilly weather:
- a -1/5% penalty to all rolls/checks when the temperature is below 50° F.
- a -2/10% penalty to all rolls/checks when the temperature is below 32° F.
- save at a -4 against Cold-related spells and effects
- suffer an extra 10% damage (rounded up) from cold related spells and effects

[4] **Treasure:** Grel carry 2d4p sp each. Grel lairs can contain vast amounts of copper, silver and trade coins as well as gems, potions and other magic items. Leaders will employ superior quality arms.

GREVAN

Also Known As: Gretan, Sar-Grevan, Har'Korri

The grevans have a term for war — "Furvann-mass", the Great Dragon. Grevans believe that war, and the many battles that comprise it, is a living creature, a great writhing god, sorting out the worthy from the unworthy like pebbles from the miner's sieve. Only through the blood-letting of fierce combat can a grevan warrior ever truly enter into fellowship with the gods and earn their favor. In this way he makes known his name to the Farr Makki — "fellowship of the departed" — ancestors who fell with honor in battles past.

Such a concept is alien to the grevan warrior's counterpart — the typical Kalamaran soldier. The legionnaire sees combat only as the means to push forth the glory of the Empire and to enforce its will. If victory is elusive and cannot be achieved, pushing the fight is a pointless endeavor. The Kalamaran would prefer to withdraw, hold his ground until an advantage presents itself or, barring that, can be engineered. It is victory, above all else that motivates the Kalamaran soldier. Although he will fight bravely, to the death if need be, he does not relish dying, nor does he drive himself toward it blindly as the grevan so often does.

In contrast, grevans do not entertain the notion of victory or defeat with such weighty regard. Grevan warlords hold council to discuss the best strategy and course of action, but the battle itself is joined solely to demonstrate the grevans' willingness — nay, his unshakable, burning desire — to embrace the Great Dragon. In the mother city of Bet Kalamar on the slopes of Savan Hill, there is a temple to the "Unknown God of Peace". It is an expression of Kalamaran hope that someday the 'nameless god' will be unveiled and she will make herself known. A hope that the countless enemies of the Empire will be quelled and in their place peace will spring eternal. To the grevans? Peace is intolerable — a weak form of death. An old grevan proverb sums it up best, "He without enemies is lost. The gods will not remember his name. It is a far better fate to look into the eyes of a foe even as he strikes you down than to grow weak by the counting of days. It is better that the whole world is set against you." - ⵎ

The history and origin of the Grevan-speaking tribes has been a subject of intense debate among historians. Standing roughly 9 feet tall, powerful and warlike, grevans strike fear in the heart of those unfortunate enough to find themselves in their path and sorrow for those unfortunates caught in their wake. Grevan height and strength (as well as the prevalence of ogres and orcs near the earliest known grevan communities) indicates the likelihood that these latter creatures form part of the grevan bloodline. However, their fluidity, intelligence, lithely build and more pleasing facial features, suggest some possible elvish blood, while their hirsute appearance, muscular structure and adaptability hint at human intermingling, with certain aspects strongly pointing to Fhokki stock. To anyone who has studied the grevans, with their culture of wandering and raiding their neighbors, it appears likely that a combination of these races blended over time to form what is now the prototypical grevan.

Although the territories of the Wild Lands felt the impact of grevan aggression for generations before the arrival of Kalamaran Emperor Kolokar, only during his reign (which began in the year 73 Imperial Reckoning; (-71 in the Fhokki Calendar)) did the grevans appear along the far northern frontier. Beforehand, the borderlands

SIGN/TRACKS

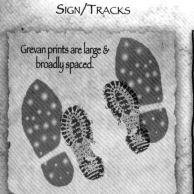

Grevan prints are large & broadly spaced.

RANGE ON TELLENE

SIZE COMPARISON

10 ft

5 ft

had been overrun for years by waves of various other races – most of whom had been displaced from their own lands by other groups who had themselves been displaced by grevan incursions. Fhokki and Dejy tribes, in particular, found themselves fighting uprooted humanoid hordes for generations – before ever encountering the grevans firsthand. In fact, some tales say it was the grevans themselves that halted Imperial advances beyond the Byth and Kakidela Mountains, prompting Kolokar to begin construction on his famous wall.

Most of what we know about the grevans today is through the writings of the Kalamaran military historian, Eradin Rilis, one of the few writers on the subject who had intimate first-hand knowledge of the race. Eradin was serving as a battle-physician for the garrison manning Kolokar's Barrier (a great stone wall stretching from the Kakidelas to the Byth Mountains) when it was overrun and sacked by grevans. Taken prisoner and enslaved, Eradin spent eight years in captivity on the Grevan Steppes. Learning the language and much about grevan culture before eventually escaping, he has written at length about his experiences among his captors. While many suspect him of embellishing his tale, he is widely regarded as the foremost authority on grevans.

According to their own oral tradition, writes Eradin, the grevans passed through 'the Forge of the Gods' before moving into the northern wastes and eventually making their way south into what some call 'the Barrens' (also north of Lake Jorakk), a sojourn that took several generations.

Although the Forge is considered by many to be a mythical setting, it is in fact a real, inhospitable icy region marked by enormous mountains, glaciers and even active volcanoes. This, of course, suggests the grevans passed over the top of the world from the other hemisphere (though even the most learned sage does not know the shape of the world or anything about these unknown lands save myth and legend). If true, it says even more about their sturdiness as a race than do their military exploits.

Other historians believe the grevans always lived on the fringes of civilization in the far northern lands and were simply prodded into migrating south as the result of famine or plague, and only later by the sheer momentum of their conquests and amazing prowess in battle.

Eradin writes that the grevans arrived in the Barrens as part of one mass exodus from the north hundreds of years ago under the guiding hand of a venerable matriarch named Varuna. As they began their drive south, they mercilessly overran many tribes of orcs, goblins and dwarves in the Deshada Mountains, forcing those races to hide within. Moving east, they swept through the lands of Torakk and then swarmed over the Jorakk Mountains in a similar manner, crushing all in their path, driving tribes of orcs, ogres and other humanoids east and south. "It was as though they [the grevans] were a great broom and the gods were sweeping the land clean with broad strokes," reported Eradin.

No one can be sure, but what is known is that the grevans were relative newcomers to the steppes, and that they rapidly changed many creatures' ranges and territories as they displaced whole populations. As the grevans advanced through the Barrens, many who stood in their way chose to flee (based on the grevans' reputation alone), creating a domino effect that stretched from the lands north of Lake Jorakk to the edges of the Khydoban, as each group displaced another. Those who chose to stand and fight were inevitably killed or enslaved.

GREVAN

HIT POINTS:	35+4d8
SIZE/WEIGHT:	H/675 lbs.
TENACITY:	Fearless
INTELLIGENCE:	Average
FATIGUE FACTOR:	-7/-6

Combat diagram:
SPEED 7 / INIT -1 / ATTACK +8 / DMG REDUCTION / DEFENSE +3 / 7 / DAMAGE by weapon +6 / medium REACH / 8 / TOP SAVE

MOVEMENT

CRAWL:	5
WALK:	10
JOG:	15
RUN:	20
SPRINT:	25

SAVES

PHYSICAL:	+9
MENTAL:	+8
DODGE:	+10

ATTACK:
Grevans use a variety of melee and ranged weapons.

SPECIAL DEFENSES:
Shield use (e.g., medium shields improve Def to +9 and increase DR).
Grevans have an unarmored DR of 2.

GENERAL INFO

ACTIVITY CYCLE:	Diurnal
NO. APPEARING:	3-12 (hunting party), 20-100 (settlement)
% CHANCE IN LAIR:	20%
FREQUENCY:	Sporadic
ALIGNMENT:	Neutral Evil
VISION TYPE:	Standard
AWARENESS/SENSES:	Standard
HABITAT:	Any
DIET:	Omnivorous
ORGANIZATION:	Individuals or clan
CLIMATE/TERRAIN:	Arctic to temperate wilderness

YIELD

MEDICINAL:	nil
SPELL COMPONENTS:	nil
HIDE/TROPHY:	heads[1]
TREASURE:	raiding plunder (often extensive)
EDIBLE:	yes
OTHER:	nil

EXPERIENCE POINT VALUE: 500

The Great Departing

The migration took many years and followed a pattern that would repeat itself again and again. The grevans would advance, then settle down in a newly conquered area (sometimes for a generation or more) and then inexplicably abandon the region and return north. For reasons unknown, as the grevans reached the center of the lands of Torakk, they split into three major migratory groups. These groups would become known as the Sar-Grevans, the Gretans and the Har'Korri.

According to Eradin, the grevans refer to this split as the 'Wurda-Meer' or 'the Great Departing.' Whether the split was by design or by chance as the grevan horde advanced and was pulled in different directions is unknown. However, it is apparent that the grevans themselves consider the split to have been an event of enormous importance, suggesting a conscious decision to part ways.

The sage Greytar concludes that the wandering tribes had grown to such great numbers as they crossed the Barrens that the sparse landscape could no longer sustain them making the splitting a calculated choice. Others propose that infighting among the tribes had become so problematic by this time that there was no other way to resolve their differences. Regardless of the reason for the parting, separated by time and distance, each group eventually became distinct from the others as each encountered new cultures and races, took on new philosophies and intermarried with those they had subjugated.

The *Sar-Grevans* gradually made their way west to the shores of Shadesh Bay, where they became embroiled in a bitter war against the elves and grel. Today, their culture reflects the mixing of those races. Several Sar-Grevan tribes are now said to be seafaring and have been reported as far west as the northern shores of Cosdol.

The second group, the *Gretan* tribes, migrated into the wilds of the Young Kingdoms. Already heavily influenced by the numerous human barbarian populations they encountered and absorbed into their bloodline, by the time of Brandobian occupation and the reign of Kruk-ma-Kali, the Gretans had almost completely disappeared. No one knows where the lost tribes went or why, but the majority opinion among scholars is that they splintered into family units and were simply assimilated into the various Dejy, Brandobian, Hobgoblin and later Kalamaran cultures. Today, what appear to be Gretan clans can sometimes be encountered in the hinterlands of the various Young Kingdom nations, but the once-mighty Gretan nation seems to be gone for good.

The third group, who refer to themselves as the *Har'Korri* ('true bloods'), is the group most commonly associated with the term 'grevan' today. This is for good reason, for they regard themselves as the only true grevans.

The Way of the Grevan

For several generations after the Great Departing, grevan culture became increasingly diluted as the conquerors moved about the Wild Lands. Each new victory brought change to the tribes, for it was common practice for warriors to choose wives from those whom they had enslaved. These wives reared and taught the children – both grevan and those of mixed blood – and brought their own interpretations of their faiths, as well as their own ways, to the hearth in the family lodge.

Further threatening the grevan way of life was the fact that their multitude of clans became increasingly fragmented as they migrated, feuding and openly warring against one another, with whole clans butchered at the hands of their neighbors. Had fate not intervened, the Har'Korri may well have suffered the same fate as the Gretans and faded into the tapestry of those they had vanquished, losing their identities completely.

In 311 F.C., a spiritual and cultural revival of sorts took place among the Har'Korri. In that year (according to Eradin), three grevan matriarchs became 'Mar'Klem' (or, 'touched with madness by the hand of the gods') and began prophesying and advocating a return to Grevus Fuun (which roughly translates to the 'Way of the Grevan' or the 'Old Way'). Although they were not actually siblings and came from different clans, the matriarchs came to be known as the Three Sisters or simply 'the Sisters.' Each represented aspects of a different god (The Battle Rager, The Unseen One and The Creator of Strife, respectively).

The Sisters called for the Har'Korri to strictly adhere to the ancient grevan laws. They called for purging their lodges of foreign ideas and embracing the Grevus Fuun. Inter-marriage outside the bloodline was offensive and those born of mixed-blood should be banished or killed outright. Nothing short of keeping the grevan bloodline 'pure' was acceptable. The message they brought stirred the grevan heart for many Har'Korri, and a movement of reawakening swept the tribes as grevans turned back to their true heritage. Many, however, were resistant to such reforms and the divisiveness among the clans increased. Eradin claims the Har-Korri refer to this period of time (which spanned an entire generation) as the 'The Honing of the Blade' – a thinning of the ranks mandated by the Sisters as the grevan bloodline was purified and 'tempered'.

Decades later, around 369 F.C., a band of Har-Korri under the instructions of the Sisters uncovered the ruins of an ancient monastic mountain retreat. Among the ruins, the band found a fragment of an ancient artifact that had once been a stone tablet. After acquiring the fragment, which they called Nangrus, the Har'Korri fought bitterly amongst themselves for decades. This fighting continued to the point where they were so weakened and fragmented that the local orcs and ogres thrived and often raided grevan homesteads.

Countless chieftains attempted to re-unify the Har'Korri under their control and seize possession of Nangrus — but old grudges ran deep and the thirst for vengeance rendered such attempts futile. It wasn't until the rise of Rangtaw, a warlord whose successes in battle had made him a living legend who fulfilled a mysterious prophecy and united the Har'Korri once again.

The Grevans Today

As a relatively new enemy to the Sovereign Lands, understanding a grevan is a difficult challenge for those who find themselves in the path of one. Grevans are unlike anything most people have ever faced – a warrior race that inexplicably attacks targets with no apparent strategic value while bypassing those that do have worth, even when they could easily take them. They are an enemy who attacks with great determination and resources to push in one direction and then suddenly shifts and advances in another direction. Furthermore, grevans seem to view diplomacy solely as a tool to deceive or to stall, and are a race that seems incapable of compromise.

Greatly feared, the true nature of the grevan has been cloaked by misperception and wildly imaginative folk tales — tales fueled by the grevans' wanton destruction and passion for aggression. Among the Drhokker, for example, it is widely believed that the grevans are cannibals. The Paruvians teach that the grevans are 'demon-spawn' sent by the gods as retribution against a kingdom that has lost its direction. Understanding the grevans is further frustrated by the fact that, as we've seen, not all grevans are woven from the same tapestry.

Although grevans love to inspire fear, and even encourage such tales, the truth is that such notions are not entirely accurate. Grevans are not cannibals (although they have been known to eat the heart of a fallen enemy) and their unquenchable thirst for conquest is not driven by the mere desire to expand borders and hold ground. Grevans thrive on war; if there are no worthy enemies to be found they will set out to look for new ones. This fact only partially explains the grevans' baffling behavior.

Nangrus, a magical stone fragment of an ancient artifact, has as much or more to do with the race's overall behavior than their own nature. Nangrus has powers that largely relate to war and the furthering of one's influence on others. Nangrus can sense the gathering of armies hundreds of miles away and detect the plotting of minds bent on doing harm to the grevans. It can strengthen armies and demoralize enemy troops. Matriarch Sheehaab is the last in a long line of grevan matriarchs who bonded with the fragment, and it is through her that the stone's powers manifest.

The grevans are always on the move because they are driven and prodded; they are constantly looking to destroy those about them while seeking the kindred fragments of Nangrus (one is rumored to be in the possession of Pekal's College of Wizardry) to increase their power. It is this aspect of the grevans' nature that their enemies simply don't and can't comprehend. Because of Nangrus, the grevans can never accept peace, and Nangrus is why they'll always be on the move and unpredictable.

Now united under the guiding hand of Nangrus, the voice of Matriarch Sheehaab and the fist of Rangtaw, the grevan masses are poised to flood out of the Jorakks and invade the southern lands.

Combat/Tactics:

A grevan war band attacks aggressively. Generally, they fire crossbows or hurl axes, knives or javelins, then close in for personal combat. They show no fear, fighting to the death even against overwhelming odds, unless commanded otherwise by a respected leader. Grevans can employ shields but are as likely to use one as not. Typical grevan weaponry runs the gantlet, although axes, clubs, warhammers, spears, bows and morning stars are most prevalent due to a general lack of skilled smiths among their populace. Swords and other higher order weapons taken from fallen foes round out their arsenal.

Habitat/Society:

Grevans prefer cooler climes, and can survive (even thrive) in sub-arctic areas. Organized into a clannish-family structure and living in large wooden or earthen lodges, grevans have no formal governing body. By far the optimal blend of size, strength, stamina and intelligence, a lack of organization (and the natural associated in-fighting) coupled with an extremely long and mostly unsuccessful birth rate has served to keep these physically superb specimens from dominating the civilized nations.

Grevans have a long life span, on average living just shy of 200 years (although grevans rarely die at a venerable age). Their gestation period is almost two full years (22 months), though females view motherhood as a nuisance; they prefer to follow the way of the warrior. While a full foot shorter than their male counterparts, females make up for their lack of stature in toughness, even to the extent of cutting off or burning out one breast to prove they can wield a bow or spear as well as a male.

Religion:

Grevans follow their three main gods, the Battle Rager, the Unseen One and the Creator of Strife. The Har'Korri believe these gods are theirs and theirs alone. The most popular has always been the Battle Rager's 'Way of the Berserk' due in no small part to the warlike teachings of his clerics, the Brothers in Blood.

On Tellene:

Small groups of grevans (of **Gretan** stock) can be found in any of the northern mountain ranges (the Deshada and Byth Mountains as well as the Legasa Peaks) and a few even appear as far south as Norga-Krangrel as well as amongst the Dejy tribes of Ek'Gakel.

Sar-Grevans can still be found in numbers on the eastern coast of Shadesh Bay, in the Brindonwood and even the slopes of Slen (as a part of the congregation).

The **Har'Korri** are by far the most influential and numerous. They hail from the Jorakk Mountains. From there they campaign as far south as Thygasha, driving humanoids and Dejy nomads before them like a wind does dry leaves. They sometimes foray west to attack the inhabitants of Torakk or Slen, venture south into Drhokker and down in Thybaj, or even far southwest past Kolokar's Barrier, deep into Paru'Bor.

The latter is no longer a great feat for the grevans since, like the Kalamaran Empire, much of Kolokar's Barrier has fallen into a state of disrepair. Large portions have crumbled or have been knocked down. Sections of the Barrier and the watch towers not controlled by Paru'Bor and O'Par are now controlled by Dejy and Fhokki barbarians. Paru'Bor controls and maintains a northern stretch of the Barrier as best it can, and it has proved invaluable in defending against the frequent skirmishes with Shynabyth, but grevans often find their way over or around it.

Fortunately, the grevan masses never seem to stay long and always return to the Jorakk Mountains. Only a few clans have chosen to stay and these can be found in permanent lodges in the Vrykarr Mountains.

[1] *The display of the heads of slain grevans is sure to win accolades from populations under pressure from these raiders. However, should local grevans learn of this outrage, their vengeance is assured.*

GRIFFYN
Also Known As: Akelone, Galausor

Once, our venture into the Elenons led us to an orc camp, where a hard-fought battle followed by a careful search rewarded us with a cache of silver ore and a crude cart. We were particularly happy to see the latter, since it meant easier transportation for the heavy ore and our wounded and unconscious cleric. Binding our wounds as best we could, we loaded the cart and set off, but our aching bodies made slow progress over the narrow, rocky trail.

After some hours, dusk began to fall and it came time to make camp. While my companions busied themselves about the task, I turned to gaze briefly back at the mountaintops, pondering the dangers through which we had come. It was then that I observed some sort of large bird silhouetted against the clouded sky. It glided down in a grand circular sweep, and I lost it among the shadows of the cliffs. Shrugging, I moved on to search the brush for suitable kindling. I had barely gone a half-dozen yards when I saw my companions suddenly cease their tasks and flee behind the nearest mass of rock. Though seeing no threat, I quickly did the same, immediately querying my allies about their strange behavior. Our mage pointed grimly back at the cart, and then I saw it.

A magnificent creature, like a giant golden eagle with the hindquarters of a powerful lion, was perched atop the cart and peering about like a robin eyeing the ground for worms. It did not seem to have noticed us, and I breathed a sigh of relief; our bruised and bloodied frames were no match for such a creature.

The beast then began a quiet assault upon the small wagon, causing oddly disquieting noises, like the snapping of twigs and the tearing of wet cloth. I could not understand what it was doing, and foolishly feared for a moment that it might build a nest there and leave us hiding betwixt the rocks. Then I turned to see the green faces of my companions and realized… we had left the cleric sleeping inside the cart.

The creature was not nesting. It was feeding. - ☖

This majestic creature combines the hindquarters of a lion with the wings, head and powerful beak of an eagle. Both the males and females of the species have eagle-like forelegs with large, powerful talons and hooked beaks that can easily rip the flesh from their prey. All griffyns possess keen eyesight that aids them in spotting potential prey from a great distance.

This broad-winged raptor has a wide variety of coloration, with shades of brown in dark ochre to light buff and generally lighter under parts being most common. However, griffyn colors can vary from almost pure white to black. Most humans consider golden-tinted griffyns to be the most beautiful and terrifying to behold.

A typical adult griffyn stands about 4 feet tall at the shoulder, with a body length of around 8 feet (not counting its 2 to 3 foot long tufted tail), a wingspan of nearly 20 feet and a weight of 350 to 400 pounds. The female is slightly larger than the male and has elongated cat-like ears on her otherwise aquiline head.

Combat/Tactics:

Griffyns can be quite fierce in combat, swooping down on adversaries with great power and fury. They can inflict 2d4p+4 hp of damage with each of their powerful talons while their massive, hooked beaks can bite for 4d8p hp of damage. They will preferentially attack whatever foe seems easiest to overpower, particularly one that has already been incapacitated.

A griffyn's call is a piercing *peea-ay*, slightly reminiscent of a

SIGN/TRACKS

Fore

Hind

RANGE ON TELLENE

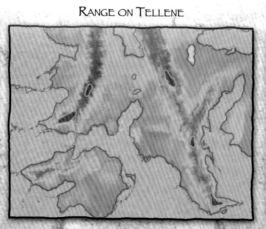

SIZE COMPARISON

8 ft

4 ft

cat's meow. This call may be given in social interactions to warn or attract other griffyns, or when the griffyn tries to scare away a foe. The difference in intent is determined by pitch, though this is rarely distinguishable by any creature that is not a griffyn.

Habitat/Society:

Griffyn breeding range extends from the temperate north to the tropical south, dwelling in large platform nests on cliff edges or, less often, elevated in tree branches sturdy enough to support their weight. They line these nests with feathers and furs from creatures they hunted and devoured, but use only the remnants that generally correspond to the substrate on which the nest sits (to thus aid in camouflaging it from other flying creatures).

Griffyns live alone or in mated pairs, and are extremely territorial. Competing pairs rarely have nests less than 15 miles apart, and often much further. Breeding occurs during the spring (or as late as fall in tropical regions), with a resulting clutch of two to three eggs. The female sits and incubates the eggs at night while the male does so during the day. Due to infertility and natural losses, it is rare for more than one egg to hatch.

Young griffyns fledge within two months after hatching, reach sexual maturity at one year and mate for life, but rarely breed before two to three years of age. A griffyn has an average lifespan of 15 years.

Ecology:

When not incubating eggs, griffyns hunt at dawn and dusk when prey is most active. A griffyn's diet consists mainly of large ungulates such as deer, wild boar, cattle and other domestic livestock, though they are capable of taking down big hunting cats, wolves and even hippos. However, they are scavengers by nature and eat carrion as readily as live prey. A griffyn rarely hunts small animals or birds, but will take an easy kill if the opportunity presents itself. A griffyn can easily consume two pounds of food per minute. The griffyn holds its prey with one talon, holds onto its perch or maintains its balance with the other and then rips away the flesh with its beak.

When griffyn and peryton territories overlap, the two species often come into conflict over food. Perytons will readily appropriate a griffyn's kill in hopes of stealing away the hearts and other internal organs, while the griffyn will steal a peryton's entire kill and even slaughter its fawns when given the chance. Thus, the two species often act aggressively toward one another even when there is no food involved.

On Tellene:

The Yan Elenon Mountains, the southwestern fork of the Elenons, is far less rugged than the connecting mountains and, consequently, are home to a wider variety of creatures. Orcs number in the thousands and their ogre allies claim mastery over the range. In truth, this is hardly the case, and the griffyns here often supplement their diet with orc meat.

[1] Griffyn blood alleviates the effects of the Fear of Heights quirk, helping the sufferer overcome this fear for 10 minutes per dose (1 ounce). The blood takes 2 seconds to take effect. Griffyn blood sells for 30 sp per ounce.

[2] Feathers from a griffyn can be used as an alternate material component in the ninth level Flight spell, increasing the duration by 20 minutes. Feathers sell for 40 sp each.

[3] The talons of a griffyn are valued by some mages for use in staves.

[4] Griffyn eggs and chicks are highly prized and fetch 500 sp or 1000 sp, respectively. During the breeding season, there is a 75% chance a nest contains d3 eggs (half of which will hatch) or one chick.

GRIFFYN

HIT POINTS:	25+7d8
SIZE/WEIGHT:	L/400 lbs.
TENACITY:	Brave
INTELLIGENCE:	Animal, High
FATIGUE FACTOR:	0

SPEED 3 — INIT -2

ATTACK +14

DEFENSE +6 — DMG REDUCTION 7

see below

DAMAGE 6

short REACH — TOP SAVE ▼

MOVEMENT

CRAWL:	2½
WALK:	5
JOG:	10
RUN:	15
FLY:	35

SAVES

PHYSICAL:	+12
MENTAL:	+12
DODGE:	+13

ATTACK:
Griffyns attack with two individual rakes of their avian foreclaws (doing 2d4p+4 points of damage each) and a vicious bite of their hooked bill (the latter inflicting 4d8p damage)

SPECIAL DEFENSES:
Flight

GENERAL INFO

ACTIVITY CYCLE:	Diurnal
NO. APPEARING:	1-2
% CHANCE IN LAIR:	5%
FREQUENCY:	Infrequent
ALIGNMENT:	Non
VISION TYPE:	Farsight
AWARENESS/SENSES:	Standard
HABITAT:	Inaccessible eyries
DIET:	Carnivorous
ORGANIZATION:	Individuals or mated pair
CLIMATE/TERRAIN:	Temperate to tropical woodlands

YIELD

MEDICINAL:	blood, alleviates Fear of Heights[1]
SPELL COMPONENTS:	feathers improve Flight spell duration[2]
HIDE/TROPHY:	talons sell for 200 sp per pair[3]
TREASURE:	incidental
EDIBLE:	yes
OTHER:	eggs sell for up to 500 sp, chicks for up to 1000 sp[4]
EXPERIENCE POINT VALUE:	1075

HAG

Also Known As: Black Annis, Crone, Yaga

If you go to a hag and ask a consultation of her, and if she deigns to place her powers at your disposal, you will certainly get what you came for – but beware the price that you will have to pay.

It was in my younger days, when I knew less of evil and cared little for danger, that I made my way to a lonely swamp hut and up its rope ladder to the open door. Inside, the hag sat in candlelight, in a huge chair, near to the farther wall. Her beaked nose and unkempt head was bent over what I believe was a book of craft, holding ancient and cruel spells that the hag delighted in. An evil vapor floated from the mouth of the potion bottle at her elbow and, circling round her head, half hid her wrinkled face and piercing eyes. A cauldron's fog likewise crept along the folds of her black garments and settled slowly about her feet, veiling them in a yellow mist. There was no doubt in my mind that this was the creature I'd been seeking. There was a certain potion that I desperately wanted, you see, and I'd been told that this hag alone knew the secrets of its brewing.

I was surprised that she priced her services so low, and happily agreed to her request that I take upon myself the simple task of gathering the components and performing certain rites with them. Certainly, I thought, I could gather toadstools and mutter cabalistic words over them if it would keep my coin purse shut. Indeed, the jobs were simple, and I soon returned to her with my prizes. It was then I learned there were more deeds to be done, and these not so easy.

Theft, consorting with imps, desecrating corpses, emboldening a drunken wretch to dance naked in a cemetery, mutilating a child's doll – I did these and worse – bile rising in my gorge with each act. The final deed I won't speak of, but to say that I am frightened of how close I came to succeeding.

The hag cackled at my weakness, chiding and mocking, but I refused to soil my hands further. Then I must pay in gold, she said, and pay well. And pay I did – the last of my small fortune and all that I could borrow from the moneylenders. Woe betide you if you ever make such a deal. –

These hideous creatures resemble old human women with unkempt gray hair, pale wrinkled skin, large eyes, long arms and claw-like hands as hard as iron. Their features are gaunt, the bones seeming to press through the flesh and their appearance is in all ways horrifying. They often dress in blackened leathers and furs, though they prefer the tanned skins of their most recent victims. Hags are exceptionally tall and thin, standing nearly 7 feet tall and weighing around 110 pounds.

Combat/Tactics:

Hags are physically weak and thus prefer to use their arcane spells from a secure distance to frighten or otherwise discourage intruders. In extremis, they can defend themselves with their claw-like hands. Hags have been known to fight with weapons (usually daggers).

A crone may often have an animal companion that doubles as a bodyguard. These can be exotic such as a such as oversized spiders or a mundane dog.

Hags are accomplished mages of at least 9th level and possibly much greater. They utilize spells just as a normal mage would and have spell points commensurate with an equivalently leveled spellcaster. Their choice of spells usually runs toward those that provide information or aid in stealth but this is not guaranteed.

Hags go to great lengths to keep their presence in an area unknown and their lairs secret, but an observant eye and a keen ear can often betray their whereabouts. A child gone missing. Certain herbs from gardens being taken (rootball and all), the discovery of small animals such as birds and rodents with certain organs harvested. Hags are forever gathering the necessary ingredients for their stew.

Size Comparison

6 ft

3 ft

Habitat/Society:

Hags dwell mostly in small mountainside caves or in swamp huts, built upon supports made from the stumps of two or three closely grown trees cut at the height of eight to 10 feet. These stumps, with their spreading roots, sometimes give the impression that the huts have chicken legs.

Hags occasionally make deals with humanoid tribes (such as orcs), allowing them to hunt her prey for her. Hags rarely associate with other hags, however, for all are obsessed with amassing power and cheating death, and with these motivations comes an extremely suspicious nature. Most hag coveys are short-term endeavors cut short by the betrayal of one of the members.

Coveys form most frequently as a matter of necessity. If a hag finds herself living in a place with high populations of other races, it may join forces with other hags as a means of survival. Where one hag is potent, a covey seems unstoppable. Multiple hags, with their physical and mystical abilities, are often able to overwhelm many opponents and use their remains for their evil purposes. However, once a covey dominates a particular area, mistrust and suspicion quickly sets in and the union of hags dissolves.

A hag has a normal lifespan of 200+2d20p years, excluding any excess granted by hag stew. How a hag reproduces is unknown and probably distasteful.

Ecology:

Hags are omnivorous three-teated monsters with a preference for the raw flesh of sapient beings, preferably young children of human and demi-human stock. These victims are also prized for their contributions to the hag's cauldron.

Hag Stew:

By using a corrupt form of alchemy, a hag can use a number of powders, herbs and organic materials to brew a concoction to extend her life even beyond its normal centuries. This stew requires a dozen different types of bloods, varying sizes of bones and organs from different races, and a dead cat soaked in aniseed, among other oddments. Although consuming the stew prolongs the hag's life by 10+d20 years, she becomes addicted to it and spends much of her life hunting for the ingredients to make more.

The stew renders hags infertile and causes their skin to wither, but it does halt the aging process. Drinking this stew proves poisonous to other races (-2 penalty to Attack, Defense and Damage for 12 hours; no effect if save is made, but a 'nat 1' on the saving throw indicates death).

After first consuming her stew, a hag must repeat the process once a month or so. Without it, she begins aging, the process accelerating to account for all the missed years. Hags often bury sealed jars in a secret location as a reserve supply.

On Tellene:

Hags exist throughout Tellene, and seem to have no specific point of origin for the species. Some of the oldest writings still extant claim that hags are the children of succubi and men, while other (slightly more recent) texts say they are a race of fey that turned to evil and associated with devils.

HAG

HIT POINTS:	18+6d8
SIZE/WEIGHT:	M/125 lbs.
TENACITY:	Cowardly
INTELLIGENCE:	Smart
FATIGUE FACTOR:	4

SPEED 7 | INIT -1
ATTACK +4
DMG REDUCTION
DEFENSE +2 | 0
see below
medium REACH | DAMAGE | TOP SAVE 4

ATTACK: Raking with her clawed fingers (one attack using both hands) deals 2d4p+4 points of damage. They are accomplished arcane spellcasters of no less than 9th level.

SPECIAL DEFENSES: Hags can create magical potions, poisoned apples, and elixirs of various (usually baneful) effects; Transmogrify into human female at will.

MOVEMENT

CRAWL:	2½
WALK:	5
JOG:	10
RUN:	15
SPRINT:	20

SAVES

PHYSICAL:	+10
MENTAL:	+12
DODGE:	+7

GENERAL INFO

ACTIVITY CYCLE:	Any
NO. APPEARING:	1-3
% CHANCE IN LAIR:	n/a
FREQUENCY:	Sporadic
ALIGNMENT:	Neutral Evil
VISION TYPE:	Low Light Vision
AWARENESS/SENSES:	Standard
HABITAT:	Caves or huts
DIET:	Omnivorous
ORGANIZATION:	Individuals or Covey
CLIMATE/TERRAIN:	Any, save arctic

YIELD

MEDICINAL:	nil
SPELL COMPONENTS:	hag homes may contain various spell components
HIDE/TROPHY:	nil
TREASURE:	hag homes are replete with potions
EDIBLE:	no
OTHER:	nil
EXPERIENCE POINT VALUE:	675

HALFLING

Also Known As: Longfellow, Amberhair, Harfoot

Rather than try to present a true history of their race, which admittedly would be quite dull since their ancestors never built huge empires or conquered great swathes of land, I shall attempt to jot down my own thoughts on halflings.

They are an insular race, interested only in their own pleasures and caring nothing for the tribulations of big folk outside their own shires. They sit quietly in their homes and busy themselves in their gardens while men fight over territory and battles rage about them as other races war against evil and seek the right to rule themselves as they choose. No, halflings watch history, but do not make history.

Their lands are often well-off, but not rich, and all have to work for a living. Work is light, however. They farm, they fish, they ranch, and they impose no taxes on their own kind, so every halfling has more than enough to eat - which you can easily discern by looking at their stout frames.

The tiny dots of halfling villages are simple places with little merit for visitors of other races, save that they are generally clean and friendly. Small ponds, wonderfully terraced gardens and wooden footbridges abound. Aside from the scenery, however, there is little reason for outsiders to travel here, and such villages are virtually independent from regional authority.

Halflings welcome others to join them in the celebrations, which they have for every stage in their lives, every major event and every passing season. Trade is simple, and you never need to know more than the value of your own wares, because that's all you have to ask for. Halflings are all shrewd judges of an item's value, and will trade you no more than what it is worth. – ⌁

Humans and other big people often mistake halflings for other little folk such as dwarves and gnomes. Anyone with even passing familiarity can easily differentiate between halflings and the other little people as, aside from their height, they bear little resemblance to the other races. Halflings are a little taller than gnomes, at about 3 foot 6 inches to maybe 3 foot 9 inches, but they weigh considerably more, nearing 100 pounds or so. Despite their considerable girth, halflings are weak, carrying their weight more in their ample pot bellies than in musculature, although less sedentary halflings are a bit trimmer and more physically fit. The greatest physical difference, though, is that most halflings are clean-shaven, owing to the fact that very few can grow facial hair of any substantial amount, although some can manage sideburns and the shortest of beards. As far as facial features themselves, halflings look similar to humans; their mouths, noses and eyes bear similar proportional size and shape to those of humans. Halflings have tough, leathery feet, requiring no footwear, even in winter as the tops of their feet also have bushy, thick fur, even on the female of the species.

Halflings take after humans in their choice of vocations as well. They make poor miners, but can learn to be adequate at most professions, including smithing. Where they truly excel is in agriculture and farming, particularly with beats, carrots, potatoes and the like. Halflings also make fine husbandmen and breed all types of animals from rabbits to ponies. They do breed milk cows, but not horses, the

SIGN/TRACKS

RANGE ON TELLENE

SIZE COMPARISON

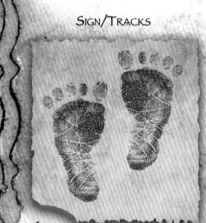

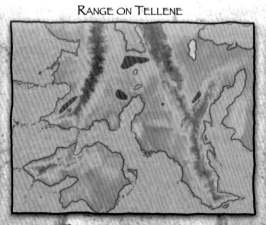

6 ft

3 ft

latter being too large and unruly (and halflings only ride ponies, and greatly prefer traveling by foot at that). Halflings have no love of monetary wealth like their cousins the gnomes and dwarves. That said, they like shiny and beautiful objects and are quite appreciative of polished gems, jewelry, fine woods and other valuables. This appreciation is one of art, rather than greed, equally enjoying a beautiful flower or a sunset as the greatest bejeweled crown of mankind's greatest emperor. Halflings also enjoy cooking, baking and brewing tasty beverages of all kinds from mead to tea, but not nearly as much as the portly little guys take pleasure in consuming such fare!

Halflings prefer a pastoral existence, dwelling in hilly meadows and other pleasant areas as long as the soil is adequate (or better) for raising crops and farm animals. In such arable lands, halflings build burrows or 'holes' into hillsides or small cozy cottages. In fact, most halfling villages are easily mistaken for a human community when viewed from afar, especially human communities with prevalent sod homes, but without the human penchant for building monuments and fortresses. Halflings build mills, bridges and the like for utilitarian purposes, not for civic or personal aggrandizement.

Among the sentient races, halflings clearly prefer the company of other halflings and tend to shy away from any other races. That said, halfling communities are often situated near human communities, owing to similar agriculturally-driven habitats. This has clearly been the case, if not forever, than for as long as anyone can remember; most halfling customs, dress and even language mirror those of their human neighbors. Halfling preference for their own kind followed by human-kind is an obvious truism, still they sometimes consort with gnomes, dwarves and elves, although the alien-nature and looks of the latter race both intrigues and frightens them, whereas the former races simply annoy either due to their dour nature in the case of dwarves or their irritating and frivolous practical jokes in the case of gnomes.

Despite their girth, halflings are quite nimble and, if they can be pried from their comfortable home-life, make excellent scouts and expert treasure-hunters. Able to sense danger and detect others better than most, halflings gain a one-die bonus to Initiative. Additionally, halflings excel in Hiding, Sneaking and the like, gaining a free mastery die roll in both of those skills. Further, when in natural surroundings such as meadows, fields and woodlands, halflings gain a +50% bonus to Hiding and Sneaking, a fact they often use to remain hidden when enemies or intimidating big folk come near. Coupled with their initiative advantage, halflings tend to remain in control of when encounters take place, remaining (or becoming) hidden when the danger seems too great or risky.

Halflings rarely leave their communities, preferring to marry and raise children. A full 55% of halfling communities are female (the difference in the sexes owing to male losses while defending against enemies or hunting accidents or the rare farming catastrophe or other similar danger.

Halflings have few trading partners, generally remaining in self-sufficient farming communities. At times, however, they trade with their human neighbors, generally proffering produce or livestock in return for (other) livestock, raw materials, wines, tobacco, rare fabrics or coinage. They have little use for monetary wealth, but do collect it for trade to gnomes or dwarves and other races that covet it, in return for tools or raw materials. Often, they spend their wealth on creature comforts, soft bedding and furniture, decorative items or spices and foodstuffs to tantalize and satisfy the palate.

HALFLING

HIT POINTS:	17+1d8
SIZE/WEIGHT:	S/100 lbs.
TENACITY:	Steady
INTELLIGENCE:	Average
FATIGUE FACTOR:	-3/-2

MOVEMENT

CRAWL:	1¼
WALK:	2½
JOG:	5
RUN:	7½
SPRINT:	10

SAVES

PHYSICAL:	+1
MENTAL:	+2
DODGE:	+3

ATTACK:
Halfling typically wear leather armor and utilize short swords and slings if battling foes; +3 Attack bonus with short bows and slings.

SPECIAL:
Hiding and Sneaking +50%; Shield use (e.g., small shields increase Defense to +8); Halflings utilize one Initiative die lower.

GENERAL INFO

ACTIVITY CYCLE:	Diurnal
NO. APPEARING:	1-6 (traveling), 3d4p+8 (warband), 24d12p (clan)
% CHANCE IN LAIR:	90%
FREQUENCY:	Frequent
ALIGNMENT:	Lawful Good
VISION TYPE:	Standard
AWARENESS/SENSES:	Standard (Initiative die type is one better)
HABITAT:	Pastoral meadows and gentle hillsides
DIET:	Omnivorous
ORGANIZATION:	Individuals, Families or Clans
CLIMATE/TERRAIN:	Any, save arctic/tropical (temperate preferred)

YIELD

MEDICINAL:	nil
SPELL COMPONENTS:	nil
HIDE/TROPHY:	carrying a halfling's foot is said to bring good luck
TREASURE:	3d4p copper and 3d4p silver[1]
EDIBLE:	yes; halfling tastes just like chicken
OTHER:	nil
EXPERIENCE POINT VALUE:	20

The standard halfling abode is a great earthen burrow, with many portals for sunlight. Such holes are never dank or damp, but rather have carefully crafted drainage and nicely paneled or plastered walls, tastefully painted or decorated with artwork of other fine items. They are filled with comfortable furniture and an always well-stocked pantry and larder. Aside from the cramped size, halfling holes are quite attractive and comfortable by human standards, not at all like they would seem from the outside. Sometimes, in particular when all of the best burrow-plots have been taken, halflings resort to cottage living. These small homes appear the same as their human counterparts, save for the size and, again, are comfortably and warmly bedecked.

Halflings dress in similar fashion to humans, but tend to remain practical, if not a bit formal. Halflings do not stay up-to-date on the latest fashions, tending to prefer more conservative human fashions. That said, they like to dress well and semi-formally. Even when traveling, a proper halfling wears a vest and coat and takes along a fancy carved-and-polished walking stick of fine wood, with appropriate trousers for the season and activity. They prefer earth tones, browns, tans and deep greens being most common, but black or even navy is not out of the question. They seldom wear hats over their ample hair (halflings are rarely bald). They exhibit excellent personal hygiene, trimming nails, hair to the good and right length and bathing regularly on an as-needed basis.

Halflings communities are fitting and orderly. They dislike intruders and are very self-sufficient and inward-looking. They are as unconcerned with the opinions of the other races as they are fretful of the opinions of their nosy neighbors. Proper halflings are never brash, nor gallivant around the countryside while their fields run fallow and their women-folk go unattended. That said, those that do fall to wanderlust or adventures tend to be good allies, genuinely caring for their companions' welfare. Optimistic and loyal by nature, halflings tend to have a never-surrender attitude, often pulling through in the darkest hour when bigger folk have long-since fallen to despair. They love stories and riddles almost as much as a good book. But tend to be rather boring when relating tales of their own. They tend to be mind-numbingly obsessed with food and dither about it constantly, adding to their dull reputation.

Combat/Tactics:

Small and weaker than the other sentient races, halflings know they stand little chance of victory in full-frontal assaults, so they tend to avoid conflict and put themselves out of sight. When overwhelming need arises, they use their superior reactions and stealthy abilities to hide, then ambush with ranged attacks, scattering when their foes return fire or advance to engage. They recognize the advantage of numbers and if they can split their foes, they lead a portion on a wild goose chase, while the majority of the halfling forces surround and overwhelm the remainder of the invaders. If forced, they engage in combat, fighting fiercely, but unless their family or friends are in need of aid, are always prepared to flee, skittering under briars, scrub or thick foliage to deter pursuit.

Owing to their small size, halflings are difficult to hit, enjoying a +4 bonus to Defense. Unfortunately, this same feature causes them to have a slow movement rate and short reach (-1 foot to the weapon type). Further, they are very weak compared to towering humans, suffering a -4 to their Strength score and suffer in the Hit Point department for the same reason. That said, while they appear to be rustic simpletons, this assesment is short of the mark for halflings possess an inherent mental toughness belied by their appearance and mannerisms (+1 to Wisdom). Further, while diminutive in stature and sedentary in form, halflings are surprisingly tough physically, gaining a +1 to Constitution as well.

When preparing for war or a skirmish of some sort, halflings tend to wear non-metal armors, with studded leather about as heavy as they prefer. Leader-types can be armored even to the point of chainmail, especially if the village in question has had opportunity to trade with dwarves. This choice of armor proves less of a hindrance than the heavier armors, a fact not lost on halflings since their little legs can only carry them at half the speed of their human counterparts. Halflings sometimes carry small shields (medium for their size) but generally do not employ them, preferring short bows and especially slings, in either case, halflings receive a +3 bonus to Attack based on their strong proficiency with such implements. For personal weaponry, halflings typically employ short swords, hand-axes, daggers and short spears.

Halfling war parties tend to be a fifty-fifty split of lightly-armored fighters and thieves, making the entire band essentially a group of scouts, saboteurs and infiltrators, especially given their advantages in Initiative, Hiding and Sneaking. For every 25 halflings encountered, there are two 2nd-5th level (d4+1) fighter/thieves. For every 100 halflings there is a warrior of 5th-6th level (50% chance of either) to lead the group. If 150 or more are encountered there are those numbers plus a major leader (fighter) of level 9th to 12th level (d4+8) and an extra 2d4p fighter/thieves of 2d4p levels each. Halfling clerics and mages are very rare, with only a 10% chance of a cleric and a 1% chance of mage per community, with their levels being roughly equal to the highest level leader (roll a d6, 1-2 = one level below, 3-4 = same level, 5-6 = one level above).

Halflings breed dogs for use as pets and pack animals. These loyal and well-trained companions fight fiercely in defense of the halfling homes and village. As a main-line of defense against their natural enemies, each halfling farmer has d4p dogs on his farm, making attacking a fully-mobilized halfling community dangerous, indeed. Dogs are considered part of the family. If a stranger can convince a halfling to sell a dog, the dog is either untrainable, diseased, or stolen.

Habitat/Society:

Halflings dwell in beautiful, rolling arable lands. Their idyllic communities nestle between and among rolling hills. They organize themselves by familial clan and township or shire. Each family is led by capable and wise adults who are generally, but not exclusively, male. These leaders comprise a council that determines public works and actions in times of crisis, but have few other responsibilities. Halfling communities are generally orderly and well-kept, requiring little governance beyond the self-policing of the citizens. Thievery of valuables is unknown, but the irritating theft of crops or food (such as a tantalizing pie left unattended to cool on a windowsill) on a petty basis is common enough.

Halflings do not have a language of their own; they speak whatever the local human dialect is, even if an elven or gnomish community is nearby. Many halflings also learn to speak kobold, their most likely and common natural competitors.

Halflings have an average lifespan roughly the same as humans, perhaps a decade longer in length. Females, who comprise about 55% of the population (although the birth rate is 51% in favor of males), gestate in about 10 months. Females tend to be homemakers, delighting in raising and teaching children, whether their own offspring or any of their neighbors or other little ones in the community. They tend flower gardens and keep a tidy home all-the-while preparing and cleaning form a half-dozen meals a day. That said, halfling communities consider females as equal partners to the males, even if both have differing roles. The males tend to be craftsman, or more often, farmers, nurturing both flock and field with great and tender care. They stand a solid 2 inches taller than their feminine counter-parts.

Whatever the number of able-bodied adults in a community, children are found at a full 50% of that quantity. These non-combatants run freely throughout the community (the older ones have studies and assigned chores, however), dining at any open home they happen to be at before returning home for the evening meal call. In times of crisis, the children are ushered into hiding with a contingent of adults to protect them.

Halflings are humble folk, rustic to the core. They care little for lasting monuments, empires and the like (although they delight in stories about such things). The quiet life is enough for most halflings and those in disagreement are considered foolish and are generally shunned by all right-thinking folk.

Ecology:

Halflings are fairly self-sufficient, growing enough crops and raising adequate livestock to sustain their tiny community. They are craftsmen enough to build their dwellings, create tools and decorate their homes with no outside assistance. That said they trade with their neighbors to supplement all of these items.

Since they do not delve the depths like their other small cousins, and generally live in proximity to humans who do not find them as a threat but rather a boon for trading, halflings generally do not find themselves in conflict with many other races. Occasionally, marauding gnoles or grel must be dealt with, but their most common foes tend to be kobolds, since the latter prefer to live in similar locales.

Subraces:

Of all the races, halflings may have the least variety. While there are technically three types of halflings, golden, longfellow, and harfoot, all three are almost indistinguishable to other races. Further, they can mix blood and often do, despite the prejudices within each society (although such intolerance ensures the maintenance of several pure families from each race).

Longfellow

The most common, or standard halfling, longfellows are the tallest of the breed. Their hair and eye coloration ranges the gamut of human, although redheads are very rare, especially in males. Most of this Hacklopedia entry focuses on longfellows.

Amberhair

Golden halflings, also known as amberhairs, claim to be the original halflings from whom the others were derived. Oral tradition tells of the birth of the first halflings, Azimen and Astemia, in a dry wasteland. They watered it with their sweat and nurtured life from the harsh land, turning it into a paradise. Halfling sages disagree about this fabled land's location, eventual fate and virtually every important detail concerning it.

Amberhairs are the same size as longfellows, but their ubiquitous rich golden locks give them away. Their eyes might be blue or even green, but a twinkling chestnut is more common than any other color. They tend to have tiny features, except for their large, observant eyes. They are the rarest of halflings, comprising less than 5% or all specimens.

Harfoot

Harfeet, also known as stouts, tend to run shorter than other halflings by about 3 inches on average, but tend to carry the same girth as the others. They tend to have thicker and longer sideburns and darker hair and eyes. Compared to the other halfling races, harfeet seem to be closer to dwarves and gnomes, perhaps sharing some blood with those races. They do not hide well in natural surroundings, but make decent smiths, gaining one bonus mastery roll in that skill.

Religion:

Halflings prefer to worship the Holy Mother above all, but the Raiser, the Bear and the Eye Opener also have followings. That said, halflings are not a very religious lot, preferring pragmatism and self-help to praying for divine aid.

On Tellene:

Halflings can be found on the outskirts of most human kingdoms, particularly where the foothills give way to the plains. Large numbers of halflings farm the Mendarn countryside, for example, especially in the valleys along the Welpremond Downs and Dopromond Hills.

Most major cities (such as Bet Rogala and Bet Seder) have a smattering of adventurous halflings, generally living in close proximity to one another, but a few have chosen complete integration into human society. The independent city-state of Daruk, for instance, has a population of mixed Fhokki and Dejy, and one citizen in five is a halfling. Halflings do not live in the Netherdeep, as they cannot abide a lack of the warm, beautiful sun on their cheeks.

Gakites tolerate most other races, and there is a large population of halfling tailors and farmers. In Kaleta, however, the nearly 1,000 halflings are suspect because they are believed to associate with the dwarves and gnomes with whom Dodera is at war. The suspicion is based completely on fact. The halflings fear that if the humans wipe out the other demi-humans, they will be killed, forced to leave, or enslaved next. In the dead of the night, dwarves sometimes come into town to visit prominent halflings, hear news, purchase weapons or food, and then leave again well before morning. Because of the suspicion, punishment given to halflings for crimes committed is often harsher than it might be for a human.

The large, yet sparse, Kalokopeli Forest is home to many halflings, who appreciate that the region is domesticated, peaceful and serene. The eastern portion of the Fyban Forest, a wooded valley sheltered from the elements by the sheer Kakidelas, is also occupied by numerous halflings.

Halflings appear in many other regions throughout the Sovereign Lands, being rarest on Svimohzia.

[1] *Halflings carry 3d4p each of silver and copper coins. Halfling communities collectively have hundreds or even thousands of most coins, some gems and jewelry and possibly some well-crafted arms and armors or magical goodies.*

HARPY

Also Known As: Aellopos

It was approaching carnival time in the ancient and once imperial, but now provincial and remote, city of Ka'uvavido. I was near 100 miles away in Sarachidu, but knew (as should all wise thieves) that festivals are fine places to make an easy profit. Looking forward to cutting the threads of a few scrips — those linen carryalls so favored by travelers — I set out on my travels. Unwisely, I decided to make haste by slipping through the Kalalali Forest rather than keeping my feet on the road.

I knew as soon as I heard the song that I was in trouble, but too late, for I was enraptured by a harpy, with whom I spent nearly a month in miserable conditions.

She was too lazy to scratch her own head, and would often make me scratch and comb it for her. At other times she would make me sharpen my dagger for hours on end, in order to better trim her hair or an errant feather. She would nest on a tree branch and make me climb up to fan her while she slept, or scratch and rub her flesh, or keep off the flies; but after a while she got sick of me, and preferred another of her thralls to do this vile business.

All the time, there was a raging hell in my heart as I struggled to resist, yet I stood there, and gazed eagerly, greedily upon her wicked face even when she slapped and cursed me for the tasks I struggled both to perform and to resist.

In time, however, her song failed to move me. I gathered myself up, and slipped quietly away into the shadows, shaking in every limb, pale, fever-lipped and haggard. When I finally arrived at Ka'uvavido, I crawled into a tavern and didn't emerge for days. As for that harpy, let me just say that a righteous and deserved judgment had fallen upon her, in which the operation of my now well-sharpened dagger was distinctly visible. - ⚒

Harpies are silent flyers and able to swoop down on selected victims without betraying their presence.

Harpies appears to be great birds of prey, but with the torso of a human female. A harpy's avian features are covered in dull and dirty feathers, most often black but occasionally brown or a dark gray.

The human form is highly varied and cannot be readily identified as characteristic of any particular race, exhibiting various coloration and bone structure. Regardless of whether their features are beautiful, hideous or even rather plain, their cruelty and malice shows through, uniformly evoking the visage of haggard females with matted, unkempt hair.

Combat/Tactics:

Wholly incongruous with their wretched appearance, harpies all possess a beautiful singing voice equal in power and timbre to the finest mezzo-soprano. Though they delight in singing for its own sake, they are capable of utilizing the power of their chorales to mentally ensnare sapient creatures. This is done to build a retinue of thralls that can be employed to perform a variety of menial tasks thereby permitting the harpy to lead a slothful and self-indulgent existence.

When chancing upon potential thralls or if confronted by individuals seeking to do bodily harm, harpies begin singing a beautiful aria. Such is the power of this magical song that

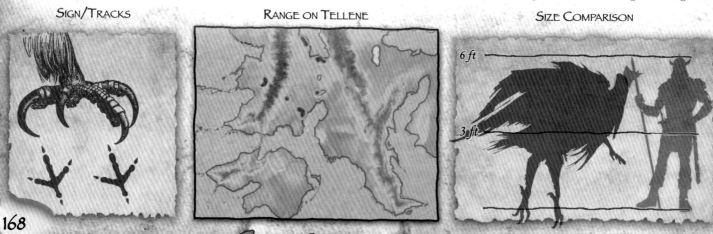

SIGN/TRACKS   RANGE ON TELLENE   SIZE COMPARISON

6 ft

3 ft

anyone hearing it must resist the allure (save vs. d20p+10) or fall under the control of the avianatrix. This song works as a Charm spell, although its effect is not broken by damage inflicted. A successful save against a lone harpy or madrigal imparts immunity to further influence by that harpy (or any member of that particular madrigal, as appropriate) for but a minute. Continued exposure to their enrapturing song necessitates additional saving throws.

The harpies prefer to send their charmed thralls against any foes that seem immune to their song, though they will attack on their own if forced, using bone clubs that deal (d6p+d4p)+4 points of damage as well as clawing with their talons.

Harpies find prey by soaring on thermals of warm, rising air, to best conserve their energy in flight. After rising on the thermal, they glide as far as possible before they need to gain altitude again. They also rely on these thermals to remain aloft while scanning the ground for their prey.

Habitat/Society:

Harpies live at the edges of civilization, isolated enough to have little fear of intrusion by armed sapients, but still close enough so that they can prey on travelers and wanderers.

They roost in groups of several individuals, who are constantly squabbling amongst each other and jockeying for a greater position in the pecking order. They lie, cheat and steal from each other, being mean-spirited and jealous even of their own kind.

Harpies consider it prestigious to have several handsome slaves; charmed males with high Looks scores are considered the most valuable. However the lives of these thralls are, were it not for the Charm effect, unbearable. Harpies use their thralls as laborers, fighters and personal groomers, henpecking them when they fail the impossible task of performing to the harpy's satisfaction, and rarely letting them out of sight. Harpies often relieve their frustrations by abusing their thralls.

Ecology:

Although feeding largely on meat, harpies do not generally kill their own prey, but leave the task to their thralls. They gorge themselves till their crop bulges, then sit (sleepy or half torpid) to digest while their thralls clean away any messes. When fresh meat is scarce, a harpy might consume plant matter or even carrion.

On Tellene:

According to Banetan legend, harpies once aided a tribe of orcs to attack the then-infant town during the time of a popular knight and dame's wedding. The nobles stood together to fight and asked the attending cleric to perform the ceremony at the same time, so that they might not die unwed. Many wedding ceremonies now take place in Baneta's cemetary, at a tranquil altar located near the couple's tomb.

Few dispute the veracity of this tale, for it is known that harpies have been reported in the nearby Kalokopeli Forest, among other woodlands of Tellene.

HARPY

HIT POINTS:	18+3d8
SIZE/WEIGHT:	M/100 lbs.
TENACITY:	Nervous
INTELLIGENCE:	Slow
FATIGUE FACTOR:	2

SPEED 5 — **INIT** -2
ATTACK +8 — **DMG REDUCTION**
DEFENSE +3 — 2
see below
medium REACH — **DAMAGE** 4
TOP SAVE ▼

MOVEMENT

CRAWL:	1¼
WALK:	2½
JOG:	5
RUN:	7½
FLY:	25

SAVES

PHYSICAL:	+7
MENTAL:	+9
DODGE:	+9

ATTACK:
Harpies sing a charming song (save vs. d20p+10) to entrance foes. In melee, they alternatively attack with their talons dealing 2d6p points of damage and bone clubs for (d6p+d4p)+4.

SPECIAL DEFENSE:
Flight

GENERAL INFO

ACTIVITY CYCLE:	Crepuscular
NO. APPEARING:	2-12
% CHANCE IN LAIR:	25%
FREQUENCY:	Infrequent
ALIGNMENT:	Chaotic Evil
VISION TYPE:	Low Light Vision
AWARENESS/SENSES:	Standard
HABITAT:	Ruins, caves and trees
DIET:	Omnivorous
ORGANIZATION:	Individuals or Madrigal Covey
CLIMATE/TERRAIN:	Temperate to semi-tropical woodlands

YIELD

MEDICINAL:	nil
SPELL COMPONENTS:	nil
HIDE/TROPHY:	nil
TREASURE:	harpies are fond of jewelry and objet d'art
EDIBLE:	yes
OTHER:	nil
EXPERIENCE POINT VALUE:	575

H

HAUNT

Also Known As: Restless Spirit, Farada

T'was the oddest form of unlife I didst ever encounter. For verily didst it appear in spectral form like unto many of its kindred malevolent spirits yet absent was the malignity one does associate with these wicked spirits of the damned. Though we did brace at the eerie approach of the phantom and I, as am wont, didst command the spirit to abay in the name of the Shining One, neither did it abscond nor didst it approach. Fearing some trickery from this seemingly powerful being, we didst wonder in confusion as it didst mince about to our fore enacting some pantomime.

Methinks upon reflection that it attempted a true parle but so befuddled at this simble-skamble performance were we that it was lost upon us. In seeming frustration it launched itself in fury upon the heraldic knight who did lead our troupe. His keen blade did seemingly wound the spirit though not, perhaps, to the degree it should were his opponent mortal.

Undeterred by the Gallant's blow, the apparition did pass its hand through the knight's shield and mail, forthwith disappearing from our sight. Though reeled by this circumstance, he soon regained composure and bade us forth with vexsome energy, though in a quite dullsome tone. Suspecting possession, though incapable of immediate remedy, we trepidatiously followed our captain.

Wanting no part in villainy, fortunate were we that none was called for. Indeed, the afflicted knight didst at day's end complete a noble quest. Thereupon the haunt didst release the knight from its bondage, a boon so little expected, and fade from sight as it bid us farewell. - 👁

Haunts appear as a slightly amorphous and diaphanous image of their former bodies. Many often mistake haunts for other forms of undead, be it a ghost or spectre. A haunt is created when a person dies prior to the completion of a significant task that he is unequivocally invested in. When this occurs, the life force becomes so strongly attached to its completion that the soul refuses to pass on into death until the task in question can be completed. This event is typically tied to a singular, and extremely powerful, emotion such as love, hate, greed, lust, revenge, and so forth.

Combat/Tactics:

In order to successfully complete its task, a haunt must first attempt to possess the body of another living creature. Most often a haunt lies in wait in an incorporeal form, near its corpse, in order to surprise a victim. On any successful attack the victim must make a Wisdom saving throw (vs. d20p+10). Failure indicates that the haunt has taken possession of the body and now has full control of the victim. Unfortunately, a haunt must touch the victim in order to take control of their body, and the touch of the undead does cause some physical damage to the living.

Once in control, a haunt may continue to inhabit the body for as long as it desires, but the victim is allowed subsequent saving throws every 24 hours. While possessing a body, the haunt is able to use the victim's weapons but does not have knowledge of their skills or abilities. As such, the haunt uses its listed combat abilities. If the host

---

It is my experience that every culture and religion maintains proper ceremonies and rituals for the interring or cremation of a corpse. After all, it is well known that death may not be the end of one's days, even among those who seek not the Harvester's touch. The haunt, that strange spirit who slips within a living body and controls it like a mere marionette, makes fools of all such rites, for neither burying nor burning can sway it from its mission.

SIZE COMPARISON

6 ft

3 ft

dies, the haunt is expunged from the body and forced to return to the site of its death.

Haunts can pass through solid material at half their movement rate, as if it didn't exist. In addition, they possess the ability to hover and are not bound by gravity or obstacles that impede the living. However, a haunt is unable to travel farther than 50 feet from the location of its physical corpse, or the place it died. Moving the remains of a haunt's former mortal remains can sometimes (10%) permit the creature to relocate, but most often the undead is tied to the place that it died. These restrictions are circumvented through possession of a mortal body.

Haunts may be physically attacked but may only be injured by silvered weapons that have received a *Bless Weapon* invocation from a priest. Their incorporeal form renders spells that inflict physical damage ineffective and the nature of their animating (i.e. being bound to the place of their death) trumps turning by a cleric. If slain, the haunt fades away never to fulfill its final quest.

In most cases, a haunt chooses to possess someone of similar alignment or perceived ideals. It judges this either by secretly listening to the conversation of a group that has entered it's abode or though use of its innate *Mind Reading* powers (as the spell but with no duration limits). Victims have the option of willingly allowing a haunt to possess their body. A successful Divine or Monster Lore skill check is required to know that this is an option once a haunt is encountered.

Once the required task is completed, a haunt passes on to the afterlife. At this time the possessed will often be enlightened as to who the haunt was in life and what why the task was so important to the haunt.

Habitat/Society:

In becoming haunts, individuals retain only hazy memories of their past lives prior to the premature termination of their vital final undertaking. Though they may recall their name and position, any recollections are purely contextual to the mission that binds them to the mortal realm. Some haunts possess the ability to speak in a whispery fashion (though only in a language they were fluent in during life) and may attempt to recruit volunteers for the task that needs to be done. This is most often employed by haunts with a moral disposition that respects the free will of other beings but may also be used by crafty haunts who seek to deceive potential dupes into volunteering for a mission by falsifying the details and context.

In rare cases, the spectral body of a haunt can be found repeatedly miming the task it needs to accomplish, although these attempts are made in vain. In these cases, the haunt simulates the act that needs to be completed, over and over, like a broken recording, but to no avail. Most haunts possess the alignment they had in life, but the irresistable urge to complete the task at hand often drives them to attack the living on sight, regardless of their alignment (perhaps justifying it as accomplishing a greater good...)

Ecology:

Haunts cling to their uncompleted task through sheer willpower. They do not feed, and they have no treasure (though some may have treasure on their corpses).

On Tellene:

Haunts may be found anywhere on Tellene where someone died before the completion of a significant task.

HAUNT

HIT POINTS:	20+3d8
SIZE/WEIGHT:	M/nil
TENACITY:	Brave
INTELLIGENCE:	Average
FATIGUE FACTOR:	n/a

SPEED		INIT
10	ATTACK +5	-1
	DEFENSE +7	DMG REDUCTION 5
short REACH	see below	n/a
	DAMAGE	TOP SAVE ▼

MOVEMENT

CRAWL:	5
WALK:	10
JOG:	15
RUN:	20
SPRINT:	25

SAVES

PHYSICAL:	+5
MENTAL:	immune
DODGE:	+5

ATTACK: A haunt's touch deals 1d3p points of damage (DR does not apply), and the victim must make a Wisdom save (vs d20p+10 or be possessed). Haunts may wield weapons when possessing a body, but use the haunt's combat statistics (except DR and ToP).

SPECIAL DEFENSES:
In ghostly form, can only be damaged by blessed silvered weapons.

GENERAL INFO

ACTIVITY CYCLE:	Nocturnal
NO. APPEARING:	1
% CHANCE IN LAIR:	n/a
FREQUENCY:	Unusual
ALIGNMENT:	Any
VISION TYPE:	Undead Sight
AWARENESS/SENSES:	Standard
HABITAT:	Any
DIET:	n/a
ORGANIZATION:	Individuals
CLIMATE/TERRAIN:	Any

YIELD

MEDICINAL:	nil
SPELL COMPONENTS:	nil
HIDE/TROPHY:	nil
TREASURE:	incidental, with corpse
EDIBLE:	no
OTHER:	nil

EXPERIENCE POINT VALUE: 275

HIPPOGRIFF
Also Known As: Wylamouranna (in Elven)

Surely the hippogriff is the most marvelous of beasts not solely for its beauty or grace and swiftness in flight. Nay, the wonder of the beast is that it exists at all. For are not horses a favored meal of the paternal griffyn? And none more savory than a young filly? Forsooth the hippogriff represents the improbable in fleshly form. A triumph of love over baser urges. One has merely to catch a glimpse of the noble beast in flight to draw inspiration. For surely if such a thing can exist, one's own predilections can be tamed in the quest for self-actualization.

As a steed, the hippogriff is greatly prized for the admixture of the equine and griffyn blood produces a mount most formidable. Nary as irascible as a true griffyn, here the creature takes after the filly. While spirited and bold, those of forceful will can master the beast and in so doing gain the companionship of a trusted ally. From its paternal lineage come the striking wings able to bear the hippogriff and rider with the swiftness of a bird. So also come the majestic beaked head and taloned forelegs which serve to make the creature a terrible foe. Surely this amalgam of flight and fury is what makes the creature the most desired of steeds.

Alas it is with a heavy heart that this venerable sage cannot personally expound upon the exhilaration of riding atop such a graceful beast and soaring amidst the clouds on high. I count myself blessed in having seen a roan hippogriff during my travels and having it's knightly master regale me with fantastic stories of airborne adventures. -

These magnificent beasts can be transformed into mounts with proper training, time and attention.

This sterile offspring of a male gryffon and female horse has the body of a horse, taloned forefeet and the head of an eagle. A muscular pair of feathery wings stretches back from its shoulders.

A hippogriff's coloration can widely vary depending on its parentage. Its equine body may exhibits the full gamut of possible horse coloration from black to roan with appaloosa or pinto marking rare but possible. The feathers are typically a uniform golden brown but again variations exist with the bald hippogriff (named so for its likeness to the bald eagle) being particularly sought after.

A typical hippogriff stands about 5 to 6 feet tall at the shoulder and weighs roughly 600 pounds. Much like mules, female hippogriffs are known as jennys while males are called jacks.

Matings of griffyns and horses are extremely rare (inspiring the expression "*to mate griffyns with horses*" as a phrase connotating unlikeliness), for horses number amongst a gryffon's prized meals.

SIGN/TRACKS

Fore

Hind

RANGE ON TELLENE

SIZE COMPARISON

12 ft

6 ft

Combat/Tactics:

Hippogriffs are seldom encountered on the ground for they have keen senses and are quick to take flight if they sense danger. They will, however, stand their ground and defend themselves or their meal in cases where flight is untenable. Should it be forced into combat, it attacks with sharp claws and hooked beak, often rearing on its hind legs to strike.

Habitat/Society:

Hippogriffs are sterile and cannot reproduce, though young jacks may become interested in fillies during the latter's breeding season. It is best to keep the two separated, for a male hippogriff has little difficulty establishing dominance over ordinary stallions, thereby resulting in ineffectual breeding and frequent maiming or death of the filly.

Wild hippogriff rakes are usually made up of several feral individuals that share a given territory. Through selective breeding, elves have managed to temper some of their most ornery characteristics, while retaining their natural fierceness, speed, alertness and endurance. The instincts of horses can be used to an elf's advantage to create a fine flying mount with a bond between master and hippogriff. These techniques vary, but are part of the art of hippogriff training.

Ecology:

The hippogriff is an omnivore desirous of meat (even carrion) but able to graze for most of its sustenance when necessary. Because of their hooved hindlegs, they do not carry food in their claws, but may disgorge it from the crop. Foolish keepers that have restricted their charge to vegetation have witnessed the beast grow weak and frail after prolonged exposure to this substandard diet.

Natural enemies include griffyns, which are nearly as fond of hippogriff flesh as they are of horse meat. Such encounters pose a great risk, however, for the hippogriff is better equipped to defend itself. Such kills usually only occur when a flying griffyn has surprised a hippogriff, or when hunger and lack of other easier prey compel it to action. Hippogriffs also hate great cats, with whom they compete for prey, and seek to kill them if threatened.

On Tellene:

Wild hippogriffs prefer the same towering peaks as their griffyn kin and may prove a nuisance to sheep and goat herders accustomed to grazing their animals on the rocky hills abutting these highlands. Their known range does not extend further south than Kalamar, and they are unknown on Svimohzia. Wild hippogriffs are sometimes visible from the taller places in P'Bapar, flying around their nesting areas in the Legasa Peaks. These creatures can be either dangerous predators or envied mounts, depending on the skill and intentions of the hunter.

The elven city of Lathlanian's military elite includes hippogriff cavalry, a tiny band of 30 to 40 fearless veterans. They often patrol the western slopes of the Legasa Peaks, keeping the city safe despite the terrible monsters of the area.

HIPPOGRIFF

HIT POINTS:	30+3d8
SIZE/WEIGHT:	L/600 lbs.
TENACITY:	Brave
INTELLIGENCE:	Semi-
FATIGUE FACTOR:	-2

SPEED		INIT
3	ATTACK +9	-1
DEFENSE +2	DMG REDUCTION 3	
short REACH	see below DAMAGE	7 TOP SAVE

ATTACK:
Two individual claw attacks deal 2d6p points of damage each, while the sharp beak inflicts 2d10p points.

SPECIAL DEFENSES:
Flight

MOVEMENT

CRAWL:	2½
WALK:	5
JOG:	10
RUN:	15
FLY:	40

SAVES

PHYSICAL:	+9
MENTAL:	+8
DODGE:	+11

GENERAL INFO

ACTIVITY CYCLE:	Diurnal
NO. APPEARING:	2-16, or as dictated by owner
% CHANCE IN LAIR:	10%
FREQUENCY:	Sporadic
ALIGNMENT:	Non
VISION TYPE:	Excellent; easily spots prey within 300 ft
AWARENESS/SENSES:	Can smell carrion from up to 1 mile away
HABITAT:	Aeries near water
DIET:	Omnivorous
ORGANIZATION:	Rakes, or as dictated by owner
CLIMATE/TERRAIN:	Temperate highlands

YIELD

MEDICINAL:	nil
SPELL COMPONENTS:	feathers, for any spell with such components
HIDE/TROPHY:	nil
TREASURE:	nil
EDIBLE:	yes
OTHER:	nil
EXPERIENCE POINT VALUE:	492

HOBGOBLIN Also Known As: Kargi, Krangi

Despite the apparent findings of certain colleagues, I hold firm in my belief that the hobgoblins' so-called 'civilization' is only an illusion brought on by over-thinking. After all, they display no sophistication or civilized tendencies that should elevate them above the other humanoids. The supposed hobgoblin culture is no more than a primitive tribal structure held together by a large military.

The idea that the hobgoblins were created by the gods as a civilized race, and have been so for all time, is untenable. Why, there is no convincing evidence in any form! To explain this obvious falsehood, hobgoblins claim that the gods, in their jealousy, destroyed their empire and forced the survivors to retreat to hills and woods. The exact method of destruction varies from story to story, of course, but plague and drought are the most common explanations. This 'catastrophe theory' maintains the belief that hobgoblins have always been civilized and explains why the hobgoblins no longer rule the known world. Foolish tripe!

Never mind the mere existence of hobgoblin kingdoms, the somewhat complex hobgoblin society, and the barely tactically and technologically sophisticated military. They prove nothing. It is merely a question of numbers. If any other monstrous race had a population equivalent to the current hobgoblin numbers, then they too would display a similar 'society.' The only reason that we do not see the kobolds, goblins and other such monsters this way is that the more powerful hobgoblins kept them in servitude, and so a similar population explosion never occurred.

Thus, the hobgoblin presence is no more perplexing than the occurrence of any other monstrous race; they are a natural fixture of the environment. In fact, it seems wise that all our fighting men should eliminate other small humanoid monster populations on the basis that they have the potential to become as powerful as the hobgoblins. - ⨎

Larger, stronger and more menacing than their smaller goblin cousins, hobgoblins are the bane of many kingdoms. They have leathery skin of a deep red, brown or ebony, with pointed teeth and ears, flat noses, prominent brows, long black hair and penetrating yellow-irised eyes. An average male stands about 6½ feet tall, but individuals can vary from 5 to 7 feet or taller. Their bodies are generally not hirsute, except for their backs and arms (both sexes). While less so than their goblin cousins, open sores, boils and skin lesions are common under their armor and sometimes on their faces. Scars from past wounds are the norm – the more numerous and greater in gravity, the older the hobgoblin. Hobgoblins stand tall and proud, hardly stooping like their smaller cousins, exhibiting posture no worse than humans. They weigh anywhere from 175 to 300 pounds, depending on height. Obesity is rare in this active and physical species, even amongst leaders.

Unlike more simple-minded monsters that dwell in their own filth, hobgoblins have well-organized, militaristic kingdoms that hold firm to their core values of strength and honor. A hobgoblin considers violence to be an acceptable

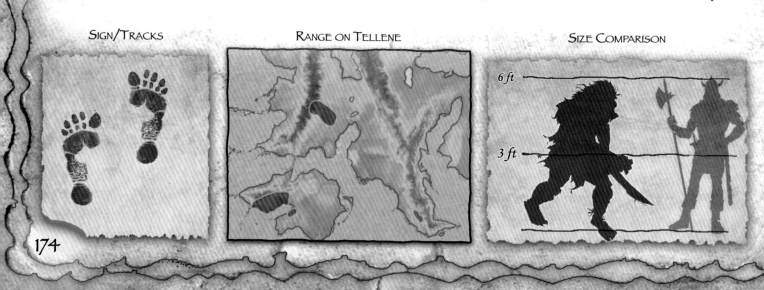

| SIGN/TRACKS | RANGE ON TELLENE | SIZE COMPARISON |

solution to every problem, providing that such an action does not break an oath or tarnish his honor in some way. Hobgoblins love warfare of all types and consider it a test of honor. They engage a known enemy even when they have fewer numbers on their side or a clear disadvantage if they think the battle is not hopeless. If given orders from their respected superior, they follow them, fighting valiantly even in hopeless conditions or against overwhelming odds. To do otherwise would cause such a loss of Honor, and they would then commit ritual suicide anyway.

Hobgoblins are more pragmatic than creative; however, they do build monuments to honor their fallen and past leaders as well as to glorify their tribe or nation. Hobgoblin military engineering is on-par with human standards. They build very functional military installations and defensive fortifications as well as offensive machinery such as siege engines and siege towers of all shapes, sizes and uses. Hobgoblins are not as prolific at building or smithing as they might otherwise be, preferring instead to spend their time fighting, even with one another.

When they do spend their energies producing arms and armor, the quality is fair to decent, on par with basic human standards. When preparing for campaign season, the hobgoblins smiths work overtime to manufacture enough goods to last through the season, as most of the armorers and weaponsmiths also hold positions in the military, whether grunt or officer.

Luckily, hobgoblins are not the most numerous humanoids. While they generally do not sustain casualties at the same rate as more primitive humanoid races, they also cannot replenish losses with rapidity. Since hobgoblins war with every known race, they have many opportunities for suffering losses and even minimal attrition can be detrimental over the course of a long campaign.

Hobgoblins dwell both above and below ground, the latter also including within the Netherdeep. Their most diverse habitations frequently brings them into competition and ultimately violent conflict with every conceivable race. Over the millennia, hobgoblins have developed a deep-seated hatred for elves and attack them on sight. They also dislike humans and dwarves, but respect these races as honorable. They view the other humanoid races, including grevans, as little more than savages at best and animals at worst. That said, hobgoblins do feel some kindred with their smaller cousins, the goblins, and sometimes join forces with them, but always as the superior. Hobgoblin warriors are sometimes loaned to goblins to lead warbands and train their soldiers.

Hobgoblins sometimes do cooperate with other humanoids, such as orcs, ogres, gnoles, bugbears and kobolds if it suits their purposes. They have little compunction about using such primitives as shock troops against mutual foes. Rival hobgoblin tribes have been known to war on each other as well.

HOBGOBLIN

HIT POINTS:	22+1d10
SIZE/WEIGHT:	M/175-300 lbs.
TENACITY:	Brave
INTELLIGENCE:	Average
FATIGUE FACTOR:	-1/-2

MOVEMENT

CRAWL:	2½
WALK:	5
JOG:	10
RUN:	15
SPRINT:	20

SAVES

PHYSICAL:	+5
MENTAL:	+5
DODGE:	+5

ATTACK: Hobgoblins prefer to employ longswords though they may wield a variety of weapons including javelins and bows; they utilize sound tactics in combat taking advantage of terrain and seizing every opportunity presented to them

SPECIAL DEFENSES: Shield use (*e.g.*, medium shields increase Defense to +4); unarmored DR is 0

GENERAL INFO

ACTIVITY CYCLE:	Nocturnal
NO. APPEARING:	1-8 (traveling), 3d4p+8 (warband), 20d12p (tribe)
% CHANCE IN LAIR:	35%
FREQUENCY:	Frequent
ALIGNMENT:	Lawful Evil
VISION TYPE:	Low light vision
AWARENESS/SENSES:	Standard
HABITAT:	Caves, fortresses, cities
DIET:	Omnivorous[1]
ORGANIZATION:	Any
CLIMATE/TERRAIN:	Any

YIELD

MEDICINAL:	nil
SPELL COMPONENTS:	nil
HIDE/TROPHY:	ears/head can be sold as bounties in many lands
TREASURE:	2d12p silver[2]
EDIBLE:	yes, though it is almost a cannibalistic act
OTHER:	armor, weapons, gear
EXPERIENCE POINT VALUE:	67

Combat/Tactics:

Hobgoblins make formidable foes. Physically imposing in battle (+1 to Damage for weapons) and with solid Hit Points (23 to 32) and decent tolerance and resistance for painful injuries, standard reach and movement rates, they can hold their own from a sheer physiological standpoint. But what sets hobgoblins apart as one of the most dangerous of humanoids is their psychological acuity.

While exhibiting merely average intelligence by human standards, their organization, discipline and advanced humanistic strategies and approach to battle make them worthy foes indeed. Further, their equipment is much better than most other humanoids, essentially equivalent to human standards, although not as superior as dwarven smithy produce. Hobgoblins fight well in darkness, possessing low light vision, but suffer no deleterious effects, even in bright sunlight.

Hobgoblins are brave and honorable combatants, much closer to humans, dwarves or even grevans than any other warrior races. They use intelligent tactics, gaining advantage from higher ground, terrain, ambush or cover if possible. They use their equipment as logic dictates, and given time, dig ditches, build ramparts and create cover. Hobgoblins have been known to train warhorses and employ advanced warfare techniques that rival those of modern humans. They use mechanical missile weapons and artillery in set-piece battles, but tend to employ hurled weapons in skirmish-level engagements. A hobgoblin never uses ranged weapons in a duel or one-on-one battle, as it may call his bravery into question.

Hobgoblins follow orders from respected superiors without question and flee only in the most dire circumstances or if ordered to do so by a ranking officer. They use the most logical combat techniques and stratagems as the situation dictates. If spying or encountering a clearly overwhelming foe, hobgoblins attempt to flee and warn others of their type, joining their brethren for an ambush or counter-attack.

Hobgoblin weapon of choice tends to be sword (of any variety) and shield, but they also like to use spears, pole arms, crossbows, bows, javelins, axes, morning stars, clubs, daggers and any other weapon that the individual prefers. They use shields as standard hobgoblin military issue, although some individuals in a skirmish setting may not have a shield (lost, destroyed or carried, but not used due to choice of weapon or combat technique). They typically wear ringmail armor, although leaders and heavy infantry are by far better armored (and light infantry, scouts, skirmishers and the like may be equipped with only leather or studded leather).

Every group of 10 hobgoblins encountered have a sergeant with maximum Hit Points. For every 30, the warband has a lieutenant wearing chainmail with +1 to Attack, Damage, Defense and a 1-point bonus to Initiative *as equipped* and having maximum hit points plus an extra d10. This is in addition to the three NCOs.

For every 90, the tribe has a captain wearing splint mail and with +2 to Attack, Damage, Defense and a 1-point bonus to Speed and Initiative *as equipped* in addition to maximum Hit Points plus two extra d10 rolls for HP. This is in addition to the 9 sergeants and 3 lieutenants.

If the tribe contains 150 or more hobgoblins, it has a powerful chieftain, serving as general, or 'kruk.' This chief has a +3 to Attack, Damage, Defense and a 2 point bonus to Speed and Initiative *as equipped*. He wears platemail or better as well as having maximum HP plus an extra 3d10 HP. This is in addition to the other officers and NCOs and an extra personal retinue of bodyguards for the chieftain (numbering 4d6p) with statistics and gear of captains.

Note: Detailed comabt statistics for Hobgoblin leaders appears on page 367.

Each tribe has at least one shaman with clerical capacity, who is generally a Knight of the Black Pit from the Church of Endless Night, but not exclusively.

Mage ability occurs in only 25% of the shamans. Their levels of spellcasting ability are not substantial by human standards, but strong compared to most humanoids, d12p-4 for clerical and d12p-6 in mage (negative and zero rounding to 1st). Roll the clerical capability for the first shaman, for every two full levels, the tribe has another shaman (rolled independently). Perform this check only once.

Habitat/Society:

Hobgoblins live in all climes and locations, although they are not as powerful as humans and thus generally live from the fringes of human civilizations to the depths of the Netherdeep and all places in-between. They have established villages, cities and even kingdoms under the sun and below-ground as well. A hobgoblin lair has sensible defensive positions and military checkpoints and installations designed to thwart and destroy invaders, but also to allow egress of units for raids on others.

Hobgoblins compete with all races and with each other. They consider it a matter of personal honor to win individual competitions of all types, from mining, to smithing to personal combat. Winners are glorified and losers scorned. Consequently, hobgoblins take their work, sports and warfare very seriously.

Hobgoblin society is organized by tribe, each further divided by warband. Tribal leaders are chosen in mortal combat, with the loser of the contest slain. Any member of the warband can challenge the leader at any time (although it is considered cowardly and dishonorable to challenge the leader while injured). Likewise, tribal leaders are chosen and displaced in a similar manner. Such fights are forbidden, however, during warfare as the chain of command must be respected for the unit to function properly in the field. In some areas, tribal leaders have further joined to create whole kingdoms, ruled by an overall hobgoblin king, again, chosen by ritual combat.

Hobgoblins speak their own language which is closely related to Dwarven. Hobgoblins sometimes pick up the languages of their neighbors, especially if involved in trade or spying. Any hobgoblin will have a 20% chance of knowing one of the following languages: Goblin, Dwarven or a local human tongue, if located near the surface and a 10% chance of knowing any other demi-human or humanoid language. Clerics and mages have a 75% and 90% chance of knowing an additional language and, if so, a 10% further chance of knowing one or more of the rest (check for each, up to d4p total).

Hobgoblins have long lifespans of up to 100-160 years. Females comprise a full 50% of the population. They appear very similar to males, but have wider hips and breasts. Females are fully liberated, able to perform any function that a male can; they fight in the military, work the smiths, mine, work as merchants and so on. Females can decline any mating overture and often do as pregnancy and child-rearing can limit their military career. Fully 40% of all warbands are female (statistically identical to males), but only 25% of sergeants, 15% or lieutenants, 5% of captains are female. No leader higher than captain has yet been female.

The hobgoblin gestation is 11 months. Young are born in litters of 2-5, although 10% of the time there is only a single birth. With twins or more, the smallest is always sacrificed to the Dark One within an hour of birth. Most females produce young but once, if at all, choosing career over motherhood. Consequently, there are only 50% as many young as there are adults.

Hobgoblins wean by 18 months and reach sexual maturity at the age of 16. By the age of four they are put to work. By adolescence, the most promising and largest join the warrior class with the others learning professions of one type or another. Those showing initiative or unusual intelligence are trained in a trade or to become spies or scouts. The remaining youths are left to toil in the mines or other manual labor.

Ecology:

Hobgoblins consider warfare a standard part of the cycle of life. They constantly fight with their neighbors, forcing them to arm and defend, flee or perish. Like orcs, they raid the countryside and all nearby communities feel their presence; unlike the other humanoids, hobgoblins are more civilized.

Those unable to defend themselves are never mindlessly butchered as there is no honor in such behavior. They are subjugated and forced to provide tribute, enslaved or forced away. *For example, a human farming settlement may be left alone and raided every two years for crops, but left enough intact to recover and provide future food, while a nearby orcish tribe is a different matter entirely.*

Orcs have no value other than as foes in battle, and are prone to raid and reduce potential hobgoblin spoils; thus, orcs are attacked mercilessly until eradicated or enslaved. Among the myriad of foes, hobgoblins hate elves the most and attack them on sight, capturing and enslaving them if at all possible.

Subraces:

Several Hobgoblin sub-races thrive, both above and below ground. They vary slightly in coloration and size, but show the least variation among the intelligent races. The more numerous nations are known as Kargi (who consider themselves the original hobgoblins), Krangi, Kors, Dazlak and Rankki. Also of note are the Sil-Karg, or half-hobgoblin. This human-hobgoblin mix is not readily accepted into either society; despised by both, they tend to wander.

Religion:

Clerics and shamans are not common, but most tribes of any significant size (100 or more members) have at least one. These spellcasters generally only serve in a cloistered capacity, never leaving the lair on raids. The priests see to the spiritual guidance of the tribe and help advise the military leaders on all matters.

Far and away the favorite religion of hobgoblins is the Church of Endless Night. All major hobgoblin kingdoms worship the Dark One and the Church is the only official, sanctioned religion of the civilized hobgoblin nations. Other Lawful Evil religions are generally tolerated, although the Courts of Inequity are not popular (or even lawfully allowed in some communities/kingdoms).

The Temple of Armed Conflict has large, fanatical followings among the military, especially the higher-ranking leaders. Most other evil religions, plus the Way of the Berserk, Parish of the Prolific Coin and the Fraternal Order of Aptitude also gain some traction among hobgoblins.

On Tellene:

Hobgoblins have formed two major nations, both having seen periods of imperial conquest as well as defeat. The oldest of the hobgoblin kingdoms, Ul-Karg, nearly conquered all of Svimohzia before being denied in a pitched two-week long struggle. They are now poised to make a second push.

The most successful hobgoblin nation is Norga-Krangrel, located in the Western reaches of the Young Kingdoms. From here, the hobgoblins crushed the Eastern Brandobian Empire and established their own Kingdom of Krangi on the central plains. The kingdom was short-lived, however, collapsing in civil war after their infamous king, Kruk-Ma-Kali was assassinated. The Krangi have since warred with their human neighbors with varying success, waiting for the right time to annihilate their enemies and re-establish their empire.

Savage hobgoblins in large numbers can also be found in the dark reaches of the Vohven and Obakasek jungles. These uncivilized hobgoblins frequently raid outside of the deep woodlands into surrounding human lands.

[1] *Higher ranking hobgoblins eat only flesh (elf, dwarf and human being the most desirable), while the weaker ones may eat nothing but mushrooms from first solid food to last.*

[2] *Hobgoblins carry 2d12p sp each. Hobgoblin lairs can contain wealth in the form of uncut gems, ores, worked precious metals, jewels, finished and worked goods of average quality and manufacture (especially arms and armor, torture implements, tools and the like). A lair that has been successful in raids will contain all types of items, even of human or demi-human manufacture as well as superior quality arms and armors (the latter, surely in-use by the leaders) and even books and other writings. Hobgoblins keep many animal pelts of all kinds and varieties.*

HUMANS
Brandobian Reanaarian
Dejy Fhokki
Kalamaran Svimohz

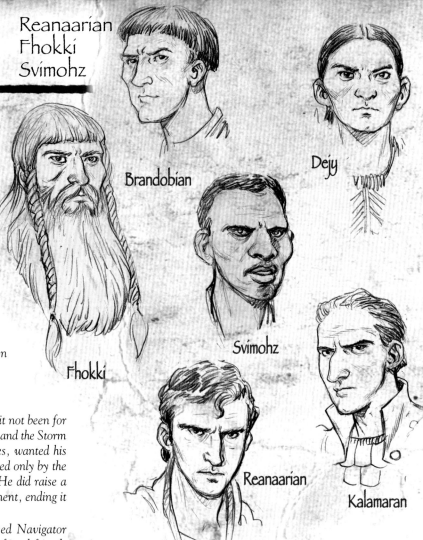

Brandobian
Dejy
Svimohz
Fhokki
Reanaarian
Kalamaran

"The Anol Fragment, named after the author who signed the work, is a portion of a large navigational map dating back over 500 years and contains the hotly contested telling of the story of human migration. Aside from the author's choice of written language (Ancient Kalamaran), the text itself betrays the author's lineage. The cursory mention of Kalamaran history (and the ignorant or perhaps arrogant assumption that recorded history began with Kalamaran expansion) indicate that the author knew well enough the then-recent Kalamaran history of expansion.

While ample evidence exists that suggests that the tale has some grounding in actual fact, the majority of the work appears to be idle speculation and several key factual events have been misstated or entirely ignored. Still, the Fragment is the oldest record of the migration events and its age alone provides a certain authority."

The Anol Fragment is as follows:

"Humans might never have reached the continent had it not been for a dispute between Rotak the Traveler, Master of the Stars, and the Storm Lord. Our wondrous Lord and Star Guide, Bright Eyes, wanted his human followers to experience the peaceful places inhabited only by the dour dwarves and joyful elves. So it came to pass that He did raise a giant causeway from the shores of Svimohzia to the continent, ending it near the mouth of the Ridara River.

Journeymen and other ardent followers of the Blessed Navigator followed the beckoning bridge and rejoiced. His people found friends among the halflings and the gnomes. Some, if they could find them, learned secrets of crafts and tools from the reticent dwarves. Others who crossed the bridge met reclusive elves and gained great knowledge from them. Truly, Rotak the Voyager had given a great gift to mankind.

When the brave travelers returned to their people on Svimohzia, they did speak of the wonders to the north and did lead masses who were unwelcome elsewhere on the island into the unknown. In this way did the Dejy come to the continent from Svimohzia.

At first the Dejy enjoyed the Ridara Valley, but they were intrigued by the towering Ka'Asas, mightier than anything on Svimohzia. Many Dejy wandered east. Some headed north in search of the headwaters of the Ridara, then continued northwest into the central lands. The Dejy enjoyed the peaceful river valleys of the Ek'Ridar, the Banader, and the Renador. They established small villages in those places, but their largest numbers learned to tame the wild horses of the Drhokker Plains and live there still. Over thousands of years, the Dejy left almost no part of the continent untouched.

And The Nimble Navigator smiled down upon his children.

The Storm Lord was enraged. First, because rage is always his initial reaction to change. Second, the land bridge slowed down his massive storms that built strength in the Kalamaran Bay and tore along the coast, wiping away any settlements along the shore. Third, he enjoyed trying to thwart and torment the Traveler and His followers with his insufferable storms. He caused the ocean to rise in anger, eroding the causeway and drowning what was left in rising seas.

Our Lord the Traveler built it again.
The Storm Lord destroyed it.
This battle repeated itself over and over.

On the second raising, the Fhokki came into the Ridara Valley. Some conquered various Dejy tribes, intermarried and became racially indistinct. Others, wanting their own lands (and not being numerous enough to force the Dejy out) rose north, where they found the Shynako Hills easy crossing into the present Wild Lands. Some tribes stayed near the headwaters of the Dodera and became plentiful. The rest continued upward until they found the Jenshyta and followed it as far as they could. It led to the Jorakk River and all the way to Lake Jorakk. They settled along both sides of its shores as their numbers increased. The Fhokki even continued once they reached the Jorakk, heading west and filling the area between the Byth Mountains and Lake Jorakk

The causeway washed away while the Fhokki explored the northeast.

The Traveler raised it again and intrepid Brandobians explored the new opening. They moved more westward than the earlier explorers and also moved more quickly. In virtually no time at all, they had skirted the Elos Bay and crossed the Legasas to settle along the warm and benevolent Brandobian Ocean. Their movement was so quick that they left virtually no legacy of their heritage in the bloodlines and place names along their path.

H

When next the bridge rose, two distinct races used it. The fewer, but bolder, Reanaarians crossed and immediately headed east, where most of them lived on the eastern shores of the Badato River. Later they crossed the P'Roruls and first saw the Bay that now carries their name.

By this time, the Storm Lord's constant destruction had wrought havoc on the Ridara's mouth. The firm valley had sunk into the warm, wet delta now known as the Alubelok Swamp.

While the Reanaarians avoided the swamp, the Kalamarans stayed long enough to learn how to use it. The Kalamarans discovered wild rice growing within and cultivated it. Within a few generations, their numbers had swelled, and they were forced to expand beyond their swampy home that nobody else wanted. They could not retreat back to the island, however; the Storm Lord had struck again.

By this time, the Traveler had grown weary of the game and chose to end it. Each time the land bridge was sunk, many of His ardent followers were destroyed. Pained at seeing so much destruction to man and earth, he allowed the Storm Lord to claim an apparent victory. The causeway remained beneath the waves.

Meanwhile, the Traveler won His war with the Storm Lord by outmaneuvering him. He simply brought another gift for man; in His infinite benevolence, He taught men and elves the secrets of sailing. Thus the Magnificent One's grateful followers could not only travel, but they would use the Storm Lord to propel them!

They already knew small boats and galleys that put to shore every night, but sailing ships were a new marvel for them, and they took to the task with great energy. The Brandobians, especially, became marine experts, exploring thousands of small islands to the west of the continent, establishing cities along the Elos Bay and bringing trade to the Kalamaran Bay while the Reanaarians were still experimenting with canoes. Filled with wanderlust, the Brandobians also explored eastward and took the lands east of the Legasas all the way to the Renador River. And the Voyager did grin.

The growing population, the new trade with the Svimohzish, and the other factors in Kalamaran history gave the Kalamarans great impetus to expand. They quickly pushed northward, driving the rest of the Fhokki out of O'Par and Dodera, then westward, shattering any resistance before them.

The expansion of the Kalamarans begins recorded history in the Sovereign Lands."

Humans are the most populous of the humanoid/demi-human races. Their adaptability has allowed them to thrive in arctic conditions as well as tropical jungles and from high mountain peaks to seaside beachfronts. Their relatively high birth rate, natural curiosity and decent engineering capabilities have allowed humans to bounce back and thrive in the face of any adversity thrown their way. As such, the fringes of human kingdoms and empires tend to be where the other intelligent races, long-since pushed aside by human expansion, can be found. There they compete, endanger and benefit the human civilization, making these fringes a hotbed of activity (often unbeknownst to the humans dwelling nearby).

Religion:

The majority of the people on Tellene are polytheistic; that is, they believe in more than one god. A person may or may not worship multiple deities, but she will most certainly acknowledge their existence. Tellene is home to magic, both divine and arcane, and a large pantheon of gods whose clerics, if not themselves, are constantly involved in the affairs of Tellene. Mages are not overly common and common people accept most unusual and seemingly inexplicable events as the work of one of the gods rather than arcane magic. In smaller communities, the townsfolk easily confuse mages with clerics, and arcane spells may be misconstrued as miracles or portents of the gods. This can work to a spellslinger's weal (or woe) depending on which god the commoners believe sent the miracle.

Subraces:

Scholars often refer to the Svimohzish Isle as the Cradle of Civilization because today's civilized humans descended from the Isle's original inhabitants. The name is a misnomer, however, because millennia before the humans of the Isle ever formed the rudimentary elements of organized society, many great demi-human and humanoid civilizations had risen and fallen on the main continent. Additionally, many sages believe that ample evidence exists of one or more great Dejy (human) empires in several areas of continental Tellene, predating any migration from the Cradle of Civilization.

Whatever troubles befell the tribesmen came and went over the course of centuries. During each of the periodic disturbances, different tribes ventured across what is believed to be a land bridge that once or periodically rose from the waves to connect the Isle of Svimohzia to the main continent. The simple clansmen crossed the bridge to reach the wetlands of the Alubelok Swamp, and were greeted with an amazing assortment of plant and animal life. They more than likely found an abundance of wild rice and edible berries, large quantities of wild honey, and flocks of waterfowl that could be easily captured.

Brandobians

The stereotypical Brandobians have brown hair, brown eyes and fair skin. Today, their hair ranges from sandy blonde to nearly black, and their skin is fair to medium in tone. Their eyes are still largely the same, ranging only from brown to black. They tend to be shorter and slighter than the other human races.

Brandobians today have the least contact with other races. They have several cultural curiosities not found in other lands. They are not affectionate people in public and generally prefer to keep contact with others to a minimum. Brandobians bury their dead face down or cut off a foot to prevent the dead from rising as undead.

The Brandobian language is used in their lands, colonies, including Miclenon, and many former colonies such as Alnarma, Vrandol and along the Elos coast. (Prompeldians now use Kalamaran or the Merchant's Tongue). The colonies like to accent it with their own spellings, pronunciations, and words, but continental Brandobians resist changing the language in any way. A few demihumans in the Young Kingdoms still understand some Brandobian, but they do not often speak it; after all, over 500 years has passed since the establishment of Eastern Brandobia. Despite the passage of time, there are still a few villages in the Young Kingdoms, especially north of P'Bapar, that speak a dialect of Brandobian because they were bypassed or for some reason never occupied by the Kalamarans.

Dejy

The Dejy are the most varied of the human races. Their division into tribes as small as a single village or the size of Bet Kalamar gave rise to diversity of appearance, tongue, and culture. They do share certain physical traits, but only to a degree. They tend to have dry black hair, deep brown eyes and yellow skin. If they grow any facial hair, it is a small tuft at their chin. Within those guidelines, they

My studies show that during the Age of Great Anguish (about 89 to 159 I.R.), the Empire crumbled into fragmented kingdoms ruled by lesser lords, each monarch attempting to assume the Imperial throne.

The victor was Prince Thedorus, a petty lord from the south, who boasted a small, loyal army of not only men, but also many dwarves from the Ka'Asa Mountains. With his troops' weapons and armor of dwarven steel, the new King Thedorus I vanquished the remaining lords and reunited the Empire, reigning for the next fifty-seven years. Yet, little more than a week after his death, the land was thrown into another civil war.

The next several years, known as the Time of Misfortune, were marked by a return to conditions not unlike those of the Age of Great Anguish. Over the next three centuries, the once-great Empire slowly deteriorated to less than half its original size.

During the last 200 years, incompetent, insane or drunken emperors dominated the Imperial dynasty. These feeble men allowed dependent duchies to openly defy the Crown, and eventually the western and northern lands began to declare independence. The provinces of Basir, Dodera, O'Par, Tarisato and Tokis remain under the nominal control or guidance of the Kalamaran Empire even today. Others, like Pekal, became completely independent. — ⚶

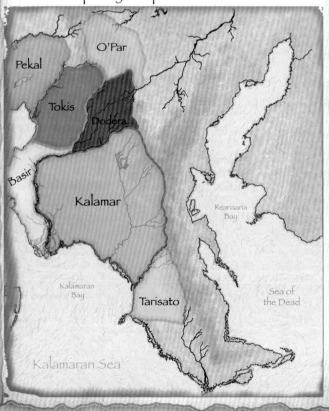

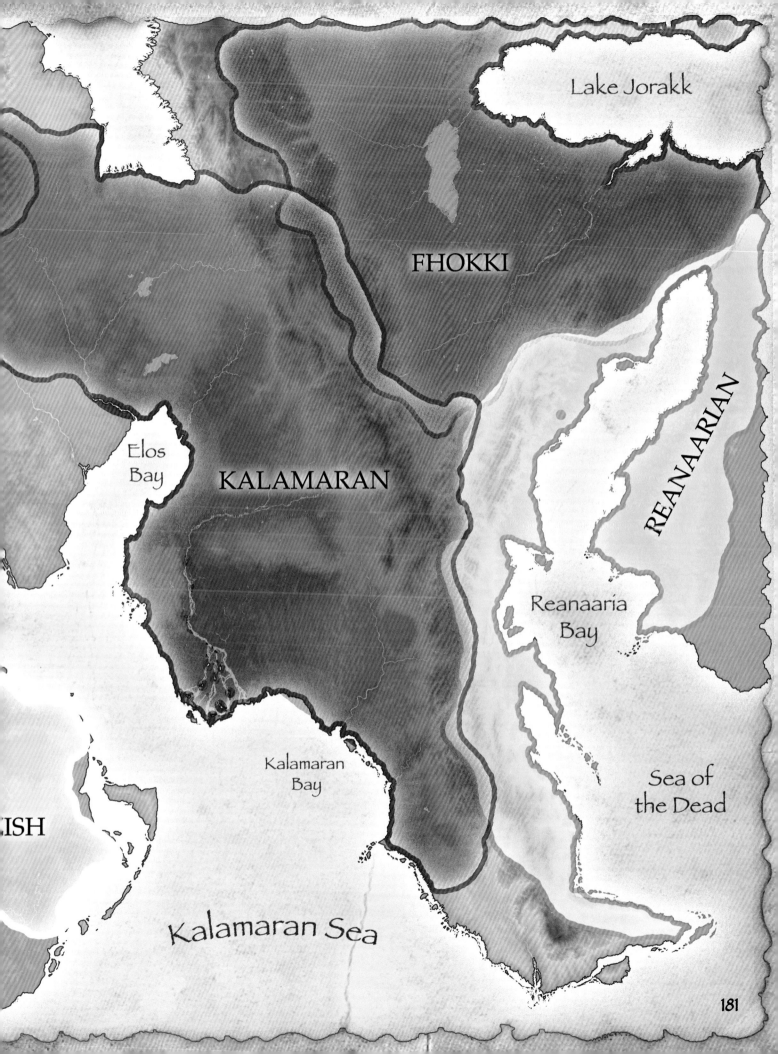

Lake Jorakk

FHOKKI

REANAARIAN

Elos
Bay

KALAMARAN

Reanaaria
Bay

ISH

Kalamaran
Bay

Sea of
the Dead

Kalamaran Sea

vary greatly in appearance. The Chors tribe, for example, are short and squat, grow their hair long, and titter quietly when they laugh. By contrast, the Defohy, currently embroiled in bitter conflict in their home in Ek'Gakel, are tall and narrow of face, with high foreheads and long limbs.

Some Dejy clans have strong traditions that have retarded their technological innovation. The social dominance of their clerics, the prevalence of certain tenets of the Conventicle of the Great Tree (even among those tribes that do not follow the Bear), their nomadic tendencies and centuries of tradition have prevented many tribes from matching the technological advances of other human cultures. Highly skilled flintworkers, powerful clerics and mages, and raging barbarian warriors have kept many Dejy tribes from being overwhelmed by their enemies. Tribes of Dejy with little outside contact still live largely apart from time, in pockets of the stone age of Tellene's past. Yet other clans have evolved into modern nations such as the great Theocracy of Slen, its warring neighbor Shynabyth, and Thybaj.

The Dejy have a long history of spoken language, and each tribe has its own tongue. Scholars might identify patterns or families of these languages, but the Dejy see little point in it. None of the tribes has any written language. The Dejy generally speak their own language among themselves and only those that must deal with outsiders learn to speak another language. With respect to the nomads and tribesmen, when they learn to speak another language, they still see no point in learning to read it. In the various nations and cities descended from Dejy, they have adopted a nearby human or demihuman language for recording history or transactions. For example, the City-State of Thygasha uses alternately Reanaarian, Fhokki, Gnome and Merchant's Tongue!

Fhokki

Fhokki have blonde hair, pale skin, and blue eyes. Due to sharing land with the Dejy for untold generations, brown eyes and slightly darker skin are now common as well, and blonde is no longer the only hair color. Those who lived in O'Par or Dodera before the Kalamarans drove them out might show some red hair; a reminder of their oppressors. Fhokki tend to be the tallest of the human races, and in areas of pure Fhokki, a man under 6 ½ feet tall is rare. Men consider beards a mark of adulthood and only the very old or certain priests may shave theirs without inviting ridicule.

Fhokki are a vibrant people. They love to laugh, they love to love, and they love to fight. When this aggressive personality is matched to a large frame, the effect shocks the peace-loving Reanaarians or the cultured Brandobians. Fhokki prefer simple log homes large enough for their extended family. They prefer working with their hands, and many Fhokki distrust mages or scholars. Fhokki burn their dead on great pyres with the possessions that best represented that person's life and desires.

The Fhokki language is surprisingly intact from ancient days, despite only recent adoption of quill and paper. Loremasters among the people painted onto stone or tree bark and have only used ink for the last hundred years or so. Fhokki is spoken in the lands of Jorakk, along the banks of the Jorakk River and in Skarrna, although its runes appear across the Wild Lands and as far South as Dodera.

Kalamarans

The ancient Kalamarans had red hair, with occasional browns and blondes. Their skin was olive in color, and their eyes were blue, hazel, or gray. Today, however, because the mighty Kalamaran Empire touched all human races, the diversity among them is great. Every combination of hair and eye coloration, skin tone and build can be

Svimohz   Reanaarian   Dejy   Fhokki   Kalamaran   Brandobian

found among the Kalamaran populace. Only the nobility, who marry chiefly among themselves, retain the classic red hair with any frequency. Their size varies greatly, with the tallest people in the north and the shortest to the west.

The Kalamaran language is spoken throughout Kalamar and the remaining elements of the former Empire. It is the native tongue of the inhabitants of the Young Kingdoms, even those who might be of Brandobian lineage or otherwise. Because of the many other peoples conquered and assimilated by the Kalamarans and the great size of the former empire, the dialects are many and varied. Natives of different regions have difficulty understanding each other's speech, although at this point in time, their written words are still nearly identical.

Reanaarians

Reanaarians have brown hair and eyes and their skin ranges from olive to darker tan. Hair spans the full range short of black–from blonde to red to brown, with medium brown being most common. The people are often shorter than Kalamarans (and much shorter than their Fhokki neighbors to the north), but their frames are strong, unlike the slender Brandobians.

Reanaarians live the closest to the demihumans of Tellene. Gnomes, halflings, dwarves, and even elves share their towns and cities. Reanaarians prefer to live in villages and govern themselves; a network of hundreds of these villages covers the Bay where they live. The Reanaarians are fond of crafts and they work hard, but they also like to enjoy themselves. Because they respect many faiths and share their lands with demihuman cultures, the Reanaarians have more holidays than any other people.

For the most part, Reanaarians speak their own language, although through trade it has lost much of its original character. Most folk speak at least a few words in a demihuman language (any of them) because they associate with these races so often. Those that live in cities tend to speak Merchant's Tongue as a primary language.

Svimohz

The Svimohz actually encompass nearly as many cultures as the widespread Dejy. Their skin is very dark brown when not actually black, and their hair is black as well. Their irises are sometimes gray, but few folk ever see anything but black and brown eyes – whether in each other or in the mirror. The average height of a Svimohz ranges from culture to culture, with the Zazahnii being generally shorter and the Meznams taller than the Ozhvins and Ahznoms.

Svimohzish culture is ancient and rich. The people are formal and have distinct social rules. Strangers are greeted warmly and guests are treated like royalty. Bargaining in the marketplace is hard, but both parties are respectful and polite. The tradition of a dowry is still alive and shows no sign of being abandoned soon. The Svimohz bury their dead in catacombs when possible, and of all the human races, save perhaps certain Dejy clans, they are most prone to become obsessed with death or the preservation of their bodies.

The Svimohzish language is spoken across the island. Many native Svimohz speak no other human language. Svimohzish is recognized in major ports because of the importance of Zha-nehzmish as a trading partner. People in port cities often speak the Merchant's Tongue. Among central Svimohzia, the hobgoblin language is widely understood because of the neighboring hobgoblin kingdom of Ul Karg.

Brandobian   Kalamaran   Fhokki   Dejy   Reanaarian   Svimohz

HUMAN: SEDENTARY (SCRIBE)

HIT POINTS:	18+1d4
SIZE/WEIGHT:	M/140 lbs.
TENACITY:	Cowardly
INTELLIGENCE:	Bright
FATIGUE FACTOR:	-1

SPEED 9 | INIT 3
ATTACK -1
DEFENSE -2 | DMG REDUCTION 0
by weapon -4 | DAMAGE 4
medium REACH | TOP SAVE ▼

MOVEMENT

CRAWL:	2½
WALK:	5
JOG:	10
RUN:	15
SPRINT:	20

SAVES

PHYSICAL:	0
MENTAL:	0
DODGE:	0

ATTACK:
Sedentary humans are not usually proficient in any weapons; statistics represent a scribe utilizing a knife to defend himself

SPECIAL DEFENSES:
none

HUMAN: MERCHANT

HIT POINTS:	21+1d6
SIZE/WEIGHT:	M/165 lbs.
TENACITY:	Nervous
INTELLIGENCE:	Average
FATIGUE FACTOR:	-3

SPEED 7 | INIT 2
ATTACK +2
DEFENSE +1 | DMG REDUCTION 0
by weapon | DAMAGE 5
medium REACH | TOP SAVE ▼

MOVEMENT

CRAWL:	2½
WALK:	5
JOG:	10
RUN:	15
SPRINT:	20

SAVES

PHYSICAL:	0
MENTAL:	0
DODGE:	0

ATTACK:
Most merchants are proficient in a small weapon such as a knife or dagger; speed varies by weapon type (dagger given)

SPECIAL DEFENSES:
none

GENERAL INFO

ACTIVITY CYCLE:	Diurnal
NO. APPEARING:	1 or 1-4
% CHANCE IN LAIR:	95%
FREQUENCY:	Frequent
ALIGNMENT:	Any (tend towards lawful)
VISION TYPE:	Standard
AWARENESS/SENSES:	Standard
HABITAT:	Any
DIET:	Omnivorous
ORGANIZATION:	Solitary or Workgroup
CLIMATE/TERRAIN:	Any

GENERAL INFO

ACTIVITY CYCLE:	Diurnal
NO. APPEARING:	1-3
% CHANCE IN LAIR:	90%
FREQUENCY:	Commonplace
ALIGNMENT:	Any
VISION TYPE:	Standard
AWARENESS/SENSES:	Standard
HABITAT:	Any
DIET:	Omnivorous
ORGANIZATION:	Enterprise
CLIMATE/TERRAIN:	Any

YIELD

MEDICINAL:	nil
SPELL COMPONENTS:	nil
HIDE/TROPHY:	nil
TREASURE:	scribes will have d8 silver coins on their person and may have scores saved up and hidden away
EDIBLE:	yes, if you do not object to cannibalism
OTHER:	nil
EXPERIENCE POINT VALUE:	5

YIELD

MEDICINAL:	nil
SPELL COMPONENTS:	nil
HIDE/TROPHY:	nil
TREASURE:	a merchant's wealth is usually tied up in his inventory with but small amount of coins for transactions
EDIBLE:	yes, if you do not object to cannibalism
OTHER:	nil
EXPERIENCE POINT VALUE:	20

HUMAN: LABORER

HIT POINTS: 23+1d8

SIZE/WEIGHT: M/180 lbs.

TENACITY: Steady

INTELLIGENCE: Slow to Average

FATIGUE FACTOR: -1

SPEED 10 | ATTACK 0 | INIT 5
DMG REDUCTION
DEFENSE -1 | 1
by weapon +2
by weapon REACH | DAMAGE | TOP SAVE 7

MOVEMENT

CRAWL: 2½

WALK: 5

JOG: 10

RUN: 15

SPRINT: 20

SAVES

PHYSICAL: 0

MENTAL: 0

DODGE: 0

ATTACK:
Workers have ready access to various implements that function as clubs; may be dangerous if intoxicated

SPECIAL DEFENSES:
Rugged work garments equivalent to thick robes; 'unarmored' DR is 0

GENERAL INFO

ACTIVITY CYCLE:	Diurnal
NO. APPEARING:	3-12
% CHANCE IN LAIR:	50%
FREQUENCY:	Ubiquitous
ALIGNMENT:	Any
VISION TYPE:	Standard
AWARENESS/SENSES:	Standard
HABITAT:	Any
DIET:	Omnivorous
ORGANIZATION:	Crew
CLIMATE/TERRAIN:	Any

YIELD

MEDICINAL:	nil
SPELL COMPONENTS:	nil
HIDE/TROPHY:	nil
TREASURE:	laborers will generally only possess a few trade coins
EDIBLE:	yes, if you do not object to cannibalism
OTHER:	nil

EXPERIENCE POINT VALUE: 25

HUMAN: MAN-AT-ARMS

HIT POINTS: 24+1d8

SIZE/WEIGHT: M/180 lbs.

TENACITY: Steady

INTELLIGENCE: Average

FATIGUE FACTOR: -3/-2 (w/ shield)

SPEED 10 | ATTACK +1 | INIT 4
DMG REDUCTION
DEFENSE -2 | 3
by weapon +1
by weapon REACH | DAMAGE | TOP SAVE 7

MOVEMENT

CRAWL: 2½

WALK: 5

JOG: 10

RUN: 15

SPRINT: 20

SAVES

PHYSICAL: 0

MENTAL: 0

DODGE: 0

ATTACK:
Men-at-arms typically are clad in studded leather and wield longswords; variant weaponry (especially missile weapons) is common and will alter speed

SPECIAL DEFENSES:
Shield use (e.g., medium shields improve Defense from -2 to +4); unarmored DR is 0

GENERAL INFO

ACTIVITY CYCLE:	Any (varies by schedule)
NO. APPEARING:	1-3 (watch), 3-30 (patrol), 50+ (fortress)
% CHANCE IN LAIR:	75%
FREQUENCY:	Ubiquitous
ALIGNMENT:	Any
VISION TYPE:	Standard
AWARENESS/SENSES:	Standard
HABITAT:	Any
DIET:	Omnivorous
ORGANIZATION:	Squads, Companies, Battles, Legions
CLIMATE/TERRAIN:	Any

YIELD

MEDICINAL:	nil
SPELL COMPONENTS:	nil
HIDE/TROPHY:	nil
TREASURE:	none if within vicinity of brothels, taverns or gambling houses
EDIBLE:	yes, if you do not object to cannibalism
OTHER:	nil

EXPERIENCE POINT VALUE: 30

HUMANS: BERSERKER

Berserkers use shouts, war cries, hand gestures and wild-eyed looks to intimidate.

These wild and highly aggressive warriors are typically of Fhokki descent and gather in bands in order to seek out combat. Most berserkers scorn armor and engage in battle in a drunken-like stupor, reveling in a battle lust that, when combined with their large frame, is both terrifying and awe-inspiring. Typical of most Fhokki, berserkers stand well over six feet in height, with seven being closer to the norm. They possess wild, loose hair ranging in color from blonde to auburn, depending on where they are found. Like all Fhokki they take great pride in their beards and view them as a sign of manhood. Berserkers rarely bathe and often exude an unmistakable stench of sweat and dried blood. Most berserkers dress in a combination of furs, leathers and hand woven clothing made by their women. When wading into battle most prefer to use two weapons, though weapon and shield is not uncommon. Fear is not an option for berserkers and they take great pride in standing up to superior, or even insurmountable, numbers.

Bands of warring berserkers can be found in groups upwards to 100 in number. For every 20 berserkers encountered there will be a champion. Each champion is a 4th – 6th level fighter equipped as his kinsmen but possessing far greater fighting skills. If 50 berserkers are encountered there will be a sub-chieftain of at least 9th level in addition to 2 champions. Bands over 75 in number are led by a war chief – a fighter of no less than 15th level. War chiefs will have 2d4 champions for bodyguards in addition to the requested number of champions in the band. Chiefs are likely to have acquired superior arms and armor as booty from their raiding.

Berserkers have no time for arcane magic though shamans and clerics hold places of honor, and leadership, in war bands. Thievery is considered not only dishonorable, but one of the worst offenses that can be committed among by a clan member. The punishment for such a crime is always death.

Combat/Tactics:

As befitting their name, berserkers enter combat with great glee, hacking and slashing at anything that moves. They give little thought to using ranged combat, weapons they consider best suited for women, and the weak. That being said they are not without tactics. Prior to combat they can be quite cunning and have been know to use elaborate battle plans when necessary. Once engaged those plans often fall to pieces as each member of the group wades indiscriminately into their enemy, hoping to score as many kills as possible.

It's always unwise to fight a berserker on his own terms. Draw him to you on your own ground.

Whenever a berserker scores a killing blow he increases his subsequent speed by one count as it drives him into a furor. This effect lasts for 10 seconds and any additional kills scored in that time further increase the speed at which a berserker attacks.

Berserkers typically wield two weapons but those that become maimed in combat will often use a shield to compensate for any loss of ability. Some clans have been known to select a weapon, or weapon and shield combination, of preference as their symbol and weapon of choice in combat.

Habitat/Society:

Over time, berserkers form clans of wandering Fhokki that migrate in search of battle. When not in combat they live simple lives, hunting and gathering food in order to subsist until such time that they can match their skill in arms against a worthy opponent. For berserkers there is nothing more important than war and combat. It is considered a great dishonor to be unable to test their

SIGN/TRACKS	RANGE ON TELLENE	SIZE COMPARISON

There's no sure way of telling if the tracks you stumble across are those of a berserker, but there are some indicators, such as footprints that wander aimlessly or that show no specific indication of purpose or direction.

6 ft

3 ft

mettle in martial prowess for a long period of time. In times of peace berserkers spend an inordinate amount of time dueling against one another.

Berserker women are not uncommon and are segregated from wives. These women are nearly indistinguishable from the men in combat, the lone exception being the lack of a beard. Wives are not warriors, but they are not without combat prowess. While they are not allowed on raids many are surprised to find that they are more than competent with weapons when the need arises. Wives tend to the day-to-day activities of the clan and hunt, gather, sew, cook and clean as needed. They perform all the requisite duties to keep the clan operational. It is a great honor to become the wife of a berserker, as such women take immense pride in their work and their role among the clan.

Berserkers speak the Fhokki tongue and have little use for the written word though they are a passionate people with a rich oral tradition. Legendary warriors are immortalized in epic songs and poems that are passed down from father to son. Few other tales are remembered and berserkers don't waste much breath on legends that don't involve combat. Berserkers are prideful and go to great lengths to maintain their honor. Those that become disgraced often go on great "war binges". The dishonored will travel into dangerous territory full of humanoids hoping to slay as many as possible before they are able to die an honorable death. In some instances these warriors will seek out others to travel with them so that their fate may be recorded and recounted to their clan at a later date.

Tribes live in temporary dwellings, or rude campsites, never staying in one location longer than needed. In peacetime, they follow flocks of sheep or herds of bison for food. Some clans evolve into mercenary bands, but it this is an uncommon occurrence. In the rare instances when berserkers settle down, they dwell in simple log homes large enough for several families. Some berserker clans live in permanent log villages where their wives and children remain. In these instances, the war clans travel a circuitous route in search of battle, returning as often as possible to rest and visit their families before the next war.

Ecology:

Sages assume that nearly all berserker clans are descendant from Fhokki, as they share a similarity in appearance and battle tactics. Where they differ is that berserkers are loyal only to their war clan, as opposed to their birth clan. If a clan were to be destroyed, or disband, the berserkers form a new one, or join with others. Migrating warriors are not entirely uncommon especially during downtimes without battle, as over-eager warriors migrate to a new, stronger war leader. As a result war bands are formed from several, if not dozens, of tribes.

Berserkers dwell in the open plains and hills of the world, though they can be found in any area where there is war, or ritualized combat. They take great pride in defending their homelands from marauding bands of humanoids, as well as human invaders. In all other aspects they are similar to typical tribes of Fhokki throughout Tellene.

On Tellene:

Like Fhokki, berserker clans can be found in the northern portions of Tellene, roaming the lands in search of war.

BERSEKKER

HIT POINTS:	25+1d10
SIZE/WEIGHT:	M/180 lbs.
TENACITY:	Brave
INTELLIGENCE:	Average
FATIGUE FACTOR:	-3/-4

MOVEMENT

CRAWL:	2½
WALK:	5
JOG:	10
RUN:	15
SPRINT:	20

SAVES

PHYSICAL:	+2
MENTAL:	+1
DODGE:	+2

ATTACK:
Berserkers attack with a variety of weapons, though preferring the battle axe (4d4p+2).

SPECIAL DEFENSES:
Shield use (*e.g.,* medium shields improve Defense from 0 to +6); unarmored Berserkers have DR 0

GENERAL INFO

ACTIVITY CYCLE:	Diurnal
NO. APPEARING:	10-100
% CHANCE IN LAIR:	5%
FREQUENCY:	Infrequent
ALIGNMENT:	Any Chaotic
VISION TYPE:	Standard
AWARENESS/SENSES:	Standard
HABITAT:	Any
DIET:	Omnivorous
ORGANIZATION:	Clan
CLIMATE/TERRAIN:	Any

YIELD

MEDICINAL:	nil
SPELL COMPONENTS:	nil
HIDE/TROPHY:	nil
TREASURE:	Berserkers may have a great deal of plunder in the form of coins and slaves if returning from raiding
EDIBLE:	yes, if you do not object to cannibalism
OTHER:	nil
EXPERIENCE POINT VALUE:	67

HUMANS: BRIGAND

Also Known As:
Bandit, Highwayman,
Cutthroat, Thug

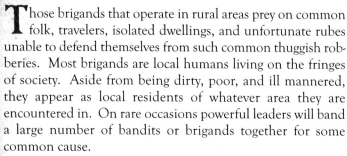

Wherever hard coin is pressed from one palm to the next or wherever horses packed down with goods pound along well-travelled routes, you can be sure of one thing —the brigand is nearby.

Like barn rats drawn to grain stores they hope to benefit from the hard labor and toil of others. These unsavory characters are constantly on the hunt. They come in all shapes and sizes and hail from every land. There's no avoiding them.

That 'cripple' perched on the wall near the front gate? He's most likely the eyes and ears for comrades nearby, reporting who has a glint of silver in his pouch or fold of silk tucked away in a saddle bag. Most likely he's not a cripple at all, but simply content to steal by falsely taking coin through misplaced charity. His beady eyes dart to and fro studying the crowds, and he often steals from the very persons who showed him compassion.

I never enter or leave a town where I don't feel their wicked prying eyes on me, sizing me up (or rather the size of my coin pouch) and making designs on how to do me in and lift my possessions.

I have several rules when it comes to traveling. Never travel alone! Never flash my coin or valuables in public and always remain armed. And never – no, never – travel the back roads. Not that such precautions have spared me from the experience of being knocked about the head, stripped and relieved of my property. Each time I'm just thankful my life wasn't taken as well.

In some areas, especially near the larger cities, travellers are often approached by individuals who express great concern over their safety. For a price, he explains, he will see to they make it to their destination unmolested. Such an individual further offers that he has the 'in' with the local thieves of the area who will not give trouble to anyone under his protection. Don't believe it!

He will take your money and lead you into an ambush to lighten your load and steal your boots. The only sure way to avoid the brigand is to stay home and keep your door locked. —

Those brigands that operate in rural areas prey on common folk, travelers, isolated dwellings, and unfortunate rubes unable to defend themselves from such common thuggish robberies. Most brigands are local humans living on the fringes of society. Aside from being dirty, poor, and ill mannered, they appear as local residents of whatever area they are encountered in. On rare occasions powerful leaders will band a large number of bandits or brigands together for some common cause.

Bandits are typically encountered in groups of no more than 20 individuals, though on rare occasions an influential leader will muster a band nearly double that.

Brigands can be encountered in groups as high as the hundreds, depending on the strength of their leader and his ability to recruit men. More organized than bandits, brigands tend to be led by high level fighters that have some military experience, or possess the leadership skills to handle, and organize, a large number of men.

For every 20 bandits or brigands encountered there will be a sub-leader with a 2-point bonus to Attack, Damage and Speed. Furthermore, this leader will be armored in studded leather armor and carry the best weapon among the lot. Groups that number 40 or more also include a fighter of no less than 6th level as a leader.

SIGN/TRACKS

One trick I've often used is to carry a bait-pouch on my belt while keeping my primary stash of coins hidden elsewhere. If confronted by brigands hopefully they take the lesser pouch and make good their escape. This tactic does carry risk — if the take isn't deemed great enough some brigands will cut your throat.

RANGE ON TELLENE

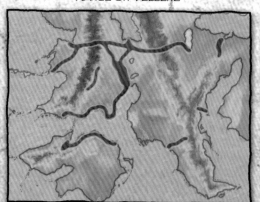

SIZE COMPARISON

Bands that number over 50 have a 25% chance that there is a cleric or mage of no less than 5th level among them. Groups of 75 or more also have a 25% chance that there are 1d4 apprentice mages, or acolyte clerics, serving with the group. In addition the leader of the band will be no less than 10th level. Assemblies of 100 or more include mounted warriors and thieves as well as those on foot. Those groups that live in rugged or mountainous terrain have less use for horses.

Combat/Tactics:

Brigands use a wide variety of tactics depending on the number encountered, but almost always attempt to ambush unwary victims in an attempt to gain the element of surprise. Small groups generally have their sights set on simple robberies. As such they wait until their quarry is nearly on top of them before springing forth to attack. Bandits prefer using ranged weapons whenever possible, along with any other dirty tactics or traps they can think up, and often times, archers will lie hidden to support their comrades.

Bandits nearly always attempt to use terrain to their advantage whenever possible, fleeing into pre-determined escape routes if the fight goes poorly. Bandits typically flee if they are out numbered or if they lose their leader (or a large portion of their force) in combat.

Habitat/Society:

Groups of brigands form on the fringes of society, banding together for a common purpose – typically to commit their crimes. These men and women are usually too lazy to work for a living, and choose to rob and steal in order to make ends meet. Whatever the reason they typically lair together in small hidden camps, old ruins, caves, or even large manors and castles, depending on the success of their group. Some countries on Tellene take a harsh stance towards banditry and will often attempt to drive large, organized groups from the region, lest they become a problem.

In-fighting and greed are typical of many bandit groups and leadership changes are common. Successful bands always have one thing in common, however – a strong, central leadership with little, if any, dissention.

Ecology:

Brigands live off the land and the spoils from their robberies. They contribute nothing to society and, since nearly all of them possess an aversion to hard work, they do not farm or herd. Some bandits have been known to trade stolen goods for services and items that they need. Those isolated in camps steal or hunt for their needs, moving on when they cannot continue their existence. In all other respects, brigands are typical of humans in the area in which they are found.

On Tellene:

Brigands can be found in the rural areas, and fringes of society, in all areas where humans live. They are particularily prevalent along trade routes.

BRIGAND

HIT POINTS:	21+1d6
SIZE/WEIGHT:	M/150 lbs
TENACITY:	Nervous
INTELLIGENCE:	Average
FATIGUE FACTOR:	-1/0

MOVEMENT

CRAWL:	2½
WALK:	5
JOG:	10
RUN:	15
SPRINT:	20

SAVES

PHYSICAL:	0
MENTAL:	+1
DODGE:	+1

ATTACK:
Brigands use a variety of weapons but favor light crossbows (2d6p, RoF 20) and short swords (2d6p); damage is by weapon type.

SPECIAL DEFENSES:
Shield use (e.g., medium shields improve Defense from +1 to +7); unarmored DR is 0

GENERAL INFO

ACTIVITY CYCLE:	Any (tend toward nocturnal)
NO. APPEARING:	2-8 (ruffians); 11-30 (camp)
% CHANCE IN LAIR:	25%
FREQUENCY:	Commonplace
ALIGNMENT:	Chaotic tending towards evil
VISION TYPE:	Standard
AWARENESS/SENSES:	Standard
HABITAT:	Trade Routes
DIET:	Omnivore
ORGANIZATION:	Band
CLIMATE/TERRAIN:	Any

YIELD

MEDICINAL:	nil
SPELL COMPONENTS:	nil
HIDE/TROPHY:	bandits often have bounties on their heads
TREASURE:	bandits may have a fair bit of treasure but they tend to spend, not hoard, so it may be fleeting
EDIBLE:	yes, if you can stomach the taste of villainy
OTHER:	nil
EXPERIENCE POINT VALUE:	34

HYDRA

Also Known As: Lernaea

As I recall, some herders claimed a big lizard was preying on the sheep in the hills near Namidu. I was recuperating from another job at the time, and so was inclined to let big lizards do as they pleased. Wouldn't you know it - the next day a band of treasure hunters rode in and tried to hire me. Seems one of the earl's sons had persuaded them to do the job, but they didn't know the area and wanted me as guide. The amount of coin they offered seemed promisin', so I agreed and we set off, accompanied by the earl's boy.

It didn't take me long to find the cave; the big lizard had left a trail a blind man could follow. The knight put his little band in formation and they slipped in as precisely as you please, while I waited a safe distance away with the youth. Well, a few minutes later, from the other direction, came this big old dragon with so many heads wavin' I couldn't get a good count of 'em. Seems it was comin' back home for a nap.

There was nothin' we could do but watch, and soon after it entered the cave came all the yellin' and clangin' armor and such you'd expect. Then it got real quiet, and I figured either the beast was dead or the hunters were, and I was just about to slip up to the cave and have a peek inside when out came the knight, clatterin' in his blood-spattered armor as he stumbled down the hill. No one followed him.

He'd pushed up his faceplate so we had no trouble hearin' him speak – which he did, I tell you, mutterin' all the way down the rocky trail. At the bottom, he stopped to lay a smack upside the head of the youth, then stomped straight fer his horse and rode off without lookin' back. I reckon I'd have done the same thing if I'd been him. - ⚔

One powerfully-beaked head would make this creature a formidable opponent. Up to twelve heads makes for a very bad day.

With a body like a huge lizard and sprouting four to twelve similar heads atop snake-like necks, the hydra is a fearsome sight to behold.

Hydras are remarkably similar in form, with bulky bodies and dorsal spines, with a base color tending to be gray-brown with lighter undersides. The jowls of males are tan and the scales around the eyes are yellow. Males also have femoral pores along each inner thigh that exude pheromones during breeding season.

The typical adult stands about 8 feet tall at the shoulder, or more than 20 feet tall with heads extended upwards. From head to tail tip, it stands roughly 30 feet long and weighs some 15,000 pounds.

Hydra heads do not each have what other species would consider a 'brain.' Instead, each head contains a loose network of nerves that connect to the rest of the central nervous system found through the body. This allows the hydra to function even when all but one of its heads is severed or otherwise so damaged as to be unable to function. When the last head is destroyed, the effect is the same as destroying a human brain.

Because of certain muscle arrangements and natural weak points in the vertebrae of the neck, a hydra can regenerate a severed head, but it grows back slowly over several weeks. The new head does not

SIGN/TRACKS

RANGE ON TELLENE

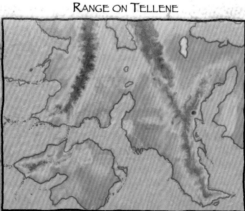

SIZE COMPARISON

get the colors or other markings of the original head and usually appears to be deep gray or jet black in color. Heads do not regenerate if removed and the neck is cauterized.

Combat/Tactics:

When hunting, the hydra simply waits in hiding for prey to pass by, and then attacks. If the prey manages to flee, the hydra follows, using its forked tongues to smell the air and track its meal.

A hydra can attack as many targets simultaneously as it has heads. Thus, a four-headed hydra can attack four different targets, while a twelve-headed hydra can battle twelve different targets simultaneously, assuming that all are within reach.

Hydras are increasingly lethal as the number of heads they possess increases. Not only do they attack more frequently but the savagery of said bites is amplified. A hydra's bite does 2d8p+X where X is the number of heads. Thus a ten-headed hydra does 2d8p+10 with each bite.

Habitat/Society:

Hydras are found in a variety of habitats across Tellene, ranging from deserts to grasslands. Most hydras are diurnal and typically bask on rocks or logs during the day (behind any available cover so as not to alert passing prey), returning to their homes in mountain or woodland caves at night.

Hydras are largely solitary, coming together only to breed and raise young. Mating begins during the month of Mustering and continues through Replanting, with the eggs laid in Reaping. About two to three eggs are incubated for seven to eight months, hatching in Declarations. Young hydras take around three to five years to mature, with siblings often fighting amongst themselves until one one remains. They are among the rare vertebrates capable of parthenogenesis, in which females may lay viable eggs if males are absent.

Hydras may live as long as 150 years.

Ecology:

Hydras are carnivores. When it comes to hunting, the hydra is very picky, preferring sheep and goats over larger unguluates but eating any type of carrion. Should other tasty prey (such as humans, demi-humans or even some of the fouler humanoids) present itself, they gladly attack this new meal with gusto.

They occasionally do battle with other great lizards and monsters for possession of a cave lair, but such occurrances are uncommon at best.

On Tellene:

Hydras can be found throughout Tellene, but are so isolated that stories of them are often confused with dragons or other giant lizards.

The dwarves from the region around Geanavue tell stories of a hydra that has taken up residence in one of the mountains, but rumors of strange creatures are common here and this may be merely another old dwarves' tale.

[1] It is easier to compute the seconds during which a hydra does not attack. By subtracting the # heads from 10, you determine the 'vacant' seconds that should be evenly spaced. For example, a seven-headed hydra attacks on 1,2,4,5,6,8 & 9 but not 3,7 or 10. 12-headed varieties attack twice on 1 & 5 and 11-headed specimens twice on 5.

[2] If fresh hydra blood is applied to a wound prior to casting a curing spell, an additional d4p Hit Points are recovered.

[3] Mounting all the heads together is the proper method to display a hydra; rakes have been known to exaggerate their prowess by adding additional heads from distinct individuals; this duplicity can be uncovered by an average Monster Lore skill check.

HYDRA

HIT POINTS:	48+(4d8/head)
SIZE/WEIGHT:	E/7+ tons
TENACITY:	Brave
INTELLIGENCE:	Animal, Low
FATIGUE FACTOR:	-1 (x # of heads)

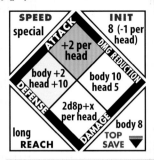

SPEED: special
INIT: 8 (-1 per head)
ATTACK: +2 per head
DMG REDUCTION: body +2 head +10 / body 10 head 5
DEFENSE: 2d8p+x per head
DAMAGE
REACH: long
TOP SAVE: body 8

MOVEMENT

CRAWL:	2½
WALK:	5
JOG:	10
RUN:	15
SPRINT:	20

SAVES

PHYSICAL:	+2/head
MENTAL:	+2/head
DODGE:	+2/head

ATTACK:
Speed is 10 divided by the number of heads (spread attacks evenly)[1].
Each head bites for 2d8p+X damage (where X=# heads); May attack multiple opponents.

SPECIAL DEFENSES:
Threshold of Pain checks do not apply to the heads.

GENERAL INFO

ACTIVITY CYCLE:	Diurnal
NO. APPEARING:	1
% CHANCE IN LAIR:	25%
FREQUENCY:	Sporadic
ALIGNMENT:	Non
VISION TYPE:	Low Light Vision
AWARENESS/SENSES:	Acute sense of smell
HABITAT:	Caves
DIET:	Carnivorous
ORGANIZATION:	Individuals
CLIMATE/TERRAIN:	Any, save arctic

YIELD

MEDICINAL:	drinking hydra blood alleviates symptoms of diabetes
SPELL COMPONENTS:	fresh blood, aids in curing spells[2]
HIDE/TROPHY:	yes[3]
TREASURE:	incidental
EDIBLE:	yes
OTHER:	nil
EXPERIENCE POINT VALUE:	492 (4 heads), 675 (5 heads), 925 (6 heads), 1242 (7 heads), 1625 (8 heads), 2075 (9 heads), 2592 (10 heads), 3175 (11 heads), 3825 (12 heads)

HYDRA, AQUATIC

Also Known As: Ladon, Borgakk, Rockworm Hydra

I've told you about runnin' into that other hydra, though I didn't know what its name was then. Well, I've learned more since then, thanks to the bad luck that gets me into these scrapes and the good luck that gets me out.

It seems that big lizards aren't the only kind of hydras out there. There's also the rockworm hydra that lives in the Netherdeep and slips outta its underground lake to hunt fer food. Now, it's bad enough that the thing can see in the dark, but this thing's also got all sorts of different ways to kill you. It don't just bite — it might sting ya, spit acid into your face, breathe fire or even squeeze ya to death.

You might think that, since this monster's got all sorts of unusual lookin' heads, that each one naturally does somethin' different. Well, that is the case. Problem is — no two of these things are the same. I've been unlucky enough to run into a handful of them over the years, and not a single encounter went the way I expected.

Most of the heads were new each time, and those I thought I did recognize weren't the same colors I remembered from before. They didn't attack the same way either. The blue spiny-crested one didn't spit acid no more. Instead, it tried to wrap itself around my body and squeeze me to death.

Take my advice — you see one of these things, just get to a distance and study how they act. Don't expect them all to do things the same way. And don't bother chippin' away at that stony body. Aim fer the heads instead. That's where the danger is. - ⌐

This bizarre creature has a stony, snake-like body with four to twelve fleshy heads budding from long, worm-like necks. Each of the protruding heads and necks is of a different color and are so dissimilar that they seem to be from separate creatures. Roughly 1 to 2 feet below each head appear two vestigial limbs or tentacles that are remnants of their ancestors' legs.

Aquatic hydras have a fragile genome that is incredibly susceptible to the natural toxins produced by fungi and other subterranean creatures or minerals. Although these toxins are not poisonous, they do cause an unusually high mutation rate among aquatic hydras. These nonlethal mutations accumulate within the gene pool and increase the amount of genetic variation among offspring, thus explaining the different colors, shapes and methods of attack. Like the landbound hydra, the aquatic hydra has a similarly developed nerve net that allows the creature to continue to function even when only one undamaged head remains.

SIGN/TRACKS

Novice trackers might easily mistake the trail of a borgakk for the slitherings of a giant snake. I've done so myself, to my eternal chagrin.
The main clue you need to remember is the depth of the track. The hydra's rocky body is much heavier than the body of a giant snake of similar size, and the impression in the earth is thus that much deeper.
On stone, you'll see the same sign, only it leaves scrapes along the floor in a manner that no giant snakeskin is tough enough to do. Also, keep your eyes open for signs of fire breath or acid spittle that might indicate a creature with those kinds of attacks.

SIZE COMPARISON

Male aquatic hydras tend to have brightly colored heads of various shades. Females sport similar colors, but are much more subdued. Both sexes have stony green-gray bodies.

From head(s) to tail tip, an adult aquatic hydra averages about 30 to 40 feet long and weighs approximately 4½ tons.

Combat/Tactics:

Each head has a different method of attack, although the creature can only attack with three heads simultaneously. Roll a d6 on the accompanying chart to determine head and attack type or devise your own.

Habitat/Society/Ecology:

Aquatic hydras are solitary carnivores that eat most living creatures. Males attract females by waving their brightly colored heads and necks, which one would think to be a mistake, since the females consume the males shortly after the breeding process occurs.

Random Body Style Chart

Head Type

1	Standard hydra
2	Crustacean-like
3	Lizard-like
4	Spiny-crested
5	Sharp-toothed
6	Multi-eyed with d6 tentacles

Attack type

1-2	Bite (as standard hydra)
3	Grab (re-roll for secondary attack mode). Grab does no damage but facilitates automatic hit with secondary attack mode every 10 seconds. Can only break hold with knock-back to the head or Feat of Strength value (*vs. d20p+12*).
4	Breathes fire at one target for 2d8p damage. Dex save versus d20p + hydra attack value results in ½ damage.
5	Paralyzing sting; Con save required versus d20 + hydra attack value to avoid paralysis for for 2d8p hours.
6	Acidic spittle directed at one target for 2d8p damage. Dex save versus d20p + hydra attack value results in no damage.

Color

1	Golden
2	Red
3	Yellow
4	Blue
5	Purple
6	Green

AQUATIC HYDRA

HIT POINTS:	40+(3d8/head)
SIZE/WEIGHT:	G/4½ tons
TENACITY:	Brave
INTELLIGENCE:	Animal, Low
FATIGUE FACTOR:	-1 (x # of heads)

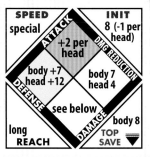

MOVEMENT

CRAWL:	2½
WALK:	5
JOG:	10
RUN:	15
SWIM:	20

SAVES

PHYSICAL:	+2/head
MENTAL:	+2/head
DODGE:	+2/head

ATTACK:
Speed is 10 divided by the number of heads (spread attacks evenly).
Each head deals a bite of 2d8p+X (where X=# heads) points of damage or a special attack. May attack multiple opponents.

SPECIAL DEFENSES:
Threshold of Pain checks do not apply to the heads.

GENERAL INFO

ACTIVITY CYCLE:	Nocturnal
NO. APPEARING:	1
% CHANCE IN LAIR:	40%
FREQUENCY:	Unusual
ALIGNMENT:	Non
VISION TYPE:	Extreme Low Light Vision
AWARENESS/SENSES:	Sensitive to vibrations within 1000 ft
HABITAT:	Lakes or larger bodies of water
DIET:	Carnivorous
ORGANIZATION:	Individuals
CLIMATE/TERRAIN:	Any wetlands or subterranean aquatic

YIELD

MEDICINAL:	nil
SPELL COMPONENTS:	unknown; further scholarly research is needed
HIDE/TROPHY:	yes (see standard hydra)
TREASURE:	incidental
EDIBLE:	no
OTHER:	nil
EXPERIENCE POINT VALUE:	492 (4 heads), 675 (5 heads), 925 (6 heads), 1242 (7 heads), 1625 (8 heads), 2075 (9 heads), 2592 (10 heads), 3175 (11 heads), 3825 (12 heads)

IMP

Also Known As: Katatra, Mangato

If thou dost chance upon an animal time and time again in thy daily activities, mind its actions. I wouldest not foster such paranoia in lay members of the community for it doth manifest itself in ways most contrary to harmonious fellowship, yet those called to a higher purpose must always be mindful of odd occurrences that mayest portent more.

Shouldest thou be suspect of a creature, act not with apprehension. If thy guess be true, thou wouldst spook the tail. Rather, playest the role of a foole and seem too pay not the slightest heed. Observeth its movements in a manner most casual. Doth it act peculiar and manifest an unusual and persistent curiosity? If so, it mayest be both a shapechanger and a spy. The imp is a likely candidate for it is a creature most sly and given to such action.

If thou be cocksure of a surreptitious watcher, know well that an evil force with resources a'plenty hath interest in thine doings. Rest easy for the odds be long that the imp itself will seek to cause bodily harm - though he may attempt to steal away small items.

Act not in haste or malice for it be apt to change form to deceive those that might seek its capture. Slaying this nefarious being mayest prove a distraction costly in time and resources and, in greatest irony, doth provide information of value dear to its master.

If thou be most clever, turnest this spy into thine unwitting ally. Ply him with information most deceptive. Feign secrecy but speak falsely of thy plans such that a listener secreted nearby may overhear. Enscribe errant charts and messages upon parchment but fail to secure them in a manner adequate. In all things act in a manner the enemy expecteth until he has laid his trump. In so doing you may mislead your foe and more easily best him. - ◉

These evil agents serve as the eyes and ears for their Hellish masters.

Imps are denizens of Hell, where they form the lowest rank of beings elevated from the writhing larval mass of tortured souls. Their appearance is reminiscent of a human child, albeit misshapen, with cloven-hooved goat legs, a sinewy tail, tiny horn nubs and proportionately large membranous wings. Do not permit their childlike appearance to cloud your perception of these creatures. They are unrepentantly evil and in every way as dedicated to the cause of tyranny as their larger and more terrifying devil-kin.

They are dispatched to Tellene with regularity to provide aid in matters for which Infernal assistance has been beseeched. This aid often proves a two-edged sword for the supplicant, in that the support rendered is informative (often cryptically so) rather than substantive. The recipient of this endowment must also contend with the fact that his progress and allegiance is continuously being reported back to those from whom he requested patronage.

When dispatched to Tellene, an imp gains the ability to transform into an animal. This will be either a rook, a giant rat, a large spider, a goat kid or a rhesus monkey, and is chosen beforehand based upon the nature of the imp's mission. Only one such form is granted and it manifests individual characteristics of the species that a trained observer may identify if repeatedly encountered. Note that if assuming the form of a large spider, the imp's natural toxin (see below) substitutes for the spider's. In other forms, it cannot employ its toxic sting.

Combat/Tactics:

On Tellene, imps serve primarily as spies, messengers and counselors (though most often serving as a mere conduit to

Shouldest thou encounter an imp, knowest that it abideth not the iconography of just gods and a goodly priest canst ward it hence.

A wicked cleric, if his idolatrous master wisheth it so, canst extract some small and fleeting measure of servitude.

WILL FACTOR
13

SIZE COMPARISON

6 ft

3 ft

their tyrannical masters than proffering their own guidance). Their combat prowess is extremely limited and generally defensive in nature permitting the imp to carry out its primary roles in the face of casual opposition.

Should it find that force is required to remove some sentient impediment, an imp utilizes its superior initiative to (hopefully) surprise its foe with a sting from its tail. Though it inflicts but a single point of damage, it injects a paralytic venom necessitating a Constitution save (*vs. d20p+5*) to avoid a bout of painful muscle seizures lasting 2d12p hours. The imp may continue attacking at two-second intervals using its claws and bite (though the former is of dubious efficacy causing but 2d3p-3 damage each). It likely thereafter attempts another stinging attack but should this also fail to immobilize its opponent, the imp endeavors to exit the encounter if possible by fighting defensively and choosing an opportune time to fly away.

Imps have a number of immunities including resistance to fire of all sorts regardless of intensity. Toxins and diseases have no effect. They are supernaturally resistant to blows from standard weapons (though silvered and greater magical ones may substantively broach this protection). When killed, their bodies dissolve into nothingness.

Though imps are not subject to Threshold of Pain checks, their diminutive size equates to an inability to sustain great physical damage. This is not an overwhelming concern as the creature can recover from the severest of wounds in short order regenerating 1 lost Hit Point per 10 seconds. The only sure method of killing an imp is to immerse it in holy water.

All imps possess the ability to Sense Magical Auras (as the spell), Translate speech (as the spell) as well as make their own verbal communication comprehensible (per the Polyglot spell).

Habitat/Society/Ecology:

Imps are strict adherents to order, discipline and hierarchy and will lawfully carry out orders of those designated as their overseer. Above all else, they respect the ruthless application of power. Should their master fail to live up to their idealized standards by being indecisive, inexact in his commands, merciful, or fail to exert firm control a subordinate imp seeks to undermine his authority by perverting his directives. Imps are masters of obeying the strictest literal interpretation of any order and notorious for withholding information not explicitly demanded of them.

On Tellene:

When dispatched from Hell to serve a mortal master, an imp's true allegiance will always be to the devil that sent him forth not his temporary superior. If the interests of the two coincide, so much the better for the imp. Should the two diverge, the imp steadfastly works to undermine the mortal using every passive-aggressive technique available.

IMP

HIT POINTS:	8+2d4
SIZE/WEIGHT:	T/25 lbs
TENACITY:	Nervous
INTELLIGENCE:	Bright
FATIGUE FACTOR:	n/a

MOVEMENT

CRAWL:	1¼
WALK:	2½
JOG:	5
RUN:	7½
FLY:	20

SAVES

PHYSICAL:	+10
MENTAL:	+16
DODGE:	+14

ATTACK:
Imps can bite for d4p points of damage, claw for 2d3p-3, or deal 1 point with their tails while inflicting a poison that paralyzes for 2d12p hours (CON save vs. d20p+5)

SPECIAL DEFENSES:
Immune to fire, toxins & diseases; regeneration
Silvered weapons reduce DR by 9.

GENERAL INFO

ACTIVITY CYCLE:	Any
NO. APPEARING:	1
% CHANCE IN LAIR:	5%
FREQUENCY:	Unusual
ALIGNMENT:	Lawful Evil
VISION TYPE:	Undead Sight
AWARENESS/SENSES:	Can sense Magical Auras
HABITAT:	Any
DIET:	None
ORGANIZATION:	Individuals or gang
CLIMATE/TERRAIN:	Any

YIELD

MEDICINAL:	nil
SPELL COMPONENTS:	nil
HIDE/TROPHY:	nil
TREASURE:	nil
EDIBLE:	no
OTHER:	nil

EXPERIENCE POINT VALUE: 242

I

KOBOLD

Also Known As: Dovurin

I've heard plenty of explorers boast about slaying kobolds. They say the critters are nothing but sword fodder; they're just nuisances that get in the way of the big game, and so on. Well, that's not wrong, but that's fighting man talk – a thief's perspective is different.

See, I'm in this business for the loot, not the battle. A good job is when I can slip across an open courtyard under cover of darkness, shimmy up a wall, slip along through dimly-lit corridors and hide in shadows until I reach the treasury. Then I just pick the lock, grab the goods and make my way out again without being detected. I don't need to bloody my blade at all.

Guards are usually the greatest variable. In my experience, most wealthy folk figure that the bigger a guard is, the fewer they need. Well, that just makes it easier for me. There's less pairs of eyes and ears that might spot me.

With kobolds, though, there's always so damn many of them. As soon as you alert one, it starts howling and yowling for reinforcements and pretty soon you've got a whole pack nipping at you. Then there's the fact that you're not just hiding from their eyes or sneaking past their ears. They've got a pretty good sense of smell, and a mere whiff of your scent might send them curiously trotting over to see what the new odor is. I recommend rubbing yourself with lemon juice or spices like red pepper. From my experience, they don't much care for those.

True, they don't have much worth robbing on their own, but dark wizards and other near-human monsters sometimes keep them as slaves to guard their lairs. Many's the time I've stumbled across a pack of kobolds where I least expected them. After all, you expect to find kobolds in a kobold den, but if you don't (or can't) reconnoiter properly, you won't expect them in that mage's tower or some other odd location. Remember – always do the best scouting you can! - ᛗ

These clever dog men often shy away from a straight-on fight and rely heavily on tricks and traps.

The smallest of the humanoid races, this hairless canid stands a mere 3 feet tall and weighs in at about 40 to 50 pounds. A kobold has a short, canine snout, largish ears and two small, impish bone protrusions or rounded horns adorn the top of his head. Its mouth contains a full set of sharp, lupine teeth used to eat raw meat, but are not large enough to be used effectively in combat (other than in a near-perfect defense situation). Its front limbs end in a strange combination of vestigial paw pads, four fingers (ending in small pads) and a dew claw along the wrist. It stands bipedal so that its odd hand-paw combinations can be used to hold tools and wield weapons. A kobold's long, snaky, hairless tail, which helps balance the creature, ends in a devilish point. Skin is dark brown, reddish brown or black. Kobold eyes are dark brown with large black pupils.

Kobolds make their dens in burrows, natural caves and gloomy woodlands. They prefer hilly landscapes with marshy valleys, but also live in mountainous terrain, bleak swamplands and lightly wooded meadowlands (where they will likely dig an underground burrow). Sometimes kobolds can be found in the Netherdeep, but they dislike mining and are not suited to that type of labor and the underground lifestyle, despite their natural low-light vision.

These creatures hate all other sentient life forms, but in

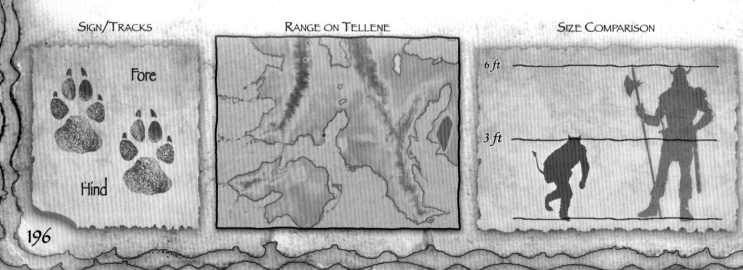

SIGN/TRACKS

Fore

Hind

RANGE ON TELLENE

SIZE COMPARISON

6 ft

3 ft

particular, they hate halflings, whom they attack on sight in preference to other targets. Sages tend to believe it is jealousy over the halfling success with canine labor on their farms and occasionally as mounts that breeds this intense hatred. Their choice of habitat also frequently brings them into conflict with gnomes, although, they dislike them slightly less than their portly cousins, but still attack them on sight. They also despise pixie-fairies, brownies, leprechauns and all small fairy and pixie-kin, and seek to capture and torture such creatures.

Kobolds dislike humans and their demi-human allies, and seek to harm them if given an opportunity with reasonably low risk. They even hate other humanoids, as those races tend to enslave and/or eat kobolds when the groups meet, even if they begin a venture as cooperative equals against a mutual foe. Gnoles are the sole exception; kobolds relate well to them as gnoles apparently dislike the taste of kobold and thus generally leave them alone after joint raids. Kobolds, like gnoles, are not far along the evolutionary path beyond animals.

Like gnomes, they enjoy the company of wild animals and can communicate directly with them. Unlike gnomes, kobolds are particularly interested in predators; foremost being dogs and weasels of all types. They are quite skilled at breeding and training them for various activities, often giving the animal free reign among the den or lair. As to the cute, smaller woodland creatures, kobolds enjoy torturing, then devouring them.

Because of their small size and quickness, kobolds are rather difficult to hit cleanly. That said, once a blow hits, it usually causes considerable effect as, owing to their undersized stature, kobolds have few Hit Points and an easily-overcome Threshold of Pain. Further, their natural hide only affords one point of Damage Reduction, and their armors tend to be thick tunics with padding sewn in or bits and pieces of animal hide (typically layers of squirrel or rabbit skins) providing just one additional point of damage protection (but easily donned in but d6p seconds). Kobolds are physically weak by human standards and suffer a -3 penalty to damage, a reason why they prefer light crossbows if they can find them. Their short arms result in poor Reach against all but equally tiny foes.

Favorite weaponry includes short swords, clubs, daggers, short spears, hand axes, small morning stars, short bows, javelins and light crossbows. Kobold hunting and war parties look for easy prey and shy away from heavily armed and armored foes unless it appears they have the upper hand.

For every 20 kobolds there is a pack leader with the equivalent of studded leather armor, a human-made weapon, a 1-point penalty to Damage (instead of -3) and 15+d6 Hit Points.

If 100 or more are encountered, there are an additional 3d12p pack leaders plus an alpha-female (with the same

KOBOLD

HIT POINTS:	13+d4
SIZE/WEIGHT:	S/40-50 lbs.
TENACITY:	Nervous
INTELLIGENCE:	Slow
FATIGUE FACTOR:	-1/0

MOVEMENT

CRAWL:	1¼
WALK:	2½
JOG:	5
RUN:	7½
SPRINT:	10

SAVES

PHYSICAL:	+2
MENTAL:	+1
DODGE:	+2

ATTACK:
Most kobolds attack with daggers (2d4p-3 due to low Strength) but may wield other weapons, especially short swords.

SPECIAL DEFENSES:
Shield use (e.g., small shields increase Defense to +8); Kobolds have a natural (unarmored) DR of 1

GENERAL INFO

ACTIVITY CYCLE:	Crepuscular
NO. APPEARING:	2-8 (hunting); 3d4p+8 (warband); 20d20p (clan)
% CHANCE IN LAIR:	35%
FREQUENCY:	Frequent
ALIGNMENT:	Lawful Evil
VISION TYPE:	Low Light Vision
AWARENESS/SENSES:	Excellent[1]
HABITAT:	Burrows, caves, trees and buildings
DIET:	Omnivorous
ORGANIZATION:	Pack
CLIMATE/TERRAIN:	Any, save arctic

YIELD

MEDICINAL:	nil
SPELL COMPONENTS:	nil
HIDE/TROPHY:	none worthy of a hero
TREASURE:	3d8p trade coins each[2]; various junk in lair
EDIBLE:	yes, but tastes like gamey dog meat
OTHER:	nil
EXPERIENCE POINT VALUE:	17

K

stats) and an alpha-male (size Medium, 20+d8 Hit Points and no penalties to Damage).

If 300 or more are encountered, the pack leader is 5 feet tall, and has combat statistics that approximate that of a gnole.

Kobolds rarely have witch-doctors, with only a 10% chance of one existing in the tribe. If so, he is a mage of moderately low level (roll a d12p-4 and divide by 2 for level, with results less than one equal to one).

Kobolds make lousy miners, but can mine if required or forced. They are generally incapable of properly working a smithy, whether armor, weapon or black (the only kobold smiths known are from the legendary kobold city of Shrogga-Pravaaz). All of their tools and weapons are either stolen or crafted from wood or stone or from parts of captured implements. They craft most of their weapons from wood and are fair-to-poor bowyers and fletchers, but they excel at weaving wicker items and can make adequately-performing shields from sticks as well as baskets and the like. They are surprisingly capable at building traps using natural surroundings, such as pits covered in sticks and leaves, vine traps, swinging logs and so on, but lack the skill to engineer homes (other than digging burrows, which they accomplish by hand sans tools).

When not chopping or killing plant life out of spite, kobolds are actually very good at nurturing them; they make decent farmers and grow their own crops to supplement their diet 35% of the time. They can also cultivate locally-native brambles and thorny briars, trimming them to fit their usage.

Combat/Tactics:

These scrappy little curs have an obvious disadvantage in combat due to their size. They prefer to lie in wait and ambush enemies, pelting them with arrows or bolts, and then fleeing through the underbrush. Sometimes they intentionally lay down tracks hoping to lure the unwary into a kill zone or elaborate trap. If forced into combat, they will fight savagely with small, wicked swords and daggers, or short spears. They can employ shields, generally of poor construction or of the wicker variety (DR4; useless after one battle) and do so to avoid suffering the full force of a blow or to catch ranged attacks. Kobolds are cowardly and try to use numbers to surround their foes.

Those facing the front of enemies put on a full defense, while those at the unguarded flank or behind nip or hack at the heels of their foes. If an enemy turns to attack their assailants, they change roles, harrying from the back whenever possible. When armed with spears, kobolds also attack from the back rank, easily poking over the heads of their allies and at the torso and head of larger opponents.

Kobolds have plenty of savage pets bred and trained to fearlessly attack their enemies and for use as an alarm system. Kobolds can communicate with these animals across long distances using yips, howls and barks of various sorts. They can also use body language for non-verbal communication if within line-of-sight, although this latter method can convey little more than emotion and danger.

Kobold favorites include weasels and dogs. They are 60% likely to have 2d4p wild dogs, 30% likely to have bred and trained 50% of them to become full-fledged war dogs; 70% likely to have 2d12p weasels; 35% likely to have 2d4p giant weasels; and 50% likely to have d4p wild boars (roll for each independently; they are not mutually exclusive). They use these animals as watch dogs/sentries, scouts, guards and shock troops. Such beasts are often more dangerous to the invader than the kobolds themselves.

Habitat/Society:

Kobolds prefer to dwell in hillside burrows, natural near-surface cave formations, dismal swamps and thickets and gnarly forests with plenty of tangled underbrush. However, their top preference is to live in an abandoned or captured halfling or gnome community; after all, the best burrow is one dug by another. They even occupy formerly cozy cottages if available. As a last resort, they dig their own burrow or build a shelter of some sort for their pack.

Kobolds share their dwellings with their pets, including boars, so they are thick with the stench of animal filth, fur and the remains of kills. Aside from food preparation tables and piles of hides used as bedding, kobold lairs are unfurnished with the sole exception of any accessories captured from gnomes or halflings (including the entire lair itself in some cases). Kobolds have no appreciation for beauty and art and toss such items aside, mark it or worse.

From their lair, kobolds launch raids and send hunting parties to the surrounding territory in search of plunder and game (in that order). Kobolds mark their home territory by leaving fecal and urine scent traces on trees, bushes, rocks and the like. They harass invaders relentlessly, but may not attack aggressively, unless they believe themselves to have the upper hand.

Kobolds have a surprisingly structured social order, with the alpha-male and alpha-female in charge of the community. Each pack consists of several extended families of kobolds, working as an integrated whole. While it is their nature to bully and enslave others, this orderly social structure and relatively peaceful order is required for such weak beings to survive in the face of opposition from larger, more powerful creatures.

Kobolds have their own language and can converse with gnoles. They are 30% likely to also speak one or more of the neighboring human, demi-human and/or humanoid languages, depending on who lives in proximity, whether ally or foe. Aside from verbal language, Kobolds also communicate with each other, with gnoles, and with other canids, by visual gestures and movements, by scent signals (left by urine, for example), and by vocalizations such as yips, barks, howls, growls and yowls. Kobolds can communicate with their pets in a similar manner. Note, relations of these types are limited to emotions and simple things such as food, water, danger and so on, including information about interlopers.

Kobolds live to be about 40 years old, although some venerable ones have lived to be 65 or more. Bitches comprise 50% of the population, fighting and sharing work with male sires, but not quite as equals. Sires are slightly larger than bitches, but aside from an inch in height and 3 to 5 pounds of weight, and the two rows of four to five nipples running down the she-torso, are otherwise indistinguishable.

Most bitches have a short mating season in late fall and bear young once a year in early spring, the typical gestation period being approximately 140 days. Litters range from 4 to 12, but typically only two to four will survive to adulthood. The young are born small and helpless and require weaning for a solid 16 weeks.

The infant mortality rate is very high, with the runts suffering until being killed by the others. The mother keeps the surviving pups in a den, most often dug into the ground for warmth and protection from the various trained animals that might eat the young if given the chance.

Until they can begin eating solid food, adults of both sexes regurgitate their meals so that the pups can lap up the half-digested foods. When they begin eating solid food, both parents and other pack members bring food back for them from the hunt. These young canids may take anywhere from 16 to 24 months to grow enough to fight for scraps among the rest of the pack. By six years they are fully grown and sexually mature.

In the female group, the oldest has alpha status over the others, so a mother retains her alpha status over her daughters until she is too weak to maintain dominance, usually around 35 years of age. For the males, in contrast, the youngest male or the sire of the other males is the strongest and most dominant. Dominance is established largely without bloodshed, as most kobolds know their place in the hierarchy, but sometimes fights to the death result from challenges. Most kobolds are cowardly enough to avoid this situation – a needed result since kobolds require superior numbers to compete effectively with the other sentient races.

Ecology:

Kobolds occupy the lowest rung on the power ladder of the sentient races. Most humanoid races consider them food or slaves, while the demi-human races regard them a nuisance to be exterminated. Because of this, they have learned to keep a tight-knit, organized group. If kobolds ever get the upper hand on any race or being, they take advantage of it, killing, maiming, torturing or capturing the creature with glee. The entire pack comes out to defile the prisoner with a wide variety of bodily fluids. Kobolds always attack halflings and gnomes on sight and with great prejudice, seldom taking prisoners, but sure to bring home a carcass if possible.

Kobolds prefer the company of their own kind and their pets, but some kobold packs trade with nearby humanoid neighbors (usually goblins and occasionally gnoles, if they happen to have anything decent to trade). They avoid bugbears for that race inevitably enslaves any kobold visitors in the area.

Sometimes they even trade with hobgoblins and orcs. Although the latter can be almost as bad as bugbears, they are not as apt to set successful ambushes and are generally too clumsy in thought and deed to pose a similar threat. They avoid grel and are deathly afraid of grevans, although that latter race generally ignores kobolds (considering them noncombatants at best and mere weak animals at worst).

Subraces:

While the majority of this entry covers the standard kobold, there is one subrace of kobold that bears mentioning – the primitive kobold. These beasts actually have a fur coat and are only found in very remote locations; they never appear in warmer-than-temperate climes. One variety even wears a thick, white fur coat and inhabits mountaintops and other frigid locations.

Primitive kobolds are a tad bigger than the common kobold, having 15+d6 Hit Points, but are still size Small. They are also stronger than standard kobolds (with only -1 Damage), but do not use weapons beyond javelins, clubs and spears and do not employ shields. They are otherwise similar to standard kobolds.

Religion:

Kobolds tend, like their alignment, towards the lawful evil religions, with the god being worshipped often depending on the pack's status among other local creatures. For instance, where kobolds rule themselves, the Overlord is a favorite, but when kobolds are slaves they seem to prefer the Corruptor or the Flaymaster. The Dark One is rarely worshipped.

On Tellene:

Kobolds have many small communities dispersed throughout the known lands, generally living in the hills on the fringes of human society, near halfling or gnomic settlements so they can most easily steal livestock and other valuables from the outlying farmhouses. Kobolds live in more remote areas as well, especially when driven out of a civilized area by a determined force. The two largest known packs are in the Arajyd Hills, and the wealthy city-state of Shrogga-Pravaaz, which is completely controlled and run by kobolds.

K

[1]Kobolds have an excellent sense of smell and hearing, along with eyesight designed to detect motion, but cannot perceive all colors and can only taste salts.

[2]Kobolds carry 3d8p local trade coins each. Their lairs can contain small amounts of wealth in the form of trade, copper coins (in the thousands), gems, and many mundane items taken in raids.

LEECH MAN
Also Known As: Shepherd's Bane

I remember one time I was in this mountain stronghold full o' soldiers — you'd reckon a place like that would be safe — and some of the local leech men slipped up outta the river and inta the stable, so they could start feedin' on the horses. The stable boys noticed a few bite marks each night, but the lazy sods didn't do anythin' about it until one of the prize stallions dropped dead at an officer's feet.

It took a few days fer them to call me in, since they figured that a guard patrol oughta spot any intruders and tried that first, but the guards had no joy at it. The horses kept gettin' bit each night even with guards watchin' the stable doors — from a safe distance, I bet.

Well, I suspected what was goin' on, so once they showed me some coin I went to work. I cleared the horses outta the stables and made right sure there was only one workin' door and one open window. Then I commissioned a couple of sheep from the main pen and tethered them up right in the center of the stable floor, and splattered a bunch of cow blood around fer good measure.

It didn't take long after night fell fer those blood thieves to come climbin' up the outer wall and slippin' in through the stable window. Once they started feedin', I slipped around and barred the window behind them. Then me and a dozen soldiers went in through the only remainin' door and slaughtered the whole lot o' them. It was a hell of a mess. Took days to get the stink out. - ⚑

These cowardly, disgusting blood thieves feed off their victims while they sleep.

Leech men can infest an area for months, going undetected while killing local livestock.

Leech men is a pejorative term given to these little bastards ('blood thieves' is another), since their true name is a mystery. These spindly creatures stand about a yard high with lanky black hair, large dark eyes and mere slits for a nose. A leech man's mouth is large and protruding, filled with razor-sharp teeth like that of a lamprey. Their hands and feet are clawed, but these are for maneuverability rather than combat.

Leech men feed on mammalian blood exclusively. Since this tends to coagulate quickly and cannot be ingested in that state, they prefer to suck the blood from a live animal.

They are nocturnal and utilize the cover of darkness to forage. They make use of low light vision to find prey from a distance and then sneak up under cover of darkness, using intervening terrain to hide their movements. They possess the Climbing/Rappelling, Hiding and Sneaking skills at 40% mastery and use both to gain silent access to their next meal. They are also unusually swift and agile, capable of better speed than many other creatures of their size. Their darting movements make them difficult to both strike and defend against in combat.

L

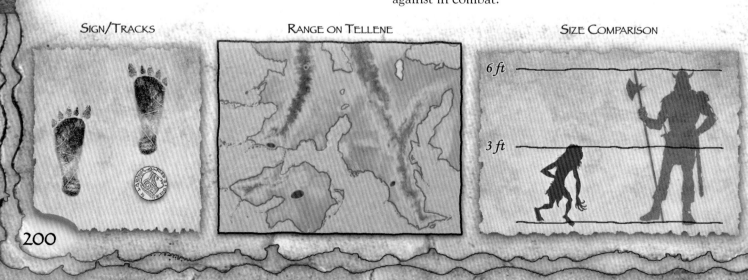

SIGN/TRACKS	RANGE ON TELLENE	SIZE COMPARISON

6 ft

3 ft

Combat/Tactics:

Leech men try to avoid battles completely, preferring not to chance injury. If forced to defend themselves from attack, they will bite fiercely. Cowards, they will seek to flee any encounter with armed foes, fighting only if cornered. Their razor maws are capable of inflicting serious wounds but, more insidiously, inject an anesthetic. Anyone bitten by a leech man must save vs. Virulence Factor 8 poison or suffer a 1-point penalty to Attack and Defense for 30 minutes. Subsequent bites compound this penalty.

They are most dangerous against sleeping or prone foes; they are just as capable as a thief of completing a coup-de-grace by biting a creature's jugular.

Habitat/Society:

Leech men seek out a good locale for feeding (a barn or corral where large animals are kept is ideal), then take up residence nearby in a thicket, a hollow old tree or even a hole in the ground and emerge at night to prey on the herd.

A leech man typically makes a small bite in a sleeping animal and then sucks the blood from the wound, draining d4p Hit Points before becoming sated. A mild anesthetic allows the leech man to go undetected in most cases. Of course, they have no qualms about feeding on humans either, emerging from the sewer at night to suck the blood of derelicts, or even being so bold as to sneak into a home through an unlocked window.

As noted previously, leech men are cowardly creatures who avoid getting embroiled in a pitched battle. However, if they are being systematically hunted, they may launch a stealthy raid in the middle of the night to murder their foes in their sleep. Though cunning and potentially malicious, they are not particularly bright. Since they must feed daily, they are quite susceptible to being baited and trapped using a readily accessible sheep or goat as a lure.

Ecology:

Leech men are parasites, living off the blood of larger creatures. They never attack a smaller animal as the effort is not worth the payoff. They can survive by eating rats, squirrels, rabbits and the like, but never willingly do so. A herdsman can detect their presence by the tell-tale round sores on the undersides or hind quarters of his larger beasts of burden (horses and cattle are favorites). Large predators that hunt similar herd animals are their main natural competitors. Lions and hyenas, for example, hunt the same prey and actively kill leech men.

On Tellene:

Leech men can be found across Tellene. They avoid colder climates and alpine settings for lack of prey, but may migrate to the valleys along with their prey as the cold weather strikes. They are very prevalent in Tarisato, Mendarn, northern Zazahni and other locations where year-round grazing is readily available for large bovines and herd animals. They avoid central Svimohzia because of the prevalence of big hunting cats.

LEECH MAN

HIT POINTS:	10+d4
SIZE/WEIGHT:	S/30 lbs.
TENACITY:	Cowardly
INTELLIGENCE:	Obtuse
FATIGUE FACTOR:	-3

SPEED 6 — INIT -1 — ATTACK +4 — DMG REDUCTION — +7 — DEFENSE — 0 — 2d4p — short REACH — DAMAGE — TOP SAVE 2

MOVEMENT

CRAWL:	2½
WALK:	5
JOG:	10
RUN:	15
SPRINT:	20

SAVES

PHYSICAL:	+3
MENTAL:	+3
DODGE:	+6

ATTACK:
Bite deals 2d4p points of damage and requires a save vs d20p+8 or suffer 1 point penalty to Attack and Defense for 30 minutes; leech men drain 1d4p HP of blood before becoming sated

SPECIAL ABILITIES:
Mastery of the Climbing, Hiding, and Sneaking skills at 40% each; can coup de gras as a thief

GENERAL INFO

ACTIVITY CYCLE:	Nocturnal
NO. APPEARING:	3-10
% CHANCE IN LAIR:	10%
FREQUENCY:	Infrequent
ALIGNMENT:	Non
VISION TYPE:	Low Light Vision
AWARENESS/SENSES:	Standard
HABITAT:	Any, usually isolated spot near prey
DIET:	Sanguivorous
ORGANIZATION:	Individuals or band
CLIMATE/TERRAIN:	Temperate to tropical, near water

L

YIELD

MEDICINAL:	healers may use leech man venom as anesthetic
SPELL COMPONENTS:	nil
HIDE/TROPHY:	nothing you'd want to hang on your wall
TREASURE:	nil
EDIBLE:	no
OTHER:	nil
EXPERIENCE POINT VALUE:	50

LEPRECHAUN

Also Known As: Tur'nylan, Jakobie

One bright day, as my companions lingered with drinks in the dimness of a local inn, I took a walk in hopes of refreshing my soul with the fine weather. It was during the course of this ramble that I heard a clacking sort of noise a little before me in a hedge.

My curiosity piqued, I peered through the leaves to see a brown pitcher, one that might hold about a gallon and a half of liquor, and a little wee bit of an old man sitting on a wooden stool. He appeared to be mending the heel of a tiny boot with equally tiny tools. Surely, I knew, no mortal man ever grew so small. Knowing that a body must never take his eyes off one of the fey, as I assumed he was, I kept my eyes affixed and stepped through the hedge, greeting the small man as kindly as if he were one of my own kin.

The little man raised up his head and thanked me kindly, whereupon I began to query him as to his purpose, all the while moving slowly closer. Could I but put my hands upon him, I thought, I might convince him to do me a good turn in exchange for his release. My old nurse once told me tales of such fey, and how they have the power to grant wishes and piles of precious coins that they've stolen from those they encounter. No doubt, I thought, my manner was pleasing enough to allay the creature's suspicions. Eyeing me coldly, he said it would be fitter for me to take care of the snake slithering over my feet than to bother decent people with foolish questions.

I was taken so by surprise with this remark that I looked down in haste, but saw no serpent of any kind. When I looked up again both the little man and his possessions were gone. Upon returning to the inn, I found it was well that I could now exchange an interesting story for drink, for the bastard sprite had taken my coin purse with him. – ẞ

Leprechauns are tiny fey, standing between 18 and 24 inches tall. They are light gray in color with reddish noses (which may originate from their strong fondness for wine), wrinkled skin and slightly in-turned feet. They claim that this abnormality gives them greater speed than other creatures of similar size, though this is but one clue to their proud character. Their chaotic nature often keeps them from associating with others of their kind, though some leprechauns have formed gangs consisting of additional leprechauns and other small fey. Most leprechauns speak the local human language.

Leprechauns are first-rate con artists who enjoy taking advantage of others. They pursue gold over any other coin or trinket, and can be very dangerous for novice adventurers to encounter. They also delight in causing trouble for vulnerable travelers. It seems the only way one is guaranteed safe from them is to travel in numbers, since rumor has it that they never waylay more than two travelers at once.

Combat/Tactics:

Leprechauns prefer to confuse and frighten their victims,

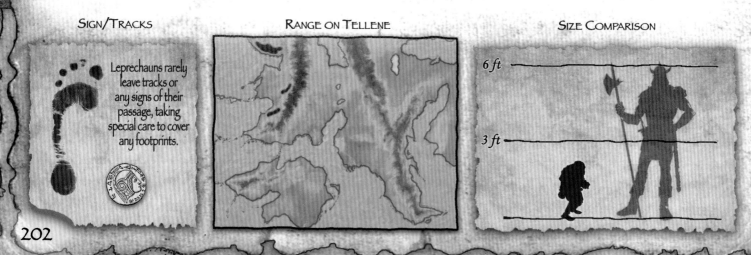

SIGN/TRACKS

Leprechauns rarely leave tracks or any signs of their passage, taking special care to cover any footprints.

RANGE ON TELLENE

SIZE COMPARISON

6 ft

3 ft

steal their coins and any other seemingly valuable or important items, and then leave the victim in a dazed and weakened state. Leprechauns can cast the Illusionary Mural, Disguise and Copycat spells. A leprechaun's Enfeeble power works like the spell of the same name, with the victim attempting an opposed saving throw immediately (*vs. d20p+8*). An individual saving against this effect is immune to any subsequent enfeebling attempts for 24 hours. A leprechaun must be able to see an opponent in order to use the spell upon him. Leprechauns often add a final touch of humiliation as they take their leave, stealing the victim's pants or pouring honey on his head.

Habitat/Society:

Leprechauns dwell in quiet, isolated locations where they have little fear of being disturbed by others. This is often a cave in a woodland glen, with a solid round door and an interior furnished with enough comforts to charm even the laziest halfling. Within this dwelling may reside up to 20 individuals all from the same family. Though they may associate with other families on occasion, leprechauns have no organizational government, and any rumors of a powerful Leprechaun King are mere guesswork.

Leprechaun sex organs and gestation are similar to those of a human, though the female ovulates only once or twice every century and continues to do so even into her old age. Twins are not uncommon, and their births are celebrated with particular joy and woe (for the chaos that mischievous twins can cause to other races, but also to their parents). Males almost never help with child rearing, even though the young remain with their parents for over a century, until they reach sexual maturity.

A typical leprechaun has a lifespan of about 500 years.

Ecology:

Leprechauns are crepuscular creatures, favoring the twilight hours in which to venture outside their lairs in search of food or entertainment. They seem to have cast-iron stomachs, able to consume any food or drink common amongst humanoids. They love pipeweed and wine (and other strong drink), perhaps more than any other race. Leprechaun ruffians have been known to ambush travelers solely for these two goods, leaving behind other items of more value but less vice.

On Tellene:

So far, leprechauns have only been encountered in Brandobia. While most favor cold climates like that of northern Cosdol, explorers in southern Mendarn have also reported encountering such creatures.

In the Narond Woods, a gang of seven pixies and three leprechaun ruffians are said to be waylaying travelers. One adventurer who claims to have met this gang states that they are mainly interested in wine (particularly vintages from Shyta-na-Dobyo), potions, and gems. It is uncertain to what uses they put their treasures, but it is surely not for the good of anyone else.

LEPRECHAUN

HIT POINTS:	6+d8
SIZE/WEIGHT:	T/20 lbs.
TENACITY:	Nervous
INTELLIGENCE:	Brilliant
FATIGUE FACTOR:	-3

SPEED	INIT
10	-3

ATTACK: +3
DEFENSE: +11
DMG REDUCTION: 0
DAMAGE: 2d4p-4
REACH: by weapon -1 foot
TOP SAVE: 2

MOVEMENT

CRAWL:	1¼
WALK:	2½
JOG:	5
RUN:	7½
SPRINT:	10

SAVES

PHYSICAL:	+27
MENTAL:	+30
DODGE:	+31

ATTACK:
Leprechauns attack with magical powers (Enfeeble; save vs. d20p+8) or daggers (2d4p-4) when cornered

SPECIAL:
Illusionary Mural, Disguise, Copycat (save vs. d20p+8); Listening mastery of 90%

GENERAL INFO

ACTIVITY CYCLE:	Crepuscular
NO. APPEARING:	1 to 20
% CHANCE IN LAIR:	5%
FREQUENCY:	Sporadic
ALIGNMENT:	Chaotic Neutral
VISION TYPE:	Standard
AWARENESS/SENSES:	Keen hearing (Listening skill 90%)
HABITAT:	Subterranean homes
DIET:	Omnivorous
ORGANIZATION:	Family or gang
CLIMATE/TERRAIN:	Cold to temperate hills and dales

YIELD

MEDICINAL:	nil
SPELL COMPONENTS:	nil
HIDE/TROPHY:	nil
TREASURE:	leprechauns are said to store pots of gold
EDIBLE:	yes, but only monsters do so
OTHER:	nil
EXPERIENCE POINT VALUE:	100

L

LINDWYRM

Also Known As: Coeruuk, Draaxin

Let me relate one of the strangest sights I ever did see. We had left Geanavue a few days earlier and were sailing south to Zoa. As we approached the Asiotuxoo Islands, something in the sky off the starboard bow caught my attention. It was a giant flying snake diving into the water! Now there was an unusual sight.

I thought much upon the encounter and desiring to learn more queried the seamen of the vessel. They informed me that this was no serpent but a Lindwyrm, a common enough mistake for a landlubber. We had little to fear from the creature for attacks upon a cog the size of which we sailed in were unheard of. The sailors guessed that it had spotted some of the seals that frequent the rocky western coasts of those isles.

When I – foolishly in retrospect – inquired if they made good sport, the gale of laughter was humbling. "Hunt 'em," one hoary old salt spat. "I seen 'em rip a grizzly to shreds. Hunt a lindwrym? You got a death wish boy? I'd sooner meet up with pirates than tangle with one of those."

"So they do assault ships?" I asked. "Well…" another mariner piped in, "I did hear tell of a whaler out a Aasaer running afoul of one once. Killed half the crew afore swimming away with their catch." – S̄

Another dragonic relative, the lindwyrm has a lithe reptilian form evocative of an enormous skink, albeit with small wings protruding from its back. Normal coloring is olive green tapering to near white on its belly.

They are terrestrial reptiles but enjoy the water and possess several adaptations to the aquatic environment. They are swift swimmers able to remain underwater for long periods. Their wings, while too small to permit flight, serve as ad hoc fins when underwater permitting the creature acrobatic grace beneath the waves. Its sinewy tail is used for propulsion.

As noted, a lindwyrm's wings cannot sustain flight. However, they do permit it to execute a gentle glide from elevation especially in the presence of favorable thermoclines. Many have mistaken a diving lindwrym for one of its more ferocious kin.

Combat/Tactics:

The lindwyrm is an aggressive predator fearing no smaller creature and few comparably sized peers. Though its legs are short and used purely for locomotion, its powerful jaws and flagellum-like tail provide ample offensive capability.

Upon spotting a potential meal, the lindwyrm rushes with amazing speed towards the target. It attacks with a powerful bite attempting to tear chunks of flesh from its prey. A lindwyrm's ferocious bite is also poisonous. Those failing a Constitution check (*vs. d20+7*) are paralyzed by the toxin while even those exceeding this check are beset by a disruption of blood clotting (the wound continues to bleed out at 1 HP/10 seconds until it is bound*).

Should anyone approach the flank or rear of the lindwyrm, it lashes out at him or her with its powerful and agile tail. This attack causes 4d4p damage.

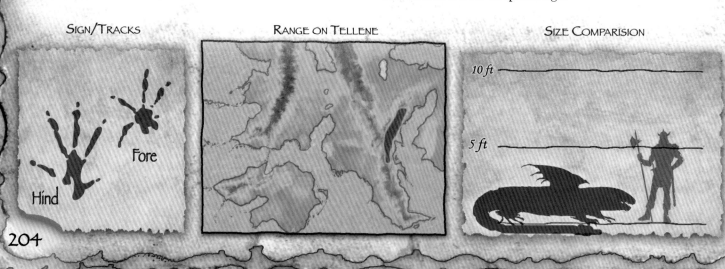

SIGN/TRACKS	RANGE ON TELLENE	SIZE COMPARISION
Fore / Hind		10 ft / 5 ft

Habitat/Society:

Lindwyrms are solitary creatures fiercely defending a large territory from other of their kind. The sole exception to this occurs during their quadrennial mating season. During this time, males become dangerously aggressive as they seek out mates. Female lindwyrms are antagonistic toward these advances compelling the male to attack and restrain a potential partner prior to coitus.

The species is ovoviviparous with the female carrying her egg internally for a year before giving birth to a single live offspring. She remains with the wyrmling for the subsequent twenty years as it slowly matures. Only when old enough to sustain itself does the mother depart and in so doing regain fertility.

These wyrms are not as intelligent as most other creatures of draconic lineage. Their nearest relative is the tetzylwyrm with which they share many morpholological features, though each is adapted to their own ecological niche. Lindwyrms have a life expectancy of two or three centuries.

Ecology:

Lindwyrms are large predators feeding on both terrestrial and marine species. Their favorite habitats are caves in high mountains in close proximity to deep water.

They are likely to maintain several abodes that facilitate their hunting – the principal one being a cave located at considerable elevation that offers an excellent vista of the seas below. From this perch the lindwyrm spies upon the both the coastline and littoral regions below always in search of large game. Sea lions and fur seals are favored marine prey while moose are hunted on land. The lindwyrm has little fear of most species and will attack other large mammals such as bears if the opportunity presents itself.

These wyrms will also assail orca and small whales though this is uncommon due more to the sparseness of these species in comparison to the lindwyrm's routine quarry. Small boats may be misidentified as such creatures and provoke a strike from the beast.

In times when food becomes scarce such as early spring, lindwyrms may take up residence at the shoreline as they transition to fish predation.

On Tellene:

Lindwyrms are most common in the mountains bordering the western edge of Reanaaria Bay. They pose a threat to fishing vessels but it is rare for them to approach a vessel with a mast. The only such reported incidents all involved a whaling vessel that was in the process of butchering a kill and likely represented an opportunistic attack.

Given their sinewy form and excellent swimming skills, they are frequently mistaken for sea serpents particularly when encountered in the spring.

It requires a successful First Aid check (Average difficulty) to bind the wound. Note that this only permits the cessation of further damage and does not remedy any lost Hit Points.

LINDWYRM

HIT POINTS:	33+7d8
SIZE/WEIGHT:	H/1 ton (23' long)
TENACITY:	Brave
INTELLIGENCE:	Animal, High
FATIGUE FACTOR:	-4

SPEED 3 · INIT 0 · ATTACK +14 · DMG REDUCTION · DEFENSE +8 · 9 · see below · medium REACH · DAMAGE · TOP SAVE 11

ATTACK:
Leads with a toxic bite that inflicts 3d8p and requires a CON check vs. d20p+7 to avoid paralysis (even if save is made wound continues to bleed out at 1 Hit Point every 10 seconds).
Individual claw attacks do 2d8p but may substitute a tail lash (4d4p) for this if an enemy approaches its rear.

MOVEMENT

CRAWL:	5
WALK:	10
JOG:	15
RUN:	20
FLY/SWIM:	25

SAVES

PHYSICAL:	+14
MENTAL:	+9
DODGE:	+10

GENERAL INFO

ACTIVITY CYCLE:	Diurnal
NO. APPEARING:	1
% CHANCE IN LAIR:	60%
FREQUENCY:	Unusual
ALIGNMENT:	Non
VISION TYPE:	Farsight
AWARENESS/SENSES:	Standard
HABITAT:	Caves
DIET:	Carnivorous
ORGANIZATION:	Individuals
CLIMATE/TERRAIN:	Temperate littoral highlands

YIELD

MEDICINAL:	skin wraps used to bandage arrow wounds
SPELL COMPONENTS:	nil
HIDE/TROPHY:	heads are prized trophies
TREASURE:	incidental, from victims
EDIBLE:	yes
OTHER:	nil
EXPERIENCE POINT VALUE:	1200

LION
Also Known As: Jungle King, Razhvar

Bound as I was, my hands and feet tied and my mouth gagged with foul-smelling rags ripped from the jungle tribesman's filthy tunic, I could not warn my captors, not that I would have. So intent were they upon drinking from the pool beneath the great nut tree, the noises of their slurping lips and gurgles of satisfaction drowned the quiet approach of the huge jungle cat behind them.

I watched as it cautiously moved closer, noiselessly placing one great paw before lifting the next. It crept closer, and the joy leapt in my heart as I watched it advance upon my captors, belly low, hind feet drawn well up beneath it and ready to spring. For an instant, it paused as if turned to stone, and then sprang upon the savages with an awful roar.

Even then, I pondered upon the foolishness of this fierce cry, at the creature warning its prey with a wild alarm. Surely, it was unwise to do so. As I watched, however, I quickly realized that the roar was not a warning. In truth, it was a perfectly timed cry intended to paralyze its victims in terror. Moreover, its reason was correct – the little fellows crouched, trembling, for the mere instant the beast needed to sink its mighty claws into their soft flesh and hold them beyond hope of escape.

It was a cruel death I witnessed, a cruel death beneath tearing claws and rending fangs, but I rejoiced in seeing it. Rejoiced, then cursed as three more of the little savages appeared from behind the tree and slowly dragged me away, leaving the lion to enjoy its meal in peace. I escaped, of course, but that is a tale for another day. -

This heavy carnivore is a powerful hunter and quite visually distinctive from other big hunting cats. Its body is obviously feline, with an average adult male standing 4 feet tall at the shoulder with a head and body length of 7 feet (plus a further 2 to 3 feet of tail) and weight of 450 pounds. Males also sport a thick mane, the color of which darkens as the lion ages.

Female lionesses lack the mane and are distinctly smaller and lighter than the males, with the typical lioness being some 3½ feet tall, 5 feet long (with 2 to 3 feet of tail) and weighing about 325 pounds. The tails of both males and females end in a hairy black tuft of fur.

Whether male or female, most lions have fur of a yellowish color, with variations ranging from light buff to ochre and lightening on the underside. The differences between subspecies of lion are mostly dependent on location, minor differences in coloration and the appearance of the mane.

The spotted lion subspecies, however, boasts leopard-like spots and (for males) a mane that is distinctly blond in coloration, in addition to its normal characteristics.

SIGN/TRACKS

Fore

Hind

RANGE ON TELLENE

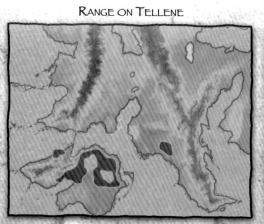

SIZE COMPARISON

6 ft

3 ft

Combat/Tactics:

Mated males fight primarily to defend their territory from invaders or protect themselves, leaving most of the hunting to the lionesses. These wily female hunters work primarily in packs, using darkness or any available cover to stalk and surround their prey. The mighty cats then rush in and leap onto the target, attacking with their claws.

If the lion lands two successive claw attacks (individually causing 2d4p+4 damage), it has grabbed its opponent and automatically inflicts a bite attack dealing 2d6p+6 points of damage every 5 seconds thereafter (superseding the claw attacks). The cat's grip can be broken with a successful knock-back or Feat of Strength (vs. d20p+14). The latter can be attempted after each bite attack. While caught, the victim can only attack with a dagger or knife.

Habitat/Society:

All lions favor warm, dry climates, though the spotted lion's territory comprises elevated woodlands, while other lions range primarily over the open savannas and grasslands. Most lions live in prides containing a single adult male, five or six related females and their cubs (though some dwell in coalitions containing two dozen individuals or more). Still other lions, particularly spotted ones and un-mated males, are nomadic and roam about singly or in pairs.

Lionesses have a gestation period of nearly four months, giving birth to a litter of up to four cubs. These cubs are weaned after several months and reach maturity when about three years old.

The average lion has a lifespan of about 12 years.

Ecology:

They feed on large herbivores, such as boars and zebras, but generally avoid creatures with massive bulk (e.g., rhinoceri, elephants) due to the greater chance of injury. Lions are also scavengers, and smart enough to realize that a flock of circling birds may mean a potential meal.

When typical prey is scarce, or when domestic livestock comes within their territory, lions often attack and scatter the herd, causing significant financial loss for the foolhardy shepherd (assuming he too is not killed in the attack).

The lion is often the dominant natural predator in its habitat, competing primarily with other cats, such as hyenas, cheetahs and leopards. Lions often claim the kills of these smaller animals, but rarely feed on the carnivores themselves. Near water, the crocodile is the greatest danger to the lion, and either creature venturing too far into the other's element may find itself in danger.

On Tellene:

Lions are native to the Svimohzish Isle, with spotted lions being most common in and around the Mizohr, Svomawhom, Whisvomi and Zamul Forests, where the woodlands meet prominent hills and mountains. Other lions dwell through the grasslands and savannas.

The only known lions outside of this continent are to be found in captivity (or having escaped from such).

LION

HIT POINTS:	24+4d8
SIZE/WEIGHT:	L/325-450 lbs.
TENACITY:	Steady
INTELLIGENCE:	Animal, High
FATIGUE FACTOR:	2

MOVEMENT

CRAWL:	5
WALK:	10
JOG:	20
RUN:	25
SPRINT:	30

SAVES

PHYSICAL:	+9
MENTAL:	+7
DODGE:	+8

SPEED 5 / INIT -3 / ATTACK +9 / DMG REDUCTION 4 / DEFENSE +4 / see below / DAMAGE 6 / medium REACH / TOP SAVE ▼

ATTACK: Lions attempt to grab prey with their claws; upon 2 successive claw hits (2d4p+4 each) they have grabbed the prey and automatically bite for 2d6p+6 every 5 seconds (superseding the claw attacks); breaking their grasp requires a Feat of Strength vs. d20p+14

SPECIAL DEFENSES: none

GENERAL INFO

ACTIVITY CYCLE:	Nocturnal
NO. APPEARING:	1-12 (lion) or 1-8 (spotted lion)
% CHANCE IN LAIR:	30%
FREQUENCY:	Infrequent
ALIGNMENT:	Non
VISION TYPE:	Standard
AWARENESS/SENSES:	Standard
HABITAT:	Open woodlands (spotted), savannas (lion)
DIET:	Carnivorous
ORGANIZATION:	Individuals or Pride
CLIMATE/TERRAIN:	Dry tropical lowlands

YIELD

MEDICINAL:	ground bones are sold as a cure for a limp libido
SPELL COMPONENTS:	nil
HIDE/TROPHY:	lion heads, pelts and claws are prized
TREASURE:	nil
EDIBLE:	yes
OTHER:	nil
EXPERIENCE POINT VALUE:	492

L

LIZARD, GIANT SUBTERRANEAN

Another menace of note when exploring the bowels of the earth are giant lizards. Oft times I have encountered these fierce reptiles – either as lone hunters or as subjugated guardians and sentries. On one excursion into the NetherDeep, I bore witness to lizardy-men employing these beasts much in the same fashion as human men do utilize fierce canines.

Despite their size, they can be difficult to discern at a distance in mere torchlight for their dark hue is dappled with lighter spotting that frequently allows them to approach their prey (to wit, my expedition compatriots) nearly within striking distance before revealing their presence.

These creatures are capable of biting through the finest armor and inflicting severe lacerating wounds. Such injuries may infrequently be so grim as to topple the doughtiest fighting man.

Their coloration permits them to excel at hiding and ambush.

One should be cautioned to focus his strikes upon the head and thorax of these reptiles. Akin to their smaller varieties that populate the surface world, these animals appear to possess a spartan ability withstand damage to the tail. I have seen one such lizard's tail shorn off with a mighty blow of a great sword to little apparent effect. ~ ⸲

Giant subterranean lizards are a ubiquitous predator within the caves and warrens that permeate the earth. Possessing adequate olfactory senses via its bifurcated tongue and low light color vision, the reptile is well suited to this terrain. Typically encountered as a solo hunter, the creature's felicitous camouflage often permits it to rapidly close upon and dispatch prey.

Their coloration is notably different from terrestrial lizards. Unlike the albinism one would expect from a denizen of lightless caverns, the giant subterranean lizard is darkly complected with individual specimens varying in color from a dark malachite to pure black. This coloration, coupled with the matte finish of their scales, makes them difficult to distinguish in poorly lit surroundings.

Combat/Tactics

Wild specimens will rush from cover taking advantage of their camouflage and quick reactions to quickly overwhelm and consume prey. If confronted by multiple opponents, they may upon overcoming a single foe grab the corpse (or incapacitated victim) and flee to a secluded spot to consume the meal. They have no means of judging the relative

L

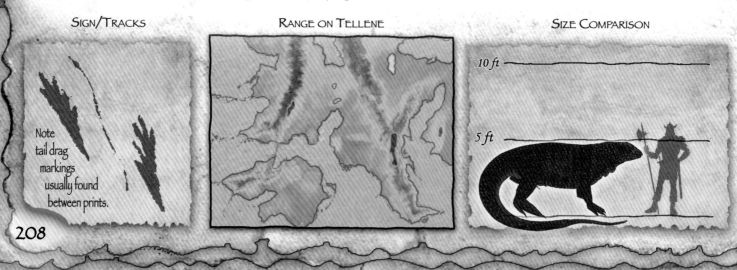

SIGN/TRACKS

Note tail drag markings usually found between prints.

RANGE ON TELLENE

SIZE COMPARISON

10 ft

5 ft

strength of opponents, other than by size. Attacks on humans and their ilk are usually at random if the lizard has the initiative or directed at the first individual bold enough to approach.

Giant Subterranean Lizards have a notable asset in that they can regrow their tail. Any damage inflicted on this appendage is not counted against the creature's hit point total (though it will be severed upon sustaining 20 hit points of damage – DR being applied to any such blows as normal). This provides a natural defense against attacks upon the creatures back (i.e. a backstab or rearward strike if the creature flees).

Domesticated lizards trained for attack are usually more aggressive than their wild kin and exhibit tactics in line with those of their trainers. Most often they are employed in a manner analogous to human use of war dogs.

Habitat/Society

These lizards exhibit a polygynous social structure within their nests, consisting of a male and 2d4 resident females. This hoarding of breeding partners by older and dominant males results in a large excess of younger male lizards left to fend for themselves as solitary hunters. These rouge males are frequently captured and domesticated by intelligent species capable of this specialized animal training. Tröglodytes in particular are said to possess these skills and reportedly make use of Giant Subterranean Lizards as sentinels and hunting companions. Though not possessed of the keen alertness of canines, their size and capacity for indoctrination in ruthless savagery can make them foes worthy of respect.

Ecology

These lizards are primarily insectivores/arachnivores and feed upon giant species of insects and spiders. Their smooth scales resist adhesion allowing them to traverse webbing with little hindrance. This adaptation, along with their noteworthy resistance to toxins (utilizing d20+20 as a saving throw against all poisons) makes them a great bane of spider-kind and the latter (if possessed of intelligence) actively avoids the hunting ranges of giant lizards.

If denied their favorite prey, this species may feed on small mammals (giant rats being the most common in no small part due to their ubiquity).

On Tellene

Giant Subterranean Lizards are encountered nearer the surface in warm mountainous climates. Sightings have been reported in the eastern foothills of the Elenon Mountains, the Arajyd Hills and unconfirmed rumors exist of encounters with giant lizards in the Ka'Asa Mountains.

GIANT SUBTERRANEAN LIZARD

HIT POINTS:	30+6d8
SIZE/WEIGHT:	L/850 lbs.
TENACITY:	Steady to Fearless
INTELLIGENCE:	Animal, Low
FATIGUE FACTOR:	-2

SPEED 7   INIT -2
ATTACK +10
DEFENSE +6   DMG REDUCTION 6
DAMAGE 4d6p
short REACH   TOP SAVE 8

MOVEMENT

CRAWL:	5
WALK:	10
JOG:	15
RUN:	20
SPRINT:	25

SAVES

PHYSICAL:	+10
MENTAL:	+7
DODGE:	+9

ATTACK:
Fierce bite inflicting 4d6p damage

SPECIAL:
immune to effects of webbing, great resistance to poison, damage to tail does not substantially hinder creature, camouflage (effective Hiding skill 35)

GENERAL INFO

ACTIVITY CYCLE:	Nocturnal
NO. APPEARING:	1 or 2d4+1
% CHANCE IN LAIR:	25%
FREQUENCY:	Infrequent
ALIGNMENT:	non
VISION TYPE:	Low Light Vision
AWARENESS/SENSES:	Standard
HABITAT:	Sunterraneans caves and warrens
DIET:	Insectivore/Arachnivore
ORGANIZATION:	nest (wild); also kept as domestics
CLIMATE/TERRAIN:	prefers warmer surroundings

L

YIELD

MEDICINAL:	blood from live lizard may be used in liquer to treat disease, asthma cure
SPELL COMPONENTS:	nil
HIDE/TROPHY:	hides substitute for leather in Netherdeep
TREASURE:	Incidental
EDIBLE:	Yes (tail is particularly fatty)
OTHER:	nil
EXPERIENCE POINT VALUE:	450

LIZARD MAN

Also Known As: Kregur, Slazeen or Zekiran

The lizard man flattens its spiny frill and extends its neck when preparing to attack.

Kregurs are an annoyance and should be eradicated upon first contact wherever they are found. Too many human settlements have tried peacefully coexisting with these brutes - some even establishing trade relations. Only later do they recognize their error. Once these creatures acquire a taste for human flesh, they will go rogue every time and become a menace.

Many believe lizard men are slow thinkers, no doubt due to the fact they are often easily taken advantage of and have difficulty picking up human tongues and grasping syntax. (I myself once traded a glass bauble broken off a cheap brooch to a Lizard man for fifty pounds of fish.)

Don't be fooled by their shy ways, animal-like hisses and tail beats — they are cunning and formidable fighters.

Lizard men often fight unarmed but prefer short jabbing weapons, clubs and swords. And even though they have tough hides, I've seen them equipped with small crude shields and body armor.

They are willing to fight toe-to-toe when they have superiority of numbers but often use the tactic of disengaging and fleeing only to return moments later to renew the attack from a different front. If you find yourself in lizard man country be sure to keep a constant watch — especially on your rear. Lizard men often attack from the front with a diversionary strike only to follow up with an attack from the rear. And watch the females — they are just as bad!

A female kregur drags its tail along the ground.

When in a pinch, lizard man flesh makes a passable meal but the meat is tough and stringy. You'll do best to boil it but be careful to drain the fat. Take the spiny barbs from the frill if you down one. They have a beautiful luster when properly polished by a skilled hand and fetch a good price at city markets where they are used to make horned dagger grips, jewelry and even buttons. The skin of a lizard man with unusual color or markings can fetch as much as a silver. Practitioners of magic and the dark arts sometimes pay hard coin for a lizard man's gizzard. - ♀

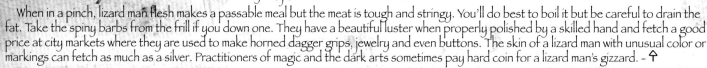

An oft overlooked, but surprisingly common race of creatures, are the lizard men. Although not hominids strictly speaking, lizard men should probably be categorized as humanoids given their bipedal nature and comparable intelligence. Most scholars steadfastly refuse to do so. Doubtlessly stemming from bigotry given the lizard man's relatively alien taxonomy, academics consistently categorize them as distinct from other bipeds (and just as erroneously classify them as analogues of the various intelligent amphibious bipeds).

In truth, 'lizard men' is an overly broad grouping as-is. Lizard men come in an astounding array of varieties and sizes, the vast majority of which are at best distant genetic cousins and typically completely different species. Indeed, these sauroids vary not simply by physical trait, but also mentally; the many tribes occupy far different locations on the evolutionary curve ranging from animalistic to civilized (although primitive by human standards). Further, their habitats and behaviors diverge as completely as their physical appearance.

L

SIGN/TRACKS

RANGE ON TELLENE

SIZE COMPARISON

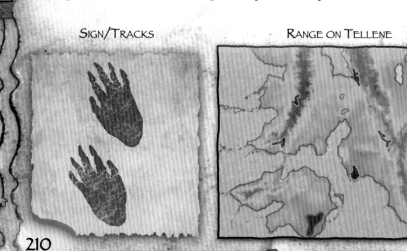

6 ft

3 ft

Certain similarities, even amongst such an assorted collection, helps categorize the lizard man group.

All members of this classification possess thick scaled hides with the toughest specimens boasting scutum. This explains the name attributed them by humans. In contrast, elves further classify them by tighter descriptive names indicating each tribe's biologic similarity to a particular reptilian class (*e.g.*, gators, lizards, snakes, turtles, etc.). While often living near or around water (but not exclusively), lizard men are, in fact, air breathers and not amphibious in nature.

The lizard man thermophysiology varies somewhat. The majority of these creatures are ectotherms, but some scholars have reported a few species living deep in the Khydoban Desert that exhibit bradymetabolism. Additionally, it has been rumored – but no clear accounts exist to support these claims – that certain lizard men living in the Netherdeep are warm-blooded. More likely, these are troglodytes exhibiting gigantothermy.

Lizard men range in size, depending on ancestry. Height ranges from lizard-gecko specimens at around 4 feet to massive crocodiline species 7 feet in height with a lengthy, powerful tail. Mass varies with height as well, with the smaller pygmy varieties sizing up with gnomes and the larger breeds roughly comparable in size and weight to bugbears.

Lizard men have surprisingly good senses, although they, too, vary with subspecies. While their serpentine cousins employ forked tongues as olfactory sensors the lacertilian saurians have nostrils near the front of their short snouts that provide a satisfactory sense of smell. Unfortunately, lizard men have poor auditory sensors (20% penalty to Listening checks), due to lack of ears, their organs located under their protective skin.

Additionally, lizard men exhibit superb tactile senses allowing them to perceive even slight movements within a body of water (where sound also travels well), tremors on the earth due to approaching enemies or victims or the shake of a tree trunk and so on.

Finally, most subspecies have decent vision, on par with humans in daylight. However, in low light conditions, they boast superior sight owing to their vertical pupils, which open wider than round ones, affording more light. Further, with eyes set wide on their head, lizard men have a 250 to 300 degree arc of vision providing almost no blind-spot. They are thus rarely surprised – one die better for Initiative rolls – and 50% of backstab attacks are actually merely rearward strikes (check randomly for each such attack).

A cleric and/or witch doctor handles the spiritual or superstitious duties for all but the smallest tribes. These spellcasters generally only serve in a cloistered capacity, never leaving the lair on raids, preferring to stay behind and manage sacrifices or other activities. However, they viciously defend the clan home with their lives. They provide knowledge and advice to leaders, as well as brewing

LIZARD MAN

HIT POINTS:	21+2d8
SIZE/WEIGHT:	M/150 lbs.
TENACITY:	Nervous
INTELLIGENCE:	Slow
FATIGUE FACTOR:	-3/-2

MOVEMENT

CRAWL:	2½
WALK:	5
JOG:	10
RUN:	15
SPRINT:	20

SAVES

PHYSICAL:	+3
MENTAL:	+2
DODGE:	+3

ATTACK: Lizard men favor morning stars (stats reflect this use) but may employ a variety of weapons; may attack unarmed with a speed of 5 alternatively clawing with both hands for 2d4p and biting for 2d6p; bite attack supersedes standard near-perfect defense

SPECIAL: Shield use (e.g, medium shields increase Defense to +6); One die better for Initiative. Wide field of sight catches backstab attempts 50% of the time & improves flank/rear defense; 20% penalty to Listening checks.

GENERAL INFO

ACTIVITY CYCLE:	Diurnal
NO. APPEARING:	d8p (hunting); 3d4p+8 (warband); 30d12p (tribe)
% CHANCE IN LAIR:	25%
FREQUENCY:	Infrequent
ALIGNMENT:	Neutral (chaotic and evil tendencies)
VISION TYPE:	Low Light Vision
AWARENESS/SENSES:	Standard (one die better for Initiative)[1]
HABITAT:	Caves and dark places[2]
DIET:	Omnivorous
ORGANIZATION:	Tribal
CLIMATE/TERRAIN:	Warm to temperate lowlands[3]

YIELD

MEDICINAL:	nil
SPELL COMPONENTS:	nil
HIDE/TROPHY:	hides make nice riding boots
TREASURE:	2d4p sp each[4]
EDIBLE:	yes, tastes like chicken
OTHER:	nil
EXPERIENCE POINT VALUE:	45

potions and salves. Finally, they provide spiritual (and superstitious) direction to the tribe, this function varying dramatically from tribe to tribe. Each tribe has at least one shaman with clerical capacity, with mage ability found in only 25% of the witch doctors. Their levels of spellcasting ability are not substantial, only d10p-4 for clerical and d10p-6 for mage (negative and zero rounding to 1st). Roll the clerical capability for the first shaman, for every two full levels, the tribe has another shaman (rolled independently). Perform this check only once.

Lizard men are not particularly evil, seeking only to hunt and live their lifestyle in most cases. They rarely raid and plunder, except if food is scarce or outside communities appear likely to threaten them or encroach on their lands. That said, lizard men certainly view humans and other sentient races as a tasty food source or even as sacrificial victims.

Lizard man tribes each speak their own strange tongue consisting of chirps, whistles, hisses and barks. Different tribes cannot natively communicate with one another (and, in fact, rarely consider one another racially the same or even similar), but they can learn new languages if given reason to do so. On rare occasion, some lizard men learn the language of their neighbors, speaking it a with heavy accent as one might imagine.

Lizard men are hard-workers, although mining is unknown to them and their weaponsmithing is crude at best. They tend to lair in dismal out-of-the-way locales, such as insect-infested bogs, dreary marshlands, harsh desert-scapes, deserted tropical islands, deep jungles or rocky coastal regions. Most primitive tribes use natural cover for housing, but more advanced tribes construct crude villages from bamboo, reeds, wood, or rude stone buildings built by simply stacking naturally-occurring rocks available in the area.

Combat/Tactics:

Lizard men have better-than-average musculature, and natural weaponry in the form of claws and powerful jaws lined with teeth. Together with their thick, scaled or scuted hide and an innate hardiness to withstand damaging blows and a determined resistance to pain, lizard men can be fearsome opponents indeed. A lizard man's defense never drops below d12p, unless surprised, even in the case of rear attacks.

Generally primitive creatures, most lizard men attack with their claws and powerful jaws. About one-in-four tribes, however, have advanced enough to replace their natural weaponry with simple weapons -- clubs, axes, morningstars, spears, daggers, blowguns, javelins and the like. They fashion these from wood, rock or bone as available. Lizard men also wear armor, typically fashioned from naturally-occurring materials such as bamboo, turtle shell, gator hide and so-on. Intelligent enough to realize the utility of superior-quality weapons forged by other races, they deploy these if obtained in some way.

Lizard man manufactured goods can hold an edge through only a few battles or hunts before becoming useless. After d3p battles, their weapons, armor and tools degrade to the point of penalties and d3p uses later fails entirely. Lizard men are diligent in servicing their gear, however, and they sharpen points and weapon heads between forays.

Every group of 10 lizard men encountered has a warrior leader with maximum Hit Points.

For every 30, the warband has a warband leader big enough to deliver a +1 to Attack, Damage, Defense and a 1-point bonus to Initiative in addition to maximum Hit Points plus an extra d8 Hit Points.

For every 90, the tribe will have a sub-chief with +2 to Attack, Damage, Defense and a 1-point bonus to Speed and Initiative in addition to maximum Hit Points plus two extra d8 rolls for Hit Points. This is in addition to the nine basic leaders and three stronger leaders.

If the tribe contains 150 or more lizard men, it has a powerful chieftain. This largest and most powerful leader has a +3 to Attack, Damage, Defense and a 2-point bonus to Speed and Initiative as well as maximum Hit Points plus three extra d8 rolls for Hit Points. This is in addition to the other leaders and an extra 4d6p warrior sub-chiefs that function as a personal retinue of bodyguards for the chieftain.

For more advanced tribes, the various leader-types employ the choicest weapons and wear various armors to provide the following improvements to Damage Reduction: warrior leader +1 DR, warband leader +2 DR, sub-chief +3 DR, chieftain +4 DR.

Lizard men prefer to attack from ambush, emerging from bog, foliage or rocky outcropping to attack with surprise. Primitive subspecies surround and close to melee with great haste, while more advanced tribes soften their enemies with a volley of hurled javelins, axes or clubs prior to engaging. Lizard men attack to defend their territories or to gather food for the tribe. In the latter case, warriors drag incapacitated or perished victims from the combat to either feast directly (if hungry) or, more often, back to the lair for a tribal banquet.

Lizard men engage with little regard to tactics, but they attempt to double-team enemy fighters and love to attack unarmored humans above all (in the hopes of gaining an easy meal). If not urged on by a tribal superior or some supernatural force, lizard men are quick to disengage if a combat turns against them, fleeing into the underbrush or other natural barrier.

In this case, the lizard men regroup at a nearby rendezvous point or back at the lair and wait for a leader to redirect them, often returning for an unexpected counter-attack in short order.

Habitat/Society:

Lizard men can be found in any temperate to tropical climate and while they sometimes live below ground, they vastly prefer living in the wilderness under the sun. When they do live in caves, they have easy avenue to the out-of-doors to access food. Lizard men prefer not to dwell in close proximity to other races, and mark their territory with warning signs to ward away others.

Lizard men live in a largely disorganized society where the strongest rule the weak. The chieftain is always the strongest, smartest or greatest hunter. Once established, the chief remains so until age dictates he hand the reins to the next in line or is forced to relinquish tribal dominance through force. As chief, his challenge is to keep the pots full of food and enemy threats at bay.

Females comprise a solid 50% of the population of the tribe (generally those with lesser Hit Points if determining randomly). The females' responsibilities include cooking, maintenance and child-rearing, as well as creating or mending weapons and armor. They hunt as well as males, but only do so when other activities do not occupy their time. They fight equal to males.

Lizard men have an average lifespan of about 50 years, but some species have shortened lifespans (20 years) while a few have been known to break the century-mark when environmental conditions are favorable and enemies rare. Most species are oviparous, laying large, tough-shelled amniotic eggs lain in clutches of six to eight that hatch in about six months. Eggs are stored in a tribal hatchery, with all eggs intermixed. Young are cared for by any female in the area or assigned that duty. Roughly one-in-four young are considered too small and are consumed by the clan in a special stew about eight weeks after birth. Certain species, however, birth their young live. This is achieved by either ovoviviparity or viviparity. Many of the viviparous species feed their fetuses through various forms of placenta analogous to those of mammals, but these are very rare.

Lizard man young occur in numbers of about 20% of the total males, half able to fight well (use orc statistics) and the other half fighting only if cornered (use kobold statistics).

Some lizard man lairs employ trained (or partially trained) animals as guard and watch beasts. There is a 50% chance that a lizard man village contains 2d6p giant lizards, a 40% chance of 2d12p giant scorpions (desert) or crocodiles (shoreline or swamplands) and a 20% chance of 2d6p giant birds or 2d4p dinosaurs (the latter only in the Obakasek Jungle).

Ecology:

Lizard men regularly feed on insects, including the giant variety, rodents, small and large game, other lizards as well as various vegetables, seaweeds, ferns and the like. Generally the dominant creature in their habitat, they brook no rival from other species, human, orc or otherwise. Such enemies are aggressively hunted and dragged back to the lizard man clan as the main course in a grisly feast. Many lizard man tribes have developed a fond liking for man-flesh and consider mankind food like any other animal to be hunted. Luckily, lizard men only occasionally raid outside their traditional tribal lands (often marked with macabre or brightly-colored warning markers). On rare occasions, an entire tribe of lizard men can be cowed into subservience by a powerful creature such as a dragon or mage, or a very powerful force of some sort.

Religion:

The religious nature of any particular lizard man clan varies dramatically from tribe to tribe. Most lizard men fear magic (both divine and arcane) and are quite superstitious, making their shamans (if any) powerful within the clan. The existence and power of a shaman relative to the lizard man chieftain determines how much sway the clergy has over the day-to-day tribal lives and activities. Lizard man spiritual leaders tend to follow neutral deities, although most evil religions and even a few good ones have representation within various tribes. The Old Oak being the most popular, but Mother of the Elements is also quite common. The Harvester of Souls, the Overlord and the Creator of Strife have significant followings.

Subraces:

This Hacklopedia entry focuses on one particular species, the iconic saurian lizard men. The reader should note well that the information may be similar to or diverge greatly from the characteristics of other lizard man species. Even within this entry, each tribe of lizard men has its own distinctive coloration, frills, plumes and so-forth, although green to yellow color palettes seem to dominate. Saurians stand about 5 to 6 feet tall and have 3-foot long to 4-foot long tails.

Lizard men come in many shapes and sizes, most of which are completely different species. Known types include the sauroids (aka saurians), croconids, aquatoids, chamelids, serpentines, turtles, and others.

On Tellene:

Lizard men can be found all across Tellene in temperate to tropical less-civilized areas. They are most numerous in warm wetlands, swampy areas, tropical jungles, islands and coastal regions, but can also be found in deserts and mountainous areas. Significant tribes occupy the Tharakka Morass and both the Vohven and Obakasek jungles.

[1] *Awareness/Senses:* Lizard men can see very well in dimly lit conditions, but cannot see in the dark. They have an average olphactory sense and excellent mechanoreception but poor auditory (-20% to Listen checks).

[2] *Habitat:* Lizard men live below ground and in dismal, dark locations above ground.

[3] *Climate/Terrain:* Highly specialized based on particular physiology; live and thrive in every climate from temperate to warmer, but also in caves and, in rare cases, in the Netherdeep as well.

[4] *Treasure:* Advanced tribal members living near other races carry 2d4p sp each and possibly some low-value gemstones found in the area. Lizard man lairs sometimes contain stashes of copper, silver and trade coins as well as gems and magical or special items depending on local raiding and trade opportunities.

MEDUSA

Also Known As: Lornae, Myrzix

The events of which I relate occurred long ago, when I was invited by a friend to pay him a visit in Meevua, a little town on the Asiotuxoo Islands. He took me about in all directions to do the few honors of the place, though my interest in architecture and statuary was little at best. Eventually seeing my flagging enthusiasm, my friend said that there was only one more thing to see, and it was the creature he had invited me to view. My excitement began to rise, though he said we must take his fishing boat, and I am not a good sailor even in the mildest weather.

After some hours of sailing, we paused at a stretch of rocky continent marked with caves and strangely decorated with statuary of men and animals. At my friend's insistence, we drifted some distance away, so far that I could see no features on the statues. My friend then began to hoot at the caves in derisive language. Suddenly, I saw it step forth – what might have been a human female, but with a head moving and wriggling in the oddest way. I peered hard but could see no better, and urged my friend to sail closer, but he refused.

As we sailed back to the island, the strange woman having retreated into her cave, my friend explained that to come too close was to fall under her sway and be turned to stone. My face must have shown some skepticism, for he suggested I take a second look at the statues in town. Did I really think, he said, that a sculptor of such magnificence would be found in tiny Meevua? ~ ←

This monstrous creature outwardly resembles a human female whose 'hair' consists of a nest of tiny, writhing, poisonous asps. Most medusae dress in robes and other feminine garments appropriate to the human style of the region, though these are often soiled and ripped from constant outdoor wear. Should she use a garment to cover her serpent companions, she may easily be mistaken for human. There are no male medusae.

Combat/Tactics:

A medusa's forced solitude reinforces a self-pitying madness, and so she delights in the death or petrifaction of all who approach her. Should a living creature within 50 feet of her be unfortunate enough to meet the medusa's gaze (she can focus on one individual per sec-

ond), he turns to inanimate stone. A successful Constitution saving throw (vs. d20p+12) resists this transformation.

Characters covering their eyes, wearing blind-folds, and so-on suffer a -8 penalty on attacks. Those that simply avert their gaze may be able to detect the Lornae via peripheral vision and thus suffer a mere -4 to their Attack. They are still susceptible to the Myrzix purposefully gazing at their eyes but gain a +4 bonus to their save. Unfortunately, those that avert their gaze or use a similar method that causes their body to contort unnaturally in combat (in contrast to simply wearing a blind-fold), suffer a -3 to all Damage rolls as well.

Approaching within striking distance subjects an assailant to two dangers. First, the Medusa can strike with a weapon (usually a dagger). Though this is hardly a formidable attack, in so doing the de-

Instead of a crown of hair, the medusa has a writhing mass of poisionous asps sprouting from her scalp. Because they see, think and move independently of the lornae, they are able to alert her of movement from behind and of lair-intruders when she is sleeping or distracted.

SIZE COMPARISON

6 ft

3 ft

fender is simultaneously exposed to her writhing coiffure of poisonous snakes. These will attempt to bite her opponent as well (roll two separate Attacks). Though her serpent mane inflicts but a single point of damage, those bitten must save versus VF 14 poison or suffer -3 to their Attack, Defense and Damage for 2d12 hours (with a natural 1 on the save indicating death).

When faced with an individual or a small group, the medusa rarely minds direct confrontation. If, however, she believes her adversary to be dangerous, she retreats or flees to terrain that cannot be easily traversed unless one is already familiar with its nature (such as a great bramble hedge or dense grove of trees where only one hidden path exists).

Habitat/Society:

Whether a medusa's appearance is beautiful, hideous or merely plain, she cannot dwell safely among other creatures and so is forced to live in isolated caves and ruins. Though some medusae have tried to live in populated settlements, such attempts have always ended in death and disaster. A medusa drinks water or other liquids common to humans but fortunately (or unfortunately, depending on your point of view), a medusa does not need to eat. Instead, she is sustained by the life energy of her victim, for it flows naturally into her as the victim turns to stone.

Gatherings of more than one medusa are rare, as even they may be turned to stone by one another's gaze (an opposed saving throw vs. d20p+3). Should two or more medusae come close together, all but one use strips of gauze to cover their eyes – thick enough so they can distinguish shapes and shadows, but not so thin as to enable one to meet the gaze of another. The final medusa remains with head unwrapped so as to keep her eyes open for signs of danger. Should two medusae be blood relatives, they are immune to each other's gaze.

Ecology:

As far as is known, new medusae appear in only one of two ways. The first occurs when a woman brings down a god's wrath or accidentally unleashes some ancient curse upon herself, then survives the fear and wrath of her family and neighbors long enough to flee to the isolated safety of the wilderness.

Medusae can also give birth, with the father typically being a barbarian who springs upon the medusa unaware and whose torments of the creature lead to the birth of a child. Medusae have also been said to conceal their hair and seduce human men, or even have men captured and blinded in order to fulfill desires that can be satisfied no other way. Children born to a medusa are always female, and have the serpentine hair and stony gaze of their mother.

Whether born as human or medusa, such a creature typically has an extended lifespan of nearly 200 years.

On Tellene:

One folktale popular in southern Reanaaria Bay tells of three sisters (Stheno, Euryle and Medusa) who were daughters of one of the first families to settle in the Bay area after the trip across the now sunken land bridge from Svimohzia. Medusa, the fairest of the three, inspired jealous aspiration in many men, including a deity often known as the Confuser of Ways. According to the tale, the deity disguised itself as a man and wooed the lovely Medusa. When she callously spurned his affections, he transformed her once beautiful hair into serpents. She fled into the woods and her family never saw her again.

In another variant of the legend, the god cursed not only the lady Medusa but also her sisters. Furthermore, the deity gave them not only serpent hair and a petrifying gaze but also immortality, so that they might suffer forever.

MEDUSA

HIT POINTS:	18+6d8
SIZE/WEIGHT:	M/120 lbs.
TENACITY:	Nervous
INTELLIGENCE:	Smart
FATIGUE FACTOR:	2

SPEED 7 INIT -4
ATTACK +9
DMG REDUCTION
DEFENSE 0 0
see below
DAMAGE 3
short REACH TOP SAVE

ATTACK: A medusa's gaze requires a save vs. d20p+12 or turn to stone (50' range); In melee, she deals 2d4p with a dagger and 1 point with a bite from her hair (plus VF 14 poison; -3 Attack, Defense and Damage for 2d12 hours on a failed save; 'nat 1' causes death; successful saves take only -1 penalty).

SPECIAL: Independently acting snake hair prevents backstabs and flanking; rolls one Initiative die lower

MOVEMENT

CRAWL:	2½
WALK:	5
JOG:	10
RUN:	15
SPRINT:	20

SAVES

PHYSICAL:	+10
MENTAL:	+14
DODGE:	+12

GENERAL INFO

ACTIVITY CYCLE:	Any
NO. APPEARING:	1-3
% CHANCE IN LAIR:	60%
FREQUENCY:	Unusual
ALIGNMENT:	Neutral Evil
VISION TYPE:	Standard (plus stony gaze within 50 ft)
AWARENESS/SENSES:	Standard
HABITAT:	Caves and ruins
DIET:	Special
ORGANIZATION:	Individuals or Coven
CLIMATE/TERRAIN:	Any, save arctic

YIELD

MEDICINAL:	nil
SPELL COMPONENTS:	nil
HIDE/TROPHY:	heads (powerless) may be trophy items
TREASURE:	works of art, magic items, gems and treasure
EDIBLE:	toxic (as per snake bite)
OTHER:	nil
EXPERIENCE POINT VALUE:	1200

M

MERMAN
Also Known As: Neaesquatilian

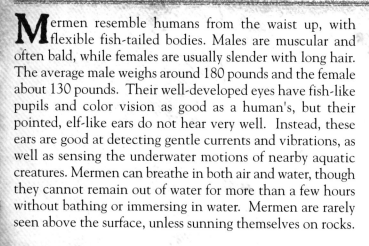

It seems odd to say that my first encounter with mermen required me to travel though the Elos Desert, but such was indeed the case. It is the inhabitants of Ehzhimahn, that bay city of great spires, who have a prosperous (if challenging) relationship with the merman of the Whimdol Bay. Of course, without the ability to use fire, the merman culture lacks many of the tools and trades common to we of the land, but they do have shellfish, mother-of-pearl, coral and other treasures of the deep to trade.

Through some maneuvering, I managed to present myself to Captain Efwhilmozh Villdensver, a merchant who knows the merman tongue. The captain, though noble, drained my coin purse nearly dry, but I must admit he fulfilled his promise of introducing me to a small party of mermen. Forgive me if I do not reveal the exact location. They were informative, if not overly friendly, and I gathered several pieces of interesting knowledge.

For instance, one of the clearest distinctions between the sexes in is their singing. Songs and singing are of extreme importance to their culture and how they convey their history and genealogies to the younger generations. However, only mermen sing history; mermaids sing for entertainment. So strong is this cultural edict that a mermaid who dares to sing history may fear for her life, as audiences have been known to throw such a 'contemptuous' mermaid up on shore, refusing her re-entry to the waters and so causing her to asphyxiate. ~

Beware the Neaesquatilian's deadly embrace.

Mermen resemble humans from the waist up, with flexible fish-tailed bodies. Males are muscular and often bald, while females are usually slender with long hair. The average male weighs around 180 pounds and the female about 130 pounds. Their well-developed eyes have fish-like pupils and color vision as good as a human's, but their pointed, elf-like ears do not hear very well. Instead, these ears are good at detecting gentle currents and vibrations, as well as sensing the underwater motions of nearby aquatic creatures. Mermen can breathe in both air and water, though they cannot remain out of water for more than a few hours without bathing or immersing in water. Mermen are rarely seen above the surface, unless sunning themselves on rocks.

Combat/Tactics:

Mermen seem to be curious about humans and demi-humans to the point of obsession. They attempt to lure ships and boats close to them by singing alluring songs, then drag the objects of their curiosity into the water for closer inspection and a 'friendly' embrace. Unfortunately, their strength is greater than they know, and their hugs are so strong as to immobilize their victim. After the embrace, the merman drags its new friend down to its underwater kingdom, not realizing that most air-breathers cannot survive underwater. (Evil mermen simply do it out of spite.) Breaking a merman's grip requires a successful knock-back or Feat of Strength (*vs. d20p+11*). The latter can be attempted every

M

Rogue mermen shunned from their society have been known to serve as guides for ships through treacherous waters, or lure ships into shallows for others where they are run aground and taken.

RANGE ON TELLENE

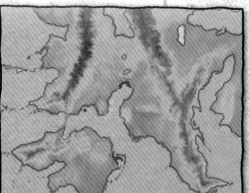

SIZE COMPARISON

6 ft

3 ft

4 seconds after the victim has been hugged. While trapped in a merman's hug, a victim can only attack effectively with a dagger or knife.

Mermen may also attack boats that they feel pose a danger to their territory. Warriors and hunters are equipped with the best weapons and armor available in the sea. Some of the most common devices are clamshell shields and sharkskin or sea serpent armor (treat as leather). They arm themselves with coral-tipped, whalebone spears and special aquatic crossbows made from various nautical materials (treat as standard light crossbows). Their nets are woven from the strongest stems of the largest sea plants and are weighted with rocks or heavy shells. Other equipment is usually made of bone or adapted from a sea creature.

Habitat/Society:

Mermen have a complex society much like that of humans, with rulers, nobles, and even criminals. Most merfolk groups are no larger than extended family units, though larger colonies and even underwater cities do exist. Some of these lie deep beneath the surface, but most are on underwater reefs where the sunlight over the water still sheds some light and warmth.

Mermen speak their own language, while those that live near the coast and trade with surface-dwellers may also speak the regional human language.

A typical merman has a lifespan of roughly 150 years.

Ecology:

Mermen live on fish, lobster, crab and other shellfish. Mermen hunt, herd fish and protect the village, while mermaids are expected to raise the children, clean the coral houses and tend to domestic affairs. However, mermaids are known for their creativity and artistry, and are the main architects and designers of their underwater homes.

On Tellene:

The best known merfolk on Tellene dwell in the underwater city of Neaesquatila, off the coast of the Elos Desert, near the human city of Ehzhimahn. The city is located just over 10 miles from the coast, and has a current population of nearly 4,000 inhabitants. Ssettlements in the regions just outside the city double this number.

Trade between the humans of Ehzhimahn and the merfolk began years ago, and mostly features bartering pearls and other undersea jewels for objects made of precious metals that do not rust underwater. Although those who trade for pearls are becoming very wealthy in Ehzhimahn, the exchange rates change rapidly and are always in favor of the merfolk.

However, the Kingdom of Neaesquatila faces new challenges on this historic threshold. Though organized trade between land and sea has begun, religious and cultural differences seek to divide the mermen, while the deep stalker menace from the depths of the sea threatens mermen and humans alike.

MERMAN

HIT POINTS:	23+d8
SIZE/WEIGHT:	M/130-180 lbs.
TENACITY:	Steady
INTELLIGENCE:	Average
FATIGUE FACTOR:	-5

MOVEMENT

CRAWL:	¼
WALK:	½
JOG:	1
RUN:	2½
SWIM:	20

SAVES

PHYSICAL:	+4
MENTAL:	+4
DODGE:	+4

ATTACK:
Mermen deal 2d6p+3 points of damage with their spears. A Feat of Strength (d20p+11) or knock-back breaks their hugs.

SPECIAL DEFENSES:
Shield use (though never underwater); unarmored mermen have DR 0

GENERAL INFO

ACTIVITY CYCLE:	Any
NO. APPEARING:	1 or 2-12 (hunters) or 20-200 (colony)
% CHANCE IN LAIR:	35%
FREQUENCY:	Infrequent
ALIGNMENT:	Neutral (lawful and good tendencies)
VISION TYPE:	Standard
AWARENESS/SENSES:	Standard
HABITAT:	Underwater reefs and communities
DIET:	Omnivorous
ORGANIZATION:	Individuals, families, colonies, cities
CLIMATE/TERRAIN:	Temperate to tropical waters

YIELD

MEDICINAL:	nil
SPELL COMPONENTS:	gills double duration of Water Breathing potions
HIDE/TROPHY:	tails, or heads with gills displayed
TREASURE:	vast riches or coral and mother of pearl
EDIBLE:	yes; tastes like whitefish
OTHER:	works of art
EXPERIENCE POINT VALUE:	67

M

MINOTAUR

Also Known As: Homatori

The lair of the minotaur is the most cunningly contrived maze that can be imagined. Its avenues are designed to confuse, full of crooked passages that wind up and down, double back upon themselves and twist and turn in all directions, while the hoarse roar of the creature itself echoes through the hollow tunnels to assault your ears.

If you dare ignore this frenzy of rage and make your way through to the center of the labyrinth, you shall see the minotaur, a creature of detestable ugliness. In some ways, he resembles a bull preposterously walking on his hind legs, but when viewed from another angle he appears to be a man with the bull's horned head.

Yet, whatever the shape, he lives only to do evil and is incapable of pity. He has no society, no companion but foul slaves of lesser races, and no love for a mate. No, he cares only for the source of his next meal.

Take care that you do not become that meal, for his sharp-bladed axe has sliced though many the limbs of men, and he knows well how to cut you down and yet keep you alive. Your screams and cries will do naught but whet his gluttony and serve as spice for his feast.

Should you be fortunate enough to have staunch allies that will aid you in your time of need, you may yet escape alive, but only if you were wise enough to mark your passage through the mizmaze in some fashion. A great length of string is said to be your best tool, but I should think that some more permanent marking of ink or wall carving would be more efficacious. - ⚷

Minotaurs are fond of capturing intelligent creatures and turning them into cringing slaves.

This man-eater appears to be some grotesque mockery of man and beast. Its muscular body, standing about 8 feet tall and weighing nearly 500 pounds, has the head, legs and hooves of a wild bull, but the torso and arms of a human. Covering the head, legs and upper torso is dense, matted under-fur as well as shaggy outer fur. Fur color ranges from brown to gray to black. A minotaur's age can be determined by its horn color, for they grow darker with age. A young bull has white or ivory horns, while a mature adult sports gray horns and an elder has black horns.

Minotaur physiology is well suited to high altitudes, for they have a relatively larger heart and lungs than do creatures at lower altitudes, as well as greater capacity for trans-porting oxygen through their blood. Minotaur sweat contains a sticky substance that keeps their under-fur matted and serves as extra insulation.

Female minotaurs exist but are rarely sighted, being more reclusive than the males. They are only slightly smaller than the males and can easily be distinguished by their multiple mammaries. Both sexes have horns.

A few explorers have reported regional variations in appearance. Thus, some scholars speculate that a second type of minotaur, one more human in appearance (with feet and flesh instead of hooves and fur), is the offspring of a minotaur and a human female rather than a simple variation in species.

SIGN/TRACKS	RANGE ON TELLENE	SIZE COMPARISON

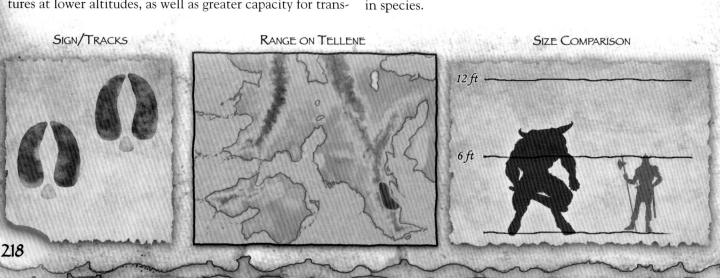

Combat/Tactics:

Minotaurs derive pleasure from confusing pursuers, leading or chasing them into dangerous areas. They are master trackers in such environments oweing to their superb hearing. Though minotaurs are not trap builders in the mechanical sense, they do know where ceiling, floor or wall are unstable, and may rig these areas to be triggered by weight or pressure.

A minotaur oft employs battle axes or clubs, though it can also attack by charging, butting with its head and then slashing with its horns. In most circumstances, they will have heard their enemies approach long before combat is initiated.

Habitat/Society:

Minotaurs live in caves or abandoned ruins. If they opt to reside permanently in a given location, they are seemingly compelled to transform this dwelling into a series of complex passages that twist and turn. The complexity is a good indication of the length of occupation. Minotaurs never get lost within their own labyrinths.

They often keep slaves (such as goblins and kobolds) to bring food and to aid in expanding the labyrinth. They rarely share their labyrinths with other minotaurs unless the lairs are of considerable size.

Minotaurs can mate with humans or other minotaurs, with any surviving offspring being fully minotaur. Females can conceive at any time of the year, though most mating occurs in early fall. They have a gestation period of eight to nine months, with a single offspring. The calf is weaned after one year and reaches sexual maturity at roughly 18 months. It then leaves to seek out its own lair.

Minotaurs have an average lifespan of 200 years.

Ecology:

Minotaurs are omnivores, though they prefer the still-warm flesh of humans and other sapient creatures. They consume grasses, lichens and other plants during times of famine. Except for their slaves, minotaurs encounter other monsters only occasionally, when expansion of the labyrinth breaks through into another lair.

On Tellene:

Legend says the first minotaur was discovered in southern Reanaaria Bay over a century ago. A ship, blown off course by a hurricane, landed along the Masau Hills. The crew took refuge in a nearby cave – a minotaur labyrinth. There was only one survivor, the captain, who left behind his log in hopes of sparing any more souls his fate. He put to sea on a makeshift raft, never to be seen again.

Twelve years later, a second crew discovered the cave in a similar manner, but had better luck in escaping. Taking the log with them, they brought the story home. Mysteriously, no one has yet been able to relocate the cave.

Since that time, rumors of other labyrinths have surfaced from all over the Sovereign Lands, though mostly in the heights of the Ka'Asa Mountains and the P'Rorul Peaks.

[1]Horn shavings can be used as an alternate material component in spells that cause mental confusion.

MINOTAUR

HIT POINTS:	32+6d8
SIZE/WEIGHT:	L/500 lbs.
TENACITY:	Brave
INTELLIGENCE:	Slow
FATIGUE FACTOR:	-7

SPEED 7 — INIT -1
ATTACK +11
DEFENSE +3 — DMG REDUCTION 6
see below
by weapon +1 foot REACH
DAMAGE 9
TOP SAVE ▼

MOVEMENT

CRAWL:	5
WALK:	10
JOG:	15
RUN:	20
SPRINT:	25

SAVES

PHYSICAL:	+13
MENTAL:	+9
DODGE:	+11

ATTACK:
Minotaurs favor battle axes or clubs, dealing +6 additional points to weapon damage, but can also deal 4d4p points of damage with their horns if unarmed (short range in this case).

SPECIAL ABILITIES:
Listening mastery of 85%.
Unerring sense of direction.

GENERAL INFO

ACTIVITY CYCLE:	Diurnal
NO. APPEARING:	1-3
% CHANCE IN LAIR:	70%
FREQUENCY:	Sporadic
ALIGNMENT:	Chaotic Evil
VISION TYPE:	Standard
AWARENESS/SENSES:	Keen hearing
HABITAT:	Labyrinthine caves and ruins
DIET:	Omnivorous (with carnivore tendencies)
ORGANIZATION:	Individuals
CLIMATE/TERRAIN:	Any, save arctic

YIELD

MEDICINAL:	ground horn, in wine, may stop bleeding (50%)
SPELL COMPONENTS:	horn shavings[1]
HIDE/TROPHY:	nil; minotaur heads look like bull heads
TREASURE:	weapons, items, all sorts of valuables
EDIBLE:	yes, though it is not a respectable meal
OTHER:	nil

EXPERIENCE POINT VALUE: 675

M

MOUNTAIN LION
Also Known As: Cougar, Mountain Screamer

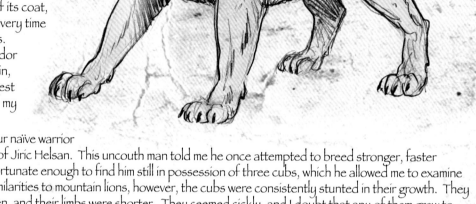

The mountain lion is such an adaptable, prodigious creature that it is the rare or the novice hunter who has never encountered one. I myself have spotted them, and suffered a few wounds from their sharp fangs, throughout the northern lands; they do not seem to appear on Svimohzia. Though they have different colorations and markings, my experienced eyes can see through the different subspecies to the consistency within. Of course, not everyone has my breadth of knowledge and experience.

Our fighter, for instance, fervently claims that the panther (a name for mountain lions that he learned in the Pel) is a great cat that can change the color of its coat, like the chameleon lizard. According to him, every time a panther feasts, it then sleeps for three days. Once it wakes, it roars out a sweet-smelling odor that attracts its prey so it can hunt, feast again, sleep for three more days, and continue the rest of its life in this strange cycle. Sadly, none of my knowledge seems to impress him.

I believe the only man of knowledge whom our naïve warrior did favor was a Baparan trapper by the name of Jiric Helsan. This uncouth man told me he once attempted to breed stronger, faster mountain lions by mixing their species. I was fortunate enough to find him still in possession of three cubs, which he allowed me to examine for only a small fee. Despite their apparent similarities to mountain lions, however, the cubs were consistently stunted in their growth. They grew only to half the size they should have been, and their limbs were shorter. They seemed sickly, and I doubt that any of them grew to maturity. Of course, they would not have lived long in any case, for Jiric no doubt intended to sell them to the Kalamaran arenas. - ⚔

This large, solitary cat is slender and quite agile, with powerful forequarters, neck and jaw serving to grasp and hold large prey. Its head is round and the ears erect, and it has five retractable claws on its forepaws and four on its hind paws.

A typical adult male is around 8 feet long from nose to tail tip and weights some 115 to 160 pounds (in rare cases over 260 pounds). Females average between 75 and 105 pounds. Mountain lion coloring is plain and spotless, but can vary greatly between individuals and regions. For instance, the mountain lion (or 'panther') of southern Brandobia is mostly solid dark brown or ebony, while the mountain lion of other regions may vary from slate gray (northern) to yellowish and sandy brown (central) to light reddish brown (southern) with lighter patches on the underside, including the jaws, chin and throat.

Much like a domestic cat, the mountain lion vocalizes low-pitched hisses, growls, and purrs, as well as chirps and whistles. It is well known for its screams, thus its "mountain screamer" nickname.

SIGN/TRACKS	RANGE ON TELLENE	SIZE COMPARISON

Fore

Hind

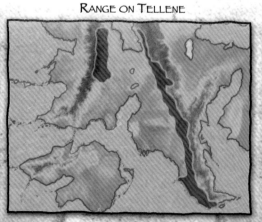

6 ft

3 ft

M

Combat/Tactics:

The mountain lion hunts by stalking through brush and trees, across ledges, or other covered spots, before delivering a powerful leap onto the back of its prey and a suffocating neck bite.

A mountain lion may attack if cornered, if a fleeing human being stimulates its instinct to chase or if a person 'plays dead.' Exaggerating the threat to the animal through intense eye contact, loud but calm shouting, and any other action to appear larger and more menacing, may make it retreat. Fighting back with sticks and rocks, or even bare hands, is often effective in spurring an attacking mountain lion to disengage.

When attacking, mountain lions use their paws to pin a victim (two successive claw attacks indicating such). Once held, it employs its characteristic neck bite, attempting to position its teeth between the vertebrae and into the spinal cord. This biting automatically succeeds in inflicting 2d6p+4 points of damage every 5 seconds thereafter. A mountain lion's grip can be broken with a successful knock-back or Feat of Strength (vs. d20p+12). The latter can be attempted after each bite attack. While being mauled, a victim can only attack with a dagger or knife.

Habitat/Society:

A mountain lion's primary food source is deer and other woodland herbivores, but domestic cattle, horses, sheep and goats are also delicious targets, should the opportunity present itself. When larger prey is not available, a mountain lion will even hunt species as small as rodents or insects.

It prefers habitats with dense underbrush for stalking, as well as rough canyons, escarpments and rim rocks, but it can survive in open areas with little vegetation. It is a reclusive cat and is most active around dawn and dusk.

Mountain lions are lone hunters, found together only when mating or caring for cubs; the latter being a purely female occupation. Litters occur about once every 2 to 3 years, with a gestation period of about 3 months and the number of offspring ranging from one to six (though two or three is most common). Kittens leave their mother when they become about 12 months old, though it is rare for more than one or two kittens to survive this first harsh year.

The lifespan for a mountain lion is about 8 to 10 years.

Ecology:

Although the mountain lion is a large predator, it is not always dominant in its range, for it competes with other animals (particularly the wolf, and less often the bear) for prey. Attacks on humans are most frequent during late spring and summer, when juvenile mountain lions leave their mothers and search for new territory.

On Tellene:

The mountain lion is found throughout Tellene (except on Svimohzia) and thus is known by many names, including the catamount, cougar, deercat, king cat, mountain screamer, panther, red tiger, silver lion and sneak cat.

MOUNTAIN LION

HIT POINTS:	20+2d8
SIZE/WEIGHT:	M/140 lbs.
TENACITY:	Nervous
INTELLIGENCE:	Animal, High
FATIGUE FACTOR:	2

SPEED	5	INIT	-3
ATTACK	+7	DMG REDUCTION	
DEFENSE	+4		3
		see below	
medium REACH		DAMAGE	5
		TOP SAVE	

MOVEMENT

CRAWL:	10
WALK:	15
JOG:	25
RUN:	25
SPRINT:	30

SAVES

PHYSICAL:	+7
MENTAL:	+6
DODGE:	+7

ATTACK: Mountain Lions attempt to pin prey with their claws (these causing 2d4p+2 damage); with 2 successive claw hits they have grabbed the prey and automatically bite for 2d6p+6 every 5 seconds (superceding the claw attacks); breaking their grasp requires a Feat of Strength vs. d20p+12

SPECIAL ABILITIES: Hiding, Listening and Sneaking at 60% mastery

GENERAL INFO

ACTIVITY CYCLE:	Crepuscular
NO. APPEARING:	1-2
% CHANCE IN LAIR:	15%
FREQUENCY:	Frequent
ALIGNMENT:	Non
VISION TYPE:	Standard
AWARENESS/SENSES:	Good hearing and sense of smell
HABITAT:	Underbrush and canyons
DIET:	Carnivorous
ORGANIZATION:	Individuals
CLIMATE/TERRAIN:	Temperate mountains

YIELD

MEDICINAL:	ground bones thought to nourish creaky joints
SPELL COMPONENTS:	nil
HIDE/TROPHY:	head, pelt and claws are common trophies
TREASURE:	nil
EDIBLE:	yes
OTHER:	nil
EXPERIENCE POINT VALUE:	350

M

MUMMY

Also Known As:
The Damned

Those given to superstition do decry mummification as an art most dark. This be most untrue for the preservation of the body of a priest or knight most good canst a righteous deed be. Preservation of these mortal remains ensureth he canst be awoken from the sleep of death shouldest a future era demand the service of a hero of such caliber.

That the process hath nonetheless acquired a reputation most sinister doth lie in the fact that it maketh a vessel that doth verily cry out for possession by a baneful entity. Shouldest this be the wicked spirit of the deceased given continued existence by dark energies, it canst become a cadaverous being most powerful. In times past, mummification was a practice of burial common to the Dejy but in subsequent centuries it hath fallen into disrepute in no small part due to its macabre association with the undead.

Mummies be likened unto zombies by some for both be corporeal bodies of the dead that moveth most slow. That they be not shadowy forms like unto wraiths provideth a false comfort. Be wary of this pitfall for this likeness be but skin-deep. The dark energies propelling this creature are strong indeed as mummification has removed the creature's organs leaving behind a mere husk beneath which is a dark power fierce.

The varnished husk of a mummy willst rot in all but the most arid of climates. The ancient dejy hadst such knowledge and thus did secrete their dead within the dusty wastes of the Elos and Khydoban deserts. Excepting of the purposeful removal of an ancient sarcophagi, it be most rare for to encounter mummies in regions beyond burial sites of antiquity.

Heedless of the danger, plundering riches of a long dead prince hath an allure irresistible for many with an adventurous spirit. It is to these latter readers that I address mine subsequent commentary.

Think not that you willst encounter but a lone mummy ensconced within its sarcophagi. Burial sites didst often contain the mummified remains of a noble or regal personage along with their retinue of servitors and minions – the latter ritually slain and mummified in order to serve the master in the afterlife. The dark force that animateth the wellborn mummy also imparteth unlife to its courtiers. Be aware then that these attendants mayest rise forthwith from the sand to defend the pyramidal tomb long before thou havest it reached. Be assured though that thine quest is well guided, for if thee be subject to such assail, know well that odds do favor a tomb be in proximal distance – though perchance lost to sight by the sand's inexorable movement.

Beware combat with mummies for the touch of them is most baneful. It causeth a rotting of the flesh which doth drain health and disfigure one's appearance. Such malady is most difficult for all but the most accomplished healer to remedy.

A mummy doth prove resilient to all save those that be silvered or bear a dweomer of magic. Mark well this power for it be but frivolity to assail a mummy with arms of other composition. The creature doth have a weakness, that being fire. Knowest that a torch canst do more harm than a sword. - ◉

M

Take note, you reckless plunderers of graves. I warn you to restrain your greed, should you be tempted to pilfer treasure from a mummy's tomb. If you but take even the smallest trinket, the mummy's curse will follow you and bring you harm. No matter where you flee, or how far, the curse will find you.

WILL FACTOR
16*
Variants Differ

SIZE COMPARISON

6 ft

3 ft

Thousands of years ago the first human inhabitants of the Sovereign Lands, the Dejy, ruled great empires. The regions that today comprise the Elos and Khydoban deserts, some scholars say, were once the verdant homelands of the greatest rival empires of these peoples. What caused their downfall millennia ago is unknown to the living sages of Tellene, though some say famine, some claim plague and others assert the cause was a great magical war. However, none argue that if such empires did exist, they exist no longer.

The mummies of these Dejy empires, like the empires themselves, stem from one of three epochs: the Early, Middle, Late and Interregnal Periods. Mummies vary with the culture and the nature of the spices, chemicals and treatments of the time.

Mummification consists of three separate processes. First comes the removal and separate preservation of major organs, including the liver, heart, stomach and brain. After this initial preparation, there is a ritualized bathing of the body in special liquids that preserve the flesh. The organs are then returned to the host in their proper orientations. Finally the body is bound in fine linen or silk, with each limb and digit wrapped separately, in order that the body might be fully articulated.

Once fully prepared, the mummies were then sealed in stone caskets and placed in special niches in either communal or clan mausoleums. Some of the more powerful and wealthy folk had full crypts of their own, replete with grave goods such as weapons, foodstuffs, cherished treasures and sundry items. Wealthier individuals also had gems, gold, jewelry and sometimes even magic items such as amulets, scrolls and wands wrapped in the linens of their mummy.

Most mausoleums are above ground affairs, built of stone and once flanked by temples, while others are subterranean and intended to offer some protection from grave robbers by virtue of their concealment. Intricate mechanical traps usually guarded these mausoleums while a few have magical wards and guardians (such as golems).

Except where noted, standard mummies (as well as each of the following subtypes) appear as a human wrapped in aged linen bandages from head to toe. Where these bandages fall away, leathery tanned skin is visible beneath. Mummies stand from 5 to 6 feet tall and weigh approximately 100 pounds.

Combat/Tactics:

Mummies have a frightening visage, enough so to cause anyone viewing them to Panic (as the 5th level mage spell). Those permitted saving throws do so vs. d20p+16.

They attack by battering opponents with their fists, raining down blows upon their target dealing out 2d8p+9 points of damage as well as the possibility for mummy rot.

On Tellene:

The typical mummy was entombed during the Interregnal Period, the years between the fall of the last major Dejy Kingdom and the rise of the barbarians from the south (the Bran-

MUMMY (Standard)

HIT POINTS:	28+6d8
SIZE/WEIGHT:	M/100 lbs.
TENACITY:	Brave
INTELLIGENCE:	Average
FATIGUE FACTOR:	n/a
WILL FACTOR:	16

SPEED	7	INIT	5
ATTACK	+16	DMG REDUCTION	
DEFENSE	+7		24
	2d8p+9		
short REACH		DAMAGE	n/a TOP SAVE ▼

MOVEMENT

CRAWL:	1½
WALK:	2½
JOG:	5
RUN:	7½
SPRINT:	10

SAVES

PHYSICAL:	+16
MENTAL:	immune
DODGE:	+12

ATTACK: Mummies deal 2d8p+9 when battering foes but such wounds may also become infected by Mummy Rot; those suffering damage from a mummy's fists must save or contract this supernatural disease (Con+d20p vs mummy's 16+d20p).

DEFENSES: Silvered or enchanted weapons reduce DR to 14; mummy takes full damage from any fire attack (cannot save for half damage)

GENERAL INFO

ACTIVITY CYCLE:	Any
NO. APPEARING:	1 or 2-8
% CHANCE IN LAIR:	80%
FREQUENCY:	Unusual
ALIGNMENT:	Lawful Evil
VISION TYPE:	Undead Sight
AWARENESS/SENSES:	Standard
HABITAT:	Ruins and tombs
DIET:	None
ORGANIZATION:	Individuals
CLIMATE/TERRAIN:	Deserts (see also 'Natural Mummies' below)

YIELD

MEDICINAL:	nil
SPELL COMPONENTS:	skulls[1]
HIDE/TROPHY:	nil
TREASURE:	mummy lairs often hold a great deal of treasure
EDIBLE:	no
OTHER:	nil

EXPERIENCE POINT VALUE: 1425

M

RATTLEBONE MUMMY

HIT POINTS:	16+3d8
SIZE/WEIGHT:	M/100 lbs.
TENACITY:	Fearless
INTELLIGENCE:	Slow
FATIGUE FACTOR:	n/a
WILL FACTOR:	8

SPEED 5 — INIT 3
ATTACK +6
DEFENSE +4 — DMG REDUCTION 12
DAMAGE 2d4p+4
REACH short — TOP SAVE n/a

MOVEMENT

CRAWL:	2½
WALK:	5
JOG:	7½
RUN:	10
SPRINT:	20

SAVES

PHYSICAL:	+5
MENTAL:	immune
DODGE:	+4

ATTACK:
Rattlebones attack by battering with their arms inflicting 2d4p+4 damage; they may also use conventional weaponry at normal weapon speed but add +4 to damage. No mummy rot.

DEFENSES:
Silvered or enchanted weapons reduce DR to 5; mummy takes full damage from any fire attack

SERVITOR MUMMY

HIT POINTS:	28+5d8
SIZE/WEIGHT:	M/100 lbs.
TENACITY:	Steady
INTELLIGENCE:	Smart
FATIGUE FACTOR:	n/a
WILL FACTOR:	13

SPEED 7 — INIT 4
ATTACK +12
DEFENSE +5 — DMG REDUCTION 19
DAMAGE 2d4p+6
REACH short — TOP SAVE n/a

MOVEMENT

CRAWL:	1½
WALK:	2½
JOG:	5
RUN:	7½
SPRINT:	10

SAVES

PHYSICAL:	+12
MENTAL:	immune
DODGE:	+9

ATTACK:
Servitor mumies either direct the actions of minions or use them as defensive screens while casting spells (if available). Battering attacks deal 2d4p+6 damage.

DEFENSES:
Silvered or enchanted weapons reduce DR to 10; mummy takes full damage from any fire attack

GENERAL INFO

ACTIVITY CYCLE:	Any
NO. APPEARING:	3-12
% CHANCE IN LAIR:	80%
FREQUENCY:	Sporadic
ALIGNMENT:	Lawful Evil
VISION TYPE:	Undead Sight
AWARENESS/SENSES:	Standard
HABITAT:	Ruins and tombs
DIET:	None
ORGANIZATION:	Troop
CLIMATE/TERRAIN:	Desert

GENERAL INFO

ACTIVITY CYCLE:	Any
NO. APPEARING:	1 or 1-4
% CHANCE IN LAIR:	80%
FREQUENCY:	Sporadic
ALIGNMENT:	Lawful Evil
VISION TYPE:	Undead Sight
AWARENESS/SENSES:	Standard
HABITAT:	Ruins and tombs
DIET:	None
ORGANIZATION:	Individuals
CLIMATE/TERRAIN:	Desert

YIELD

MEDICINAL:	nil
SPELL COMPONENTS:	nil
HIDE/TROPHY:	nil
TREASURE:	none of their own, but master's tombs have much
EDIBLE:	no
OTHER:	nil

EXPERIENCE POINT VALUE: 200

YIELD

MEDICINAL:	nil
SPELL COMPONENTS:	skull[1]
HIDE/TROPHY:	nil
TREASURE:	may wield magic items
EDIBLE:	no
OTHER:	nil

EXPERIENCE POINT VALUE: 975

M

dobians and Fhokki in the early centuries, Reanaarians and Kalamarans in the later centuries), when the Dejy faced migrations, wars, interracial strife, chaos and destruction.

The hidden subterranean tomb predominated throughout this period, for barbarian invasions and thievery were common occurrences that threatened to disturb the sanctity of these graves. Commoners were buried in situ, as most could not afford even the least embalming; only nobles and royalty were mummified during this era. Most tomb complexes were simply cut out of the side of a hill, with little care to the style and décor, though notable exceptions can be found. Some folktales state that mummification inexorably links the subject to a specific location; such a loss of mobility would certainly interfere with one's plans in the afterlife.

Mummification has fallen out of favor as a burial practice and is not currently utilized by any cultural group on Tellene. As such, knowledge of the actual processes involved to properly mummify a corpse is something of a lost art. It is rumored within certain clerical orders that the Congregation of the Dead has retained this knowledge and some members of this vile sect are capable of returning from death as hideous animated mummies.

Mummy Subtypes

The types of mummies that appear throughout Tellene depend heavily on their time of origin (mummification), culture and region. Included are the blood mummy, noble mummy, rattlebone mummy, royal mummy, and servitor mummies.

Mummy Rot

The mere touch of a mummy is enough to inflict a rotting disease on its foe; the victim must make an opposed Con check (Con plus d20p) versus a d20p plus the mummy's Will Factor, or contract a rotting disease. Once contracted, Mummy Rot forces the victim to make another opposed Con check each day. Failure indicates the loss of one point of Constitution; the next failure causes a loss of Looks, then back to Constitution and so forth. Once a character's Constitution drops to zero, he dies. A successful save does not stop the progress, and multiple hits are cumulative.

Mummy Rot can only be cured magically by a cleric's Remove Curse spell followed by a Cure Disease spell. The cleric makes a successful turn check against the mummy's Will Factor. If the cleric succeeds, the survivor's lost ability points can be regained with rest. For each day of complete rest, the victim may attempt a Con check (using his original, undrained Con score) against the mummy's Will Factor. Success indicates one point returns. A critical failure ('nat 1') indicates the loss of that point is permanent. The process continues until all points have been returned (save any losses due to critical failures — these points are lost permanently).

Lesser Orders

Rattlebone Mummies

Thinchejany (rattlebone mummies) safeguard the tombs of their long deceased masters. Often they were members of the royal praetorian bodyguard ritually slaughtered and hastily mummified when their liege died. Their bodies were placed within the tomb proper as well as interspersed in the immediate vicinity.

Poor initial preparation of the remains has frequently resulted in rattlebone mummies having sparse residual flesh, potentially leading to misidentification as some sort of skeletal undead.

Combat/Tactics:

These mummies are unusually swift for their kind and are able to move at speeds comparable to an unladen human. When moving faster than a walk though, their bones shake and rattle inside their wrappings, often providing an auditory herald of their arrival.

Rattlebone mummies are dogged in their assaults against tomb raiders fighting until destroyed. However, unlike the automatonic undead, they retain some intelligence – particularly that related to small unit tactics. As such, they will seek to gather up their peers and set up ambushes where they can best make use of their numbers rather than hurling themselves in dribs and drabs at a superior foe. They can be extremely patient, and will hold still for hours on end while lying in wait.

They attack by battering opponents with their limbs, their otherworldly strength permitting said blows to impact with considerable force. Rattlebone mummies may also employ standard weapons if available, attacking at the implement's normal speed but adding +4 to damage.

The rattlebone mummy does not impart mummy rot.

On Tellene:

Rattlebone mummies and Early Period burial sites are usually found only in the western Elos Desert region and the western Young Kingdoms, though a few have been discovered as far south and east as Tokis and Dodera.

Servitor Mummies

When an important noble or royal personage died or was otherwise removed from his position of authority, his personal courtiers were frequently ritually strangled and mummified along with their patron. Interned in his tomb, their symbolic role was to continue their service to their departed master. In truth, this ceremony was often just a ritual veil over the some brutal housecleaning by the new regime eager to ensure that no ties to the former sovereign remained and that the new cadre of attendants was aware in no uncertain terms that their very lives depended upon complete loyalty and devotion to the current ruler.

When their patron was invigorated with malevolent unlife, these *jhurijany* (or servitor mummies) were similarly animated and now truly fulfill the role they were, in theory, assigned at

M

their death (despite it being mere court theater at the time).

Though not as powerful as true mummies, many servitors functioned in roles such as court astrologer, magician or seer. As undead beings they retain these skills with the result that many can possess the powers of a mage – some even a highly skilled ones. Aptitude in divine magic is less common but possible as well.

Combat/Tactics:

Servitor mummies can shamble forward and batter opponents much as standard mummies do (including transmission of the dreaded mummy rot). This is a last resort though, for servitors are quite intelligent and, if forewarned (possibly by magical means), will mount a coordinated defense of the master's tomb.

They will rally rattlebones mummies and assign them the routine task of perimeter defense while coordinating the actions of several of these groups to maximize their collective effectiveness at repelling intruders. If possessed of the ability to employ magic, they seek primarily to gain intelligence on the actions and whereabouts of interlopers or to enhance the passive defenses of the complex. In extremis, they can also support the guards by direct application of destructive force. Note that servitors will never employ dweomers that produce flame or fire.

On Tellene:

Servitor mummies are found exclusively in the burial sites of noble and royal mummies, ranging from the Elenon Mountains to the Khydoban Desert.

Blood Mummies

The *hijarjany* is a rogue not typically affiliated with a greater mummy. It claims a territory of its own and assails the living who dare trespass, draining them of their life-blood. Though possible to originate from the Middle Period, it is also the most common manifestation of so-called 'natural' mummies.

Blood mummies are sanguivores utilizing fresh blood to rejuvenate their withered form. When fed, their mortal corpulence is restored permitting them to (at least in silhouette) give the impression of mortality. Viewed up close though, it is clearly evident from their dark brown to bronze red skin and misshapen features that something is amiss.

They seek to disguise such tell-tale characteristics by shrouding themselves in loose and concealing clothing typical of the region. Those encountered in arid regions dress from head to toe in robes, incidentally protecting themselves from the scorching sun. Thus, from a distance, travelers may think it a simple desert nomad.

Similarly, arctic mummies wear an anorak or parka while blood bog mummies dress in leather or fur overcoats all in an effort to avoid alerting their quarry.

Combat/Tactics:

Blood mummies are vicious creatures and will attempt to feed on anyone who enters their territory. Their preference is allow their prey to approach closely, often feigning deafness if mis-

BLOOD MUMMY

HIT POINTS:	30+5d8
SIZE/WEIGHT:	M/100 lbs.
TENACITY:	Brave
INTELLIGENCE:	Average
FATIGUE FACTOR:	n/a
WILL FACTOR:	14

MOVEMENT

CRAWL:	1½
WALK:	2½
JOG:	5
RUN:	7½
SPRINT:	10

SAVES

PHYSICAL:	+13
MENTAL:	immune
DODGE:	+10

SPEED 7   INIT 2   ATTACK +14   DMG REDUCTION +6   20   DEFENSE   DAMAGE 2d6p+5   short REACH   TOP SAVE n/a

ATTACK:
Blood mummies prefer potential prey to closely approach for it is generally incapable of pursuit; Attacks by battering opponents with arms for 2d6p+5 damage

DEFENSES:
Silvered or enchanted weapons reduce DR to 9; mummy takes full damage from any fire attack

GENERAL INFO

ACTIVITY CYCLE:	Always Active
NO. APPEARING:	1
% CHANCE IN LAIR:	0%
FREQUENCY:	Sporadic
ALIGNMENT:	Neutral Evil
VISION TYPE:	Undead Sight
AWARENESS/SENSES:	Standard
HABITAT:	Very arid or cold areas; bogs
DIET:	Sanguivorous
ORGANIZATION:	Solitary
CLIMATE/TERRAIN:	Desert, arctic or cold temperate

YIELD

MEDICINAL:	nil
SPELL COMPONENTS:	nil
HIDE/TROPHY:	nil
TREASURE:	rare, due to their method of preservation
EDIBLE:	no
OTHER:	nil

EXPERIENCE POINT VALUE: 825

M

Natural Mummies

Not all mummies are the result of deliberate action by mankind. It is possible for exceptional environmental conditions to mummify a corpse as well. Extreme and persistent cold may freeze-dry a body preserving it for millennia while those buried (or perhaps simply perishing) in severely arid regions may desiccate leaving behind remains that persist for centuries. Cold bogs are another source of naturally occurring mummies. The combination of low temperatures, highly acidic water and lack of oxygen serves to preserve cadavers though tanning their skin in the process.

All of these mummies may become animated as undead creatures statistically identical to either blood or standard mummies. Their appearance, though, will be distinct as they obviously lack the burial linens employed in deliberate mummification. Instead, they appear to be an emaciated corpse of uniform dark brown or black coloration.

Natural mummies are not grossly flammable & receive standard saving throws versus such attacks.

taken for a benign traveler or peasant.

Though they share a sanguivorous diet with vampires, their feeding habits are far cruder. Rather than directly siphoning lifeblood via the arteries, a blood mummy employs the same techniques it employs in combat – namely battering a body into a bloody pulp. Once left alone to feed, it guzzles the fluids (phlegm, choler, blood and black bile) indiscriminately.

Rough contact with a blood mummy presents a strong likelihood of contracting the dreaded mummy rot.

Ecology:

A blood mummy must feed upon living creatures to sustain itself and retain its corpulence. A starving blood mummy's flesh will begin to desiccate should it not feed for an extended period of time. For each continuous week it does not imbibe sufficient plasma, it suffers -1 to its Attack bonus. Should this reach zero, the mummy falls dormant.

If in an environment favorable to preservation of tissue, it may lay dormant for centuries until revived by dousing or infusing the husk with warm, fresh blood. If a blood mummy undergoes starvation-induced hibernation in a less favorable climate, the creature decomposes within a month.

On Tellene:

Blood mummies can be found from the Elenon Mountains in the west to the Khydoban Desert in the east. Naturally occurring blood mummies have been reported in the DuKem'p swamp and amongst the highest elevations of the Legasa Peaks.

Greater Orders

Noble Mummies

The *shojarijany*, or "noble mummy," were lesser princes or sundry members of an Imperial lineage. They may also have been lesser monarchs subservient to an emperor. Regardless of their circumstances in life, they were interred as the principal oc-

NOBLE MUMMY

HIT POINTS:	28+8d8
SIZE/WEIGHT:	M/100 lbs.
TENACITY:	Brave
INTELLIGENCE:	Bright
FATIGUE FACTOR:	n/a
WILL FACTOR:	18

SPEED	INIT
7	2
ATTACK	+18
DR (DICE REDUCTION)	
+7	26
DEFENSE	DAMAGE 2d12p+6
short REACH	TOP SAVE ▼ n/a

MOVEMENT

CRAWL:	1½
WALK:	2½
JOG:	5
RUN:	7½
SPRINT:	10

SAVES

PHYSICAL:	+18
MENTAL:	immune
DODGE:	+15

ATTACK: Noble mummies deal 2d12p+6 when battering foes but such wounds may also become infected by Mummy Rot; nobles will utilize their thralls to fight and act as screens while utilizing its magical powers.

DEFENSES: Silvered or enchanted weapons reduce DR to 16; mummy takes full damage from any fire attack (cannot save for half damage)

GENERAL INFO

ACTIVITY CYCLE:	Any
NO. APPEARING:	2-8
% CHANCE IN LAIR:	80%
FREQUENCY:	Exotic
ALIGNMENT:	Lawful Evil
VISION TYPE:	Undead Sight
AWARENESS/SENSES:	Standard
HABITAT:	Ruins and tombs
DIET:	None
ORGANIZATION:	Individuals
CLIMATE/TERRAIN:	Any, save arctic

YIELD

MEDICINAL:	nil
SPELL COMPONENTS:	skull[1]
HIDE/TROPHY:	nil
TREASURE:	may wield magic items
EDIBLE:	no
OTHER:	nil
EXPERIENCE POINT VALUE:	1850

cupant in a mausoleum or crypt. These structures were never as grand or imposing as those of the royal mummies but nonetheless ape the latter in having a retinue of servants and guards that were mummified along with the noble personage to serve his needs in the hereafter. They may also contain the mummified remains of siblings and other relations who passed during the often lengthy periods it may have taken to build these structures.

Combat/Tactics:

In death, as it did in life, the noble mummy serves in the role of executive. Servitor and rattlebone mummies will act with some measure of independence to carry out their assigned duties within the tomb, reacting to intruders with vigorous determination in the case of rattlebones while the servitors rouse their master from his slumber. Once awakened, the noble, perhaps with assistance from other family members (these being standard mummies), will conspire to destroy intruders.

The *shojarijany* is a capable magician able to utilize the following spell-like powers once per day (at baseline spell point effect if applicable): Bedazzle, Clairvoyance, Fracture Object, Induce Fatigue , Induce Fratricide , Mass Influence, Panic, Paralysis, Pestilent Swarm, Righteous Cursing, Sense Invisible Beings, Wizard's Lock. Creatures may attempt a saving throw versus these powers (if the spell would normally allow it) versus the mummy's d20p+18. It will utilize these power to best effect before personally engaging in combat. *Note that these powers do not induce spell fatigue but cannot be employed more frequently than one effect per 10 seconds.*

Noble mummies also have the mummy rot ability.

On Tellene:

Mummification and entombment of lesser nobility in large structures gradually tapered off in later years as resources were siphoned off in every increasing amounts to build the grand edifices of the emperors. Many of the existing noble tombs were also plundered for building materials during the last great age of mummification, thus sparing the builders of these prohibitively expensive monuments some effort in quarrying new stone. As such, intact noble tombs tend to be located along the fringes of the Elos and Khydoban deserts where their very distance from the seat of power ensured their survival.

Many, if not most, of these structures were impressive above ground buildings when initially built. That is no longer the case. Many – and surely most that remain intact – were gradually subsumed by shifting sand that buried them and, in so doing, transformed them into subterranean lairs for the dead that rest within their bowels. Often it is but the peak of the highest minaret that stands above the surface – unrecognizable for what it truly is (or was).

Royal Mummies

Shijarinjany (royal mummies) were kings during the Late Period and consequently received the best mummification process available. They can be readily distinguished by the golden death masks they wear.

Royal mummies are rarely found alone. They inhabit massive pyramidal tombs with many servitors and minions to attend to any need including defense of the regal personage.

Combat/Tactics:

Royal mummies are extremely formidable combatants. Yet, for all their prowess, this is a last resort employed only when all other attempt to dislodge tomb raiders have failed.

Having in life been at the pinnacle of an entire society, royal mummies were buried with fantastic works of artistry - many of which carry powerful magical enchantments. While it is impossible to give any but the broadest guidance, these regal mummies will at a minimum have access to a bevy of protective amulets, pectorals, and rings. These will certainly be used to their full effectiveness.

A royal mummy's preference is to use its opponents as instruments of its will rather than destroy them. This is facilitated by its power to dominate any creature within 30 feet that meets its gaze. This works as the Charm spell, but its effect is not broken by damage inflicted. Those subject to the royal mummy's domineering gaze (which may be employed once per 10 seconds) must succeed at an opposed Wisdom (vs. d20p+20) or fall under his control. Resisting this tyrannical mastery provides proof against subsequent attempts.

Those whom it cannot command, it will destroy.

Royal mummies can transmit a virulent form of mummy rot. Any it touches must make an opposed Con check (Con plus d20p *vs.* d20p+20) or contract the rotting disease.

On Tellene:

Royal mummies are exclusively found in large ornate tombs located in either the Elos or Khydoban deserts. Some of these structures may present a distinct and unmistakable silhouette against the otherwise featureless wastes. Others may be almost completely buried beneath centuries of blowing sand.

These tombs are almost certainly protected by lethal mechanical traps of ingenious design. Beneath this first passive layer of defense lies further obstacles all designed to thwart the most clever and determined of grave robbers.

---

[1]*Some mummy skulls, when used as an additional material component for any Animate spells to revive the undead, permit the cleric to animate additional undead (one for every four full levels the presiding cleric possesses).*

M

Mummy Scarabs

Royal Mummies are always in possession of a most powerful item, their mummy scarab. It may appear most plain and ordinary or be fit with gemstones of phenomenal beauty. Regardless of its appearance, it is their most treasured possession and usually kept near.

This scarab acts as a conduit for dark energy and provides the animating force to not only the Regal mummy but also to all those within his sphere of control – to wit all lesser mummies within the immediate vicinity of his tomb. It may also provide structural integrity to the tomb itself if the passage of time has rendered it unstable.

Holding the scarab permits the possessor to control the royal mummy. It is thus a tremendous weapon in the wrong hands and it is not unheard of for there to be a command word restricting access.

Smashing this scarab severs the flow of dark energies and with them the power of the Royal mummy. A brilliant flash of light (actually a receding stream of negative energy) will issue from the point of breakage and withdraw the animating force from all mummies within the tomb leaving only husks behind. If the scarab was responsible for or contributed to the structural integrity of the tomb, it begins to creak and crumble possibly collapsing in on itself as gravity reclaims the building.

Mummy Curses

While a mummy's raw powers are frightening enough, many of these creatures have another terrifying weapon to bring to bear on their foes: the mummy's curse. Many tombs, and certainly all those associated with royalty, have some sort of curse placed upon them to ward off would-be grave robbers. Every mummy curse is unique to that mummy and will relate somehow to its former life, its desires or the wishes of its followers. Typical curses involve retribution in the form of violent death. Some force such as snakes or insects that will preferentially attack the cursed individuals or crocodiles that will hunt them and so forth generally accomplishes this. Each curse will specify not only the method of retribution but also the requirements for enacting the curse, such as breaking the seal of the tomb, removing anything from the tomb, touching the mummy or its family's remains and so on.

All royal mummies have an additional curse: anyone so foolhardy as to steal the mummy's scarab or remains will be pursued relentlessly by the guardians of the tomb (i.e., the lesser mummies). They will pursue the defilers relentlessly, the pilfered goods a silent beacon somehow calling to its guardians - clear to them but imperceptible to all others. Only return of the item(s) will halt pursuit.

ROYAL MUMMY

HIT POINTS:	30+10d8
SIZE/WEIGHT:	M/100 lbs.
TENACITY:	Fearless
INTELLIGENCE:	Brilliant
FATIGUE FACTOR:	n/a
WILL FACTOR:	20

MOVEMENT

CRAWL:	1½
WALK:	2½
JOG:	5
RUN:	7½
SPRINT:	10

SAVES

PHYSICAL:	+21
MENTAL:	immune
DODGE:	+17

SPEED		INIT
6	ATTACK +20	0
DEFENSE +12	DMG REDUCTION 28	
short REACH	DAMAGE 2d12p +10	n/a TOP SAVE ▼

ATTACK: Royal mummies first try to *Dominate* (save vs. d20p+20) opponents; failing that, they employ any magical resources as best fits the situation, relying on their servitors and minions to provide a defensive screen. Melee is a last resort.

DEFENSES: Silvered or enchanted weapons reduce DR to 18; takes full damage from any fire attack (cannot save for half damage)

GENERAL INFO

ACTIVITY CYCLE:	Always active
NO. APPEARING:	1
% CHANCE IN LAIR:	100%
FREQUENCY:	Exotic
ALIGNMENT:	Lawful Evil
VISION TYPE:	Undead Sight
AWARENESS/SENSES:	Standard
HABITAT:	Tombs
DIET:	None
ORGANIZATION:	Leader
CLIMATE/TERRAIN:	Desert

YIELD

MEDICINAL:	nil
SPELL COMPONENTS:	skull[1]
HIDE/TROPHY:	nil
TREASURE:	potentially a king's ransom
EDIBLE:	no
OTHER:	nil
EXPERIENCE POINT VALUE:	2300

M

OGRE

Also Known As: Aanaagrugr (in Orcish)

The psychology of an ogre is only describable as evil personified. No act of terror, violence or debauchery is too low for an ogre to perform. Ogres are also inherently greedy and always desire more than they already possess. So, you see, material possessions are a measure of status amongst ogres, but not in the way you might think. An ogre does not want a fine mansion with luxurious finery so that he can impress the other ogres. No, owning things is not a sign of wealth in the traditional sense, but a sign of virility and strength. Yes, ogres do occasionally trade, but that rarely gains them much wealth. You can have no doubt that an ogre wielding a silvered weapon did not purchase it from a mage. Instead, he fought its owner, or looted it from a fallen body that someone else killed, for the right of possession. Regardless of how it gained the prize, to an ogre the simple act of wielding the weapon is a clear sign that he is powerful and should be feared.

Although ogres may ally themselves with rival humanoids, it is never for long. All other races are inferior in ogre eyes and any alliance is often at the expense of their ally, weakening him so that the ogre may finish the job later. Even powerful allies such as giants are merely tools to use and then relieve themselves of in the proven manner of slaughter and feeding. Yes, it is quite true — flesh is all an ogre sees in another race. An easy meal.

Can you imagine man killing his wounded neighbor and eating his flesh? An ogre would, and gladly. There is no place for the weak in their society, and famine is a constant danger for ogres, given their propensity for eating as oft as they may. Of course, without a proper diet they will never achieve the perfection of man and will remain firmly rooted amongst the animals. - ☩

These large, monstrous humanoids are hideous to behold. An ogre appears to be mostly human, but has a long, low skull with protruding brows and an unusually wide mouth that bears the cruelest of expressions. These mouths also sport slightly protruding tusks. Its back is slightly hunched, and it runs in a rather clumsy manner.

Ogre hide has a light greenish tint, though this can be more or less prominent in certain individuals or families. Ogres are no more hairy than an average human and have heads topped with thick, black hair. They tend to wear furs or crudely sewn cloth (when they wear anything at all), and are known to decorate their lairs with the most grotesque of ornamentation – namely the rotting heads or skulls of their victims.

Their bodies are massive, with the typical adult ogre standing over 9 feet tall and weighing at least 550 pounds. When specifically referring to a female ogre, most scholars use the term ogress.

Combat/Tactics:

Ogres possess great brute strength and are formidable opponents. They live to kill and devour victims, being brutal in all aspects of life. Ogres attack with massive clubs or other large weapons. Their skin is thick and acts as a natural armor, so they often see no need of wearing armor or using shields. Some may learn the value of defensive armament though – particularily if exposed to more structured battle tactics.

SIGN/TRACKS

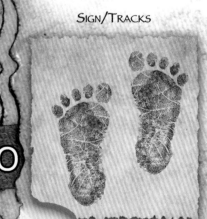

RANGE ON TELLENE

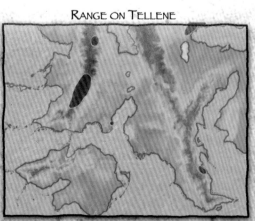

SIZE COMPARISON

12 ft

6 ft

Once an ogre has rendered a victim helpless, it proceeds to gobble the poor wretch up with great delight. There is a 10% chance that an ogre attempts to capture a victim alive for use as a slave that it can later devour at its leisure, should its voracious appetite drive it to do so.

Habitat/Society:

Ogre tribes live in places many other races consider inhospitable, particularly the rough, rocky lands where they (or more often, their slaves) mine for minerals. Contrary to popular belief, ogres can interact with members of other races for trade or other economic reasons and may even be open to diplomacy. However, popular belief is also correct when it states that ogres prefer to rape and pillage.

There is little hierarchy in ogre society between males and females, although they each have their roles. Male ogres tend to be the hunters while females manage slaves and household duties. The female ogress, however, is just as fierce as any male. The ability to fight and hunt seems to be inbred in them as naturally as breathing. They don't seem to undergo much formal training in fighting; they don't need to. It is inconceivable for an ogress to not know how to fight.

Ogres and ogresses mate at will, with pregnancies lasting for about 12 months before a baby ogre is born. Ogres reach maturity at the age of 10 and have a natural lifespan of around 95 years.

Ecology:

The ogre's diet includes many of the same foods as those of the human and demi-humans races, depending upon climate, terrain and whatever the ogre or his clan can forcibly take in a raid. Of course, the ogre also gladly consumes those same human and demi-humans (particularly dwarves). Ogres are carnivores that may or may not cook their food. As a general rule, the more rotten the meat is, the more likely an ogre is to roast it in order to remove the putrid taste.

Ogres are raised to believe that all members of 'lesser races' (i.e., anyone smaller and/or weaker than the ogre race) are enemies to be squashed and used at their will. However, they are also very lazy, and many ogres gladly serve any master who can provide a regular supply of meat, drink and slaves. They have some respect for their giant kin and often find themselves 'cooperating' with them (most likely as thralls).

On Tellene:

Many tribes and even greater numbers of ogres call the Jorakk and Elenon ranges home, but they can be found throughout the Neebau Cliffs and other temperate hills and mountains of Tellene.

For instance, the Duchy of Bandran claims all of the Sanakir Hills, but his protection is minimal and the hardy shepherds who live there often turn to P'Bapar for help fighting the wolves, wargs, werewolves, ogres and hill giants.

A handful of ogres have even settled into Shrogga-pravaaz, the desert 'City of Giants.'

OGRE

HIT POINTS:	34+4d8
SIZE/WEIGHT:	H/550+ lbs.
TENACITY:	Steady
INTELLIGENCE:	Obtuse
FATIGUE FACTOR:	-2/-1

SPEED	INIT
8	4

ATTACK: +5
DEFENSE: -1
DMG REDUCTION: 4
DAMAGE by weapon +6
long REACH
TOP SAVE: 9

MOVEMENT

CRAWL:	5
WALK:	10
JOG:	15
RUN:	20
SPRINT:	25

SAVES

PHYSICAL:	+8
MENTAL:	+2
DODGE:	+4

ATTACK:
Ogres attack with their large weapons (usually an oversized club with which they inflict 2d10p+6).

SPECIAL DEFENSES:
Shield use (e.g., medium shield increases Defense to +5); an Ogre's DR is 3 sans skins or furs

GENERAL INFO

ACTIVITY CYCLE:	Diurnal
NO. APPEARING:	1, 2-10 (band), 11-20 (war band)
% CHANCE IN LAIR:	25%
FREQUENCY:	Infrequent
ALIGNMENT:	Chaotic Evil
VISION TYPE:	Standard
AWARENESS/SENSES:	Standard
HABITAT:	Caves, and crude log or stone homes
DIET:	Carnivorous
ORGANIZATION:	Individuals or Band
CLIMATE/TERRAIN:	Any, save arctic

YIELD

MEDICINAL:	nil
SPELL COMPONENTS:	nil
HIDE/TROPHY:	nil
TREASURE:	much ogre treasure comes in the form of tribute from lesser races and is thus generally large quantities of low value coins
EDIBLE:	yes, but it tastes incredibly foul
OTHER:	nil
EXPERIENCE POINT VALUE:	242

O

Ooze, Corrosive

Also Known As: Peragic, Vorkkus

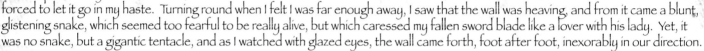

For several hours we followed the path easily, for the tunnel walls were still blazed with the marks I inscribed on our previous descent. We had been walking at a swift pace, despite the roughness of the stone floor, when I saw to my dismay that the tunnel ahead came to an abrupt end. My companions immediately set upon me with their complaints, saying that no doubt I had mis-marked one of the earlier turnings and thus put us upon this detour.

As I argued, I unwittingly tapped at the wall with the point of my short sword. Seeing our thief's eyes staring in surprise at that point directly behind me, I tried to scramble away, not knowing what lay behind me but still determined not to give Risk any aid that day. Yet, the point of my sword held fast, and I was forced to let it go in my haste. Turning round when I felt I was far enough away, I saw that the wall was heaving, and from it came a blunt, glistening snake, which seemed too fearful to be really alive, but which caressed my fallen sword blade like a lover with his lady. Yet, it was no snake, but a gigantic tentacle, and as I watched with glazed eyes, the wall came forth, foot after foot, inexorably in our direction.

As we quickly withdrew back the way we had come, the wall came with us, not as a rough boulder or square frame, but a gelatinous blob that slowly, blindly crept towards us with its ugly, fat body creasing and elongating. We picked up rocks and threw them, but it showed no interest in them, nor in the hurled magicks of our cleric or mage. At length, one of our casters produced a wand that arced lightning from its tip — the only thing so far that halted the creature — scorching the grayish mass and, only after repeated strikes, killing it. It was my first encounter with one of the gelatinous subterranean creatures, but woe betide that it was not my last… -

Slow moving ooze can detect sources of metal nearby and will seek it out.

Corrosive ooze varies in color from gray to black and may resemble any sediment from wet mortar to moistened basalt, due to alterations in diet and moisture levels. Because of the biogenic content of the creature, it is always glistening (which helps to distinguish it from any surrounding but inanimate sediment).

As befits its moniker, corrosive ooze is a slow moving blob that moves by slow rhythmic waves of contraction, simultaneously secreting a thin layer of mucus on which it travels; this mucus helps prevent unwanted foreign objects from sticking to its body as well as aiding it in retaining moisture. However, the fact that this mucus must be continually re-placed, limits the distance to which the ooze travels in search of food or a mate.

Most species of corrosive oozes grow to be roughly 10 feet in diameter and weigh about 600 pounds.

Combat/Tactics:

Corrosive ooze poses the greatest hazard when undetected, for it has little capability (or indeed interest) in pursing living prey. However, its senses are well attuned to the presence of metals and it will swat out with a pseudopod at any sizeable metallic object. A suit of armor certainly merits its attention.

Corrosive ooze is very dense, resulting in blows that pack a wallop. They are, obviously, highly corrosive. Metal armor

SIGN/TRACKS

Ooze leaves what looks to me like thousands of slimy snail trails.

Such sign can remain for days after its passing.

RANGE ON TELLENE

SIZE COMPARISON

12 ft

6 ft

struck by corrosive ooze is reduced by 1 DR per blow while any weapon hitting the ooze becomes pitted (assess a 1-point penalty to Attack and Damage thereafter). Stabbing the ooze multiple times compounds the penalty.

Corrosive ooze is immune to fire and cold attacks. Electricity is exceptionally effective and any such spells inflict an additional point of damage per die rolled.

Habitat/Society:

Corrosive ooze is most likely to be found in abandoned mines or other subterranean regions rich in ore. Its metabolism requires high concentrations of metal ions that must be constantly replenished. Its gelatinous nature is limited by certain abiotic factors such as the need for moisture and a cool, relatively constant, temperature.

The corrosive ooze is rarely encountered aboveground or in urban areas, but when it appears thereat it does so almost exclusively within a combined set of guidelines: at higher elevations, within foundries and other such metal workshops, where moisture is prevalent and in spaces filled with deposits and sludge piles. Their bodies are prone to desiccation and retreat to damp hiding places when the weather is dry. Such surface-dwelling corrosive oozes often migrate underground during the winter months.

Corrosive oozes are hermaphrodites, having both female and male reproductive organs. Once an ooze locates its mate, they encircle each other and exchange fluids through their protruded genitalia. A few days later, each ooze lays roughly a dozen small, gelatinous 'eggs' into a hole or crevice along a metal seam. These eggs are actually miniature oozes and, depending on the quantity and type of metal, grow to reach maturity within six to nine months.

A typical specimen has a lifespan of seven years, when it becomes unable to maintain its internal moisture levels and suffers a drying out period of eight to 10 weeks, followed by desiccation (to 60% of its former mass) and death.

Ecology:

Corrosive oozes play an important role in the natural ecosystem of Tellene, by not only eating useful metals such as iron, but also those that can cause toxic effects on man and most other living creatures (e.g., arsenic, antimony, mercury, nickel, chromium, etc.). The oozes have little to no natural competition for the consumption of these minerals, save for others of their species. However, they do sometimes come into conflict with miners and treasure hunters that arrive bearing tasty metal tools, weapons, and/or armor.

On Tellene:

Anarvis of Nenehi is a specialist in the field of slimes and oozes, and wears the stump of his right arm as a token of his studies. He claims to have encountered over two-dozen amorphous creatures, including several species of corrosive ooze. The dwarven miners of the Ka'Asa Mountains, he says, have given him a great deal of useful information. Anarvis even hints that he might pay well for a few specimens, despite the obvious illegality of storing them in town.

CORROSIVE OOZE

HIT POINTS:	30+4d8
SIZE/WEIGHT:	L/600 lbs.
TENACITY:	Brave
INTELLIGENCE:	Animal, Low
FATIGUE FACTOR:	n/a

SPEED		INIT
10	+8	-2
	0	see below
short REACH	4d6p	n/a TOP SAVE

ATTACK:
Strikes reduce armor DR by 1 per blow, while weapons become pitted (-1 to Atk and Damage thereafter).

DEFENSES/WEAKNESSES:
DR varies (12 vs. crushing, 8 vs. piercing & 2 vs. hacking weapons); Immune to fire and cold; Electricity inflicts +1 point of damage per die rolled.

MOVEMENT

CRAWL:	¼
WALK:	½
JOG:	1
RUN:	2¼
SPRINT:	3½

SAVES

PHYSICAL:	+10
MENTAL:	immune
DODGE:	+2

GENERAL INFO

ACTIVITY CYCLE:	Any
NO. APPEARING:	1-3
% CHANCE IN LAIR:	n/a
FREQUENCY:	Infrequent
ALIGNMENT:	Non
VISION TYPE:	n/a
AWARENESS/SENSES:	Can detect vibrations/metal within 30 ft
HABITAT:	Caves, dungeons, and similar locations
DIET:	Metallivorous
ORGANIZATION:	Individuals
CLIMATE/TERRAIN:	Subterranean

YIELD

MEDICINAL:	slime can treat warts and other skin conditions
SPELL COMPONENTS:	nil
HIDE/TROPHY:	nil
TREASURE:	incidental
EDIBLE:	no
OTHER:	nil
EXPERIENCE POINT VALUE:	325

ORC

Also Known As: Ork, Ukak

The beginning of the orc race is shrouded in times so distant that even the most long-lived elf has no true memory of their creation. The orcs themselves care nothing for their past and do not dwell on the matter, for too much evil dwells in their hearts and their strongest desire is only to rule the future. Yet, there are some scholars such as myself who actively debate their history and the reasoning behind their creation.

I believe the oldest records regarding orcs to be in the hands of the elves of Lendelwood, which date back over ten millennia and tell of how their ancient forest was attacked and burned. It is written — or so I am told, for I am not allowed access to those musty tomes — that the assailants were a previously unknown race that crawled from the earth like maggots or beetles and showed no thought of peaceful contact. Few orcs survived the elf counter-attacks, the text mentioning that they were low in numbers at that early stage, but those that did spoke only an unknown guttural tongue to their captors. All the elves could make any sense of was the word "uk", or "uc" in their own tongue, which to their ears sounded like "orc", a suitable term given that in Low Elven it means "fell being."

Whatever their method of creation, the orcs are now as much a part of the world as any of the other races, and over the millennia have spread to threaten us all. Fortunately, my scrolls also tell me that orcs fear sunlight and are weakened by it, for as a subterranean race they are unused to its glare. So long as the sun is shining, you are safe from orcs. Trust me. - ᚠ

The pig-faced orc is a stranger to peace and determined to subjugate anything in its path.

The most numerous and prolific of the evil humanoid races, orcs are also the most violent and savage. Aggressive, sadistic, strong and stupid, orcs are born for the fight. They vary dramatically in size from about 5 feet to over 6 feet, but most specimens exhibit a stooped posture that masks their true height. They have lanky builds and many drag their knuckles when walking.

Because orc blood has mixed with almost every conceivable combination of human, demi-human and humanoid race, orcish facial features run the gamut of possibilities, but the pure orc shows signs of a porcine quality, a trait that runs common among the vast majority of offspring, even those of mixed breed. The pure orc is hairless, but those with mixed parentage possess greasy black or dark brown tangled locks, typically in patches, but sometimes a full head. They have pointy, animalistic ears.

Orcs weigh between 120 and 250 pounds, depending on their height and build. Generally, only the subchiefs or chiefs show any signs of obesity, although as orcs age they can gain a round belly, despite spindly appendages.

Although low on the evolutionary chain, orcs have senses that easily outstrip those of humans and even some demi-humans. Blessed with superior audition, olfaction and gustation, and vision in the near-dark, orcs can generally sense opponents before they themselves are spotted (20% bonus to Listening and Observation checks). Because they are lazy, dumb and cowardly, orcs suffer with their slow reaction times.

From the perspective of civilized races, they have no other redeeming qualities, although their better-than-average strength can make them fearsome opponents. They are a fairly stout and

SIGN/TRACKS	RANGE ON TELLENE	SIZE COMPARISON

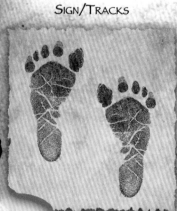

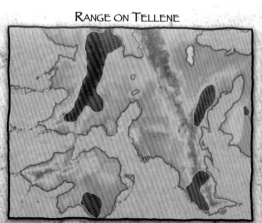

hearty race, with plenty of Hit Points to withstand damaging blows, and a fairly solid threshold of pain and resulting save, should an adversary manage to land a powerful hit.

Clerics and shamans are fairly rare, at least on a per-capita basis, but since orcs are so numerous each tribe of any significant size (100 or more members) has at least one. These spellcasters generally only serve in a cloistered capacity, never leaving the lair on raids. They are valuable because only they can perform the necessary rituals to create Black Orcs. They also provide knowledge and advice to leaders as well as brew potions and salves. Finally, they provide spiritual (and superstitious) direction to the tribe, this function varying dramatically from tribe to tribe.

Each tribe has at least one shaman with clerical capacity, with mage ability found in only 25% of the shamans (both abilities are required for creating Black Orcs, but only clerical ability is required to create the spawning pool). Their levels of spellcasting ability are not substantial, only d10p-4 for clerical and d10p-6 in mage (negative and zero rounding to 1st). Roll the clerical capability for the first shaman, for every 2 full levels, the tribe will have another shaman (rolled independently). Perform this check only once.

Orcs are thoroughly wicked and malicious, deriving joy from violent acts. They take no pleasure even in plunder, which they gather at the behest of their leaders and because monetary gains can further personal (and tribal) power. They do love acquiring prisoners and enslaving others. They always capture enemies when able; even a stupid orc recognizes the value of forcing another to do the menial work so that it does not have to. Orcs hate all forms of art and beautiful things and go out of their way to crush and destroy any living thing they encounter. Orcs eat any type of meat, but vastly prefer to eat sentient races over other varieties such as cattle.

Orcs place no value on beauty or personal hygiene, actually despising both. They dress in parasite-infested rags or furs as long as such clothing has some form of utility (such as offering protection from the elements or weaponry). Orcs never willingly bathe.

While orcs are not industrious, they are fair miners and sometimes delve their own complexes. They vastly prefer, however, to capture another lair by force and live off the fruits of another group's labors. Thus, orcs can be found above or below ground including in caves, cave complexes, deep in the Netherdeep or in abandoned areas, crude villages and ruins left (or surrendered) by other races. If a tribe manages to create a birthing pool for black orcs, it tries to retain that lair permanently, protecting the source of great orcs at all costs.

Combat/Tactics:

Being classic bullies, orcs intimidate and subjugate all those weaker than themselves, but are easily cowed by more powerful creatures. Orc war bands flee from enemies that seem more powerful or more numerous than they, but attack wildly and ferociously when they feel they have an advantage in numbers, strength, equipment, or all of the above. They use any conceivable weapon available to them (even makeshift), but the following are most common: scimitar, javelin, short bow, great axe, spear, pole arm, crossbow, dagger, flail.

Orcs employ shields of all shapes, varieties, and makes. Each

ORC

HIT POINTS:	23+1d8
SIZE/WEIGHT:	M/175 lbs.
TENACITY:	Steady
INTELLIGENCE:	Slow
FATIGUE FACTOR:	-1/0

SPEED 9 · INIT 5 · ATTACK +3 · DMG REDUCTION · -4 · 3 · DEFENSE · by weapon +2 · DAMAGE · medium REACH · TOP SAVE 6

MOVEMENT

CRAWL:	2½
WALK:	5
JOG:	10
RUN:	15
SPRINT:	20

SAVES

PHYSICAL:	+4
MENTAL:	+1
DODGE:	+3

ATTACK: Ranged weapons followed by melee weapons (usually scimitars that in orc hands deal 2d8p+2).

SPECIAL: Shield use (e.g., medium shields provide a +6 bonus, increasing Defense to +2); Orcs get 20% bonuses to Listening and Observation skill checks; -2 Attack/Defense in sunlight and -1 Attack/Defense in dimmer natural light; unarmored DR is 0

GENERAL INFO

ACTIVITY CYCLE:	Nocturnal
NO. APPEARING:	d8p (gang); 3d4p+8 (war band), 30d12p (clan)
% CHANCE IN LAIR:	25%
FREQUENCY:	Frequent
ALIGNMENT:	Neutral Evil
VISION TYPE:	Extreme Low Light Vision
AWARENESS/SENSES:	Good vision (in dim light), smell, taste, and hearing
HABITAT:	Dismal, dark locations and underground
DIET:	Carnivorous
ORGANIZATION:	Tribal; ruled by the strongest
CLIMATE/TERRAIN:	Any

YIELD

MEDICINAL:	nil
SPELL COMPONENTS:	digits, for replacement Stinking spell components
HIDE/TROPHY:	ears make nice trophies and fun playthings
TREASURE:	2d4p sp each; lairs can contain vast amounts[1]
EDIBLE:	yes, but so foul that that elves and fey spit it out
OTHER:	nil
EXPERIENCE POINT VALUE:	34

has one, even if using a two-handed weapon (in this case, strapped to their back and ready for use if it switches to a smaller weapon). Orcish-manufactured weapons and shields are serviceable only for a few battles and must then be discarded, but anywhere from 10% to 60% of a band's weapons were taken from fallen foes, so these may exhibit human or better manufacture 20% of the time.

Despite their indolence, orcs have some smithing ability (although they are far inferior to goblins in skill) and can churn out massive quantities of arms, armors and gear. This equipment is good enough to hold an edge or protect the wearer, but not for long. After every d4 battles, orcish-made gear degrades to such an extent that it imposes a 1-point penalty to DR (for armor) or Attack and Damage (for weapons), eventually becoming so damaged or dull that the orc simply discards the ruined gear and grabs new equipment from the smithies.

Orcs have hides similar to humans and demi-humans, and thus derive any Damage Reduction solely from their armor (typically studded leather, although leather, padded and ringmail can be found amongst the rank-and-file as well). Leaders are better equipped as described below.

Every group of 10 orcs encountered has a leader clad in ringmail, with maximum Hit Points. For every 30, the war band has a leader with a 1-point bonus to Attack, Damage, Defense and Initiative *as equipped* in addition to maximum HP plus an extra d8 HP. Such a leader wears chainmail.

For every 90 orcs, the tribe has a sub-chief wearing banded splint and with a 2-point bonus to Attack, Damage, Defense and a 1-point bonus to Speed and Initiative *as equipped* in addition to maximum HP plus two extra d8 rolls for HP. This is in addition to the nine basic leaders and three stronger leaders.

If the tribe contains 150 or more orcs, it has a powerful chieftain. This leader has a 3-point bonus to Attack, Damage, Defense and a 2-point bonus to Speed and Initiative *as equipped*. He wears platemail and has maximum HP plus three extra d8 rolls for HP. This is in addition to the other leaders and an extra 4d6p sub-chiefs that function as a personal retinue of bodyguards for the chieftain.

There is a 10% chance that any leader of a war band is a black orc. The odds increase to 30% for any subchief (or bodyguard) and 75% for a chief, respectively. Black orcs have an extra 2-point bonus to Attack, Damage, Defense and a 1-point bonus to Speed and Initiative beyond any other bonuses already mentioned.

Orcs war with all races, even their own. Unless a leader whom they fear is within sight or has taskmasters within reach, whenever orcs meet another group, the orcs fight 90% of the time (70% if the other group is another orc tribe and 50% if from their own orc tribe). On rare occasions, orcs cooperate with other humanoid races such as grel, goblins and especially ogres. In these cases, there must be a viable clear and present goal – generally a community or other tribe to plunder.

Orcs hate elves and always attack them on sight (unless outnumbered). Defeated foes are taken as slaves 75% of the time, but only 25% for elves (the other 75% are slain immediately). Determine this chance on a per-captive basis, rather than on an aggregate/group basis (*i.e.*, for large conquered groups, some slaves will always be taken).

Orcs like to hurt others and do not really care much how. They generally fire ranged weapons first as the fastest, most efficient way to inflict casualties. They genuinely enjoy the adrenalin-charged thrill of hand-to-hand combat and never hesitate to engage an inferior foe or group of victims. They attack seemingly weaker or known enemies remorselessly with little regard to self-preservation, but change their tune as soon as they suffer from a lack of success, if the odds change meaningfully in the enemy's favor, or if an individual receives a serious wound.

Orcs engage with little regard to tactics, but attempt to flank enemy fighters and love to attack unarmed foes above all. Many orcs hang back on the first attack, in order to get an idea of who the weaker opponents are before attacking, or to wait for the more powerful adversaries to become engaged so they can move in and attack from behind. If not urged on by a superior, orcs are quick to flee if a combat turns against them, routing in a disorderly every-orc-for-itself manner.

Orcs fight well in the darkness, having twice the range of low light vision than other races, but have great difficulty fighting in very bright light. Sunlight causes them to suffer a -2 to Attack and Defense rolls, while dark, cloudy conditions or twilight forces a -1 penalty on Attack rolls (but no penalty for Defense). Orcs suffer no penalties under storm clouds and see perfectly well in starlight, even if all moons are new and the sky is overcast.

Habitat/Society:

Orcs can be found in any climate and are equally at home above or below ground, but when above-ground will only be active at night due to their intense dislike of the sun. Their lairs will generally have some underground component, even if just a series of basements, but this is not a requirement unless the tribe plans to have or has a spawning pool. Orcs will always live in close proximity to other races, as they cannot survive without targets for their raids.

Orcs live in a largely disorganized society where the strongest rule the weak. The chieftain is always the strongest, wiliest and most underhanded. The chieftain's position is under constant threat from rivals seeking to murder him and seize control for themselves. These rivals may be sub-chiefs or younger, foolish orcs. As chief, his challenge is to supplicate his sub-chiefs and make life easy enough for them to enjoy the status quo, but not so easy as to appear weak. Because of their larger size, greater strength and superior intellect, black orcs tend to populate the sub-chief and chieftain ranks within society.

Females comprise a solid 50% of the population of the tribe, but few of these are actually orcish females; the vast majority are slaves taken in raids. Unless the tribe suffers from recent heavy losses or a shortage of females, male orcs dash she-orc runts on the ground shortly after birth and devour them. The females (orc or other race), called 'breeders' by the orcs, are held captive in an unlit cavern. Cold, naked and half-starved, when a male orc enters the breedery, whether to feed them or otherwise, all females must prostate themselves, facing away from the male. The only attention shown them is an occasional sack of half-rotten food or violent rape by males, both happenings occur at random and unpredictable times. Clearly, females are non-combatants and can seldom be saved, even if rescued. Their life expectancy ranges from weeks to years once imprisoned.

Orcs have an average lifespan of only about 30 to 40 years, but could live to almost 60 if with proper diet and cowardly neighbors. Most die when young and many more die as young adults in battle. Gestation period varies by the parent, but generally occurs from four to six months. Orc young are born in litters of three to five, but as stated previously, only the males are generally saved. Many of those are murdered by their mothers and only a few survive to wean (around 6 months). Once weaned, they are moved from the breedery and begin survival and combat training by fighting with one another for scraps of food. Only the strongest survive. The youngest comprise only 20% or a tribe's numbers, half fighting as kobolds (and only if cornered) and the other half fighting as goblins.

Orcs speak their own language, thought to be a perversion of Dwarven. Thirty percent of them can speak a goblin or kobold tongue, and 10% might speak some other language of a nearby tribe, be it human, humanoid or demi-human.

An orc lair typically has slaves equal to 50% of the adult orc population. Aside from breeders, these slaves provide a source of labor as well as fresh food. Ogres may serve orcs as guards in return for food (50% chance of d4p ogres per lair).

Most orc lairs employ trained (or partially trained) animals as guard and watch beasts. There is a 50% chance that an orc warren contains 2d12p wild boars, a 40% chance of 2d12p lesser orkin wardawgs, and a 20% chance of greater orkin wardawgs (roll for each independently).

Ecology:

Orcs are not the most physically powerful humanoids, nor do they have the organizational skills of hobgoblins or even goblins. Nevertheless, orcs are often the most dangerous threat to civilized races and the local ecology. This is due to their vast numbers and ability to replenish those numbers far faster than the other races. An orc tribe may disappear after suffering complete annihilation in battle, only to return a decade or two later with a new host of equal numbers. An orc tribe considers every living thing to be a possible food source.

Subraces:

Having originated from the same racial stock, all orcs belong to the same species. They can create fertile offspring with one another, except black orcs and simian orcs, who seem to have diverged enough to be their own species. Orcs can breed with any race, including elves, although the results of an elf-orc union inevitably results in a stillborn runt. Due to the many disparate orc tribes, and how quickly they can produce new generations within a tribe, several orc subraces with distinct features exist.

Half-orcs

While not technically a sub-species, their prevalence among orc society necessitates some discussion. Since male orcs regularly mate with every conceivable race (kept as breeders), their offspring are overwhelmingly a mix. For reasons not fully understood, the offspring tend to take after the orcish parents, with only a 10-20% chance that the runt has any resemblance to the mother. Those few that retain some features of their maternal side are considered half-orcs. They are generally born into slavery in orc-society and despised if born into a non-orc community.

Black (Great) Orcs

Black orcs are the dominant strain in orc society and brook no rivals. Artificially bred from magical slime-filled pools (in combination with the sacrifice of a sentient being), and unable to reproduce, black orcs are technically not even an orc species or sub-species. Immortal, black orcs never age, succumbing only to wounds and similar downfalls. Possessing enhanced stamina, strength and intelligence, they can survive in harsh and adverse condition and have no physical aversion to sunlight (though they dislike it). Generally found as leaders of a tribe, black orcs hate being subservient to any being. Black orcs have little tolerance for failure from their minions.

Gray (Deep) Orcs

Living deep within the earth, gray orcs possess keener low light vision than even standard orcs, but suffer stronger adverse effects in sunlight because of this (double range low light vision, completely blind in sunlight with other penalties reflective of dimmer light – treat overcast as direct sunlight, etc.). They lack some of the orcish strength commonly found in other breeds, but are more nimble. However, they are slow of thought and are extremely crude, even by orc standards. Such orcs are generally found serving more powerful subterranean creatures, (dark elves and such) and their weak willpower makes them ideal servants.

White (Highland) Orcs

White orcs spend their time living high on snow-capped mountains and because of the constant glare of the sun off the snow and ice they have adapted well to direct sunlight. However, they lack the extreme low light vision common to other types of orcs. While not as strong as common orcs, they possess remarkable stamina. They lack advanced cognitive abilities, have low willpower and are unsociable creatures.

Brown (Desert) Orcs

Brown orcs spend much of their lives in the open desert. While they have not yet developed a full resistance to the adverse effects of sunlight that affects many of their orcish kin, they suffer only half the penalty for full-sunlight and no penalties for lesser lighting conditions. They are not as strong as common orcs, they have no advanced cognitive abilities, suffer from poor willpower and are unsavory creatures.

Simian Orcs

Simian orcs are the result of a bizarre mix of ape and orc. No one cares to consider how the initial breeding took place, but the fact that they persist in large numbers, especially in jungle terrain, leads scholars to conclude that they thrive as a viable new race and possibly a new species. They are strong, but very dumb.

Religion:

While orcs fear magic (both divine or arcane) and are quite superstitious, the religious nature of any particular orc group varies dramatically from tribe to tribe. The existence and power of a shaman, relative to the orc chieftain's power, determines how much sway the clergy has over the day-to-day tribal lives and activities. Orc shamans tend to follow the Seller of Souls or the Emperor of Scorn. That said, the Harvester of Souls, the Overlord and the Creator of Strife have significant followings. In fact, any evil deity can have a following.

On Tellene:

Orcs can be found all across Tellene but they are most numerous in less civilized areas where they face no organized resistance. Major tribes occupy the Krond Heights, Elenon Mountains, Counai Heights, P'Roral Peaks, Northwestern Brindonwood, Jorakk Mountains, Vrykarr Mountains, Neebau Cliffs, and both the Vohven and Obakasek jungles.

[1]Orcs carry 2d4p sp each; lairs can contain vast amounts of copper, silver and trade coins as well as gems and potions (typically Orcish Steadfastness, but others are possible depending on the tribal shaman's powers).

ORKIN WARDAWG

GREATER ORKIN WARDAWG
LESSER ORKIN WARDAWG

Also Known As: Goraz, Pig-Dog, Shronhund

It was some time ago that I was on the east side of the Byth mountains, in company with four men who had hunted over the country. We came down the Deshada river in two canoes, and shantied on the Upper Byth, just below the site where the Deshada empties itself into it. We hid our canoes and struck into the Rytarr Woods, traveling about for three weeks, so we were ready for a rest when we got back to our shantying ground.

Few survive the death-pounce of the shronhund.

It was early on one of these morns, when my companions were asleep, that I got up and paddled across the river after a deer, for we wanted venison for breakfast. I slew a buck, and was returning, when what should I see but an orkin wardawg watching me from the bank.

Well, I couldn't very well use my crossbow and paddle at the same time, and my longsword was useless at that distance, so I thought I'd just continue on downstream for a bit and avoid it. Darned if it didn't follow my canoe along the bank, lookin' at me and slavering like it was imagining what I was gonna taste like. I didn't offer any opinion on the subject, but just continued to paddle, pondering what I should do.

I suppose I might be there paddling still, had I not spotted our thief gesturing silently to me from the shadows on that very bank. He seemed to be indicating that he would slip up behind that creature and slit its throat. Quick as a flash, he rushed at it, and threw himself into the very face of the desperate brute as it turned to meet him. Unfortunately, he made a great mistake when he calculated he was a match for that beast, for, with one quick counter-attack the wardawg sent him end over end down the bank, nearly into the water. Well, the little time that was so occupied saved me a deal of trouble and danger, for it lasted just long enough for me to bring my canoe ashore and draw my crossbow, which I did about the quickest, you may bet your life on that.

I ran my eye along the bolt, sighted the wardawg between the eyes, and loosed it. The bolt flew into its side, a bit wide, and it turned to look at me with a face that said I was sure to be next. Somehow, I managed to put another bolt into it before it reached me, with a perfect shot into its head that caused the beast to tumble to its feet. It gave a spiteful bite at my ankles as it did so, before I could give it a fine kick and sent it too rolling down the bank and into the water's edge.

I looked over, and saw the thief staggering to his feet, looking about at the wardawg's still body in a bewildered way, as if not quite understanding how he came there. I went round a little way, and got down into the water where I found the wardawg only knocked senseless, not quite dead, and our thief with two ribs broken, a broken leg and his shoulder out of joint. I quickly took my blade to the wardawg and put it down for good, then set the thief's shoulder as well as I could. I hustled back to the shanty and left the thief there in the canoe with the buck and the wardawg, so he could push off if something came to assault him before I returned with aid.

It was near on a fortnight before we left the area, but our thief learned a little piece of wisdom by that cuff that sent him down the bank, and got more than a little insight into the nature of an angry orkin wardawg. ~ Š

SIGN/TRACKS	RANGE ON TELLENE	SIZE COMPARISON

Fore
Hind

6 ft
3 ft

LESSER ORKIN WARDAWG

HIT POINTS: 30+3d8

SIZE/WEIGHT: M/250 lbs.

TENACITY: Steady

INTELLIGENCE: Animal, High

FATIGUE FACTOR: 2

SPEED **9**	ATTACK	INIT **0**
	+7	DMG REDUCTION
DEFENSE **+3**		**4**
short REACH	DAMAGE **4d4p+1**	TOP SAVE ▼ **8**

MOVEMENT

CRAWL: 10

WALK: 15

JOG: 20

RUN: 25

SPRINT: 30

SAVES

PHYSICAL: +7

MENTAL: +5

DODGE: +7

ATTACK:
Bites for 4d4p+1 points of damage.

SPECIAL ABILITIES:
Listening 70%, Tracking 70%

GENERAL INFO

ACTIVITY CYCLE:	Crepuscular, or as dictated by owner
NO. APPEARING:	1-12 (wild), or dictated by owner
% CHANCE IN LAIR:	20% (wild), or 100% dictated by owner
FREQUENCY:	Frequent
ALIGNMENT:	Non
VISION TYPE:	Extreme Low Light Vision
AWARENESS/SENSES:	Listening 70%, Tracking 70%
HABITAT:	Woodlands, or as dictated by owner
DIET:	Omnivorous
ORGANIZATION:	Solitary, Pack, or dictated by owner
CLIMATE/TERRAIN:	Any, save arctic

YIELD

MEDICINAL:	nil
SPELL COMPONENTS:	nil
HIDE/TROPHY:	heads make trophies, while pelts make clothing
TREASURE:	incidental
EDIBLE:	yes
OTHER:	pups may sell to animal trainers or arenas

EXPERIENCE POINT VALUE: 122

GREATER ORKIN WARDAWG

HIT POINTS: 38+4d8

SIZE/WEIGHT: L/450 lbs.

TENACITY: Steady

INTELLIGENCE: Animal, High

FATIGUE FACTOR: 2

SPEED **7**	ATTACK	INIT **1**
	+9	DMG REDUCTION
DEFENSE **+5**		**5**
short REACH	DAMAGE **4d4p+5**	TOP SAVE ▼ **9**

MOVEMENT

CRAWL: 10

WALK: 15

JOG: 20

RUN: 25

SPRINT: 30

SAVES

PHYSICAL: +9

MENTAL: +7

DODGE: +9

ATTACK:
Bites deal 4d4p+5 points of damage.

SPECIAL ABILITIES:
Listening 80%, Tracking 60%

GENERAL INFO

ACTIVITY CYCLE:	Crepuscular, or as dictated by owner
NO. APPEARING:	1-12 (wild), or dictated by owner
% CHANCE IN LAIR:	20% (wild), or 100% dictated by owner
FREQUENCY:	Infrequent
ALIGNMENT:	Non
VISION TYPE:	Extreme Low Light Vision
AWARENESS/SENSES:	Listening 80%, Tracking 60%
HABITAT:	Woodlands, or as dictated by owner
DIET:	Omnivorous
ORGANIZATION:	Solitary, Pack, or dictated by owner
CLIMATE/TERRAIN:	Any, save arctic

YIELD

MEDICINAL:	nil
SPELL COMPONENTS:	nil
HIDE/TROPHY:	as lesser orkin wardawgs, but more prized
TREASURE:	incidental
EDIBLE:	yes
OTHER:	pups may sell to animal trainers or arenas

EXPERIENCE POINT VALUE: 350

These merciless beasts resemble a bizarre combination of a large canine body with the front claws of a cat and a tough snout like a pig. Their teeth are similar to those of any other large meat-eaters. Fur color is usually a grizzled brown, with a noticeable red tint in the females (sow bitches), but may vary from dark gray to black. Mature males have a slight ridge of hair along the spine, though this ridge is barely noticeable in orkin wardawgs of domesticated stock.

There are two subspecies, known simply as greater and lesser variations. Most greater orkin wardawg adults stand roughly 4 feet tall at the shoulder, with a body length of about 7 feet and weight of around 450 pounds. When born, they have light brown hair with longitudinal darker stripes. These stripes fade when the creature is half-grown, at which point the coat takes on an adult's solid color.

Lesser orkin wardawg adults usually stand about 3 feet tall at the shoulder, with a body length averaging between 4 to 5 feet and weigh around 250 pounds. Unlike their greater kin, they retain their youthful stripes through adulthood, causing outsiders to sometimes mistake them for greater orkin wardawg puplets.

Orkin wardawgs are prized heavily by orcs who employ them to hunt game and other sapient creatures. Although an orkin wardawg's olfactory sense is relatively weak when compared to a hunting dog, it can still follow fresh tracks. As an independent hunter, the orkin wardawg sights its prey from a distance, quietly stalking it until a final, quick pursuit brings it down. When domesticated, orkin wardawgs hunt alongside orcs, though their primary function is to flush prey on command. When the victim flees, the orc orders his wardawg to either to chase it down and kill it, or wait until the orc has his fun with the prey – and then chase it down and kill it.

Domesticated wardawgs can spend hours waiting in ambush and can spot and remember the locations of downed prey. A trained orkin wardawg understands the hand, verbal and/or whistled commands of the orc. These domesticated wardawgs may hunt in packs and even squeal to alert that creatures are nearby.

Combat/Tactics:

If surprised or cornered, an orkin wardawg (and particularly a sow bitch with her puplets) defends itself by lowering its head, charging and then slashing with its claws. One can spot an aggressive or self-assertive wardawg by its slow and deliberate movements, high body posture and raised hackles.

In packs, orkin wardawgs stalk their prey, and then strike when the target is distracted. Their sharp teeth target the hips and legs primarily, to bring the prey down to the ground. At that point, the wardawgs rip open the prey's throat and belly, feeding on the internal organs first.

Habitat/Society:

Domesticated orkin wardawgs live wherever orcs can be found. Wild orkin wardawgs dwell in plains and broadleaved woodlands, often near farms, monasteries and other relatively isolated locations where crops and livestock can be found. They are easily adaptable to other climates, and encroachments on new territories or unexpected population increases are routine. Local governments are usually quick to offer bounties on a pair of orkin wardawg ears.

In the wild, orkin wardawgs usually live and hunt in packs of 2d4 individuals, with the strongest or most aggressive male (generally a greater orkin wardawg) serving as leader. This group structure changes routinely due to the coming and going of pregnant sow bitches, and the departure of maturing males hoping to form their own packs.

In regions where wild wardawg density is low, the beasts tend toward monogamy, with mated pairs remaining together for life. Sow bitches are capable of breeding every spring. Pregnancy lasts approximately 80 days, with a typical litter size ranging from four to six puplets. These puplets can eat solid food after only 2 weeks, can flee from danger after a month, are fully weaned after 3 to 4 months and reach puberty at two years of age. Wild orkin wardawgs have a typical lifespan of 8 years, though domesticated ones can live for up to 15 years.

Ecology:

Orkin wardawgs are omnivores, feeding on a variety of plants, animals and sapient creatures. Solitary wardawgs use their snouts to root up their primary diet of fungus, mushrooms and earthworms, while foraging amongst the foliage for grasshoppers, berries, fallen fruits and nuts. In packs, orkin wardawgs prey mostly on deer, elk, moose and the other hoofed herbivores of the forests and plains. All wardawgs are opportunistic feeders and if given a chance eat any carrion or living prey that crosses their path. Wild wardawgs feel no natural kinship with orcs and attack them without even a hint of bestial remorse.

Orkin wardawgs often trouble farmers foolish enough to build within the creature's territory. Besides digging up crops searching for roots, the orkin wardawg may slaughter sheep, pigs, chickens and even the farmer's children.

The natural predators of an orkin wardawg include big hunting cats (e.g., mountain lions, tigers), wolves, bears, crocodiles and large snakes, though the latter favor puplets over adults. Although orkin wardawgs, dogs and boars may seem genetically close and often share vast portions of their ranges, they do not voluntarily interbreed in the wild.

On Tellene:

Orkin wardawgs are most common in Cosdol, the northern Young Kingdoms and the Wild Lands, though they can be found wherever orcs have gathered in number. Domesticated wardawgs are loyal only to their masters.

Their masters rarely mistreat orkin wardawgs, although what an orc considers mistreatment is different from most humans' idea of the same. Few orcs have affection for their wardawgs, but they do respect their ferocity. The adjective 'goraz' (meaning 'wardawg' in Orcish) is sometimes added to an orc's name to show his bravery and courage.

The horns of a great horned owlbeast are highly prized as trophies.

A mature owlbeast sow in an attack stance.

Also Known As: Alucrel, Feranoc, Strovia, Thelkk

Bound as I was with no hope of release, I could only watch in horror. Yet, I saw that hope remained; if the brigand could but reach his dagger, even with his arms pinioned to his sides, he might still be able to plunge it into the creature's side. Even so slight a wound could force the great bird-thing to loosen its hold. If it did not drop the man to the ground, it might at least give an opportunity for him to wrench himself away and strike a second time.

The man wriggled in the creature's grip, his fingers finally grasping the dagger hilt, but each movement brought blood-curdling shrieks from the glistening beak and an obvious tightening of its powerful arms. Amidst the sounds of cracking ribs and screams, the dagger fell to earth, but bounced lightly off a tree root to land within my grasp.

It was yet another of those strange happenings that further emphasized the absurdity of the situation, and I silently cursed the whims of Queen Destiny that led this cursed highwayman to my person and, mere minutes later, the owlbeast to us both.

Although I tried to focus on maneuvering the blade to cut my hands free, I could not help but hear the pitiful gasps and sobs as the crushing arms tightened. A quick glance upwards showed me the protruding tongue, bulging eyes and the drops of blood that trickled from the brigand's nostrils.

He seemed to be working up to his final spasm, but he never finished it, as the creature opened its pointy beak and with a single bite severed the limp neck.

The blood poured out in streams, splashing onto the ground and spattering my feet even as I cut the last strand of rope that bound me. Dropping on all fours, I scuttled backwards behind the nearest tree before standing and fleeing into the gloom, leaving the horrific sounds of savage dining to fade behind me. - ⨍

This frightening quadruped has a strigiform head with a hawk's sharp, pointed beak. Its ursine body is covered with downy plumage that closely resembles fur and is well adapted for cold climates. Owlbeasts also have a hump of muscle on the upper back; this gives their forelegs incredible clawing and digging power. It also has vestigial wing flaps under the armpits, though these down-covered leathery membranes are noticeable only when the owlbeast stretches out a foreleg at a certain angle. These membranes are perhaps the most delicate part of an owlbeast's anatomy, but the tissue is able to regrow and tears in them heal quickly.

They have exceptional eyesight, particularly in low light and darkness. With one exception, owlbeasts have a poor sense of smell; a female owlbeast can easily follow the pheromones given off by her eggs. In fact, so potent is the drive to track that she can follow an egg's trail for over 130 miles.

Most owlbeasts have predominantly drab brown plumage that aids them in camouflaging their massive bodies against the earth, though certain individuals or subspecies may range from white to black and all shades in between; reddish-brown, sandy or gray are most common. Some also have stiff-feathered manes, tufts and crests.

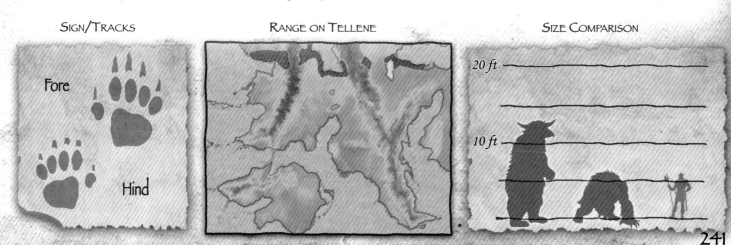

SIGN/TRACKS	RANGE ON TELLENE	SIZE COMPARISON
Fore / Hind		20 ft / 10 ft

OWLBEAST

HIT POINTS:	34+6d8
SIZE/WEIGHT:	H/1,500 lbs.
TENACITY:	Brave
INTELLIGENCE:	Animal, Low
FATIGUE FACTOR:	-5

SPEED 3 | **INIT** 0
ATTACK +12 | **DMG REDUCTION**
DEFENSE +2 | 11
short REACH | see below | **DAMAGE** 13 | **TOP SAVE** ▼

MOVEMENT

CRAWL:	5
WALK:	10
JOG:	15
RUN:	20
SPRINT:	25

SAVES

PHYSICAL:	+14
MENTAL:	+8
DODGE:	+11

ATTACK: Owlbeasts initially attack with their claws attempting to grab prey. Two consecutive claw hits (2d8p+7 each) indicates it has grabbed a foe and will attempt to crush it to death in its embrace. This hug automatically deals 2d8p+7 points of damage every 5 seconds thereafter. Escape is possible via a knockback of the Owlbeast or a Feat of Strength (vs d20p+16). The squeeze of death supercedes all other attacks.
If it fails to grab an opponent, it will peck at it (inflicting 2d4p+7 points) before attempting another round of grabbing.

GENERAL INFO

ACTIVITY CYCLE:	Nocturnal
NO. APPEARING:	1-2
% CHANCE IN LAIR:	35%
FREQUENCY:	Infrequent
ALIGNMENT:	Non
VISION TYPE:	Extreme low light vision
AWARENESS/SENSES:	Listening 60%
HABITAT:	Forest caves
DIET:	Carnivorous
ORGANIZATION:	Individuals or small groups
CLIMATE/TERRAIN:	Sub-arctic to Temperate woodlands

YIELD

MEDICINAL:	boiled eyes are said to cure cataracts
SPELL COMPONENTS:	unknown[1]
HIDE/TROPHY:	a stuffed owlbear is an impressive prize; claws may be worth 10 silver or more to interested parties
TREASURE:	incidental
EDIBLE:	yes
OTHER:	eggs or young[2]

EXPERIENCE POINT VALUE: 810

GREAT HORNED OWLBEAST

HIT POINTS:	39+8d8
SIZE/WEIGHT:	G/2,000 lbs.
TENACITY:	Fearless
INTELLIGENCE:	Animal, High
FATIGUE FACTOR:	-5

SPEED 3 | **INIT** 1
ATTACK +14 | **DMG REDUCTION**
DEFENSE +3 | 12
medium REACH | see below | **DAMAGE** 14 | **TOP SAVE** ▼

MOVEMENT

CRAWL:	5
WALK:	10
JOG:	15
RUN:	20
SPRINT:	25

SAVES

PHYSICAL:	+16
MENTAL:	+8
DODGE:	+11

ATTACK:
It initially charges a foe if space permits. Horns deal 2d10p+8 damage (it uses this attack mode as a substitute for pecking; thus: butt, claw, claw, butt, etc.). Its two claws deal 2d8p+8 points each.
Does not hug and crush foes.

GENERAL INFO

ACTIVITY CYCLE:	Nocturnal
NO. APPEARING:	1-2
% CHANCE IN LAIR:	35%
FREQUENCY:	Sporadic
ALIGNMENT:	Non
VISION TYPE:	Extreme low light vision
AWARENESS/SENSES:	Listening 60%
HABITAT:	Groves and caves
DIET:	Carnivorous
ORGANIZATION:	Individuals or small groups
CLIMATE/TERRAIN:	Sub-arctic to Temperate woodlands

YIELD

MEDICINAL:	ground horn is said to increase man's fertility
SPELL COMPONENTS:	unknown[1]
HIDE/TROPHY:	a mounted head is a tribute to the hunter's skill; claws may be worth 10 silver or more to interested parties
TREASURE:	incidental
EDIBLE:	yes
OTHER:	eggs or young[2]

EXPERIENCE POINT VALUE: 925

Females can be easily differentiated from males by their stiff back feathers. Though the male's entire back is covered in the beast's natural hair-like plumage, the female's upper back sprouts a stiff feathery growth in a roughly triangular shape, tapering from immediately behind the feathered head to the upper back where the feathers start to lose their stiffness, blending rapidly into the downy plumage.

One subspecies of owlbeast, known colloquially as the great horned owlbeast, is morphologically similar to the standard owlbeast but bears a distinctive pair of bovine horns. Great horned owlbeasts cannot interbreed with other owlbeasts.

Most adult owlbeasts stand about 5 feet tall at the shoulder when on all fours, with a body of up to 9 feet long and weighing around 1,500 pounds. When rearing up on its hind legs, an owlbeast stands roughly 12 feet tall.

Combat/Tactics:

These temperamental monsters attack at the slightest provocation. Owlbeast sows are particularly aggressive when their nest or eggs are threatened.

Owlbeasts utilize two claw attacks of 2d8p+7 each, typically followed by a bite of 2d4p+7 points. However, if an owlbeast successfully attacks with two consecutive claw attacks, it traps its opponent in a crushing hug, inflicting 2d8p+7 points every 5 seconds thereafter (DR applies). The owlbeast uses no other attacks until the victim stops wriggling. The hug can be broken with a successful knock-back or Feat of Strength (vs. d20p+16). A Feat of Strength can be attempted every 5 seconds after the victim is enveloped in the hug attack. While trapped in a crushing hug, a victim can only attack with a dagger or knife.

The great horned owlbeast charges opponents, lowering its head slightly in order to gore with its horns. It prefers to gore rather than peck, and does not attempt to hug and crush its foes.

Like their parents, owlbeast chicks use claw/claw/bite tactics, but are too small and inexperienced to effectively hug. Great horned owlbeast chicks attack in a similar manner, for their horns are not sufficiently grown to be used as weapons.

If outnumbered and facing death from a tenacious enemy, an owlbeast may feign a mortal wound and collapse in seeming death throes. It will lie unstirring - patiently waiting for an opportunity to renew the attack when the foes have turned their backs.

Habitat/Society:

Most owlbeasts live in cold to temperate zones where the summers are mildest, preferring coniferous, deciduous or mixed forests from sea level to 8,000 feet in elevation. These deep forests are usually notable for an abundance of dense undergrowth. Some owlbeasts prefer caves, particularly those with access to a subterranean pool or other water source. Great horned owlbeasts prefer open ground, but breed in caves above the tree line in the mountains and the far north.

Most owlbeasts live in mated pairs with a home range of

OWLBEAST CHICK

HIT POINTS:	24+2d8
SIZE/WEIGHT:	M/275 lbs.
TENACITY:	Nervous
INTELLIGENCE:	Animal, Low
FATIGUE FACTOR:	-1

SPEED 3 — INIT 2
ATTACK +5
DR REDUCTION
DEFENSE +5 — 5
see below
short REACH
DAMAGE
TOP SAVE 8

MOVEMENT

CRAWL:	2½
WALK:	5
JOG:	10
RUN:	15
SPRINT:	20

SAVES

PHYSICAL:	+7
MENTAL:	+2
DODGE:	+6

ATTACK:
Owlbeast chicks use two consecutive claw attacks of 2d4p+4 damage each, followed by a bite attack of d6p+4.

GENERAL INFO

ACTIVITY CYCLE:	Nocturnal
NO. APPEARING:	1-6
% CHANCE IN LAIR:	80%
FREQUENCY:	Sporadic
ALIGNMENT:	Non
VISION TYPE:	Extreme low light vision
AWARENESS/SENSES:	Listening 60%
HABITAT:	Nest
DIET:	Carnivorous
ORGANIZATION:	Solitary or Brood
CLIMATE/TERRAIN:	Sub-arctic to Temperate woodlands

YIELD

MEDICINAL:	as appropriate for parental owlbeast
SPELL COMPONENTS:	unknown[1]
HIDE/TROPHY:	only novice fighting men stuff and mount these
TREASURE:	none
EDIBLE:	yes
OTHER:	nil
EXPERIENCE POINT VALUE:	225

roughly 15 square miles, though the actual range size varies depending upon the location, season, age and sex of the owlbeast, and the availability of food, water and shelter. In areas where the local food and resources are abundant, two to four mated pairs may live together. These groups have a typical home range of 25 to 40 square miles; should their territory become so depleted that 100 or more square miles are required to support their dietary needs, the group disbands and the mated pairs go their own way. Owlbeast territories are clearly distinguishable by the many claw marks on trees, rocky outcroppings and soil.

Gestation lasts nearly four months, with a clutch size of one to six leathery eggs laid in a hollow of earth or vegetation followed by an incubation period of another two months. The mated pair shares the nesting duties between them, with the male incubating the eggs during the day and the female at night.

Owlbeast chicks are born with feathers and within the first few hours are up and walking. Afterwards, chicks mature slowly, not reaching sexual maturity for at least the first 20 years of their life. There is a 25% chance that between one and six eggs are incubating in a nest or a 25% chance that one to six immature owlbeast chicks are present in and around the nest. These immature chicks stand about 4½ to 5 feet tall and weigh between 250 to 300 lbs.

The average lifespan of an owlbeast is 150 to 200 years.

Ecology:

Owlbeasts are nocturnal creatures, hunting at night and rarely venturing away from their nests during the day. An owlbeast's diet consists mainly of smaller mammals and giant insects, though owlbeasts that live near pools or lakes also supplement their meals with fish. Owlbeasts are also attracted by the sounds of livestock and may raid isolated camps or farms in the middle of the night.

When feeding, the owlbeast uses its sharp claws and beak to rip apart its prey, swallowing great chunks of it whole. Any indigestible bits (bone, teeth, hair, feathers and so forth) are later regurgitated as wet, slimy pellets.

An owlbeast's most common natural foes are the wolf pack and grizzly bear, though it may come into conflict with any creature that shares its habitat.

On Tellene:

Owlbeasts range primarily throughout the northern portions of the Sovereign Lands, particularly the woodlands and mountain ranges in Cosdol, Ek'Gakel, Shynabyth, Torakk and Drhokker.

Some Dejy and Fhokki tribes or clans consider the procuring of an owlbeast egg to be a rite of manhood through which all warriors must pass to be considered truly worthy.

[1] No mage has yet determined the possible uses of its fur, feathers, bone, horn, blood or eggs, though they suspect it to be a very magical creature indeed.

[2] Owlbeast eggs may be worth several hundred silver pieces, depending on the buyer, though it is assuredly a top end price in that most eggs sell for around 200 sp or so. Live young may fetch a price double that of an egg.

THE BEAST IN THE ROCKS

I gave the small stack of silver coins in my palm a quick toss to produce a satisfying jingle but could only frown with disappointment. Not much to show for two weeks work in the wilds. I hoped the half-dozen rotting kobold heads I had hauled back to Frandor's Keep would fetch a more sizeable bounty. This meager sum was hardly enough to tie on a good drink — let alone bed down a whore.

I stepped out of the paymaster's shop into a drizzling rain and began negotiating the narrow streets of the lower bailey. My feet knew the way to go, so I focused on shoving aside the human vermin I so despise. It didn't take long before I reached my destination, the Broken Hilt.

As I entered the tavern shaking the wet from my coat, I was annoyed to see that a red-bearded dwarf was busy finishing off a platter of roast pheasant and a bottle of waxberry wine at my regular corner table.

Deciding not to make an issue of it, I turned and stepped up to the bar. I laid my trappings across the oaken planks and settled down on a stool throwing down the three coins I had just received in payment and gave them a soft pat.

A toothless grin flashed across Vikira the barkeep's face as he noticed the glint of silver in the flickering light.

"Larz! Been a spell," he commented. "You've been busy by the looks of it."

"I've been thirsty," I snapped. I then looked over my shoulder

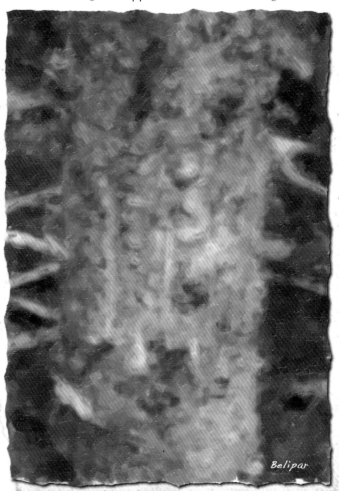

Belipar

Owlbeast Markings

at the dwarf in the corner unable to shake my annoyance.

"I see the fresh air hasn't tempered your tongue any," replied the barkeep. "So, what was it this time? Orcs? Gnoles…? Any sign of that hill giant you were…?"

"Why don't you just pour me some mead," I again snapped, turning my attention back to the barkeep. "And keep pouring 'til the coin runs out."

"That I can do," Vikira muttered picking up the coins, "'Course, two of these will go toward settling that little debt you promised to repay. A month ago…."

I fumed. I really should have gone to the Prancing Pegasus.

"Just pour, old man. Preferably with yer mouth shut. And make sure it's the good stuff. Not the gutter-swill you serve the guards."

Vikira quickly produced a full tankard and placed it before me. I grabbed it, threw my head back and quickly emptied it, the suds filling my beard and running down the front of my tunic.

As I lowered the stein back to the table, my eyes paused on something peculiar hanging on the wall behind Vikira's head.

It was the skin of an enormous animal, hanging heavy from three iron spikes driven into the plank wall. I immediately recognized the orange-brown fur peppered with feathers to be that of a great horned owlbeast. But it was the jagged scar across the beak and left side of the head that drew my attention and held it fast.

Noticing my reaction the barkeep smiled proudly. "Aaahh… I see you've noticed my latest trophy. She's a beaut isn't she?"

"W-where did ya get that…?", I asked without looking away from the skin.

"You're not the only one who's been busy, my friend." Vikira smiled proudly as he slung the dirty rag in his hand over his shoulder. "I felled that beast on my trip down to Vew last week. Was quite the battle."

I grabbed him by the collar and pulled him across the bar growling, "I asked you a question…"

"I-I told ya — I had to make a trip down trail to fetch some new girls. It tried takin' our horses when we were camping at…"

I drew a dagger with my free hand and pressed its finely honed edge to the sweating barkeep's neck. "The truth… or by the gods I WILL cut you."

Fear welled up in Vikira's eyes as he strained to pull away from the blade, but my hold on him was fast and he only increased the pressure. Finally he blurted out, "All right… ALL RIGHT… I — gasp — I bartered for it. I got it from a merchant laying over at Kar Mardri."

I released my grip and sat back, still feeling the veins on my forehead throb. This damned temper — it will be the ruin of me one day. "S-sorry," he stammered after a few moments of gathering his thoughts.

Losing my temper with a no-account merchant was one thing, but as a former soldier, Vikira was popular with the Keep guards. He could make a lot of trouble for me.

Vikira swiped at the trickle of blood running down his neck with the dirty rag and stared hard at me. "W-What in the nine Hells has gotten into you…? You could've killed me!!"

"You can steal a man's kill," I yelled pointing to the skin on the wall. "But I'll be damned if anyone's goin' to steal my braggin' rights."

Vikira looked at the skin, then back to me and finally to the skin again. "Y-you….?" he asked, his face flush with astonishment. YOU killed THAT…?!""

"I did," I replied. "Three seasons ago. After it nearly killed me. Unfortunately, I weren't able to take the skin."

Vikira poured another tankard of ale and set it before me. Placing his elbows on the bar and leaning in he motioned toward trophy with his head. "How can you be so sure…? One looks about the same as the rest. Wouldn't you say?"

"You see that scar…? Just across the beak?"

"Aye, that I do."

"Well, I'm the fella who put it there."

"Fine. You want the bragging rights? You can have 'em. But it'll take more than that silver you have there if plan on taking the skin from me. I paid good money for…"

"Keep yer rotten skin," I barked. "Leave me in peace".

The barkeep knew when to shut up, and moved down the bar to another customer.

I cradled the tankard of mead in my hands and bowed my head. After a long while I turned my gaze back to the trophy hanging on the wall and stared at the empty slits where menacing eyes had once stared through. A flood of painful memories began to resurface. Memories I'd been runnin' from for years.

Suddenly my thoughts were interrupted by a voice thick with a dwarvish accent.

"Well? How 'bout it then…?"

I turned to face the bearded dwarf in the corner. "How 'bout what?"

The dwarf raised his hands, "How 'bout finishing the story?"

Again my temper began to flare but this time I forced myself to relax and decided to take a different tack.

"Friend dwarf," I said raising his tankard and turning in my stool. "Fer THAT to happen I would need several more of these."

A grin broke across the dwarf's face as he fished behind his broad leather belt and produced a coin pouch. Dropping it on the table he motioned to Vikira. "Til he's had his fill!!"

Feeling pleased with myself, I picked up my drink and moved over to the corner table and sat across from the dwarf. A half dozen other patrons crowded around us as I ran my hand across my beard and gathered the words.

Finally….

"Thirteen seasons ago, a group of us were trekkin' up a goat trail 'bout a week's journey west of here. We'd been drawing coin from the Earl scoutin' out the whereabouts of a group of bugbears that had been harassin' patrols. Two weeks up in the heights scouring the limits of the tree line and not a sign of 'em.

Well, we were fixin' to head back down the mountain and return to the Keep when the weather turned and all signs pointed to a heavy snow a-comin'.

We pitched our tent on a shelf of rock on the forest's edge where a rock pile formed a natural windbreak. We built up a good fire, broke out a bottle of ale and then retreated into our tents fer the night.

I thought dawn would never come. It was bitter cold and a wind whipped up that I thought would surely blow us off that shelf.

In the morning when I threw back the flap of my tent it crackled like dry leaves underfoot. A deep snow had settled over the camp during the night. As I stepped outside, the poor man's ale from the jug passed around the night before was havin' its revenge — my head was throbbin' and my stomach was threatenin' to purge itself right then and there.

As I cupped my hands and breathed into 'em to warm my fingers, the first thing I noticed was that the fire had long gone out. The first business of the day had been decided — namely to gather more wood and get it goin' again.

I thought about wakin' the others to set them about preparin' for the day but decided to let 'em grab a few more minutes of sleep. No doubt they were feelin' no better than I.

So, slingin' my bow and grabbin' my axe I set off down the slope a short distance toward a fallen tree that looked to have an abundance of deadfall about it fer easy gathering.

I'd barely taken a dozen steps when I noticed deep tracks cuttin' across our campsite from north to south.

Stooping to examine 'em, I took them to be bear tracks though it was hard to be sure since they weren't real well defined. But they were fresh – made after the snow that fell early in the night — and that worried me.

I tensed, realizing that some dangerous creature had paid us a visit. Readyin' my axe, I turned my attention back toward the tents and froze.

Nurvarii's tent, which was pitched just behind my own, was torn and spread about like a soiled handkerchief. A big ol' crimson trail of blood stained the snow leadin' from his tent into the forest's edge — and the tracks at my feet led in that direction. By the gods!!

Runnin' back toward the tent I shouted out an alarm to rouse the others. Drunken sods, all of us. How could we not have heard the commotion?

Reaching Nurvarii's tent, my heart sank. To my eye the bloody trail looked to be a kill-drag. The dwarf was most likely taken in his sleep and his body dragged into the trees.

By this time Hurn and Fargus had been roused and were scramblin' out of their tents and pullin' on their clothing.

"What's the matter?" one of them shouted out. There was then a gasp, and I knew I needn't bother answerin'.

Both were at my side as fast as their shaky legs could take 'em.

"Poor bastard…" Fargus finally muttered under his breath. "He'd have wanted to go out with a fight. Not…. Not like this."

That's when I spotted the dwarf's axe propped up in the snow as though it'd been tossed or knocked aside. Takin' a few steps forward, I retrieved it. After pattin' off the accumulated snow I saw that its broad blade was coated with the poor fella's congealed blood.

"I'd say he got his wish" I said as I held it up for them to see. "He got at least one good bite on the beast."

Hurn turned his attention to the blood trail and then let his gaze follow it to the dark wall of mountain pine and the veil of their low hanging branches.

"Then let's finish it."

Without a word, the three of us headed toward the forest, our eyes dartin' back and forth takin' in every detail around us. A dozen yards and we were in murky shadow. A dozen yards more and it was like night again, the snow-laden branches of the pines chokin' out the sunlight.

Following the blood trail a bit further, we came upon a gruesome scene.

'Twas the body of our comrade — or at least what was left of it. Naught but a rib cage stained pink with laid back shreds of skin and muscle surroundin' it, a bloodied head with the skull-top exposed

nearby, a leg cast aside in one direction and a half eaten arm in the other.

Again we found ourselves standin' in silence. Any glimmer of hope in finding our friend alive, albeit wounded, had sure enough been dashed.

I turned my attention to Hurn, who was pointin' to the area 'round us. It was jumbled up with tracks, splattered blood and bits of broken branches. Clearly a life-and-death battle took place here.

"Looks like he gave the beast a good fight!"

I weren't so sure for not a single boot print was visible. Nurvarii had surely been dragged to the spot, and it didn't look to me that he had ever regained his footing.

As my eyes danced about and took in the details, somethin' caused them to lock and focus. A shadow loomed nearby darker than the rest.

I then realized it wasn't a shadow at all but a heap of black fur, perhaps five yards away lyin' at the base of a large tree but largely obscured by a fallen limb.

"There!" I pointed.

With weapons raised, the three of us spread out as we approached the figure from different directions.

As we closed on it, I soon realized it was a large black bear. A black bear? They're pesky creatures to be sure but I was nonetheless surprised. They typically don't have much fight in 'em, particularly when confronted by a combative foe.

Assumin' it had just fed and was slumbering with a full belly, I raised my axe and braced myself. To my left I saw Fargus notching an arrow.

Yet, somethin' didn't feel right.

The bear was motionless, showin' neither sign of its sides rising as it inhaled nor the foggy exhalation of breath the frigid morning air would surely compel.

As I studied the critter's form a moment longer I saw the reason for these peculiarities. It was lyin' in a pool of its own blood with four exposed ribs visible through a gapin' wound in its side.

"I don't get it…." Fargus muttered. "What the hell happened to…?"

These would be the last words he ever spoke.

Out of the corner of my eye I saw a blur of motion followed by a "Tha-rummp!!" and a clickin' hiss that seemed louder and more frightenin' in the confines of them tightly grouped trees than anythin' I've ever heard before or since.

Fargus was thrown quite literally a dozen feet like he'd been catapulted. With a sickenin' thud his body impacted a tree trunk where he hung fer a moment as though suspended, afore droppin' in a heap to the ground.

Where he had just stood was a wall of fur, feather, beak and claw — an enormous great horned owlbeast! Nine feet o' terror filled the small clearing like a mountain.

Its soulless golden yellow eyes flashed in the shadows like two burning embers. Shoulders thrown back, it roared again nearly bucklin' my knees with fear.

I call it a roar but the cry of an owlbeast ain't like that of any other animal. It's not the low guttural snarl of the bear but a reverberation of pure intimidation you can feel against the chest and that makes yer knees quake and yer bladder evacuate.

Both Hurn and I were frozen with inaction fer several seconds as we contemplated our certain deaths. Fortunately, the owlbeast threat-postured just long enough fer me to regain my senses. I knew we could never outrun the beast and we most certainly couldn't outfight it. Our only chance was to buy some time, if only a few seconds.

Mutterin' a prayer to the Great Huntress and beseechin' her to aid my weapon in strikin' its mark, I hurled my axe directly at the owlbeast's head.

Not waitin' to see if my plea was answered, I turned and bolted intending to yell, "Run!!" to Hurn as I passed. I never got the chance fer Hurn was already running.

As we ran through the treesm takin' a beating from the low hanging branches, I could hear the owlbeast behind me shriekin' in pain. I'd hit the damn thing!

I panted fer breath as I followed closely on Hurn's heels.

Any feelin' of hope fostered by the owlbeast's cries were suddenly replaced with dread as the cracklin' of branches and heavy footfalls told of an ominous pursuit.

We'd just broken into the clearing at the edge of our camp when Hurn pointed toward the broken rocks nearby. Usin' them as a windbreak was one of the reasons we'd chosen to camp on the site.

Well, we ran fer the stones and I swear we'd barely gotten half way when the owlbeast broke through the brush behind us. Glancin' over my shoulder I could see it was on all fours. With blood pourin' down its face, the enraged beast let loose another bone-chillin' howl as it spotted us and continued the chase.

Hurn made the rocks first. I was envious of him as he leapt up on top of the largest boulder and quickly dropped down into a gap, disappearing from sight. I weren't far behind. I'd just made it up onto the rocks and was about to follow suit when my right foot took a bone crushing claw-swipe that sent me spinnin' around on my back. I hit the rocks hard, my head reelin' and the wind knocked out of me.

The owlbeast was towerin' over me with the remnants of my right boot caught on his claw. It shook its wing furiously to dislodge the boot and was startin' to raise its other claw to finish me off when I felt a pair of hands on my shoulders.

My head struck a sharp outcropping as I was roughly pulled in among the rocks, and I found myself leanin' against Harn in the dark with a trickle of warm blood running down my cheek. Mere feet away, the owlbeast was roarin' with anger at being robbed of revenge. It began savagely tearin' at the rocks as the two of us retreated into our rocky prison. It was at that moment I realized that my right foot was damn well shattered and useless.

To our miscontent, the void in the rocks where we'd sought refuge barely extended seven or eight feet. The owlbeast alternated from shovin' its one good eye up to the opening to peer in at us to tearin' at the rocks with its powerful claws. We feared it would be successful if it kept goin', so massive were its forearms. As if intent on confirmin' our anxiety, it managed to displace a great deal of loose stone and widen the hole.

Praise be to Kalenadil that them large stones buttressin' our fortress proved immovable!

And so there we sat imprisoned, sentenced to do nothin' but watch our would-be executioner tear at our cell, tryin' its utmost to carry out Fate's verdict.

The critter was relentless and threw itself at this task for most of the day, breakin' off its assault only occasionally to either rest or continue feeding on our poor comrades before renewin' its efforts.

Finally, just after dusk, it retreated and didn't return.

So terrified were we of the monster that we decided not to emerge from our hidey-hole until noon the next day, and then only long enough fer a spy-peep, fearin' to venture more than a few feet from the rocks.

Since I couldn't rightly walk, Hurn gathered sufficient food and water fer me to survive for a week among the rocks. He then left me so he could go fetch help from a clan of itinerant miners about two day's walk down slope.

I tell you rightly, it was the longest five days I've ever endured. Though the owlbeast never showed its head again, every noise from the forest or glimpse of a foragin' rat or squirrel gave me a jolt.

When Hurn finally returned in the company of a half dozen sturdy men to pull me out of the rocks, I felt reborn. We gathered what was left of Nurvii and Fargus and placed them among the broken rocks, pilin' loose stones high atop their remains. Hurn and I were both silently grateful we weren't entombed with them and had lived to see another day."

I paused for dramatic effect and then stated, "But the story doesn't end there."

"Three years later, on a narrow mountain cliffside trail 'bout thirty miles further south, I'd just rounded a blind spot on a bend in the trail and was huggin' the rock face with my back when I caught glimpse of some movement barely 30 feet up ahead. It was an owlbeast!

It had been negotiatin' the narrow trail on all fours, but when it caught sight of me it immediately reared up on two legs and let out a roar that made me quake at the knees. I can't say it recognized me then and there, but I certainly recognized it. The jagged scar, slashin' across one pale lifeless eye and cuttin' across its beak made its identity a sure thing.

I barely had time to react and draw my axe before it had closed on me. Its great girth forced it to cling to the rock face with one great claw as it swung with the other. And swing it did, catchin' me across my shoulder and nearly dislodgin' me, intent, it seemed, upon sendin' me tumblin' over to my death.

Somehow I managed to regain my footing, but my axe was gone. Desperate, I fumbled around and found a sharp-edged rock to use as a makeshift weapon. I doubted it would do much good but still, it was better than nothin'. The beast swung awkwardly at me several more times but I avoided the blows, narrowly so as one came close enough to my eye that I it blinded me fer a moment. Lashin' out in an emotional wave of fear and fury driven by the bloodied corpses of my friends flashing in my brain, I let loose a cry, the very same battle cry I had yelled so long time ago on a distant field. I hurled that stone with all my might. Again, the Merry Marksman must have been looking out fer me 'cause the rock flew true, strikin' the owlbeast in its one good eye. The beast flailed in pain, forgettin' that it was clingin' to a cliff face hundreds of feet up. It let go of the wall and in its writhing became unbalanced, so it took to tumblin' and screamin' over the edge. I reckon it was still only focused on its pain as it hit the jagged rocks below. I weren't about to go down there to get the skin, though it woulda been a great trophy. I was just happy to be alive at that point and scrambled back to safety — and a bottle of good, stout ale to drown the fear."

I've always despised weakness and particularly the admission of such, but I will confess that to this day I have a morbid fear of owlbeasts. It is a fear so palpable that fer years it's caused me to seize up every time I even catch the scent of one in an abandoned lair or stumble across an occasional nesting area.

I know, deep in my heart, that it was only through blind dumb luck or divine providence that I'm alive to tell you the story and drink this mead. I sure ain't about to push that luck any further.

PEGASUS

Also Known As: Neeloor

If your mother was like mine, I daresay you heard stories about the pegasus in your childhood. I have not let learned the truth, but I have come across a tale with which to further my annals.

I believe it was on the last 28th of Famine when I was idly studying the old winged horse carvings in the temple when Soother Vledin walked up beside me. He put a hand on my shoulder, the way so many priests seem to do when imparting wisdom, and we began to talk. Noticing the object of my interest, the conversation wandered to his childhood days and tales of the pegasus.

According to Vledin, his mother used to lure him and his sister to sleep at night with the story of the winged horse, and how it watched over them as they slept, covering them with its great wings so that they would stay safe through the night. Eventually, as some curious children do, the siblings decided to search the forest just to glimpse that supposedly fantastic being. The sister, seemingly as bold then as her brother is meek now, told him that she was determined to find and ride a pegasus. Despite the sister's determination, the boy eventually grew weary of the search and began to doubt whether the pegasus truly existed. His sister refused to give sway and badgered her brother into more searchings throughout the forest. Her favorite spot, it seemed, was near a hillside spring, for she had been told that pegasi love to drink spring water.

My interest was flagging, but I remained polite as the priest continued with his tale, finally interjecting with a query of whether he or his sister had ever gotten a glimpse of the fabled beast. The old priest got a strange look on his face – seemingly one of hidden amusement, but I cannot be sure.

The next event occurred on the 13th year after his sister's birth - on that very anniversary, in fact. She grabbed her brother's arm and dragged him back to explore those woods once again. As they neared the spring, he was amazed to see a Pegasus land at the very point where the spring water reached the bottom of the hill and formed a small pool in the ground.

She then moved quickly forward, brazenly daring all, then walked over to the white winged horse that stood silently watching her. It was there she placed a hand on its nose, and it bowed down to her like she was a queen. His sister then climbed on the pegasus' back and they flew away. She was gone for three years, he claimed, and thought he should never see her again. Then, one day, she walked into the cottage with a sword in her hand and told him all about her many amazing adventures, and the battles she had fought on the back of that mighty winged pegasus.

Fortunately, a parishioner approached him with a question of doctrine, and I was able to extract myself before he could continue with his little epic. A fine story, but I'm sure he was pulling my leg. Perhaps the temple of the True would be a better place for my next investigation of old carvings. - ☦

A feather from a pegasus wing is said to bring good fortune.

A pegasus appears to be a magnificent, wild, winged horse. Most stand between 14 and 16 hands tall (56 to 64 inches) and weigh around half a ton. Pegasi are generally white-haired on coat and tail, though some are light gray or pale chestnut in color. Pegasi have predominantly pink skin (a rare trait in horses) and anatomy similar to most light riding equines. An adult pegasus generally has a wingspan of about 30 feet across and can fly up to 50 miles before needing a rest.

Combat/Tactics:

Pegasi are often seen as mounts to great warriors or pure, virginal maidens. Those who have been chosen by a pegasus (for these beings select their own riders, and do so very carefully), say there is not a better mount to have when in combat. The magnificent beast is highly maneuverable, absolutely loyal to its rider, and always courageous and honorable.

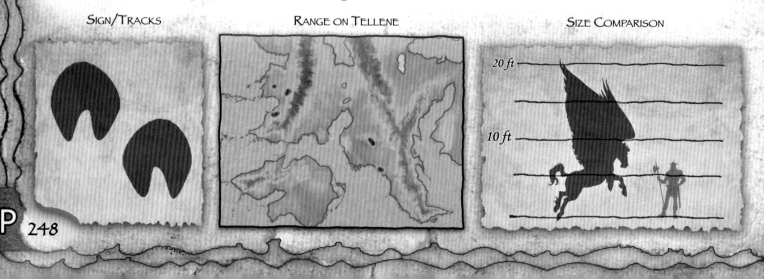

SIGN/TRACKS   RANGE ON TELLENE   SIZE COMPARISON

20 ft
10 ft

Although a pegasus is not a vicious, or usually dangerous animal, it can attack enemies and those who threaten it or its rider. If possible, they prefer not to fight, instead using their speed to escape enemies, but if necessary can use their strong legs to kick a foe for 4d4p+2 points of damage. A pegasus may also drop an enemy from a great height, if that person somehow manages to climb upon its back.

If a pegasus is in danger of being mortally wounded, or if its rider is in desperate need, it escapes by flying to safety.

Habitat/Society:

Like horses, pegasi favor grassy plains with abundant water sources, though they may be spotted in a variety of habitats, including semi-arid deserts, tropical rainforests and other climes.

Pegasi live alone or in small herds of up to 10 individuals of various sexes. Such herds are often small groups of two to three families. Female pegasi carry their young for around 11 months, with gestation usually resulting in one foal; twins are rare. Foals can stand and run shortly following birth. They quickly learn how to fly and can do so within 4 to 8 weeks after birth. They reach maturity at age 5.

When a person is chosen by a pegasus to become its mount, it is a monumental occasion. A pegasus does not make the choice lightly. It will often study its potential rider for months, flying above him, watching his comings and goings, before deciding to approach him.

Pegasi are well known to live over 200 years, but their average lifespan is unknown.

Ecology:

Pegasi graze on grasses and other vegetation. In arid lands or when food resources are scarce, herds may migrate up to 700 miles for food. They are rarely found more than 20 miles from a water source.

Their main natural enemies include other flying creatures such as griffyns, though some large ground-based predators (mostly big hunting cats) do target pegasus foals that cannot yet fly.

On Tellene:

Pegasi have been spotted in (or flying over) a variety of sparsely populated plains near rivers and forests, such as those south of the Paliba and Rytarr woodlands. They have also been reported landing in (or emerging from) groves amidst the Crondor Woods, the Lendelwood, and the Brindonwood, usually near a spring or brook.

Over the last decade, these magnificent and rare creatures have become the target of evil religious orders and cults. Some have even been captured and sacrificed in dark and hideous rituals. Because of this, many pegasi have become extremely careful about who they approach.

[1] *Feathers, when used as a material component in the mage's fifth level Levitation spell (among other flight spells) doubles the standard duration.*

PEGASUS

HIT POINTS:	27+6d8
SIZE/WEIGHT:	H/about ½ ton
TENACITY:	Steady
INTELLIGENCE:	Average
FATIGUE FACTOR:	-6

SPEED 5 • INIT -2 • ATTACK +9 • DMG REDUCTION +5 • 6 • DEFENSE • 4d4p+2 • 7 • medium REACH • DAMAGE • TOP SAVE ▼

MOVEMENT

CRAWL:	10
WALK:	15
JOG:	20
RUN:	25
FLY:	40

SAVES

PHYSICAL:	+9
MENTAL:	+11
DODGE:	+12

ATTACK:
Pegasi kick with both hooves, dealing a total 4d4p+2 points of damage. If facing an opponent, they may bite for d4+1 damage but their preference is to wheel about and kick.

SPECIAL DEFENSES:
Flight

GENERAL INFO

ACTIVITY CYCLE:	Diurnal
NO. APPEARING:	1-10
% CHANCE IN LAIR:	20%
FREQUENCY:	Unusual
ALIGNMENT:	Lawful Good
VISION TYPE:	Standard
AWARENESS/SENSES:	Standard
HABITAT:	Plains, savannas, forest groves
DIET:	Herbivorous
ORGANIZATION:	Individuals or Herd
CLIMATE/TERRAIN:	Temperate to Tropical wilderness

YIELD

MEDICINAL:	nil
SPELL COMPONENTS:	feathers, in Levitation or other flight spells[1]
HIDE/TROPHY:	feathers are prized gifts between lovers
TREASURE:	nil
EDIBLE:	yes
OTHER:	nil
EXPERIENCE POINT VALUE:	675

PIXIE-FAIRY

Also Known As: Faeriefolk

Tellene is home to many mysterious races, but I know of few that are more magical and intriguing than the pixie-fairy. Well do I recall my first encounter with them, when my companions and I were trekking through the Lendelwood. We stood hidden amongst the trees at the edge of a glade, watching a dozen or more of the tiny creatures flitting about the green with the sunlight glistening on their wings. As I stared, my mind wondered at their intent.

Not less than a twelvemonth before, you see, I'd been told the tale of a tiny village beset by pixie-fairies with dark hearts and evil powers to match. In the guise of helpful aides, they had been torturing other creatures for fun and performing other horrific acts. It was said that one even went so far as to advise a distraught young man to kill a young woman, then put some of her blood on the forehead and palms of his dying wife, in order to restore her to health. The poor obsessed fool did so, but with no good result and the cackling laughter of the winged evil in his ears. He took his own life shortly thereafter, or so the storyteller said.

Fortunately, I learned the falsity of such tales. The fey we met that day were noble and gentle, as willing to assist travelers through the woods as they would have been to make war upon us, had we seemed to possess malicious intent. They were at first reluctant to allow us approach, but the persuasive powers of our elf cleric (as well as mine own knowledge of nature) eventually broke through their mistrust, and we spent a pleasant night drinking acorn tea, eating bark soup and sleeping on soft peat moss beds.

Human children sometimes say that if you see the glimmer of a pixie-fairy's wings in the moonlight, your wish will come true. This is, of course, nonsense. Do not waste your time. - ℟

Rarely seen unless they desire it to be so, the pixie-fairy is perhaps the least understood of the civilized races.

Asked to envisage a pixie-fairy, images of tiny, blonde winged elves in brightly colored clothes and a whimsical attitude come to mind. In truth, pixie-fairies come in many forms, not all of which fit the stereotypical image. The variety of pixie-fairies is nearly as wide as that of the human races.

Their skin tones vary from snow white to mauve to orange, and two pairs of beautiful, shimmering, dragonfly-like wings also spring from the back to grace each side of their bodies. These wings are folded and soft at birth, expanding within hours to about ⅘ of the pixie-fairy's height. The wings attach to either side of the spine, with internal flight muscles attached to the rib cage. The primary wings are slightly larger, and are atop the secondary wings. Pixie-fairies use the primary wings to gain lift and propulsion, while the secondary, smaller wings to help maneuver. These wings come in a variety of hues, but most are brightly colored with an iridescent sheen.

The face of a typical pixie-fairy combines angular bone structure with features similar to small human children (such as large, innocent looking eyes and pouting lips). They also possess two antennae, which sprout upwards from their heads. A pixie-fairy's antennae grow in one of three different locations – from the inner edge of either eyebrow, at the hairline, or between the hairline and the crown of the skull. Human sages debate on whether the placement of antennae is hereditary or due to the amount of magical energy a pixie-fairy possesses. When asked, the pixie-fairies simply give the interviewer a bemused look, as a scholar may give a child who asks an unusual question. To them, the exact location of their antennae matters only when being fitted for headgear. Biologically, the antennae have a core of cartilage protecting the antennal nerves and then covered with skin. These sense organs efficiently detect the minute traces of magical energy that are the pixie-fairy diet.

SIGN/TRACKS

RANGE ON TELLENE

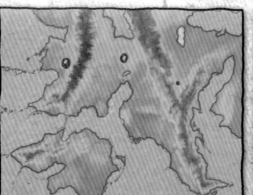

SIZE COMPARISION

6 ft

3 ft

The female of the species has slightly larger antennae, and men and other sapients often use this characteristic to distinguish the sex of a pixie-fairy (since to them the pixie-fairy often appears androgynous, just as a halfling might appear androgynous from a giant's point of view). Upon closer inspection, however, the physical features of male and female pixie-fairies can be determined, when two conditions exist. Firstly, that the pixie-fairy is not heavily clothed, and secondly, that the pixie-fairy allows the viewer to come within a few feet. Pixie-fairies are careful by nature, and prefer to keep well out of arm's reach of any stranger. Some sages claim that all pixie-fairies are androgynous, but that the greater a pixie-fairy's beauty, the more feminine (or masculine) it appears to outsiders. Others state that certain clans are simply more androgynous than others. In fact, both arguments hold a bit of truth, for androgyny varies by clan and individual.

Pixie-fairies do not have individual teeth, but rather have two crescent-shaped bony ridges that span the upper and lower jaw, as would rows of teeth. Though these partially segmented ridges can easily be mistaken for rows of individual teeth, they are actually all of one piece.

Pixie-fairy clothing comes in as many styles and colors as human clothing, if not more. Lone pixie-fairies encountered are typically dressed in outdoor clothes, comprising soft leather boots or shoes, knee-length trousers, and a short-sleeved shirt, normally finely spun wool or cotton. These garments are generally brown or green, which help with concealment in wooded areas.

However, in the safety of their settlements, pixie-fairies often go barefoot and wear very short trousers or loincloths. Males go barechested, as do females, or wear a small shirt or strip of clothing that leaves little to the imagination. What little clothing they do wear is colored in bright hues, often orange, yellow, pink or light blue or green. Darker shades are more common among magic-users or the more somber clerics. Only nobles wear purple. Pixie-fairies may or may not wear undergarments, depending on the weather.

A typical adult pixie-fairy stands between 18 and 24 inches tall, and weighs roughly 8 to 15 pounds.

Combat/Tactics:

Pixie-fairies keep track of intruders through scouts and animal spies. Scouts make frequent reports, passing on details on numbers, composition and the best place to set an ambush. Any party entering pixie-fairy territory is usually detected within a few hours and is watched closely until they decide what action to take.

Their usual tactic is to wait invisibly in ambush until the enemy stumbles into a pre-set trap, then utilizing a variety of ranged attacks from behind cover. These ambushes often include a dozen or more individuals led by an experienced leader (typically a 4th to 6th level mage). When the majority of the intruders are cowed or incapacitated, the pixie-fairies emerge from their hiding places, ready to fire. An enemy receives one verbal order to surrender; refusal is met with a rain of diminuative arrows or spells (or both!) against the trapped forces.

For every band of pixie-fairies encountered, approximately 25% to 50% will be mages. The larger the group, the higher is the level and the greater is the quantity of mages. Among groups of 4 pixie-fairies, one will usually be a 2nd level mage. For every dozen, there will be an additional 4th to 6th level mage leader. Among bands of 20 pixie-fairies, a mage of 6th to 8th level leads the band, accompanied by a thief of at least half the mage's level.

PIXIE-FAIRY

HIT POINTS:	7+d4
SIZE/WEIGHT:	T/15 lbs.
TENACITY:	Nervous
INTELLIGENCE:	Average
FATIGUE FACTOR:	2

SPEED	5		INIT	-2
	ATTACK	+4	DMG REDUCTION	
DEFENSE	+11		0	
		1d4p		2
short REACH			DAMAGE	TOP SAVE

MOVEMENT

CRAWL:	⅝
WALK:	1¼
JOG:	2½
RUN:	3¾
FLY:	30

SAVES

PHYSICAL:	0
MENTAL:	+4
DODGE:	+6

ATTACK: Pixie-Faries are usually aware of the approach of enemies through their animal spy network; they will wait in ambush initiating combat with wee bows (RoF 7, Range as Javelin, D 1d4p per missile) and spells; utilize a variety of small weapons that all inflict 1d4p damage in melee but will disperse readily if serious resistance is offered

SPECIAL DEFENSES: May become Invisible 1/day; Flight

GENERAL INFO

ACTIVITY CYCLE:	Any
NO. APPEARING:	d10p (gang); 4d4p+8 (war band); 30d12p (clan)
% CHANCE IN LAIR:	10%
FREQUENCY:	Infrequent
ALIGNMENT:	Chaotic Good
VISION TYPE:	Standard
AWARENESS/SENSES:	Standard
HABITAT:	Treetop homes
DIET:	Omnivorous
ORGANIZATION:	Solitary to Clan
CLIMATE/TERRAIN:	Any, save arctic

YIELD

MEDICINAL:	dust doubles the effectiveness of healing potions
SPELL COMPONENTS:	dandruff or flakes substitute for common material
HIDE/TROPHY:	preserved bodies are trophies of the truly evil
TREASURE:	gems worth 5d4p silver[1]
EDIBLE:	yes[2]
OTHER:	nil
EXPERIENCE POINT VALUE: 20	

For every 50 pixie-fairies, there is a mage leader of 12th-13th level (50% chance of either) and a 6th level thief. For 100 or more, there are those numbers plus a mage of level 15th to 18th level (d4+14) and an extra 2d6p thieves of 2d6p levels each. Pixie-fairy clerics are uncommon and fighters are rare, with only a 20% chance of a cleric and a 10% chance of a fighter accompanying any dozen; their levels are roughly equal to the highest level leader (roll a d6, 1-2 = one level below, 3-4 = same level, 5-6 = one level above).

Pixie-fairies are skilled at scare tactics, and an enemy force camping in the woods is a sitting target for such. A small number of pixie-fairies penetrate the camp, leave a warning by the commander's head (such as an arrow or a dagger) and then retreat into the night. The clear threat that the pixie-fairies could have killed the commander in his sleep is usually enough to rattle even hardened veterans.

Pixie-fairies also have access to a tribal tattoo magic that comes down from ages past. These magical tattoos serve as focal points, allowing the pixie-fairy to draw from its own inherent magical energy to achieve perpetual spell-like results. The pixie-fairies do not speak of tattoo magic to outsiders.

While humans favor large quadrupeds for their steeds, pixie-fairies may ally themselves with birds or monstrous insects, dangerous predators like wolves and wolverines, or simple creatures like the fox, rabbit, raccoon, squirrel, etc.. These woodland thralls can also serve as reinforcements when pixie-fairies are threatened.

Habitat/Society:

While most humans assume that pixie-fairies live only in temperate woodland homes, pixie-fairy settlements actually exist in many lands, from the deep hearts of jungles to the cold and bitter northern regions. Of course, they are most common in well-forested lands, for all pixie-fairies prefer to build their homes high in the trees, away from the ground.

These treetop settlements are difficult to detect, especially from the ground. As pixie-fairies are flying creatures, no paths lead into the communities, except for recent trails used by woodland thralls and local game. Most are constructed near bodies of water.

Strangers making camp close to the pixie-fairy settlement must be investigated, for a large number may signify a raiding party or group of loggers come to destroy their home. If the defenses are weak, the pixie-fairies attack immediately, using surprise and stealth to slaughter the intruders before they can muster a consolidated defense. Even should the clans be forced to search for a new home, they return to enact revenge on the intruders.

The area between the trees is strung with trip wires, small pits full of sharp spikes, and snares, all designed to thwart an enemy attack. Further out from the center are still more traps, though these are fewer in number to avoid trapping animals. Sentries sit in the trees, their eyes scanning the forest for unusual sounds or sights, their weapons ready to defend their kinfolk. Pixie-fairies do not build sentry posts in the trees; they simply find a comfortable spot with a good view of any approaching trails and wait.

Locating a settlement is not easy, for most are isolated on islands, in deep valleys or in areas where the trees form a living maze. Minor cultivation of the forest encourages creepers and vines to shadow their habitats from casual observers on the ground. All one sees when looking up is thick vegetation.

Within these settlements are individual clans and families. When multiple clans live in close proximity, the nominal ruler of the joint settlement is usually the eldest female mage or cleric. Clans vary in size from a few pixie-fairies to many dozen, and may comprise several families that claim to be derived from a common ancestor. A settlement may have many clans or only one.

Associated families that either sought the protection of the clan at some point in history, or were tenants or vassals of its patriarch, may also be members of the clan. Allegiance is generally given to a father's clan, but there is also a strong sense of descent through, and loyalty to, the mother's line as well.

Pixie-fairies have at least two names. The first is the personal name, given to each newborn upon birth, while the surname is the father's clan name. Upon reaching adolescence, the character also chooses a nickname to use when among other races. Nicknames are usually highly descriptive and refer to something arboreal, colorful or seasonal, or a combination of the above. This nickname may be one word (such as Peaseblossom) or two words (such as Pease Blossom), depending on the pixie-fairy's whim.

Pixie-fairy gestation lasts only four months, with the newborn weighing little more than a pound. Twins are exceptionally rare and are viewed as great blessings. Pixie-fairy children, like those of larger races, are helpless at birth and rely on adults for everything they need to survive. Most pixie-fairies are born with white hair, which alters to black, blonde, brunette or redhead within a few weeks. The natural offspring of two pixie-fairies is always another pixie-fairy, with no tendencies towards either pixie or fairy blood. A child enters adolescence at the age of three and maturity at the age of four.

A typical pixie-fairy has a natural lifespan of 10 to 12 years, and its mental state reflects this. Matters of long-term import seem insignificant to many; they are mere distractions in the pursuit of living life to the fullest. Pixie-fairies know that their life is short and often make snap judgments about friends or enemies. However, this does not mean that they are friendly creatures that immediately forgive and forget. A pixie-fairy may wait months to enact revenge, but you can rest assured he will strike back. After all, he wants to be sure to get revenge before he or his intended victim die.

Ecology:

Because of their metabolism and the fact that they are magical creatures, pixie-fairy sustenance requirements differ from other races. Pixie-fairies actually feed on errant magical energies (the residual energies left behind by magical spells, items, etc.) that tend to accumulate in certain rare plants and insects. Although they eat less food as compared to their larger counterparts, their diet is so selective and restrictive that they spend a good deal of time acquiring provisions. However, a pixie-fairy is able to forage enough food to sustain itself in any environment where plant and insect life are plentiful. Some sages speculate – but have been unable to prove – that pixie-fairy consumption of free magical energy prevents environmental magic levels from rising to the point that formerly harmless species mutate into monstrous forms.

Topping the pixie-fairy's list of natural enemies are the grel, who seek pixie-fairies out and devour them in hopes of gaining magical energy from their corpses. When the two races encounter one another, combat is usually constant and savage. Only the most foolish pixie-fairies trust a grel.

Throughout their history, pixie-fairies have had several beneficial dealings with elves, and often make a token payment of goods or services to elven rulers, if the pixie-fairy settlement lies in elven lands. For the most part, however, they are content to remain in their own isolated territories and let the other races 'live and let live.' They seem to like most halflings and tolerate dwarves (even if they do not understand why they live beneath the ground). They dislike humans, for history teaches them that the race of man is filled with excellent liars and deceivers.

Pixie-fairies tend to view most other fey in the same way as they would a distant cousin. Few rise through the pixie-fairy clan structure, but pixie-fairies are willing to give them a chance to prove themselves worthy. After all, they share a common bond of heritage.

Pixie Meet:

Once every six years, all pixie-fairies must make a pilgrimage of sorts back to the Village of the Elders (the traditional founding village or homeland of their particular clan) for a week-long festival. Pixie Meet is a matter of tradition and paying homage to the clan. The entire month leading up to Pixie Meet is referred to as the Gathering. During this time, pixie-fairies begin to arrive and the organizers set up pavilions, tables and other facilities in preparation.

The opening ceremony is a remarkable sight. The high priest (or priestess) is carried to the center of the Meet by flying pixie-fairy clerics of the highest ranks. The high priest rides in a special basket-chair called the 'arboredan.' As the high priest enters, every musician plays a lively tune written specially for the occasion and circulated six months before the Meet. Once he lands, the high priest speaks to the assemblage, extolling the clan(s) and the virtues of pixie-fairy life. After the speech, most pixie-fairies mingle to seek out old friends or partners for entertainment (songs, poetry, sex and so on).

The second day of Pixie Meet is known as the Casting of Blessings. On this day, the clerics bless all present and may join to summon great blessings on entire clans, settlements or kingdoms. Otherwise, this day is much like the first, and drinking and partying continues unabated.

Only during the third day of the Meet, the Forging of Friendship, are intercourse and other such intimate acts forbidden. Instead, all present socialize in order to meet as many others as possible. Neutral representatives try to resolves disputes between individuals and clans. For those not involved in disputes, many art displays, magical entertainment, plays and games take place during this time. The Forging of Friendship is when pixie-fairies draw together.

The fourth day, the Feast of Joy, is a huge party with every delicacy possible. The feast lasts for hours and includes entertainers trying to outdo each other for the amusement of the crowd. Dancing, singing and the playing of musical instruments are constant themes. The first course is always accompanied by the traditional aria "Bounty of the Glen" (or Bounty of the Isle, or so on, depending on the location of the Meet). After the feast, from midnight on the fourth day until dawn of the fifth, is the Revel. The Revel involves drinking massive amounts of dandelion wine while singing silly limericks.

The fifth day is the Dispensing of Honors, where the clan ruler grants special positions within the clan, and other honors, including appointing the organizer of the next clan Pixie Meet. The sixth day includes more festivities and feasts. Closing ceremonies beginning at dusk, when the magic-users create an impressive display filled with illusions and other magical pyrotechnics.

On the seventh day, the festival culminates with all the attendees participating in a unique magical ceremony never witnessed by outsiders. To begin, clerics sing a somber hymn as rows of pixie-kin kneel respectfully in a circle. The high priests then lead the company in a special chant. As the chant and song continue, visible streams of magical energy swirl from the assembled crowd and slowly gather in the clearing at the center of the circle. As the chant continues, the energy continues to gather and spin until it resembles a slowly spinning energy orb of an amber color.

When visible energy no longer flows from the assembled faerie-kind, the music becomes livelier and more melodious. The Amber Horde orb slowly begins to spin in the other direction, and the magical energy streams return and spread forth into the assembled multitude. After several more minutes, the orb dissipates entirely and both chant and song end. Each pixie-fairy then rests for several moments in silence, until the high priest steps forward and declares that both the ceremony and the Pixie Meet are at an end. Most pixie-fairies spend the next few hours saying goodbyes and partings to distant friends, before returning home.

Religion:

The deity most commonly worshiped is Raconteur, although the Guardian, the Holy Mother, the Bear, the Laugher and the Riftmaster all have followers among the pixie-fairies. They generally avoid the Mule, the Landlord and the Overlord.

Pixie-fairies also believe in the Realm of Faerie, an outer plane whose exact relationship to other planes remains unclear and unproven. Those who claim to have visited this realm report it as a lush, beautiful garden stretching as far as the eye can see. Great stone castles sit in distant vales and atop immense mountains, yet it seems to take only a few steps to reach them. The sun is a pale yellow orb, but still provides good light and comfortable warmth. Others claim it to be a harsh, snowswept land ruled over by a dark queen. Some pixie-fairies believe that the land's appearance depends upon the viewer, while others argue that the realm's magical nature means that alternate versions exist simultaneously, and that by somehow 'shifting sideways,' one may be able to visit the alternate Faerie realms. Like the land, the native creatures seem to vary with each story. Most are said to resemble the fey of Tellene, but with more powerful aspects of beauty, good and evil.

Regardless, time is said to flow strangely in this land, and visitors not of the fey blood should be prepared, for they may find that a hundred years have passed in a single day. Even worse, they may age one or more decades upon their exit.

On Tellene:

Pixie-fairies hold no known lands, save for a few small acres deep in vast wooded areas. They are most common in the Kalalali Forest, the Fyban Forest and the Lendelwood. It was once said that all pixie-fairies left the Edosi Forest in a mass exodus, due to the murders of their kind by the Kalamaran Empire, intent on expanding its logging and shipbuilding industry. Rumor has it that a militaristic clan of pixie-fairies assists the guerilla tactics of the Edosi elves.

The pixie-fairy name for a member of his or her own species is 'paelifa,' which roughly translates into Merchant's Tongue as 'the joined ones.'

---

[1]*Each pixie-fairy carries gems valuing 5d4p sp. Settlements can contain small amounts of wealth in the form of precious gems and jewels of all types.*

[2]*According to grel mages, pixie-fairies are magically delicious. Furthermore, a mage of any race can consume a pixie-fairy to restore up to 140 spent Spell Points.*

RAKSHASA

Also Known As: Rakkosh, Srinpo

As we burst into the cargo hold, an unexpected sight met our eyes. A number of thin, dusky-skinned men wearing loincloths, burlap jerkins, rope belts and tattered brown cloaks knelt before a figure on a wooden throne — a great tiger that stood, walked and wore robed finery like a man. Its servants (as I felt the men must be) stood swiftly to their feet, grabbed the scimitars lying by their sides and rushed at us, screaming in their strange Dejy dialect that I could not understand.

The battle was a fierce one, as my companions and I fought both the fanatical cultists and their great man-tiger leader, the latter of whom easily outlasted his servants. Finally, a lucky shot from my arcane-touched crossbow took down the strange beast and ended the fight, in time enough for the cleric to heal our dying friends. As he did so, I cautiously approached the creature with dagger in hand, ready to slash its throat and ensure the fight was well and truly over.

And so it was, but I was fortunate enough to also hear the monster's dying words. "Man-ape," he choked up at me in crude Svimohzish, "you are foolish, but not so foolish as monkeys, I think. Perhaps I should have stayed in old Shwimajomwhi [or so I can best transcribe the name] and been content to rule over such a kingdom. Perhaps you will—" He never finished these words, and expired without need of my dagger to send him on his dark path.

So far, my researches into the place-name of Shwimajomwhi have yielded no results. I can only surmise is that it is a city or ruin occupied by monkeys either of common stock or unusual simian intelligence, and that it lies somewhere deep inside the Vohven Jungle or another of the dark, dangerous woodlands of the Svimohzish Isle. - ⚕

Rakshasas are supernatural humanoids with sharp teeth and long nails, the urge to defile and desecrate holy places and a taste for human and demi-human flesh. Though it can transmogrify into other beings, a rakshasa's true form is a bipedal feline creature with a tiger's head, a fur-covered body and arms ending in a tiger's claws. When transforming from human to feline, any clothes or gear worn are either shredded or fall away from the body as if removed by hand.

In any shape, a rakshasa's hands are palm backwards (the reverse of a human hand), though the creature can turn his wrist enough to pass for a human when in that form.

Most rakshasas stand about 6 feet tall and weigh around 175 pounds. A female rakshasa is called a rakshasi.

Combat/Tactics:

Rakshasas are cunning, reading the minds of potential enemies (as the mage's sixth level *Mind Reading* spell, at will) and *Transmogrifying* into whatever that foe considers friendly or innocuous. In addition, all Rakkosk have mage abilities of at least 12th level. They prefer to use these magical abilities foremost, resorting to conventional attacks as a last resort.

In its tiger-headed form, a rakshasa can grab a foe with its feline claws inflicting 2d4p+5 damage. Two successive hits

SIZE COMPARISON

A rakshasa often engages its foe in seemingly harmless conversation — but beware. For this cunning adversary has the ability to read minds and extract secrets from such chattering. Although evil, they are highly charismatic and masters of manipulation. A rakshasa is only ever faithful to one cause — himself.

6 ft

3 ft

means it has ensnared an opponent in its grasp and will subsequently bite at its neck. This latter attack automatically succeeds and causes a d6+5 point wound against which armor DR does not apply. A rakshasa's grip can be broken with a successful knock-back or Feat of Strength (vs. d20p+10).

In any other guise, they will employ an appropriate melee weapon gaining +4 damage. If disarmed or in desperate straits, they may resort to natural weaponry (long nails capable of inflicting d3p+5 per hand) but prefer not to bite considering it uncivilized.

Habitat/Society:

Rakshasas can be found in many climes, though they seem to prefer forests and grasslands where they can dwell in isolated lairs. Though they are mostly solitary creatures, they do keep a variety of slaves or followers to attend to their needs. Mating occurs as desired, on the rare occasions that a rakshasa and a rakshasi meet.

The exact length of a rakshasa's lifespan is unknown, but certainly lasts for hundreds of years.

Ecology:

Rakshasa often ally themselves with other powerful evil beings in exchange for frequent opportunities to kill and dine on human and demi-human flesh. However, a rakshasa will twist the wording of any agreement to its own ends, hardly maintaining the letter of the agreement and rarely the spirit.

The origins of the rakshasa are obscure, spoken of only in the scattered passages of certain ancient, worm-eaten tomes. Unfortunately, these are often contradictory. The Canto of Zorvhan, for instance, notes that the rakshasa are spirits bound in magically crafted flesh of their own designs, while the Scroll of Saint Boravir states that they are forest-dwelling creatures descended from a coupling between man and demon. Other folktales claim they are spirits encased in flesh, while others even state that they were created from the foot of the deity known as the Great Huntress.

What is truly known is that rakshasas are notorious for desecrating graves and holy sites of good and even neutral-aligned temples, shrines and churches. It is also true that they are vicious villains who take great joy in the slaughter of humans and demi-humans, particularly clerics.

On Tellene:

Treasure hunters have reported battling rakshasas in several areas of Tellene, including southern Brandobia. However, the greater number of appearances in the southern Imperial lands of Tarisato over the last three decades, with rakshasas supposedly forming alliances with the local lords of dubious reputation, seems to place their primary territory in the Obakasek Jungle.

There are folktales of creatures like rakshasas but with white (rather than orange) fur, living above the steppes north of Lake Jorakk, but these are surely naught but stories.

[1] When used as an additional material component in any illusionary spell (with a duration longer than instantaneous), a rakshasa claw increases the spell duration by 50%.

RAKSHASA

HIT POINTS:	22+7d8
SIZE/WEIGHT:	M/175 lbs.
TENACITY:	Steady
INTELLIGENCE:	Smart
FATIGUE FACTOR:	1

SPEED 5 — ATTACK +12 — INIT -4 — DMG REDUCTION
+9 — 25
DEFENSE — see below
medium REACH — DAMAGE — 8 — TOP SAVE ▼

MOVEMENT

CRAWL:	10
WALK:	15
JOG:	20
RUN:	25
SPRINT:	30

SAVES

PHYSICAL:	+27
MENTAL:	+33
DODGE:	+30

ATTACK: Claws or nails deal 2d4p+5 each; held victim subject to d6p+5 bite attack (no armor DR); may use melee weapons with a +4 Dmg bonus; Casts spells as a mage of 12th+ level; Initiative roll is two dice types lower

SPECIAL DEFENSES: Against true magical weapons (+6 and greater), rakshasas have DR 6. Can read minds and transmogrify at will.

GENERAL INFO

ACTIVITY CYCLE:	Any
NO. APPEARING:	1
% CHANCE IN LAIR:	25%
FREQUENCY:	Scarce
ALIGNMENT:	Neutral Evil
VISION TYPE:	Standard
AWARENESS/SENSES:	Standard (Initiative die type is two better)
HABITAT:	Richly appointed lairs
DIET:	Carnivorous
ORGANIZATION:	Leader
CLIMATE/TERRAIN:	Any

YIELD

MEDICINAL:	nil
SPELL COMPONENTS:	claw, in illusion spells[1]
HIDE/TROPHY:	yes, in feline form
TREASURE:	valuable works of art
EDIBLE:	yes, but considered close to cannibalism
OTHER:	nil
EXPERIENCE POINT VALUE:	1425

R

RAT, GIANT

Also Known As: Sumatran

When I first saw the preserved carcass of a giant rat, I thought it must surely be an aberration, or else some rare and exotic species that dwelt in only one particular habitat. Its silver-brown coat of thick long fur had been handled well by the taxidermist, and I deduced that this creature came from a cold or wet location at a high altitude — a speculation that its owner quickly confirmed.

The next day, whilst I still smarted over the high price I paid the man for that unique specimen of rodent, my companions and I ventured into the Geanavese undercity. I know not whether it was the sweat running down my face, the foul vapors in my nose or the intriguing moss growing on the opposite wall, but I confess I was not paying attention to my feet. Suddenly, I put my foot down on the back of, yes, a giant rat identical to the one I'd seen the previous night. This one had not yet suffered the taxidermist's art, however, and sank its teeth into my leg with ferocious glee. As I battered it in hopes of loosing its grip, still more continued to appear until we were completely surrounded. In the end, I gained more giant rat corpses than I could ever care to dissect, but I never found that rat seller again. - ᚠ

Wherever people settle and congregate these nasty vermin are sure to be found.

Giant rats have the large incisors, flattened ears, beady eyes, pointed nose, whiskers, hairless tail, four elongated feet and rough fur of the common rat. However, giant rats are by definition much larger. They grow to about three feet in length, excluding the tail, which stretches out another two to three feet. They weigh in at about 20 pounds.

As with common rats, giant rats can stand on their hind feet and use their front paws to grasp food, although they can neither attack nor wield items with these digits.

In color, giant rats range from black to brown to gray. There are even some who display the albino trait and are pure white with pink eyes.

Combat/Tactics:

The biggest danger that giant rats pose is of disease. They live, eat and revel in filth, and because of this are prime carriers for every type of deadly disease. Not all rats, and certainly not all swarms, are diseased, but when one rat carries disease then so does the entire swarm.

Giant rats can also be aggressive, and will generally attack people, either out of fear or hunger. Their teeth can inflict d4p+1 points of damage. Anyone bitten must also make a saving throw or become infected with a disease.

Giant rats are somewhat intelligent, and they cooperate during an attack, so that they try to surround a person or group of foes.

SIGN/TRACKS

SIZE COMPARISON

Note the opposable thumb on the front paw.

Fore
Hind

Always a nuisance, the giant rat poses even more of a threat when food is in short supply. These vermin will stop at nothing to get sustenance and can be extremely aggressive. I have heard stories of giant rats dragging away dogs as well as small children!

6 ft
3 ft

They can be kept at bay with fire, which they are instinctually afraid of.

Rat Bite Fever:

The most common disease is rat bite fever, a contagion with a communicability of d20p-2 and a severity of d20p+7. If the PC fails his saving throw (d20p+CON) against communicability, he contracts the disease and must check for severity. If this second saving throw succeeds, the PC suffers only the Minor Effect. If failed, he suffers the Major Effect.

Minor Effect: Within d3p hours, a bitten individual sees a rash appear around the wound. Within another hour, it spreads over the entire body. For the next 24+3d12p hours, the victim suffers a 1-point penalty to Attack, Defense and Damage, after which the rash begins to dissipate.

Major Effect: As above, but the rash grows more severe and irritating. For 3d3p days, the victim suffers a 3-point penalty to Attack, Defense and Damage. The rash then begins to dissipate.

Habitat/Society:

They are social animals, living in swarms of 3-30, roaming attics, walls, roofs, trees and burrows. However, they can also be found in caves, in forests near rivers, and even in dungeons and other structures. They are good diggers, and can excavate burrows quite quickly. They often cause structural damage in buildings as they dig through walls.

Giant rats like damp areas, so they are usually found not too far away from a source of water. Some types of giant rats have made some of the swamps on Tellene their homes and seem entrenched in that habitat.

Because of their love of decay and dank conditions, these vermin are scarce (but not unheard of) in deserts or any areas with a dry climate and little vegetation. They like to have some sort of cover in which to hide and sleep during the daylight hours.

Giant rats are active breeders, and female rats can produce up to five litters per year. Gestation is one month. A litter usually consists of seven pups.

Because rat pups are born blind, they use ultrasonic vocalizations to locate their mothers, but, as they grow older, the use of this ability decreases as a defense against male rats that will undoubtedly eat them. Adult males use ultrasonic vocalizations when they feel threatened, and adult females will use this ability during mating.

They may also emit audible chirps that sound a bit like eerie laughter, when they are actively enjoying mating or a meal.

Ecology:

Giant rats are omnivorous and opportune scavengers, feasting primarily upon carrion, grain and other livestock food, but will eat almost anything. In some of the poorer or more remote settlements, they have been known to snatch babies from their cradles and devour them.

On Tellene:

They can be found all over Tellene in temperate, or warmer, regions. Some of the cities with the largest known giant rat infestations are: Balelido, Ashakulagh, P'Bapar, Giilia, Xaarum, Monam-Ahnozh, Burzumagh, and Ronazagh.

GIANT RAT

HIT POINTS:	6+1d4
SIZE/WEIGHT:	S/20 lbs.
TENACITY:	Cowardly
INTELLIGENCE:	Animal, High
FATIGUE FACTOR:	-3

SPEED		INIT
10	ATTACK 0	DMG REDUCTION 0
DEFENSE -1		1
short REACH	d4p+1 DAMAGE	TOP SAVE 7

ATTACK:
Any bite from a disease-carrying rat necessitates a communicability check. Multiple bites increase the chance of contracting a disease but not not increase its severity.

MOVEMENT

CRAWL:	1¼
WALK:	2½
JOG:	5
RUN:	7½
SPRINT:	10

SAVES

PHYSICAL:	+0
MENTAL:	+0
DODGE:	+3

GENERAL INFO

ACTIVITY CYCLE:	Nocturnal
NO. APPEARING:	3-30
% CHANCE IN LAIR:	10%
FREQUENCY:	Ubiquitous
ALIGNMENT:	Non
VISION TYPE:	Poor, avoid bright lights
AWARENESS/SENSES:	Enhanced taste, touch, smell
HABITAT:	Wetlands, sewers, ruins, and similar
DIET:	Omnivorous
ORGANIZATION:	Swarm
CLIMATE/TERRAIN:	Any, save arctic

YIELD

MEDICINAL:	nil
SPELL COMPONENTS:	nil
HIDE/TROPHY:	stuffed bodies may be sold as curiousity pieces
TREASURE:	incidental
EDIBLE:	yes, but possible disease unless cooked to well-done
OTHER:	nil

EXPERIENCE POINT VALUE: 12

R

ROC Also Known As: Rukh

The roc is a wonderful predator in that it frequently gathers items of value while hunting, yet cares little for these treasures. This speaks to me of an opportunity for some victimless larceny.

Certainly there are dangers in such an endeavor but no less so than stealing from a creature or individual acutely aware of its fortune and dedicated to one degree or another in maintaining control over said possessions. Frankly, I am too old to relish the danger of a big heist. Let the young and foolish engage in jobs that too often devolve into armed robbery.

The most important portion of a heist is surveillance and this type of operation is no different. Obviously you need to locate the roc's nest. This is a more difficult task than it might appear at first as the giant bird usually roosts at significant altitude. Be prepared for some camping in the mountains.

Once you've located a nest, you now need to ascertain whether or not it consists of a nesting pair. Again, this can be accomplished by reconnoitering. Above all else, you want to make absolutely certain that there are neither eggs nor hatchlings in the aerie. While rocs may not care one bit for sundry baubles their prey may have carried, they most definitely are alert to the threat of predators that could harm their young. You do not want to be misidentified as a weasel and face the wrath of a seven-ton mother bird!

Obviously, rocs nest in high mountain eyries. This in itself should prove but a minor inconvenience to an experienced thief as it requires climbing skills that should have long ago been mastered. The time to strike is when the birds are out hunting. I do realize that by this point you have likely grown tired of bird watching but – to be honest – there are worse ways to spend one's time. Knuckle down, we're almost there.

You're only going to get one shot at it because the bird's gonna know someone's been prowling around. Take the time to search the nest but don't dally. If you're lucky, you may come across some nice bits of gold or silver treasure. More likely though is elephant or mammoth ivory – not as portable but a nice find regardless. - ⚶

During my stay in Meznamish, I once saw a rukh carry away a bull elephant!

The roc is one of the most impressive beasts anyone might see on Tellene. Its wingspan, some 75 feet across, is enough to give anyone pause. Some of the creature's wing feathers are over 10 feet long and it weighs in at a whopping 15,000 pounds, with a body at least 25 feet long.

Its talons are strong and tipped with razor sharp claws. Most rocs are of an overall white in color, while others have light golden-brown plumage on their heads and necks. Like smaller birds of prey, its hooked beak can easily tear flesh from bone. Its legs are about the size of tree trunks.

A roc's eyes have large pupils, causing minimal light diffraction and giving them incredibly keen eyesight. They can see clearly for up to 3 miles.

Combat/Tactics:

When hunting, the rukh's giant wings enable it to travel swiftly and easily scan vast areas for prey. When it spots likely quarry, the gigantic bird swoops down digging its talons into the victim's flesh A hit deals 12d6p points of damage and ensnares the victim in the bird's talons. Escape requires a Feat of Strength (vs d20p+19). If this attack incapacitates the

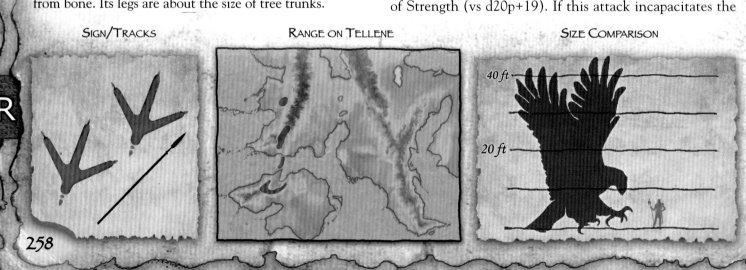

SIGN/TRACKS   RANGE ON TELLENE   SIZE COMPARISON

40 ft

20 ft

prey then and there, the roc may stop to eat, each bite inflicting 7d6p points of damage. Alternatively, it may fly away and drop the victim from a great height, so as to break it apart and make for easier feeding.

If compelled to fight terrestrially, a roc pecks with its enormous beak (for 7d6p) and then alternatively slashes foes with its taloned feet – the latter attack inflicting 6d6p damage per successful slash.

Though fierce creatures, rocs are unlikely to engage in a protracted fight on the ground in which they forfeit numerous advantages. In such a contest, they are wont to fly off and seek less determined prey. They may, however, simply be biding their time and awaiting another opportunity to swoop down and snatch away a victim.

Habitat/Society:

Rukh maintain territories that may extend over several hundred square miles. They nest in high places including cliffs and the largest of trees, building massive nests to which they may return for several breeding years.

Rocs are monogamous and may remain together for several decades or possibly for life. If a roc's mate is killed, it eventually finds another, but often lives for decades in solitude. These single rukh are often the ones adventurers meet, for they tend to be more aggressive and unpredictable.

Females lay one to two eggs, and both parents incubate them for two to three months. Female rocs are extremely protective over their eggs. Anything that threatens an egg is immediately attacked. When the eggs hatch, the dominant chick kills its sibling and eats it. The lone chick fledges within four months and grows its full adult plumage within its sixth year.

The average roc lives roughly 90 years.

Ecology:

A roc's prey is predominantly large herd animals of the equine or bovine variety, though they also feed upon bears, elephants, hippopotami and other large animals.

As avian apex predators, they fear little, and with good cause; their mere size is enough to ensure that no simple-minded predator would dare try to prey on a roc.

They occasionally compete with other large avians (e.g., griffyns) for nesting space. Unless outnumbered, however, the roc is rarely the loser in these battles.

On Tellene:

Sailors claim that rocs nest on the Dragon's Teeth, those peaks of once fierce mountains that protrude from the watery Straits of Svimohzia. It does seem that rocs are most often found in the lands to the immediate north (the Elenon mountains and Eldrose forest) and south (the Dashahn and Tanezh mountains) of the straits. Rocs have also been reported flying above Sentinel's Grove, where mammoth trees grow tall within the heart of the Lendelwood.

[1] *Adding a roc feather as an additional material component in the casting of the mage's fifth level Levitation spell (or other flight spells) increases the spell duration by 25%.*

ROC

HIT POINTS:	40+18d8
SIZE/WEIGHT:	E/7½ tons
TENACITY:	Brave
INTELLIGENCE:	Animal, High
FATIGUE FACTOR:	-1

MOVEMENT

CRAWL:	5
WALK:	10
JOG:	15
RUN:	20
FLY:	50

SAVES

PHYSICAL:	+31
MENTAL:	+19
DODGE:	+27

ATTACK:
Rocs employ a twin claw grab (12d6p) from altitude that also tightly ensnares its prey – may either peck at trapped prey or drop it from a great height; if fighting terrestrially, its enormous beak can deal 7d6p points of damage and each of its sharp taloned feet 6d6

SPECIAL DEFENSES:
Flight

GENERAL INFO

ACTIVITY CYCLE:	Crepuscular
NO. APPEARING:	1-2
% CHANCE IN LAIR:	15%
FREQUENCY:	Unusual
ALIGNMENT:	Non
VISION TYPE:	Farsight; can spot prey up to 3 miles
AWARENESS/SENSES:	Standard
HABITAT:	Nests in mountains or mammoth trees
DIET:	Carnivorous
ORGANIZATION:	Individuals
CLIMATE/TERRAIN:	Temperate to tropical highlands

YIELD

MEDICINAL:	nil
SPELL COMPONENTS:	feather, in levitating and flight spells[1]
HIDE/TROPHY:	a giant roc feather is an impressive token
TREASURE:	incidental
EDIBLE:	yes
OTHER:	nil
EXPERIENCE POINT VALUE:	2500

R

RUSALKA

Also Known As: Swamp Witch

As an acolyte yet ensconced within my tender years, I hadeth cause to accompany my mentor into the Eb'Sareb Swamp. To what end I was scarce appraised yet joyous was I at prospects of adventure. There foul fortune didst us waylay, for our barge didst founder and carry our precious stores to the murky bottom.

As prospects of reaching our goal didst sink as surely as our vessel, we made haste to call upon the nearest village to replace what the swamp gremlins didst rob us of.

T'was the second night our most arduous trek back when I did sit still and quiet on a mossy log it being my role to watch for any manner of swamp-being that mightest seek to take our encampment unawares. The fire was but a dull flame as struggle it did with the vaporous fog. The endemic insects hadest ceased their noisesome chatter, and I heardest nary a sound about the camp save the low breathing my companions did issue.

Recallest these details in specificity do I for it was then that a cool, damp mist issued forth from the gloomy distance, thickening what I had perchanced to believe was already air most humid. Thereupon the soft voice of a woman breached the silence, crying out from a distance. "Man, yonder, by the fire," she began. "I am lost and you must save me."

"No man am I but a maiden fair and true," replied I.

I was taken as unaware as a dozing babe when through the fog the image of her face did break. A matron of some 40 summers did make her way timorously through the swamp. In my state of bewilderment, I couldst but gaze upon the wind tousling her long hair. As if compelled, I then strode most briskly towards her for reasons I couldest not fathom. She too reached for me in kind, but her hands fell upon my neck and grasped me tight but released before doing me harm. "In truth you are but a lass," said she. "No harm would I do you. Be gone and return not." - ◉

Many a would-be rescuer has fallen prey to these damsels in 'distress.'

Rusalka are the undead spirits of women who met an untimely end through drowning, whether by murder or suicide. These creatures now haunt the waters where they met their tragic end.

The face of a rusalka always appears proud and haughty, occasionally distorted with the cruelty of their final moments. Rusalkas have pale white skin, disheveled white hair, long dirty nails and drooping breasts. Rusalkas cloak themselves in mists and light white fogs, drifting along the banks of rivers or over the marshes that are their homes. On rarer occasions, rusalkas may be found in wells or mills, where they terrorize the locals with their seductive calls.

The rusalka mist is always cool and very damp, leaving thick traces of water on gear and clothing. As the mist settles on the hapless victims, the rusalka makes her appearance. She rises slowly from the water, her face alone breaking the surface. Those who see her glimpse what looks much like a corpse in the water. In a sing-song voice, she then calls out to those present, asking for aid against the perils of the river. Her voice appears caught up by the mist, seemingly coming from one direction and then another. A rusalka never attacks women except in defense, unless it was a woman who was the cause of her death.

Whether the evil creature uses her charm or false beauty, many a poor fool has moved off into the water to rescue her - only to meet a tragic end. The rusalka waits until her victim comes within reach, so as to attack from close quarters. She wraps her arms around the victim, waiting for him to pull her from the water, then tries to throttle him. She chokes her victims slowly, often allowing them a respite only to commence again. She also may hold the victim under the water, lift-

Take heed when ye doth hear the beckoning call of a damsel in distress. Be not the randy lad eager for a grateful maiden's private succor but gather thine companions. For if the plea be true, surely it is better to share the laud as gentlemen. And if it prove false, a group doth prove less desirous prey...

WILL FACTOR
12

SIZE COMPARISON

6 ft

3 ft

ing them back from a watery death seemingly at the last minute.

On other occasions, the rusalka assumes a pleasing form and offers herself as reward for her rescue. She is always gentle in her lovemaking, taking great pains to prove that she means no harm. Alas, her nature is too strong, and eventually she kills these men, strangling or drowning them without sufferance.

If more than one person approaches the rusalka, she slips beneath the water, moves off a little and rises again. She calls more ardently, trying to separate at least one person from the party or group. She often succeeds, as few can resist offering aid to a woman in need.

Should an enterprising mercenary deliver the villain that originally killed the rusalka, and allow her to slay him, she is mollified and the curse of her creation is broken. Before vanishing into true death, the rusalka grants her champion the one thing she can give – any knowledge of her life or of the region.

Combat/Tactics:

Rusalka go to great pains to separate individuals from the group, usually targeting the most handsome or the one who seems most arrogant. At this point, she tries to charm him (opposed save *vs. d20p+10*) and pull him into the water to kill.

If her charming fails, she attacks by grabbing. After the second successful grab attack, the rusalka begins choking her victim for an automatic d4p, ignoring any armor (though not natural defenses such as a thick hide, etc.). Every 10 seconds thereafter, the rusalka continues to deal an additional d4p points of strangulation damage.

Women are never deliberately targeted by Swamp Witches and are immune to their charming powers. If attacked by a woman, a Rusalka will defend herself – possibly resulting in the death of the female assailant.

On Tellene:

Some Kalamaran scholars say that the ancient origins of the rusalka lie in the Ep'Sarab Swampland, where three witches lay buried in three separate, but adjoining mounds. In the year 458 IR, river pirates led by the famous brigand Caran Bluetooth plundered the mounds. When they did so they roused the souls of the three witches. These evil incarnations rose from the dead in raging madness, hounding the greater part of the crew to death. Only a few escaped, fleeing south down the Badato River. One of these, Caran's brother Malaran, is thought to have escaped with a powerful magic ring. He fled into the swamps and wandered listlessly, without home or any kind of shelter. The witches, not satisfied with destroying the pirates, lay a curse on the swamp and all the water that earned the pirates their livelihood.

The curse had greater impact than the witches ever dared hope and soon the spirits of women tormented in life rose from the surrounding wetlands; the rusalka had come to Kalamar. The plague soon spread, being reported as far north as the Otekapu Swamps and the E'Liral River, and as far south as the E'Korus River. They have become a serious plague on certain stretches of these rivers and merchants grumble and complain about their loses in ship's captains and crew. The merchant guilds are clamoring for the local rulers to hire soldiers to destroy these creatures, but few respond. The guilds, left to their own devices, are hiring men and priests to wage war on these strange creatures.

It is thought by the learned that if the items stolen from the women, particularly the ring, are returned and the bodies set back in their mounds that the curse will end. If there is truth to these tales, none may say.

RUSALKA

HIT POINTS:	19+4d8
SIZE/WEIGHT:	M/120 lbs.
TENACITY:	Steady
INTELLIGENCE:	Average
FATIGUE FACTOR:	n/a

SPEED 5 — INIT -1
ATTACK +8 — DMG REDUCTION
DEFENSE +6 — 9
see below
medium REACH — DAMAGE — TOP SAVE n/a

MOVEMENT

CRAWL:	2½
WALK:	5
JOG:	10
RUN:	15
SWIM:	20

SAVES

PHYSICAL:	+7
MENTAL:	immune
DODGE:	+8

ATTACK: Rusalkas first use their Charm (*vs. d20p+10*). If unsuccessful, they grab and deal strangulation damage of d4p (ignoring armor DR) every 10 seconds; (*a successful clerical turning will naturally force her to release her grasp as she is repelled - a knockback though will not; a victim may break her grasp with a Feat of Strength vs. d20p+15*); women are immune to the Swamp Witch's charm powers are never attacked except in self-defense

GENERAL INFO

ACTIVITY CYCLE:	Any
NO. APPEARING:	1
% CHANCE IN LAIR:	70%
FREQUENCY:	Unusual
ALIGNMENT:	Neutral Evil
VISION TYPE:	Undead Sight
AWARENESS/SENSES:	Standard
HABITAT:	Swamps, rivers, lakes
DIET:	n/a
ORGANIZATION:	Individuals
CLIMATE/TERRAIN:	Any wetlands, save frozen

YIELD

MEDICINAL:	nil
SPELL COMPONENTS:	nil
HIDE/TROPHY:	nil
TREASURE:	incidental
EDIBLE:	no
OTHER:	nil
EXPERIENCE POINT VALUE:	575

R

SATYR

Also Known As: Byrein, Tovine

The lively joyous notes from a satyr's panpipes can have a powerful enchanting effect.

Perhaps the most telling comment about satyrs is that they are mentioned in a series of Dejy drinking songs so perverse that certain communities actually ban them. In fact, the songs happen to be quite accurate. Satyrs think of nothing but participating in wild drinking binges and writhing in lengthy, sordid orgies. They seem to always have, if not an abundance, at least an adequate supply of wine or women. Human women — respectable women — even innocent maidens, seem to be spellbound by the creatures. I've seen them follow a group of the randy fellows into the woods, leaving behind husbands, children, and even religious vows to take part in unrestricted acts of hedonism.

My taxonomic analysis of the hairy men agrees with the anecdotal evidence that relates them to the goat. They sport two horns of various shapes and sizes, no doubt depending on age and family relation. They also have the hind legs of a goat, though only the youngest children cavort about on all fours. The adults stand erect and seem quite dextrous, consuming food and drink with great rapidity and relish even while they dance about the fire pit. I note also that their eyes have horizontal slit-shaped pupils, and wonder if they also hold a four-chambered goat stomach within their bellies.

The horns of a mature saytr.

I end these preliminary notes here, as the woodland folk are keen to carouse with us here in our wooded camp, and my companions show no hesitation to join in their drinking, songs and personal gratification. Myself, I find the music of the hairy men soothing, but it does not inspire in me this urge for revelry. Perhaps I am simply too in tune with my higher nature to be swayed. I shall listen again and see if my opinion changes with a fresh hearing. - ⚘

These roguish folk have the lower body and hind legs of a goat and the naked upper body of a human man or woman, with elongated, animalistic ears and two horns on their foreheads. Their hair is long and curly and usually brown or black. Male satyrs sport beards, which some say resembles the hair on the chin of a billy goat.

Young satyrs start out with nubby horns that grow longer as they mature. Along with this horn growth, most male satyrs also lose the hair from their heads upon reaching middle age. Older males tend to have chubbier bodies – a symptom of excessive drinking and celebrating.

Most adults stand 5 feet tall and weigh about 100 pounds.

Combat/Tactics:

Satyrs carry panpipes, which they play to produce enchanting music. Anyone hearing this music must make a saving throw (*vs. d20p+5*) or fall under the effects of the music (which is equivalent to a Charm spell).

Male satyrs can be dangerous to human women who refuse their advances and who do not fall under the charming sway of the flute music. Satyrs refuse to take no for an answer. They may force their advances or abduct a woman who resists.

Satyrs sometimes wield daggers, though they may use other weapons as needed. Female satyrs, for instance, often utilize bows to hunt for food.

SIGN/TRACKS

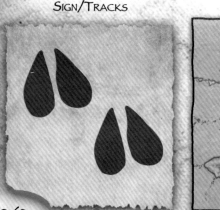

RANGE ON TELLENE

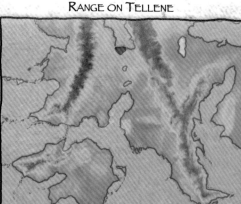

SIZE COMPARISON

6 ft

3 ft

Habitat/Society:

Satyrs live in temperate to tropical climes, avoiding the cold north steppes, and are active throughout the year. They make their homes in caves or sheltered groves in the woods, preferring to live in the open rather than expend the effort to construct even the simplest of lean-tos.

Males tend to roam about, almost constantly, seeking pleasure throughout the day, sleeping as little as possible. When they encounter other sapient creatures, they may attempt to lure them to a party, charm them, steal their valuables and seduce women who are especially comely. Female satyrs seem to be somewhat more sober-minded than males, for they do care for their offspring and even serve as hunters and gatherers when other resources are scarce. Male satyr behavior seems to be tolerated by females and admired by children growing up.

Male and female satyrs do mate in order to produce offspring, but the relationships between the males and females are not monogamous or affectionate. Young satyrs are quite playful, full of energy and possessing great curiosity. The children mature at the age of 40, when the boys join the older males in their exploits and the girls join the older females to be taught any hunting and survival skills.

A satyr has an average lifespan of 300 years.

Ecology:

Satyrs are omnivorous feeders, eating vegetation and animals alike, though they never take or kill more than they can consume before it spoils. They are particularly fond of wine and other spirits and may barter, cheat or steal to get it.

During the day, their lives are full of playfulness and indulgence, while at night this frivolity is replaced with maliciousness (or at least mischievousness) and cunning. Even the tunes played by their panpipes sound different.

Under the cover of darkness, satyrs may ambush travelers, as well as raid homes and farms. By using their pipes on victims, the satyr can gain both food and wealth. Any lonely building or traveler is at risk of becoming a victim in a night-time raid. After all, a life of idleness requires other, innocent creatures for it to take advantage of.

On Tellene:

Most of the major forests on Tellene have housed a drove of satyrs at one time or another. Pekal's Brindonwood, for example, has seen more satyrs than perhaps any other region.

In 493 I.R. (Imperial Reckoning), farmers north of Lake Eb'Sobet claimed that a drove was teasing their cattle to the point they would not give milk. Worse, constant stampedes in the middle of the night did damage to both property and nerves. Although a small military contingent was sent to deal with the matter, they failed to eliminate even a single satyr.

In 463 I.R., a Dejy merchant named Sharyth claimed to have lost his entire caravan to a satyr drove. When passing through the Nanakary Forest one night, Sharyth and all his guards fell victim to the creatures. A local druid found them a few days later tied to the trees, stripped of their valuables and their cargo of wine but fortunately still alive.

SATYR

HIT POINTS:	13+2d8	
SIZE/WEIGHT:	S/100 lbs.	
TENACITY:	Nervous	
INTELLIGENCE:	Bright	
FATIGUE FACTOR:	3	

SPEED		INIT
10	ATTACK +3	0
DEFENSE 0		DMG REDUCTION 2
by weapon REACH	by weapon -1	3
	DAMAGE	TOP SAVE ▼

MOVEMENT

CRAWL:	2½
WALK:	5
JOG:	10
RUN:	15
SPRINT:	20

SAVES

PHYSICAL:	+2
MENTAL:	+5
DODGE:	+3

ATTACK:
Most satyrs wield daggers (2d4p-1), but can use other weapons. Those hearing satyr music must make a saving throw (vs. d20p+5) or fall under the effects of a Charm spell.

SPECIAL DEFENSES:
none

GENERAL INFO

ACTIVITY CYCLE:	Any
NO. APPEARING:	2-8
% CHANCE IN LAIR:	45%
FREQUENCY:	Infrequent
ALIGNMENT:	Chaotic Neutral
VISION TYPE:	Standard
AWARENESS/SENSES:	Standard
HABITAT:	Caves or groves
DIET:	Omnivorous
ORGANIZATION:	Familial
CLIMATE/TERRAIN:	Temperate to tropical woodlands

YIELD

MEDICINAL:	nil
SPELL COMPONENTS:	horn, increases Charm spell's save period to 28 days
HIDE/TROPHY:	nil
TREASURE:	usually possess several rare vintages
EDIBLE:	yes; ogres often do so while drinking satyr wine
OTHER:	nil
EXPERIENCE POINT VALUE:	242

S

SCORPION, GIANT

Also Known As: Agaroshy, Vezano

My companions and I had been lately exploring a ruined chapel and its catacombs, but the falling dusk compelled us to halt our studies and we began to make our camp among its heaps of stones. As our scout took his turn at building the fire, I saw in one of those lateral recesses made by the collapse of the temple walls, two large pedipalps — black, glistening in the low firelight, armed with a great double claw. I stood staring in horror, struck dumb by the grim countenance of the thing, watching as its mouth parts, its prosoma flanked by powerful legs, then its abdomen and finally its awful stinger emerged noiselessly from the crevice, within a few feet of my ally's back.

He must have noticed my countenance, with the blood drained from my face and my hair standing up, for he whirled about to face the arthropod, whose eyes somehow seemed as fixed on his own shape as mine own eyes were on it. For a few moments he stood as stock still as I myself — then with a cry he threw out his hand and let slip a hidden knife from his sleeve. The blade shot past the creature back into the cranny from which it had come, but shook me from my fascination, permitting me to grab a flaming branch and keep the snapping claws at bay until that Fhokki lout grabbed his broadsword. His engaging it in battle allowed us time to grab our weapons from where they lay and assist him, at last putting blade into its shell with a metallic, crunching sound that at last put paid to this mortal fear. I hope I shall not soon look upon its like again. - ✦

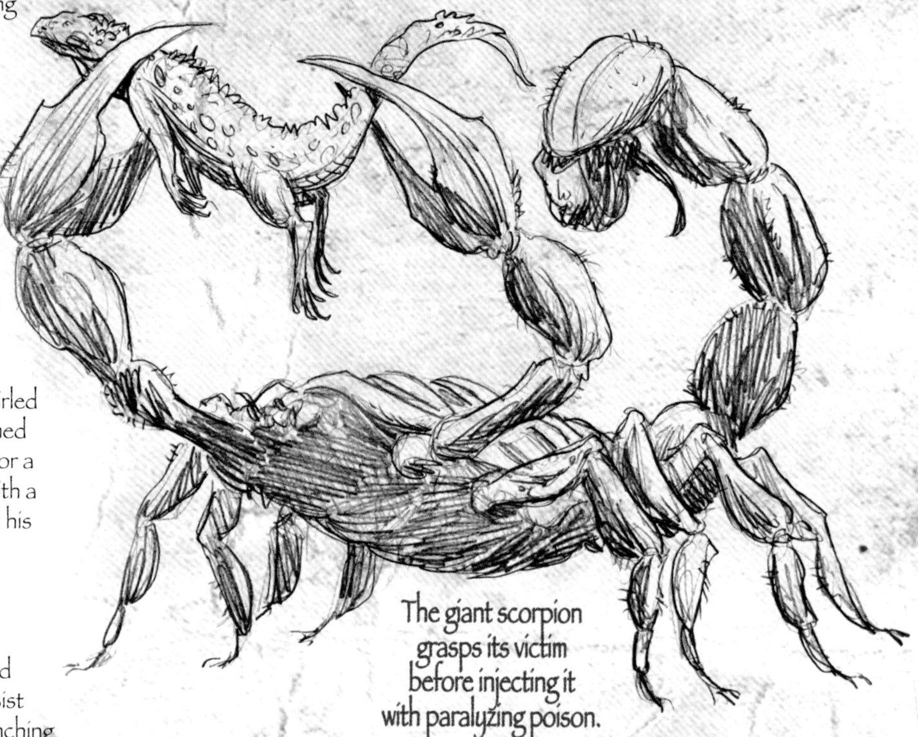

The giant scorpion grasps its victim before injecting it with paralyzing poison.

Except for size, a giant scorpion is identical to a common scorpion. This arachnid, related to spiders and mites, has eight legs, a two-part body with a cephalothorax (head), and the abdomen. The cephalothorax contains the carapace, eyes, chelicerae (mouth parts), pedipalps (claws) and the legs. The exoskeleton of the creature is tough and durable, protecting it nicely from predators.

Scorpions have two eyes atop their heads and two to five pairs of eyes along the corners. The number and positioning of the eyes depends upon the terrain they live in. There are even rumors of giant scorpions that live in dark caverns and have no eyes at all.

The tail is divided into six sections, the last of which contains its venom and the barb that it uses to inject this venom. Giant scorpion coloring ranges from light to dark brown, to yellow, light red, pink or, as in the case of cave-dwelling scorpions, off-white.

A typical giant scorpion is 2 to 3 feet long and weighs in at about 50 pounds.

Combat/Tactics:

Agaroshy hunt by rushing from concealment and attempting to grab prey with their pincers. A successful attack inflicts 2d4+3 damage and restricts its prey's movement preventing retreat and imposing a -3 Defense penalty (-6 if grabbed by both pincers).

SIGN/TRACKS	RANGE ON TELLENE	SIZE COMPARISON

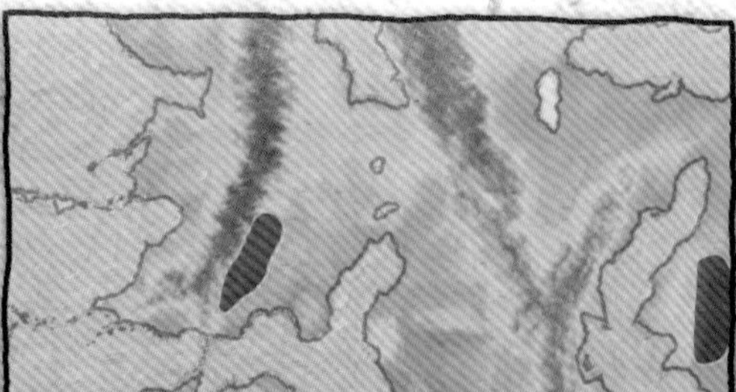

Giant scorpion tracks are often confused with those of the giant ant.

6 ft

3 ft

This grip can be broken by a Feat of Strength (vs. d20p+2 if held by one pincer or vs. d20p+8 if restrained by both) but such action precludes counterattacking for five seconds.

Once it has grabbed a victim, the vezano will substitute an attack with its stinger for the pincer (thus a foe held by one pincer will be attacked on alternate five second intervals by a stinger and pincer but one held by both pincers is subjects to the stinger every five sconds). The stinger causes only 1 point of damage, but injects a neurotoxin. A successful saving throw versus this Virulence Factor 12 poison indicates the victim suffers weakness, dizziness, headache, difficulty breathing and nausea (imposing a 2-point penalty to Attack, Defense and Damage for 2d12p hours). A failed save results in paralysis for 10+d20p minutes followed 2d12p hours of the aforementioned weakness. A natural '1' on the victim's saving throw indicates death; characters that are allergic to insect stings die automatically with no saving throw.

Note that this toxin is cumulative and multiple stings may result in severe enfeeblement. Duration is not, however, additive and is simply the highest result of those generated by individual stings.

Once the scorpion's prey is paralyzed, it employs its mouth-parts that contain two protruding claw-like structures. These structures are used to rip and pulverize the victim's flesh for digestion - incidentally inflicting d4p+2 points of damage every 10 seconds.

Scorpions can only digest food in liquid form. Any solid matter, such as hair and bone, is discarded.

Habitat/Society:

Giant scorpions can live in temperatures from 68 degrees Fahrenheit and warmer. They are found in the desert and in some rocky, mountainous regions, such as the Arajyd Hills. During daylight hours, they seek shelter in cool underground holes, the undersides of rocks or inside caves. They are solitary animals, except during mating and while the females are raising their offspring.

Giant scorpions reproduce sexually. The young are born one by one, and the brood is carried around on its mother's back. The litter is usually made up of about eight scorplings. They stay on their mother's back until they achieve at least one molt.

Growth is accomplished by periodic shedding of the exoskeleton, and a giant scorpion will usually go through five or six molts before reaching maturity. When it emerges, its exoskeleton is soft for d6 days, making the arthropod much more vulnerable (no Damage Reduction).

The average giant scorpion has a lifespan of 25 years.

Ecology:

They are nocturnal and opportunistic hunters, feeding primarily on lizard, rodents and insects (including the giant variety). Should a larger creature present itself as an unwitting target, however, the creature may slip up behind its prey and sting it into submission.

On Tellene:

Giant scorpions are widely spread over Tellene, but are most common in the deserts and adjacent hills and mountains (such as the Arajyd Hills near the Khydoban Desert, and the Elenon Mountains near the Elos Desert).

GIANT SCORPION

HIT POINTS:	14+d8
SIZE/WEIGHT:	S/60 lbs.
TENACITY:	Steady
INTELLIGENCE:	Semi
FATIGUE FACTOR:	n/a

SPEED	INIT
5	0

ATTACK +5
DMG REDUCTION

DEFENSE 0 | DAMAGE 2

see below

medium REACH | nil TOP SAVE

ATTACK: Pincers inflict 2d4p+3 points and grasp prey restricting movement and lessening Defense by 3 (or 6 if held by both); substitutes stinger attack for pincer once prey is held; stinger deals 1 point of damage plus VF 12 poison resulting in enfeeblement or paralysis (see text)

SPECIAL ABILTIES: Hiding 90% in natural surroundings.

MOVEMENT

CRAWL:	1¼
WALK:	2½
JOG:	5
RUN:	7½
SPRINT:	10

SAVES

PHYSICAL:	+5
MENTAL:	+5
DODGE:	+5

GENERAL INFO

ACTIVITY CYCLE:	Nocturnal
NO. APPEARING:	1-4
% CHANCE IN LAIR:	50%
FREQUENCY:	Infrequent
ALIGNMENT:	Non
VISION TYPE:	Standard
AWARENESS/SENSES:	Standard
HABITAT:	Burrows and caves
DIET:	Carnivorous
ORGANIZATION:	Individuals or nest
CLIMATE/TERRAIN:	Arid deserts and highlands

YIELD

MEDICINAL:	diluted venom, thought to cure chest pains
SPELL COMPONENTS:	nil
HIDE/TROPHY:	nil
TREASURE:	incidental
EDIBLE:	yes, except for the tail which is poisonous
OTHER:	nil
EXPERIENCE POINT VALUE: 242	

S

SCREECHER   Also Known As: Akana

Screechers we called 'em for that is what they did. And make no mistake, it weren't no tolerable sound likin' to stepping on a cat. No sir, it were loud, almost painful, and piercin' sure enough to drive a man crazy if'in he stood too long near the blasted thing. And we was certain loud enough to let any beast know we'd come a'knockin'.

Now locatin' the source of the racket ain't nearly as straightforward as ya might think. That caterwauling was so durn loud and echoing every which way. Took me quite a bit a time swiping with my saber afore I literally struck upon the infernal toadstool that was wailing so. And it were nearly the size of our crotchety old dwarf! Silencing the thing took me the better part of a minute fer it were a mighty mushroom and with a tough bark.

Now good fortune was with us fer nothin' came out to greet us. Figurin' we knew what to look fer, we had that skitterin' druid keep a special eye out fer any sign o' these fungus harpies — them fellers knowin' 'bout plants and such and having a good eye for things.

Well wouldn't ya know it but we was creeping down some tunnel and something commences to screechin' again. Only this time the sound was different. Sure it was every bit as loud and irritatin' as afore 'ceptin' it kinda warbled like some crazy bird. We was pokin' around tryin' to find the durned thing when we was attacked by a mess load of goblins. Seems like they was just waitin' fer us because a hailstorm of arrows came flyin' at us from beyond our torchlight. Several of the fellas was hit before we could form a shield wall and charge the sneaky bastards. - ⚥

Beauty and death intertwined.

Screechers are a variety of organisms collectively belonging to the screecher genus, so named because they emit a loud screech if approached by flame (heat), bright light or when sensing the movement of nearby creatures. Discernable species and patterns probably exist and can be mapped, but few scholars have the inclination, patience or enough ear plugs to warrant such a deep investigation.

Because this genus is so physically varied, screechers may look just like roughly 4-foot tall (or long) versions of almost any fungus or lichen, although giant mushrooms and toadstools seem to be the most common. Their coloration varies across the spectrum, but red tones seem to dominate.

Many varieties also exhibit a pattern of one type or another, with mottled or spotted being most common, but solid colors and patches are also frequently encountered. Some varieties can move and relocate themselves, but they do this at a very slow, almost imperceptible rate. If screechers have any sort of intelligence, no one has witnessed signs of it, or at least not reported it in any case. However, they seem to have a sense of touch, or something akin to it, because touching a screecher will also set off its intense shriek.

Combat/Tactics:

Screechers are immobile megafungi with no defense other than a cacophonous wail triggered by nearby movement, bright

Because screeching plants come in so many varieties, they often go undetected until it is too late. They shun light and are usually found growing underground. Occasionally, they may also be found growing in dark forest labyrinths cloaked by perpetual shadow.

SIZE COMPARISON

6 ft

3 ft

light, open flames or even body heat or touch. Their howl can be an effective defense as it can serve to draw curious creatures in the area, particularly any local predators that are hungry for a meal.

How long it takes for the cause to trigger the screeching can even vary depending on the amount of humidity, light, size of prey, and general growing conditions. The speed with which screechers wail can be used as an indicator of the plant's general health, though this is usually of interest only to botanists.

Once triggered, a screecher will bellow for anywhere from 5 to 10 minutes after the irritant is removed, further increasing the odds that some unsavory wandering beast takes notice. While a lone screecher is easy to distinguish, one or more camouflaged within a growth of similar-looking fungi may be nearly impossible to differentiate. Even when screeching, a Listening check (Average difficulty) is required to determine the sound's precise source due to its volume and echoing acoustics common to confined subterranean areas.

Other than the passage of time, slicing a screecher to bits is the only sure way of silencing the thing. However, its fibrous casing and inordinate size often preclude doing this swiftly.

Habitat/Society:

Given their sensitivity to light, screechers are rarely found growing on the surface world (those who have attempted transplanting this fungi have discovered that the plant soon withers and dies as it is overstimulated by incident sunlight).

The few exceptions seem to be varieties that grow in north-facing shallow caves, deep valleys or, more commonly, amongst giant ferns in rain forests where the thick canopy protects them from direct sunlight. A few varieties can also be found in dismal swamps or even growing within large, hollowed-out, felled tree trunks.

Ecology:

Like all fungi, screechers feed upon decaying organic matter leading many to believe they have evolved in such a way as to create a symbiotic relationship with aggressive predators; the screecher identifies the passage and location of prey to the predator, which slays the creature. After the grisly feast, the screecher is free to soak up any nutrients left nearby. Should chunks of flesh actually land atop or in the plant itself, it can digest these in several days, leaving only a tiny husk of chitin behind.

On Tellene:

Screechers are not uncommon in dark caves, warrens and the vast Netherdeep beneath the ground. While they pop up in a variety of locations, their value as a passive security alarm has been recognized by residents of these dark realms and many have taken to purposely cultivating this fungi for said purpose. Occasionally, lizard men may also strategically plant these creatures if the right conditions exist.

SCREECHER

HIT POINTS:	10+3d8
SIZE/WEIGHT:	S/~50 lbs.
TENACITY:	n/a
INTELLIGENCE:	Non
FATIGUE FACTOR:	n/a

SPEED 0 | INIT 0
ATTACK 0
-6 | DMG REDUCTION 4
DEFENSE 0
none REACH | DAMAGE n/a
TOP SAVE ▼

MOVEMENT

CRAWL:	0
WALK:	0
JOG:	0
RUN:	0
SPRINT:	0

SAVES

PHYSICAL:	+4
MENTAL:	n/a
DODGE:	-6

ATTACK:
none

SPECIAL DEFENSES:
Noise; screechers emit a loud wail that can be triggered by movement, light, heat or touch within 10 feet; a Listening check (average difficulty) is required to determine the precise source of the screeching

GENERAL INFO

ACTIVITY CYCLE:	Any
NO. APPEARING:	2-8
% CHANCE IN LAIR:	100%
FREQUENCY:	Commonplace
ALIGNMENT:	Non
VISION TYPE:	n/a
AWARENESS/SENSES:	Very sensitive to movement, light, heat, touch
HABITAT:	Dark caves, valleys or deep forests
DIET:	Carnivorous
ORGANIZATION:	n/a
CLIMATE/TERRAIN:	Warm to Tropical lowlands or subterranean

YIELD

MEDICINAL:	nil
SPELL COMPONENTS:	nil
HIDE/TROPHY:	nil
TREASURE:	incidental, from corpses consumed
EDIBLE:	yes, but taste like mushrooms dipped in dung
OTHER:	nil

EXPERIENCE POINT VALUE: 5

S

SHADOW

Also Known As: Shadowmen, Darklings

I canst name no greater affront to The Shining One than these beings we callest Shadows. For in truth it is only by the prigging of a scantling portion of The Lantern's wondrous endowment that these loathsome wretches doth manifest themselves.

One needeth but half a wit for to deduct the longsome presence of shadow men. Unharried by those set upon their foiliture, they killest all beings which draw breath. Silence like unto a mausoleum doth cover the land into which these darklings do skulk.

If thou thinkest the shadow an ardent foe thou misappraisest thine enemy. They are a cowish lot that doth prey on those most feeble – the younglings, the grayhairs, and those infirm. They robbest them of life and damn the poor souls into an accursed transmogrification into darklings themselves.

Ridding a place of their villianry is no foole's errand. Knowest that in such an endeavor it is the quality not the quantity of thine allies that is of greatest import. When I didst encounter such a foe, I dispatched my acolytes to shepherd the yeomen as far afield as they couldest travel go and to light bonfires at night. "Flee far away." I didst tell them. "Ye be but a hindrance to me!"

Takest not cheer upon dispersing this foe once they have been spit upon thine sabers. They willst flee from stout men – be most assured of this. But they willst return time and time again always springing forth from darkest hollows thine strength to sap. Be vigilant lest ye be taken unawares. Sleepest not if they be near for ye willst surely awaken incarnate as a darkling.

Ensure thine blades are silvered for ordinary steel hath but minor effect upon their shadowy form. But know well in thine hearts that thy greatest ally be the power of light. Call upon thine faith and illuminate their darkened hideaways. Open wide doors and shutters. Burn the structure if thou must. Deprivest them of the dark. Deprivest them of the dark. - 👁

Shadows are wicked, undead beings whose physical manifestation is the source of their eponymous name. In poor lighting, they are virtually indistinguishable from the ambient gloom. In daylight, they can clearly be seen as incongruous shadows either on the ground or against a vertical surface.

They are likely encountered in abandoned ruins, for they prey upon the living. Cohabitation with mortals is likely temporary or under auspices of powerfully evil divine magic.

Shadowmen invoke a special dread among sentient races. Both an orc and a Dejy tribesman may find common ground in their fear and hatred of these creatures. Such shared animosity has formed unlikely, if temporary, alliances in the past.

Combat/Tactics:

Shadows are able to perfectly mask themselves in poor lighting conditions, blending in with natural shadows created by torch or lantern light (effectively gaining Hiding and Sneaking masteries of 100%). Only careful Observation (a Very Difficult check) reveals their presence before they strike.

Shadowmen operate as packs, stealthily surrounding an opponent and then attacking en mass from every direction. They are intelligent enough to recognize weakness and, if given time to assess the results of their assault, will focus their efforts on individuals most susceptible to their frigid jabs.

A darkling's chilling touch drains its victim's strength

SIGN/TRACKS

If you ever venture into an area with long shadows where light is wont to break through, and feel as though you are being watched... there's a good chance you are. Shadows evoke their own particular brand of fear and their reputations are well deserved. Early detecton is crucial to your success. - ✦

WILL FACTOR
9*
0 in bright light

SIZE COMPARISON

6 ft

3 ft

(reducing its Strength score commensurate to the damage inflicted). Creatures sapped of all strength (i.e., their Strength score is reduced to zero) become shadows themselves. Silvered weapons are unquestioningly superior at injuring darklings.

Shadow packs are not particularly brave, preferring to slip away into the shadows when resolutely confronted. What they lack in bravery though, they more than make up for in perseverance. The creatures will continue to stalk a foe that has bested them seeking an opportune time to reengage. As the creatures do not tire, one of their favorite times to mount an additional attack is when their foes have set up camp and let down their guard to sleep.

Bright light (e.g., sunlight) has a deleterious effect on shadowmen. Not only can they be readily seen but also their powers are significantly diminished. They become more susceptible to ordinary weaponry, their defense is significantly compromised and their attacks are far easier to resist.

Ecology:

The transformation to shadowform is both literal and figurative for not only is the creature's physical form dissipated to a nearly insubstantial shadow but its mind too is stripped of all memories and most cognitive reasoning leaving only a malicious beast hateful of all life.

Unless exterminated or ruthlessly controlled by a powerful master, shadows kill all living creatures within striking distance of their lair. Battling a shadow pack is a difficult task and should be undertaken only by a uniformly strong group, as auxiliaries are frequently a detriment. Shadows target these weaker individuals and bolster their numbers by killing them.

Most targets of a shadow pack abandon their villages, strongholds or lairs after it becomes clear that they cannot endure these continuing attacks. The creatures' tactics of preferentially attacking the weak, young and infirm merely add to their sinister reputations. Once any organized resistance has been eliminated or driven off, the shadows proceed to kill all remaining fauna. A sure sign of the presence of a shadow pack is the complete absence of any noise save the rustling of the wind. Nary a bird's chirp or even the buzzing of a flying insect bears witness to the horrible depredations of these undead villains.

This insatiable hatred for life is, in the end, a shadow's undoing for in methodically killing everything within their range they end up depriving themselves of the *elan vital* necessary to sustain their existence. Though the process is slow, eventually a shadow will simply fade from the mortal world if it cannot feed upon the living.

On Tellene:

The Khydoban Desert is said to be home to many abandoned settlements from a vanished era. Rumors persist that the dead still walk amongst them. Were this true, it certainly would be the height of irony for shadows to dwell in the recesses of ruins within the blazing sunlight of this desert.

SHADOW

HIT POINTS:	26+3d8
SIZE/WEIGHT:	M/insubstantial
TENACITY:	Brave
INTELLIGENCE:	Slow
FATIGUE FACTOR:	n/a

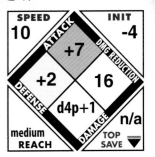

SPEED	INIT
10	-4
ATTACK +7	DMG REDUCTION
DEFENSE +2	16
d4p+1	
medium REACH	DAMAGE	n/a TOP SAVE

MOVEMENT

CRAWL:	20
WALK:	25
JOG:	30
RUN:	35
FLY:	40

SAVES

PHYSICAL:	+7
MENTAL:	immune
DODGE:	+7

ATTACK:
A shadow's touch drains STR equal to damage (save for half); creatures reduced to zero (0) STR become shadows.

SPECIAL DEFENSES:
Silvered weapons reduce DR to 8.
Almost indistinguishable in dim light.
In bright light, a shadow's Defense drops to -4, Will Factor 9 drops to 0 and DR bcomes 8 versus any type of weapon.
Hiding and Sneaking 100% in poor light.

GENERAL INFO

ACTIVITY CYCLE:	Any
NO. APPEARING:	2-20
% CHANCE IN LAIR:	50%
FREQUENCY:	Infrequent
ALIGNMENT:	Neutral Evil
VISION TYPE:	Undead Sight
AWARENESS/SENSES:	Standard
HABITAT:	Dark ruins and caverns
DIET:	n/a
ORGANIZATION:	Individuals or Pack
CLIMATE/TERRAIN:	Any

YIELD

MEDICINAL:	nil
SPELL COMPONENTS:	nil
HIDE/TROPHY:	nil
TREASURE:	retains small items of value from their victims
EDIBLE:	no
OTHER:	nil
EXPERIENCE POINT VALUE:	417

S

SIREN

Also Known As: Sirines, Sea Maidens, Mariners' Bane, Sea Nymphs

I write this story only second-hand; but I feel I have it in substance — and he wasted few words over it—as the man Rolon told it me only yesterday. This fellow, though he now lives in a monastery operated by the Church of Everlasting Hope, was once a lowly deckhand on a Zoan merchant ship.

It seems the lookout had spotted an uncharted island, and the captain sent a longboat of his men, including this Rolon, to investigate it. As the longboat grew ever closer to shore, Rolon became conscious of a music that seemed to resonate in his head, and a greater and greater desire to reach it, even before he saw what awaited him there. For seated atop the rocks that decorated the shore were many fine young damsels dressed in the faintest garments, or even not dressed at all, baring their charms for all to see.

The song, he says, grew more insistent and his desire grew stronger. He tried to call to them, but his tongue would not move. He tried to spring out of the boat and swim towards shore, to thrust out his arms and touch them, but found his limbs paralyzed. And then… he remembers nothing else but the faint memory of sweet caresses, interrupted by hideous cries and shrieks, his ears being stuffed with wax and the bearded face of his captain shouting noiselessly into his own. Rolon's next memory was, he said, of waking on the deck of his ship, now missing its captain and manned by a smaller crew of blood-spattered men who refused to speak of the incident again. -

"Where is father, e's been gone so long?
Hush child, he was lured by the siren's song."
~ Old seaman's ditty

Members of this immortal race are few in number and live mostly on small islands distant from active shipping lanes. Although their race does not age or require food, they can still die by violent means like any mortal. All known sirens are female. They wear little to no garments and appear as beautiful human women, with their lower legs covered in scales of nearly any color, with green, blue and gold the most common. Hair colors range from white to black, and all colors in between.

Combat/Tactics:

A siren's voice is incredibly bewitching and they possess the ability to charm all non-sirens who hear them[1] (opposed save vs. d20p+10 immediately upon hearing; only one save needed per encounter). In addition to their song, all sirens have mage abilities of at least 5th level. Sirens prefer to avoid melee combat whenever possible, as they are often overmatched in a physical sense. They attempt to use magic, and their ability to charm, in order to subdue potential attackers. If forced to engage in melee combat, they will use a small weapon (if available) or strike with their hands in feeble self-defense.

Those succumbing to their Charm may eventually break free of this enchantment (see the 2nd level Mage's *Charm* spell).

Habitat/Society:

Sirens are almost universally found in isolated islands far from heavily trafficked shipping lanes, living alone or in small

Legend has it that one of the small islands south of Zoa was once the home of four sirens known as 'The Sisters.' The story has it they lured over a hundred ships (along with their crews) to disaster on the rocky shoals.

RANGE ON TELLENE

SIZE COMPARISON

6 ft

3 ft

groups of up to four. Sirens lair in sheltered areas of their island homes, be it caves or other natural features that protect them from the elements. Some sirens will lair in the wreckage of the ships that crash on the rocky shores of their islands. They do not create elaborate or intricate living spaces.

Sirens often use their songs to lure lost sailors to their islands. Whether this is to cruelly wreck the ship upon the rocks or because the sirens want to try and repopulate their race depends on the nature of the sirens involved. Even if the sirens are extremely friendly, the sailors may still be in great danger. If the island has no food, the men will be too enraptured to leave and so die of starvation.

Those sirens found in groups possess an intimate knowledge of one another and each considers themselves a sister to the others, even if they differ in alignment. Sirens never attack one another, instead parting ways before coming to blows.

Sirens breed with captured or charmed human males in order to procreate. Once they become impregnated, they sever any ties with the father in order to raise the children on their own or among their own kind. Gestation time is similar to that of a human, but sirens always give birth in the water. Often times this can be dangerous as the birthing process is bloody and can draw natural sea predators (such as sharks) to the area. Sirens always give birth to female children.

Sirens speak whatever human language is most common to the region in which they live. They have the ability to quickly learn new languages and often times inadvertently pick up such languages from their captives without much thought. As such, a siren is likely to know d4+1 random human languages common to the area in which they are found.

Since they are immortal, time means very little to them and they tend to be extremely patient.

Ecology:

Though they have no need to eat, many sirens enjoy a diet of fish, oysters, mussels and kelp found near their island homes. Unlike humans, sirens can consume salt water with no ill effects, though they have no need to do so.

Sirens were once the handmaidens of the Pure One but were banished to Tellene when they inexplicably attempted to charm several deities with their song. At several times in their lives sirens are consumed by a great desire to breed, or enjoy intercourse, but for the most part they revel in solitude away from the men of the world.

Few sirens collect any sort of treasure, though they have a fondness for jewelry, especially pieces made of coral or pearl. Vast wealth can often be found near their island homes in the wreckages of ships lured to their doom.

On Tellene:

Sirens are most often found in sub-tropical to tropical island areas removed from shipping lanes. Most reports of sirens come from sailors once lost in southern Reanaaria Bay and the Sea of the Dead.

[1] *Effective range is 100 yards*

SIREN

HIT POINTS:	16+d8
SIZE/WEIGHT:	M/120 lbs.
TENACITY:	Nervous
INTELLIGENCE:	Bright to Brilliant
FATIGUE FACTOR:	2

MOVEMENT

CRAWL:	2½
WALK:	5
JOG:	10
RUN:	15
SPRINT:	20

SAVES

PHYSICAL:	-1
MENTAL:	+6
DODGE:	+4

SPEED 7 **INIT** -2 **ATTACK** -1 **DMG REDUCTION** 0 **DEFENSE** -2 **see below by weapon REACH** **DAMAGE** 2 **TOP SAVE** ▼

ATTACK:
Charming songs bewitch others (save vs d20p+10; only one save per encounter). Sirens have inherent spellcasting abilities equivalent to a mage of at least 5th level but do not employ spellbooks; they may use a knife (d6p-4) in close quarter combat but this is extremely unusual

SPECIAL DEFENSES:
None, other than disarming beauty.

GENERAL INFO

ACTIVITY CYCLE:	Diurnal
NO. APPEARING:	1-8
% CHANCE IN LAIR:	40%
FREQUENCY:	Scarce
ALIGNMENT:	Chaotic Good to Chaotic Evil
VISION TYPE:	Standard
AWARENESS/SENSES:	Standard
HABITAT:	Isolated islands
DIET:	Omnivorous
ORGANIZATION:	Individuals
CLIMATE/TERRAIN:	Temperate to tropical islands and aquatic

YIELD

MEDICINAL:	nil
SPELL COMPONENTS:	nil
HIDE/TROPHY:	nil
TREASURE:	sirens often keep the valuables of their victims
EDIBLE:	yes; large aquatic predators may prey on sirens
OTHER:	nil
EXPERIENCE POINT VALUE:	575

SKELETON Also Known As: Creth, Trondak

A horrible sight to behold, these animated bones of the long departed. Nary a trace of flesh remains on the skeleton yet they are swift afoot as any man. Beware these creatures for they are resolute opponents incapable of tiring and unlike mortals heedlessly assailest a foe without regard to loss until utterly destroyed. They wield blades with a fair bit of skill but those not so armed will ravenous tear at ye with their bony digits. Many wear the tattered remnants of mail and utilize shields compounding the difficulty of dispatching them.

Methinks the greater number of these creatures are vivified from orkin charnel mounds for the curved blade so prized by that vile race is frequently wielded in their bony hands. In truth, the frequency with which the orcs make war and the perfunctory manner they dispensest with their slain warriors provideth an ample fodder of accessible corpses for the evil priest intent on creating undead minions. Certainly not all skeletons are raised from such stock for I hath encountered these beings in the form of the bones of men, goblinoids and other such creatures that in life walked upright.

One must pay heed to the creature's unique defenses lest a grave error be made. Spears, arrows and quarrels prove nigh useless in hindering skeletons and even stout blades and axes carry not their full effect. It is the mace, flail and hammer one should employ to ensure a resounding blow. An experienced warrior doth ensure he can heft one of these bludgeoning armaments should one anticipate venturing into crypts.

Ye mustn't be afeared, for skeletons are the most base of the unliving and often cannot readily abide even a mere acolyte's invocation of his deity's scorn for such abominations. - ◉

Employing piercing weapons against these evil monstrosities will put you at a disadvantage.

Skeletons are animated, fleshless corpses under the magical command of some evil being. Their macabre appearance alone is sufficient to frighten those not hardened to such unnatural things. Skeletons are clad in tattered bits of armor and may use shields. Most have been armed with melee weapons (often a scimitar) by their master or creator, but they are not limited to this weapon. Even grisly skeletal archers have been encountered, although how they can draw a longbow lacking the requisite musculature is a mystery. Unless under the active control of an evil cleric (an infrequent occurrence), skeletons operate under a simple and fixed instruction set such as "Attack anyone entering this chamber." Only patently obvious caveats may be appended to their instructions ("…except those clad in black robes" being such an example). They have no ability to discern the difference between races nor do they possess any extraordinary Observation skill, although they seem to completely ignore, or are unable to perceive, the non-living.

Combat/Tactics:

When attacking, they simply rush at the closest available target. Only when it is fully engaged will they proceed to harass any other nearby victims. A few skeletons may be equipped as archers. When deployed as such, their tactics are elementary firing at the nearest target regardless of circumstance. As these creatures are incapable of feeling pain or fear, they must be

When faced with skeletons, rid yourselves of bladed weapons, bows and the like. Find yourself a crushing weapon. Hammer, mace. Improvise a club if in a pinch. Keep your lines tight. Fighting shoulder to shoulder against these vile creatures is more effective than splitting ranks.

WILL FACTOR
1*
2 *Animal Skeleton*
5 *Monster Skeleton*

SIZE COMPARISON

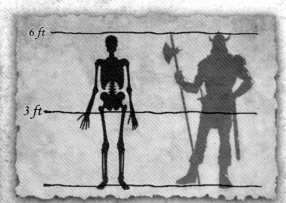

6 ft

3 ft

physically destroyed to cease their attacks. This makes them far deadlier opponents than comparable living beings. Lacking any physical incarnation beyond bones, a skeletal target is a difficult one to injure with most puncturing arms as more often than not a solid attack with such a weapon simply passes right between the skeletons ribs, for example. Crushing weapons, with their larger surface, tend to be much better implements, as a solid hit to the ribcage will shatter bones rather than pass through ineffectually. Hacking weapons provide somewhat mixed results, being larger and more sweeping than puncturing weapons, but not as large and effective as a crushing weapon, like mace, club or hammer. To reflect these properties, skeletons have a +10 DR bonus when attacked by piercing weapons and a +6 DR bonus when attacked by hacking implements.

Skeletons are essentially automatons with no consciousness beyond their programming. Magic seeking to influence emotions or biological functions (such as sleep) are wholly ineffective. The dark energy sustaining these creatures in unlife is, however, most tenuous.

Though perfectly loyal minions who will faithfully execute their master's commands to the best of their ability or comprehension, they have no ability to reason. This latter deficiency may be taken advantage of by feigning retreat or otherwise compelling skeletons to enter a hazardous area – be it a prepared ambush, trap or off the side of a cliff (for example, whilst chasing an individual capable of flight).

Note that the tattered bits of armor worn by most skeletons account for 3 points of the creature's DR rating. Should they not be so armored, their rating should be adjusted accordingly. If deprived of a weapon, a skeleton may alternatively scratch and claw with its bony digits inflicting d4p+1 damage.

Habitat/Society/Ecology:

Skeletons are unnatural creatures inspirited by dark energy. As such, they have no need of nourishment or sleep. These qualities make them excellent guards for evil beings comfortable with horrific mannequins of living beings. It must be stated that nearly all sentient beings, regardless of moral values, loathe the undead. Even most evil humanoids shun their presence. Integrating undead guardians or soldiery with far more flexible human, orkin or goblin thralls requires severe means of compulsion.

As these monsters have no fear (or even cognition) of daylight, their presence at the perimeters of supposedly haunted sites may be indicative of a more powerful undead presence within. It is not uncommon for such creatures to be deployed by spectres or wraiths to protect areas into which they themselves cannot pass.

Skeletons may be raised from the bones of any humanoid creature. The source material is irrelevant, for the evil enchantment providing the vigor to these bones supersedes any species differentiation. Thus an animated goblin skeleton is functionally equivalent to that of a human. That being said, the types of beings used as feedstock for this

SKELETON

HIT POINTS:	27+1d8
SIZE/WEIGHT:	M/25 lbs.
TENACITY:	Fearless
INTELLIGENCE:	Non
FATIGUE FACTOR:	n/a

MOVEMENT

CRAWL:	2½
WALK:	5
JOG:	10
RUN:	15
SPRINT:	20

SAVES

PHYSICAL:	+1
MENTAL:	immune
DODGE:	+1

ATTACK:
Skeletons wield scimitars (2d8p-1) or other melee weapons. Bony digits deal d4p+1 damage, if weaponless.

SPECIAL DEFENSES:
Shield use (*e.g.*, medium shields increase Def to +7). Effective DR altered by weapon type (+0 crushing, +6 hacking, +10 piercing); unarmored skeletons have a base DR of 0

GENERAL INFO

ACTIVITY CYCLE:	Any
NO. APPEARING:	1-30
% CHANCE IN LAIR:	n/a
FREQUENCY:	Infrequent
ALIGNMENT:	Non
VISION TYPE:	Standard
AWARENESS/SENSES:	Standard
HABITAT:	Any
DIET:	n/a
ORGANIZATION:	Thralls
CLIMATE/TERRAIN:	Any

YIELD

MEDICINAL:	nil
SPELL COMPONENTS:	bodies, for 10th level Animate Skeletons spell
HIDE/TROPHY:	nil
TREASURE:	incidental
EDIBLE:	no
OTHER:	nil
EXPERIENCE POINT VALUE:	67

S

ANIMAL SKELETON

HIT POINTS:	15+1d8
SIZE/WEIGHT:	S/varies
TENACITY:	Fearless
INTELLIGENCE:	Non
FATIGUE FACTOR:	n/a

MOVEMENT

CRAWL:	5
WALK:	10
JOG:	15
RUN:	20
SPRINT:	25

SAVES

PHYSICAL:	0
MENTAL:	immune
DODGE:	0

SPEED 10 | **INIT** 0
ATTACK +2
DMG REDUCTION
+1 | 0
DEFENSE
3d4p
DAMAGE
short **REACH** | **TOP SAVE** n/a ▼

ATTACK:
Animal skeletons attack with natural weapons of teeth and claws, dealing 3d4p points of damage.

SPECIAL DEFENSES:
Effective DR altered by weapon type (+0 crushing, +6 hacking, +10 piercing);

GENERAL INFO

ACTIVITY CYCLE:	Any
NO. APPEARING:	1-20
% CHANCE IN LAIR:	n/a
FREQUENCY:	Sporadic
ALIGNMENT:	Non
VISION TYPE:	Standard
AWARENESS/SENSES:	Standard
HABITAT:	Any
DIET:	n/a
ORGANIZATION:	Thralls
CLIMATE/TERRAIN:	Any

YIELD

MEDICINAL:	nil
SPELL COMPONENTS:	bodies, for 10th level Animate Skeletons spell
HIDE/TROPHY:	nil
TREASURE:	incidental
EDIBLE:	no
OTHER:	nil
EXPERIENCE POINT VALUE:	100

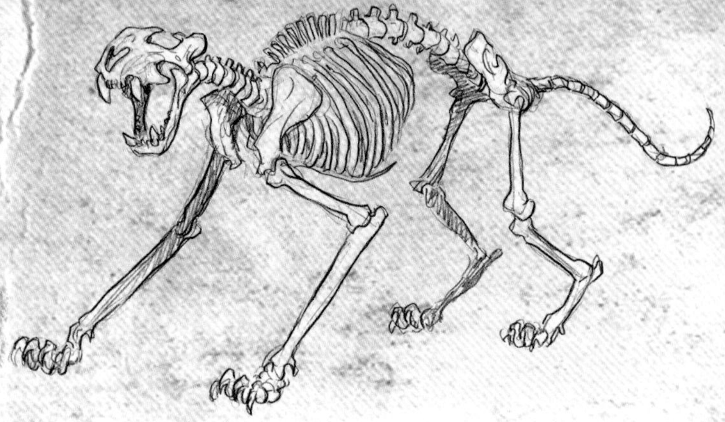

S

Animal skeletons can be unnerving. I've seen grown men break ranks and flee at the sight of one. Stand your ground and steady your nerves. There's more fright and less fight in these aberrations.

unholy ritual may provide some contextual clues as to the circumstances surrounding their current placement.

Skeleton Variants:

The bones of humanoids are not alone in being subject to reanimation. Animals too, as well as the remains of larger creatures, are not infrequently inspirited as obedient – if expendable – sentinels and warriors. Much of what has been written with respect to 'ordinary' skeletons holds true for these creatures as well. However, there are some notable caveats.

Animal Skeletons

Unquestioningly easier to commandeer, the bones of animals such as dogs can be animated to serve as tireless guardians. Animal remains of a roughly comparable size (like wolves, boars, mountain lions or small black bears) may be used as analogues. However, like standard skeletons, the creature's capabilities in life do not translate to its revivified form. Rather, these bones are merely a template upon which is layered a standardized set of capabilities.

In many ways, animal skeletons are poor substitutes for living creatures as they do not possess the former animal's typically keen senses of smell and hearing – features that aid living creatures immensely in their ability to perceive and react to intruders. The undead are far less capable combatants, as the animating enchantment is rather weak and produces but a pale mockery of the original creature.

These creatures are typically created as a stop-gap measure when a sufficient pool of humanoid skeletons is unavailable, for they are in most respects inferior. Lacking the means to employ weapons, they are limited to a solitary biting attack capable of only modest harm. Their one advantage is speed. Having the means to outrun humans and being relentless in pursuit, they are difficult to escape from.

Monster Skeletons

The bones of larger bipeds such as bugbears and ogres may, via more powerful dark magic, be similarly animated. The combination of a stronger enchantment and the sheer physical size of these constructs results in a far more formidable undead creature. Though subject to the same restrictions inherent to all skeletons, these variants are appreciably faster and tougher than smaller varieties. In addition, they are more difficult for a cleric to disperse.

These monstrous skeletons are usually armed with rusty axes and swords, clad in scavenged armor and possibly shields as well. Deprived of these accoutrements, their DR rating is reduced by 4 and they may only claw at foes (inflicting 2d4p damage in so doing).

On Tellene:

Skeletons are most commonly found as passive guardians in crypts or tombs. Without need for food, water or sleep, they may maintain their silent vigil for centuries.

More common though is their employment by followers of the Harvester of Souls. These evil priests of death make ample use of these creatures in roles befitting their strengths, at times raising entire legions of these expendable but blindly obedient automatons to wage war.

The appearance of skeletons is not limited to terrestrial encounters. Indeed the Xaaboemio Sea (also known as 'the Sea of the Dead') is reportedly haunted by ghost vessels manned by skeletal crews. While the presence of any such ship has never been substantiated, in turn leading to the conclusion by many learned folk that they are merely the drunken ramblings of superstitious seamen or tales meant to frighten competitors away from prime sea lanes, their continued persistence leads others to question whether or not there is some truth behind these tales.

A minotaur skeleton
I once met, left to guard
against would-be tomb
robbers.

MONSTER SKELETON

HIT POINTS:	30+3d8
SIZE/WEIGHT:	L/varies
TENACITY:	Fearless
INTELLIGENCE:	Non
FATIGUE FACTOR:	n/a

SPEED 8 — INIT -1
ATTACK +5 — DMG REDUCTION
DEFENSE +5 — by weapon +3 — 4
by weapon +1 foot — REACH — DAMAGE n/a — TOP SAVE

MOVEMENT

CRAWL:	5
WALK:	10
JOG:	15
RUN:	20
SPRINT:	25

SAVES

PHYSICAL:	+5
MENTAL:	immune
DODGE:	+5

ATTACK: Monstrous skeletons attack with weapons they used in life; unarmed their bony claws deal 2d4p points of damage.

SPECIAL DEFENSES: Shield use (*e.g.,* medium shields increase Defense to +11). Effective DR altered by weapon type (+0 crushing, +6 hacking, +10 piercing); unarmored monster skeletons have a base DR of 1.

GENERAL INFO

ACTIVITY CYCLE:	Any
NO. APPEARING:	1-6
% CHANCE IN LAIR:	n/a
FREQUENCY:	Sporadic
ALIGNMENT:	Non
VISION TYPE:	Standard
AWARENESS/SENSES:	Standard
HABITAT:	Any
DIET:	n/a
ORGANIZATION:	Thralls
CLIMATE/TERRAIN:	Any

YIELD

MEDICINAL:	nil
SPELL COMPONENTS:	bodies, for 10th level Animate Skeletons spell
HIDE/TROPHY:	nil
TREASURE:	incidental
EDIBLE:	no
OTHER:	nil
EXPERIENCE POINT VALUE:	230

S

SKITTER-RAT Also Known As: Cave Squirrel, Shadow Scurry, Skuridar

Skitter-rats are horrid creatures. To the unlearned they appear no more a threat then a common squirrel. Make no mistake — there is murder in these tiny creatures.

Having a ravenous appetite for flesh of all sorts, they have been equipped by the gods with the means to obtain it. Their razor sharp teeth and merciless articulated claws are used to reach into gaps in armor, and at the eyes, cheeks and hands of any poor bastard unfortunate enough to draw their ire.

They are always encountered in dark places for they shun the daylight. Keeping torches raised high when traveling and a raging fire when camping will keep the beasts at bay. Beware though for they are patient hunters. I once had a porter killed by a pack of scurries after moving into the shadows of a great oak by the camp's edge to relieve himself. An old Brolenese hunter once told me that skitter rats hate the smell of owlbeast musk. He recommended rubbing the stuff on any exposed flesh when going into an area known to be infested with these rodents. - ⚓

Creatures tend to ferret out gaps in armor and go for any exposed flesh.

Jerking tail motion with an accompanying bark — a sure sign the skuridar is about to pounce.

Sharp claws rend flesh easily with rapid raking motions once contact is made.

Skitter-rats are large feral rodents that resemble horrid squirrels. Their rat-like fur (considered beautiful by some clienteles) and ranges from blue gray to coal black. It is often speckled with patches of various colors that match the surrounding rock and textures of the lair in question.

Combat/Tactics:

Cave squirrels are able to climb and cling to any surface (even ceilings) and scurry about at their full movement rate while doing so. They also have a natural ability to move silently (possessing a Sneaking mastery of 75%). The unique quality of their fur effectively camouflages them from sight (granting an effective 80% mastery in the Hiding skill).

Skitter-rats have excellent senses of hearing and smell which allows them to detect most creatures within 100 feet (corresponding to an Listening mastery of 70%). This allows them to to utilize an Initiative die two better than their opponents. It also gives them the ability to position themselves so that they are out of the line of sight of all but the most astute observers.

Skuridar love to position themselves on stone columns, pillars, stalagtites and stalagmites on which they can scurry from side to side to avoid detection. In this way they may frequently attack victims from behind.

These fierce creatures always attempt to attack from the rear on their first attack, in ambush fashion. They target any parts of the victim that are not protected by armor, such as the back of the neck, ankles, hamstrings, etc. Once they have attacked and drawn blood, they go into a blood-frenzy, often singling out a victim and attacking en masse. Once surprise has been lost, they go for the eyes, face, hands and attempt to disable and immobilize their victim so they can feed.

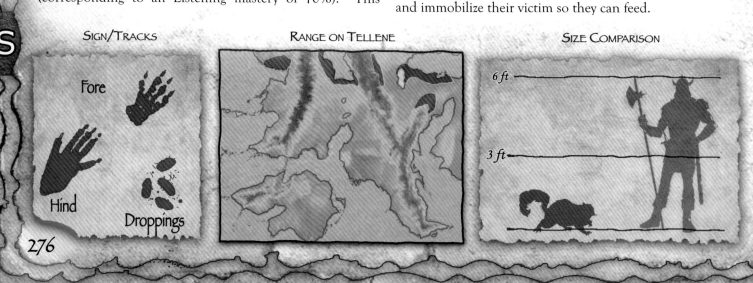

SIGN/TRACKS

Fore

Hind

Droppings

RANGE ON TELLENE

SIZE COMPARISON

6 ft

3 ft

When attacking from behind, skitter-rats emulate a thief's Rearward Strike ability and reduce an opponent's effective DR by 2.

Habitat/Society:

These much-feared creatures can be found in virtually any subterranean complex. They can also be found in abandoned structures or ruins which provide adequate darkness (shadow scurries shun daylight).

Skitter-rats are social animals who live in large warrens. Warrens meander throughout large subterranean areas in which they hunt and mark their territory. When a warren grows large enough (around 40 individuals), it splits with the new colony going off in search of new territory to claim as its own. Such migratory groups can be encountered out of doors, but only in the dark of night.

Each warren has a large female skitter-rat matriarch. The queen skitter-rat has 12+1d8 Hit Points and is capable of inflicting d8p+1 points of damage. She is given the choicest pieces of meat and is also protected by 1d6 guardian skitter-rats who fight to the death to protect her.

Ecology:

Skitter-rats are voracious eaters. They prefer fresh meat but will also scavenge (and steal) the kills of others. They have a fondness for both pixie-fairy and halfling flesh and will always target individuals of these races first when encountered.

Cave squirrels mate three times a year. Females give birth to d8 young at a time. Young skitter-rats are cared for communally by the warren and kept in a large brooding nest. The brooding nest is always protected by d4 female skitter-rats who fight to the death to protect the young. Scraps of meat from any kill are dragged to the nest for the young to feed on. Skitter-rat females love to bring wounded prey back to the nest so that their young may practice their disabling attacks on them before feeding.

On Tellene:

Skitter-rats are a pestilence common to forested uplands particularly in the more northerly climates. Fur garments made from skitter-rats are a mark of status amongst the Slen. A wholly different attitude prevails in the southwest, where the Brolenese consider such creatures pure vermin.

Skitter-rat saliva is festering with diseases.

Those who survive a skitter-rat swarm often meet their fates weeks later racked with pain and death-fever.

SKITTER-RAT

HIT POINTS:	8+1d4
SIZE/WEIGHT:	T/3 lbs.
TENACITY:	Steady
INTELLIGENCE:	Animal, High
FATIGUE FACTOR:	-2

SPEED	INIT
10	-1

ATTACK 0
DMG REDUCTION
DEFENSE +4 | 1
d6p+1
short REACH | DAMAGE | TOP SAVE 8

MOVEMENT

CRAWL:	5
WALK:	10
JOG:	15
RUN:	20
SPRINT:	25

SAVES

PHYSICAL:	0
MENTAL:	0
DODGE:	+3

ATTACK:
Claws & bites (one unified attack) deal d6p+1 points of damage (or 1d8p+1 for queen); Rear attacks ignore 2 points of foe's DR; utilize two initiative dice lower

SPECIAL ABILITIES:
Hiding 80%, Listening 70%, Sneaking 75%, climb any surface at full movement rate

GENERAL INFO

ACTIVITY CYCLE:	Nocturnal
NO. APPEARING:	4-40
% CHANCE IN LAIR:	30%
FREQUENCY:	Frequent
ALIGNMENT:	Non
VISION TYPE:	Standard
AWARENESS/SENSES:	Keen hearing and smell (Initiative die are two better)
HABITAT:	Warrens
DIET:	Carnivorous
ORGANIZATION:	Pack
CLIMATE/TERRAIN:	Temperate to Tropical subterranean

S

YIELD

MEDICINAL:	nil
SPELL COMPONENTS:	nil
HIDE/TROPHY:	fur, used for clothing in some areas
TREASURE:	incidental
EDIBLE:	yes
OTHER:	nil
EXPERIENCE POINT VALUE:	30

SLIME, FLESH-EATING

Also Known As: Nik'Lo, Vuulaan

It was after some subterranean travel, including a quite perilous descent down a cliff face, that my companions and I encountered an immense iron door of obvious dwarven construction, but with no obvious handle, lock or keyhole. Even the moss that flourished on the walls and ceiling was unable to penetrate its almost invisible seams. We spent some time checking the barrier against danger, but found nothing. Then, so quickly that it robbed me of my senses, two things happened.

Our hired guide, he who worshipped the Discordant One, became frustrated at our lack of progress and kicked the door savagely with his hobnailed boot. The sound, small though it was, became so amplified by the rock around us that it seemed The Thunderer himself was raging in my head; every nerve and fiber of my body throbbed and tingled with the hellish vibration.

Suddenly, the air came alive with rain, pattering lightly over us all but heavy like a flood upon our hired villein. Under the thick green downpour, our flesh began to burn, and for some time we thought only of ourselves, discarding our clothes and scraping off the rain that continued to strike us as we fled like rats to the potential safety of a nearby tunnel. Even as I ran, the man's agonized scream rattled the diaphragms of my ears with horrible, deafening intensity, and I heard his torch fall hissing upon the rocks under a rain of green fire.

When we had at last recovered our senses, we returned with quiet tread to the door, as silent as mice. There were no sounds now, only a vague, ringing silence in my head. At the door, I drew back with a shudder. A heap of disconnected bones and a mishmash of reddish slush, onto which the occasional drop of green still fell, were all that remained. ~

Words cannot describe the pain and terror of having one's limb exposed to flesh-eating slime.

Flesh-eating slime flourishes in damp subterranean areas. It feeds off of organic material by means of potent enzymes that can rapidly break down wood, leather and animal tissue. Its green color may lead inexperienced explorers to dismiss these growths as relatively benign moss – that is, until they lose a hand after brushing up against the stuff.

Combat/Tactics:

This slime has a proclivity to grow in large masses along underground ceilings. Such growths frequently become so large as to have only a tenuous anchor and may be easily dislodged – even by the vibrations of a man walking beneath.

Should anyone disturb a growth, a globule equal to 3d6p Hit Points* falls on him. A failed attack against the victim indicates the PC is only splashed with d4p HP of slime; otherwise he is coated. Using a shield to defend guarantees a dousing, but reduces the amount of slime touching the PC by the shield's DR (if the shield is immediately discarded).

* This is the most common sized globule based upon field research. Particular environmental conditions may result in globules differing from this median range.

SIZE COMPARISON

I once observed a pack bearer's hand dissolve into a bloody stub in the space of a few seconds. The poor bastard dipped it into what he thought was a pool of stagnant water to retrieve a dropped dagger. ~

6 ft

3 ft

S

Once in contact with organic material, the slime quickly begins to break it down. This process is excruciatingly painful and results in damage every 10 seconds equivalent to the quantity of slime in contact with the person. Leather, padded, studded leather and ringmail armors absorb the first 2 points of this damage before being destroyed while thick robes absorb 1 point.

Slime cannot be damaged by weapons but may be destroyed by fire. A torch burns up 1d4 HP worth of slime every 10 seconds while fire spells automatically inflict damage (the slime is not permitted a saving throw). In both of these instances, the character having the slime burned off his hide suffers equivalent damage.

The victim (and his allies) may also attempt to scrape the slime off. Assuming they have a blade handy, 1d3 HP can be scraped off every 10 seconds by each person attempting to do so (though the victim suffers 1 point of damage as he is inevitably nicked by the presumably sharp blades). These ad hoc scraping tools must themselves be burned to remove the slime before being able to be used for their primary function.

Example: Grekar the fighter (clad in leather armor and employing a medium shield) walks beneath some flesh-eating slime and dislodges a 13 HP globule. He employs his shield for defense and is thus covered in slime – though 6 HP worth is coating his shield. He immediately discards it taking 1d4p seconds to do so. The remaining slime begins to eat away at his skin – inflicting 7 points of damage every 10 seconds

The party torchbearer immediately runs to his aid and begins burning the slime. He manages to burn away 2 HP worth of the goo during the first 10 seconds – incidentally burning Grekar for 2 points as well. 5 HP of slime thus remains. Grekar would ordinarily sustain 5 points of damage but only takes 3 as the remaining 2 is absorbed by his armor as it is dissolved.

In the following 10 seconds, the torchbearer again jabs at the slime covering Grekar this time burning away another 2 HP worth (and inflicting a 2 point burn on Grekar). Grekar himself spends the time using his short sword to scrape off goo and manages to remove an additional 2 HP worth (but nicks himself for 1 point). Since 2 HP of slime remain, Grekar takes 2 points of damage as his skin is being transformed into slime.

The torchbearer and Grekar continue in their actions for an additional 10 seconds. The torch burns 3 HP worth of slime (the balance and then some) but inflicts a 3 point burn. Since Grekar had stated he would continue to try scraping the slime off, he efforts are wasted but he manages to cut himself again for another hit point.

After the fighter casts aside his slime coated sword, he takes stock of his health. He's suffered 5 points of damage from the slime but 7 points from being burned by the torchbearer and another 2 points from cutting himself. He's also lost his shield and armor, and his sword is useless until the slime is burned off the blade.

On Tellene:

Flesh-eating slime can be found in many subterranean areas through Tellene, but is most common in warmer climes.

[1] *A single ounce of flesh-eating slime, if used as an additional material component in the mage's fifth level Munz's Bolt of Acid spell, extends the duration of acid seepage by 10 seconds.*

FLESH-EATING SLIME

HIT POINTS:	50
SIZE/WEIGHT:	M/100+ lbs.
TENACITY:	n/a
INTELLIGENCE:	Non
FATIGUE FACTOR:	n/a

SPEED		INIT
0		n/a
	ATTACK +3	DMG REDUCTION
	n/a	0
DEFENSE	see below	DAMAGE
n/a		n/a
REACH		TOP SAVE ▼

MOVEMENT

CRAWL:	0
WALK:	0
JOG:	0
RUN:	0
SPRINT:	0

SAVES

PHYSICAL:	+3
MENTAL:	immune
DODGE:	n/a

ATTACK:
This slime deals damage equal to the appropriate HP quantity (typically 3d6p) every 10 seconds. A failed attack roll (by the slime) only splashes the victim with 1d4p HP.

SPECIAL DEFENSES:
Corrosive to the touch.

GENERAL INFO

ACTIVITY CYCLE:	Any
NO. APPEARING:	1-3
% CHANCE IN LAIR:	n/a
FREQUENCY:	Commonplace
ALIGNMENT:	Non
VISION TYPE:	n/a
AWARENESS/SENSES:	n/a
HABITAT:	Caverns and catacombs
DIET:	Omnivorous
ORGANIZATION:	n/a
CLIMATE/TERRAIN:	Temperate to tropical subterranean

YIELD

MEDICINAL:	slime may be used to dissolve warts and growths
SPELL COMPONENTS:	1 ounce of slime, for Munz's Bolt of Acid[1]
HIDE/TROPHY:	nil
TREASURE:	incidental
EDIBLE:	no
OTHER:	nil
EXPERIENCE POINT VALUE:	200

S

SMILODON

Also Known As: Dythnar, Sabre-Toothed Tiger, Shindri

Though I must admit to having only viewed a live smilodon from a safe distance atop a rocky shelf, and that the lone corpse I studied was badly mangled by a great lizard beforehand, I am confident you will benefit from my anatomical studies. This magnificent feline exudes power from its long maxillary canines down its muscular neck and robust body to the tip of its short, thick tail.

The limbs are more massive and yet shorter than those of other felines, indicating that although it is not a great runner, it is strong enough to pull down and wrestle the largest of prey. Its canine teeth, too, are much longer than those of other big hunting cats, and it can open its jaws almost twice as wide, using its great neck muscles to stab its prey with great force.

One of the most feared of the big cats, the smilodon has massive claws and fangs powered by powerful muscles that can inflict horrendous wounds.

A fighting man of my acquaintance once learned this to his great disadvantage, when he gave a captured smilodon cub to a farmer's daughter as a means of strengthening the relationship. Of course, you can no doubt guess what happened. The cub grew quickly to a significant size, escaped, and attacked the local livestock and farmers. Sadly, the fighter's romance was quashed as the young woman was mauled to death. I don't believe they ever captured the creature. - ⚘

A typical adult smilodon is a massively built creature weighing nearly half a ton. It stands over 4 feet tall at the shoulder and has a total body length of about 8 feet (including the nearly foot-long tail), with few to no markings on its thick reddish-brown or yellowish-brown fur. This fur coat consists of two layers; the first is composed of guard hairs that keep out water and dirt, with the second layer being a thick undercoat that helps keep out cold and damp.

It has powerful legs, with the hind ones being shorter than its forelimbs. This gives it a sloped back and slower running speed but also a powerful claw attack. Smilodon paws have a slight webbing between each toe, which helps them to tread easily on a variety of terrains (snow, particularly).

They are also distinguished by their muscular neck and extremely long upper canines, which can grow to be as much as 11 inches long and protrude over 6 inches from the mouth. Furthermore, these teeth have some ductility which keeps them from breaking off in the bodies of their struggling prey. Unlike most other big hunting cats that can only open their mouths to 65°, the smilodon can open its mouth to an impressive 120°, giving the beast a frightening jaw extension and the ability to use its large canine teeth to the best advantage.

Body size and canine length are similar in both sexes.

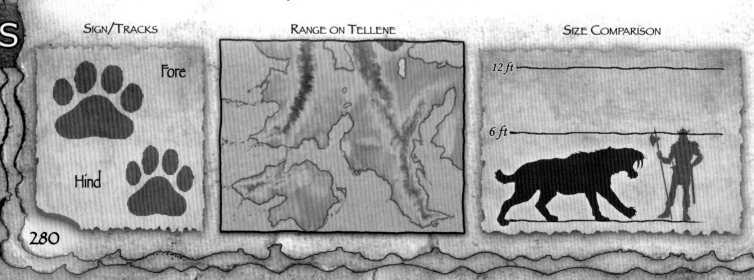

SIGN/TRACKS

Fore

Hind

RANGE ON TELLENE

SIZE COMPARISON

12 ft

6 ft

Combat/Tactics:

When hunting, smilodons often position themselves from the leeward side of a rock or fallen tree, waiting for prey to pass by. When it does so, the smilodon springs from an overhead position and grabs the prey under the chin with one forepaw and the throat with the other, then bites.

If the sabre-toothed tiger lands two successive claw attacks, it has grabbed its opponent and automatically inflicts a deep, piercing bite attack on the target's neck causing 2d10p+8 points of damage. Its jaws remain closed as it continues to press its canines into the prey, dealing an additional bite attack every 5 seconds thereafter (superseding the claw attacks).

The shindri's grip can be broken by anyone striking it severely enough to cause a knock-back or by the overborn victim succeeding at a Feat of Strength (*vs. d20p+18*). The latter can be attempted after each bite attack. While held, prey can only attack with a dagger, knife or claws.

Habitat/Society:

Smilodons dwell in grasslands where the winters are long, living and hunting in packs containing at least one dominant male, five or six related females and their cubs, though some dwell in coalitions containing two dozen individuals or more. The dominant male and his current mated female eat first during feeding, with lesser smilodons following in order of pack dominance.

Smilodons may mate in any season. Females have a gestation period of nearly 4 months, giving birth to a litter of up to four cubs. These cubs are weaned after several months and reach maturity when about 3 years old.

The average smilodon has a lifespan of about 15 years.

Ecology:

A smilodon pack is semi-nomadic, favoring lowland forests and mountain river valleys overgrown with shrubs and trees and thus supporting a wide variety of prey. Here, they claim a particular territory marked by feces, urine and scent. When food is scarce, a pack may leave its normal territory and roam over a wider area in search of nourishment. Smilodons are carnivores, preying on the local wildlife (primarily elk, wild horses, boars, brown bears and other large game) as well as any other game that can provide enough food to keep their bulky frames active. A smilodon pack will also scavenge kills from other predators if given a chance.

A smilodon's main rival is the dire wolf, with whom it competes for prey. As a general rule, the two species avoid each other, with the occasional skirmish occuring when in defense of young or in disputes over carcasses. A smilodon pack that stumbles across a wolf den will most likely raid it and kill any pups inside.

On Tellene:

Smilodons dwell mainly in the northern lands above Lake Jorakk, although they occasionally venture south into the lands of Torakk.

[1]*A smilodon tooth or claw can be used as an alternate material component for the mage's sixth level Boost Strength spell. It is not eaten, but is consumed in the casting.*

SMILODON

HIT POINTS:	32+8d8
SIZE/WEIGHT:	H/nearly ½ ton
TENACITY:	Brave
INTELLIGENCE:	Animal, Low
FATIGUE FACTOR:	1

SPEED 4 **INIT** -1
ATTACK +16
DAMAGE REDUCTION
DEFENSE +9 5
see below
medium **REACH** **TOP SAVE** 8

MOVEMENT

CRAWL:	10
WALK:	15
JOG:	20
RUN:	25
SPRINT:	30

SAVES

PHYSICAL:	+16
MENTAL:	+14
DODGE:	+15

ATTACK:
Smilodons attempt to grab prey with their claws; upon 2 successive claw hits (2d6p+5 each) they have grabbed the prey and automatically bite for 2d10p+8 every 5 seconds (superseding the claw attacks); breaking their grasp requires a Feat of Strength vs. d20p+18

SPECIAL ABILITIES:
Listening 35%, Sneaking 25%

GENERAL INFO

ACTIVITY CYCLE:	Diurnal
NO. APPEARING:	1-2
% CHANCE IN LAIR:	10%
FREQUENCY:	Sporadic
ALIGNMENT:	Non
VISION TYPE:	Standard
AWARENESS/SENSES:	Excellent sense of smell
HABITAT:	Woodlands and valleys
DIET:	Carnivorous
ORGANIZATION:	Individuals
CLIMATE/TERRAIN:	Cold to temperate lowlands

YIELD

MEDICINAL:	nil
SPELL COMPONENTS:	tooth or claw, for Boost Strength spell[1]
HIDE/TROPHY:	hide, head, teeth and claws
TREASURE:	nil
EDIBLE:	yes
OTHER:	items made from bone thought to imbue courage
EXPERIENCE POINT VALUE:	1100

S

Snake

Boa Constrictor, Asp
Rattlesnake, Xullith

That day, my companions and I celebrated the day's victories in the manor house we had claimed for our own. Being the most sober — a rare instance in our group — I was chosen to fetch more wine, and so trotted along to our meager store room. The sun had set and I wore no boots, but my familiarity with the room was such that I needed no candle or lamp. Stepping onto a stool to reach the shelf, I soon realized only one bottle of a very rare and valuable vintage remained. Thus, I stood there for a few seconds pondering whether I ought to take it, before putting my foot to the floor. As I did so, however, I knew that I had stepped on a snake.

The reptile began writhing, flogging at my ankle and instep, and coiling round my leg, but I kept my wits about me. I realized the snake's head was too close to my foot for the use of its fangs, but that to step off could mean instant death. Worse, I had no tool or weapon, nor dared I bring my other bare foot too close to its head. I could perhaps squat down and smash the bottle on it, but my heart sank at the thought of wasting such a valuable wine.

I called for aid, but my companions were too far and too much in their cups to hear me. I yelled for help until my voice was hoarse, all the while feeling the snake lash out at my leg in frustration. Finally, I bent carefully down and shattered the bottle upon its head. The serpent soon went limp, and I left the room with a cask of ale upon my shoulder and no worse venom in my blood than the cheap wine that already coursed through it.

Yet, I will never forgive that snake for causing me to kill it in that fashion. - 𝔖

These elongated reptiles are scaled, legless and lack eyelids or external ears, using a forked tongue to give a directional sense of smell and taste. Most can dislocate their lower jaw to swallow prey larger than their head.

Perhaps the best-known constricting snake is the aptly named boa constrictor. These frighteningly large snakes can grow up to 13 feet long and weigh over 100 pounds, although larger specimens have certainly been rumored to exist. Most boas have a light brown or tan body patterned with dark brown or reddish-brown 'saddle' shapes.

The venomous snakes include the asp, or cobra, a long, slender snake able to raise the front quarter of its body off the ground to display a flattened neck that sticks out on the sides like a hood. The typical asp is dark or light brown, 3 to 5 feet in length and weighs between 6 and 10 pounds.

Another venomous snake is the rattlesnake, which varies widely in coloration depending on region. The most common pattern is a series of dark brown or black bands over a background color of yellow or brown. They have an average length of 3 to 6 feet and weigh about 6 to 12 pounds.

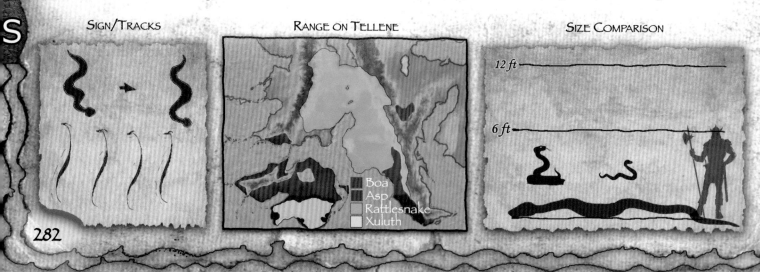

SIGN/TRACKS	RANGE ON TELLENE	SIZE COMPARISON

Boa
Asp
Rattlesnake
Xuluth

12 ft

6 ft

S

BOA CONSTRICTOR

HIT POINTS:	19+2d8
SIZE/WEIGHT:	M/100 lbs.
TENACITY:	Cowardly
INTELLIGENCE:	Animal, Low
FATIGUE FACTOR:	2

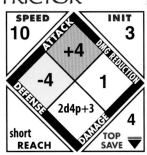

SPEED 10 / INIT 3 / ATTACK +4 / -4 / DMG REDUCTION 1 / DAMAGE 2d4p+3 / short REACH / TOP SAVE 4

MOVEMENT

CRAWL:	1¼
WALK:	2½
JOG:	5
RUN:	7½
SPRINT:	10

SAVES

PHYSICAL:	+4
MENTAL:	+2
DODGE:	+3

ATTACK: Boa constrictors do not have a substantive bite in combat, but deal 2d4p+3 points of damage when constricting their prey; armor DR does not apply to this damage

SPECIAL DEFENSES: Enveloped victims may be inadvertently hit; on any missed attack on a boa engaged in constriction roll again vs. its victim with a +4 bonus to reflect inability to dodge

ASP

HIT POINTS:	2+1d4
SIZE/WEIGHT:	T/8 lbs.
TENACITY:	Nervous
INTELLIGENCE:	Animal, Low
FATIGUE FACTOR:	2

SPEED 10 / INIT -2 / ATTACK +6 / +4 / DMG REDUCTION 0 / DAMAGE 1+ poison / short REACH / TOP SAVE 4

MOVEMENT

CRAWL:	1¼
WALK:	2½
JOG:	5
RUN:	7½
SPRINT:	10

SAVES

PHYSICAL:	+1
MENTAL:	+1
DODGE:	+6

ATTACK:
An asp's fangs inflict 1 point of damage, plus VF 9 poison (failed saves have -2 to Attack, Defense and Damage for 2d12 hours; a 'nat 1' is instant death); may spit venom up to five feet at at target's eyes (save or make CON check to avoid ToP & temporarily blinded)

GENERAL INFO

ACTIVITY CYCLE:	Nocturnal
NO. APPEARING:	1-2
% CHANCE IN LAIR:	5%
FREQUENCY:	Frequent
ALIGNMENT:	Non
VISION TYPE:	Standard
AWARENESS/SENSES:	Can sense body heat within 15 ft
HABITAT:	Tree branches and cave mouths
DIET:	Carnivorous
ORGANIZATION:	Individuals
CLIMATE/TERRAIN:	Tropical woodlands

GENERAL INFO

ACTIVITY CYCLE:	Nocturnal
NO. APPEARING:	1-6
% CHANCE IN LAIR:	5%
FREQUENCY:	Frequent
ALIGNMENT:	Non
VISION TYPE:	Excellent eyesight up to 30 ft
AWARENESS/SENSES:	Senses vibrations/presence of creatures within 15 ft
HABITAT:	Rat holes near lakes and streams
DIET:	Carnivorous
ORGANIZATION:	Individuals
CLIMATE/TERRAIN:	Temperate to tropical woodlands and savannas

YIELD

MEDICINAL:	fats believed to cure joint pain
SPELL COMPONENTS:	can be used in any spell that requires snake parts
HIDE/TROPHY:	yes
TREASURE:	nil
EDIBLE:	yes
OTHER:	nil
EXPERIENCE POINT VALUE:	100

YIELD

MEDICINAL:	purified venom used to treat pain
SPELL COMPONENTS:	can be used in any spell that requires snake parts
HIDE/TROPHY:	yes
TREASURE:	nil
EDIBLE:	yes, but the head is poisonous
OTHER:	nil
EXPERIENCE POINT VALUE:	133

S

RATTLESNAKE

HIT POINTS:	2+1d4
SIZE/WEIGHT:	T/9 lbs.
TENACITY:	Cowardly
INTELLIGENCE:	Animal, Low
FATIGUE FACTOR:	2

SPEED 10 — **INIT** -2
ATTACK +3
DMG REDUCTION 0
DEFENSE +2
DAMAGE 1+ poison
REACH short
TOP SAVE 4

MOVEMENT

CRAWL:	1¼
WALK:	2½
JOG:	5
RUN:	7½
SPRINT:	10

SAVES

PHYSICAL:	+1
MENTAL:	+1
DODGE:	+5

ATTACK:
Rattlesnake fangs deal 1 point of damage, plus VF 8 poison (failed saves have -2 to Attack, Defense and Damage for 2d12 hours; a 'nat 1' is instant death).

XULLITH

HIT POINTS:	27+4d8
SIZE/WEIGHT:	L/500 lbs.
TENACITY:	Brave
INTELLIGENCE:	Animal, High
FATIGUE FACTOR:	3

SPEED 7 — **INIT** -1
ATTACK +12
DMG REDUCTION 4
DEFENSE +5
DAMAGE 3d4p + poison
REACH medium
TOP SAVE 7

MOVEMENT

CRAWL:	2½
WALK:	5
JOG:	10
RUN:	15
SPRINT:	20

SAVES

PHYSICAL:	+7
MENTAL:	+5
DODGE:	+9

ATTACK:
Bites deal 3d4p points of damage plus VF 13 poison; failed saves result in a cumulative -2 CON and -2 penalty to Attack, Defense and Damage every 5 minutes until dead

GENERAL INFO

ACTIVITY CYCLE:	Nocturnal
NO. APPEARING:	1-6
% CHANCE IN LAIR:	5%
FREQUENCY:	Commonplace
ALIGNMENT:	Non
VISION TYPE:	Standard
AWARENESS/SENSES:	Senses vibrations/presence of creatures within 20 ft
HABITAT:	Rocky ledges
DIET:	Carnivorous
ORGANIZATION:	Individuals
CLIMATE/TERRAIN:	Various warm temperate biomes and elevations

GENERAL INFO

ACTIVITY CYCLE:	Nocturnal
NO. APPEARING:	1
% CHANCE IN LAIR:	5%
FREQUENCY:	Sporadic
ALIGNMENT:	Non
VISION TYPE:	Keen eyesight within 60 feet
AWARENESS/SENSES:	Senses body heat within 20 ft
HABITAT:	Dens near slow-moving/shallow water
DIET:	Carnivorous
ORGANIZATION:	Individuals
CLIMATE/TERRAIN:	Temperate to tropical wetlands

YIELD

MEDICINAL:	fats believed to regrow hair in balding humans
SPELL COMPONENTS:	can be used in any spell that requires snake parts
HIDE/TROPHY:	yes
TREASURE:	nil
EDIBLE:	yes, but the head is poisonous
OTHER:	nil

EXPERIENCE POINT VALUE: 84

YIELD

MEDICINAL:	unknown
SPELL COMPONENTS:	can be used in any spell that requires snake parts
HIDE/TROPHY:	yes
TREASURE:	nil
EDIBLE:	yes, but the head is poisonous
OTHER:	nil

EXPERIENCE POINT VALUE: 725

The xullith, known colloquially as the purple adder, is perhaps the largest venomous snake, with an average length of 20 feet and a weight of around 500 pounds. Its name actually comes from the distinct royal purple interior of its mouth; its skin actually varies in color from a dull yellow-green to a grayish-brown. Its belly is white, yellowish white or tan, marked with dark spots that grow darker the closer one gets to the tail. The xullith has a broad head that is distinct from the neck, with a blunt, angled snout (the top of which extends forwards slightly further than the mouth).

Each of these snake species displays some form of sexual dimorphism, with females generally having larger length and girth than males.

Combat/Tactics:

Constrictors, such as the boa, attack with a mouth full of small, hooked teeth, holding its prey until its can wrap its body around the prey and squeeze it to death. If the boa attacks successfully, it has coiled around its prey, inflicting automatic constriction damage thereafter every 10 seconds. Constriction can be broken with a successful knock-back or Feat of Strength (vs. d20p+18; can attempt every 10 seconds). While trapped, a victim can only attack with daggers or smaller weapons.

When hunting small animals, most venomous snakes deliver a single bite and retreat slightly, waiting for the venom to bring down its prey. If the target is a bird, the snake may hang on to it with its fangs while it waits for the neurotoxin to take effect. Otherwise, the bird might fly away and die where the snake cannot find it, thus temporarily diminishing the snake's limited supply of venom without providing any survival benefit in terms of food. If fighting off a threat, a venomous snake may deliver multiple strikes to its foe.

The asp may attack either with its venomous fangs or by spitting venom (VF 9) at an enemy's eyes up to 5 feet away. The latter attack is considered ranged with the Asp rolling a straight d20p. If it hits, the victim is entitled to a saving throw. Failure results in great pain (requiring a Constitution check to avoid effects identical to a failed threshold of pain check) and blindness until 30 seconds are spent cleansing the venom from one's eyes (the blindness being permanent if the poisonous irritant is not washed out within 5 minutes).

The rattlesnake shakes its tail tip when threatened, the ring of loosely attached bead-like scales creating a rapid, crisp vibration that resembles a loudly buzzing insect or the rustle of dry leaves. This rattle may become muted or indistinct should the scales become wet or suffer from excessively damp weather. Similiar to the asp, it injects venom (VF 8) through its fanged bite.

If stressed, the xullith throws its head back with its mouth open to display the intense purple interior, while pulling its neck and the front part of the body into an 'S' shape. Alternatively, it may flatten itself to the ground and secrete a pungent musk through its anal glands. Though this is not a debilitating stench, it does serve to deter most creatures from attempting to consume it.

Habitat/Society:

Most snakes prefer warm or temperate climates (particularly woodlands), though they are rarely exclusive to such locations. For instance, the boa constrictor thrives in warm, humid woodlands near rivers or streams, but can survive in even arid semi-desert conditions. Asps favor warm climates with savannas or prairies near standing or slow-moving water, while rattlesnakes range from desert flats to rocky hillsides, prairies and woodlands. The xullith are highly adaptable, dwelling in temperate or warm lands in or near water and woodlands, particularly where slow-moving and shallow waters (e.g., lowland swamps, streams, lakes, canals, rice fields) are present.

When a male snake battles another male for the mating rights to a female, the two wrap their bodies around each other, rearing and slamming their foe against the ground until one of them concedes defeat. After mating, the female snake has a certain gestation period (one to two months for the asp, four to eight months for boa constrictors, rattlesnakes and xullith), after which she bears an average litter of 25 live young that are independent at birth. All venomous snakes are born complete with fangs and venom.

Snakes leave behind evidence of their existence not just by any slight tracks in the earth, but by their molted scales. Snakes shed their entire layer of scales together, as a complete outer layer during each molt much like a sock being turned inside out. Younger snakes may molt as much as four times annually, though older snakes do so only once or twice per year.

Ecology:

Boa constrictors, asps and rattlesnakes are carnivorous, consuming a variety of tiny and small mammals (primarily rodents) and birds, as well as bats, lizards and amphibians. With no teeth appropriate to chewing food, snakes swallow their prey whole (by flexing out the lower jaw and various skull joints) even if the prey is somewhat bigger than the snake itself.

Boa constrictors expand their diet to include creatures as large as a halfling, should the opportunity arise, while asps prefer frogs over other prey. Rattlesnakes seem to consume more rodents than anything else.

The diet of the purple adder includes the varied prey preferred by other snakes, but also consists of local monsters and other sapient creatures. It may even include carrion in its diet.

Most snakes' natural enemies include the mongoose and various birds of prey, such as the giant eagle. Other large carnivores may catch and eat snakes, but rarely do so. Snakes also prey on other snakes when necessary, consuming them as easily as they would a rat. Xullith are targeted by giant eagles and other beasts more confident of attacking something that size.

On Tellene:

Giant constrictors can be found at least as far north as Shyta-Thybaj, where they prey on monsters as well as the occasional murder victim dumped into the city's old granite quarry.

The holy symbol of the Imposters, clerics of the Confuser of Ways (god of lies, deceit and mischief) is a snake head with extended tongue. Thus, Impostors are fond of snakes and will often be found raising them or in possession of one.

S

SPECTRE Also Known As: Ciguld, Karigon

It hast been my experience that the spectre is like unto pernicious weeds. When first thou doth note their presence, they be but a trifling concern. The farmer hath much to do and it seemeth correct to attend to matters which doth press more urgent. Such is a common error of judgment, for left alone the weed doth in secret wind its tendrils betwixt stalk and loam. Having thusly ensconced itself most thoroughly, it resists all but the most grueling efforts.

The spectre is a enemy that brimmest over with danger – maketh not such a fallacious error in thine assessment shouldest thou consider him unworthy of the awe due the mightiest of the unliving. Forsooth, it is not by might of arms that he wieldeth power. Indeed his chill touch may be less severe than that of the barrowed wight. Rather, it is the crafty and determined nature of the spirit that must be afeared. Many have the power of Seers for they do so frequently seem to read one's very thoughts from afar and have laid on contingencies one could scarcely expect from a foe without intimate knowledge of thine planning. This doth surprise me but little for I have witnessed a spectre employ the wizard's tools of wand and ring to trenchant effect.

It behooves the brave souls who dare stalk this fiend to know that he doth cast but little care upon thine presence. Most haveth a far-reaching schemata that doth all their focus command. Little will they trouble ye until thine actions seemest to interfere – inefficacious meddling will draw but the lowest minions. This is their greatest weakness for it is possible to whittle away at these allies and resources before the spirit is himself goaded into personal action.

Be wary though for once ye've interfered with his plans, ye've gained a vengeful enemy who will act with disregard. Having ruined his life's toils, he hath little left to retain and thus focuseth all his ire upon you. Ye must with all assurity kill him. Shouldest ye fail, thine demise willst become his newest obsession… - ◉

Spectres are the spirits of wickedly obdurate beings who failed in life to complete to fruition their grand evil schemes. Force of will coupled with supernatural assistance has permitted their continued existence as agents of evil.

Their visual appearance is that of a translucent replicate of the being they were in life. Most often, this is an elderly man with accoutrements befitting a person of wealth and status.

Combat/Tactics:

Spectres, by and large, were not powerful combatants in life, being more of the nefarious schemer than doughty warrior. Despite the far greater resilience unlife bestowed upon them, few have fully embraced this enhanced capacity, instead relying upon guile, trickery and bluff when confronting armed foes.

While not immaterial, they can seemingly pass through doors or walls (their wispy form may pass though any barrier not absolutely airtight). Spectres use this ability to both frighten opponents as well as to gain a tactical advantage.

Should circumstances dictate their direct involvement in combat, they are reluctant to engage in a toe-to-toe melee with sword-wielding knights. Rather, they focus their efforts on a secondary combatant (most frequently a despised cleric). They are likely to engage in repeated probing attacks in order to gauge an opponent's strength and tactics while allowing for an escape route passable only to themselves

S

Takest heed when venture thou dost in darkest night within boewls of manors and castles lang ruined, for oftimes be the evil manor lord about, dead but ever waiting in his home.
It be not cowage for flight to be foremost in thine thoughts. Be not a foole to think a barred door provest a ward for it canst filtre through the wee cracks if thine soul it wisheth for to consume.

WILL FACTOR
14

SIZE COMPARISON

6 ft

3 ft

A spectre's chilling touch drains both Constitution and Dexterity from its victims in equal measure (randomly determine odd results, a 3-point hit reduces one of either Con or Dex and two of the other statistic). Should it completely devour the life essence[1], it may command the slain individual to rise as a new spectre itself. Upon so rising, it immediately seeks out its undead master for service; it assumes the statistics of a full spectre but retains any skills and proficiencies from life.

Spectres cannot employ weapons; their diaphanous form cannot exert sufficient force to make the endeavor worthwhile. However, they may wear jewelry and rings, and possibly make use of magical items if their background permits. Note that such material items may be left behind should a spectre pass through a tiny crack in a wall.

The creature's essence is truly tied to the night, deriving their vitality from dark energy. As such, they despise light of any sort and seek to extinguish any source of illumination they encounter. The merest contact with sunlight drives the creature off rendering it unable to attack and applying a -6 penalty to its Defense while so fluoresced.

Habitat/Society/Ecology:

As has been insinuated, spectres are highly intelligent and seek to deal with intruders in direct relation to the threat they pose to the fiend's plans. Though unrepentantly wicked and evil, spectres are constrained in both time and resources and do not permit themselves to engage in petty hate crimes (utilizing minions for random acts of terror if that serves their greater purpose).

Many spectres possess a variety of skills carried over from life that directly benefit their macabre purposes. These are usually of the sort that permits them to gather information or to manipulate their enemies (these may include Arcane Lore, Glean Information, Interrogation, Intimidation, Salesmanship, and Art of Seduction). More than a few are also spell casters – some of considerable proficiency – and most are competent administrators.

Spectres are thus often dread foes being highly motivated, organized and well informed with a capacity to react intelligently to any force that dares oppose them. If they have a weakness, it is the tendency for them to develop a monomania with respect to their schemes – certainly abetted by their undead form's lack of need for sleep, rest, or nourishment. They also have a marked tendency to allow thoughts of vengeance to warp their plans – subtly revising them to allow for revenge against those who may have interceded to foil them in life.

On Tellene

It is an accepted belief that binding a corpse with ropes constructed of yarn wrapped in a band of high content silver filé prevents the dead from rising as a spectre. This is often the practice with notorious masterminds or other disreputable persons of note executed by central authorities. The danger is that the burial crew or grave robbers may pilfer these ropes, thus circumventing these wise precautions and possibly facilitating the creation of a master spectre.

[1] If a spectre's touch drains either Constitution or Dexterity to zero, the victim is slain.

SPECTRE

HIT POINTS:	25+5d8
SIZE/WEIGHT:	M/nil
TENACITY:	Nervous
INTELLIGENCE:	Smart to Brilliant
FATIGUE FACTOR:	n/a

SPEED		INIT
10	+13	-4
+6	21	
medium REACH	d6p	TOP SAVE ▼

(ATTACK +13, DMG REDUCTION, DEFENSE +6, DAMAGE d6p)

ATTACK:
Touch drains CON and DEX in equal measure (randomly determine odd results; a 3 point hit reduces 1 point from either and 2 points from the other). Slain foes rise as spectres in service to their killer.

DEFENSES:
Can only be damaged fully by silvered weapons (reduces DR to 11).

MOVEMENT

CRAWL:	2½
WALK:	5
JOG:	10
RUN:	15
SPRINT:	20

SAVES

PHYSICAL:	+13
MENTAL:	immune
DODGE:	+13

GENERAL INFO

ACTIVITY CYCLE:	Any, but shun daylight
NO. APPEARING:	1-6
% CHANCE IN LAIR:	25%
FREQUENCY:	Unusual
ALIGNMENT:	Lawful Evil
VISION TYPE:	Undead Sight
AWARENESS/SENSES:	Standard
HABITAT:	Caverns, tombs and dungeons
DIET:	n/a
ORGANIZATION:	Individuals
CLIMATE/TERRAIN:	Any subterranean

YIELD

MEDICINAL:	nil
SPELL COMPONENTS:	nil
HIDE/TROPHY:	nil
TREASURE:	spectres are often near their former life's treasures
EDIBLE:	no
OTHER:	nil
EXPERIENCE POINT VALUE:	1075

S

SPHINX
ANDROSPHINX
GYNOSPHINX

Fierce, noble and headstrong is how I would describe the androsphinx. Unlike others of its kind that can be vexatious to mankind, this creature truly seems to revel in the company of certain brave and audacious men whose bold natures mirror its own.

Though I, alas, cannot number myself amongst those souls who have experienced the company of an androsphinx, I have it on good authority – no less than the Patriarch of Miclenon's Face of the Free – that it is an experience unparalleled.

Though I was forced to shout through my interview with the priest for he was hard of hearing, he related a tale of his adventure with one such creature. Though he recalled this decades-old trek with a wistful gleam in his eye, I could not help but to think that the sphinx did truly lead his human compatriots into a hornet's nest of villainy from which they were lucky to have escaped with their lives… ⸙

This regal creature has the body of a lion and the wings of an eagle, with a head resembling that of a human. The female sphinx also bears the shoulders, upper arms and breasts of a human woman. The male, on the other hand, is much more leonine in appearance, with a thoroughly feline body and a head that resembles a strange hybrid of lion and man. Even from behind, a male sphinx is easily recognized by its heavy mane, which grows thickly to cover its upper back, shoulders and much of its chest. When sages discuss the matter amongst themselves, they often refer to male sphinxes as androsphinxes and females as gynosphinxes.

Hair coloration between both sexes varies from light buff to yellowish, reddish, or dark ochraceous brown with generally lighter underparts. Flesh tones are light tan to deep bronze, and serves as a potential indicator of age. Older sphinxes are naturally darker after centuries of basking in the sun. Should a sphinx open its mouth to speak, the viewer may catch sight of its sharp, leonine teeth.

Ancient sites often display statuary of these creatures. Whether this paid tribute to their service as counselors or was merely an aspiration for long-departed kings is unclear. One thing is certain, it points to the longevity and wisdom these creatures possess.

SIGN/TRACKS	RANGE ON TELLENE	SIZE COMPARISON

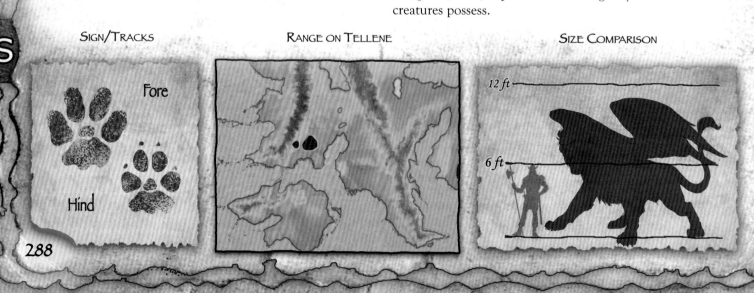

Fore

Hind

12 ft

6 ft

ANDROSPHINX

HIT POINTS:	38+12d8
SIZE/WEIGHT:	G/2 tons
TENACITY:	Fearless
INTELLIGENCE:	Smart
FATIGUE FACTOR:	-6

SPEED 5 | INIT -2
ATTACK +22
DEFENSE +13 | DMG REDUCTION 14
see below
medium REACH | DAMAGE | TOP SAVE 12

MOVEMENT

CRAWL:	5
WALK:	10
JOG:	15
RUN:	20
FLY:	30

SAVES

PHYSICAL:	+24
MENTAL:	+22
DODGE:	+21

ATTACK: Androsphinxes can cast spells as a 12th+ level cleric; They also have a frightening roar [see text]; In close quarter combat, claws deal 3d12p+3 points of damage each.

SPECIAL DEFENSES:
Flight

GENERAL INFO

ACTIVITY CYCLE:	Diurnal
NO. APPEARING:	1
% CHANCE IN LAIR:	35%
FREQUENCY:	Unusual
ALIGNMENT:	Chaotic Good
VISION TYPE:	Standard
AWARENESS/SENSES:	Standard
HABITAT:	Abandoned Structures
DIET:	Carnivorous
ORGANIZATION:	Solitary
CLIMATE/TERRAIN:	Arid desert to semi-desert

YIELD

MEDICINAL:	nil
SPELL COMPONENTS:	unknown
HIDE/TROPHY:	displaying corpse as trophy may result in retribution as Androsphinx are well-liked by locals
TREASURE:	antiques of great value, magic
EDIBLE:	yes
OTHER:	nil
EXPERIENCE POINT VALUE:	1850

GYNOSPHINX

HIT POINTS:	30+8d8
SIZE/WEIGHT:	H/1 ton
TENACITY:	Steady
INTELLIGENCE:	Brilliant
FATIGUE FACTOR:	-2

SPEED 5 | INIT -3
ATTACK +16
DEFENSE +14 | DMG REDUCTION 11
5d4p
medium REACH | DAMAGE | TOP SAVE 11

MOVEMENT

CRAWL:	5
WALK:	10
JOG:	15
RUN:	20
FLY:	25

SAVES

PHYSICAL:	+16
MENTAL:	+25
DODGE:	+20

ATTACK: Gynosphinxes can cast spells as a 18th+ level mage; In close quarter combat, claws deal 5d4p points of damage.

SPECIAL DEFENSES:
Flight

GENERAL INFO

ACTIVITY CYCLE:	Diurnal
NO. APPEARING:	1
% CHANCE IN LAIR:	65%
FREQUENCY:	Unusual
ALIGNMENT:	Neutral
VISION TYPE:	Standard
AWARENESS/SENSES:	Standard
HABITAT:	Abandoned Structures
DIET:	Omnivorous
ORGANIZATION:	Solitary
CLIMATE/TERRAIN:	Arid desert to semi-desert

YIELD

MEDICINAL:	nil
SPELL COMPONENTS:	unknown
HIDE/TROPHY:	nil
TREASURE:	objet d'art, exquisite jewelry, magic
EDIBLE:	yes
OTHER:	nil
EXPERIENCE POINT VALUE:	1500

S

Combat/Tactics:

Sphinxes are powerful combatants (particularly the androsphinx) and highly intelligent beings whose first inclination is to utilize their power of flight, craftiness and magical capabilities (including the near-certain possession of magical devices) to forestall or avoid physical combat on any but their own terms.

Androsphinxes are divine spellcasters with the capabilities of at least a 12th level cleric, though they are not priests per se. More fearsome, though – and readily employed when angered – is their dreadful roar. This roar can be audible for miles and, when first unleashed, all creatures within 300 feet must succeed at a magic saving throw vs. d20p+15 or flee in stark terror for 30 minutes. After this flight, any creature so affected must succeed at a morale check to approach the sphinx again.

Should its initial roar fail to dissuade opponents, the androsphinx can bellow again, this vocalization being yet louder. Those within 30 feet are deafened for 15 minutes (and have ringing in their ears for another day). In addition, any creatures within 150 feet must save vs. d20p+15 or be rendered paralyzed with fright for 4d12p seconds and then succumb to fear (as above). Individuals farther away (up to 350 feet) are affected as the first roar.

If completely enraged by extremely resolute opponents, the sphinx issues its final roar. This roar is so loud that it cracks stone within 30 feet (incidentally shattering glass vials or ceramic containers as well). The sonic force of this roar inflicts 2d12p points of physical damage to creatures within this radius (and counts triple for knock-back purposes). This roar also inflicts deafness until the character succeeds at a Constitution check (may attempt once per hour – a 'nat 1' on any check indicates permanent deafness). Those further away are affected as described in the first or second roar depending on distance from the sphinx.

Should it deign to engage in physical combat, an androsphinx can rend foes with powerful slashes of its razor sharp talons for 3d12p+3 every 5 seconds.

Gynosphinxes are astute magi with a spell arsenal of no less than 18th level. As would be expected from any creature with such capabilities, they prefer to remain at a safe distance from potential adversaries, while utilizing their formidable arcane spellcasting powers to harry the impudent thugs seeking to do them harm. Should worse come to worse, a gynosphinx can defend herself by lacerating opponents with her forepaws every 5 seconds (causing 5d4p points of damage with a successful hit).

Despite their size and visual similarity to the paws of great cats, those of both sexes of sphinx possess incredible manual dexterity, permitting them to manipulate small objects as easily as a human might. They are thus capable of using precision instruments, reading books and scrolls, and may also utilize wands, potions and other magical devices.

Habitat/Society:

Sphinxes are desert dwellers, though it is uncertain if this is a climatic preference or a means of isolating themselves from 'lesser' beings. They usually dwell in long-forgotten ruins of past civilizations, seeking out the former abodes of kings or princes in which to live. Many of these palaces have been spared the ravages of time by the continued maintenance of these creatures, and can resemble a museum of sorts (for the sphinxes are wont to gather items of historical relevance from the surrounding region).

Though the sphinx race has male and female counterparts, relations between the androsphinx and gynosphinx are seldom harmonious (and even then, only briefly). When together, they invariably bicker over everything. Eventually, the androsphinx storms off in a huff while vowing never to return (though he always does, albeit sometimes after a very prolonged absence).

This quarreling is attributable to the very different personalities of the two sphinxes. The androsphinx is an ardent libertarian, advocating personal freedom and repudiating any strictures on an individual's rights save those that would transgress the rights of others. Unfortunately, in its personal life, this translates to a hatred of being told what to do and when to be home. Androsphinxes are a gregarious lot and feel compelled to become involved in the affairs of others. They often enter into quixotic adventures while seeking to right perceived injustices.

They are not fond of elvenkind, despite an often-similar ethical philosophy and extended lifespan. They see the former as being too passive and overly concerned with art and aesthetics (perhaps manifesting in this scorn some misplaced antipathy towards females of their kind). It is humans to whom they are most often drawn, in part for their vitality and eagerness to take action. Few high priests of the Guardian have not had the opportunity to seek the council of an androsphinx, and many have collaborated with a sphinx on some crusade.

Gynosphinxes, conversely, are self-absorbed narcissists. They care little for companions other than for what they can offer the sphinx (though the sphinx is seldom appreciative). In the case of androsphinxes, they desire his burly good looks, physical companionship, protection from other males (particularly the heinous hieracosphinx) and the possibility of children. In exchange, they offer little but haranguing.

Other individuals seeking her favor must offer her comparably valuable gifts. Gynosphinxes are shrewd bargainers and demand both exceptional quality and lavish attention. This makes them difficult clients for even the rarified artisans capable of producing the exquisite jewelry they prize most dearly.

Despite their renowned intransigence, persons seeking knowledge of historical or cryptic information occasionally seek out gynosphinxes. As venerable geniuses, all are accomplished lore masters possessing immeasurable knowledge. However, they are also very cognizant of their superiority and treat supplicants with condescension for their enfeebled intellect. One manifestation of this sardonic attitude is their em-

S

ployment of riddles. However, it must be said that not all gynosphinx are riddlers; individuals may employ other methods such as mathematical or linguistic games, logic puzzles or even trivia contests.

Gynosphinxes love all sorts of mind games and utilize them both for personal amusement as well as a 'screening process.' At the very least, to be engaged by a sphinx in such a contest ensures that the sphinx does not consider that person to be an immediate threat. Solving the puzzle she proffers does merit some modicum of respect from the sphinx, and disposes her to consider the such a person to be possessed of sufficient intelligence (and not a waste of her time spent communicating with him). Any service rendered, though, will be dearly paid for.

Sphinxes do not age once mature, with lifespans that traverse the centuries, though they are mortal and may be felled by various forms of corporeal injury.

Ecology:

Although sphinxes are undoubtedly carnivorous, they seem to subsist on the merest morsels of food and may go for years between meals. They can also withstand long periods without water, visiting the local oasis only every month or so. Living as they do among the isolated desert ruins of old, they have little natural competition for food or resources.

The androsphinx is an intimidating presence and, except for the occasional encounter with other desert monsters, has few troubles with other local predators. The gynosphinx must deal with these foes as well, but her main persecutions come from the males of her species. While the androsphinx is an acceptable mate in most circumstances, the criosphinx and hieracosphinx are constant tormentors. A criosphinx's crude attempts at mating include presenting her with gifts and frequently badgering her with over-attention until she becomes sexually receptive. Hieracosphinxes, however, form alliances of multiple males (usually no more than two or three) and aggressively surround or chase the female for minutes, days or even weeks at a time, using all manner of violence until she mates with each male.

Most births of criosphinxes or hieracosphinxes are the result of a mating with such a creature when the gynosphinx was at the beginning of her estrus cycle. There is a small chance that a mating between andro- and gynosphinx may produce a crio- or hieracosphinx offspring, though these are rare. Female offspring are always gynosphinxes.

On Tellene:

It is said that sphinxes have been encountered most often in the vicinity of the Elos Desert city of Dijishy. This harbor of learning and research is perhaps unique in human society for its appeal to the sphinxes' core interests.

It is rumored that the Khydoban Desert is also an abode of sphinxes. If true, it is almost certain that they know the true location of the City of the Dead and whether or not there is some truth to the tales of long-dead residents still inhabiting that fabled city.

S

SPHINX, CRIO~

The secret to successful treasure hunting is information. That's a pure and simple fact. Step one of any plan is knowin' what you're after and step two is knowin' where it's at.

I personally favor liberating wealth from the dearly departed – leastwise 'cause they aren't around to take personal offense at your actions. Sure, some of them go to great lengths hiding their tombs but that's where information comes into play.

Anyone experienced in the trade knows that the Elos Desert has the greatest concentration of cairns on the face of Tellene, but Hells if I'm going to go wandering about like a crazy nomad looking for them.

I got in good with a couple of criosphix livin' outside of Dijishy. Greedy bastards all right, but they know the lay of the land. Extortionist rates was what they were charging, but I got them by the horns sure enough. Turns out these guys are crazy for riddles and word games. To each his own I say.

Now I got a halfling buddy that's all into that same kind of nonsense. Waste of time if you ask me but you're not, right? So for an evening of pickin' his brain I get a load of riddles. And whouldn't you know but the ram headed beasts just loved 'em. Gave me everything I wanted and then some! - ☥

This bruiser loves to charge and charge hard. Loosen up your rank or front line to let him pass through and minimize the number of targets.

The criosphinx is one of the three male sphinx phenotypes. Atop its lionesque body is the head of a mouflon ram with large curved horns, while large wings resembling those of an owl sprout from its shoulders. Its coloration is typically a deep reddish-brown interspersed with patches of black though its snout is usually white. Its plumage is usually a matte brown.

Criosphinx are haughty creatures and fully expect anyone who deigns to enter their presence to treat them in an reverent manner. Failure to acquiesce to their vanity ensures at best a tepid reaction and possibly enrages them.

Combat/Tactics:

If angered, a criosphinx charges at an opponent head down to butt with its great curved horns. Having gained sufficient speed via this charge, it then soars into the air and wheels around to gauge the effectiveness of its attack.

If this demonstration of its prowess was insufficient to cow its adversaries, it maneuvers to position itself for another head-butt – this time diving from altitude. Once grounded, it rears up to deliver another butt while employing both its mighty clawed paws to rend its enemies.

Habitat/Society:

Much as with their bestial hieracosphinx kin, criosphinxes are aroused by the scent of the gynosphinx. However, they are not malevolent and sadistic hunters like the latter and thus utilize less rapacious means of snaring a mate.

Although gynosphinx find them repugnant, they do not live

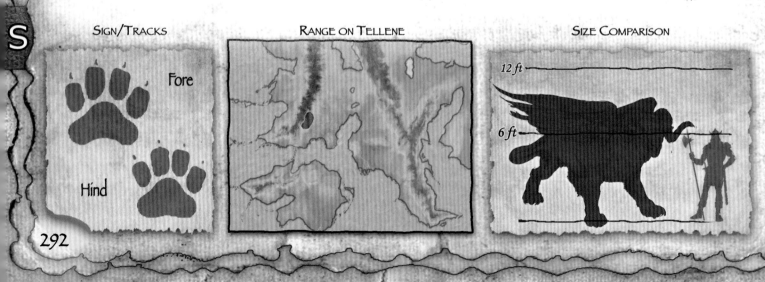

| SIGN/TRACKS | RANGE ON TELLENE | SIZE COMPARISON |

Fore

Hind

12 ft

6 ft

in mortal fear of the ram-headed sphinx and thus the two can often reach a détente. From this point forward, the criosphinx flatters and lavishes attention upon the gynosphinx as well as showering her with precious gifts. Though she may pine for the aloof and distant androsphinx, the criosphinx will always be there to comfort and console. In a moment of weakness or self-doubt, she may decide to settle for the criosphinx (particularly a seemingly wealthy one). Once he has had his way with her, a criosphinx quickly loses interest and leaves.

Though not bloodthirsty creatures, the criosphinx is known for exceptional avarice (though not for personal enrichment but rather for use in seducing the next gynospinx it meets). It may seek to intimidate travelers, extorting them for a bribe to permit safe passage through its territory.

These sphinx are long-lived and reasonably observant, permitting them to gather a vast amount of intelligence with regard to the area in which they dwell. Unlike many xenophobic sylvan creatures that avoid human contact, a criosphinx's greed makes it amenable to interacting with anyone willing to buy its services.

If approached with due deference to its elevated sense of self-importance, criosphinx are willing to entertain any reasonable offer (though they demand an exorbitant fee for any information provided or service rendered). The sole exception is when riddles are offered in trade. Although they know many riddles themselves, they are completely outclassed by the gynosphinx. Acquiring new riddles (especially very clever ones) with which to impress a future paramour is one of their highest goals. An adept riddler may often bargain with them from a position of power and obtain far more than mere bribery would secure.

One has to be careful when dealing with these sphinx, for they are completely self-centered and have no qualms about betraying the presumed trust of a deal. They tend to be very talkative without revealing anything of value, all the while seeking to gather as much information about the other party as possible.

Ecology:

Criosphinxes are usually solitary creatures given to leading a lonesome existence in hilly scrubland abutting deserts. Despite their size and ferocity, they are herbivorous.

Although they live in regions simultaneously populated with hieracosphinxes, the two seldom come into conflict. Each begrudgingly respects the danger of severe injury or death in confronting another of its kind, leading them to actively avoid one another. Androsphinx regard them as sniveling duplicitous worms and rarely have anything to do with them.

On Tellene

A number of criosphinx live on the western fringes of the Elos Desert, most notably in the vicinity of Dijishy. Though hardly numerous, many are well known to residents of the city – particularly followers of the Lord of Intuition.

CRIOSPHINX

HIT POINTS:	32+10d8
SIZE/WEIGHT:	H/1 ton
TENACITY:	Brave
INTELLIGENCE:	Average
FATIGUE FACTOR:	-7

SPEED 3   INIT -2

ATTACK +19

DMG REDUCTION

DEFENSE +12   13

see below

medium REACH   DAMAGE   11 TOP SAVE

MOVEMENT

CRAWL:	5
WALK:	10
JOG:	15
RUN:	20
FLY:	25

SAVES

PHYSICAL:	+21
MENTAL:	+17
DODGE:	+18

ATTACK:
Criosphinxes deal 6d6p points of damage with a butt from their horns, or 5d4p with each of their claws.

SPECIAL DEFENSES:
Flight

GENERAL INFO

ACTIVITY CYCLE:	Diurnal
NO. APPEARING:	1-4
% CHANCE IN LAIR:	25%
FREQUENCY:	Unusual
ALIGNMENT:	Neutral
VISION TYPE:	Standard
AWARENESS/SENSES:	Standard
HABITAT:	Rocky ledges
DIET:	Herbivorous
ORGANIZATION:	Individuals
CLIMATE/TERRAIN:	Deserts and surrounding territory

YIELD

MEDICINAL:	nil
SPELL COMPONENTS:	nil
HIDE/TROPHY:	nil
TREASURE:	criosphinxes prize treasure for seducing mates; as such it tends to be beautiful & valuable
EDIBLE:	yes
OTHER:	nil
EXPERIENCE POINT VALUE:	1425

S

Sphinx, Hieraco

As a professional hunter for bounty, I am privy to a certain degree of rumor, innuendo and outright lies regarding dastardly beasts that prey upon the common ranks of mankind. I consider bona fide stories of a great winged hawk with a large and unfamiliar silhouette. Should these be accompanied by tales of rapacious killing where corpses are left to rot mangled and broken but uneaten, my suspicions naturally run to the presence of a heiracosphinx.

I am not by nature motivated by a crusading spirit nor do I seek to be an arbiter of justice. Avoidance of these high-minded but impractical notions has doubtless served to extend my life. One of the few exceptions I tolerate is the case of the great falcon cat. These creatures exhibit such intolerably capricious and murderous temperament that even a world weary and jaded soul as myself cannot but be moved to assist those subject to its predation.

Keen eyesight and the ability to soar high above the ground make this sphinx a deadly predator.

Hunting this beast is a task for which combined action is a necessity for it is both a deadly combatant and capable of extricating itself skyward in great rapidity should one weather its onslaught. There are those that advocate employment of fishing nets seeded with barbed hooks to ground the creature. This I cannot recommend for too often such tactics ensnare allies in proximity to the beast. My preference is to set packs of trained hounds upon the sphinx. It is fortunate that the creature does not recognize the danger of this threat for wardogs can quite ably ground it by seizing its wings while serving to divert its attention as they gnaw upon its flanks. These tactics have served me in good stead. - ↑

The hieracosphinx possesses the same leonine body as its sphinx kin albeit topped with an avian head resembling that of a brown falcon in all aspects save size. Its large wings too resemble those of a bird of prey.

Its body coloration is generally an ochraceous brown often with faint darker rosettes. The underparts tend to be lighter hued but the tail tuft is always black. Its plumage displays similar brown colors, but strongly patterned in a manner reminiscent of hawks. Notably, their underwings have a lengthwise pattern of blotches, lines or arrowhead marks.

Though all hieracosphinx are male, none possess a mane.

Combat/Tactics:

The hieracosphinx is the least anthropomorphic of the species and in many regards more similar to a predator. In this role, it is certainly an effective hunter combining speedy and agile flight with the brawn of a great cat.

Its normal hunting method is to fly high over the hills of its territory employing its exceptional eyesight to scan for prey. The latter can be large game animals – or indeed anything else that this malicious beast might enjoy killing. Of particular interest to it are groups of humans that may have gold and silver objects that it cherishes.

It may dive from altitude seeking to surprise and incapacitate its quarry. Alternatively, it may land nearby and spring from ambush utilizing flight to reach its target in a single bound. Once engaged, it employs both powerful leonine forepaws and its oversized beak to brutal effect.

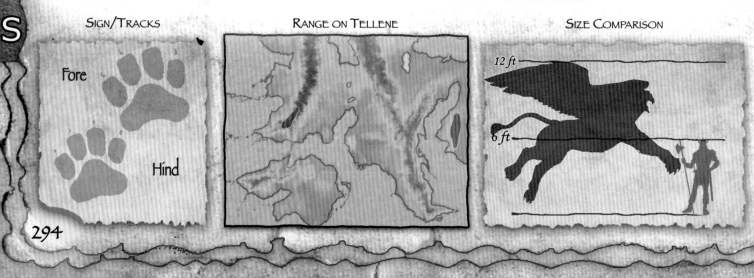

SIGN/TRACKS — Fore — Hind

RANGE ON TELLENE

SIZE COMPARISON — 12 ft — 6 ft

Habitat/Society:

The hieracosphinx is one of three male sphinx phenotypes (the others being the androsphinx and criosphinx). While desirous of the gynosphinx when her scent is detected, the latter considers the falcon-headed sphinx a dangerous and repellant aberrant to avoid at all costs.

Successful mating can only be accomplished by group force. When a female sphinx is located, hieracosphinxes gather together into a flock of up to six individuals and actively stalk her (and systematically killing any potential competitors such as an androsphinx). When they eventually attack, this flock will attempt to beat the gynosphinx into submission before inseminating her in turn via an established pecking order.

Whilst not aroused by a female, the hieracosphinx often simply reverts to the role of a predator navigating the thermals at the fringes of deserts and scanning for prey.

Like others of their species, they value treasure of all sorts and are rapacious in collecting anything of perceived value often accumulating a large, if disheveled, hoard of objects (many of which may be of dubious value). It is this impulse which may lead the sphinx into a collaboration with wealthy and powerful individuals, occasionally suffering the indignity of serving as a steed.

Hieracosphinx are most commonly encountered along the periphery of a large desert, often in highlands that facilitate a thermal gradient.

Ecology

Hieracosphinx are brutal predators killing both for sustenance as well as sport. These creatures are just as likely to attack with a full belly as not. These frequently are unprovoked attacks of opportunity done to assert territorial dominance or merely to relieve boredom. Thus as vicious and unpredictable hunters, the appearance of a hieracosphinx is a true cause for alarm.

Though much has been written to denigrate this creature's intelligence, it is only in comparison to their kin that they appear fascile. Despite falling short of median human intellectual capacity (if only moderately so), they are sentient beings and no mere animal. They are fully capable of planning and all can comprehend human speech (though proficiency in any given language is not assured).

Griffyns and hieracosphinxes are natural enemies occupying a similar ecological niche. Though the latter is predominantly found in hot and arid climes, where their territories overlap both creatures are vehement in their efforts to exterminate the other.

On Tellene

Hieracosphinxes dwell in the Arajyd Hills and the western Elenon Mountain slopes. In the former, they are a notorious pestilence greatly feared by gnome and kobold alike. In their western range along the Elos Desert, rumors persist of their employment by Pel Brolenon's soldiery. While this is unsubstantiated, it cannot be denied that the preconditions to facilitate such a union are in place.

HIERACOSPHINX

HIT POINTS:	35+9d8
SIZE/WEIGHT:	H/ ¾ ton
TENACITY:	Brave
INTELLIGENCE:	Slow
FATIGUE FACTOR:	-3

SPEED			INIT
3	ATTACK +17	DMG REDUCTION	-3
DEFENSE +11		12	
medium REACH	see below	DAMAGE	11 TOP SAVE ▼

MOVEMENT

CRAWL:	2½
WALK:	5
JOG:	10
RUN:	15
FLY:	40

SAVES

PHYSICAL:	+17
MENTAL:	+13
DODGE:	+17

ATTACK:
Hieracosphinxes have a claw/claw/bite attack, with claws dealing 6d4p each and a bite doing 4d8p points. Unlike great cats, they do not grab prey preferring to simply tear it to pieces

SPECIAL DEFENSES:
Flight

GENERAL INFO

ACTIVITY CYCLE:	Diurnal
NO. APPEARING:	1-6
% CHANCE IN LAIR:	20%
FREQUENCY:	Unusual
ALIGNMENT:	Chaotic Evil
VISION TYPE:	Farsight
AWARENESS/SENSES:	Standard
HABITAT:	Scrubland
DIET:	Carnivorous
ORGANIZATION:	Individuals
CLIMATE/TERRAIN:	Deserts and surrounding territory

YIELD

MEDICINAL:	nil
SPELL COMPONENTS:	nil
HIDE/TROPHY:	yes
TREASURE:	favor very shiny objects
EDIBLE:	yes
OTHER:	nil
EXPERIENCE POINT VALUE:	1425

S

SPIDER

BIG SPIDER   **GARGANTUAN SPIDER**   **GIGANTIC SPIDER**
HUGE SPIDER   **LARGE SPIDER**   **MASSIVE SPIDER**
VERY LARGE SPIDER

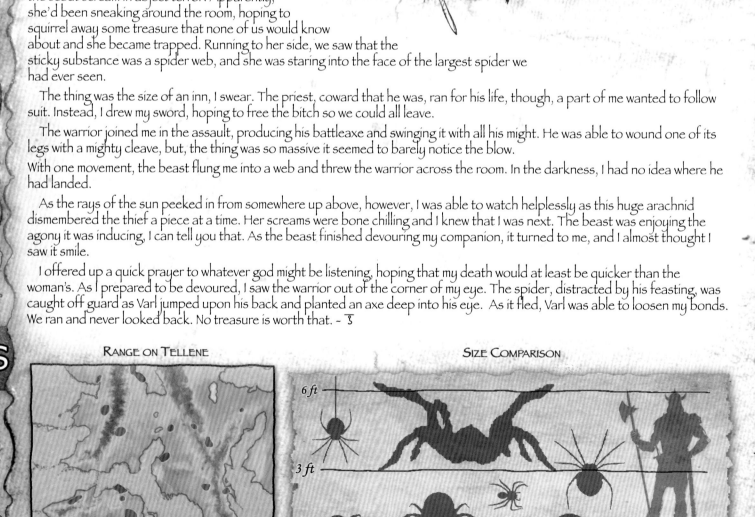

So, there we were: me, some Fhokki warrior with a name I couldn't pronounce so we all called him Varl, a 'scout' with a limp, and some priest with body odor that could clear a room. We had found some secret tunnels underneath the Krond Heights, where Varl said there was some lost treasure that we really just had to see for ourselves.

As we inched our way through, the tunnels began to get larger, and more serpentine until we stumbled into a large cavern that smelled of death. The walls of the cavern were covered with some sort of sticky substance that we couldn't see very well due to the size of the cavern and the weakness of our torch. Some sort of stinking breeze wafted through on occasion, causing our torch to flicker wildly, adding to our trepidation. Suddenly, we heard the scout scream in abject terror. Apparently, she'd been sneaking around the room, hoping to squirrel away some treasure that none of us would know about and she became trapped. Running to her side, we saw that the sticky substance was a spider web, and she was staring into the face of the largest spider we had ever seen.

The thing was the size of an inn, I swear. The priest, coward that he was, ran for his life, though, a part of me wanted to follow suit. Instead, I drew my sword, hoping to free the bitch so we could all leave.

The warrior joined me in the assault, producing his battleaxe and swinging it with all his might. He was able to wound one of its legs with a mighty cleave, but, the thing was so massive it seemed to barely notice the blow. With one movement, the beast flung me into a web and threw the warrior across the room. In the darkness, I had no idea where he had landed.

As the rays of the sun peeked in from somewhere up above, however, I was able to watch helplessly as this huge arachnid dismembered the thief a piece at a time. Her screams were bone chilling and I knew that I was next. The beast was enjoying the agony it was inducing, I can tell you that. As the beast finished devouring my companion, it turned to me, and I almost thought I saw it smile.

I offered up a quick prayer to whatever god might be listening, hoping that my death would at least be quicker than the woman's. As I prepared to be devoured, I saw the warrior out of the corner of my eye. The spider, distracted by his feasting, was caught off guard as Varl jumped upon his back and planted an axe deep into his eye. As it fled, Varl was able to loosen my bonds. We ran and never looked back. No treasure is worth that. - ℨ

RANGE ON TELLENE

SIZE COMPARISON

6 ft

3 ft

BIG SPIDER

HIT POINTS:	d3+1
SIZE/WEIGHT:	T/1 lb.
TENACITY:	Nervous
INTELLIGENCE:	Non
FATIGUE FACTOR:	n/a

SPEED 10 | **INIT** -4
ATTACK -2
DEFENSE +4 | DICE REDUCTION 2
poison
short REACH | DAMAGE | TOP SAVE ▼ | n/a

MOVEMENT

CRAWL:	1¼
WALK:	2½
JOG:	5
RUN:	7½
SPRINT:	10

SAVES

PHYSICAL:	-2
MENTAL:	-2
DODGE:	-2

ATTACK:
Big spider bites do not reduce Hit Points, but inject VF 5 poison that causes -1 to Attack, Defense, and Damage for 2d6 hours on a failed save; Huge and larger creatures are unaffected.

SPECIAL DEFENSES:
Initiative die type is one better.

GENERAL INFO

ACTIVITY CYCLE:	Nocturnal
NO. APPEARING:	3-30
% CHANCE IN LAIR:	50%
FREQUENCY:	Commonplace
ALIGNMENT:	Non
VISION TYPE:	Low Light Vision
AWARENESS/SENSES:	Sensitive to web vibrations within 100 ft
HABITAT:	Dark ruins, rubble and urban areas
DIET:	Carnivorous
ORGANIZATION:	Cluster
CLIMATE/TERRAIN:	Any, save arctic

YIELD

MEDICINAL:	diluted venom often used to treat chest pain
SPELL COMPONENTS:	spinneret organ, for Viscous Webbing spell[1]
HIDE/TROPHY:	bodies can be preserved and displayed
TREASURE:	incidental
EDIBLE:	yes, but poisonous if eaten raw
OTHER:	webbing has many uses

EXPERIENCE POINT VALUE: 25

LARGE SPIDER

HIT POINTS:	5+1d6
SIZE/WEIGHT:	T/5 lbs.
TENACITY:	Nervous
INTELLIGENCE:	Non
FATIGUE FACTOR:	n/a

SPEED 10 | **INIT** -4
ATTACK -1
DEFENSE +3 | DICE REDUCTION 2
1+ poison
short REACH | DAMAGE | TOP SAVE ▼ | n/a

MOVEMENT

CRAWL:	1¼
WALK:	2½
JOG:	5
RUN:	7½
SPRINT:	10

SAVES

PHYSICAL:	-1
MENTAL:	-1
DODGE:	-1

ATTACK:
Large spiders bite for 1 point of damage and inflict poison (VF 6) that causes -1 to Attack, Defense, and Damage for 2d12 hours on a failed save.

SPECIAL DEFENSES:
Initiative die type is one better.

GENERAL INFO

ACTIVITY CYCLE:	Nocturnal
NO. APPEARING:	2-20
% CHANCE IN LAIR:	50%
FREQUENCY:	Frequent
ALIGNMENT:	Non
VISION TYPE:	Low Light Vision
AWARENESS/SENSES:	Sensitive to web vibrations within 200 ft
HABITAT:	Warm, dry, dark ruins and woodlands
DIET:	Carnivorous
ORGANIZATION:	Pair or cluster
CLIMATE/TERRAIN:	Any, save arctic

YIELD

MEDICINAL:	diluted venom often used to treat chest pain
SPELL COMPONENTS:	spinneret organ, for Viscous Webbing spell[1]
HIDE/TROPHY:	bodies can be preserved and displayed
TREASURE:	incidental
EDIBLE:	yes, but poisonous if eaten raw
OTHER:	webbing has many uses

EXPERIENCE POINT VALUE: 45

S

VERY LARGE SPIDER

HIT POINTS: 10+1d8

SIZE/WEIGHT: S/18 lbs.

TENACITY: Steady

INTELLIGENCE: Non

FATIGUE FACTOR: n/a

	SPEED		INIT
	10	ATTACK +1	-4
DEFENSE +2		DMG REDUCTION 2	
short REACH		1d3p + poison DAMAGE	TOP SAVE ▼ n/a

MOVEMENT

CRAWL: 1¼

WALK: 2½

JOG: 5

RUN: 7½

SPRINT: 10

SAVES

PHYSICAL: +1

MENTAL: +1

DODGE: +1

ATTACK:
Very large spiders bite for 1d3p points of damage and inflict poison (VF 7) that causes -2 to Attack, Defense, and Damage for 2d12 hours on a failed save; a 'nat 1' indicates death.

SPECIAL DEFENSES:
Initiative die type is one better.

GENERAL INFO

ACTIVITY CYCLE:	Nocturnal
NO. APPEARING:	2-12
% CHANCE IN LAIR:	50%
FREQUENCY:	Frequent
ALIGNMENT:	Non
VISION TYPE:	Low Light Vision
AWARENESS/SENSES:	Sensitive to web vibrations within 300 ft
HABITAT:	Crevices and brush
DIET:	Carnivorous
ORGANIZATION:	Pair or cluster
CLIMATE/TERRAIN:	Any, save arctic

YIELD

MEDICINAL:	diluted venom thought to cure chest pain
SPELL COMPONENTS:	spinneret organ, for Viscous Webbing spell[1]
HIDE/TROPHY:	body may be preserved and displayed
TREASURE:	incidental
EDIBLE:	yes, but poisonous if eaten raw
OTHER:	webbing has many uses

EXPERIENCE POINT VALUE: 100

HUGE SPIDER

HIT POINTS: 15+3d8

SIZE/WEIGHT: S/35 lbs.

TENACITY: Steady

INTELLIGENCE: Semi

FATIGUE FACTOR: n/a

	SPEED		INIT
	9	ATTACK +4	-4
DEFENSE +2		DMG REDUCTION 2	
short REACH		2d4p + poison DAMAGE	TOP SAVE ▼ n/a

MOVEMENT

CRAWL: 2½

WALK: 5

JOG: 10

RUN: 15

SPRINT: 20

SAVES

PHYSICAL: +4

MENTAL: +4

DODGE: +4

ATTACK:
Huge spider bites cause 2d4p points of damage and inflict poison (VF 10) that causes -3 to Attack, Defense, and Damage for 2d12 hours on a failed save; a 'nat 1' indicates death. Successful saves have only a -1 penalty.

SPECIAL DEFENSES:
Initiative die type is one better.

GENERAL INFO

ACTIVITY CYCLE:	Nocturnal
NO. APPEARING:	1-8
% CHANCE IN LAIR:	50%
FREQUENCY:	Infrequent
ALIGNMENT:	Non
VISION TYPE:	Low Light Vision with keen eyesight
AWARENESS/SENSES:	Sensitive to web vibrations within 300 ft
HABITAT:	Burrows
DIET:	Carnivorous
ORGANIZATION:	Individuals or cluster
CLIMATE/TERRAIN:	Any, save arctic

YIELD

MEDICINAL:	diluted venom thought to cure chest pain
SPELL COMPONENTS:	spinneret organ, for Viscous Webbing spell[1]
HIDE/TROPHY:	body may be preserved and displayed
TREASURE:	incidental
EDIBLE:	yes, but poisonous if eaten raw
OTHER:	webbing has many uses

EXPERIENCE POINT VALUE: 200

These oversized arachnids outwardly resemble normal spiders except with respect to sheer size. Giant spiders range from about one to 20 feet in length (including their leg spans) and are fairly common in the wild, though some live in or near settlements and towns. There are a variety of different spiders across Tellene.

Big Spider: While large compared to common spiders (their bodies have a 1-foot diameter), the big spiders are still small enough to dwell unnoticed in some urban areas. These arachnids often resemble brown recluse spiders with dark brown mottling on the undersides of their abdomens and three pairs of eyes on their cephalothoraxes. Their bodies are covered with numerous fine brown hairs, giving them a velvety appearance. Males are slightly smaller than females.

Large Spider: These dangerous arachnids are about 2 feet in diameter, with shiny round abdomens and long, spindly legs. Like the black widow spiders that they tend to resemble, females are slightly larger and often distinguished from males by a particular marking on their backs. Males and young large spiders have different markings (or none at all; it varies by species). Their bodies are mostly black or brown in color. They are comb-footed spiders, meaning that their back legs have bristles, which they use to spread silk over their prey once it has been trapped.

Very Large Spider: These species often resemble crab spiders, with two front pairs of legs that angle outward and flattened, angular bodies. They also can move sideways or backwards. They are able to change color from white to yellow and green to blend in with their surroundings, where they wait for prey to approach. Adults grow to 3 feet in diameter.

Huge Spider: These 4-foot long monstrosities have eight eyes, arranged in three rows with the middle row possessing two very large eyes. These are incredibly eerie to view but give them extremely keen eyesight. Their eyes reflect light very well, and that is one way of locating them, for any light shone toward their eyes glints back toward the light source.

They mostly resemble wolf spiders, being nearly solid dark brown in coloration and relying on camouflage for protection. They produce messy-looking, but very strong, webs.

Gigantic Spider: This roughly 6-foot long spider has a large, orb-shaped abdomen, mottled in color, and fairly long, thin legs much like those of a tangleweb spider. Color ranges from light orange to dusty brown. They also have bristles on their back legs for spreading silk and they possess fangs.

Massive Spider: These arachnids grow to about 10 feet in length, with males growing a bit longer than females, but females growing much greater in girth. Their tarantula-like bodies are covered in hair, and most are brown, but great variety in color is possible. Cobalt blue massive spiders have been spotted in the Vohven Jungle.

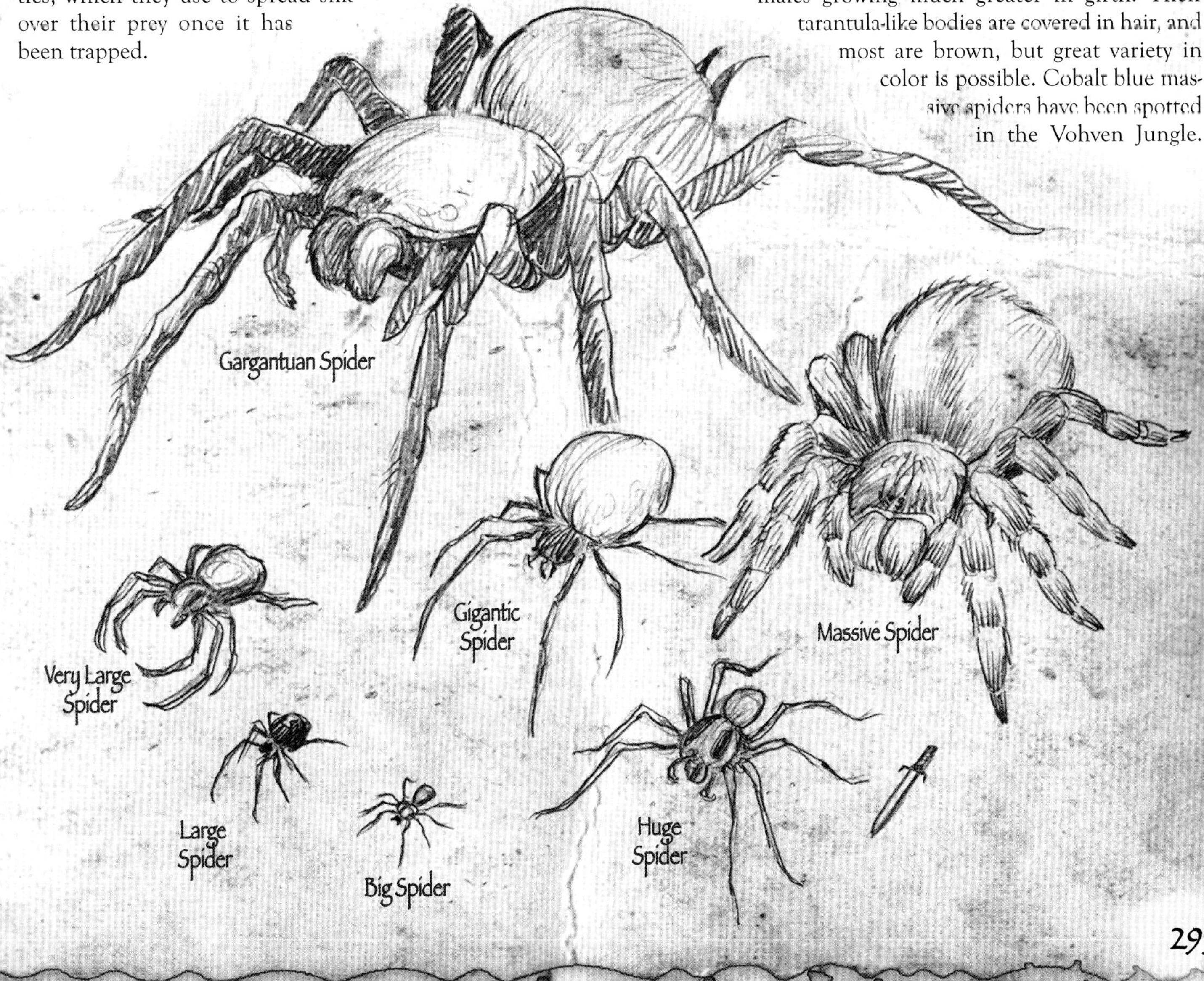

Gargantuan Spider

Gigantic Spider

Massive Spider

Very Large Spider

Large Spider

Big Spider

Huge Spider

Other massive spiders are black with white stripes, and still others are brown with yellow leg markings. They possess articulated fangs, which extend when attacking and fold back when resting, and are used to inject venom into prey.

Their legs are divided into seven segments with two claws at the end of each of their eight legs. Surrounding these claws are hairs that help the spider grasp and climb. Its mouth is a tube-like structure which can only be used to suck liquefied food. The hairs on this spider's body act as its sensory organs, therefore its sense of touch is its keenest sense.

Gargantuan Spider: These 20-foot long spiders have leathery looking heads and abdomens that are generally reddish-brown in color, much like tunnelweb spiders. They have prominent spinnerets that extend behind the abdomen and resemble feelers.

Combat/Tactics:

Most spin webs, feeding on whatever prey is hapless enough to become stuck in them, though they also have two sharp fangs for injecting venom.

Spider bites are obvious, as the skin around the site erupts into a volcano-shaped wound within minutes of being bitten. The size of the bite varies depending upon the size of the spider, but often ranges from that of a thumbnail to the size of a human hand. The skin around the bite begins to die and slough off, leaving a deep wound. There is chance that the wound leaves a scar even after it heals.

To eat, the spider grinds its victim into pulp or pumps in digestive juices before sucking out the liquefied tissue – a grisly death in either case. Each type of giant spider, however, has its own unique methods that are noted here. All poison effects are cumulative.

Big Spider: These spiders usually hunt insects or small animals during the hours of the night. However, if surprised or threatened by a larger creature, they bite. Their bite is not particularly dangerous, dealing no physical damage, but injects a VF 5 poison that causes -1 to Attack, Defense and Damage for 2d6 hours on a failed saving throw. Huge and larger creatures are unaffected.

Large Spider: They are quite deadly and aggressive, even with one another. A successful bite inflicts its target with 1 point of damage and VF 6 poison. This venom causes weakness, nausea, and paralysis of the diaphragm, making breathing difficult and thus imposing a 2-point penalty to Attack, Defense and Damage for 2d12 hours on a failed saving throw.

They are solitary except for when they come together to mate in a violent way. Once a female mates with a male large spider, she liquefies the body and ingests it.

Large spiders hunt during the night, hiding in the thickest part of its web, near the center. There, they hang upside down motionlessly waiting patiently for prey to become entangled in the web, after which they move swiftly to attack.

Very Large Spider: This spider does not build webs to trap prey. It is a hunter and an ambusher. It sits in places where it can find concealment in vegetation, or inside the crevices of dead trees or rocky areas.

A successful bite inflicts 1d3p points of damage and VF 7 poison, causing a 2-point penalty to Attack, Defense and Damage for 2d12 hours on a failed saving throw. A roll of '1' on the saving throw die indicates death.

Huge Spider: These spiders are solitary wanderers, pouncing on prey as they find it or chasing it short distances. They have excellent eyesight and their sense of touch is extremely acute. Some wait near the mouths of subterranean burrows where they wait for prey to pass so they can jump out and attack.

A bite attack causes 2d4p points of damage and injects VF 10 poison, imposing a 3-point penalty to Attack, Defense and Damage for 2d12 hours on a failed saving throw. A roll of '1' on the saving throw die indicates death. Successful saves receive only a 1-point penalty to the statistics noted.

Gigantic Spider: They often drop down on prey from trees, but have also been encountered on the ground, where they jump on their prey with great power.

A successful bite attack inflicts VF 14 poison, with failed saves suffering a loss of 2d6p Hit Points (losing 1 point every 10 seconds until rolled damage is reached). Successful saves suffer only d4p lost Hit Points. Gigantic spiders have legs so pliable as to be immune from piercing and crushing damage.

Massive Spider: These spiders are quite intelligent (for a spider), attacking any creature it thinks it can overcome. Massive spider species usually dwell alone in caves, typically in mountainous regions. While they may hunt prey, most prefer to use the diabolical method of constructing silk 'welcome mats' extending from their lairs. When they feel the vibration of a creature stepping on or touching this silk floor covering, they hurry from deep within their burrows to strike. Most of their homes are lined with this silk, so that they can feel approaching prey from anywhere within the lair. Their eyes are not keen, and they see light and movement poorly.

When they attack, their bite deals 2d6p+7 points of damage and injects VF 19 poison. Failed saves cause death, while success results in paralysis for d4 hours. A massive spider's legs are immune to damage from piercing and crushing weapons as they are able to absorb the impact.

Gargantuan Spider: They dwell in deep, dark lairs near underground sources of water, often in mountainous regions. They are unrepentantly cruel in their attacks on prey. Unlike other spiders, who liquefy their meal before eating, these spiders have large, gaping maws that they can use to swallow prey whole, where it dissolves slowly and painfully from acidic digestive juices. Often, with malice, they trap their food in silken webbing and dismember the victim slowly and painfully, clicking gleefully as it screams.

Gargantuan spider bites cause 2d6p+10 points of damage and inflict VF 25 poison. Failed saves cause death, while successes are paralyzed for d12 hours. Their legs are immune

GIGANTIC SPIDER

HIT POINTS: 25+4d8

SIZE/WEIGHT: M/100 lbs.

TENACITY: Steady

INTELLIGENCE: Animal, High

FATIGUE FACTOR: n/a

SPEED 8   **INIT** -4

ATTACK +8

DMG REDUCTION

body +4 legs +2   body 2 legs 6

2d6p + poison

short REACH   DEFENSE   DAMAGE   TOP SAVE ▼   n/a

MOVEMENT

CRAWL: 5

WALK: 10

JOG: 15

RUN: 20

SPRINT: 25

SAVES

PHYSICAL: +8

MENTAL: +8

DODGE: +8

ATTACK:
Bites cause 2d6p and inject poison (VF 14) that deals 2d6p (at a rate of 1 HP loss per 10 seconds until rolled damage is reached). Successful saves suffer only 1d4p points of poison damage.

SPECIAL DEFENSES:
Legs are immune to damage from piercing and crushing weapons. Initiative die type is one better.

GENERAL INFO

ACTIVITY CYCLE: Nocturnal

NO. APPEARING: 1-4

% CHANCE IN LAIR: 60%

FREQUENCY: Sporadic

ALIGNMENT: Non

VISION TYPE: Low Light Vision

AWARENESS/SENSES: Sensitive to web vibrations within 300 ft

HABITAT: Caves and trees

DIET: Carnivorous

ORGANIZATION: Individuals

CLIMATE/TERRAIN: Temperate to tropical foothills and subterranean

YIELD

MEDICINAL: diluted venom ingested to relieve chest pain

SPELL COMPONENTS: spinneret organ, for Viscous Webbing spell[1]

HIDE/TROPHY: bodies can be preserved and displayed

TREASURE: incidental

EDIBLE: yes, but poisonous if eaten raw

OTHER: webbing has many uses

EXPERIENCE POINT VALUE: 417

MASSIVE SPIDER

HIT POINTS: 30+6d8

SIZE/WEIGHT: L/250 lbs.

TENACITY: Brave

INTELLIGENCE: Obtuse

FATIGUE FACTOR: n/a

SPEED 7   **INIT** -4

ATTACK +13

DMG REDUCTION

body +6 legs +2   body 3 legs 8

see below

short REACH   DEFENSE   DAMAGE   TOP SAVE ▼   n/a

MOVEMENT

CRAWL: 5

WALK: 10

JOG: 15

RUN: 20

SPRINT: 25

SAVES

PHYSICAL: +13

MENTAL: +13

DODGE: +13

ATTACK:
Massive spider bites deal 2d6p+7 points of damage and are so venomous (VF 19) as to cause instant death on a failed saving throw. Successful saves result in paralysis for 1d4 hours.

SPECIAL DEFENSES:
Legs are immune to damage from piercing and crushing weapons. Initiative die type is one better.

GENERAL INFO

ACTIVITY CYCLE: Nocturnal

NO. APPEARING: 1-2

% CHANCE IN LAIR: 70%

FREQUENCY: Unusual

ALIGNMENT: Non

VISION TYPE: Low Light Vision (half normal range)

AWARENESS/SENSES: Sensitive to web vibrations within 300 ft

HABITAT: Caves and burrows

DIET: Carnivorous

ORGANIZATION: Individuals

CLIMATE/TERRAIN: Temperate to tropical mountains

YIELD

MEDICINAL: diluted venom ingested to relieve chest pain

SPELL COMPONENTS: spinneret organ, for Viscous Webbing spell[1]

HIDE/TROPHY: can be preserved, but difficult to transport

TREASURE: may hoard shiny objects

EDIBLE: yes, but poisonous if eaten raw

OTHER: webbing has many uses

EXPERIENCE POINT VALUE: 925

GARGANTUAN SPIDER

HIT POINTS:	40+10d8
SIZE/WEIGHT:	H/500 lbs.
TENACITY:	Brave
INTELLIGENCE:	Average
FATIGUE FACTOR:	n/a

SPEED 6
INIT -4
ATTACK +19
DMG REDUCTION
body +10 legs +2
body 3 legs 8
DEFENSE
see below
DAMAGE n/a
short REACH
TOP SAVE ▼

MOVEMENT

CRAWL:	10
WALK:	15
JOG:	20
RUN:	25
SPRINT:	30

SAVES

PHYSICAL:	+19
MENTAL:	+19
DODGE:	+19

ATTACK:
Gargantuan spider bites deal 2d6p+10 points of damage and are so venomous (VF 25) as to cause instant death on a failed saving throw. Successful saves result in paralysis for 1d12 hours.

SPECIAL DEFENSES:
Legs are immune to damage from piercing and crushing weapons; Initiative die type is one better.

GENERAL INFO

ACTIVITY CYCLE:	Nocturnal
NO. APPEARING:	1
% CHANCE IN LAIR:	100%
FREQUENCY:	Scarce
ALIGNMENT:	Chaotic Evil
VISION TYPE:	Extreme Low Light Vision
AWARENESS/SENSES:	Sensitive to web vibrations within 300 ft
HABITAT:	Deep Forests, Subterranean
DIET:	Carnivorous
ORGANIZATION:	Solitary or Leader of lesser spiders
CLIMATE/TERRAIN:	Any subterranean, save arctic

YIELD

MEDICINAL:	diluted venom used to treat chest pain
SPELL COMPONENTS:	spinneret organ, for Viscous Webbing spell[1]
HIDE/TROPHY:	can be preserved, but quite difficult to transport
TREASURE:	collects objects of obvious or apparent value
EDIBLE:	no
OTHER:	webbing has many uses
EXPERIENCE POINT VALUE:	2075

S

to damage from piercing and crushing weapons (these types of blows merely knocking aside the limb without appreciably injuring the creature), making them quite difficult to disable.

Habitat/Society/Ecology:

Big Spiders: These spiders generally live in dark places within human dwellings, such as attics, cellars, barns or outhouses. They also may live in woodpiles, in dead leaves or piles of stones. They are not aggressive, and often eat dead insects.

Egg laying primarily occurs in the summer months. The female of the species typically lays about 50 eggs, encased in a white, silken sac. Maturity is slow. It takes a year for a spider to become a full adult from the time of hatching. Adults live about two years. These spiders can live for as long as six months without food or water. Unlike most spiders, this spider spins a web to act as a retreat, not to trap prey.

Large Spiders: The large spiders live primarily in abandoned buildings, trash heaps, piles of dead leaves, lumber stacks, quarries, subterranean lairs (in the desert) or in pits or depressions in wooded areas. Females often spin webs in low-hanging trees or in warm, dark, dry places. Adult males often wander in search of mates. After mating occurs, females often kill and eat their mates.

When ready, females then lay several batches of eggs, up to 250 at a time. This occurs during summer months. The egg case is suspended in the female spider's web. The incubation period of eggs is between 14 and 30 days, but only one in 12 young survive due to cannibalism. Female large spiders mature in about 90 days and live another six months to a year after emergence. Males mature in about 70 days, but only live a month or two after emerging from the egg sac.

Very Large Spiders: They live in forested regions, in any climate except for extremely dry deserts or very frigid climes, hiding in dead trees, ground debris such as dead leaves, or in thick, lush vegetation. They blend in with their surroundings by changing their body color so that they can surprise prey and also remain safe from danger.

During the autumn mating season, males of the species attempt to attract mates by tapping on dry leaves, a sound that can be heard quite some distance away (between 1 to 6 miles). Once a male finds a female he intends to mate with, he wraps her in silk, imprisoning her until mating is complete. Females lay hundreds of tiny eggs in cocoons, attaching the cocoons inside dead trees, or high up in living trees where there are ample branches for concealment. The female typically dies soon after laying her eggs.

Huge Spiders: These creatures are especially amorous during summer months. When approaching a female to mate, a male huge spider waves his front legs at her to signal his intentions. This is partially because he is somewhat smaller than she and he wants to ensure that she knows he is coming as a mate and not a meal. He then begins to raise and lower his palp, drumming on it with his front legs before jumping on the back of the female, where he stays for several hours. Sometimes, a female huge spider casually continues to hunt even with the male on her back.

When ready, she seeks a secluded spot to lay approximately 100 eggs, guarding them ferociously while she encases them in silk. Once they are surrounded by the egg sac, she carries them around on her abdomen for two to three months. On warm, sunny days, she often sits in the burrow she's constructed, keeping her head in the burrow and her abdomen, along with her eggs, warming in the sun.

When time comes for hatching, she rips open the sac to allow the young to swarm out, covering her body and clinging to her for several days until they are ready to drop off and live independently. Even juvenile huge spiders have the bite and venom of their mother.

Gigantic Spiders: These live in forested regions, in trees, in piles of leaves or brush, and even underground. Females are much sought after, and males may even fight to the death for a chance to mate with a prized female. Females are much larger than males, and after mating, usually devour their mates. They often have many webs in the area where they dwell, and carry their egg sacs, filled with about 50 eggs, from web to web to discourage predators. If hungry, the female may eat some of her own eggs, so that only about two or three spiders emerge alive every summer. Female gigantic spiders live for nearly three decades after maturing while males live about half that time.

Massive Spiders: They reside in caves, often found in forested mountain foothills. They have been known to construct their own burrows, should they be unable to find suitable caves in which to dwell. They line their lairs with silk to stabilize them and to make it easier for them to climb up and down, as well as to facilitate prey capture.

Males are much smaller and duller in coloration than females. They also have a much shorter lifespan than females, dying soon after maturation. Males are more likely to be seen outside of the burrows, where they sometimes wander about, while females tend to stay hidden.

Females lay between 50 and 200 eggs, in egg sacs that they guard for six to seven months, turning the sacs frequently to prevent deformation. Females are very aggressive while guarding their egg sacs. The young spiderlings may stay in the nesting area for a month or more, surviving by consuming the remains of their egg sac, before dispersing.

Females can live as long as a century, during which time they mate with many generations of male massive spiders.

Gargantuan Spiders: Gargantuan spiders are a breed apart. No mere oversized arachnid, they are self-aware and possess intelligence comparable to mankind. All are uniformly wicked beings savoring cruelty for its own sake.

These creatures can live for centuries and appear as recurring villains in tales related by both deep delving dwarves and isolated wood elves. Woe to those who fall prey to the spider mistresses for a quick death at the hands of their minions is salvation from the far crueler fate than can await.

Gargantuan spiders are likely to be encountered as the nexus of a huge conglomeration of all varieties of smaller breeds that venerate her (or infrequently, him) as their god. These communities may be found deep within primeval forests or far underground. In either case, the surrounding region is desolate and littered with webbing.

These spiders are capable of human speech as well as being able to communicate with their arachnid minions. It is unclear by what means the latter feat is accomplished save that it seemingly is effective for many stories relate how an evil spider mustered its spider thralls to attack.

Some gargantuan spiders seem not to crave power choosing instead to live in solitude ensconced within some secret lair long lost to memory. These may be the most evil and depraved of all spider-kind and are fastidious in retaining their secrets.

On Tellene:

Big, large and huge spiders can be found in most civilized areas of Tellene, although huge spiders are more common in the Young Kingdoms. Very large spiders are found in the jungles of Tellene. Gigantic spiders are most common in the woodlands of Svimohzia, and in the Edosi Forest in Kalamar.

Massive and gargantuan spiders can be found in any mountainous region, but, the massive have been encountered more often in the Ka'Asa and Kakidela Mountains as well as the Legasa Peaks. Gargantuan spiders have been reported more frequently around the Elenon and Dashahn Mountains, plus a few sightings in the area surrounding Krond Heights.

[1]*Some giant spiders' spinnerets, when used as a replacement material component in the mage's sixth level Viscous Webbing spell, alter the spell effects in some fashion. Big, large, very large and huge spiders increase the spell duration by 1, 4, 7 and 10 minutes, respectively. Gigantic spiders increase the movement difficulty, with size M and smaller creatures needing at least 15 Str to move through the web, 16 to 19 Str to move at a rate of 1 ft/10 seconds, and 21+ Str to move 1 ft/5 seconds. Massive spiders increase the area of effect to 9000 cubic feet. Gargantuan spider spinnerets impose all of the above variant effects as well as slowing size L creatures to 1 ft/4 seconds, size H to 1 ft/2 seconds, and size G to 1 ft/second.*

Down in the Netherdeep, resources we take for granted up here on the surface — like wood, cloth, and the like — are rare. Instead, they've got substitutes like stone, tanned hides, and giant spider silk. Why, I've been told that there's even different kinds of silk in the same spider — and that each strand is as strong as a steel rod of the same size. Of course, you've got to know the secret of drying it out and treating it to get rid of just the right amount of moisture and stickiness depending on what you're gonna be crafting. Not to mention facing the danger of gathering it in the first place! You can't 'farm' spiders like you would silkworms - they'll bite each others' (and your) head off if you try it.

Still, if you can gather up a fair supply, and happen to be in the know on how to work it, you can make all sorts of things. In my travels of the deep, I've seen spider silk cloaks, tunics and clothing of all varieties, ropes, bedding, belt pouches and bags, and even a kind of silken 'vellum.' ~

STRIX

Also Known As: Bloodbeak, Maulsquito, Strzyga

Strix swarms are one of the most feared flying terrors.

Some years ago, my then-companions and I were visitors to the great elven city of Doulathanorian, and witnesses to the birth of a beautiful infant girl given the name of Jenneriaeclycalina. Though assured that this was an abbreviated name transliterated for our Kalamaran tongue, even our halfling comrade, not a fellow often pressed for time, shortened it to "Jenneria" in conversation. Among we of other races it was infallibly docked down to "Jen".

Jenneria was the second daughter of an old alchemist, Teleseineatin, concerning whom I have little to report, except that he had formerly loved two women who met unexpected deaths, had by them two children each, and that I thought him an ass. His wife at the time was a beauty named Wylameianarei, though her beauty lasted no great time we were there, and it was only the fourth day after the child's birth that she and her husband died. Though only our elven traveling companion was allowed to view the bodies, it was enough, for he was able to tell us of the punctures on the bodies and the strange absence of blood on the floor beneath. Suspecting some manner of vampire, we waited with anticipation for further activities, but the corpses did not rise, nor did we discover any evidence of undead.

I am ashamed to admit it was mere fortune that we discovered the true culprit, as we stood guard outside the child's room. The scream of her nurse brought us rapidly into the bedchamber, where our startled eyes met a half-dozen striges stabbing at the lady with vicious accuracy, and three more landing atop the cradle like malevolent spirits. I still recall with vivid horror the sight of that repulsive trio, seeming to polish their beaks in lusty anticipation of the infant beneath them. Fortunately, I can report that our weapons soon slew the foul creatures and ended the threat with not a scratch on the child, though one of our number lost a bit of his own vital fluid in the process. - ℞

This bizarre winged creature resembles a mangy feathered owl with the wings and undercarriage of a bat, plus four to six bat-like legs (depending on species). Its most striking physical characteristic, however, is the two-part beak composed of an elongated, forward-projecting proboscis well adapted for piercing the skin of plants and animals, and a hideous four-fanged mouth that collects airborne particles and examines them to give the strix a directional sense of smell and taste simultaneously. Thus, a strix (*pl. strixes or striges*) can scent the chemicals contained in the breath and sweat of creatures from 30 feet away, enabling them to locate their prey in any habitat.

Coloration varies by species, though most sport brownish hues, sometimes with a lighter underside and/or face that helps camouflage the creature on tree trunks. Other striges are polymorphic, appearing in gray and reddish-brown colors.

Striges range from 8 to 14 inches long with a wingspan of 15 to 26 inches and a weight of roughly 5 pounds. Among most species, the females are larger than the males.

Combat/Tactics:

A successful attack (inflicting d4p+4 damage) indicates that the strix has inserted its proboscis into its victim and thereafter can automatically suck blood at a rate of d4p Hit Points per every 10 seconds it is attached (DR does not apply towards this blood drain). It is considered engorged after consuming blood equal to its maximum HP. A strix can be removed by a successful knock-back, Feat of Strength (*vs. d20p+12*) or death.

A victim may attack an attached strix with a dagger or smaller weapon at a -2 penalty (with care) or at +6 (without

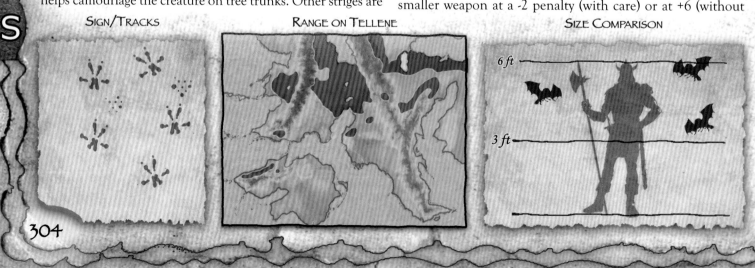

SIGN/TRACKS	RANGE ON TELLENE	SIZE COMPARISON

6 ft

3 ft

care). Attacks without care or by allies wielding weapons have a 50% chance of injuring the victim (roll the attack and then a d6 – on a 1-3 the maulsquito is the true target while on a 4-6 the victim is accidentally targeted and must make a defense roll versus the attack). In addition, the victim sustains any damage to a stryga beyond its remaining HP total. Allies attempting to manually remove a strix must first make a successful attack with their bare hands prior to attempting the Feat of Strength.

Habitat/Society:

Although thought to originate in the Nine Hells, most bloodbeaks dwell in semi-open forests home to other mammals and birds, though they may also be found in swamps, caves, plains or pastures (provided there are a few old wells, hollow trees or other such nesting places). Few live in high elevations or in dry, arid lands, but they adapt easily to living in urban or suburban areas. Striges are adept at infiltration and have been known to find their way into barns and farmhouses, where they feed on the inhabitants therein.

Maulsquito social structure varies, with some living in pairs or small groups and others living in colonies of dozens of individuals. A female strix may have one to three litters each spring, depending on the species and the availability of food and roost sites. Female striges also require a blood meal in order to reproduce. After mating and feeding, the female rests for two to three days, digesting and using the proteins in the blood as building blocks to begin egg production. The female strix usually lays between three and 13 eggs, with incubation lasting for about 25 days. The female brings small mammals for her offspring to feed upon for the next 5 to 6 weeks, after which they can fly and fend for themselves. Striges reach maturity at about 10 months old.

Ecology:

Most species of strix are crepuscular feeders, roosting in cool places during the heat of the day and waiting until the cooler twilight hours to feed. When they do feed, they drink the blood of other living creatures, though striges can subsist on fruit nectar when victims are scarce. While consuming blood, a strix injects saliva into the body to serve as an anticoagulant. Otherwise, the creature's proboscis would quickly become clogged with blood clots. Its anatomy rapidly begins processing and digesting the blood, so that even a blood-bloated strix can take flight within 2 minutes after feeding. After consuming a blood meal, the strix usually returns to its roost and continues digesting.

A typical bloodbeak has a natural lifespan of 5 to 7 years, though this varies somewhat by species (and the creature's ability to feed while avoiding the host's defenses).

On Tellene:

Striges on Tellene seem to favor the northern lands, except for a single species from Pel Brolenon. These "Pel Striges" have four legs, greenish-yellow feathers, and lay no more than three eggs at a time. Unlike other striges, they are migratory, leaving Pel Brolenon in the fall to winter in northwest Svimohzia, in a range from Monam-Ahnozh to Vrandol. Some sages speculate they may also exist in the Vohven Jungle, but none have yet been reported.

STRIX

HIT POINTS:	10+1d8
SIZE/WEIGHT:	T/5 lb.
TENACITY:	Cowardly
INTELLIGENCE:	Animal, Low
FATIGUE FACTOR:	0

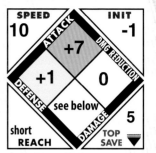

SPEED 10   INIT -1
ATTACK +7
DMG REDUCTION
DEFENSE +1   0
see below
short REACH   DAMAGE   TOP SAVE 5

MOVEMENT

CRAWL:	¼
WALK:	½
JOG:	1
RUN:	2
FLY:	20

SAVES

PHYSICAL:	+2
MENTAL:	+0
DODGE:	+4

ATTACK:
With a successful attack (inflicting d4p+4 damage), a strix latches onto its foe and drains d4p hit points in vital fluids per 10 seconds attached. A knock-back or Feat of Strength (vs. d20p+12) removes the strix. Attacks against affected characters have a 50% chance to injure the victim (damage to the strix beyond its remaining HP also injures the victim).

SPECIAL DEFENSES:
Flight

GENERAL INFO

ACTIVITY CYCLE:	Crepuscular
NO. APPEARING:	2-40
% CHANCE IN LAIR:	55%
FREQUENCY:	Frequent
ALIGNMENT:	Non
VISION TYPE:	Standard
AWARENESS/SENSES:	Can scent creatures from 30 feet away
HABITAT:	Caves and trees
DIET:	Sanguivorous
ORGANIZATION:	Colony
CLIMATE/TERRAIN:	Temperate to tropical lowlands

YIELD

MEDICINAL:	nil
SPELL COMPONENTS:	nil
HIDE/TROPHY:	the hideous strix is not a popular trophy
TREASURE:	incidental
EDIBLE:	no
OTHER:	proboscis may be carved into needles or darts
EXPERIENCE POINT VALUE:	67

S

STURM-WOLF

Also Known As: Thalnarkk

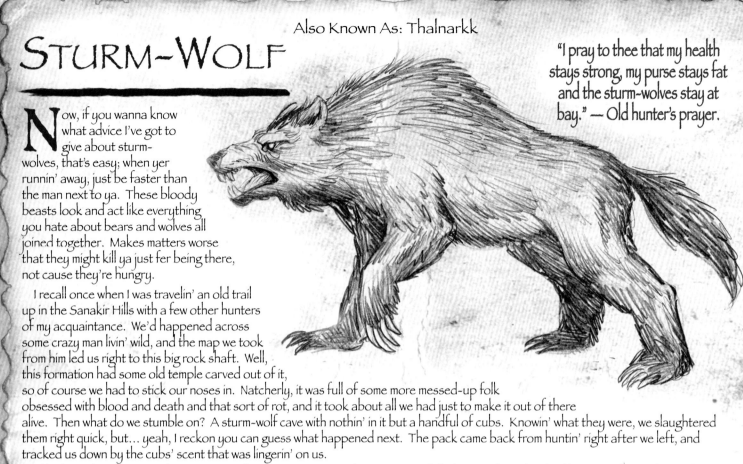

"I pray to thee that my health stays strong, my purse stays fat and the sturm-wolves stay at bay." — Old hunter's prayer.

Now, if you wanna know what advice I've got to give about sturm-wolves, that's easy; when yer runnin' away, just be faster than the man next to ya. These bloody beasts look and act like everything you hate about bears and wolves all joined together. Makes matters worse that they might kill ya just fer being there, not cause they're hungry.

I recall once when I was travelin' an old trail up in the Sanakir Hills with a few other hunters of my acquaintance. We'd happened across some crazy man livin' wild, and the map we took from him led us right to this big rock shaft. Well, this formation had some old temple carved out of it, so of course we had to stick our noses in. Natcherly, it was full of some more messed-up folk obsessed with blood and death and that sort of rot, and it took about all we had just to make it out of there alive. Then what do we stumble on? A sturm-wolf cave with nothin' in it but a handful of cubs. Knowin' what they were, we slaughtered them right quick, but... yeah, I reckon you can guess what happened next. The pack came back from huntin' right after we left, and tracked us down by the cubs' scent that was lingerin' on us.

The damn thing gives me shivers just recallin' it. Four sturm-wolves runnin' at full tilt towards us, howlin' like spirits being dragged to the Nine Hells, their mouths slobberin' and their eyes on fire. I was the only one to make it out of there alive, and that was for no better reason than the monsters havin' slowed down to slaughter my friends. - ᛉ

This highly aggressive carnivore resembles a wolf with the sturdy frame and powerful claws of a bear. Most sturm-wolves stand about 4 to 5 feet tall at the shoulder, with a body length of just over 8 feet and weighing around half a ton. In the dark, a sturm-wolf can be mistaken for a cave bear. The coat of a sturm-wolf is usually coal black, though some have various shades and patterns of multiple colors.

Sturm-wolves have an excellent sense of smell. They can normally detect the scent of any large game in a given area up to miles away. Sturm-wolves can communicate very effectively with barks and high-pitched howls. They use these to reveal themselves to other sturm-wolves in the area.

Combat/Tactics:

Sturm-wolves are notorious for overkill; not always killing just to feed, but for the sake of a kill alone. Sturm-wolves have the habit of becoming enraged when wounded, and severe blows, shouting and so on will drive the creatures into a fever pitch. From this point, they will not withdraw until either their wounds prevent them from carrying on the attack or they are killed.

The powerful jaws of the sturm-wolf are used to snap the neck of large game animals. The beast lunges at its prey, locking its jaws about the animal's throat and using its massive weight to aid in breaking the neck.

SIGN/TRACKS — Fore — Hind

RANGE ON TELLENE

SIZE COMPARISON — 6 ft — 3 ft

Habitat/Society:

Social creatures by nature, a Sturm-wolf is rarely found alone or away from its pack (three to eight adults, plus up to half that many young). As it takes a relatively large number of game animals to support a pack, they have very large territories, averaging from 25 to 50 square miles. Often the chosen territory will be bordered by a large stream or river, where game animals tend to congregate. The pack will constantly roam within the bounds of its territory, rarely spending more than a day at the same location. The main exception is during mating season, usually early spring, when the pack disperses for short periods of time. It is during this time that sturm-wolves, especially the males, are encountered alone or in mating pairs.

Normally the males (particlarly the leader) of a pack will be required to vie for leadership numerous times, as their status in the pack will be constantly challenged. When the pack reforms after mating season, a series of ritual fights break out between the males. Those who were too young or inexperienced to beat their competitors during the previous season will try again. If the current leader has grown too old or slow, he will be quickly dislodged from his role. After losing within their own pack, some males venture into another pack's territory to challenge its males.

Sturm-wolves have an average lifespan of 15 years.

Ecology:

Sturm-wolves prefer large grazing game such as deer, bison, and when the opportunity affords itself, sheep and cattle. They will, however, attack any animal they happen to encounter within their territory.

Due to their tendency to overkill, sturm-wolves often deplete their territories of game to the point that a pack cannot support itself. It may then attempt to expand its territory or abandon it in favor of new ranges. Depending on the size and strength of a pack, it may be able to force another pack from its territory. If not, a pack may become uprooted and roam for months in search of a hunting range it can control – it is packs of this sort that humans most often encounter. A pack often encroaches upon human lands and attack livestock as well as the human inhabitants.

On Tellene:

A few sturm-wolf cubs have been successfully domesticated and trained. Some Dejy tribes and Fhokki clans have used them as war-dogs. There is a danger, however.

No amount of training or bond between master and sturm-wolf seems to be able to overcome the wolf's tendency to become outraged when attacked or provoked. When sufficiently enraged, the sturm-wolf often becomes oblivious to friend or foe, and many a trainer has found himself the victim of his own 'loyal' pet.

[1]If used as an additional material component for the mage's seventh level Induce Fratricide spell, a sturm-wolf's cuspid (a.k.a. canine tooth or fang) extends the duration by 10 seconds.

STURM-WOLF

HIT POINTS:	43+5d8
SIZE/WEIGHT:	H/1000 lbs.
TENACITY:	Brave
INTELLIGENCE:	Animal, High
FATIGUE FACTOR:	-2

SPEED 4 — INIT -1

ATTACK +13

DEFENSE +9 — DMG REDUCTION 6

DAMAGE 4d4p+8

short REACH — TOP SAVE 12

MOVEMENT

CRAWL:	10
WALK:	15
JOG:	20
RUN:	25
SPRINT:	30

SAVES

PHYSICAL:	+15
MENTAL:	+12
DODGE:	+13

ATTACK: Sturm wolves lunge at their prey and inflict massive wounds (4d4p+8) as their weight and massive shoulders and neck permit their jaws to rip chunks of raw meat from an opponent. They can bite and tear with great rapidity.

SPECIAL ABILITIES: Listening and Tracking mastery of 75%

GENERAL INFO

ACTIVITY CYCLE:	Crepuscular
NO. APPEARING:	1-8
% CHANCE IN LAIR:	10%
FREQUENCY:	Sporadic
ALIGNMENT:	Chaotic Evil
VISION TYPE:	Standard
AWARENESS/SENSES:	Can scent game up to 2 miles away
HABITAT:	Cave dens
DIET:	Carnivorous
ORGANIZATION:	Pack
CLIMATE/TERRAIN:	Subalpine plains, forests and tundra

YIELD

MEDICINAL:	nil
SPELL COMPONENTS:	canine tooth, for Induce Fratricide spell
HIDE/TROPHY:	teeth, claws and hide are prized trophies
TREASURE:	incidental
EDIBLE:	yes
OTHER:	nil
EXPERIENCE POINT VALUE:	925

S

SWAMP DEATH

Also Known As: Bolog, Shazvim, Living Bog

I once believed that it was not a question of how many species of plant life could be domesticated, for to a botanist with sufficient time and patience all things are possible, but how many varieties are worth the attempt. After all, a particular species may not be decorative, useful or interesting away from its native haunts; it may also may be quite difficult to transplant the soil akin to that from which it came. Yet, I must now add another consideration — whether the plant life will feed on the botanist rather than, as is so common, the reverse.

In the deep Alubelok swamp and the great Vohven jungle, you may know, there is luxuriance in every natural detail and a lavish exuberance of plant and animal life. There are some areas, however, where the soil does not compare and the plants grow pale and yellow-tinged for lack of certain nutrients. It is here you may find the ambulatory plant species, of which the living bogs are but one.

Faced with a lack of nutrients in the soil, these plants have adapted themselves to take their needs from living beings. Unfortunately, the treasure hunter, in his nature, disdains plants. To his way of thinking, these imposing creatures should simply be mown down with the scythe. The sturdy limb-roots, the dextrous tentacle-vines, and potential to engulf and consume its sustenance are all dismissed as 'monstrous' rather than being appreciated for their ability.

Of course, I should not like to approach one too closely myself, but that is surely beside the point. - ⚕

The swamp death is a vegetable creature found naturally enough in swamps, bogs and similar waterlogged areas. Fully capable of locomotion, it can best be described as a roughly-conical shambling mound of dense tangles and vines some 8 feet tall and no less than 6 feet in diameter at its base.

A swamp death is capable of moving at a speed comparable to a dwarf by means of an oscillating contraction of its constituent vines or foot-like roots. In so doing, it seems to erratically bulge and contract as it shambles forward.

The creature has no animal-like central nervous system but nonetheless has sensory capabilities for light, touch and even chemical receptors attuned to animal pheromones. When stimulated to activity by sufficient concentrations of animal scent (a level far below human acuity), a swamp death shuffles toward the source.

When in surroundings with thick vegetation, they are almost undetectible (Hiding 90%; elves receive a 25% bonus to any competing checks).

S

SIGN/TRACKS	RANGE ON TELLENE	SIZE COMPARISON

If it looks like a great mass was dragged along the ground, leaving bits of rotten leaves and other such foliage in its wake, you've most likely found yourself a swamp death. Be wary if you follow the trail, for it may have doubled back upon your own path.

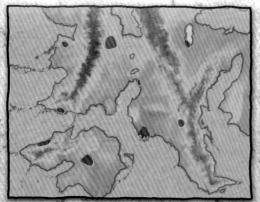

12 ft

6 ft

Combat/Tactics:

Upon encountering animal prey, it lashes out with surprisingly dense clusters of 6-inch thick vines. These are able to inflict powerful crushing blows capable of killing a man. However, should two consecutive blows be landed, it indicates the creature ensnared its prey.

It then drags it into the slimy foliage unless able to muscle out (Feat of Strength *vs. d20p+8*). Creatures unable to break free will be dragged into the center of the beast in 10 seconds unless the tendrils can be hewed with a hacking weapon for 20 damage or more in one blow, severing one of the limbs (*note: the vegetable-creature will simply produce another, so this will thwart an attack, but does no damage to the creature and does not limit its attacks*). Those unable to be saved in time will be engulfed by vines, muck and piles of rotting vegetation, suffering strangulation or suffocation in 2d4p x 10 seconds. Such is the strength of these vines that, once swallowed up, a heroic Feat of Strength (*vs. d20p+16*) is required to wriggle free, the matter taking 15 full seconds and while multiple attempts can be made, each succeeding one with a 2-point cumulative penalty to the Feat of Strength attempt.

Alternatively, the creature can be hacked apart by allies, although this places the entrapped victim in further danger as any damage delivered to the swamp-thing will also injure the trapped ally for up to 75% of the damage rolled (d4p-1 times 25%). Once prey has been drawn into the main body, the swamp thing can continue to attack with its thick appendages.

The creature attacks solely to feed and has no conception of tactics per se. As such it continues to seek to devour an opponent rendered and not chase other available food until its meal is completely entrapped and no longer struggling. It will, however, continue to defend itself with blows to would-be attackers and is fully willing and capable of devouring multiple foes; in fact, it may consume up to four man-sized creatures at once.

Crushing weapons are nearly useless in damaging this green horror and puncturing implements hardly fare better. Its build is such that it has no vulnerable backside, rendering moot an attempt to exploit this weakness.

As a plant creature, the swamp death is immune to most spells that do not cause physical damage. Its soggy mass is also highly resistant to flames imparting a 20 DR against any such effect used upon it. Cold is likewise ineffective (20 DR), but cold damage of 20 or more reduces the creature's Damage Resistance to crushing weapons to the same as hacking weapons for 20 seconds. Cold damage in excess of 30 points also slows the creature by half (both movements and attack Speed) for 20 seconds.

Habitat/Society/Ecology:

Swamp deaths grow in fetid surroundings with extremely poor soils deficient in nitrogen and other trace elements. Digesting meat is simply an adaptation to this environment.

They are never found in regions subject to seasonal frosts for even a day or two of freezing temperatures is sufficient to kill these creatures.

On Tellene:

Tellene's mild climate provides a relatively large range for these horrible creatures. The Alubelok Swamp is a notorious harborer of swamp deaths.

SWAMP DEATH

HIT POINTS:	35+9d8
SIZE/WEIGHT:	L/1 ton
TENACITY:	Fearless
INTELLIGENCE:	Semi-
FATIGUE FACTOR:	n/a

MOVEMENT

CRAWL:	1¼
WALK:	2½
JOG:	5
RUN:	7½
SPRINT:	10

SAVES

PHYSICAL:	+16
MENTAL:	immune
DODGE:	+16

SPEED 4 | INIT -1
ATTACK +16 / +8
DMG REDUCTION see below
DAMAGE 4d8p
DEFENSE / medium REACH / TOP SAVE n/a

ATTACK: Vines deal 4d8p damage, with two successful attacks ensnaring (break out with Feat of Strength vs d20p+8) and engulfing in 10 seconds (suffocate in 2d4p(x10) seconds without Feat of Strength (vs d20p+16)).

SPECIAL: DR varies by weapon (7 hacking, 16 crushing or piercing). Hiding skill mastery of 90%; many spells are of limited use against a Swamp Death (see text)

GENERAL INFO

ACTIVITY CYCLE:	Any
NO. APPEARING:	1-3
% CHANCE IN LAIR:	40%
FREQUENCY:	Sporadic
ALIGNMENT:	Non
VISION TYPE:	n/a
AWARENESS/SENSES:	Senses pheromones within 30 feet
HABITAT:	Wetlands
DIET:	Carnivorous
ORGANIZATION:	Individuals
CLIMATE/TERRAIN:	Temperate to tropical wilderness

YIELD

MEDICINAL:	nil
SPELL COMPONENTS:	unknown
HIDE/TROPHY:	nil
TREASURE:	nil
EDIBLE:	no
OTHER:	nil

EXPERIENCE POINT VALUE: 1500

TARANTUBAT

Also Known As:
Tel-tulmeramika
(in Low Elven)

Tarantubats seem to be fist-sized spiders sporting bat-like wings with a wingspan a couple of feet across. Though they are trivial to kill as individuals, we encountered them as a swarm, where they overwhelmed our expedition with sheer numbers. All team members suffered bites that proved minor. However, the creatures apparently are venomous – the poison seeming to sap physical strength from individuals not of a true warrior's mettle.

These winged vermin are very territorial when it comes to their cocoons and may attack larger creatures without provocation.

As alluded to, our expedition opted to seek refuge some distance from the cavern in which we encountered these creatures. When we performed a quick headcount, we discovered to our horror that one of the porters was missing. We dispatched our halfling scout to reconnoiter the route we had traversed subsequent to our run in with the flying vermin. He retraced our steps all the way to the hideous creatures' cave where he observed the unfortunate porter encased in a cocoon presumably of silken fibers. A dozen or so tarantubats were crawling on the corpse, apparently feeding.

With the mystery of the porter's whereabouts solved, the expedition proceeded apace. We were blessed with great fortune that the lost porter was not bearing essential equipment that might have mandated a rescue attempt. In our subsequent subterranean trekking we discovered that the spider venom appears to be of relatively brief duration for after a couple of hours we were once again our jocular old selves. – S

These creatures have dull-black, hairy bodies about 4 inches in diameter and 2 inches tall, weighing less than 1 pound. They have four pairs of legs, the first three being webbed and allowing them to fly in a fluttering, deceptively clumsy manner. The wingspan is roughly 2 feet and, along with the creature's rodent-like ears, gives it a batlike appearance when seen from a distance or in dim light.

Combat/Tactics:

Tarantubats hunt larger opponents by swarming them from all sides and gradually wearing them down by delivering numerous poisonous bites. This venom has a Virulence Factor 9, and creatures that fail their saving throws lose 1 point of Strength (no effect on a successful save. Victims reduced to 0 Strength become paralyzed for 2d6p hours. Lost Strength is restored at a rate of 1 point every 30 minutes.

Those who become paralyzed by Strength loss are usually encased in a cocoon. The tarantubats then feed upon the encased victim at their leisure, sometimes taking days to completely drain the fluids from a large kill before beginning the process of consuming the flesh.

Even if a victim becomes paralyzed due to their poison, tarantubats

SIGN/TRACKS

Tarantubats have a natural fear of fire and can be repelled by smoke as well. If you find yourself in the middle of a swarm swing a torch high and wide to keep them at bay.

RANGE ON TELLENE

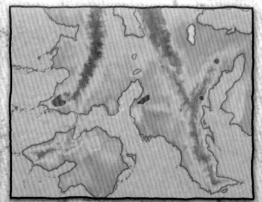

SIZE COMPARISON

6 ft

3 ft

only begin the process of building the cocoon if not threatened by other creatures. If they successfully paralyze an opponent and are driven away, they return as soon as they are able, in order to assess if the victim is still available for cocooning.

Habitat/Society:

Many tarantubats make their webbed nests high in trees or caves, though those in climes where trees and caves are scarce prefer small underground burrows or rock crevices. Tarantubats line the areas around their nests with their silken webbing. These threads are quite sticky and vibrate easily, serving the tarantubat as both passive trap and active warning device.

Tarantubats rarely fight amongst themselves, save when two males become rivals over the same female. In such events, tarantubats usually limit their attacks to 'dry' bites that deal damage but do not pump venom into the wound.

They may be encountered alone or in small flocks, depending how many tarantubats the local fauna can sustain. Tarantubats mate in the warmer months, with gestation lasting only a few weeks, after which the female produces her egg sac. If possible, the female lays this egg sac inside a fresh corpse, so as to provide food for the hundreds of tiny tarantubats that will hatch two weeks later.

If a resting (i.e., not flying) tarantubat wishes to warn away an approaching threat, it raises its body and spreads its wings. If the intruder ignores the warning, the tarantubat may flee or leap off its perch and attempt to bite.

Males have a potential lifespan of 12 years, though females may live for as much as three decades.

Ecology:

Tarantubats are accomplished predators, feeding primarily on birds, frogs, snakes and rodents, though their diet also includes insects (including wasps, bees and other arachnids) and occasionally much larger creatures. As noted in the combat section, they use their poisonous bite in an attempt to paralyze creatures larger than themselves. However, when it comes to smaller creatures, a single tarantubat can catch its prey in mid-air and begin feeding almost immediately.

After desiccating their prey, tarantubats may consume the flesh as well. They do this by vomiting up digestive juices (in order to liquefy the flesh) or slowly masticating and grinding up the solid flesh. In times of famine, they can even consume their own webs directly from their own abdomens; this can sustain a tarantubat for nearly a month without food.

Occasionally, a pair or group of tarantubats may take flight with strands of webbing hanging from their bodies. They can use these to gather up flying insects or foul the wings of birds, much like a fisherman trawls the sea with his net.

Tarantubats are preyed upon by large snakes, lizards and giant wasps.

On Tellene:

Tarantubats are also known as 'tel-tulmeramika,' which means 'half-spider, half-bat' when loosely translated from Low Elven. Significant colonies are said to be located in a cave within the Rokk Woods, a deep cavern near the city of Giilia, the foothills of the Yan Elenon Mountains and the northern Edosi Forest.

[1] Tarantubat blood can enhance the fifth level Levitation spell when used as an additional material component. By smearing the blood on one's shoulders, vertical movement is increased to 15 feet/second.

[2] Tarantubats can be quite tasty. Preparation requires a difficult Cooking/Baking skill to avoid poisoning (a failed check resulting in meals that cause d3p lost points of Strength for 2d6p hours).

TARANTUBAT

HIT POINTS:	1d6
SIZE/WEIGHT:	T/1 lb.
TENACITY:	Steady
INTELLIGENCE:	Non
FATIGUE FACTOR:	2

SPEED		INIT
10	ATTACK -1	0
DEFENSE +8	DMG REDUCTION 0	
short REACH	1 + poison DAMAGE	2
		TOP SAVE ▼

MOVEMENT

CRAWL:	¾
WALK:	1¼
JOG:	2½
RUN:	5
FLY:	25

SAVES

PHYSICAL:	-2
MENTAL:	-1
DODGE:	+3

ATTACK: Tarantubats deliver a poisonous bite that results in the loss of 1 point of Strength if not resisted (VF 9 toxin). Though not formidible as individuals, these creatures often attack in great numbers, overwhelming the defenders and wearing down larger prey with multiple bites to the rear and flanks.

SPECIAL DEFENSES: Flight

GENERAL INFO

ACTIVITY CYCLE:	Nocturnal
NO. APPEARING:	10+3d8
% CHANCE IN LAIR:	60%
FREQUENCY:	Infrequent
ALIGNMENT:	Non
VISION TYPE:	Standard
AWARENESS/SENSES:	Senses vibrations in webbing or within 30 feet
HABITAT:	Cave ceilings and treetops
DIET:	Carnivorous
ORGANIZATION:	Individuals or flock
CLIMATE/TERRAIN:	Temperate to tropical woodlands

YIELD

MEDICINAL:	nil
SPELL COMPONENTS:	blood, for the Levitation spell[1]
HIDE/TROPHY:	nil
TREASURE:	incidental
EDIBLE:	yes[2]
OTHER:	nil
EXPERIENCE POINT VALUE:	20

T

Tentaslug

Also Known As:
Killer Snail, Vrazz

Attacking the eye stalks on these monsters may seem like a good ideam but avoid the grasping tentacles.

When first approached about killing slugs I guffawed and told my perspective client, "I'm a bounty hunter, not a gardener. I'm afraid someone has played a practical joke on you." His terse reply "It's already eaten the gardeners" got my attention there and then. Perhaps this would prove an interesting diversion.

Upon reaching my employer's estate, I began to grasp the enormity of the problem, for I was shown the creature's slimy trail that led down to the drainage system. Its five foot breadth implied a truly massive beast lurking somewhere near the sewage cistern.

After we settled upon an elevated price for my services, I made what preparations I could hoping that the giant mollusc would prove vulnerable to the same deterrents employed by gardeners when combatting ordinary slugs. I settled upon a powered mixture of ground salt and copper filling several linen sacks with the mixture before returning to the hunt.

Tracking the creature initially proved a trivial affair for its distinctive trail was unmistakable. Once below ground though, several inches of most noxious liquid filled the drainage tunnels and disguised any history of the beast's passage. Soon enough I learned that I was not the only hunter for tentacles lashed out at me from a side passage seemingly too small to warrant closer inspection.

Ensnared as I was, my great sword proved impossible to employ. I reached for the salt packets and tore one open haphazardly flinging the contents about hoping for a miracle. In this I was rewarded for the tentacles loosed with alacrity. -ϯ

These massive mollusks bear a close resemblance to giant shell-less snails, but with a pair of massive grasping tentacles and a gaping maw of sharp, rasping teeth. These gastropods shuffle along with an extension-contraction motion, leaving a slimy trail as evidence of their passing.

In addition to the larger tentacles, which it uses to grasp larger prey, the tentaslug has two sensory small tentacles near its mouth and two larger optical eyestalks located atop its head. Tentaslugs prefer damp, dark environments and have difficulty seeing in bright light, although their sensitivity to vibrations make this a non-issue. A tentaslug's organs of smell are in its tentacles and enable it to detect food several hundred feet away. Worse, they can pursue prey through small openings,

their bodies adjusting to fit as needed. They can also cross with ease any barrier, such as a crevasse, that is two-thirds their length or shorter.

A hole on the right side of the tentaslug's head is its pneumostome. This is like the slug's nose, allowing entry to its respiratory system. The slug has the ability to close this hole.

Combat/Tactics:
Tentaslugs track their prey by scent and vibration. When within reach (10'), they attack with their large tentacles. Each can strike every 12 seconds (thus getting a single attack every 6 sec); any hit inflicts 4d4p+5 dmg and firmly grasps its opponents; held foes do not sustain further damage but are dragged to the maw in 10 seconds where they are bitten (Atk

SIGN/TRACKS

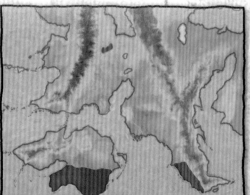

When a tentaslug took up residence among the ruins of an old watchtower near Hezmahn, Ahznomahnii troopers were able to eradicate the beast by dousing it with flasks of salt water and driving it out into the open where it could be deal with.

RANGE ON TELLENE

SIZE COMPARISON

12 ft
6 ft

+14, Dmg 6d6p) until dead, then consumed. This biting attack substitutes for one or both tentacles and thus occurs either every 12 or 6 seconds. Breaking the grasp of a tentacle requires a Feat of Strength (*vs. d20p+11*). Such a feat may be attempted once per 5 seconds.

Their bodies are most resistant to crushing weapons. Puncturing weapons are also of little use, except with a lucky hit that might damage an innard. Hacking weapons are most effective.

Tentaslugs are mostly water and pouring 5 pounds of salt on them or any form of dehydration spell deals 4d8p damage per attack (with no DR or saving throw, as appropriate). Lesser quantities of salt causes proportionately lesser injury. They also suffer a -10 penalty to saves against gaseous attacks because their slimy hides readily absorb gases.

Habitat/Society:

As water is quickly lost from the tentaslug's soft, moist and unprotected body it lives in damp places in the soil and among debris. When living above ground, it emerges only at night or on wet days. When dry or during bright sunlight hours, tentaslugs burrow into the soil and remain safely there in a state of hibernation until conditions change. When hibernating, a tentaslug can be safely slain. Tentaslugs do not live in deserts or tundras.

Killer Snails are hermaphroditic, meaning they have both male and female reproductive systems. The genitalia are covered by the massive body. Although a hermaphrodite, the tentaslug rarely fertilizes itself, and usually mates with another after an elaborate courtship that takes days.

Mates are attracted by the tentaslug's slime trail, which contains pheromones to attract other slugs. After mating, each tentaslug departs. In the following weeks they produce up to 75 translucent eggs, laid in a bed of rotting vegetation or a dead animal. The latter is typically slain by the tentaslug rather than found. Tentaslugs mate and lay eggs throughout the year. The adults provide no further care for their eggs beyond finding a suitable hiding spot and body and the eggs are abandoned as soon as the clutch is laid.

Ecology:

Vrazz are detritivores, or decomposers. They process leaves, animal droppings, plant material and animal proteins (alive or dead) and then recycle them into soil humus. They seem to have a fondness for mushrooms, and they spread seeds and spores when they eat, making them an important part of the ecology of the Netherdeep.

They may supplement their diet with meat when they can get it. Whether fresh or carrion, it matters not. These voracious beasts will eat moss or plant life, but when they sense movement (through ground vibrations), the tentaslug moves toward the source.

On Tellene:

Tentaslugs can be found in subterranean settings or in any dank, dark environment. They are plentiful in both the Obakasek and Vohven jungles.

[1] *Tentaslug slime protects open wounds from infection and may even (25%) counter the disease effects of a fresh wound from a lycanthrope.*

[2] *The slime from a tentaslug, when used as an additional material component in a Slippery Surface spell, causes any affected by it to make saving throws with an additional -2 penalty.*

TENTASLUG

HIT POINTS:	30+6d8
SIZE/WEIGHT:	L/400 lbs.
TENACITY:	Brave
INTELLIGENCE:	Semi
FATIGUE FACTOR:	n/a

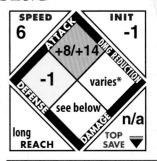

SPEED	INIT
6	-1
ATTACK	+8/+14
DEFENSE	-1
	varies*
	see below
long REACH	DAMAGE
	n/a
	TOP SAVE ▼

MOVEMENT

CRAWL:	1¼
WALK:	2½
JOG:	5
RUN:	10
SPRINT:	15

SAVES

PHYSICAL:	+13
MENTAL:	+6
DODGE:	+7

ATTACK: Tentaslugs lash out with their tentacles attacking with each every 12 sec (thus getting a single attack every 6 sec); any hit inflicts 4d4p+5 dmg and firmly grasps its opponents; held foes are drawn to the mouth in 10 seconds where they are bitten (Atk +14, Dmg 6d6p) until dead, then consumed.

DEFENSES: *DR is 16 (vs crushing), 12 (piercing), 9 (hacking); 5 lb salt inflicts 4d8p damage to tentaslug (no DR)

GENERAL INFO

ACTIVITY CYCLE:	Nocturnal
NO. APPEARING:	1
% CHANCE IN LAIR:	20%
FREQUENCY:	Sporadic
ALIGNMENT:	Non
VISION TYPE:	Poor vision
AWARENESS/SENSES:	Sense of smell up to 300 feet; Tracking 85%
HABITAT:	Wetlands; other regions with moist soil
DIET:	Detritivorous
ORGANIZATION:	Individuals
CLIMATE/TERRAIN:	Warm temperate to tropical wilderness

T

YIELD

MEDICINAL:	slime, as antibiotic for wounds and lycanthropy[1]
SPELL COMPONENTS:	slime, for Slippery Surface spell[2]
HIDE/TROPHY:	nil
TREASURE:	incidental
EDIBLE:	no
OTHER:	nil
EXPERIENCE POINT VALUE:	533

TETZYLWYRM

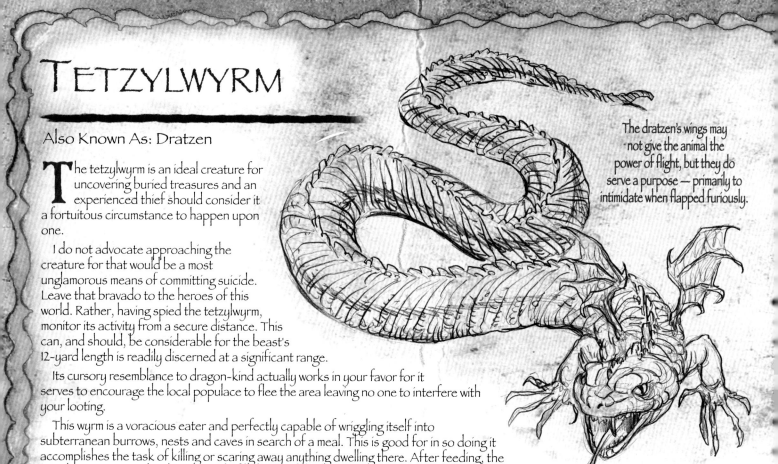

The dratzen's wings may not give the animal the power of flight, but they do serve a purpose — primarily to intimidate when flapped furiously.

Also Known As: Dratzen

The tetzylwyrm is an ideal creature for uncovering buried treasures and an experienced thief should consider it a fortuitous circumstance to happen upon one.

I do not advocate approaching the creature for that would be a most unglamorous means of committing suicide. Leave that bravado to the heroes of this world. Rather, having spied the tetzylwyrm, monitor its activity from a secure distance. This can, and should, be considerable for the beast's 12-yard length is readily discerned at a significant range.

Its cursory resemblance to dragon-kind actually works in your favor for it serves to encourage the local populace to flee the area leaving no one to interfere with your looting.

This wyrm is a voracious eater and perfectly capable of wriggling itself into subterranean burrows, nests and caves in search of a meal. This is good for in so doing it accomplishes the task of killing or scaring away anything dwelling there. After feeding, the tetzylwyrm enters a day-long period of lethargy while digesting its meal – most often while lying upon bare rocks and sunning itself.

Unlike dragons, tetzylwyrms are mere animals lacking such higher emotions as avarice and greed. Having cleared the way, you are now free to sneak in and search around for all manner of valuables. Just don't get greedy. I suggest collecting high value coins, gems and jewelry. Leave the bulky stuff for it slows you down and risks making noise. Although the wyrm won't take personal offense at this thievery, its keen sense of smell may detect you. Hopefully it won't be too eager for a chase if you're quick to scamper away. -✗

A tetzylwyrm, or snake dragon, appears as a large, thick serpent some 40 feet long with a line of bony ridges along its spine. The creature has a pair of scaly vestigial wings that perform no known function but hint perhaps at a traditional draconic past. The wyrm's clawed forearms protrude near the skull, but the creature has no hind legs. The lacertine head is set with powerful jaws. Its body is metallic blue-gray, with the ridges and wings a darker charcoal. The bifurcated tongue constantly darts in and out, making use of this excellent scent receptor to locate prey. Its eyes are set wide on its head giving it an excellent field of view but hardly stellar depth perception. Protected by nictitating membranes, the eyes have vertical pupils. Tetzylwryms appear to possess a very thick neck as broad as their head. Packed with coiled musculature, it is able to extend the head forward at remarkable speed permitting the creature to bite at opponents up to ten feet distant.

Though it appears to be a dragon of some type, the tetzylwyrm is not dragon-kind; most sages agree that it is a distant relation, as it evidences certain similar characteristics. In truth, it is not even a sapient monster, merely a large reptilian predator. It normally propels itself by slithering but may use its forelegs as well for short bursts of speed.

RANGE ON TELLENE

SIZE COMPARISON

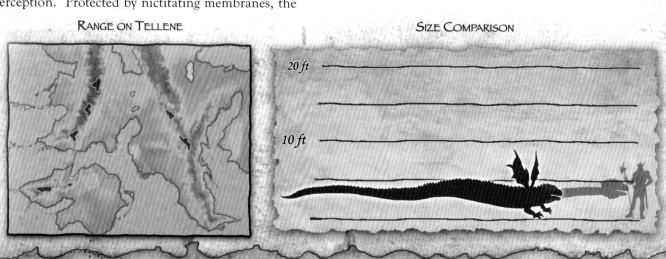

20 ft

10 ft

Combat/Tactics:

When it locates quarry, it scampers forward using its arms for acceleration (and, incidentally, madly flutters its wings to no effect other than intimidation). It attacks by darting with its head at targets up to 10 feet distant. Despite the size of their head, these strikes are lightning quick and difficult to both defend from and respond to. Its body is easier to attack but is defended by the creature's two claws.

Habitat/Society:

Tetzylwyrms are aggressive carnivores preying on a wide variety of large animals. Because they are poikilotherms, they do not need to feed with the regularity of warm-blooded creatures and thus are less active than many similarly-sized predators. After feeding on a large creature, a tetzylwyrm remains inactive for a day or more. A tetzylwyrm in such a state can be identified by the large lump in its body, similar to a recently-fed snake.

Dratzen prefer to dwell in hilly or mountainous terrain. They are susceptible to a fungus found in warm, stagnant waters of swamps and boglands, and so are seldom encountered in such regions. They can get into surprisingly tight spaces for a creature their size and so frequently are found underground where they've managed to worm themselves through passageways barely larger than their own girth.

These slithering beasts have fairly long lifespans with some specimens living for many scores of years. They are solitary, pairing up only to mate every decade or so. Females seek out some dark sheltered hole in which to lay a clutch of about a dozen 1-foot long eggs, but promptly abandon them. Assuming no predator has found and eaten the eggs, they hatch in about 6 months. The young are almost 6 feet long at birth. These small (for their species) tetzylwyrms fend for themselves, seeking out insects and arachnids, their natural prey. Only one in 20 survive the first year, the others falling prey to eagles (within a month) and other predators. They reach sexual maturity in about 4 years and full size in 5 years.

Ecology:

These predators are meat eaters with a taste for giant insects and spiders. In areas where human civilization has encroached upon these creatures' natural range, some have adapted to feeding on flocks of sheep and goats.

Their slight visual similarity to dragons has both advantages and disadvantages. Although excellent at instilling a great deal of fear in an unsophisticated opponent, repeated sightings may cause settlers to abandon their homesteads, thinking a far more powerful foe dwells in the area, and thus depriving the creature of a relatively easy food source.

On Tellene:

Tetzylwyrms cannot abide areas that are too damp or stagnant. In the Obakasek Jungle, they are only found at elevation, where the water drains away and sunlight can warm the ground directly.

[1] *Tetzylwyrm fang, when used as an alternate material component in the mage's fourth level Magic Projectile of Skewering spell, increases damage by 2d4p+2.*

TETZYLWYRM

HIT POINTS:	35+6d8
SIZE/WEIGHT:	H/900 lbs.
TENACITY:	Brave
INTELLIGENCE:	Animal, Low
FATIGUE FACTOR:	-4

SPEED	INIT
10*	-4

ATTACK +12
DMG REDUCTION
DEFENSE +8
10
long REACH
see below
DAMAGE n/a
TOP SAVE ▼

MOVEMENT

CRAWL:	5
WALK:	10
JOG:	15
RUN:	20
SPRINT:	25

SAVES

PHYSICAL:	+10
MENTAL:	+8
DODGE:	+11

ATTACK: Tetzylwyrms prefer to maintain a 10 foot distance from prey and strike out with their head to bite - this attack is at +12, inflicts 2d12p+4 damage and defends against opponents at +8; it retreats to maintain distance from a foe; if opponents close in they can attack the body (Def +3) but are also subject to claw attacks - the wyrm's speed increases to 3 (claw, claw, bite); clawing attacks are made with a +8 bonus and inflict 4d4p+2 damage

GENERAL INFO

ACTIVITY CYCLE:	Diurnal
NO. APPEARING:	1
% CHANCE IN LAIR:	15%
FREQUENCY:	Unusual
ALIGNMENT:	Non
VISION TYPE:	Standard
AWARENESS/SENSES:	Standard
HABITAT:	Caves
DIET:	Carnivorous
ORGANIZATION:	Individuals
CLIMATE/TERRAIN:	Temperate to tropical highlands

YIELD

MEDICINAL:	nil
SPELL COMPONENTS:	fang, in Magic Projectile of Skewering spell[1]
HIDE/TROPHY:	tetzylwyrm heads make great wall trophies
TREASURE:	incidental
EDIBLE:	yes, if marinated in water for three days
OTHER:	nil
EXPERIENCE POINT VALUE:	815

TICK, GIANT

Also Known As: Blood Gorger, Grypt

When I wrote my absey-book of insects and their kin, I noted that the giant tick, like the mite-sized nuisance familiar to most of us, moves from larvae to nymph to adult stage over a series of hosts, only producing eggs after blood-boltering its mandibles on the third host. However, it is now my contention that the giant tick is a one-host parasite with a life cycle of only a few weeks or months, feeding on a single victim before mating or dropping off to lay its eggs. It is truth that, although I have not yet been able to study a giant tick female in the egg-laying stage, I feel confident that it lays dozens, if not hundreds, of these eggs.

In my last shriving-time, I recalled to my new clerical ally a frightening incident when last my companions and I delved into an abandoned mine. We stepped over many the corky shards of man and beast, but found nothing else in the winding tunnels until we reached a great cavern several hundred yards beyond the entrance. As we moved into the center of the room and our torches played across the many cracks and crevices throughout, we were suddenly frozen in terror as thousands of flat-bodied, giant ticks came rushing towards us in a great swarm. My cheeks grow hot even now as I say that my survival is due mainly to the slowness of the two dwarves, whose short stance and heavy armor engrossed the ticks long enough for the rest of us to scape the tumult. - ℵ

Removing a tick that has attached itself to a victim can be a dicey affair. Care must be taken not to break off the proboscis within the victim's flesh. Applying a torch to a tick can sometimes force it to release its grip.

Giant ticks are eight-legged monstrosities about 30 inches in length with rounded and leathery bodies. When engorged with blood, their bodies swell, giving them a near spherical appearance. Their mouthparts are on the underside of their bodies, just beneath their mandibles.

They have black legs and bodies when they are flat (not engorged), but when filled with blood, their abdomens may take on a pinkish or red color.

Combat/Tactics:

When a giant tick makes a successful attack, it buries its head in the victim and begins to suck blood (ignoring all Damage Reduction) at a rate of d4p Hit Points for every 10 seconds so attached. A tick can be removed by a successful knock-back attack, a Feat of Strength (vs. *d20p+18*) or death. A victim may attack an attached tick with a dagger or knife at a -2 penalty (with care) or at +6 (without care). Note that if its initial attack does not exceed the target's DR, it can't attach itself and the

SIGN/TRACKS

Ticks love to hide in high grass, under brush and dark, shadowy places.

Small oblong prints about the size of a man's thumb can indicate giant ticks in an area.

RANGE ON TELLENE

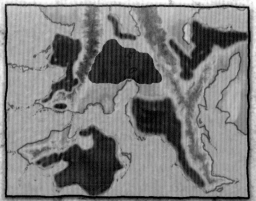

SIZE COMPARISON

6 ft

3 ft

attack was for naught.

Attacks without care or by allies wielding weapons have a 25% chance of accidentally striking the victim instead of the giant tick (any damage to a tick beyond its remaining Hit Point total goes to the victim as well). Allies attempting a Feat of Strength must first make a successful barehanded attack.

If a steady flame is held to an embedded tick (such as if burning it with a torch), it must make a morale check every 10 seconds or voluntarily withdraw from its host.

Ticks are disease carriers and may infect a victim with a variety of illnesses should they not kill him outright (a giant tick ceases to suck blood once gorged – a point reached when blood drain is equivalent to the tick's maximum HP).

Ticks cannot jump or fly, and thus prefer to conceal themselves at ground level and wait for prey to pass by so they can attach themselves.

Habitat/Society/Ecology:

Ticks have a wide range of habitats and live in mountain regions, grasslands, woodlands, shady areas with lots of vegetation and/or dry leaves and tropical regions.

Giant ticks have four life cycle stages. The female must have a blood meal to develop eggs. These eggs are laid in leaf litter, or in the soil, after the female drops off its host. The eggs hatch into larva. As a larva, a giant tick has only three pairs of legs. (Females lay about 40 eggs per day.)

These larva are produced in significant numbers, and are known as seed ticks. These ticks must find a host so they can change into the next stage – the nymph. If the nymph finds a host to feed on, it becomes an adult.

Immature ticks generally feed on small mammals, such as squirrels and chipmunks. Adults usually seek out cattle, deer, people and other animals.

Most giant ticks have a lifespan of about one year.

On Tellene:

Ticks are found almost everywhere on Tellene. They can live in temperate regions, though they cannot survive frigid temperatures. In regions where winter is very cold, they often seek shelter inside structures.

They do not generally inhabit desert regions, though they have been found there. It is believed any ticks found in those regions came as parasites on the mounts and pack animals of nomads.

They do not live in the tundra of the highlands in the Ka'Asa range, the rocky barren tundra of the upper Elenons, or the lands of Torakk. They also do not live in the high mountains or the ice fields or glaciers in the Krond, Deshada and Jorakk ranges.

They are common in the Brindonwood, Rytarr Woods and the Khorren Woods, the forests north of Tarisato and Zazahni, and the Kalokopeli Forest. They also infest areas of the Young Kingdoms and Drhokker, where there are grasslands in abundance.

[1] Employing a giant tick's head as an alternate material component in the Vampiric Touch spell increases damage by 1d4p points.

GIANT TICK

HIT POINTS:	12+3d8
SIZE/WEIGHT:	S/20 lbs.
TENACITY:	Nervous
INTELLIGENCE:	Non
FATIGUE FACTOR:	n/a

MOVEMENT

CRAWL:	1¼
WALK:	2½
JOG:	5
RUN:	10
SPRINT:	15

SAVES

PHYSICAL:	+5
MENTAL:	+3
DODGE:	+4

ATTACK: Giants ticks attack by attempting to bury their heads into a victim (causing 2d4p damage in the process); once embedded, they suck blood draining d4p HP every 10 seconds until sated or the victims dies

SPECIAL DEFENSES: attacking an embedded tick risks injury to its host; Feat of Strength (vs. d20p+18) is required to remove an embedded tick

GENERAL INFO

ACTIVITY CYCLE:	Diurnal
NO. APPEARING:	3-12
% CHANCE IN LAIR:	n/a
FREQUENCY:	Frequent
ALIGNMENT:	Non
VISION TYPE:	Standard
AWARENESS/SENSES:	Standard
HABITAT:	Forests, grasslands
DIET:	Sanguivorous
ORGANIZATION:	Individuals or brood
CLIMATE/TERRAIN:	Temperate to tropical lowlands

T

YIELD

MEDICINAL:	nil
SPELL COMPONENTS:	head, in the Vampiric Touch spell[1]
HIDE/TROPHY:	insignificant
TREASURE:	incidental
EDIBLE:	no
OTHER:	nil
EXPERIENCE POINT VALUE:	67

TIGER

Also Known As: Tigris, Vigral

My colleagues have mentioned to me that I should record my observations on the vocalization of tigers. No doubt this is due to the recent incident wherein our sentinel mistook the friendly meeting of two tigers in the brush as the moans of a zombie. What happened when he rushed upon the scene is not a matter I care to discuss so soon after my meal, so let me proceed with my notes.

Two tigers meeting each other in a friendly fashion (as our thief interrupted) vocalize a light brrrr, which oft comes out as a low moan punctuated with a sort of soft snort. This chuffing is only audible at close range, and it was our thief's misfortune that his ability to listen far outstripped his restraint.

The mating call of the tiger is a slightly subdued roar, occasionally interspersed with a growl. However, tigers also moan when calmly padding along the ground with their heads downwards. Neither of these sounds travels further than 300 or 400 yards, unlike the loud roar that carries over a mile. This great cry not only signals its presence or victory over its prey, but also serves to call its cubs home.

Tigers also communicate through their tails, like any common housecat, as well as by scent. Perhaps a ranger with an exceptional nose can distinguish the individual scents of feline urine, but I cannot. Nor have I any interest in trying. – ✍

The pelt of a tiger is highly prized, both as a trophy and for trade.

These big hunting cats are quick to anger, their growl serving as a warning sign that all would do well to heed. In appearance, most tigers have a yellow-orange coat marked with dark brown or black stripes, white underbelly and a 3-foot long white tail with black rings.

However, color variations do appear; perhaps the most notable is the white tiger with its brown stripes, blue eyes and pink nose, although there is also a 'golden' tiger with light gold fur, orange stripes and a white underbelly and legs, as well as a 'blue' tiger with slate gray fur and black stripes.

The typical adult male weighs roughly 475 pounds, with a total body length of around 9 feet (including the tail) and stands just over 3 feet tall at the shoulder. Females are slightly smaller and lighter.

Combat/Tactics:

Tigers fight to take down prey, defend their territory or themselves. They are particularly aggressive if encountered while already on the hunt for prey or when with cubs. They are also clever; a tiger may stalk a group and attack stragglers, or obviously weaker or wounded prey, first.

When attacking, tigers use a claw/claw/bite routine. If a tiger lands two successive claw attacks, it has grabbed its opponent and automatically inflicts a bite attack every 5

SIGN/TRACKS

Fore

Hind

RANGE ON TELLENE

SIZE COMPARISON

12 ft

6 ft

seconds thereafter. A tiger's grip can be broken with a successful knock-back or Feat of Strength (*vs. d20p+16*). The latter can be attempted after each bite attack. While caught, a victim can only attack with a dagger or knife.

Habitat/Society:

Tigers are usually found in warm or temperate forests and grasslands close to or containing water sources as well as an abundance of prey. However, there are breeds that are adapted to far more northerly climates.

Most are solitary creatures, living in individual territories of 8 to 70 square miles (with female territories typically being smaller than those of the male). A tiger marks its territory with urine and feces, as well as gland secretions rubbed onto various inanimate objects (*e.g.*, rocks and trees). Should a male tiger encounter another male in its territory, it may allow the newcomer to remain, provided it shows proper submission and does not remain in proximity. Otherwise, death results for the loser of the inevitable fight. Female intruders are more likely to be tolerated.

Tigers may mate at anytime during the year, though most do so in the winter months. A successful pregnancy has a gestation time of about 3 months, with the female giving birth to a litter of up to four cubs in her hidden den. Tiger cubs are able to hunt after roughly 18 months, but may wait another year before setting off on their own.

The average tiger has a lifespan of about 10 years.

Ecology:

Tigers are carnivores, preying on the local wildlife (primarily deer, boars and other large game) and any other creature foolish enough to get in the way of a hungry tiger. Their main rivals are other tigers but, while most predators avoid each other, they do occasionally come into conflict with aarnz hounds and brown bears (even to the extent of making them a part of their diet). Tigers have been seen to kill crocodiles, large snakes and other big hunting cats.

Humans rarely encounter tigers, save for those explorers who unknowingly step into a tiger's territory. However, when a tiger does taste the flesh of man (or other near-human creatures), it develops a taste for it. Such tigers often lurk in forests at the edge of small settlements, waiting for another tasty meal to leave the safety of the village walls and enter the dark woods.

On Tellene:

The largest known tiger population is in the Obakasek Jungle and its eastern hills, where they prey on jungle wildlife as well as the local goblin population. In fact, the tiger is such a danger to these goblins that more than one tribe has integrated the big hunting cat into their crude stories and legends, often giving it the intelligence and powers of a near-deity.

Tiger pelts are greatly prized in Tarisato and nearby Kalamar, where nobles and royalty often integrate them into fancy costumes and other garments.

[1] *Tiger bone, as an alternative material component in the mage's sixth level Boost Strength spell, increases that attribute by d8 points instead of d6.*

TIGER

HIT POINTS:	30+6d8
SIZE/WEIGHT:	L/475 lbs.
TENACITY:	Steady
INTELLIGENCE:	Animal. High
FATIGUE FACTOR:	1

SPEED		INIT
5	ATTACK +13	-2
	DMG REDUCTION	
DEFENSE +8	3	
	see below	
medium REACH	DAMAGE	TOP SAVE 6

MOVEMENT

CRAWL:	10
WALK:	15
JOG:	20
RUN:	25
SPRINT:	30

SAVES

PHYSICAL:	+14
MENTAL:	+11
DODGE:	+14

ATTACK: Tigers attack with powerful forepaws (2d4p+5 damage) and attempt to bring down their prey (two successive hits indicating this); thereafter they automatically inflict a bite (2d8p+7) every 5 seconds; breaking their grasp requires a Feat of Strength vs. d20p+16

SPECIAL ABILITIES:
Listening 45%, Sneaking 40%

GENERAL INFO

ACTIVITY CYCLE:	Any
NO. APPEARING:	1
% CHANCE IN LAIR:	5%
FREQUENCY:	Infrequent
ALIGNMENT:	Non
VISION TYPE:	Standard
AWARENESS/SENSES:	Good hearing and sense of smell
HABITAT:	Grasslands, forests
DIET:	Carnivorous
ORGANIZATION:	Individuals
CLIMATE/TERRAIN:	Subarctic to tropical lowlands

YIELD

MEDICINAL:	bone, used to treat pain and strengthen muscles
SPELL COMPONENTS:	bone, in the Boost Strength spell[1]
HIDE/TROPHY:	heads and pelts are prized
TREASURE:	incidental
EDIBLE:	yes
OTHER:	nil
EXPERIENCE POINT VALUE:	925

TOAD

GIANT TOAD
POISONOUS TOAD

Also Known As: Great Paddock, Rizhor

My companions misdoubt my sobriety when I provision that the giant toad will one day conquer the world, and no doubt you who read these notes will also take me for a ninny. Yet, mistake me not. I do not play the termagant, ranting about an empire of giant toads ruling over human slaves, as evocative a picture as that creates in my head. No, I merely mean that my recent studies of the giant toad have identified multiple adaptive traits that predict large distributional range expansion in leaps and bounds. For instance, certain lineage-specific range-shifting abilities include its independence from constant access to water and even humidity, as well as its capacity to propagate a great number of fast-hatching eggs. The poisonous giant toad has an even greater propensity for expansion, as its glands protect it from most predators that would otherwise consider it a slow-moving snack.

On the other hand, I have witnessed certain birds (such as the ousel-cock) eating poisonous toads without ill effect. Could any of our land's giant avian species do so with the poisonous giant toad? As much as I admire their beauty and plumage, I think I should afear an flight of giant birds more than the mass spawning of giant toads. At least I should be able to better see the toads closing in upon me. ~ ℵ

The giant poisonous toad can be distinguished from its non-poisonous cousin by looking at the tongue and mouth. They display a slight purple hue.

These squat, stocky reptiles stand roughly 5 feet tall and weigh nearly 300 pounds. A giant toad's dry skin is usually rough and warty in appearance, in colors ranging from green to brown. (Poisonous toads have no characteristics distinguishing them from non-poisonous varieties.) Giant toads can hop up to 10 feet forward (or 5 feet vertically) from a standstill.

Combat/Tactics:

If a giant toad bites a Small or Tiny creature and its attack roll exceeds the defender's result by 7 or more, it swallows the creature whole. The trapped creature automatically suffers 1d4p damage (from asphyxia) every 10 seconds thereafter. While caught, a victim cannot attack and must be rescued by others.

Giant poisonous toads are far deadlier in that their bite carries a virulence factor 12 toxin (*see sidebar on following page for details*). Even skin-to-skin contact with such a toad subjects one to their bitter-smelling poison, but with a reduced Virulence Factor of 9. Opting to execute a near-perfect defense will expose the defender to this poison unless one is armed with a small weapon.

Habitat/Society/Ecology:

Giant toads are often most active at night and particularly so in damp or wet weather. Most toads are amphibians and so live near swamps, ponds and other still, freshwater bodies where the females lay their eggs. A giant toad's favorite meal consists of giant insects, reptiles and rodents, but when hungry it can swallow almost any creature smaller than itself.

On Tellene:

Many cultures on Tellene associate toads (even giant ones) with fertility and harmony. In the Kingdom of Cosdol, for instance, the toad is seen as a symbol of luck and good fortune (so much so that stone toads are a common feature in household gardens and are often given as gifts). Interestingly, toads are also associated with evil female mages (oft referred to as witches) and the same Cosdolites speak of witches being marked with the symbol of the toad's foot.

[1] *Giant toad hide may be used as a remedy for patients suffering a variety of illness. This treatment reduces the disease's severity by 1.*

[2] *A giant toad leg, when substituting for an ordinary toad's leg, enhances the Springing spell permitting an extra 5' jumping distance.*

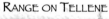
SIGN/TRACKS

RANGE ON TELLENE

SIZE COMPARISON

Fore

Hind

6 ft

3 ft

GIANT TOAD

HIT POINTS:	20+4d8
SIZE/WEIGHT:	M/160 lbs.
TENACITY:	Nervous
INTELLIGENCE:	Animal. Low
FATIGUE FACTOR:	2

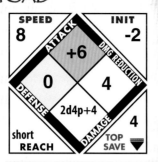

SPEED 8 • INIT -2 • ATTACK +6 • DMG REDUCTION • 0 • 4 • DAMAGE 2d4p+4 • short REACH • TOP SAVE 4

MOVEMENT

CRAWL:	1¼
WALK:	2½
JOG:	5
RUN:	10
HOP:	15

SAVES

PHYSICAL:	+6
MENTAL:	+4
DODGE:	+6

ATTACK: Hop forward to attack, preferentially targeting size T or S opponents (possibly leapfrogging creatures in their way); exceeding oppont's Defense by 7 or better permits them to swallow size T or S foes.

SPECIAL DEFENSES:
Can hop up to 10' from standstill (clearing 5' height)

GENERAL INFO

ACTIVITY CYCLE:	Nocturnal
NO. APPEARING:	1-12
% CHANCE IN LAIR:	n/a
FREQUENCY:	Frequent
ALIGNMENT:	Non
VISION TYPE:	Standard
AWARENESS/SENSES:	Standard
HABITAT:	Wetlands
DIET:	Carnivorous
ORGANIZATION:	Individuals or nest
CLIMATE/TERRAIN:	Temperate to tropical lowlands

Giant Toad Poison

Virulence Factor: 12 (or 9)

Effect if Save Failed: Victim is incapacitated by seizures and convulsions for 5d4p minutes (treat as a failed Threshold of Pain check). A natural 1 or 2 on the saving throw results in death from cardiac arrest at the end of the seizure.

Effect if Save Made: -1 penalty to Attack, Defense and Damage for 5d4p minutes (cumulative if repeatedly poisoned).

GIANT POISONOUS TOAD

HIT POINTS:	25+6d8
SIZE/WEIGHT:	L/300 lbs.
TENACITY:	Steady
INTELLIGENCE:	Animal. Low
FATIGUE FACTOR:	2

SPEED 5 • INIT -1 • ATTACK +10 • DMG REDUCTION • +6 • 8 • DAMAGE 2d8p+6 • short REACH • TOP SAVE 7

MOVEMENT

CRAWL:	1¼
WALK:	2½
JOG:	5
RUN:	10
HOP:	15

SAVES

PHYSICAL:	+9
MENTAL:	+6
DODGE:	+12

ATTACK: Hop forward to attack, preferentially targeting size T or S opponents (possibly leapfrogging creatures in their way); exceeding oppont's Defense by 7 or better permits them to swallow size T or S foes. Bite is VF 12 poison causing incapacitation and possibly death.

SPECIAL DEFENSES: Can hop up to 10' from standstill (clearing 5' height)

GENERAL INFO

ACTIVITY CYCLE:	Nocturnal
NO. APPEARING:	1-6
% CHANCE IN LAIR:	n/a
FREQUENCY:	Sporadic
ALIGNMENT:	Non
VISION TYPE:	Standard
AWARENESS/SENSES:	Standard
HABITAT:	Wetlands
DIET:	Carnivorous
ORGANIZATION:	Individuals or nest
CLIMATE/TERRAIN:	Temperate to tropical lowlands

YIELD

MEDICINAL:	hide eases illnesses[1] (giant toad only)
SPELL COMPONENTS:	leg, for the Springing spell[2]
HIDE/TROPHY:	nil
TREASURE:	incidental
EDIBLE:	yes (giant toad); no (poisonous toad)
OTHER:	nil

EXPERIENCE POINT VALUE: 275 (giant toad); 800 (giant poisonous toad)

TRÖGLODYTE

Also Known As: Sleestack

The barbed-crest of a sleestack will be fully extended when it is angered and about to attack — without fail!

Sleestack stench can permeate hair and clothing for days.

I well recall the explorations of the Miclenon caves, when a great gust of wind extinguished our torches and I, tumbling down a steep slope, became somewhat separated from my companions. Fortunately, I did not roll out of their hearing, and after coming to my feet and assuring them of my safety, fumbled for flint and steel. My hands had barely drawn them from my belt pouch when I felt hands plucking at my clothing and became sensible of a horrible stench.

Even as I shouted in fear, I struck a spark and saw in a flash two dazzled reptilian faces recoiling from the sudden light. You can scarce imagine how frightening those pale, toothy countenances looked even as they startled in bewilderment. I did not stay to look further, I promise you, but retreated on my backside up the smooth stone, again and again striking the sparks that the beasts seemed not to like. Still, they continued to advance in between the timing of my flashes, so that they seemed to move in heartbeats of time rather than by any continuous motion. Suddenly, from the tops of their heads sprouted spiny frills, appearing in the light as if by magic, and giving them an even more menacing appearance than they already possessed.

Once, I stumbled, and as I did so, my feet were grasped and my right boot claimed as a trophy. Yanking my foot out of the leather, I tried again to strike a spark in the eyes of my pursuers, but both flint and steel flew from my hand and clattered against the rock. Fortunately, I could now feel rougher stone beneath me and, kicking violently, was able to free myself and clamber upwards. The last I remember is slipping again, falling insensible at my companions' feet even as their torches sprang again into brightness and the light glinted off their soon-to-be-bloodied blades. - S

These primitive relatives of lizardmen are natural albinos though their diet colors their scaly hides in varying shades of mustard, green and olive. Like their lizardman cousins, tröglodytes should probably be categorized as humanoids, although not hominids strictly speaking, given their bipedal nature and comparable intelligence, but again, most scholars steadfastly refuse to do so. Ironically, the first academics to classify tröglodytes, thought them to be mammalian relatives of the orc based solely on skeletal remains; likely the tröglodyte name has its origins in this earliest research. Once the connection was made between the live specimens and the first studied remains, scholars reclassified these creatures as simple lacertilian beasts, outside the class of the other intelligent bipeds. Most accurately, trögs should be classified as cousins to the surface-dwelling lizardman species and a bit more distant cousin to the various intelligent amphibious creatures.

Atop its reptilian head, each tröglodyte sports a crest that it can raise or lower at will. This crest is comprised mainly of flaps of skin, supported by cartilaginous spines, the whole of which is usually of a complementary color to its hide. A trög typically raises its frills when battling for territory, attracting a mate, or when making itself seem bigger when threatened.

On average, the male tröglodyte stands between 5 and 6 feet tall, and is heavily built with robust bone structure and particularly strong arms and hands. A two to two-and-a-half foot tail juts from their hindquarters. A thick scaled hide completely protects the tröglodyte's body. The typical male trög

SIGN/TRACKS

RANGE

12° east

12° west

SIZE COMPARISON

6 ft

3 ft

weighs roughly 175 pounds, while female trögs stand about 5 feet tall and weigh between 125 and 150 pounds.

While often but not exclusively living near or around underground lakes or water sources (including seepage), tröglodytes are, in fact, air breathers and not amphibious in nature. Tröglodyte thermophysiology is interesting. While technically cold blooded ectotherms, tröglodytes exhibit a form of gigantothermy, likely due to a blubber layer just under their scaly skin. This form of metabolism, coupled with the warmth permeating the Netherdeep at the depth generally inhabited by trögs, allows them to be as active as most warm-blooded creatures despite far lower levels of caloric intake.

Tröglodytes can see well in very dimly lit conditions. Generally functioning with vegetable-generated luminescence or fires as small as burning coals or embers, trögs have extreme low-light vision, but are completely blind in daylight. Relatively weak compared to other primitive bipeds such as orcs, their olfactory sensors are merely on-par with humans. Additionally, due to a lack of ears, tröglodytes possess fairly weak auditory sensors (-20% to hearing checks), although the fact that sound travels well and magnifies in their underground habitat tends to lessen the impact of this deficit. Their superb tactile senses further mitigate these deficiencies; tröglodytes can perceive even faint vibrations.

Tröglodytes are surprisingly strong and, like their lizardman cousins, boast natural weaponry in the form of claws and powerful, sharp-toothed jaws. If unarmed, trögs have a speed of 5 and alternatively claw with both hands for 2d4p and then bite for d8p. (A near-perfect defense permits them to use the biting attack even if employing a weapon.) While they have there are no recorded instances of a trög donning armor of any type, their thick, scaled hide serves that purpose well. That said, certain tribes do employ primitive shields. Further, an innate hardiness to withstand damaging blows and a determined resistance to pain make tröglodytes hardy foes, indeed. But their best defense is their famous stench. When excited or filled with adrenaline, they excrete a moist perspiration with a pungent, noxious odor, capable of repelling even determined foes. Most sages believe that this ability is related somehow to the musk glands exhibited by skunks, but occurring in smaller nodules tied to sweat and adrenal glands.

Tröglodytes possess a chameleon-like ability to blend with their surroundings. Through specialized cells intermixed with their outer scales both above and under, they can camouflage themselves to the local environment. When aroused or angered, they will exhibit a hot, glowing reddish hue between scales, giving them a frightful demonic appearance. Trögs control their pigmentation to conceal themselves, gaining an impressive 80% hide skill. Completely changing color, however, requires roughly five minutes of concentration. Hasty changes such as when hiding from pursuit requires no time at all but affords a mere 40% hide skill.

After twenty seconds of intense excitement (such as mating, fear or combat), tröglodytes begin to excrete a disgustingly putrid musk, thoroughly repulsive to all non-tröglodytes. Accordingly, any non-tröglodyte within thirty feet must make a Constitution check (vs. d20p+7) or

TRÖGLODYTE

HIT POINTS:	20+2d8
SIZE/WEIGHT:	M/175 lbs.
TENACITY:	Steady
INTELLIGENCE:	Obtuse
FATIGUE FACTOR:	0/+1

SPEED 10 · INIT 0 · ATTACK +3 · DEFENSE 0 · DMG REDUCTION 2 · by weapon +2 · DAMAGE 6 · medium REACH · TOP SAVE

MOVEMENT

CRAWL:	2½
WALK:	5
JOG:	10
RUN:	15
SPRINT:	20

SAVES

PHYSICAL:	+4
MENTAL:	+1
DODGE:	+3

ATTACK: Tröglodytes are very fond of employing javelins and each warrior has 3 or more of these to hurl before engaging in close order combat; axes and spears are typical weapons; may attack unarmed with a speed of 5 alternatively clawing for 2d4p and biting for d8p; bite attack supersedes standard near-perfect defense

SPECIAL DEFENSES: Foul (and possibly debilitating) stench. Shield use (e.g., medium shield increases Def to +6.

GENERAL INFO

ACTIVITY CYCLE:	Nocturnal
NO. APPEARING:	d6p (traveling, hunting); 2d4p+8 (warband); 15d12p (clan)
% CHANCE IN LAIR:	25%
FREQUENCY:	Infrequent
ALIGNMENT:	Neutral Evil
VISION TYPE:	Extreme Low light vision
AWARENESS/SENSES:	Poor sight in darkness and hearing[1]
HABITAT:	Subterranean cave and tunnel systems
DIET:	Omnivorous
ORGANIZATION:	Tribal
CLIMATE/TERRAIN:	Netherdeep

YIELD

MEDICINAL:	nil
SPELL COMPONENTS:	scent glands, for Stink Bomb spell[2]
HIDE/TROPHY:	troglodyte frills make impressive trophies
TREASURE:	on trading missions[3]
EDIBLE:	yes, but it's an acquired taste (glands are mildly toxic)
OTHER:	nil
EXPERIENCE POINT VALUE:	60

suffer nausea that weakens the character (-1d4p to Constitution, but no corresponding hit point loss). Any character remaining in range of the stench must make such a Constitution check every ten seconds. Any poor soul who's Constitution drops to zero or lower immediately falls prone, vomiting uncontrollably. Once all tröglodytes have calmed or left the area, the stench remains for one minute before dissipating. Characters removed from the reeking area regain lost Constitution at a rate of one point per minute.

Tröglodytes have weak intellects, ranking in intelligence somewhere between the great apes and orcs, probably just under gnoles on the evolutionary scale with one notable exception. Every tribe has one leader, an intelligent brown tröglodyte. These leaders seem to have some sort of collective tribal ancestral knowledge that somehow passes from one leader to another. These clan chiefs live far longer than their subjects, surviving until a new dun specimen is born and reaches maturity. These leader types influence their clan in all areas, from better living conditions to superior tactics, defense works, weaponry, although the latter still created exclusively from stone materials. Tröglodytes wield stone-tipped spears, clubs and axes. They can sometimes hurl throwing axes, darts or javelins before engaging foes.

Tröglodytes war with all races, save their own and will not cooperate with even evil humanoid races or lizardmen (whom they rarely encounter anyhow due to such disparate habitats). Cooperation is theoretically possible, but far from the norm and must certainly be imposed against the tröglodyte nature by their ruler.

For every group of 10 tröglodytes encountered, a stronger one with maximum hit points will lead (in the loosest sense of the word). He'll enjoy a +1 to Attack, Damage, Defense and a -1 bonus to Initiative as well. For every 30, the warband will have an even larger trög with a +2 to Attack, Damage, Defense and a -2 bonus to Initiative in addition to maximum hit points plus an extra d8 hit points. For every 90, the tribe will have a sub-chief, a massive specimen with +3 to Attack, Damage, Defense and a -2 bonus to Speed and Initiative in addition to maximum hit points plus two extra d8 rolls for hit points. This is in addition to the 9 basic leaders and 3 stronger leaders. Finally, each tribe will have their powerful chieftain. This leader will always be male and will have maximum hit points and a +5 to Attack, 4 Defense and a -4 bonus to Initiative, but no additional hit dice or bonus to Damage. He will always have an extra 4d6p sub-chiefs at his disposal at all times. Though physically no larger than a standard trög, this chieftain has genius-level intelligence, speaks several languages and possesses spellcasting ability of level d12p-2 for clerical and d12p-2 in mage (negative and zero indicating no ability).

By human standards, tröglodytes act with immoral intent. They enjoy feasting on other intelligent beings, eating their enemies live, often keeping live prisoners as a fresh food source only finishing the torso days after the limbs have been consumed. Tröglodytes choose their victims indiscriminately from amongst their neighbors, but clearly revel in the suffering of their meals. Tröglodytes do not generally loot or pillage, other than taking fresh meals. They will, however, carry off spoils if

directed by their leader whom they follow without question or even any thought, frankly; his instruction and wishes are simply commands to be followed the same as food should be eaten when the body is hungry. Beauty and art have no meaning in tröglodyte society. Any accouterment worn carries only a utilitarian purpose.

While tröglodytes work assiduously, such efforts involve only food preparation, weapon-making, fire maintenance and other primitive tasks. They do not mine, preferring to dwell in natural-occurring caves and tunnels, but sometimes live in areas mined or created by other subterranean races. Likewise, they have no smithing ability. They make their own weapons from any material available, although some trögs will use weapons taken from fallen foes (generally when directed by their tribal leader). Their stone-tipped, tröglodyte-manufactured weapons and tools must constantly be maintained. After d3p uses, trög-made weapons, tools and paraphernalia degrade to the point of penalties and d3p uses later will fail entirely unless maintained by a tröglodyte.

Combat/Tactics

Tröglodytes prefer to lie in wait for victims, using their chameleon abilities to gain the drop on their foes. They deploy few tactics beyond that, perhaps firing a volley of ranged weapons prior to attacking the closest and easiest foes to reach. They use their musk to weaken foes and to take prisoners, binding and dragging helpless victims back to their lair. Prisoners may be taken even during the heat of battle, though even the dimmest tröglodyte understands not to endanger himself to capture a prisoner; they do so when the opportunity presents itself, but only if it is relatively safe to do so.

Habitat/Society

Exclusively subterranean, tröglodytes dwell in moist caverns and tunnel systems that contain underground lakes or streams. Because tröglodytes consume a great deal of fungus, the size of the water source and the wetness of the cave (and thus the amount of fungus growing therein) greatly affect the number of tröglodytes in any location. While they prefer the heat of the Netherdeep, some tröglodyte tribes thrive in the chillier reaches far closer to the surface world. These latter tribes, of course, rely on various forms of combustion for warmth.

Trögs have a loosely tribal society, with the family unit being more important than the tribe. However, a tröglodyte family unit is characterized only as a male and female with immature offspring. Once any offspring reach maturity, the family unit simply disbands and its members move to seek other mates. That said, each tröglodyte family lives in close proximity to the overall tribe, generally in a small cave, niche or area adjacent to the main food source, water source and so-on. Therefore, as each family disbands, another simply reforms as new mates are chosen. Survival is the greatest motivator for a trög, with the degree of cooperation among a tribe depending heavily on the frequency of threats from outsiders.

In all known cases, an auburn or dun specimen leads the tribe. This leader rules absolutely and unchallenged, but rarely exerts his authority preferring to keep to his own devices. Further, the orders directing tribal activity rarely change, even decades later, leaving this brown tribal leader little to command. For example, the methods of tool and weapon creation or even food production may remain stable with no change necessary or even desired even after generations. Besides this uninterested ruler, tribal society has no order; the stronger rule the weak and generally do as they please.

Though they do not forge weapons or work metal, and their bone industry is relatively simple, tröglodytes construct Neolithic tools and weapons made of obsidian, flint and other chipped stone. Tröglodytes routinely sharpen the blades by careful flaking away from the cutting edge, repolishing or a combination of both. This makes their weapons very sharp, even more so than the iron blades so common to surface dwellers. Due to the limitations of the material, tröglodytes cannot craft swords or similar weapons with long, straight blades, but can construct sophisticated axes, spear points and the like.

Females comprise fully 50% of the population of the tribe. Tröglodyte females are smaller than males, having only one hit die and a -1 to all rolls relative to males. Females generally do not participate in raids; they produce and rear young, fashion weapons, farm and prepare meals, although smaller males also perform these chores.

After a gestation period of a few months, oviparous tröglodytes lay tough-shelled, large amniotic eggs. The eggs require no specific care and hatch in a few months. Each tribe will have a special chamber dedicated to such eggs, with keepers assigned to assist in the hatching process, clearing debris and removing young that appear weak or deformed (such young are taken to the food preparation area and fed to the tribe). The hatchlings receive care in the form of food tossed to them from the custodians assigned the task but otherwise fend and survive on their own. There exists only notable exception; if an immature trög grows a brown hide, it is removed and taken to the tribal leader for private care and upbringing. This youth will become the new tribal leader upon reaching sexual maturity.

The youngest are equal in number to the adults, half (those four and under) fighting with a -4 to all rolls (and only if cornered) and the other half (the adolescents) fighting with a -2 to all rolls. Tröglodytes reach sexual maturity in eight years. Tröglodytes have an average lifespan of only about 60 years, but survive for less than twelve months in captivity on the surface.

Tröglodytes speak their own primitive language that appears to be unique and unrelated to any other. Advanced concepts are difficult if not impossible to communicate. They have no alphabet, written word and the arts simply do not exist. The leader, however, always speaks multiple languages and is literate in many as well. Generally these languages are those of intelligent species living in close-proximity, but also ones that once did but have since perished or moved-on.

Tröglodytes do not keep slaves, but a typical lair will have prisoners equal to about 10% of the population. These prisoners will range from unharmed to missing portions or complete limbs.

Most tröglodyte lairs employ trained (or at least allied) creatures as sentries or reserves. There is a 50% chance that a warren will contain 1d4p giant subterranean lizards.

Ecology

A tröglodyte's diet is composed primarily of fungi and algae, which they supplement with fish, meat and insects when they can find it. As the spores of many fungal species are robust, however, they can pass undamaged through the trög's digestive system and out with the feces; thus the tröglodyte helps disperse the fungal spores with little worry of a food shortage due to over consumption. The coloration of a trög is due heavily to pigments in its diet, so that the tint of an individual's hide is determined by the local fungus. The smell of a tröglodyte is also heavily influenced by this diet.

A tröglodyte's natural enemies include any other subterranean creature with which it competes for food and shelter. Should two tribes with different diets encounter each other, they can easily determine identity by the other's coloration and/or the smell.

Religion:

Tröglodytes fear magic (both divine or arcane) and are quite superstitious and easily frightened by flashy displays. Tröglodytes themselves do not follow any particular religion, probably lacking the intellect to grasp such concepts. The same cannot be said for the leader. The trög tribal chief will likely follow the teachings of some god, typically one that is evil in nature. The most popular are the House of Scorn, the House of Hunger or the Conventicle of Affliction. Any tröglodyte participating in a religious ceremony does so at the behest of the chieftain, simply following whatever instructions have been ordered but having little interest in any religious significance one way or another. That said, the average trög does enjoy partaking in the behaviors extolled and required among the darker aspects of these religions.

On Tellene

Because of the reluctance of man to enter the deep caves beneath Tellene, not much is known about the tröglodytes. Their range seems to lie primarily between the 12th meridian west and the 12th meridian east, for none have yet been reported outside, only within.

The furthest known reporting to the west came from the hobgoblins of Norga-Krangrel, while rangers have encountered trögs as far east as the caves of the Rytarr woods. To the south, soldiers occasionally battle tröglodytes in the numerous limestone caves on Miclenon's shores.

[1]*Awareness/Senses:* Troglodytes can see very well in dimly lit conditions, but cannot see in the dark. They have well-developed sense of mechanoreception but poor hearing.

[2]*Spell Components:* Tröglodyte scent glands, if used as an alternative material component in the mage's sixth level Stink Bomb spell, increases the strength of the dweomer by adding +2 to the caster's d20 roll.

[3]*Treasure:* Troglodytes carry 3d4p sp if on a trading mission, otherwise they have no personal treasure. Lairs can contain variable amounts of copper, silver and trade coins as well as gems. The leader will have many books, scrolls and possibly several magical items.

TROLL

Also Known As: Jotunn

It was some years ago now that the genius of the painter Varama fell upon the noble community of Bet Bireli like a plague. None could travel among the wealthy houses without hearing one thing or another of the artist's skill, and how each family had some portrait or other commissioned to his brush. My companions and I never anticipated a meeting with the artist, until the fortnight he refused to appear for any clients and we were ourselves commissioned to investigate his absence.

We had but barely knocked upon his door when it was flung open and the man himself rushed us in from the twilight streets to see the finish of his latest work – a large painting of an unnamed monster he had seen lightly sketched in some dark book and was determined to re-create. I tell you truth, a mere glimpse of his artistry was enough to make the blood curdle. The creature was over two heads taller than I, staring out at us from an oversized canvas lit only by dim candlelight. Its wide, staring black eyes seemed totally devoid of soul. The emaciated, hunched body wore dark-green skin like parchment in its tautness over ribs, an eruption of warts covering all flesh. The mouth was a cavern of sharpened, gnashing teeth beneath a large nose, and a hint of blood showed on its sharpened claws. It was hideous, filled with an almost palpable aura of danger.

Even as I stared in shock, I unthinkingly slipped my hand onto my crossbow. I doubt not that had the wind shifted the canvas, my frayed nerves would have shot a bolt straight into it. I eyed my friends, and saw they were no better than I. Fright and disgust stood on each face. My halfling friend, whom I soon learned had personal experience of the creature, was worst. His hands were twitching, his eyes were like bright glass, his face bleached and drawn. "Troll," he stammered, and quickly retreated from the room. -€

Be sure to burn all troll flesh, even the smallest scrap!

This brutal killer is a seemingly anorexic humanoid with a long nose, black soulless eyes, a toothy maw, long arms ending in clawed hands and (except for a head topped with long black hair) hairless skin covered in fungal warts that seem to quiver of their own accord. Their true stature is disguised by their universal tendency to walk with a stooped posture, dragging their long nails along the ground. Troll hide varies in color from light to very dark green, but is generally lighter in younger individuals, darkening with maturity.

Trolls may use tools and weapons to acquire food and attack rivals, but these are limited to those found or taken off the corpses of past victims; they do not craft nor forge items of their own design. Though capable of speech, their vocabulary is extremely limited and employ pantomime even when communicating amongst their own kind. Their limited reasoning faculties also preclude systematic planning. This, coupled with an inherent disregard for authority and a predilection for disruptive cruelty, make them vexing allies for even the most powerful of nefarious masters.

An average male or female troll stands about 8 feet tall, though it walks with a stoop and appears much shorter. While tall, they rarely weigh more than 300 pounds due to their wiry frames. Despite their frail appearance, trolls are very strong.

SIGN/TRACKS

One scholarly theory is that trolls are sexless, walking fungus creatures, but since all the sages I've known prefer to talk about trolls rather than go hunting for them, it's still naught but a theory.
Seems like foolishness to me. Look at their tracks — quite a bit like yours or mine, just longer and skinnier, and with prominent nails. No fungus I know walks like a man.

SIZE COMPARISON

12 ft

6 ft

Combat/Tactics:

Trolls are notoriously difficult to kill. When smashed, pierced, slashed or otherwise damaged, its body knits back together with amazing speed (recovering 1 Hit Point every 3 seconds); even severed limbs crawl or wriggle their way back to the main body and reattach themselves and may even attack on their own! Only fire seems able to obliterate this threat (burn damage does not regenerate).

Perhaps due to the leanness of their frame, trolls are extremely susceptible to having their limbs hacked off. Any critical hit, regardless of severity, will sever a limb (or even lop off its head). Such strikes do no greater damage. Severed limbs will continue to claw, bite or kick at an opponent (though doing only 2d4p damage due to the lack of leverage that can be applied by the loose arm or leg).

Trolls attacks are not planned or well orchestrated. They simply attack the first person they can. Once they defeat their enemies, they may continue to fight one another for the spoils.

Habitat/Society:

Trolls are subterranean creatures found in the deep caverns and tunnel systems beneath the surface. Most trolls are solitary, though sprawling underground caves with bountiful food sources may contain a tribal grouping with one or more of the following packs: all-male, adult females and offspring, both sexes, or one female and her offspring. Where they do occur, tribes and packs live in a dominance hierarchy where the strongest individual (male or female) may do as it pleases and each individual is responsible for its own food. Trolls are highly territorial and are known to fight off other trolls as well as intruders of other races.

Ecology:

Trolls feed primarily on insects, molds and slime, though the taste of flesh is more to their liking. They are scavengers and opportunistic hunters with keen senses of smell that they use to detect their food. Due in no small measure to their regenerative abilities, trolls have few natural enemies.

All trolls have one overriding fear, that being sunlight. Any troll touched by the rays of the sun immediately turns to stone. This alone keeps trolls from becoming an insurmountable menace. Any troll venturing forth on the surface is certain to have a hidey-hole nearby where it can sequester themselves during daylight hours.

Trolls have an average lifespan of 200 to 300 years. In its extreme old age, a troll's regenerative abilities slowly cease to function, after which it dies within several months (and is quickly consumed by other trolls).

On Tellene:

Trolls can be found almost anywhere that chill underground caverns and tunnel systems exist. Known reports of trolls come from such locations as the Byth and Sliv Elenon Mountains, the Vohven Jungle and the Shynako Hills.

[1] Trolls value treasure and may have a variety of coins and weapons pilfered from creatures they have slain.

TROLL

HIT POINTS:	36+6d8
SIZE/WEIGHT:	L/300 lbs.
TENACITY:	Fearless
INTELLIGENCE:	Obtuse
FATIGUE FACTOR:	n/a

SPEED 3 — INIT -2 — ATTACK +13 — DMG REDUCTION — DEFENSE +5 — 6 — see below — DAMAGE n/a — long REACH — TOP SAVE ▼

MOVEMENT

CRAWL:	5
WALK:	10
JOG:	15
RUN:	20
SPRINT:	25

SAVES

PHYSICAL:	+16
MENTAL:	+8
DODGE:	+14

ATTACK: Trolls attack in a predictable and straightforward manner seeking to tear the nearest opponent to shreds; they attack with two swipes of their clawed hands (each doing 2d4p+8 damage) and a bite for 4d6p damage.

SPECIAL DEFENSES: Trolls can regenerate wounds at a rate of 1 HP every 3 seconds; burns recuperate at the normal rate.

GENERAL INFO

ACTIVITY CYCLE:	Nocturnal
NO. APPEARING:	1-12
% CHANCE IN LAIR:	33%
FREQUENCY:	Sporadic
ALIGNMENT:	Chaotic Evil
VISION TYPE:	Extreme Low Light Vision
AWARENESS/SENSES:	Standard
HABITAT:	Caverns and tunnels
DIET:	Omnivorous (meat preferred)
ORGANIZATION:	Individual, pack, tribal
CLIMATE/TERRAIN:	Subterranean

YIELD

MEDICINAL:	nil
SPELL COMPONENTS:	boiled troll blood adds +1 HP to any Cure spell
HIDE/TROPHY:	none (any such trophy eventually regenerates)
TREASURE:	yes[1]
EDIBLE:	no
OTHER:	nil
EXPERIENCE POINT VALUE:	925

VAMPIRE
Also Known As: Upyr, Vampir, Vampyr

Sunlight is the vampyr's natural enemy, but darkness is its fast ally!

Vampyres be creatures of the night most unlike their evil kin. Whilst other such automatons and phantoms displayeth an abomination of the human form that doth repel those who live, the vampyre canst be a romantic figure pleasant both in appearance and manner. Shouldest it so desire, its style, grace and sophistication canst rival any noble gentleman.

Whether this is but an act to lure the unwary or the creature's natural manner I cannot ascertain. I doth assume the latter for the sole time I didst confront a vampyre, his mansion was adorned with true art objects of the highest value and craftswork.

Lest ye be deceived, knowest that behind this façade lies a creature of the purest evil. Permiteth not thyself to be put off thy guard by its grace. For in so doing ye doth become vulnerable to the vampyre's most powerful skill to mesmer. Even those of stout will do easily become a willing thrall.

Those it cannot seduce shall witness the creature's true wrath. All such pretense of gentility doth vanish as the creature's eyes do glow red as if the hate within cannot be contained. In this vexed state, the vampire is a ferocious opponent both strong and fleet afoot. If he doth lay his hands upon thee, he will hold fast sinking fangs into thine neck to drink the warm blood and sap thine élan vital.

Slaying the creature is a vexatious task for common blades do leave little mark and silvered ones often land but a minor wound. Even these pinpricks do close rapidly of their own accord. Shouldest the vampyre be set upon by warriors of great skill and ferocity, he canst assume the form of a wolf or bat and escape so. Even if prevented from such flight, slaying his mortal form merely compeleth him into a vaporous entity allowing him to seek his coffin and regenerate.

The vampyre canst only be slain by driving a wooden stake 'twixt his breast. Think not that you can accomplish this manually for even a brute of a man wouldst be challenged to perform this task on a mortal corpse. Nay, it must be driven in with a mallet while the creature lies helpless. - 👁

Some folk say a vampyr leaves no footprints and casts no reflection.

This evil human corpse rises from the grave to feed on the blood of the living. However, the vampire is no mindless undead horror, but a highly intelligent and elegant individual; most were once of an aristocratic bloodline. Thus, while a newly risen vampire can be found clad in its burial shroud or other funereal clothing, they eventually discard this for finery more befitting someone of noble birth. Indeed, they appear as normal humans in many respects, and may pass as such.

A vampire has a strikingly pallid countenance, though its flesh gains a ruby-red undertone for several hours after consuming blood. Its lips, too, become quite red at this time, while its youth seems partially restored (e.g., white hairs become dark, cheeks become fuller, wrinkles lighten, etc.). The vampire also has two peculiarly sharp upper canine teeth. These protuberant teeth are scalpel sharp such that the bite is virtually painless, and allow the vampire to pierce the flesh of its victim (usually on the neck, atop the jugular vein) in order to drink its lifeblood. Its fingernails are long and fine.

A vampire may not walk in sunlight, for its rays burn like fire, and its image does not appear in mirrors or similarly reflective surfaces. It cannot cross running water (e.g., rivers) unless transported in some conveyance by a third party, and it recoils from garlic and divine icons. When angered, an almost palpable sense of dread manifests around it and its irises turn red with fury.

This sinister creature has an eloquent voice and can converse knowledgeably on a variety of topics, though it frequently does so utilizing anachronistic words and idioms, perhaps belying its true age.

Combat/Tactics:

All vampires possess hypnotic powers similar to that of the Charm spell and are thus able to mesmerize by engaging the victim in conversation, however brief (save vs. d20p+19).

SIZE COMPARISON

Be not enamoured of this insideous creature ye foolish young ladies though he mightest appear most comely and speakest with honeyed words of love. Nay, he desires not thy heart but the blood which that organ doth course through thine body. Abide not his approach, for he may ensnare thee to thine mortal peril.

WILL FACTOR
20

6 ft

3 ft

V

Should it become involved in physical melee, a vampire attempts to restrain its foe as a prelude to draining its blood. Any hit in melee (incidentally inflicting d4p+4 damage) indicates it has grabbed a foe. After two successful attacks, the vampire has bound its opponent fast and may automatically bite him with its next attack and every 5 seconds thereafter. This mighty hold can be broken by anyone striking the Vampir severely enough to cause a knock-back or via an opposed Feat of Strength (vs. d20p+16) on the part of the victim (the latter may be attempted once per 5 seconds any time after the Vampyr's initial grab but precludes other actions). Once fully held fast, a victim is powerless to attack.

The fearsome bite of a vampire causes d6p+4 damage (armor DR does not apply) and drains and equivalent number of Constitution points from the living (though a save vs. the Vampire's Will Factor reduces this loss by half); charmed persons allow the bite and this action does not break the charm.

Vampires fear holy water, garlic and divine icons. Strongly presenting the latter two can hold it at bay or compel its withdrawal from a victim, though garlic does not prevent the undead from employing its charm powers. Divine icons must be brandished by an anointed follower of that goodly religion, and such use forces the vampire to turn its gaze (and frustrates attempts to charm).

A vampyr may summon creatures to execute its will (particularly if held at bay by icon wielding trespassers). 3d6p Dire Wolves and/or 4d20p Giant Rats will daily answer their master's summons and savagely attack his enemies heedless of their own lives. The vampyr may himself assume the form of either of these animals (or that of a bat or large spider) if and when he desires. Alternatively, he may sublimate into gaseous form if that better suits his purpose.

Damage reducing a vampire to zero (0) Hit Points forces it into a gaseous form and compels it to retreat to its coffin until such time as it recovers half or more of its original HP. Silvered weapons fare better at wounding the creature than steel. Regardless of their source, a vampire regenerates 1 Hit Point every 5 seconds. A vampire can only be killed by exposure to direct sunlight, hammering a stake into its heart while it sleeps, or severing its head and stuffing its mouth with garlic.

Habitat/Society:

Vampires are native to all lands and climes, though they must remain hidden from daylight. This leads the vampire to make its lair in a sealed chamber, such as its family burial crypt. When a vampire can lay claim to a larger residence, like a castle or manor house, it utilizes the cellars or other series of windowless rooms. In this dark lair is the vampire's coffin. Even in undeath, the vampire prizes his coffin as another indicator of its once-noble status (since few people who are not wealthy can afford one), and may sleep in it as a bed. However, the vampire is perfectly comfortable resting wherever it happens to be, provided the bottom of this berth is (like its coffin) layered with a scattering of the creature's native soil.

Each dawn, a vampire retreats to his lair to rest for a full 8 hours in his coffin (or equivalent). This daily sleep is crucial to a vampire, so much that it loses its regenerative ability for as long as it is deprived of this repose.

Where the vampire has a large, secure lair and an ample supply of blood (in the form of local citizens), one to three other vampires and at least one enthralled servant may accompany it. These covens usually contain one dominant male and three female vampires, though various other combinations are possible.

When meeting the living, the vampire is usually a gracious host, abiding by the social conventions it learned in life and conducting itself in a fashion that conforms to the position and reputation it once had. When not sleeping or feeding, it spends much of its time reading or otherwise expanding its knowledge of the world.

Ecology:

The vampire's principal foes are those who, after years of suffering under its predation, unite and oppose his reign (often calling upon some external champion or patron of a virtuous faith). It may also have monstrous rivals that desire the vampire's wealth and power.

On Tellene:

Frequent tales of vampires come from Svimohzia, though the undead have been reported throughout the Kalamaran Empire, even within Bet Urala and the dwarven kingdom of Draska. Rumors from Reanaaria Bay tell of a powerful vampire in the city of Giilia, but its citizens are either too frightened or distrustful to talk to strangers.

VAMPIRE

HIT POINTS:	26+8d8
SIZE/WEIGHT:	M/170 lbs.
TENACITY:	Fearless
INTELLIGENCE:	Brilliant
FATIGUE FACTOR:	n/a

SPEED		INIT
5		-6

ATTACK +19

DEFENSE +10

DMG REDUCTION 25

see below

short REACH

DAMAGE

TOP SAVE ▼ n/a

MOVEMENT

CRAWL:	2½
WALK:	5
JOG:	10
RUN:	15
FLY:	25 (as bat)

SAVES

PHYSICAL:	+19
MENTAL:	immune
DODGE:	+19

ATTACK: Charm (save vs. d20p+19), then grabbing (two d4p+4 attacks to hold); held victims automatically bitten (d6p+4 damage and CON drain, no armor DR, save for half ability drain). Knock-back or FoS (vs. d20p+16) breaks hold.

SPECIAL DEFENSES: Silvered weapons reduce DR to 13. Regenerates 1 HP/5 sec if it had 8 hours rest previously. Transmogrify into bat, rat, wolf or big spider (with no poison) at will.

GENERAL INFO

ACTIVITY CYCLE:	Nocturnal
NO. APPEARING:	1-4
% CHANCE IN LAIR:	30%
FREQUENCY:	Unusual
ALIGNMENT:	Lawful Evil
VISION TYPE:	Undead Sight
AWARENESS/SENSES:	Standard
HABITAT:	Crypts, ruins, castles
DIET:	Sanguivorous
ORGANIZATION:	Leader
CLIMATE/TERRAIN:	Any

YIELD

MEDICINAL:	nil
SPELL COMPONENTS:	nil
HIDE/TROPHY:	nil
TREASURE:	vampires prize objet d'art and monetary wealth
EDIBLE:	no
OTHER:	nil
EXPERIENCE POINT VALUE:	2275

WARG

Also Known As: Vargr, Wearg, Wyrg

My companions and I had been making our way through one of the dense northern forests, when we came upon a small clearing overgrown with a thorny thicket. The wry-necked shrubs and stunted thistles reared aloft as if in menace to all living things, choking the young trees that attempted to grow therein. We began to make our way around and, of course, I took the liberty of clipping a few specimens for later study.

Suddenly, our fighter gave a cry of surprise and wheeled about with blade in hand. You can imagine my surprise when we followed his example and found ourselves gazing at a semicircle of what I took to be three great wolves. Each of them was nearly the size of a bison, squatting on their haunches with their wicked eyes fixed upon us and their mouths growling and salivating.

A glance at our fighter, in turn, showed great beads of sweat trickling down his forehead and little more color in his face than a peeled turnip. His great sword shook in his grip like a young willow caught by the breeze, and his tremulous whisper of "Wargs…" nearly inaudible.

It was then that I realized the truth, and began to shake no less than my well-armored comrade beside me. Indeed, I now saw the powerfully muscular build, the ominously intelligent eyes and the sharply angled teeth (enabling the creatures to eat bone and flesh) so common to the legends.

For a space that seemed to last an eternity, both groups maintained a solemn silence. Then, almost without knowing that I spoke, I requested a boon of passage. Truly, I did not expect the wargs to answer in voice, but it somehow did not seem ridiculous for them to do so.

Then, in a rough speech that I immediately recognized as Orcish, the foremost warg barked "No." And the battle was joined. - ℜ

Wargs are well known to have a taste for human flesh.

These large, carnivorous canines resemble massive wolves in appearance, with cruel, intelligent eyes and snarling, salivating mouths. Warg coloration seems to vary by environment - those living in more temperate climes have colors ranging from white to black with gray dominating. Those found in colder climates tend to be gray, white, or a combination thereof. The southernmost wargs are commonly red-brown, black, gray, or a combination of those colors. Like normal wolves, wargs have powerful jaws filled with jagged teeth used to tear apart prey.

Combat/Tactics:

Wargs often lead packs of wolves, or other wargs, and use pack-like tactics in combat. They prefer overwhelming numbers and herding prey into areas where they cannot escape. When hunting they often pick out the sick, the weak, or the slow to attack first. Unlike the normal variety of wolves, wargs have no fear of attacking humanoids if they are hungry. Once they run down their prey, they bite with their powerful jaws in an attempt to snap the creature's spine.

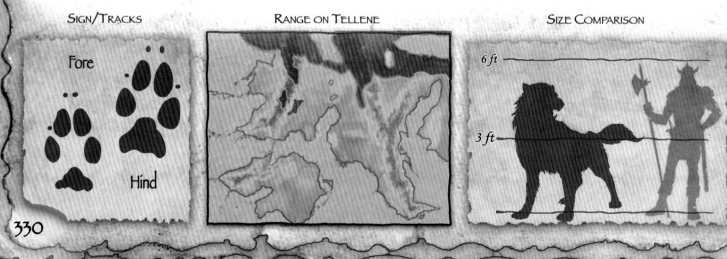

SIGN/TRACKS — Fore / Hind

RANGE ON TELLENE

SIZE COMPARISON — 6 ft / 3 ft

W

Wargs often ally themselves with orcs or goblins and sometimes willingly serve as mounts to the latter. They never consider themselves servants, or pets, to these creatures. When fighting alongside humanoids, wargs attempt to strike at whatever their rider is attacking.

Habitat/Society:

Among their own kind, wargs act in nearly the same manner as a pack of normal wolves would. There is generally one dominate alpha male and female, and each pack has a clearly defined social structure. Packs range in size from a lone warg to two to four individuals. When they are found in packs consisting mostly of wolves, the warg is always the alpha. Alpha males and females are the only wargs allowed to breed among a pack. Mating occurs mostly in the winter months and unlike normal wolves, wargs only sire one or two pups after a gestation period of roughly 60 days. The mother kills any pups born with a birth defect, or those that have trouble eating or gaining weight.

Wargs can be, and often are, domesticated by those who have the will to control them. They respect only strength and it takes a firm – and often abusive – hand to keep them under control. A broken warg is a handy companion but any sign of weakness, kindness or mercy by the master causes the warg to lose any respect it may have had for its controller.

The preference of the warg is to live in a den, but many make their lair in secluded woodland areas that are hard to access. Briars, thick undergrowth, rocky outcroppings and any other natural areas that provide some shelter for the elements make good homes for wargs. Some wargs will move into the ruins of human settlements when they discover them abandoned. Wargs detest humans, elves and halflings and generally attack them on sight.

Ecology:

Wargs are intelligent and capable of a guttural barking speech. They are aggressive and territorial creatures. They hunt everything from field mice to bears, depending on how desperate they are for food. Wargs take particular pleasure in killing humans and have been known to overrun small, isolated farmsteads, terrorizing the livestock before eventually killing the farmers.

At their core wargs are inherently evil. They do not have enough intelligence, or desire, to form ambitious plans but they enjoy cruelty and malice when they find it in other creatures. This explains their penchant for living in and around orcs and goblins. When living among humanoids wargs take on a symbiotic relationship. They expect to be treated like an equal and not a subservient animal. Those that fail to do so often regret this decision at a later date.

On Tellene:

Wargs can be found in any sub-artic to temperate wilderness on Tellene. Packs of wargs thrive in many areas, including forests, grasslands, deserts and mountains. Wargs are featured in many human cultures throughout Tellene. Some tribes hold a place of great honor for the warg, while others fear them, and rightly so.

WARG

HIT POINTS:	35+4d8	
SIZE/WEIGHT:	L/425 lbs.	
TENACITY:	Brave	
INTELLIGENCE:	Obtuse	
FATIGUE FACTOR:	-3	

SPEED 6   **INIT** -1
ATTACK +7
DMG REDUCTION +7   4
DEFENSE +7
DAMAGE 4d4p+4
short REACH   TOP SAVE 10

MOVEMENT

CRAWL:	10
WALK:	15
JOG:	20
RUN:	25
SPRINT:	30

SAVES

PHYSICAL:	+8
MENTAL:	+6
DODGE:	+7

ATTACK:
Bite for 4d4p+4 points of damage.

SPECIAL ABILITIES:
Listening and Tracking mastery of 65%.

GENERAL INFO

ACTIVITY CYCLE:	Nocturnal
NO. APPEARING:	3-12
% CHANCE IN LAIR:	10%
FREQUENCY:	Sporadic
ALIGNMENT:	Neutral Evil
VISION TYPE:	Good eyesight
AWARENESS/SENSES:	Good hearing and sense of smell
HABITAT:	Dens, undergrowth, caves, ruins
DIET:	Carnivorous
ORGANIZATION:	Pack
CLIMATE/TERRAIN:	Cold to temperate wilderness

YIELD

MEDICINAL:	nil
SPELL COMPONENTS:	nil
HIDE/TROPHY:	a pelt with attached head can sell for up to 36 sp
TREASURE:	incidental
EDIBLE:	yes
OTHER:	nil
EXPERIENCE POINT VALUE:	350

WASP, GIANT

Also Known As: Dolicho, Vespula

Though this perhaps seems an outrageous number, I have documented over 44 species of wasp, and feel sure that there must be well over 100! Of course, such categorization is of less interest to most people, who are uninquisitive about the nature of the insects around them. Only true scholars like myself, who see a great deal of variation in anatomy, social behaviors and other characteristics, can appreciate these flying creatures.

The only occasion I can recall when my companions appreciated my knowledge of wasps was, unfortunately, rather early in my career when I was particularly thrasonical. We encountered a single giant wasp that my sword-wielding comrades, being newly refreshed from our stay in a very pleasant roadside inn, slew with relative ease. I knew from my studies that giant wasps live and operate alone, and do not construct nests, and I said so, stating plainly that we need not worry about disturbing any more. However, I was not aware that some giant wasp species are not solitary, but social, plantationing up to several hundred strong. What followed was not a pleasant experience, and even today my fellows still weary me with their gibes about it. - ⚸

Giant wasps look similar to common wasps, with two pairs of wings, a stinger, hard exoskeleton, antennae and compound eyes. Their bodies are divided into three sections: the head and a two-part abdomen made up of the metasoma and the mesosoma. Giant wasps can grow up to 2 feet long, and have proportionate wingspans for the size of their bodies. They weigh about 5 pounds each.

Dolicho have a variety of colorations, depending on what part of Tellene they are native to. Most have black bodies overall, with certain distinctive alternating bands of colors (usually brown, red or yellow) that indicate a particular subspecies and/or region.

Combat/Tactics:

Giant wasps are very aggressive and easily provoked into stinging. When they sting, their stinger inflicts 1d4p points of damage and injects a VF 9 neurotoxin. They sting multiple times, and may continue to sting until they or their target is incapacitated.

A failed saving throw versus giant wasp poison indicates the victim suffers weakness, dizziness, headache, difficulty breathing and nausea (imposing a 2-point penalty to Attack, Defense and Damage for 2d12p hours). These effects are cumulative for multiple stings (excepting duration). A natural '1' on the victim's saving throw indicates death; characters that are allergic to insect stings die automatically with no saving throw.

SIGN/TRACKS

RANGE ON TELLENE

SIZE COMPARISON

Giant wasp nests are rather easy to detect if one is alert. A half dozen or so wasps are tending to the nest at all times while others come and go constantly bringing food and building material.

6 ft

3 ft

Dolicho flee from fire and are unable to attack in clouds of smoke. One wasp-hunting trick is to flood a wasp nest with smoke, so as to confuse the senses of the wasps and make them easier to attack. However, it is often difficult to flood the nest without awakening any wasps or without setting the nest on fire.

Habitat/Society:

Vespula nests and colonies can be found under the overhangs of large wooden buildings, in barn lofts, hanging from tree limbs and in caves or other dark, out of the way locations. There are some who live in subterranean colonies and some who live in cellars or the dungeons of various estates.

While solitary giant wasps favor nests of mud in sheltered locations, colonies form nests of paper, made from wood pulp. They gather this pulp by using their mandibles to strip wood from buildings, trees, fences, or they will use any parchment they might encounter. They chew the wood pulp, where it mixes with their saliva, then expel it. In its dampened state it becomes adhesive, and the giant wasp spreads it with its legs and mandibles. Once this material dries, it becomes quite tough and durable.

Giant wasp reproduction is a complex affair. Mating occurs between a fertile queen and several males. The sperm is stored inside the queen's body until spring. The bulk of each wasp colony dies every year, leaving mainly the queen. This queen then leaves the nest and searches for a place to hibernate for winter. In the spring, she emerges, searches for a suitable nesting sight, and then builds a small nest, where she lays her eggs and uses the stored sperm to fertilize the eggs.

The queen first raises a series of sterile female wasps as workers to help construct a bigger nest. The rest of the eggs then transform into fertile males and additional fertile female queens. The colony grows and then spreads out, perpetuating the species across Tellene.

Alternatively, solitary giant wasps may insert one or more eggs into a larger host or deposit them upon the host's body. The host remains alive until the larvae are mature, dying as the parasitoids pupate or when they emerge as adults.

Ecology:

These large winged insects feed primarily on fruit, gigantic spiders and other insects, but do not readily distinguish humans and their ilk from the latter. Some sages speculate that almost every giant spider or insect species has at least one giant wasp species that preys upon it.

On Tellene:

Giant wasps can be found throughout much of Tellene, with certain markings and coloration being more common (but not exclusive) to certain regions.

The giant wasps that are native to Brandobia and the western Young Kingdoms often have yellow or white body markings, respectively, while those found throughout the eastern kingdoms are commonly orange. Giant wasps around Reanaaria Bay are brown. Around Voldor Bay, the giant wasps are completely black with an orangish tint to their wings, and in the southern Kalamaran Empire and Svimohzish Isle, the wasps tend to have reddish-orange blotches, rather than stripes, all over their bodies.

GIANT WASP

HIT POINTS:	8+1d4
SIZE/WEIGHT:	T/5 lbs.
TENACITY:	Fearless
INTELLIGENCE:	Non
FATIGUE FACTOR:	n/a

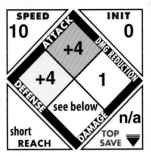

SPEED		INIT
10	ATTACK +4 / DMG REDUCTION	0
DEFENSE +4	1	
short	see below	n/a
REACH	DAMAGE	TOP SAVE

MOVEMENT

CRAWL:	1½
WALK:	2½
JOG:	5
RUN:	7½
FLY:	30

SAVES

PHYSICAL:	+1
MENTAL:	+2
DODGE:	+7

ATTACK:
Stingers deal d4p damage plus VF 9 poison (failed save suffers -2 to Attack, Defense and Damage for 2d12 hours; 'nat 1' indicates death; no effect on a successful save); those allergic to insect stings die with no save permitted

SPECIAL DEFENSES:
Flight

GENERAL INFO

ACTIVITY CYCLE:	Diurnal
NO. APPEARING:	1-20
% CHANCE IN LAIR:	20%
FREQUENCY:	Frequent
ALIGNMENT:	Non
VISION TYPE:	Standard
AWARENESS/SENSES:	Standard
HABITAT:	Trees, buildings, ruins
DIET:	Omnivorous
ORGANIZATION:	Individuals or Colony
CLIMATE/TERRAIN:	Any Temperate to Tropical

YIELD

MEDICINAL:	nil
SPELL COMPONENTS:	nil
HIDE/TROPHY:	giant wasp bodies make frightening trophies
TREASURE:	incidental
EDIBLE:	no
OTHER:	nil
EXPERIENCE POINT VALUE:	20

WEASEL

COMMON WEASEL
GIANT WEASEL

Also Known As: Ermelin

Weasels are surprisingly intelligent and adaptive when it comes to combat.

Weasels are inquisitive and playful creatures. They are typically not a threat to humans, as they tend to hunt significantly smaller prey. Over the years I've encountered them many times, usually quietly observing while I set up camp or racing through a thicket along the trail's edge and shadowing me as I pass through their territory. Most times that was the extent of such encounters.

But make no mistake — giant weasels can be deadly threats. If you make the mistake of encroaching upon a pack or getting too close to a weasel's kit, they will not hesitate to attack. Woe to you if you find yourself in such a predicament.

An old Fhokki myth I recall goes something like, "To the wolf the gods gave pink-stained teeth that bite and to the eagle grand talons that hold prey tight. Dominion of the shallow seas they gave to the shark but to the weasel they gave a wicked heart."

Weasels may be trained as guard animals, attacking when certain commands are issued or when an invisible line is crossed. Kobolds, for example, are particularly fond of using weasels for perimeter defense around their warrens.

They are fast animals with astounding agility permitting them to seemingly be anywhere other than where you are swinging in any particular second. As assailants, they create what can only be described as unified confusion by darting to and fro, crawling or leaping over individuals, scurrying between legs and so forth. Within this furry maelstrom, one can honestly believe it to be just as likely for you to strike your sword brother fighting next to you as one of these obstreperous polecats. If you suspect the presence of weasels and wish to draw them out, here's an old trick I picked up from some fur trappers many years ago. Give a shrill whistle and then carefully observe the location you believe contains weasels. If there are any present, they will stand on their hind legs and look about sharply, thus revealing their position. - S

Common and giant weasels are of similar appearance except with regards to size. The former are about 18 inches long at full maturity with tails some 9 inches in length whilst the giant variety easily doubles these measurements. Many giant weasels are often mis-identified as common ones due to morphological measurements, either falling outside known ranges for each species or inside ordered ranges common to both.

Weasels have long bodies and necks but small heads and short legs. They usually have a red or brown upper coat with a white belly, but colors and patterns may vary widely with climate and region. For instance, species living in climates with winter snow cover often molt in autumn and then turn snow white in winter. These white weasel pelts are often the most prized by furriers, though this is dependent on the area's current fashion.

SIGN/TRACKS

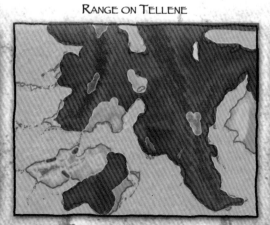

Fore

Hind

RANGE ON TELLENE

SIZE COMPARISON

6 ft

3 ft

WEASEL

Hit Points:	6+1d4
Size/Weight:	S/1 lb.
Tenacity:	Nervous
Intelligence:	Animal, High
Fatigue Factor:	1

SPEED 10 · INIT -2 · ATTACK +1 · DMG REDUCTION 1 · DEFENSE 0 · DAMAGE d3p · REACH short · TOP SAVE 5

MOVEMENT

Crawl:	1¼
Walk:	2½
Jog:	5
Run:	7½
Sprint:	10

SAVES

Physical:	+1
Mental:	+1
Dodge:	+2

ATTACK:
Bites deal d3p points of damage.

SPECIAL ABILITIES:
Climbing 60%, Listening 80%.
Immune to cockatrice gaze.

GENERAL INFO

Activity Cycle:	Nocturnal
No. Appearing:	1 (wild), or as dictated by owner
% Chance in Lair:	10%
Frequency:	Ubiquitous
Alignment:	Non
Vision Type:	Keen eyesight
Awareness/Senses:	Keen senses of smell and hearing
Habitat:	Farmlands, meadows, brush, forests
Diet:	Omnivorous (but prefer meat)
Organization:	Individuals
Climate/Terrain:	Temperate to subtropical wilderness

YIELD

Medicinal:	nil
Spell Components:	leg, in the Springing spell[1]
Hide/Trophy:	pelts worth up to 1 sp each[2]
Treasure:	incidental
Edible:	yes
Other:	urine and glands[3]
Experience Point Value:	10

GIANT WEASEL

Hit Points:	21+2d8
Size/Weight:	M/25 lbs.
Tenacity:	Steady
Intelligence:	Animal, High
Fatigue Factor:	1

SPEED 7 · INIT -2 · ATTACK +3 · DMG REDUCTION 2 · DEFENSE +3 · DAMAGE 2d4p+2 · REACH short · TOP SAVE 7

MOVEMENT

Crawl:	5
Walk:	10
Jog:	15
Run:	20
Sprint:	25

SAVES

Physical:	+3
Mental:	+3
Dodge:	+5

ATTACK:
Bites deal 2d4p+2 points of damage.

SPECIAL ABILITIES:
Climbing 45%, Listening 80%.
Immune to cockatrice gaze.

GENERAL INFO

Activity Cycle:	Nocturnal
No. Appearing:	1 (wild), or as dictated by owner
% Chance in Lair:	10%
Frequency:	Infrequent
Alignment:	Non
Vision Type:	Keen eyesight
Awareness/Senses:	Keen senses of smell and hearing
Habitat:	Farmlands, meadows, brush, forests
Diet:	Omnivorous (but prefer meat)
Organization:	Individuals
Climate/Terrain:	Temperate to subtropical wilderness

YIELD

Medicinal:	nil
Spell Components:	leg, in the Springing spell[1]
Hide/Trophy:	pelts worth up to 6 sp each[2]
Treasure:	incidental
Edible:	yes
Other:	urine and glands[3]
Experience Point Value:	84

Combat/Tactics:

Although small, weasels are clever and nimble fighters. Once they have a target sighted, they go after it relentlessly, and use their long, sharp canine teeth to bite (crushing the skulls of smaller animals). When threatened, a weasel often emits a loud 'chirring' sound and excretes a pungent odor from its anal glands (the latter intended to deceive the opponent into believing the weasel flesh is foul and unappetizing).

Humans and their ilk, given their size, are not usually targeted for attack, though they do prey upon weasels for their pelts. However, domesticated weasels may be trained (relying upon their natural aggressiveness when their territory is invaded) to do so with an appropriate Animal Training check.

Weasel urine is a Virulence Factor 12 poison for both basilisks and a cockatrices, killing either on contact if the monster fails its saving throw (*vs. d20p+12*). They are immune to the touch and toxic breath of a cockatrice as well as the gaze, poisonous bite and paralytic blood of a basilisk. The latter's bite though is fully effective and certainly capable of killing a weasel.

Habitat/Society:

Weasels occupy a wide variety of habitats; woodlands, thickets, open areas and even farmland. They are most active at night, but also come out in the day.

Weasels make multiple dens out of grass and leaves and line them with fur, locating them in the abandoned burrows of other mammals, in rotting logs, under rocks or tree roots, and usually near a source of water. They move swiftly through tunnels and brush, but can also climb trees and are good swimmers (at jogging speed).

Weasels mate in summer, when the males begin their mesmerizing 'courting dance.' After mating, the eggs inside the female gestate for 200 to over 300 days and do not begin to develop until about a month before she gives birth. Young weasels are born in the spring, with litters consisting of between four and eight offspring. Infants are born blind, with only a light covering of fur. Assuming they survive (the young are particularly vulnerable to predators), they usually become independent at about eight weeks of age and leave the litter in the autumn.

Common weasels have an average lifespan of about three years (or 10 in captivity), while giant weasels may live up to six years (or 15 in captivity).

Ecology:

Weasels are aggressive hunters owing to high metabolism and consequent caloric needs. Common weasels hunt small mammals such as frogs, mice, voles and lemmings, while a giant weasel's diet also includes larger beasts such as rabbits, possums, and even their own kind.

Common and giant weasels are highly destructive predators of eggs both avian and reptilian, though they do so cautiously in full knowledge that they are stealing from predators that would gobble them up in an instant. Fortunately, both varieties of weasels have long, thin bodies that are very quick, allowing them to scamper through burrows after prey (or away from predators) with deft precision.

Weasels are the natural prey of many larger predators, though they most often fall the victims of wolves, cats, snakes, foxes, various birds of prey and, of course, mankind and man-like creatures.

On Tellene:

Weasels are widespread and can be found in most climates, excepting deserts. Some hunters swear that the Avdoron Mires is a good place to hunt and that the wetlands there are thick with weasels.

Other good hunting areas for weasels are the Edosi Forest, the DuKem'p Swamp near the Banader River, the Hadaf Highlands, the Miznoh Forest, Keenoa Tors, the Ehniven Marsh, the Fyban Forest and the P'Rudekela Forest.

Farmers near Aroroleta, Sisalasido and some of the smaller villages near Thygasha report problems with weasels killing barnyard fowl. There are small bounties for weasels in these parts.

[1] *A common weasel leg can be used as an alternate material component in the apprentice level Springing spell. A giant weasel leg, alternatively, extends the spell duration by 30 seconds.*

[2] *Weasel coats are both luxurious and beautiful and can fetch a decent price at market. In some areas, weasel pelts may be the exclusive wear of nobles and royalty, despite the weasel's reputation as a villainous vermin. Unscrupulous furriers sometimes use painted or dyed rabbit fur and falsely sell their works at the same price as garments of weasel fur.*

[3] *As noted, weasel urine is toxic to both the basilisk and cockatrice. The weasel's anus glands can also be harvested to act as a scent bait for foxes, as well as wolves and mountain lions.*

W

WEASELS OF WOE
A Hard Lesson Learned

Though one might think of ordinary weasels as harmless beasts, I can relate a quite frightening tale of woe associated with the vile creatures. It all began when my adventuring companions and I came upon a thicket of brambles on the side of the dirt path upon which we were walking. The thick vegetation was an ideal natural barrier for the hostile brigands that lurked above the brambles in the trees.

Before we knew something was amiss we were assaulted with tiny arrows. Instinctively, we ran past the brambles and out of harm's way to look for a less daunting entry point to engage with the highway robbers, for so we surely thought them to be. With a bit of casual searching we were in luck, or so I thought at the time, for we had found a tiny passage through the undergrowth that clearly looked traveled. In fact, it was littered with tiny bits of clothing and tufts of fur, which demonstrated that living beings definitely used this as a thoroughfare.

With little trepidation the hearty warriors led the way, eager to exact revenge on our bold attackers. Within a short distance, however, we found that the entry hole narrowed considerably and wound around in a tortuous path such that it was slow going. In our eagerness to penetrate the wall of vegetation we lined up on our hands and knees behind our leaders in bulky armor.

As I belly crawled and did my best to avoid the sharp thorns and points of the bushes, I wondered to what end this difficult journey would come. It was then that the chattering began. Almost at once, the briar became alive with movement. A stench wafted into my nostrils. It was musky and damp and odorous with offal. Within seconds the sleek little vagabonds set upon us like trained circus animals. They seemed to move through the undergrowth with ease, bending their slender bodies to curl around the wiry branches.

Those in my troop who sported daggers drew them to defend themselves, for this was the only weapon one could wield in such a tight space. Of course I normally relied upon my magic as my main source of physical defense, but in such tight quarters and with the nipping, scratching beasts crawling all over me,

the arcane arts were quite out of the question. So I too was left with nothing but a dagger and a backpack with which to defend myself.

As an aside, I will point out also that on this particular excursion I was dressed in my summer ensemble. The weather was warm so I foolishly neglected to go without the thick robes that are more traditional for practitioners of my art when delving into the dank dungeons of the Netherdeep. I feel certain that had I done so they would have afforded me considerable protection from the gnawing teeth of the ravenous weasels lacerating my skin like a butcher slaughtering a pig. From that day forward I vowed to never again be caught without my sturdy robes while out in the wilderness.

Needless to say, the battle went poorly. Our ability to dodge the beasts was virtually nil due to the close quarters and their speed and numbers meant that they landed considerably more blows than we were capable of. As I felt I was being eaten alive, someone among our number had the brilliant idea to abandon the attack and simply continue to crawl through the brambles, perhaps to find more hospitable ground on which to conduct our defense.

The main drawback of the 'simply continue on the path' defense was that I was stuck behind heavily encumbered fighters who made the push for freedom slow going. Eventually, several of our number were able to stand clear of the dense bushes. By this time, however, I had suffered a myriad of wounds all over my body and was profusely bleeding from a particularly nasty bite that made me go pale from the sight of it.

As I struggled to slither those last few feet to freedom I felt cold and weak. The slicing pain was numbing now and the will to go on just drifted out of me. Then everything went black.

I awoke some time later, with no knowledge of how I was saved, though relieved to still be alive. The pain returned and I knew I was injured badly, though now bandaged and seemingly safe for a time. I eventually found out that my dear friends had pulled me to safety. Our cleric was able to apply aid to most of my wounds, which allowed them to quickly heal shortly thereafter.

Oh yes, my encounter with the common weasel is not one that I shall ever forget. - ⊱

WERERAT

Also Known As: Rat-Man

The sewers of Geanavue are no place for persons who value clean clothes and pleasant smells, but they do offer certain opportunities for conducting unobserved meetings. It was such an event that I speak of now, when we ventured in search of an undercity dweller with particular information.

Finding a ledge relatively free of debris and tying our skiffs to a convenient metal hook, we clambered up and made our way towards the rendezvous. At this time, our cleric hissed that he heard something following. We all listened intently but could hear nothing. In the near-darkness, I heard clearly his sharp sigh of disgust, followed by the soft jingling of buckles as he took something from his gear. In a moment, a flickering light shone from his lantern and the thing menacing us was revealed.

A hairy rat-man, clad only in loincloth and carrying a wicked-looking sword, chittered some unintelligible words and turned on its heels. Our thief quickly shot a crossbow bolt, but it only nicked the creature's right ear and caused it to stumble. However, it did not fall and was quickly out of sight.

Rather than pursue, we continued towards the rendezvous, but our contact never arrived. The next evening, we were surprised to find him at our rooms and apologizing sycophantically for his absence. I was exasperated, even while congratulating myself that, although I was not most ladies' favor, I was still more handsome than this peculiar man. His being had a disagreeable air I could not place, from the deep wrinkles that moated in his wide mouth, his beady eyes, a contorted nose with pointed tip and those almost tulip-shaped large ears. The right ear, I saw, had a slight incision no doubt earned in some disagreement over money. Hopefully, I mused, whatever associates had so marked him would not come to do business with us. - ❧

Wererats can be unpredictable in a fight, often disengaging only to reappear moments later from a completely different direction.

A wererat is a shapechanger that resembles a normal human, only with a short coat of gray or black fur, a rat-like face, hands and feet ending in short claws, and a long, hairless tail. The creature may keep this appearance, change into the form of a giant rat or even change to its original human form. During the night of the full moon, wererats change shape to wander cities and sewers to further whatever agenda they have. Wererats in human form slowly take on rat-like characteristics as they age, growing short, thin facial hair and slowly becoming shorter and thinning.

Some wererats develop unexplainable nervous twitches or find that rodents are drawn to them. These changes take place over the course of years and are extremely subtle to the point of being nearly imperceptible. Not all wererats change in this manner and there seems to be little reason as to why one will suffer these traits while another does not.

Combat/Tactics:

Rat-Men tend to employ tactics that either rely on overwhelming numbers or some cunning plan if the former cannot

SIGN/TRACKS

Fight enough of these little creeps and you'll soon learn to identify them even in their human form. Those little quill-thin mustaches are a dead giveaway. Don't bother putting out a plate of cheese to tempt them into revealing themselves, though. Just like any common rat, a wererat will eat just about anything it can get its dirty little paws into.

SIZE COMPARISON

6 ft

3 ft

be achieved. They generally detest facing off against a foe in a fair fight and attempt to use terrain to their advantage, preferring to live and fight another day over risking death in battle.

Whenever possible, wererats summon or employ the use of giant rats to bolster their numbers in combat. When faced with no other option, wererats engage in melee combat with small, fast weapons such as short swords (gaining a -1 Speed bonus but inflicting damage by weapon type) and small shields, biting whenever they are presented with an opportunity (certainly in the case of a near-perfect defense).

Wererats are very resistant to blows from non-silvered weapons and this knowledge bolsters their morale. Conversely, they are apt to flee upon seeing multiple argentite blades drawn sensing their foes are knowledgeable opponents capable of inflicting severe harm.

Humans bitten by a wererat must make a Constitution check against the Virulence Factor of the disease (VF 8) or turn into a wererat on the next full moon. Demi-humans, on the other hand, suffer an agonizing death lasting several hours during the next full moon, if they fail that same Constitution check.

Habitat/Society:

Wererats tend to serve as bottom feeders of large cities, devising elaborate plans to lure unsuspecting victims in dark sewers so they can be captured and held for ransom or killed for sport. Many wererats plot and scheme, attempting to think up grand ways to prosper at the expense of others.

Wererats rarely travel alone. They live in swarms in subterranean lairs, preferring dingy sewers and dusty catacombs. Most wererats prefer to live in or near cities, especially those with large sewer systems. When flush with coin they prefer to linger in the worst possible bars and brothels. Many wererats become packrats, collecting all manner of odd items, most of it junk. Wererats detest the presence of cats but most can control their outrage when needed. They flee from dogs, wolves and big hunting cats (e.g., lions, tigers).

Ecology:

Wererats subsist on the scraps of the city in which they live. They can eat any type of food, even if it becomes old and moldy. If needed, wererats can survive on wood, paper or even human waste.

On each full moon, and sometimes the days leading up to one, a human recently infected with lycanthropy changes form to become some hybrid half-man/half-rat, roaming the streets and sewers plotting and killing. In the morning they will retain very little knowledge of what happened the night prior. Those infected may wake in tattered clothing covered in water, sewage and blood, reeking of feces and with no reasonable explanation of what happened the night before.

Those born with the disease can control it, changing forms at will. Those that become infected can learn to control their disease over time, but it is an arduous process often taking years. Such wererats can retains their spellcasting or other abilities even when in rat-man form.

On Tellene:

Wererats can be found on Tellene anywhere that men and rats are found together.

WERERAT

HIT POINTS:	21+3d8
SIZE/WEIGHT:	M/150 lbs.
TENACITY:	Nervous
INTELLIGENCE:	Average
FATIGUE FACTOR:	0

SPEED	INIT
7	-2
ATTACK +7	DMG REDUCTION
DEFENSE +2	13*
by weapon or short	see below
REACH	8
	TOP SAVE ▼

MOVEMENT

CRAWL:	5
WALK:	10
JOG:	15
RUN:	20
SPRINT:	25

SAVES

PHYSICAL:	+5
MENTAL:	+7
DODGE:	+10

ATTACK: Rat-Men favor weapon use (typically short swords) with which they inflict standard damage; often use small shields (increasing Defense to +6); bites deal 2d6p damage and compel CON check vs VF 8 (or turn into wererat on next full moon; demi-humans die on next full moon); wererats use a die type two less than their opponents when determining initiative

SPECIAL: Shield use (e.g., small shields increase Defense to +6). Shapechange. *Silvered weapons reduce DR to 3. Listening, Hearing and Sneaking 75%.

GENERAL INFO

ACTIVITY CYCLE:	Nocturnal
NO. APPEARING:	2-20
% CHANCE IN LAIR:	25%
FREQUENCY:	Infrequent
ALIGNMENT:	Neutral Evil
VISION TYPE:	Low Light Vision (wererat form only)
AWARENESS/SENSES:	Keen hearing (Initiative die type is two better)
HABITAT:	Sewers, catacombs, places of filth
DIET:	Omnivorous
ORGANIZATION:	Individuals
CLIMATE/TERRAIN:	Any

YIELD

MEDICINAL:	nil
SPELL COMPONENTS:	nil
HIDE/TROPHY:	nil
TREASURE:	may collect anything from junk to magic
EDIBLE:	yes, but only monsters do so
OTHER:	nil
EXPERIENCE POINT VALUE:	350

W

Werewolf Also Known As: Wolfman, Man-Wolf

I was lodging with a noble acquaintance one winter night when, not quite dozing in an overstuffed chair, I witnessed him slipping behind a tapestry. Curious, I waited some moments and then followed into a hidden passageway.

I cautiously made my way down the dusty stone stairs, taking a torch from the wall to guide my way. In a short time, I spotted an iron-barred door with a small window in its frame. Hearing some noise, I stopped and peered within. Horrified, I saw my host's brother sleeping on a wooden cot, locked in this cell like some convict awaiting the hangman's noose on the morrow. I called softly to him, afraid to shout in case of alerting my host, but the unconscious figure did not stir.

I had barely begun a second attempt when Veshemo's light shone through the outer window and the change began. In times past, I knew the man inside as tall, pale and silent with dark, close hair and one forelock as bright as silver. Yet, even as I watched his hair grew gray, strangely full and spreading irregularly over his entire body. He seemed wracked with pain, and rent his clothes in madness. His face drew out to a portentous length, while his limbs too lengthened and his hand and feet became clawed. I saw the truth then; he was a man-wolf.

I do not know how long I stood there, watching the ferocious creature rage and buffet the sturdy door, but in time he seemed to calm somewhat. Then, another body-wracking change took place. After it ceased, there stood a hairy four-legged canine with wide paws, a narrow muzzle, broad forehead, and a muscular body broad over the back and shoulders while slender and tapering towards the hind legs; yes, he now bore all the aspects of the common wolf. Only one thing betrayed his countenance; the white hair that grew from the forehead of the man also marked the head of both wolf and man-wolf. ~

"Avoid the moors on a moonlit night ~ lest you find yourself in the wolfman's bite."

Each night a full moon rises, these humans transform into bipedal creatures with a wolflike head, fur-covered body and long limbs ending in clawed hands and feet. Clothes or gear worn are either shredded or fall away from the body as if removed by hand. This form typically retains the intelligence and cunning of the original being, but little to none of the personality, recognizing friends and family only as prey. After the shift into a werewolf, it may remain in this shape or shift again into a common wolf. A werewolf may easily endure wounds delivered by iron and steel blades but those with a silvern patina can gravely injure the beast.

Combat/Tactics:

Werewolves give little thought to battle tactics and hunt in an instinctual manner similar to a wolf stalking prey. Where they differ is that they posses a human intellect and can readily take countermeasures to defensive tactics employed by their opponents. Wolfmen are naturally sly and always attempt to pick apart groups one by one rather than face a united force. Once engaged in melee, a werewolf launches a terrifying onslaught of claw and bite attacks as it attempts to tear a foe to pieces. These occur at five-second intervals with rakes of their claws and biting each inflicting 4d4p+6 damage.

Wolfmen are very resistant to blows from non-silvered weapons. When outnumbered or facing a determined foe armed with sterling implements, werewolves retreat but often return to stalk prey, attacking hours later when their foes have let down their guard.

SIGN/TRACKS

Trust not the protestations of one claiming not to be a werewolf for certainly that is the surest sign. Be mindful of unexplained absences, lost memories and suspicious wounds. Do not put this off to drink as naïve souls are apt to do. Trust no one ~ neither your family nor men you've known for years. The lycanthrope is sly and will stop at nothing to deceive you.

SIZE COMPARISON

6 ft

3 ft

Humans wounded by a werewolf must make a Constitution check against the Virulence Factor of the disease (VF 12) or turn into a werewolf on the next full moon. Demi-humans, however, suffer a drawn-out, agonizing death during the next full moon, if they fail that same Constitution check.

Habitat/Society:

Naturally-born werewolves can be found as either humans or wolves, each preferring their natural state (thus, wolves typically live as wolves and humans as humans), despite the fact that they can shapechange at will. On the full moon, and the sometimes the nights leading up to it, werewolves shapechange to their hybrid form of half-man/half-wolf and prowl the night in search of prey.

As humans, werewolves tend to be loners, keeping their social circles small and never getting too close to those they love, lest they be injured. In their natural wolf form werewolves tend to act as any other wolf, though they retain their intelligence and tend to be larger than normal wolves. Only those born with the disease have any control over it; those who were bitten are at the mercy of the moons. It is rumored that, over time, those bitten can learn to control the process of changing but no one knows for sure if this is true.

On the day after its escapade, the human form awakes completely naked, often covered in blood and gore, with no memory of the previous night save what he may recall as disturbing dreams. Though most werewolves have enough sense to return to an area near their home, many find themselves miles from their homes on the morning following a full moon.

Werewolves may travel in packs or families. These are mostly naturally-born werewolves and not those that have become infected through a bite. In such cases, they live as a typical family of humans or wolves. Packs consist of a male and female and d4 young of either sex. As humans, these groups are often inbred in order to preserve their secret and the pure bloodline.

Ecology:

Lycanthropy is considered a terrible curse and many cultures rightly fear the disease. However, those that become infected are not without some hope. Consuming a number of belladonna berries equal to or greater than 1/2 CON will cure the disease if taken within 12 hours of being infected, but also acts as a VF 13 toxin causing -2 to Attack, Defense and Damage for 2d12 hours on a successful save (a failed save equals death).

Werewolves prefer to eat meat and game (in either human or wolf form) and abstain from other forms of food unless they have no choice. As humans they tend to consume raw, or nearly raw, meat when presented with the opportunity. Those that become infected may grow alarmed to learn that over time they develop a taste for bloody meat.

There are many legends and misconceptions involving the origins and legends about werewolves. In truth, lycanthropy is a permanent viral disease that can be passed on to offspring. Even those that become infected through a bite may find that any future children are born with the disease. In the case of infected males, there is a 25% chance that any offspring from this sire are born with the disease. Any children birthed by a female werewolf are always born with the disease. This event is so tragic that, upon discovery, parents may abandon or kill their young.

On Tellene:

Werewolves can be found on Tellene anywhere that other men are found. They seem to be more common among the Fhokki than other races.

WEREWOLF

HIT POINTS:	26+5d8
SIZE/WEIGHT:	M/250 lbs.
TENACITY:	Steady
INTELLIGENCE:	Average
FATIGUE FACTOR:	-4

SPEED 5 — INIT -2 — ATTACK +10 — DMG REDUCTION — DEFENSE +7 — 14* — see below — short REACH — DAMAGE — TOP SAVE — 10

ATTACK:
Bites and claws (*the latter a single attack*) each deal 4d4p+6 damage and necessitate a CON check vs VF 12 (or turn into werewolf on next full moon; demi-humans die on next full moon).

SPECIAL:
*Silvered weapons reduce DR to 4. Shapechange. Listening +30% in werewolf and wolf form only.

MOVEMENT

CRAWL:	10
WALK:	15
JOG:	20
RUN:	25
SPRINT:	30

SAVES

PHYSICAL:	+12
MENTAL:	+9
DODGE:	+10

GENERAL INFO

ACTIVITY CYCLE:	Nocturnal
NO. APPEARING:	1-12
% CHANCE IN LAIR:	20%
FREQUENCY:	Sporadic
ALIGNMENT:	Chaotic Evil
VISION TYPE:	Low Light Vision (wolf/werewolf only)
AWARENESS/SENSES:	Keen hearing
HABITAT:	Anywhere humans are found
DIET:	Carnivorous
ORGANIZATION:	Individuals or family
CLIMATE/TERRAIN:	Any

YIELD

MEDICINAL:	nil
SPELL COMPONENTS:	nil
HIDE/TROPHY:	nil
TREASURE:	naturally born werewolves care little for treasure
EDIBLE:	yes, but only monsters do so
OTHER:	nil
EXPERIENCE POINT VALUE:	575

WILL-O'-THE-WISP

Also Known As: Corpse Candle, Fool's Fire, Will-O-Wisp

I recall one solemn twilight, in a particularly humid and oppressive Ozhvinmishii summer, when Zhodin and I rode west along the great coastal road. Not a breath stirred in the trees, and we saw not a movement in hedge or ditch. The horizon was narrowing quickly with the coming of night and we had just come upon a small boneyard, no doubt set apart from the next village on our route. We passed it without incident until, when I happened to glance back over my shoulder, I noticed the light.

It might have been nothing more than some gravedigger going about his work with barely adequate candlelight, yet it seemed somehow much more ghostly than any translucent figure clad in a burial shroud. Then another light appeared, seemingly to float only a few feet away from the first. When a third appeared, I halted my horse and stopped to watch.

The lights came slowly towards us, though they stopped too far short for me to see their bearers and then slowly retreated again. It seemed an invitation, and though I resisted, Zhodin persuaded me that no harm could come to us if we were careful. Though he was merely my hired villein and so far knew nothing of adventure, his words shamed me. Indeed, I thought, the lights might be no more than the tiny glowing insects so common in this time and season. It was not until we had dismounted and made our way to the edge of the boneyard that the lights struck, each with its own miniature discharge of lightning.

Zhodin's hair seemed to stiffen on his head like the bristles of a pig while the cold sweat ran off his face and a great tremor wracked his bones, 'til he fell silent at my feet. The next I knew, I was astride my horse and galloping madly west again, the other horse following behind with empty saddle. - ₣

These tiny, floating phosphorescent spheres are no mere fireflies or glimpses of spontaneously ignited swamp gas. No, the will-o'-the-wisp is an intelligent spirit composed entirely of light. A will-o'-the-wisp varies in size from that of a candle flame to that of an adult human's head (the largest size has maximum possible Hit Points, and the smallest has minimum HP).

The brightness of this spirit serves to indicate how 'hungry' it is and thus how dangerous it might be, with bright will-o'-the-wisps being recently fed, and dim, barely visible lights being voracious.

Will-o'-the-wisps appear in a variety of colors, with white or yellowish light being the most common. Some folktales say that this color indicates intent, with will-o'-the-wisps of light blue coloration tending to be benevolent (and even guiding living creatures to hidden treasures), while glowing green will-o'-the-wisps favor malice and mischief. Of course, relying on such speculations could be quite dangerous.

WILL FACTOR 18

RANGE ON TELLENE

SIZE COMPARISON

6 ft

3 ft

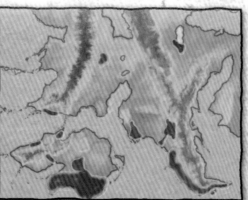

Combat/Tactics:

A will-o'-the-wisp can emit a crackling surge of energy that ignores Damage Reduction from armor and shields and deals damage directly to the target. However, the will-o'-the-wisp rarely attacks its target directly, instead preferring to dance just at the reach of vision, luring the intended victim(s) onwards into a treacherous bog of quicksand, a deadly pit or some other dangerous location.

Fool's Fire is extremely difficult to damage with weaponry, as it is capable of nearly instantaneous shifts of position easily maneuvering out of harm's way. This defensive bonus applies to missile weapons as well.

Will-o'-the-wisps cannot tolerate direct sunlight, and appear only in the dark or on heavily overcast days. Dim and shadowy sunlight (including that of dusk, dawn, and those heavily overcast days) confers a -4 penalty to a will-o'-the-wisp's attack and defense rolls.

Habitat/Society:

Will-o'-the-wisps are nocturnal creatures, haunting swamps, moors, catacombs, graveyards, coastal areas and other damp places during the dark and twilight hours. They are mostly solitary but, when faced with multiple targets, they may cooperate in order to divide and conquer, or simply to provide greater incentive for their prey to follow them. When in pairs, will-o'-the-wisps may keep in close proximity and precisely synchronize their light emissions in an attempt to appear as the eyes of a larger, single creature.

Ecology:

Will-o'-the-wisps survive by draining the life force from dying humans, demi-humans and other sapient creatures. Without such living energy to draw upon, the will-o'-the-wisp's spirit fades into nothingness.

On Tellene:

The most common tale of the will-o'-the-wisp concerns a blacksmith in a war-torn, impoverished land. In unthinking desperation, he offers his daughter to any god or being that will bless his skill at the forge and so bring him coin with which he can support the remainder of his large family. The gods did not respond, but a being from the Nine Hells did.

This devil (or demon, depending upon the tale being told) quickly came to collect the girl, but the smith realized his own wickedness and decided not to give away his daughter. Instead, he tricked the devil by bragging about the hotness of his fire and claiming that the devil's home could surely not be as hot. The devil jumped willingly into the smith's hottest fire to prove his point, whereupon the smith doused him with a bucket of frigid water. The thermal stress shattered the devil into tiny fragments, which the smith later discarded in a nearby swamp.

Each individual fragment retained a bit of the devil's mind and eventually became known as a will-o'-the-wisp among the locals – or so the story is often told.

If you should find yourself in the woods during the black of night, best that you ignore any dancing lights that beckon, for the fool's candle will lead the unwary to their demise. Pull your collar tight and look the other way.

WILL-O'-THE-WISP

HIT POINTS:	10+7d8
SIZE/WEIGHT:	T/insubstantial
TENACITY:	Cowardly
INTELLIGENCE:	Brilliant
FATIGUE FACTOR:	n/a

SPEED	INIT
5	-1

ATTACK: +9
DEFENSE: +26
DMG REDUCTION: 7
DAMAGE: 2d8p
TOP SAVE: n/a
REACH: short

MOVEMENT

CRAWL:	n/a
WALK:	n/a
JOG:	n/a
RUN:	n/a
FLY:	15

SAVES

PHYSICAL:	+9
MENTAL:	immune
DODGE:	+26

ATTACK:
Energy attacks deal 2d8p damage (no armor DR applies).

WEAKNESSES:
Defense bonus applies to *both* melee and when targeted by missile fire; Suffers a -4 penalty to Attack and Defense in dim sunlight; flees from direct sunlight.

GENERAL INFO

ACTIVITY CYCLE:	Nocturnal
NO. APPEARING:	1-4
% CHANCE IN LAIR:	n/a
FREQUENCY:	Unusual
ALIGNMENT:	Neutral Evil
VISION TYPE:	Undead Sight
AWARENESS/SENSES:	Standard
HABITAT:	Swamps, rivers
DIET:	Special
ORGANIZATION:	Individuals
CLIMATE/TERRAIN:	Temperate to tropical wetlands

YIELD

MEDICINAL:	nil
SPELL COMPONENTS:	nil
HIDE/TROPHY:	nil
TREASURE:	swamps may be filled with valuable remains
EDIBLE:	no
OTHER:	nil
EXPERIENCE POINT VALUE:	625

WOLF

WOLF
DIRE WOLF

Also Known As: Lukos

If you have read my treatise on the subject of wolves, you know how fascinating I find these wild predators. Sitting as they do sit at the apex of their ecosystem, they are one of the most widely distributed mammals across the continent and thus have afforded me many opportunities to study them. I have even been graced with the opportunity to study the great dire wolf, whose skull I am sure is morphologically distinct from that of the common lupine, having a bigger rostrum, a wider occiput and larger teeth. All of this surely points toward greater slicing capability and perhaps a hypercarnivorous desire for meat.

Many fellow academics feel much less kindly to the wolf than do I. I suppose this is understandable, considering the fate of all too many mages whose curiosity compelled them to wander far off into the primeval forest bereft of bodyguards. Regardless, I still maintain that such a savage behavior is not common to all wolves, only certain packs that have learned to include humans in their catalog of prey based on prior experiences. That many goblin tribes have inculcated this behavior into their kept wolves only speaks to the former's evil nature, not some inherent predilection for savagery on the part of the animals themselves. - ⚶

These predatory canines have narrow chests and powerful backs and legs, with paws able to tread easily on a wide variety of terrains, especially snow. Coloration varies greatly, running from gray to gray-brown, all the way through the canine spectrum of white, red, brown, and black. Aging wolves acquire a grayish tint in their muzzles and coats. A typical wolf stands about 2½ feet tall at the shoulder, is roughly 4½ feet long with a further 16-inch tail, and weighs around 80 pounds.

The dire wolf is superficially similar to a large wolf with proportionally shorter and sturdier legs, standing over 3 feet tall at the shoulder, with a body length of more than 5 feet (plus 20 inches of tail) and a weight of nearly 200 pounds. Most dire wolves also have a clue to their identity in the tail, which is usually (but not always) tipped with black.

Regardless of species, the female is physically similar to the male, only slightly smaller and weighing roughly 20% less.

Combat/Tactics:

Wolves hunt their prey by stalking in packs, then striking when the target is distracted, using their teeth to tear at the hips and legs. Once the prey has been downed, the wolves tear open its guts and begin to feed even while the target lives.

Packs of wolves cooperatively hunt any large herbivores in their range, such as deer, moose or even bison. Pack hunting revolves around the chase, as wolves are able to run for long periods before relenting. It requires careful cooperation for a pack to bring down large prey, and the rate of success for such chases is very low. Wolves, in the interest of saving energy, only chase one potential victim for the first half mile or so before giving up and trying at a different time against a

W

SIGN/TRACKS

Fore

Hind

RANGE ON TELLENE

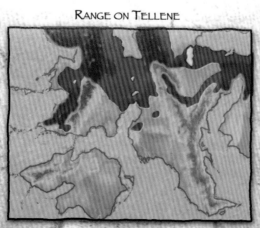

SIZE COMPARISON

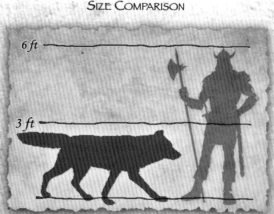

6 ft

3 ft

WOLF

HIT POINTS:	21+2d8
SIZE/WEIGHT:	M/80 lbs.
TENACITY:	Nervous
INTELLIGENCE:	Animal, Low
FATIGUE FACTOR:	-2

MOVEMENT

CRAWL:	10
WALK:	15
JOG:	20
RUN:	25
SPRINT:	30

SAVES

PHYSICAL:	+5
MENTAL:	+2
DODGE:	+4

ATTACK:
Bites deal 2d4p+2 points of damage.

SPECIAL ABILITIES:
Listening mastery of 65%, Tracking mastery is 50%

GENERAL INFO

ACTIVITY CYCLE:	Nocturnal
NO. APPEARING:	2-20
% CHANCE IN LAIR:	10%
FREQUENCY:	Ubiquitous
ALIGNMENT:	Non
VISION TYPE:	Good eyesight; Low Light Vision
AWARENESS/SENSES:	Good hearing and sense of smell
HABITAT:	Dens, burrows, forests, plains
DIET:	Carnivorous
ORGANIZATION:	Pack
CLIMATE/TERRAIN:	Arctic to Temperate wilderness

YIELD

MEDICINAL:	nil
SPELL COMPONENTS:	nil
HIDE/TROPHY:	pelts worth up to 2 sp
TREASURE:	incidental
EDIBLE:	yes
OTHER:	nil
EXPERIENCE POINT VALUE:	84

DIRE WOLF

HIT POINTS:	27+3d8
SIZE/WEIGHT:	M/200 lbs.
TENACITY:	Steady
INTELLIGENCE:	Animal, High
FATIGUE FACTOR:	-2

MOVEMENT

CRAWL:	10
WALK:	15
JOG:	20
RUN:	25
SPRINT:	30

SAVES

PHYSICAL:	+7
MENTAL:	+2
DODGE:	+5

ATTACK:
Bites deal 4d4p points of damage.

SPECIAL ABILITIES:
Listening mastery of 65%, Tracking mastery is 45%

GENERAL INFO

ACTIVITY CYCLE:	Nocturnal
NO. APPEARING:	3-12
% CHANCE IN LAIR:	10%
FREQUENCY:	Frequent
ALIGNMENT:	Non
VISION TYPE:	Good eyesight; Low Light Vision
AWARENESS/SENSES:	Good hearing and sense of smell
HABITAT:	Dens, burrows, forests, plains
DIET:	Carnivorous
ORGANIZATION:	Pack
CLIMATE/TERRAIN:	Arctic to Temperate wilderness

YIELD

MEDICINAL:	nil
SPELL COMPONENTS:	nil
HIDE/TROPHY:	pelts worth up to 3 sp
TREASURE:	incidental
EDIBLE:	yes
OTHER:	nil
EXPERIENCE POINT VALUE:	122

W

different target. Solitary wolves depend more on smaller animals (like rodents or foxes), which they capture by pouncing and pinning them to the ground with their front paws. When pursuing large prey, wolves generally attack as a pack from all angles, targeting the necks and flanks as noted above.

Habitat/Society:

Most wolves hunt in packs of two to 12 individuals, led by a dominant pair. They feed primarily on animals about the same size or larger than themselves (*e.g.*, sheep, goats, pigs, moose and deer).

Wolf packs test large herds by initiating a chase, targeting less-fit prey such as the elderly, diseased, or young. Healthy animals may also succumb through circumstance. However, most healthy, fit individuals stand their ground against wolves, increasing the possibility of injury to the preying wolves; thus, the weaker members of a group are easier and safer to hunt.

Both wolves and dire wolves hunt and feed in the same manner.

Ecology:

Wolves are intolerant of mountain lions and other similar predators in their territory, seeing them as competitors for food and as threats to their cubs. A wolf pack steals their kills and eats mountain lion cubs, but the adult mountain lion is usually at an advantage on a 1-to-1 basis, considering it can effectively use both claws and teeth, while the wolf relies on its teeth alone.

As long as there is sufficient prey, wolves seem to avoid taking livestock, often ignoring them entirely. However, some wolves or packs can specialize in hunting livestock once the behavior is learned despite natural prey abundance. In such situations, sheep are usually the most vulnerable, but horses and cattle are also at risk.

It was several years ago that I was sitting in the Gabled Drake tavern in Vew, staring at my last – and increasingly out of focus – copper coin lying on the table before me. By this point, I'd already thrown back numerous tankards of cheap ale. A fat man with a drooping eye had the temerity to disturb my repose by sitting down beside me and then proceeded to offer employment.

He proposed paying twenty-five silver denarii if I were to run a string of mules on the three-day journey up the borderland road to Frandor's Keep. The obese fellow stated that he was under a contractual obligation to deliver these beasts of burden to the garrison there but that his shiftless mule skinners had ran out on him after hearing rumors of a silver strike in the Krond Heights. He was in dire straights and had just made the error of revealing his hand to me.

I held out for fifty and he reluctantly obliged. I was to receive twenty-five coins up front with the balance paid upon delivery by his agent at the fortress. After shaking hands to formalize the deal, he presented me a letter bearing his seal authorizing me as his agent pro temp and documenting the terms of our arrangement.

Now the thing is, I had already been heading in that direction when my last remaining funds slipped through my fingers as they were so often wont to do. I took the job offer as a sign that the fates had finally deigned to smile on me. This was certainly easy money. Or so I thought for I had no idea what I had gotten myself into.

After following the merchant to a pen a few streets away, I learned that his "string of mules" was actually a full dozen animals. To makes matters worse, they were the most stubborn, contrary, ornery and generally most difficult beasts I've ever worked with. They preferred to remain motionless and nothing short of cracking a whip over their haunches and yelling until I was hoarse would get them to take a step.

The first day on the trail I spent most of my time pushing and shoving the braying mules only taking a break from this labor to hunt through the brush in search of those who had broken loose. In hindsight, their reluctance to move into the wilds probably should have told me something.

I made poor time that day, not even reaching the first way station at Kar Darkan. When the sun began setting behind the mountains and the shadows grew longer, I cursed my brash stupidity at not staying in the company of the caravan I had passed making

W

HOWLIN' WOLVES
A Pack Attack

camp several hours previously.

As darkness set, I hobbled the mules with rope and weight stones beneath the drooping branches of an ancient twisted willow by the roadside. I then set out to gather up wood to make a fire. It was while engaged in this task some twenty yards or so into the forest's edge that I heard the first wolf. It was a mournful howl, perhaps a half-mile to the east, and caused me to freeze in my tracks.

If I was nervous, the mules were absolutely terrified. They protested loudly by tugging at their ropes, their eyes wide with fear and nostrils flaring. I immediately took what little wood I had managed to gather and ran to the center of camp. There I dumped it and dropped to my knees. I was retrieving my flint and tinder from my kit when I heard the second howl.

This one was much closer — issuing as it did from the trees' shadows not more than a stone's throw away. The hair on the back of my neck bristled as I stared hard.

Then there was a blur of movement, a patch of gray and white. Suddenly a snarl erupted from the other end of camp followed by another howl several hundred yards to my right. A reply came a few seconds later much closer and from the left. A wolf pack was moving in and they were coming fast.

Realizing my dire predicament, I stood to my feet and drew my short sword. My eyes darted to and fro looking for a defendable spot. My focus had just settled on the low branches of the willow when a large wolf stode out of the foliage, it's teeth bared and head hanging low as it snarled. Stepping carefully away from it, my blood ran cold. I then heard snarling coming from behind me.

Glancing over my shoulder, I noticed an even larger wolf closing the distance between us. Turning so as to keep both wolves in my peripheral vision, I knelt slowly to pick up one of the large sticks I had gathered for the fire thinking to wield it like a club in my free hand. The wolf on my right protested when I did so, lunging forward with a feint and growling loudly.

I swung at him with my sword trying hard not to take my eyes off his comrade. As if my predicament couldn't get any worse, a third wolf arrived on the scene then a fourth and finally a fifth. It was a hunting pack and they looked hungry.

Feeling like I was being herded, I found myself backing away toward the mules who were now absolutely insane with terror. Shoving at one another, braying and pawing, they wanted nothing more than to flee. If I approached the writhing mass much closer, their jostling threatened to knock me down and if that occurred I knew I'd be in for it. Acting in a moment of inspirational clarity, I suddenly slashed my sword at the ropes binding the mules. Bolting for freedom, the mules cried out through the valley as a pair of the wolves instantly gave chase.

I wasn't in the clear yet. The sudden rush of mule flesh had, as I feared, knocked me off balance and I fell onto my back. One of the howling beasts ran across my chest to get to the mules and painfully lacerated my chest. Two others turned toward me, heads down, jaws open, fangs dripping with anticipation of a meal.

I didn't know what to do so in desperation I made like the mules, bolted to my feet and ran for my life. I was no match for the two lupine hunters who had chosen me for a meal and could almost feel their hot breath on my skin as they closed teeth slashing the air. Luckily, a tree with good climbing branches was mere paces away. I had never seen a sight so beautiful as that tree and scrambled up it like I had been born in one. I didn't stop climbing until I'd gotten near to the top and then just hugged that trunk for dear life. The two wolves below paced in anxious fury for a good ten or fifteen minutes before giving up and heading for the mules.

When I finally mustered the courage to climb back down, I made a vain attempt to look for the mules. When I found the remains, there wasn't much left of the poor beasts save tails and hooves. Needless to say, I didn't get paid for delivering those burros.

WORM, TITANIC
Also Known As: Grandfather Worm, Shahul

I hear the Netherdeep is plagued by these giant plum-colored worms, and that they're the reason for all those tunnels underground. Given their size it doesn't surprise me at all. I've been lucky enough not to meet one down there.

Oh, sure, once I fought a titantic dun-colored worm in the desert. It was tough, but not like fighting them underground. You run into one of these things underground and you're dead. Sorry, but that's it. Nowhere to run and nowhere to hide.

Worse, there's nothing to be gained by fighting them. They don't keep treasure, and fighting them is instant death on their home terrain. You can't get away from them in a tunnel, after all. When one comes at you there's only one way to run because nothing's going to stop it — not caltrops, flaming oil or even a slow dwarf for a companion. - ᛉ

The enormous maw of a shahul can swallow up horse and cart with room enough for the man driving it to clear his head.

The tunnel network in the Elenons is actually worm tubes created by shahul. An ally of mine once attempted to explore the system. He mapped 15 miles of passageways before giving up.

Titanic worms are a gigantic species of segmented worm that burrow deep within the bowels of the earth. These creatures are truly immense measuring 6 to 12 feet in diameter and as much as 60 feet in length. Most tend towards a plum or violet hue, but reds, blacks, blues, browns and tans are not uncommon. While these creatures lack a brain, they do possess nerve centers and photoreceptors. Both light and vibrations (as from footfalls) serve as beacons.

Combat/Tactics:

The creature's front end is essentially one giant maw, with row upon row of teeth the size of mining picks, much like a great lamprey, only a short distance down its gullet. In the most likely scenario - that in which the creature is encountered fill-ing a passageway – the worm wriggles forward seeking to swallow whole any tasty morsels in its path. Such is the creature's mass that any before it must give ground or be crushed beneath its bulk (assuming there is minimal clearance on either side of the worm). Those failing to give way are killed as the creature advances.

If faced with multiple opponents before its mouth, the worm rolls but once for attack, comparing its score to each defender's roll. Any it exceeds are simultaneously abraded by the cutting teeth. If the worm exceeds any Defense roll by 6, that defender has been swallowed whole, suffering 6d12p damage as it passes through the multiple rings of teeth within the enormous maw. Once swallowed, a creature suffers d12p damage every 10 seconds from a combination of suffocation and constriction,

---

SIGN/TRACKS

Entrances to titanic worm tubes are often mistaken for mine shafts. There are clues, however, that betray their true nature — the lack of tailings and debris piles being foremost. Uniform, rounded walls that twist and turn abruptly are another.
During the rainy season, titanic worms may come to the surface to mate amidst the pelting drops. Should you come upon a great patch of ground with trenches seemingly formed by the battering of giant ropes, look sharp, for the grandfather worms may still be nearby.

SIZE COMPARISON

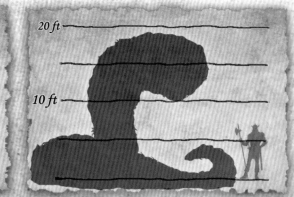

20 ft

10 ft

Damage Reduction from armor and like protections notwithstanding. If the victim held a knife or dagger in his hands prior to being swallowed, he may attempt to cut his way out. These attacks succeed automatically (at the trapped individual's normal speed), but no Strength bonus is applicable and half the creature's Damage Reduction applies. It is necessary to inflict 20 points of damage from within the worm to extricate one's self.

The worm possesses a stinger in its tail that likely developed to thwart attacks to its unprotected rear, since the beast cannot turn after burrowing through rock. This stinger may only be employed against opponents attacking it from the rear, except if in a large open cavern. In that instance it may bring this surprisingly supple weapon to bear. Successful strikes inflict 4d4p damage and inject a virulent paralytic poison (VF 16) that incapacitates a victim for 2d4 hours if a save is failed. Incapacitated victims are eaten during this time.

Habitat/Society:

Titanic worms fill a parallel role to their miniscule cousin but on a different scale. Their size, specially adapted mouth and incredible musculature permits them to burrow through stone (at a rate too glacially slow to matter in combat). Although they do this in search of food, a result was the creation of a vast subterranean tunnel network criss-crossing the Netherdeep. These are filled with the pea gravel remnants excreted by the worm, but subsequent excavation is much easier than burrowing through igneous rock.

Generations of deep dwelling gnomes and dwarves (along with creatures less fair) have been permitted far easier access to mineral wealth greatly enriching both these races. Humans and other surface races have benefited as well for ample stocks of gold, silver and copper have been liberated for use in currency facilitating a continent-wide repudiation of the inefficient barter system.

Ecology:

Titanic worms are quite rare for their habitat is relatively scarce in food sources. The creatures are hermaphrodites, but still require a mate to produce offspring. They are capable of sexual reproduction and always do so on the rare instance of encountering another of their species. Such events are earth shattering (literally!) and can cause cave-ins and severe damage to any unfortunate creatures nearby.

These creatures are extremely long lived – one centuries-old dwarven book describes in exacting detail the features of a purpuraceous worm that would periodically return to wreck havoc on the clan. In each instance the creature bore remarkable similarity to the bane of old – down to scars received in previous encounters.

On Tellene:

These titanic worms have been burrowing within the Netherdeep for untold ages. They can be found deep below the surface in all areas of the continent, with a sand variety sometimes surfacing in the Khydoban Desert.

Some of the Netherdeep races have folktales about a massive albino, twice as large and four times as long as the largest known titanic worm.

TITANIC WORM

HIT POINTS:	40+15d8
SIZE/WEIGHT:	C/18 tons
TENACITY:	Steady
INTELLIGENCE:	Semi-
FATIGUE FACTOR:	n/a

SPEED		INIT
5	ATTACK +20	3
DEFENSE +6		DMG REDUCTION 16
medium REACH	see below	n/a
	DAMAGE	TOP SAVE ▼

MOVEMENT

CRAWL:	1¼
WALK:	2½
JOG:	5
RUN:	7½
SPRINT:	10

SAVES

PHYSICAL:	+31
MENTAL:	+8
DODGE:	+11

ATTACK: Single bite attack rolled against all before it; this deals 4d12p and swallows on 6 over; those swallowed take 6d12p from teeth & d12p/10s thereafter; Bite occurs once/10s; Stinger attack (usually rear only) occurs 1/10s staggered by 5s from bite; this inflicts 4d4p plus VF 16 poison that incapacitates for 2d4 hours if save failed.

WEAKNESSES: Rear stinger may often be unemployable

GENERAL INFO

ACTIVITY CYCLE:	Nocturnal
NO. APPEARING:	1
% CHANCE IN LAIR:	n/a
FREQUENCY:	Unusual
ALIGNMENT:	Non
VISION TYPE:	Standard
AWARENESS/SENSES:	Senses movement within 75 feet
HABITAT:	Subterranean
DIET:	Omnivorous
ORGANIZATION:	Individuals
CLIMATE/TERRAIN:	Any, save arctic

YIELD

MEDICINAL:	nil
SPELL COMPONENTS:	nil
HIDE/TROPHY:	none except for teeth
TREASURE:	incidental
EDIBLE:	no
OTHER:	nil
EXPERIENCE POINT VALUE:	2000

WRAITH

Also Known As: Eternal Wrath

Wraiths be spirits of men most powerful and bounteous of ambition bewitched by powers nefarious to lead an eternal existence of malice and hatred. Though they giveth the perception of having the form of men, this is but a guise. Though having shape, it is a nebulous one only given form by that attire they choose to clothe themselves in. Shorn of these garments, the wraith appearest as but a globe of inky darkness.

Though a combatant most fearsome, a wraith doth possess the intellect and fortitude to accomplish purposes far-reaching in scope. Know well that wraiths mayest be agents both trusted and capable acting in the stead of creatures far more severe.

The true power of a wraith is its power to command. Whether through force of will or via fear of its unhallowed existence, many a wraith hath the knowledge of generalship and the power to hold dominion over rapacious armies of evil men and humanoids.

Most devilish of all is that the creature canst trod upon the earth in the full radiance of sunlight. It is a far more dangerous foe that is not resigned to the hours of darkness in which to discharge its evil deeds.

Though the creature may seem to wield great weapons, these be but illusions or phantoms for they in truth pass through the stoutest of armor yet the wounds so inflicted are but little. Of paramount concern is their ability to sap the life of any so injured for any physical damage is accompanied by a loss of health and vigor that is slow to return, if at all. - 👁

A wraith is a fearsome undead creature inhabited by the spirit of an incredibly wicked mortal. It draws strongly on dark energy such that its physical manifestation is nearly invisible. Wraiths clothe themselves in garments they once wore in life in order to present an intimidating appearance when interacting with the living. Many carry weapons, decorated in frightening images, in order to cast forth an imposing and haunting image.

Wraiths possess the ability to speak in whatever languages they used in life; their voices are always cold, hollow and unpleasant to the living.

Combat/Tactics:

When confronted by the living, wraiths often first command their minions to attack. They retain much of the memories and habits that they had in life, including battle tactics and combat strategies. They have no fear of the living, or anything else for that matter, and willingly enter combat against superior numbers if need be.

The touch of a wraith drains life energy in the form of lost Constitution (1 point for every point of damage inflicted). Those slain are forever dead. A wraith can only be fully damaged by silvered weapons. Wraiths cannot enter, or pass over, consecrated ground.

SIGN/TRACKS

SIZE COMPARISON

Know that the sight of a black-cloaked figure in brightest day may well be a wraith on some villainous errand. They fear not the light and may challenge ye with the sun directly overhead. Thou must beware but make this encounter known to those who mayest gauge if it be a harbinger of events most foul.

WILL FACTOR
18

6 ft

3 ft

Habitat/Society:

Most wraiths were powerful and capable men in life. These traits carry over to undeath, making them extremely dogged and resourceful servants or commanders to an overlord, or even leaders in their own right. Since most wraiths were once men of means, or power, they often command other undead, and even living creatures. Some wraiths will willingly serve as guardians and servants to powerful creatures or lords, both living and undead. In such instances those that command the wraiths must themselves be heinous creatures of incredible power.

Wraiths inhabit the dark and forgotten places of the world, where they reign over their minions as powerful lords and leaders existing much as they did in life. Some wraiths are seemingly tied to their former homes, or places of death, but this is likely due to some unknown advantage the region affords rather than sentimentality.

Wraiths have a great hatred for the living. Barring more urgent tasks they may be charged with accomplishing, they seek to destroy all living creatures. That being said, they are not wonton slayers. Rather, they delight in the fear, terror and hopelessness a victim displays before meeting death.

Ecology:

It is unknown how an individual becomes a wraith. Some sages postulate that great men who in life exhibited hatred, malice, and depravity of legendary proportions received this fate as punishment for their wickedness while others insist that these same lords bartered their souls for earthly power. What is certain is that wraiths exist between two worlds, drawing upon dark energy to enable them to manifest a physical presence in the mortal realm. Wraiths are incredibly evil, hateful, and cruel, possessing no redeeming qualities or traits.

As wraiths are undead they do not need to eat or sleep, however they do have a slight aversion to sunlight. They are fully able to function in sun but given a choice prefer to operate during the nighttime hours. In instances where it is required wraiths have been known to enter into society for some purpose or another. In such cases they don heavy clothes and robes in order to obscure their true identity.

It is suggested that wraiths possess an extraordinary sense of smell in regards to detecting the living. Those that have been hunted by these terrifying creatures have observed at times that they will stop and sniff at the air when they loose their quarry, before moving on. No one knows for certain if they can actually smell the living or not.

Many animals can sense a wraith's presence. Horses will become nervous when a wraith is near, fleeing in terror at their visage. Dogs bark incessantly at their approach but run and hide when they come near.

On Tellene:

Wraiths may be encountered anywhere on Tellene where men live, or once lived, but are more commonly found in long abandoned ruins than anywhere else. However, if obeying a dictum of their overlord, they may be dispatched to the unlikeliest of places where one might otherwise consider himself safe from such nightmarish intrusion.

WRAITH

HIT POINTS:	27+9d8
SIZE/WEIGHT:	M/insubstantial
TENACITY:	Fearless
INTELLIGENCE:	Smart
FATIGUE FACTOR:	n/a

SPEED 10 — INIT -4 — ATTACK +17 — DMG REDUCTION — DEFENSE +8 — 25 — see below — DAMAGE nil — medium REACH — TOP SAVE

MOVEMENT

CRAWL:	2½
WALK:	5
JOG:	10
RUN:	15
SPRINT:	20

SAVES

PHYSICAL:	+17
MENTAL:	immune
DODGE:	+17

ATTACK:
Touch deals d8p CON drain (save for half); may employ standard weaponry with a +4 damage and +2 speed bonus but this substitutes for their touch attack

WEAKNESSES:
Silvered weapons reduce DR to 13

GENERAL INFO

ACTIVITY CYCLE:	Nocturnal
NO. APPEARING:	1 or 2-12
% CHANCE IN LAIR:	20%
FREQUENCY:	Unusual
ALIGNMENT:	Lawful Evil
VISION TYPE:	Undead Sight
AWARENESS/SENSES:	Standard
HABITAT:	Any
DIET:	n/a
ORGANIZATION:	Individuals
CLIMATE/TERRAIN:	Any

YIELD

MEDICINAL:	nil
SPELL COMPONENTS:	nil
HIDE/TROPHY:	nil
TREASURE:	rings, crowns and other bejeweled or gilded emblems of rank, power and authority
EDIBLE:	no
OTHER:	nil
EXPERIENCE POINT VALUE:	1842

WYRM

Also Known As: Drakon, Harkoon, Drakus

First time I ran across a wyrm was years ago when I walked into this village that claimed they were being terrorized by a dragon. They begged for my help, I'm no fool. There weren't any way I'd be setting one foot anywhere near a dragon's lair, and I only stuck there long enough to rest my horse and refresh my provisions.

It was a few months after that when, well, I hit a little rough patch. All the monsters seemed to be hiding their heads and bounties were few and far between, while certain parties were hounding me for a few small debts I owed. I'd even taken to visiting the local taverns all day, merely to keep my ears open for opportunities, of course.

Didn't take too long afore my creditors took offense to my shortfall and, against my better judgement, I rode back to that upset village and took on the dragonslayer job — with the stipulation that I got a nice fat payment up front so I could concentrate on the task without being trouble over my small debts.

It only took a bit of investigation afore I realized that this dragon didn't behave quite like what you'd expect from a dragon. It seemed content just to cause terror, and hadn't struck any deals with the nobility for tributes and princesses and such. Plus, the locals said it flew like a wounded partridge. I stalked the beast for a few days, and pretty quickly figured out that it weren't no dragon, but a wyrm. A formidable monster and nothing to be lax about, but not the godsawful terror of a dragon. I played it smart, took my time, played out a few of my cleverest tricks and cunningly managed to slay that beast, earning enough reward to get the damn moneylenders off my back for good.

It did slip my mind to disclose the true nature of the beast, but why ruin a good story the villagers could tell for generations to come? - ♀

A wyrm's diet can affect the color of its scales. I've seen hues ranging from gray to red and even blue and green.

A wyrm is a gigantic reptilian beast with a lizard's torso but proportionately longer neck and legs. A pair of smaller membranous wings jut from the creature's muscled back, seemingly too small to carry such a huge beast aloft. Atop the neck rests an outsized lacertine head with huge eyes and rupicaprine horns. The body is covered in thick but supple scales, with irregular small plates dotting the hide. The base hide coloration is a light gray, but the wyrm's diet may impart a reddish, bluish, greenish or other hue.

Wyrms are intelligent and capable of speech, though the physiology of their larynx is such that they cannot produce all vocalizations of which humans are capable. Naturally, this makes conversation a difficult task.

Wyrms may be mistaken for dragons for they are indeed a closely related genus. None, though, possess the latter's horrific breath weapon, although some can produce a small cloud of acrid smoke. The color variation of their hides also causes frequent mis-identification of the creature.

SIGN/TRACKS	RANGE ON TELLENE	SIZE COMPARISON

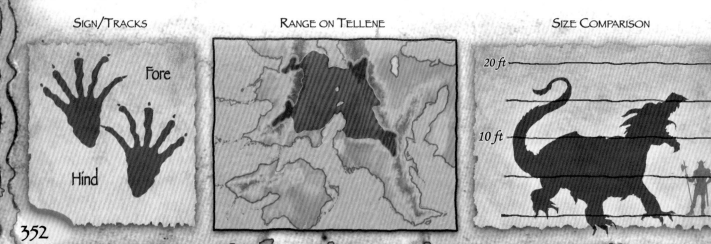

Combat/Tactics:

A wyrm is able to savagely rend foes as well as slash with its powerful clawed feet. Though able to fly for short distances, it requires a significant running start to become airborne (and is quite an ungainly flier even then). Flight from battle, both literally and figuratively, is not an option.

The average wyrm is the veteran of many battles and fights craftily, seeking to destroy opponents in-turn rather than piecemeal. They are aware of the power of magic and seek preferentially to kill any mages should the latter prove an annoying threat. Its enormous size permits it to traverse the battleground at will (and those in its way had best retreat or be squashed). Size M or L creatures cannot hope to deny a wyrm freedom of movement and it puts this advantage – as well as its substantial reach – to best use.

Wyrms are not crafty by nature and only of moderate intelligence. As such, they are subject to manipulation. They generally take well to any offer that provides a modicum of comfort and ease rather than having to go through the effort of carrying through on a threat.

Habitat/Society:

Wyrms are very similar to dragons with respect to their haughty attitude and sense of superiority. They are solitary and jealous of their territory though prizing it for its abundance of nourishment rather than exploitable wealth. In this they show their difference for they are more interested in eating than in wealth and power. Their evil is more of a brutish variety than sinister.

If a male hears the female's mating screech, it approaches with an appearance of strength, spreading its wings and tail a bit before bowing to the female. After coupling, the two separate. One year later, when the female is ready to lay her eggs (usually two or three), she digs a nest in the earth and remains with the eggs until they hatch in another 13 to 14 months. A brood of wyrms remains with the mother for several years, until they strike out on their own or are killed by their siblings or mother. They are not sexually mature for 40 to 50 years, despite being seemingly full grown.

A wyrm has a lifespan of well over 200 years.

Ecology:

Wyrms can live anywhere, but their enormous caloric requirements and general sloth often draw them into the realms of man where they live along the fringes as a brigandish parasite. They are frequently appeased by fearful villagers anxious to curry a wyrm's favor by sacrificing a portion of their flocks.

On Tellene:

In one tale common among clerics of the Valiant, a Servant of the Swift Sword confronted a dragon that swallowed all the children of a village. The dragon let out a mighty roar and the cleric leaped into its mouth, made his way to the belly and cut it open to free the children. Critics of this story claim that it actually involves a wyrm, due to the lack of fire breath and obvious intelligence on the part of the dragon.

WYRM

HIT POINTS:	35+10d8
SIZE/WEIGHT:	G/3-4 tons
TENACITY:	Brave
INTELLIGENCE:	Slow
FATIGUE FACTOR:	-5

SPEED 3 · INIT 3 · ATTACK +17 · DMG REDUCTION 11 · DEFENSE +7 · see below · long REACH · DAMAGE 12 · TOP SAVE ▼

MOVEMENT

CRAWL:	5
WALK:	10
JOG:	15
RUN:	20
FLY:	30 (ungainly)

SAVES

PHYSICAL:	+23
MENTAL:	+15
DODGE:	+18

ATTACK:
Wyrms attack by raking with their forepaws (two claw attacks each doing 2d10p damage) and then biting (4d10p). They are intelligent enough to focus their efforts on a single opponent (preferring obvious spellcasters).
It guards against being attacked from the rear by sweeping its posterior with the tail (an attack with long reach dealing 3d12p damage).

GENERAL INFO

ACTIVITY CYCLE:	Diurnal
NO. APPEARING:	1
% CHANCE IN LAIR:	75%
FREQUENCY:	Scarce
ALIGNMENT:	Chaotic Evil
VISION TYPE:	Standard
AWARENESS/SENSES:	Standard
HABITAT:	Caves
DIET:	Carnivorous
ORGANIZATION:	Individuals
CLIMATE/TERRAIN:	Temperate highlands

YIELD

MEDICINAL:	bathing in its blood is said to neutralize poisons
SPELL COMPONENTS:	unknown; scholarly research is needed
HIDE/TROPHY:	hide for clothing, bone for tools, head for trophy
TREASURE:	hoard of coins and miscellaneous valuables
EDIBLE:	yes
OTHER:	eggs may be worth much to the right buyer
EXPERIENCE POINT VALUE:	1700

WYVERN

Also Known As: Sky Viper, Wyvere

The earliest known carving of a wyvern is, perhaps, the small statue that now rests upon the table in front of me. I was fortunate enough to come upon it half-buried in some Elos Desert ruins, and somehow managed to return it still undamaged to my little workshop several hundred miles away.

The statue, composed of some sort of reddish clay, consists of the forepart of a four-legged, toothless lizard with the hindpart of a scorpion and the wings of a bat. Of course, it is not the true wyvern, as I can speak of from my own glimpse of the reality and my taxonomic sketches upon the subject. However, this rare carving is perhaps the best symbolic representation of one, for it captures all the essential elements of the wyvern even without being an exact copy of the beast itself.

For instance, the wyvern is certainly not lacking in sharp teeth, for my own left arm still bears the scars of a wyvern's sharp, daggerlike maw. Likewise does its tail have more flexibility than that of a scorpion, and is not limited to merely one direction, as our thief can well recall from his brash attempt at a rear assault. Furthermore, the true wyvern has only two legs, as do birds and bats and many other such creatures of the air.

Interestingly, I now recall that some old alchemist tales speak of the gods fashioning sapient life from clay and presented their own blood to the images in order to give them life and consciousness. Of course, this could not be one of those images; the idea is absurd. Yet, I believe I can spare a bit of my own blood for a small experiment... ~

Wyverns, though kin to dragons, are less intelligent and more numerous than their larger relatives. They have powerful flattened jaws, rows of sharp teeth and two short legs that enable it to take flight from the ground with a jumping start. Its wings, head and neck are glossy black with a metallic violet sheen, with the underside of the wings and body dull instead of glossy. Its legs and tail are black. The wyvern's tail is distinguished by a bulbous venom gland and the viscious, curved venom-injecting barb.

The wyvern's ears are covered with thin, slightly transparent skin, and are visible in a shallow depression on each side of the head. Interestingly, the wyvern has no eyelids; it uses its tongue to clear away debris, while a transparent scale keeps its black-pupiled eyes moist.

A typical adult female wyvern has a total length of over 30 feet, with a massive wingspan of around 40 feet and a weight of about a ton. The male wyvern is slightly smaller and lighter than the female (roughly 10%), but otherwise determining a wyvern's sex is difficult to say the least.

Combat/Tactics:

Sky Vipers may make an initial attack by diving at prey tearing with their claws and buffeting them with their sheer bulk and momentum for a total of 4d10p damage. If this aerial assault is successful, the wyvern remains on the ground to consume its meal. If its

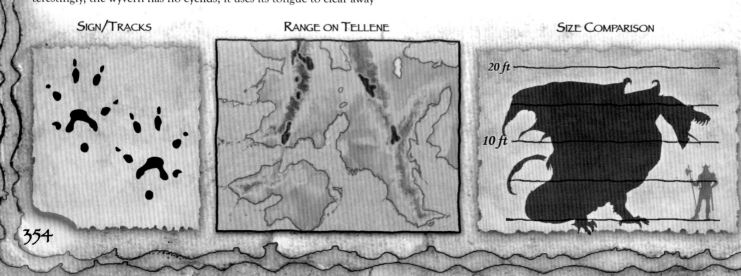

SIGN/TRACKS   RANGE ON TELLENE   SIZE COMPARISON

20 ft

10 ft

victim is merely incapacitated, the wyvere may either bite (for 4d6p) or grab it in its talons flying away to drop the hapless victim to its death.

If compelled to fight terrestrially, either due to being encountered in restricted territory or if faced with a stalwart opponent, a wyvern utilizes both its bite and a lethal stinger protruding from its whip-like tail. On the ground it must use its legs for balance and movement and thus cannot attack with these taloned appendages.

Those struck by the tail stinger suffer 1d6p+3 damage and must save vs. VF 14 poison. Failure indicates that the target suffers a loss of 2d6p Hit Points at a rate of 1 HP/second and is incapacitated by seizures and convulsions for 6d4p minutes (treat as a failed Threshold of Pain check). A natural 1 or 2 on the saving throw results in death from cardiac arrest at the end of the seizure. Success results in a mere loss of 1d6p hit point at the rate above plus a -1 penalty to Attack, Defense and Damage for 6d4p minutes (cumulative if repeatedly poisoned).

Habitat/Society:

Wyverns make their lairs in mountainous caves, preferably those adjoining or within deserts and other similar temperate climes, though sightings have also been reported in tropical regions as well as in the cold north. Their ability to fly also allows them to range across oceanic island chains as well as continents. Wyvern nests are littered with coins, gems and other shiny items

Wyverns are territorial and tend to remain in what they consider their range. They are found mostly alone or in pairs, but may come together in small groups of three to eight related individuals (usually siblings or cousins) at the start of each breeding season. Mated pairs are briefly monogamous, remaining together only until the hatchlings mature. Should one of the two die, the survivor searches out a new partner.

The breeding season is determined by cycles of hatching, rainfall and availability of food, but generally takes place twice each year in early spring and late summer. Female wyverns generally lay five to eight almost spherical eggs that hatch 4 to 5 months after they are laid. Multiple hatchlings of less than 1-foot long are born, though only the most aggressive one survives for long (as it kills and consumes its brothers or sisters shortly after hatching). Wyverns are quick to mature for dragonkind, taking only 20 or 30 years to do so.

A wyvern's natural lifespan lasts for several centuries.

Ecology:

Wyverns are omnivores, but prefer meat (even carrion) to grains and other vegetable substances. When feeding, a wyvern will gorge itself until its gullet bulges to overflowing. Afterwards, the wyvern sits in a torpid stupor for well over an hour while the food digests (giving the creature a -4 penalty to Defense rolls during that time).

Although mainly active during twilight, wyverns may also be active during the day, particularly during mating seasons.

On Tellene:

The Sliv Elenon mountains are known to be a primary habitat of wyverns, among other dangerous creatures. One interesting superstition regarding wyverns is common to Alnarma and other desert settlements. The superstition goes that, as well as being dangerous predators, the sighting of a number of wyverns is also a herald that someone in the settlement will die an unusual death before the morning dawn.

WYVERN

HIT POINTS:	35+7d8
SIZE/WEIGHT:	G/1 ton
TENACITY:	Brave
INTELLIGENCE:	Obtuse
FATIGUE FACTOR:	-3

SPEED 5 — INIT -2
ATTACK +13
DMG REDUCTION
DEFENSE +6 — 9
see below
medium REACH — DAMAGE
TOP SAVE ▼ 12

MOVEMENT

CRAWL:	5
WALK:	10
JOG:	15
RUN:	20
FLY:	30

SAVES

PHYSICAL:	+14
MENTAL:	+10
DODGE:	+13

ATTACK:
May attack from flight doing 4d10p if successful; terrestrially attacks every 5 seconds with either 4d6p bite or 1d6p+3 stinger. Stinger also has VF 14 poison (see text for details).

SPECIAL ABILITIES:
Listening mastery of 60%; Flight

GENERAL INFO

ACTIVITY CYCLE:	Crepuscular
NO. APPEARING:	1-8
% CHANCE IN LAIR:	25%
FREQUENCY:	Sporadic
ALIGNMENT:	Neutral Evil
VISION TYPE:	Can spot targets up to 1000 feet away
AWARENESS/SENSES:	Good hearing (Listening 60%)
HABITAT:	Caves
DIET:	Omnivorous
ORGANIZATION:	Individuals or familial
CLIMATE/TERRAIN:	Any wilderness, save arctic

YIELD

MEDICINAL:	nil
SPELL COMPONENTS:	unknown; scholarly research is needed
HIDE/TROPHY:	hide for clothing, bone for tools, head for trophy
TREASURE:	hoard of coins and miscellanous valuables
EDIBLE:	no, meat is foul and inedible
OTHER:	nil
EXPERIENCE POINT VALUE:	925

W

YETI
Also Known As: The Abominable

These strange creatures do not appear to use tools or weapons.

The abominable is expert at avoiding detection and blending into its environment.

We were scouting in the Deshada mountains, looking for a cave where this old magic stone tablet was supposed to be hidden, when I saw my first yeti. To be fair, I guess it saw me first — that white fur gives them a big advantage hiding in the snow and on snow-covered boulders. I was alone, since we had all split up to try and find this cave faster, which was a bad idea to start with. Never go off on your own if you can help it.

So, I felt this big eruption of snow behind me that hit the back of my head, and I turned to look just as what I thought was a white furry troll leaped out of the snow. It swung its long, clawed arms and crushed the breath from my body before I could even grab the hilt of my sword. That's another thing - wear gloves when you go up the mountains. If you don't, you should have your sword drawn anyway. Better a couple of frozen fingers stuck to its metal hilt than your dead body lying in the snow.

When I woke up I was hanging upside down with my back against an icy cave wall somewhere inside the mountain. Seems the yeti had stuck my legs in a hole in the wall and packed it with snow so it hardened around them — and there was nothing I could do. I could see my sword on the ground below, spotted with what looked like a lot of my blood, near a pile of old bones, but I couldn't reach it.

If I had been a mage then maybe I could have teleported my sword into my hand. You can bet it would have been a fair fight then. I'd have been the one to decorate my nice warm drawing room with a stuffed yeti corpse. See how he likes it.

As it was, I had to wait for rescue, and didn't even get the pleasure of killing the beast myself. - §

A yeti resembles a tall, muscular human with an ape-like face and limbs, and a body covered in long white fur. Its long limbs end in clawed hands and feet, and its mouth is full of sharp teeth. The typical adult stands about 8 feet tall and weighs around 450 pounds. During the summer months, a yeti will often molt and take on a more gray-brown color. This is especially true anytime a yeti spends an inordinate amount of time at lower elevations lacking in snow.

Combat/Tactics:

Yetis prefer to ambush prey. They burrow in the snow, pounce from advantageous heights, or follow prey through snowstorms so that they cannot be detected. When attacking at twilight, they approach from the direction of the sun (if possible) to hide their presence until it is too late. Despite their size, yetis are experts at hiding. Should man-like victims approach, the yeti leaps out of hiding, using strong arms to crush its victim in a nigh-unbreakable hug. Abominables always use one initiative die lower.

SIGN/TRACKS	RANGE ON TELLENE	SIZE COMPARISON

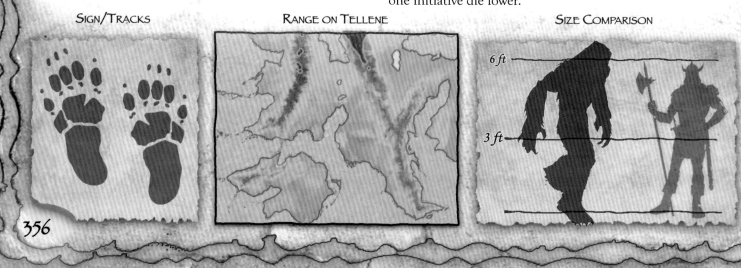

6 ft

3 ft

They attack with their bear-like claws (2d4p+5 each). Two successful consecutive attacks indicate they have grabbed their opponents and can crush them in their embrace inflicting an automatic 2d4p+5 damage every 5 seconds thereafter. The Yeti's hug can be broken by anyone striking it severely enough to cause a knock-back or by the held victim succeeding at a Feat of Strength (*vs. d20p+15*). The latter can be attempted every five seconds. Held prey is incapable of fighting back.

Habitat/Society:

This mysterious beast lives a mostly isolated life in cold mountainous regions, keeping its ravenous hunger at bay by feeding on small mammals and plants. Food sources are often scarce and yetis have been known to roam great distances in search of prey. Yetis are primitive creatures; they possess no knowledge of tools and can often be outsmarted. They hunt and live as animals. Despite this they are still extremely dangerous creatures when encountered.

Yetis live in small bands, or families, numbering up to six. Larger groups have a difficult time finding a reliable food source and most often break apart in order to survive. Yetis freely mate and fight with others of their kind as they desire. Generally there is one alpha male but the pecking order changes often, as battles for dominance are common. Young yetis mature in three years and generally leave their family upon maturation in search of food and to start their own family.

Ecology:

A yeti subsists primarily on the meat of small mammals that live high in the reaches of the mountains of Tellene. They hunt caribou, bear, wolves, mountain goats, cougars and even men when the opportunity presents itself. Large mountain cats and other monstrous creatures may compete for food with yetis.

Yetis are covered by a coat of thick, long, white fur with several thin layers of specialized fat underneath. As a result they are completely immune to the natural elements of cold. They are extremely patient hunters and can lie in wait, unmoving for hours at a time. During these periods of inactivity their heart rate slows to a nearly catatonic state. The same is true when a yeti sleeps after consuming a large meal, and is as close as a yeti comes to hibernating.

On Tellene:

Yetis are found in sub-artic, and artic mountainous regions on Tellene. They have been spotted in the highest reaches of the Krond Heights and Legasa Peaks, but are most commonly found in the Deshada Mountains.

Many sages say that yeti enjoy the screams of torment from prey. Those that have survived yeti encounters recount tales of being wounded or maimed by the beasts, then left to die, knowing the yeti was stalking them through the snow as they ran screaming for their lives. Others claim the howl of a yeti is so powerful and terrifying as to paralyze those that hear it.

[1]*A fistful of yeti fur, used as an additional material component in the cleric's second level Endure Temperature spell (Endure Cold only), increases the spell duration by 20% (round down).*

YETI

HIT POINTS:	30+5d8
SIZE/WEIGHT:	L/450 lbs.
TENACITY:	Brave
INTELLIGENCE:	Animal, High
FATIGUE FACTOR:	-2

SPEED	INIT
5	-2
ATTACK +8	DMG REDUCTION
DEFENSE +6	10
see below	
medium REACH	DAMAGE 9
	TOP SAVE

MOVEMENT

CRAWL:	2½
WALK:	5
JOG:	10
RUN:	15
SPRINT:	20

SAVES

PHYSICAL:	+11
MENTAL:	+5
DODGE:	+7

ATTACK:
Attack with claw for 2d4p+5 points of damage. If both claws hit consecutively, yeti hugs for 2d4p+5 points every 5 sec (break with Feat of Strength *vs d20p+15* or knock-back).

SPECIAL:
DR 15 versus any cold-based attack. Hiding mastery of 80%.; Initiative die one better

GENERAL INFO

ACTIVITY CYCLE:	Diurnal
NO. APPEARING:	1-6
% CHANCE IN LAIR:	50
FREQUENCY:	Sporadic
ALIGNMENT:	Non
VISION TYPE:	Standard
AWARENESS/SENSES:	Standard
HABITAT:	Caves
DIET:	Carnivorous
ORGANIZATION:	Individuals or Family
CLIMATE/TERRAIN:	Artic to subarctic mountains

YIELD

MEDICINAL:	bathing in yeti blood is said to cure frostbite
SPELL COMPONENTS:	fur, in Endure Temperature (Cold only) spell[1]
HIDE/TROPHY:	some folk value yeti hides as rugs
TREASURE:	incidental
EDIBLE:	yes, but tough and stringy
OTHER:	nil
EXPERIENCE POINT VALUE:	417

Y

ZOMBIE

ZOMBIE
MONSTER ZOMBIE

Also Known As:
Zuvembie

Slowly they came on upon us, I knew not if the horrors were attracted by our torchlight or the cacophony of noises our band made as we explored the ruins. Numerous quarrels seemed to have scant effect on the pack as the bolts lodged themselves within their putrid flesh.

Undeterred by our fusillade, the zombies staggered into our midst seeking to grab ahold of limbs, cloaks, armor, hair, anything they could grasp or, failing that, overbear those who would bar their advance. Only numerous heavy blows proved effective in dispatching these animated corpses for incidental, painful-looking wounds did not deter the creatures in the least.

When a zombie did grasp one of our number, it held fast necessitating he to focus his energy upon breaking the hold of the corpse. Upon failing to do so, the warrior was further beset by the zombie, which upon gaining further hold on the fighting man proceeded to gnaw upon his flesh. His heavy mail coat offered scant protection from the ravenous creature as it chose to bite his face, hands and any other exposed flesh. Ensnarement in the creature's grasp severely hindered my ally's ability to deliver the stout blows required to harm his attacker. Once grappled, several additional living corpses best upon him and, owing to the man's compromised defenses, were able to easily latch on to his person and tear, bend and rend his flesh.

Indeed it was only the divine grace of the Shining One, blessed be He, that spared our young comrade that day, for zombies have but a minor bond with the dark energies sustaining their unnatural existence. When finally able to proffer my divine icon, the wretches immediately released their victim and shambled away. We made haste to depart the region for we did know that speed and distance offered us the greatest measure of protection. - ◉ 〇

"A'gin all that's holy and right, beware my child the zombie at night" - old Deju saying.

Most zombies are mindless human or near-human (e.g., various man-sized humanoids or demi-humans) corpses stolen or risen from their graves. Some evil priests favor the cadavers of large bipedal monsters (e.g., bugbears, gnoles, and minotaurs), should they have access to them.

Many zombies make a soft groaning sound when advancing toward their victims, but they cannot speak and have no memory of their former lives. They walk with a slow, shambling gait, moving their putrid corpses onward like the grim inevitability of approaching death.

Though they are generally devoid of treasure or belongings, zombies do wear their burial garments; fresher zombies may be in finery or even jewelry. While they walk the earth under their master's orders, they tend to ruin or lose anything of value.

Except in very dry areas where they desiccate, or in the extreme cold where they freeze, zombies decompose over time and may look much like skeletons (but never become them). Once their tendons and muscles deteriorate completely, they collapse in a pile of bones, never to rise again (although the proper ritual can be used to raise them as skeletons).

SIGN/TRACKS

Little is to be gained by battling zombies save if they serve as a ward to bar thine approach to an unhallowed shrine whose destruction ye are charged with. They are not swift afoot thus lead them on a chase most merry until thou shouldest reach an obstacle whose circumvention they are incapable of.

WILL FACTOR
3*
© Monster Zombie

SIZE COMPARISON

6 ft

3 ft

ZOMBIE

HIT POINTS: 24+2d8

SIZE/WEIGHT: M/150 lbs.

TENACITY: Fearless

INTELLIGENCE: Non

FATIGUE FACTOR: n/a

SPEED 10 | INIT 6
ATTACK +4
DEFENSE 0 | DMG REDUCTION 8
DAMAGE d4p
REACH short | TOP SAVE ▼ | n/a

MOVEMENT

CRAWL: 1¼

WALK: 2½

JOG: 5

RUN: 7½

SPRINT: 10

SAVES

PHYSICAL: +4

MENTAL: immune

DODGE: +0

ATTACK:
Automatic bite damage after two successful grab attacks, and every 10 seconds thereafter. Break free with Feat of Strength (vs d20p+12) or knock-back.

SPECIAL DEFENSES:
Grabbed characters attacking with weapon larger than a dagger/knife are limited to d6p base weapon damage.

GENERAL INFO

ACTIVITY CYCLE:	Any
NO. APPEARING:	1-20
% CHANCE IN LAIR:	n/a
FREQUENCY:	Infrequent
ALIGNMENT:	Non
VISION TYPE:	Standard
AWARENESS/SENSES:	Standard
HABITAT:	Any, as dictated by master
DIET:	n/a
ORGANIZATION:	Thralls
CLIMATE/TERRAIN:	Any, as dictated by master

YIELD

MEDICINAL:	nil
SPELL COMPONENTS:	bodies, for 12th level Animate Zombies spell
HIDE/TROPHY:	nil
TREASURE:	incidental
EDIBLE:	no
OTHER:	nil
EXPERIENCE POINT VALUE:	100

MONSTER ZOMBIE

HIT POINTS: 30+4d8

SIZE/WEIGHT: L/250+ lbs.

TENACITY: Fearless

INTELLIGENCE: Non

FATIGUE FACTOR: n/a

SPEED 10 | INIT 6
ATTACK +8
DEFENSE 0 | DMG REDUCTION 12
DAMAGE 2d4p
REACH short | TOP SAVE ▼ | n/a

MOVEMENT

CRAWL: 1¼

WALK: 2½

JOG: 5

RUN: 7½

SPRINT: 10

SAVES

PHYSICAL: +8

MENTAL: immune

DODGE: +0

ATTACK:
Automatic bite damage after two successful grab attacks, and every 10 seconds thereafter. Break free with Feat of Strength (vs d20p+16) or knock-back.

SPECIAL DEFENSES:
Grabbed characters attacking with weapon larger than a dagger/knife are limited to d6p base weapon damage.

GENERAL INFO

ACTIVITY CYCLE:	Any
NO. APPEARING:	1-10
% CHANCE IN LAIR:	n/a
FREQUENCY:	Sporadic
ALIGNMENT:	Non
VISION TYPE:	Standard
AWARENESS/SENSES:	Standard
HABITAT:	Any, as dictated by master
DIET:	n/a
ORGANIZATION:	Thralls
CLIMATE/TERRAIN:	Any, as dictated by master

YIELD

MEDICINAL:	nil
SPELL COMPONENTS:	bodies, for 12th level Animate Zombies spell
HIDE/TROPHY:	nil
TREASURE:	incidental
EDIBLE:	no
OTHER:	nil
EXPERIENCE POINT VALUE:	266

Z

Combat/Tactics:

A zombie attacks by grabbing its foe. Immediately after the second successful grab attack, any adjacent zombie (including, but not limited to any zombies grabbing on) bites the victim for an automatic d4p (or 2d4p for monster zombies), ignoring any armor (but not natural defenses such as a thick hide, etc.). Every 10 seconds thereafter, each such zombie does an automatic bite attack and grabs hold as well!

Multiple zombies can feed on a grabbed foe and only two grab attacks are necessary from any combination of zombies attacking. A zombie that has grabbed a character can be removed with a successful knock-back or Feat of Strength (vs. *d20p+12* for normal zombies, or vs. *d20p+16* for monsterous). Monster zombies, being appreciably larger and stronger, are harder to knock-back or break free of, making them even more dangerous than they might first appear.

While caught, a victim can attack most effectively with a dagger or knife. Trying to attack with other weapons is feasible, but such base weapon damage is limited to d6p (plus Strength and other relevant factors).

Though sluggish, zombies do not tire. A sustained battle with a pack of zombies may prove a harrowing experience as the creatures relentless attack unfettered by fatigue or pain and able to shrug off all but the more severe of wounds. As with skeletons, a zombie is no more than an evil automaton and so unaffected by magic seeking to influence the will or more basic functions of biology.

Zombies have a Strength of 12 (or 16 for monster zombies) when determining Feat of Strength checks, such as battering down a door. Note that zombies are relentless and eventually destroy most obstacles in their way, but tend to give up after an hour or so and merely stand in place to await new orders or the re-appearance of their victims.

Habitat/Society:

Zombies are unnaturally invigorated corpses with no natural role. Many are animated by evil clergy for some particular function – usually to spread fear and chaos as marauders, for they are not as easily controlled than skeletons and so less suited to passive tasks.

Left to its own devices, a zombie shambles about aimlessly until it succumbs to some natural hazard such as being swept away by a river or tumbling down a cliff face. Barring such destruction, its spirit eventually wanes (in 2d4 weeks). The zombie simply ceases moving and becomes once again the corpse it was prior to animation, collapsing in a heap on the spot where it stands.

Ecology:

Zombies controlled by an evil priest do not need to eat to survive. Few creatures can abide their presence, and only larger and more powerful carrion-eaters turn the tables and seek them out as prey.

On Tellene:

The Congregation of the Dead is ultimately responsible for many of the zombies found in the world, frequently employing them to sow terror in locals who would otherwise not countenance their presence. However, it must be noted that spontaneous mass risings of the dead have been recorded by scholars without the seeming intervention of these unholy covens.

It is rumored that zombies abound in the 'city of the dead,' a fabled lost ruin deep within the Khydoban Desert. Wilder tales declare that the entire population of the city was cursed and transformed into zombies who survive to this very day in a desiccated but very animated state.

My Night of the Walking Dead

It was several years ago that I found myself allied with a band of treasure hunters, gazing down at the bleeding corpse of a high-ranking Harvester priest. Though I normally try to avoid direct confrontations, I'd been assured that I'd only be responsible for getting this little group into his subterranean temple, and could leave the fighting to them. Naturally, it didn't work out that way. I'd actually been the one to strike the final blow, thrust deep into the evil one's back.

That meant I was the only one to hear the priest's last words — a mumbled prayer to his dark god — before the endless sleep took him. So, while my erstwhile allies celebrated by looting the chamber, I remained uneasy and watchful, and was the first to see his slain guards stiffen, touched by the last of his power as it thinned out to cover the temple, like water flowing down the stone steps.

I cried a warning even as I slipped into the dark, while the dead-alive — a dozen zuvembies still in armor — stood upward in one accord and moved to attack the living who remained in the light. I helped as I could, moving from shadow to shadow and striking blows that would have felled a living man, but it soon became clear to me that it was futile.

One by one my companions fell and I realized that I would soon be next, since the undead stood between me and the door. Then, suddenly, the last fighting man turned and fled down the stairs. The undead followed, and I found myself alone save for the broken, still-dead bodies of my companions.

Quickly filling my packs with the best and lightest valuables that were now rightfully mine, I prostrated myself against the wall and quietly followed the shambling horrors down the steps. If I made a single noise, I knew, they would turn and spot me with their unmoving eyes, even in the darkest of shadows.

In the distance, I heard the fighter's death scream, so hideous it nearly made me miss my footing on the narrow stairs. I could not understand it, since those dead creatures were still in my sight and none were fast enough to have caught a fleeing man.

Eventually, the plodding creatures continued on into the temple proper, and I took the opportunity to slip from the corridor into the sacristy, where I watched though the keyhole.

Here and there amongst the pews had lain the dozens of cultists we slew on our way in. Now, however, they stood with their heads lifted and bloodied husks risen to their feet on uncertain limbs. All surrounded the fighter's body, as if his now unmoving corpse was the final altar in this temple of the dead. It seemed the high priest's final prayer had more power than I expected, to reach his followers outside the room of his death.

The thought jarred any lingering fear from my head. If I was going to escape, now would be the time. All I needed to do was keep quiet and out of sight. I stood, ignoring the cramped stiffness of my legs from where I'd been kneeling to peer through the keyhole, and ever so slowly inched the door open again. It seemed to be well-oiled, such a gift that I almost breathed a prayer of thanks to Risk but, realizing where I was, decided better for it. He might choose this moment to test me if I were foolish enough to show my peril.

With all my senses taut, I snuck quietly out into what had once been the main place of worship, sticking quietly to the shadows and pausing frequently to listen for the slightest scrape of boot upon stone. A scattering of areas were still lit by torchlight, but only when I was certain that none of the undead faces were turned in my direction did I dare slip through the light.

Then, as I neared a low window, an idea struck me. There was naught beneath but a hundred foot drop — and zuvembies, I knew, could not climb.

Shouting my loudest, I leaped into the sill as the undead faces turned toward me. There was no intelligence in the vacuous eyes, no thought, and little life in the wide-mouthed stares. Still, they ambled towards me like a tidal wave of death.

When they were nearly upon me, I easily climbed out the window and sideways along the crude stone. As I suspected, each one attempted to follow and so fell to a shattered pulp on the rocks below. Even when no more appeared, I waited until my arms were weary and ready to fail before slipping back inside and looting the temple at my leisure. —

ZOMBIE, BRAIN-EATING

Are they truly foul undead or merely men under a vile curse?

Also Known As: Infected, Living Dead, Zombii

I used to enjoy killing zombies — though I guess 'killing' isn't the right word since they were already dead to start with. They're scary for sure, but they're dumb and have to follow whatever orders their master gave them. They're really slow, too, easy to get away from unless you are fool enough to let yourself get surrounded. That's an easy way to end up dead, but you will probably be okay if you keep moving, and especially if you have a cleric with you.

That's what I used to think, anyway. The last time I ran into zombies it was lot different. I heard our druid say that the same kinds of monsters may have different habits if they live in different places. Maybe the zombies I saw were like that. I hope so — if the Harvester has blessed zombies so they can start running and getting smarter then we're all in trouble.

Oh, what happened last time was when me and my party were hired to investigate this family crypt on the outskirts of the city. Strange lights had been seen there at night and everyone else was too scared to go near it. Well, we ransacked the crypt and smashed up all the bodies inside so we wouldn't have to worry about undead while we were hiding out and waiting for the lights. And you know what, the family was not happy about it when they found out. They just didn't understand the logic of it all and kept complaining about desecration. Some people.

In the end it turned out that the culprit was just a will-o'-the-wisp, and it wasn't too hard to deal with. The real problem came when we went back to the inn for the night. After a few drinks paid for with crypt loot, the innkeeper locked up early, complaining he felt sick, so we went to bed.

Downstairs we came the next morning to find a whole room of dead people — the innkeeper and his family, and a bunch of villagers we'd been drinking with. As we poked at them, they rose up, moaning like zombies. Our cleric stepped up with his holy icon to keep them back — and for a second it seemed to work. Then their moans turned into screams and they ran up to him at full speed, swarming and pulling him to the ground while they ripped him apart.

The last I saw before I ran up the stairs and out the upstairs window was the innkeeper and his daughter digging at the cleric like he was a berry pie. I used to like berry pie. - ☩

Brain-eating zombies are diseased individuals with a monstrous craving to feed on the brains of other sapient creatures. They are not actually undead, but may easily be mistaken for true zombies.

As well as being drawn toward any living creature they can sense, brain-eating zombies are also attracted by loud noises and bright lights. Consequently, a noisy scuffle with a lone brain-eater is bound to attract the attention of any others nearby and permit them the time to close in.

Combat/Tactics:

Brain-eating zombies attack by grabbing their foe. Once two successful (albeit non-injurious) attacks have been made, the brain-eating zombie has overborn its victim. It inflicts an automatic d6p bite immediately after the second successful grab attack and every 10 seconds thereafter. This bite ignores armor (but not natural defenses such as thick hide). Brain-eaters can be removed with a knock-back or Feat of Strength (vs. d20p+13). Multiple brain-eaters can feed on a grabbed foe and

If you get bit by a zombii, get your comrades to tie you up right quick. Tell them to pour some water and ale in your mouth every day so you don't die of thirst, and you might be restored within a week. If not, they might as well kill you right away.

RANGE ON TELLENE

SIZE COMPARISON

6 ft

3 ft

only two grab attacks are necessary from any combination of attacking zombies.

A held victim can attack most effectively with a dagger or knife. Trying to attack with other weapons is feasible, but such base weapon damage is limited to d6p (plus Strength and other relevant factors).

These diseased creatures have a Strength of 13 for determining Feat of Strength checks, such as battering down a door. Unlike true zombies, brain-eaters retain enough cognitive ability to work simple items (such as pulling shutters or turning doorknobs) and to discern alternative access routes to blocked areas that would frustrate a true undead zombie.

Because brain-eating zombies are not true undead, they cannot be turned.

Living Death Disease:

Also known as 'the wandering sickness,' this disease causes memory loss and inflicts a raging madness upon its host's brain as it destroys brain cells over time. It is typically transmitted by the bite of an infected individual, but occasionally by other unknown forms of contact.

The living death disease has a communicability of d20p+12 and a severity of d20p+12. If the PC fails his saving throw (d20p+CON) against communicability, he contracts the disease and must check for severity. If this second saving throw succeeds, the PC suffers only the Minor Effect. If failed, he suffers the Major Effect.

Minor Effect: Within 1d4 hours, depending on the distance the virus must travel to reach the central nervous system, an infected individual suffers intense nerve pain throughout his entire body and becomes a rage-crazed homicidal maniac desiring only to kill and eat brains. This madness lasts for 36+2d12p hours, after which the pain and madness begins to dissipate over a further 12 hours.

Major Effect: As above, but the effect is permanent. Necrosis begins to affect the body within days, eventually making the victim impossible to differentiate from a true zombie. Death occurs within three months, after which the body may be animated as a true zombie (or skeleton, depending on the condition of the corpse).

Habitat/Society:

These brain-devourering creatures appear wherever the living death disease manifests itself. If left unchecked, a single brain-eating zombie could spread the disease so rapidly that a city of one million residents becomes overrun in no more than seven to 10 days.

Ecology:

The brain-eaters have an instinctive lust for any brain matter, at least 5 pounds of which serves as an opiate for their constant neuropathic pain (but does not alleviate their madness).

On Tellene:

As far as is known, the living death has never caused a pandemic at any time in the history of the Sovereign Lands. Only the most favored clerics of the Rotlord are blessed with its knowledge, and their schemes for spreading it have so far been thwarted by the forces of good.

BRAIN-EATING ZOMBIE

HIT POINTS:	20+3d8
SIZE/WEIGHT:	M/175 lbs.
TENACITY:	Fearless
INTELLIGENCE:	Obtuse
FATIGUE FACTOR:	n/a

MOVEMENT

CRAWL:	2½
WALK:	5
JOG:	10
RUN:	15
SPRINT:	20

SAVES

PHYSICAL:	+7
MENTAL:	immune
DODGE:	+2

ATTACK: Automatic bite damage after two successful grab attacks, and every 10 seconds thereafter. Break free with FoS (vs d20p+13) or knock-back. Bite inflicts living death disease (communicability 12, severity 12).

SPECIAL DEFENSES: Cannot be turned. Consuming at least 5 pounds of brains regenerates 5 HP; consuming less provides no benefit.

GENERAL INFO

ACTIVITY CYCLE:	Any
NO. APPEARING:	3-24
% CHANCE IN LAIR:	n/a
FREQUENCY:	Unusual
ALIGNMENT:	Non
VISION TYPE:	Standard
AWARENESS/SENSES:	Standard
HABITAT:	Any
DIET:	Carnivorous
ORGANIZATION:	Individuals
CLIMATE/TERRAIN:	Any

YIELD

MEDICINAL:	nil
SPELL COMPONENTS:	nil
HIDE/TROPHY:	nil
TREASURE:	incidental
EDIBLE:	yes, but automatic communicability (no save)
OTHER:	nil
EXPERIENCE POINT VALUE:	180

Customizing Humanoids

The humanoid creatures presented in this book are given game statistics that reflect their most commonly used compliment of armor and weaponry. This is a satisfactory solution for most encounters with said creatures and accurately reflects the humanoids' natural predilections for implements of butchery.

There may, however, be special circumstances wherein it is desirable to alter these norms. Designating a fraction of these creatures as lightly armed archers or conversely as heavily armored shock troops may serve to add variety and unexpected surprises for your players as they venture into a humanoid lair. The following discussion provides guidance on accomplishing these ends by changing the typical battle load.

Humanoid Ability Scores

The chart below provides a comparison of the baseline ability scores of humanoid bipeds. These figures are of necessity human-centric and reflect mean attributes for the race expressed in terms meaningful for comparison to *homo sapiens*. Intelligence, Wisdom and to a lesser degree, Charisma are certainly approximations for we are dealing with minds with a cognition and neurological makeup alien to our own and can only measure performance in similar acts of reasoning. Looks too are based on *human* ideals of beauty (those creatures listed as n/a are simply too fundamentally different for this score to have any meaning in the eyes of humanity).

Race	STR	INT	WIS	DEX	CON	LKS	CHA
Bugbear	17	10	10	16	17	7	8
Dwarf	11	11	11	11	15	9	8
Elf	9	11	11	13	7	13	14
Gnole	16	7	3	15	15	3	3
Gnome	9	11	11	13	11	9	12
Goblin	8	10	8	13	12	7	9
Grel	11	10	11	12	11	10	11
Halfling	7	11	12	13	12	11	11
Hobgoblin	13	10	11	13	12	9	11
Human	11	11	11	11	11	11	11
Kobold	6	12	10	12	8	9	8
Lizard Man	14	8	10	11	11	n/a	8
Orc	15	7	5	12	13	6	5
Pixie Fairy	3	13	10	15	7	15	11
Tröglodyte	14	6	5	10	10	n/a	8

Note also that just as with mankind, exceptional individuals with traits superior to the norm may be encountered. Such creatures are always atypical and should be handled on a case-by-case basis. Should you desire the inclusion of such a specimen, any benefits these enhanced scores yield should be added to the base combat abilities detailed hereafter.

Tread lightly before dramatically altering any individual creature's abilities and bear in mind the race's baseline. While there may indeed be a gnole with 15 Intelligence, this savant is likely the Einstein of his entire species.

Humanoid Raw Combat Scores

This chart lists combat scores sans armor and weapons. Using these base statistics, you can generate final combat abilities by designating armor and weapons and applying appropriate adjustments to Initiative, Speed and Defense.

Some may balk at these base statistics by comparing them to their own novice player characters and reverse-engineering the bonuses (or penalties) derived from the creature's ability scores alone. In so doing they reveal their utter narcissism and naiveté by presuming that the typical NPC dwarf (for example) has a comparable background to their own young and novice character. They cry foul without taking into account the possible experience that said dwarf might have had. Given his extended lifespan and incessant warfare with humanoids, said dwarf may well have (in contemporary American terms) fought in the Battles of Antietam and Gettysburg, crested San Juan Hill with Teddy Roosevelt, endured gas attacks at the Battle of the Marne, slogged through Guadalcanal, nearly froze at the Battle of Chosin Reservoir and participated in the Tet Offensive.

Likewise humanoids are more than a template of ability scores applied to a small, medium or large frame. While most are not as long-lived as their dwarven or elven foes, they have been engaging in combat since pubescence. With the exception of hobgoblins, this generally is not formal martial training but rather years of bitter skirmishing with rival clans. Adding to this battle experience are daily and frequently mortal clashes with their own kin for humanoids are not given to settling disputes via jurisprudence. It should be of no surprise that those surviving this environment are capable fighters. That such competence manifests itself differently from the stepwise progression of a human fighter is merely a reflection of the obvious fact that they are neither physiologically, psychologically nor socially human.

Base Combat Statistics (sans armor & weapons)

Race	Initiative	Speed	Attack	Defense	Damage	DR
Bugbear*	-1	-1	7	2	+4	3
Dwarf	3	-1	4	3	+1	0
Elf	0	-1	5	5	0	0
Gnole*	3	-2	5	-1	+3	2
Gnome	2	0	3	7	-1	0
Goblin	3	0	3	4	-1	0
Grel	0	-3/-1	6	5	+3	0
Halfling	1	0	1	6	-2	0
Hobgoblin	1	-1	5	2	+1	0
Human						0
Kobold	3	-1	2	5	-3	1
Lizard Man[A]	1	-2	3	0	+2	2
Orc	4	0	3	-1	+2	0
Pixie Fairy[A]	-1	see below	4	11	see below	0
Troglodyte[A]	1	-2	3	0	+2	2

* Bugbears and Gnoles typically both wear body armor giving them an additional 3 or 4 DR. However, as size L creatures, this only assesses defense and initiative penalties equivalent to leather or studded leather armor. The adjustments for any armor worn by these creatures should always be that of one armor type lighter. For example, a bugbear clad in chainmail and wielding a short sword would have the following combat statistics: Init 0; Speed 9; Attack 7; Defense -2; Damage 2d6p+4; DR 8.

[A]These creatures normally wear no armor. The initiative modifier for this condition (i.e. a -1 initiative modifier) is not incorporated into these base combat statistics. Bear this in mind should you designate any creature as unarmored.

Pixie Faries may employ a variety of tiny weapons. However, they are statistically indistinguishable. These weapons have a speed of 5 and inflict 1d4p damage on a successful hit regardless of the Pixie Faries' strength.

Customizing Humanoids

Utilizing the creature's base combat statistics, it is a simple matter to customize their armor and weaponry to suit your needs. For example, should you wish to designate a small band of orc thugs to challenge your novice players, you may wish to have them be unarmored and employ clubs. Knowing that wearing no armor provides them a -1 initiative bonus and a club has a base speed of 10, these orcs have the following combat statistics: Init 3; Speed 10; Attack 3; Defense -1; Damage 1d6p+1d4p+2; DR 0. As an additional example,

let's suppose you wished to make an elite squad of goblins wearing scalemail, employing small shields and using warhammers (perhaps all scavenged from an unfortunate band of dwarven miners). Scalemail provides excellent damage reduction but at a high defensive penalty. These particular goblins have the following combat statistics: Init 6; Speed 10; Attack 3; Defense 2; Damage 2d6p-1; DR 5.

Bugbear Leaders

Bugbear Leader

HIT POINTS:	48+d8
SIZE/WEIGHT:	L/375 lbs.
TENACITY:	Brave
INTELLIGENCE:	Average
FATIGUE FACTOR:	-5/-4

MOVEMENT

CRAWL:	2½
WALK:	5
JOG:	10
RUN:	15
SPRINT:	20

SAVES

PHYSICAL:	+8
MENTAL:	+7
DODGE:	+8

SPEED 11 | INIT -1
ATTACK +8 | DMG REDUCTION 7
DEFENSE +1 | DAMAGE by weapon +5
REACH: by weapon +1 foot | TOP SAVE 9

ATTACK:
Damage by human-type weapons with +5 bonus. They prefer great swords.

SPECIAL:
Possible shield use (e.g., medium shields increase Defense from +1 to +7). Body armor provides 4 DR. Hiding 50%, Listening 40%, Observation 55%, Sneaking 50%.

EPV: 280

Bugbear Chief

HIT POINTS:	56+d8
SIZE/WEIGHT:	L/400 lbs.
TENACITY:	Brave
INTELLIGENCE:	Average
FATIGUE FACTOR:	-5/-4

MOVEMENT

CRAWL:	2½
WALK:	5
JOG:	10
RUN:	15
SPRINT:	20

SAVES

PHYSICAL:	+9
MENTAL:	+8
DODGE:	+9

SPEED 11 | INIT -1
ATTACK +9 | DMG REDUCTION 8
DEFENSE +2 | DAMAGE by weapon +6
REACH: by weapon +1 foot | TOP SAVE 9

ATTACK:
Damage by human-type weapons with +6 bonus. They prefer great swords.

SPECIAL:
Possible shield use (e.g., medium shields increase Defense from +2 to +8). Body armor provides 5 DR. Hiding 50%, Listening 40%, Observation 60%, Sneaking 50%.

EPV: 425

Humanoid Leaders Base Combat Statistics (sans armor & weapons)

Race	Initiative	Speed	Attack	Defense	Damage	natural DR	Hit Points	Preferred Armor
Bugbear Leader	-2	-1	+8	+4	+5	3	48+d8	*better armor (total DR 7)*
Bugbear Chief	-2	-1	+9	+6	+6	3	56+d8	*better armor (total DR 8)*
Gnole Leader	1	-2	+6	0	+4	2	46	*ringmail equivalent*
Gnole Praetorian	-1	-3	+7	+2	+5	2	46+d8	*chainmail*
Gnole Clan Chief	-1	-3	+7	+2	+5	2	54	*chainmail*
Goblin Sergeant	2	0	+4	+6	0	0	23	*studded*
Goblin Captain	1	-1	+5	+7	+1	0	23+d8	*ringmail*
Goblin Sub-Chief	0	-2	+6	+7	+2	0	23+2d8	*chainmail*
Goblin Chief	-2	-2	+7	+5	+4	0	28+3d8	*plate mail*
Hobgoblin Sergeant	1	-1	+5	+2	+1	0	32	*standard armor*
Hobgoblin Lieutenant	-1	-2	+6	+4	+2	0	32+d10	*chainmail*
Hobgoblin Captain	-1	-3	+7	+5	+3	0	32+2d10	*splint mail*
Hobgoblin "Kruk"	-2	-4	+8	+6	+4	0	32+3d10	*plate mail*
Kobold Pack Leader	2	-1	+2	+6	-1	1	15+d6	*studded*
Kobold Alpha Male	2	-1	+4	+5	0	1	20+d8	*studded*
Kobold AlphaPlus Male	1	-2	+5	+6	+3	2	26+2d8	*ringmail*
Lizard Man Warrior Leader[A]	1	-2	+3	0	+2	2	37	*may wear armor if intelligent*
Lizard Man Warband Leader[A]	0	-2	+4	+1	+3	2	37+d8	*may wear armor if intelligent*
Lizard Man Sub-Chief[A]	0	-3	+5	+2	+4	2	37+2d8	*may wear armor if intelligent*
Lizard Man Chieftain[A]	-1	-4	+6	+3	+5	2	37+3d8	*may wear armor if intelligent*
Orc Leader	4	-1	+3	0	+2	0	31	*ringmail*
Orc Warband Leader	2	-2	+4	+2	+3	0	31+d8	*chainmail*
Orc Sub-Chief	2	-3	+5	+3	+4	0	31+2d8	*splint mail*
Orc Chieftain	1	-4	+6	+4	+5	0	31+3d8	*plate mail*
Black Orc (additional bonus)	-1	-1	+2	+2	+2			
Tröglodyte Leader[A]	0	-2	+4	+1	+3	2	36	*none*
Tröglodyte Warband Leader[A]	-1	-2	+5	+2	+4	2	36+d8	*none*
Tröglodyte Sub-Chief[A]	-1	-4	+6	+3	+5	2	36+2d8	*none*
Tröglodyte Chieftain[A]	-3	-2	+8	+4	+2	2	36	*none*

Bugbear Female

HIT POINTS: 32+d8
SIZE/WEIGHT: L/250 lbs.
TENACITY: Steady
INTELLIGENCE: Average
FATIGUE FACTOR: -5/-4

MOVEMENT
CRAWL: 2½
WALK: 5
JOG: 10
RUN: 15
SPRINT: 20

SAVES
PHYSICAL: +7
MENTAL: +6
DODGE: +7

SPEED 10 | INIT -1
ATTACK +7
DEFENSE +1 | DMG REDUCTION 5
REACH by weapon +1 foot | by weapon +2 | DAMAGE | TOP SAVE 7

ATTACK: Damage by human-type weapons with +2 bonus. They usually wield morning stars.

SPECIAL: Possible shield use (*e.g.*, medium shields increase Defense from +1 to +7). Minimal body armor provides 2 DR. Hiding 50%, Listening 40%, Observation 50%, Sneaking 50%.

EPV: 115

Bugbear Youth (stronger)

HIT POINTS: 20+d8
SIZE/WEIGHT: M/200 lbs.
TENACITY: Nervous
INTELLIGENCE: Average
FATIGUE FACTOR: -5/-4

MOVEMENT
CRAWL: 2½
WALK: 5
JOG: 10
RUN: 15
SPRINT: 20

SAVES
PHYSICAL: +4
MENTAL: +3
DODGE: +4

SPEED 10 | INIT -1
ATTACK +4
DEFENSE -2 | DMG REDUCTION 5
REACH by weapon | by weapon +1 | DAMAGE | TOP SAVE 7

ATTACK: Damage by human-type weapons with +1 bonus. They usually wield morning stars.

SPECIAL: Possible shield use (*e.g.*, medium shields increase Defense from -2 to +4). Minimal body armor provides 2 DR. Hiding 40%, Listening 30%, Observation 30%, Sneaking 35%.

EPV: 80

Gnole Leaders

Gnole Leader

HIT POINTS: 46
SIZE/WEIGHT: L/275 lbs.
TENACITY: Fearless
INTELLIGENCE: Slow
FATIGUE FACTOR: -2/-1

MOVEMENT
CRAWL: 5
WALK: 10
JOG: 15
RUN: 20
SPRINT: 25

SAVES
PHYSICAL: +7
MENTAL: +3
DODGE: +6

SPEED 10 | INIT 2
ATTACK +6
DEFENSE -3 | DMG REDUCTION 6
REACH by weapon +1 foot | by weapon +4 | DAMAGE | TOP SAVE 8

ATTACK: Gnoles can hurl axes and javelins to gain +4 damage while they advance on a foe. In melee they prefer great swords (d8p+d10p+4)

SPECIAL: Possible shield use (*e.g.*, shields increase Defense from -3 to +3). Body armor provides 4 DR.

EPV: 160

Gnole Praetorian/Clan Chief

HIT POINTS: 46+d8 or 54
SIZE/WEIGHT: L/300 lbs.
TENACITY: Fearless
INTELLIGENCE: Slow
FATIGUE FACTOR: -2/-1

MOVEMENT
CRAWL: 5
WALK: 10
JOG: 15
RUN: 20
SPRINT: 25

SAVES
PHYSICAL: +8
MENTAL: +4
DODGE: +7

SPEED 10 | INIT 0
ATTACK +7
DEFENSE -2 | DMG REDUCTION 7
REACH by weapon +1 foot | by weapon +5 | DAMAGE | TOP SAVE 8

ATTACK: These leader-types prefer great swords (d8p+d10p+5).

SPECIAL: Possible shield use (*e.g.*, shields increase Defense from -2 to +4). Body armor provides 5 DR.

EPV: 215

Goblin Leaders

Goblin Sergeant

HIT POINTS:	23
SIZE/WEIGHT:	S/90 lbs.
TENACITY:	Steady
INTELLIGENCE:	Slow
FATIGUE FACTOR:	-2/-1

MOVEMENT

CRAWL:	1¼
WALK:	2½
JOG:	5
RUN:	10
SPRINT:	15

SAVES

PHYSICAL:	+4
MENTAL:	+3
DODGE:	+5

SPEED 8 | INIT 3
ATTACK +4
DEFENSE +3
DMG REDUCTION 3
by weapon -1 foot
REACH
by weapon
DAMAGE
TOP SAVE 6

ATTACK: Goblin sergeants typically have a short sword (2d6p), studded leather armor and small shield.

DEFENSES: None explicitly, but most goblins are ingenious trap makers. *Shield use (e.g., small shields increases Defense from +3 to +7).

EPV: 32

Goblin Captain

HIT POINTS:	23+d8
SIZE/WEIGHT:	S/100 lbs.
TENACITY:	Steady
INTELLIGENCE:	Slow
FATIGUE FACTOR:	-2/-1

MOVEMENT

CRAWL:	1¼
WALK:	2½
JOG:	5
RUN:	10
SPRINT:	15

SAVES

PHYSICAL:	+5
MENTAL:	+3
DODGE:	+5

SPEED 8 | INIT 2
ATTACK +5
DEFENSE +3
DMG REDUCTION 4
by weapon -1 foot
REACH
by weapon +1
DAMAGE
TOP SAVE 6

ATTACK: Goblin sergeants typically have a short sword (2d6p), ringmail armor and small shield.

DEFENSES: None explicitly, but most goblins are ingenious trap makers. *Shield use (e.g., small shields increases Defense from +3 to +7).

EPV: 55

Goblin Sub-Chief

HIT POINTS:	23+2d8
SIZE/WEIGHT:	M/115 lbs.
TENACITY:	Brave
INTELLIGENCE:	Slow
FATIGUE FACTOR:	-2/-1

MOVEMENT

CRAWL:	2½
WALK:	5
JOG:	10
RUN:	15
SPRINT:	20

SAVES

PHYSICAL:	+6
MENTAL:	+5
DODGE:	+7

SPEED 10 | INIT 2
ATTACK +6
DEFENSE +2
DMG REDUCTION 5
by weapon
REACH
by weapon +2
DAMAGE
TOP SAVE 7

ATTACK: Goblin sub-chiefs typically have a long sword (2d8p), chainmail armor and small shield.

DEFENSES: None explicitly, but most goblins are ingenious trap makers. *Shield use (e.g., small shields increases Defense from +2 to +6).

EPV: 90

Goblin Chieftain

HIT POINTS:	28+3d8
SIZE/WEIGHT:	M/225 lbs.
TENACITY:	Brave
INTELLIGENCE:	Average
FATIGUE FACTOR:	-2/-1

MOVEMENT

CRAWL:	2½
WALK:	5
JOG:	10
RUN:	15
SPRINT:	20

SAVES

PHYSICAL:	+8
MENTAL:	+7
DODGE:	+7

SPEED 10 | INIT 0
ATTACK +7
DEFENSE 0
DMG REDUCTION 7
by weapon
REACH
by weapon +4
DAMAGE
TOP SAVE 7

ATTACK: Goblin chiefs typically have a long sword (2d8p), plate mail armor and medium shield.

DEFENSES: Shield use (e.g., shield increases Defense from 0 to +6).

EPV: 170

Hobgoblin Leaders

Hobgoblin Sergeant

HIT POINTS:	32
SIZE/WEIGHT:	M/175-300 lbs.
TENACITY:	Brave
INTELLIGENCE:	Average
FATIGUE FACTOR:	-1/-2

MOVEMENT

CRAWL:	2½
WALK:	5
JOG:	10
RUN:	15
SPRINT:	20

SAVES

PHYSICAL:	+5
MENTAL:	+5
DODGE:	+5

SPEED 10 — INIT 2 — ATTACK +5 — DMG REDUCTION 4 — DEFENSE -2 — DAMAGE by weapon +1 — REACH by weapon — TOP SAVE 6

ATTACK: Hobgoblin sergeants typically utilize armaments of their subordinates (longswords) but may use other weapons. Speed listed is for such weapon.

SPECIAL DEFENSES: Shield use (*e.g.*, medium shields increase Defense to +4)

EPV: 80

Hobgoblin Lieutenant

HIT POINTS:	32+d10
SIZE/WEIGHT:	M/175-300 lbs.
TENACITY:	Fearless
INTELLIGENCE:	Average
FATIGUE FACTOR:	-1/-2

MOVEMENT

CRAWL:	2½
WALK:	5
JOG:	10
RUN:	15
SPRINT:	20

SAVES

PHYSICAL:	+6
MENTAL:	+6
DODGE:	+6

SPEED 10 — INIT 1 — ATTACK +6 — DMG REDUCTION 5 — DEFENSE -1 — DAMAGE by weapon +2 — REACH by weapon — TOP SAVE 6

ATTACK: Hobgoblin lieutenants typically utilize armaments of their subordinates (longswords) but may use other weapons. Speed listed is for such weapon.

SPECIAL DEFENSES: Shield use (*e.g.*, medium shields increase Defense to +5); chainmail

EPV: 121

Hobgoblin Captain

HIT POINTS:	32+2d10
SIZE/WEIGHT:	M/175-300 lbs.
TENACITY:	Fearless
INTELLIGENCE:	Average
FATIGUE FACTOR:	-1/-2

MOVEMENT

CRAWL:	2½
WALK:	5
JOG:	10
RUN:	15
SPRINT:	20

SAVES

PHYSICAL:	+7
MENTAL:	+7
DODGE:	+7

SPEED 9 — INIT 1 — ATTACK +7 — DMG REDUCTION 6 — DEFENSE 0 — DAMAGE by weapon +3 — REACH by weapon — TOP SAVE 7

ATTACK: Hobgoblin captains typically utilize armaments of their subordinates (longswords) but may use other weapons. Speed listed is for such weapon.

SPECIAL DEFENSES: Shield use (*e.g.*, medium shields increase Defense to +6); splint mail

EPV: 188

Hobgoblin 'Kruk'

HIT POINTS:	32+3d10
SIZE/WEIGHT:	M/175-300 lbs.
TENACITY:	Fearless
INTELLIGENCE:	Average
FATIGUE FACTOR:	-1/-2

MOVEMENT

CRAWL:	2½
WALK:	5
JOG:	10
RUN:	15
SPRINT:	20

SAVES

PHYSICAL:	+8
MENTAL:	+8
DODGE:	+8

SPEED 8 — INIT 0 — ATTACK +8 — DMG REDUCTION 7 — DEFENSE +1 — DAMAGE by weapon +4 — REACH by weapon — TOP SAVE 8

ATTACK: Hobgoblin chiefs typically utilize armaments of their subordinates (longswords) but may use other weapons. Speed listed is for such weapon.

SPECIAL DEFENSES: Shield use (*e.g.*, medium shields increase Defense to +7); plate mail

EPV: 300

Lizard Man Leaders

Lizard Man Warrior Leader

HIT POINTS:	37
SIZE/WEIGHT:	M/150 lbs.
TENACITY:	Steady
INTELLIGENCE:	Slow
FATIGUE FACTOR:	-3/-2

SPEED 9 — INIT 0
ATTACK +3
DEFENSE 0 — DMG REDUCTION 2
REACH by weapon — DAMAGE by weapon +2
TOP SAVE 6

MOVEMENT

CRAWL:	2½
WALK:	5
JOG:	10
RUN:	15
SPRINT:	20

SAVES

PHYSICAL:	+3
MENTAL:	+2
DODGE:	+3

ATTACK: Lizard men favor morning stars that allow them to deal 2d8p+2 damage.

SPECIAL: Shield use (e.g, medium shields increase Defense to +6). One die better for Initiative. 20% penalty to Listening checks.

EPV: 36

Lizard Man Warband Leader

HIT POINTS:	37+d8
SIZE/WEIGHT:	M/150 lbs.
TENACITY:	Steady
INTELLIGENCE:	Slow
FATIGUE FACTOR:	-3/-2

SPEED 9 — INIT -1
ATTACK +4
DEFENSE +1 — DMG REDUCTION 2
REACH by weapon — DAMAGE by weapon +3
TOP SAVE 6

MOVEMENT

CRAWL:	2½
WALK:	5
JOG:	10
RUN:	15
SPRINT:	20

SAVES

PHYSICAL:	+3
MENTAL:	+2
DODGE:	+3

ATTACK: Lizard men favor morning stars that allow them to deal 2d8p+2 damage.

SPECIAL: Shield use (e.g, medium shields increase Defense to +6). One die better for Initiative. 20% penalty to Listening checks.

EPV: 67

Lizard Man Sub-Chief

HIT POINTS:	37+2d8
SIZE/WEIGHT:	M/150 lbs.
TENACITY:	Brave
INTELLIGENCE:	Slow
FATIGUE FACTOR:	-3/-2

SPEED 8 — INIT -1
ATTACK +5
DEFENSE +2 — DMG REDUCTION 2
REACH by weapon — DAMAGE by weapon +4
TOP SAVE 6

MOVEMENT

CRAWL:	2½
WALK:	5
JOG:	10
RUN:	15
SPRINT:	20

SAVES

PHYSICAL:	+3
MENTAL:	+2
DODGE:	+3

ATTACK: Lizard men favor morning stars that allow them to deal 2d8p+2 damage.

SPECIAL: Shield use (e.g, medium shields increase Defense to +6). One die better for Initiative. 20% penalty to Listening checks.

EPV: 150

Lizard Man Chief

HIT POINTS:	37+3d8
SIZE/WEIGHT:	M/150 lbs.
TENACITY:	Brave
INTELLIGENCE:	Average
FATIGUE FACTOR:	-3/-2

SPEED 7 — INIT -2
ATTACK +6
DEFENSE +3 — DMG REDUCTION 2
REACH by weapon — DAMAGE by weapon +5
TOP SAVE 6

MOVEMENT

CRAWL:	2½
WALK:	5
JOG:	10
RUN:	15
SPRINT:	20

SAVES

PHYSICAL:	+3
MENTAL:	+2
DODGE:	+3

ATTACK: Lizard men favor morning stars that allow them to deal 2d8p+2 damage.

SPECIAL: Shield use (e.g, medium shields increase Defense to +6). One die better for Initiative. 20% penalty to Listening checks.

EPV: 200

Lizard Man Leaders
(Intelligent Variety)

Lizard Man Warrior Leader (Intelligent)

HIT POINTS: 37
SIZE/WEIGHT: M/150 lbs.
TENACITY: Nervous
INTELLIGENCE: Slow
FATIGUE FACTOR: -3/-2

SPEED 9	ATTACK +3	INIT 1
DEFENSE -1	DMG REDUCTION 3	
REACH by weapon	DAMAGE by weapon +2	TOP SAVE 6 ▼

MOVEMENT

CRAWL: 2½
WALK: 5
JOG: 10
RUN: 15
SPRINT: 20

SAVES

PHYSICAL: +3
MENTAL: +2
DODGE: +3

ATTACK: Lizard men favor morning stars that allow them to deal 2d8p+2 damage.

SPECIAL: Shield use (e.g, medium shields increase Defense to +6). One die better for Initiative. 20% penalty to Listening checks.

EPV: 36

Lizard Man Warband Leader (Intelligent)

HIT POINTS: 37+d8
SIZE/WEIGHT: M/150 lbs.
TENACITY: Nervous
INTELLIGENCE: Average
FATIGUE FACTOR: -3/-2

SPEED 9	ATTACK +4	INIT 0
DEFENSE -1	DMG REDUCTION 4	
REACH by weapon	DAMAGE by weapon +3	TOP SAVE 6 ▼

MOVEMENT

CRAWL: 2½
WALK: 5
JOG: 10
RUN: 15
SPRINT: 20

SAVES

PHYSICAL: +3
MENTAL: +2
DODGE: +3

ATTACK: Lizard men favor morning stars that allow them to deal 2d8p+2 damage.

SPECIAL: Shield use (e.g, medium shields increase Defense to +6). One die better for Initiative. 20% penalty to Listening checks.

EPV: 67

Lizard Man Sub-Chief (Intelligent)

HIT POINTS: 37+2d8
SIZE/WEIGHT: M/150 lbs.
TENACITY: Steady
INTELLIGENCE: Bright
FATIGUE FACTOR: -3/-2

SPEED 8	ATTACK +5	INIT 0
DEFENSE -1	DMG REDUCTION 5	
REACH by weapon	DAMAGE by weapon +4	TOP SAVE 6 ▼

MOVEMENT

CRAWL: 2½
WALK: 5
JOG: 10
RUN: 15
SPRINT: 20

SAVES

PHYSICAL: +3
MENTAL: +2
DODGE: +3

ATTACK: Lizard men favor morning stars that allow them to deal 2d8p+2 damage.

SPECIAL: Shield use (e.g, medium shields increase Defense to +6). One die better for Initiative. 20% penalty to Listening checks.

EPV: 150

Lizard Man Chief (Intelligent)

HIT POINTS: 37+3d8
SIZE/WEIGHT: M/150 lbs.
TENACITY: Steady
INTELLIGENCE: Bright
FATIGUE FACTOR: -3/-2

SPEED 8	ATTACK +6	INIT -1
DEFENSE -1	DMG REDUCTION 6	
REACH by weapon	DAMAGE by weapon +5	TOP SAVE 6 ▼

MOVEMENT

CRAWL: 2½
WALK: 5
JOG: 10
RUN: 15
SPRINT: 20

SAVES

PHYSICAL: +3
MENTAL: +2
DODGE: +3

ATTACK: Lizard men favor morning stars that allow them to deal 2d8p+2 damage.

SPECIAL: Shield use (e.g, medium shields increase Defense to +6). One die better for Initiative. 20% penalty to Listening checks.

EPV: 200

Orc Leaders

Orc Leader

HIT POINTS:	31
SIZE/WEIGHT:	M/200 lbs.
TENACITY:	Nervous
INTELLIGENCE:	Slow
FATIGUE FACTOR:	-1/0

SPEED 9 · INIT 5
ATTACK +3
DEFENSE -4 · DMG REDUCTION 4
REACH by weapon · DAMAGE by weapon +2 · TOP SAVE 6

MOVEMENT

CRAWL:	2½
WALK:	5
JOG:	10
RUN:	15
SPRINT:	20

SAVES

PHYSICAL:	+4
MENTAL:	+1
DODGE:	+3

ATTACK: Orc leaders employ the same weapons as their troops (usually scimitars doing 2d8p) and wear ringmail armor. Stats reflect this equipment.

SPECIAL: Shield use (*e.g.*, medium shields provide a +6 bonus, increasing Defense to +2). Orcs get 20% bonuses to Listening and Observation skill checks.

EPV: 37

Orc Warband Leader

HIT POINTS:	31+d8
SIZE/WEIGHT:	M/225 lbs.
TENACITY:	Steady
INTELLIGENCE:	Slow
FATIGUE FACTOR:	-1/0

SPEED 9 · INIT 4
ATTACK +4
DEFENSE -3 · DMG REDUCTION 5
REACH by weapon · DAMAGE by weapon +3 · TOP SAVE 7

MOVEMENT

CRAWL:	2½
WALK:	5
JOG:	10
RUN:	15
SPRINT:	20

SAVES

PHYSICAL:	+5
MENTAL:	+2
DODGE:	+4

ATTACK: Orc warband leaders employ the same weapons as their troops (usually scimitars doing 2d8p) and wear chainmail armor. Stats reflect this equipment.

SPECIAL: Shield use (*e.g.*, medium shields provide a +6 bonus, increasing Defense to +3). Orcs get 20% bonuses to Listening and Observation skill checks.

EPV: 50

Orc Sub-Chief

HIT POINTS:	31+2d8
SIZE/WEIGHT:	M/250 lbs.
TENACITY:	Steady
INTELLIGENCE:	Slow
FATIGUE FACTOR:	-1/0

SPEED 8 · INIT 4
ATTACK +5
DEFENSE -2 · DMG REDUCTION 6
REACH by weapon · DAMAGE by weapon +4 · TOP SAVE 7

MOVEMENT

CRAWL:	2½
WALK:	5
JOG:	10
RUN:	15
SPRINT:	20

SAVES

PHYSICAL:	+6
MENTAL:	+4
DODGE:	+5

ATTACK: Orc sub-chiefs employ the same weapons as their troops (usually scimitars doing 2d8p) and wear splint mail armor. Stats reflect this equipment.

SPECIAL: Shield use (*e.g.*, medium shields provide a +6 bonus, increasing Defense to +4). Orcs get 20% bonuses to Listening and Observation skill checks.

EPV: 125

Orc Chieftain

HIT POINTS:	31+3d8
SIZE/WEIGHT:	M/275 lbs.
TENACITY:	Brave
INTELLIGENCE:	Slow
FATIGUE FACTOR:	-1/0

SPEED 7 · INIT 3
ATTACK +6
DEFENSE -1 · DMG REDUCTION 7
REACH by weapon · DAMAGE by weapon +5 · TOP SAVE 8

MOVEMENT

CRAWL:	2½
WALK:	5
JOG:	10
RUN:	15
SPRINT:	20

SAVES

PHYSICAL:	+7
MENTAL:	+5
DODGE:	+6

ATTACK: Orc chieftains employ the same weapons as their troops (usually scimitars doing 2d8p) and wear plate mail armor. Stats reflect this equipment. Will substitute high quality weapons if available.

SPECIAL: Shield use (*e.g.*, medium shields provide a +6 bonus, increasing Defense to +5). Orcs get 20% bonuses to Listening and Observation skill checks.

EPV: 170

Black Orc Leaders

Black Orc Leader

HIT POINTS:	31
SIZE/WEIGHT:	M/220 lbs.
TENACITY:	Fearless
INTELLIGENCE:	Slow
FATIGUE FACTOR:	-1/0

MOVEMENT

CRAWL:	2½
WALK:	5
JOG:	10
RUN:	15
SPRINT:	20

SAVES

PHYSICAL:	+6
MENTAL:	+3
DODGE:	+5

SPEED 8 / INIT 4 / ATTACK +5 / -2 / DMG REDUCTION 4 / DEFENSE / by weapon +4 / by weapon REACH / DAMAGE / TOP SAVE 7

ATTACK: Black orc leaders employ the same weapons as their troops (usually scimitars doing 2d8p) and wear ringmail armor. Stats reflect this equipment.

SPECIAL: Shield use (*e.g.*, medium shields provide a +6 bonus, increasing Defense to +1). Orcs get 20% bonuses to Listening and Observation skill checks.

EPV: 85

Black Orc Warband Leader

HIT POINTS:	31+d8
SIZE/WEIGHT:	M/250 lbs.
TENACITY:	Fearless
INTELLIGENCE:	Slow
FATIGUE FACTOR:	-1/0

MOVEMENT

CRAWL:	2½
WALK:	5
JOG:	10
RUN:	15
SPRINT:	20

SAVES

PHYSICAL:	+7
MENTAL:	+4
DODGE:	+6

SPEED 8 / INIT 3 / ATTACK +6 / -1 / DMG REDUCTION 5 / DEFENSE / by weapon +5 / by weapon REACH / DAMAGE / TOP SAVE 8

ATTACK: Orc warband leaders employ the same weapons as their troops (usually scimitars doing 2d8p) and wear chainmail armor. Stats reflect this equipment.

SPECIAL: Shield use (*e.g.*, medium shields provide a +6 bonus, increasing Defense to +2). Orcs get 20% bonuses to Listening and Observation skill checks.

EPV: 125

Black Orc Sub-Chief

HIT POINTS:	31+2d8
SIZE/WEIGHT:	M/270 lbs.
TENACITY:	Fearless
INTELLIGENCE:	Slow
FATIGUE FACTOR:	-1/0

MOVEMENT

CRAWL:	2½
WALK:	5
JOG:	10
RUN:	15
SPRINT:	20

SAVES

PHYSICAL:	+8
MENTAL:	+6
DODGE:	+7

SPEED 7 / INIT 3 / ATTACK +7 / 0 / DMG REDUCTION 6 / DEFENSE / by weapon +6 / by weapon REACH / DAMAGE / TOP SAVE 8

ATTACK: Black orc sub-chiefs leaders employ the same weapons as their troops (usually scimitars doing 2d8p) and wear splint mail armor. Stats reflect this equipment.

SPECIAL: Shield use (*e.g.*, medium shields provide a +6 bonus, increasing Defense to +5). Orcs get 20% bonuses to Listening and Observation skill checks.

EPV: 165

Black Orc Chieftain

HIT POINTS:	31+3d8
SIZE/WEIGHT:	M/290 lbs.
TENACITY:	Fearless
INTELLIGENCE:	Slow
FATIGUE FACTOR:	-1/0

MOVEMENT

CRAWL:	2½
WALK:	5
JOG:	10
RUN:	15
SPRINT:	20

SAVES

PHYSICAL:	+9
MENTAL:	+7
DODGE:	+8

SPEED 6 / INIT 2 / ATTACK +8 / +1 / DMG REDUCTION 7 / DEFENSE / by weapon +7 / by weapon REACH / DAMAGE / TOP SAVE 9

ATTACK: Black orc chiefs employ the same weapons as their troops (usually scimitars doing 2d8p) but will substitute high quality weapons if available. They wear plate mail armor and stats reflect this equipment.

SPECIAL: Shield use (*e.g.*, medium shields provide a +6 bonus, increasing Defense to +6). Orcs get 20% bonuses to Listening and Observation skill checks.

EPV: 375

Kobold Leaders

Kobold Pack Leader

HIT POINTS:	15+d6
SIZE/WEIGHT:	S/60 lbs.
TENACITY:	Steady
INTELLIGENCE:	Slow
FATIGUE FACTOR:	-1/0

MOVEMENT

CRAWL:	1¼
WALK:	2½
JOG:	5
RUN:	7½
SPRINT:	10

SAVES

PHYSICAL:	+3
MENTAL:	+2
DODGE:	+2

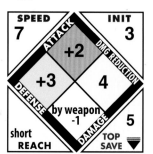

SPEED **7** — INIT **3**
ATTACK **+2**
DMG REDUCTION **4**
DEFENSE **+3**
by weapon **-1**
DAMAGE
short REACH — TOP SAVE **5**

ATTACK:
Kobolds pack leaders will wield the best weapons available to the kobold band (typically a human-made short sword). Combat statistics reflect this fact.

SPECIAL DEFENSES:
Shield use (*e.g.*, small shields increase Defense to +8).

EPV: 30

Kobold Alpha Male

HIT POINTS:	20+d8
SIZE/WEIGHT:	M/100 lbs.
TENACITY:	Brave
INTELLIGENCE:	Slow
FATIGUE FACTOR:	-1/0

MOVEMENT

CRAWL:	2½
WALK:	5
JOG:	7½
RUN:	10
SPRINT:	15

SAVES

PHYSICAL:	+5
MENTAL:	+4
DODGE:	+4

SPEED **9** — INIT **3**
ATTACK **+4**
DMG REDUCTION **4**
DEFENSE **+2**
by weapon
DAMAGE **6**
medium REACH — TOP SAVE

ATTACK: Kobold alpha males will wield the best weapons available to the kobold band (typically a human-made long sword) and wear studded leather armor. Combat statistics reflect this fact.

SPECIAL DEFENSES:
Shield use (*e.g.*, medium shield increases Defense to +8).

EPV: 50

Kobold Alpha-Plus Male

HIT POINTS:	26+2d8
SIZE/WEIGHT:	M/150 lbs.
TENACITY:	Brave
INTELLIGENCE:	Slow
FATIGUE FACTOR:	-1/0

MOVEMENT

CRAWL:	2½
WALK:	5
JOG:	7½
RUN:	10
SPRINT:	15

SAVES

PHYSICAL:	+6
MENTAL:	+5
DODGE:	+5

SPEED **9** — INIT **2**
ATTACK **+5**
DMG REDUCTION **6**
DEFENSE **+2**
by weapon **+3**
DAMAGE **7**
medium REACH — TOP SAVE

ATTACK: Kobold alpha+ males will wield the best weapons available to the kobold band (typically a human-made long sword) and wear ringmail. Combat statistics reflect this fact.

SPECIAL DEFENSES:
Shield use (*e.g.*, medium shield increases Defense to +8).

EPV: 150

Tröglodyte Leaders

Tröglodyte Leader

HIT POINTS:	36
SIZE/WEIGHT:	M/185 lbs.
TENACITY:	Steady
INTELLIGENCE:	Obtuse
FATIGUE FACTOR:	0/+1

SPEED 10 — INIT -1
ATTACK +4
DEFENSE +1
DMG REDUCTION 2
REACH by weapon
DAMAGE by weapon +3
TOP SAVE 6

MOVEMENT
CRAWL:	2½
WALK:	5
JOG:	10
RUN:	15
SPRINT:	20

SAVES
PHYSICAL:	+5
MENTAL:	+1
DODGE:	+3

ATTACK. Tröglodytes are very fond of employing javelins and each warrior has 3 or more of these to hurl before engaging in close order combat; stone-headed battle axes are typical weapons.

SPECIAL DEFENSES: Foul (and possibly debilitating) stench. Shield use (*e.g.*, medium shield increases Def to +7).

EPV: 95

Tröglodyte Warband Leader

HIT POINTS:	36+d8
SIZE/WEIGHT:	M/210 lbs.
TENACITY:	Steady
INTELLIGENCE:	Obtuse
FATIGUE FACTOR:	0/+1

SPEED 10 — INIT -2
ATTACK +5
DEFENSE +2
DMG REDUCTION 2
REACH by weapon
DAMAGE by weapon +4
TOP SAVE 7

MOVEMENT
CRAWL:	2½
WALK:	5
JOG:	10
RUN:	15
SPRINT:	20

SAVES
PHYSICAL:	+6
MENTAL:	+2
DODGE:	+4

ATTACK: Tröglodytes are very fond of employing javelins and each warrior has 3 or more of these to hurl before engaging in close order combat; stone-headed battle axes are typical weapons.

SPECIAL DEFENSES: Foul (and possibly debilitating) stench. Shield use (*e.g.*, medium shield increases Def to +8).

EPV: 133

Tröglodyte Sub-Chief

HIT POINTS:	36+2d8
SIZE/WEIGHT:	M/230 lbs.
TENACITY:	Fearless
INTELLIGENCE:	Slow
FATIGUE FACTOR:	0/+1

SPEED 8 — INIT -2
ATTACK +6
DEFENSE +3
DMG REDUCTION 2
REACH by weapon
DAMAGE by weapon +5
TOP SAVE 8

MOVEMENT
CRAWL:	2½
WALK:	5
JOG:	10
RUN:	15
SPRINT:	20

SAVES
PHYSICAL:	+7
MENTAL:	+3
DODGE:	+5

ATTACK: Tröglodytes are very fond of employing javelins and each warrior has 3 or more of these to hurl before engaging in close order combat; stone-headed battle axes are typical weapons.

SPECIAL DEFENSES: Foul (and possibly debilitating) stench. Shield use (*e.g.*, medium shield increases Def to +8).

EPV: 165

Tröglodyte Chief

HIT POINTS:	36
SIZE/WEIGHT:	M/170 lbs.
TENACITY:	Steady
INTELLIGENCE:	Genius
FATIGUE FACTOR:	0/+1

SPEED 5 — INIT -4
ATTACK +8
DEFENSE +4
DMG REDUCTION 2
REACH by weapon
DAMAGE by weapon +2
TOP SAVE 6

MOVEMENT
CRAWL:	2½
WALK:	5
JOG:	10
RUN:	15
SPRINT:	20

SAVES
PHYSICAL:	+4
MENTAL:	+12
DODGE:	+3

ATTACK: Tröglodytes chiefs possess spellcasting ability of level d12p-2 for clerical and d12p-2 in mage (negative and zero indicating no ability). They typically have only a dagger for self-defense.

SPECIAL DEFENSES: Foul (and possibly debilitating) stench. Spellcasting ability.

EPV: 417

Glossary

Abay: To stop; to cease moving, operating, etc., either permanently or temporarily.

Adroit: Skillful or nimble

Aggregates: coarse material particles

Amalgam: Combination of different things

Amorphous: having no distinct form

Anthropomorphic: having human characteristics

Apex: The summit; apex predators reside at or near the top of their respective food chains, having no natural predators of their own.

Aquatoid: A species of lizard man.

Arthropod: Invertebrates with an exoskeleton, a segmented body and jointed appendages.

Automatonic: an object or creature able to perform assigned tasks without continous supervision but without the intelligence to deduce or reason; it is sentient but not sapient.

Avianatrix: A feminine creature that is not a bird but has obvious bird-like anatomy, such as feathered wings and bird-like legs and feet.

Bifurcated: Divided into two branches or parts.

Bioluminescence: natural ability to glow

Bodies of Water: Adesh, Lake; Brandobian Ocean; Eb'Sobet, Lake; Edros Bay; Elos Bay; Fanateen, Lake; Jorakk, Lake; Kalamaran Bay; Kalamaran Sea; Mewzhano Bay; Reanaaria Bay; Renador Lakes; Shadesh Bay; Svimohzia, Sea of; Svimohzia, Straits of; Voldor Bay; Whimdol Bay; Xaaboemio Sea (Sea of the Dead); Yordon Sound; Zhano-Mewhi Bay . . . .

Bradymetabolism: having a high active metabolism but a low resting metabolism

Brandobia: The western side of Tellene, named after the people who live there. It is divided into three separate kingdoms – Cosdol, Eldor and Medarn – of a shared bloodline plus a fourth realm to the south that is known as Pel Brolenon. The elven city of Lathlanian can also be found in this region.

Cabalistic: occult or secret

Cairn: An often-conical pile of stones erected to mark a burial site, commemorate an event, indicate a path, or for some other practical use.

Carnivorous: Feeding on flesh, such as animal tissue, through predation or scavenging.

Cautelous: A term that, depending on context, may mean cautious, cunning or treacherous.

Chamelid: A species of lizard man.

Chitin: A tough, protective, semitransparent substance that is the main component of arthropod exoskeletons and the cell walls of certain fungi.

Cilorea: Elven nation in the Kalalali Forest.

Cilorealon: Elven city, on the shores of the largest of the Renador Lakes in the Kalalali Forest.

Commodious: spacious

Coragio: Courage

Corpuses: main body or mass of an individual

Countries: Ahznomahn, Basir, Cosdol, Dodera, Drhokker, Ek'Gakel, Eldor, Kalamar, Korak, Mendarn, Meznamish, Norga-Krangrel, O'Par, Ozhvinmish, Paru'Bor, Pekal, Pel Brolenon, Shynabyth, Skarrna, Slen, Tarisato, Tharggy, Thybaj, Tokis, Torakk, Ul-Karg, Zazahni

Covey: A flock

Cowage: The lack of courage to face danger, difficulty, opposition, pain, etc.

Credent: Capable of being believed; plausible.

Crepuscular: Term used to describe creatures that are primarily active during twilight (*i.e.,* at dawn and at dusk).

Croconid: A species of lizard man.

Cytoplasm: A thick, clear liquid residing between the cell membrane in giant amoebae, and able to change between solid and liquid. The fluid state of the cytoplasm is called plasmasol; the more solid state is called plasmashell.

Deciduous: trees that lose their leaves

Dejy: Language of the Dejy, a human race.

Deserts: Elos, Khydoban

Desiccate: Dry up

Diadolai: The smallest of Tellene's three moons.

Diaphanous: delicate, sheer material that one can see through

Dichromatic: A form of color-blindness where only two light wavelengths are distinguished instead of the usual three.

Dimorphism, Sexual: The difference in form between individuals of different sex within the same species. Size, color, and the presence or absence of certain body parts (*e.g.,* ornamental feathers, horns, antlers, or tusks) are common examples.

Diurnal: Term used to describe creatures that are primarily active during the daytime.

Doulathanorian: Elven kingdom located deep in the Edosi Forest of Basir.

Draska: Dwarven kingdom located in the Byth Mountains.

Dullsome: Depending on context, this word may indicate dullness in the form of bluntness or sluggishness, or being boring, overcast, unclear or intellectually weak.

e.g.: Abbreviation for the Latin phrase "exempli gratia," translating as "for example." Often confused with *i.e.*

Ectothermic: cold-blooded

Efficacious: capable of producing a desired result

Effluvium: unpleasant vapor

Elan vital: A term meaning "vital impetus" or "vital force," often indicating a creature's soul or will to live.

Elemental contact points: Locations that are rumored to dimensionally overlap the elemental planes.

Estrus: periodic sexual excitement, usually in female animals

Exoskeleton: An external skeleton that supports and protects an creature's body.

Fhokki: Language of the Fhokki, a human race.

Forests: Ashul Weald, Awhom, Brindonwood, Brolador, Crondor Woods, Edosi, Eldrose, Fautee, Fyban, Kalalali, Kalasali Woods, Kalokopeli, Khorren Woods, Lendelwood, Miznoh, Mizohr Woodlands, Nanakary, Narrajy, Obakasek Jungle, Paliba Woods, Pipitul Woodlands, P'Rudekela, Rokk Woods, Rolutel, Ryakk Woods, Rytarr Woods, Svomawhom, Vohven Jungle, Voldorwoods, Whisvomi, Zamul

Furvann-mass: A grevan term for war that loosely translates as "the great dragon."

Garrulous: An individual in the habit of making pointless or annoyingly talkative conversation.

Genome: The total genetic material inherited by an organism through its parents or ancestors.

Gigantothermy: describes a creature that is so large it exchanges little heat with its surroundings

Giwhani: Svimozhish term loosely translating as "hill of the unwary."

Grevus fuun: A grevan term roughly translating as "way of the grevan" or "the old way."

Gustation: The act or sensation of tasting.

Herbivorous: Feeding on plants.

Hijarjany: Dejy term for blood mummies.

Hills: Adiv, Alufalik, Arajyd, Aggar Rise, Bisibopaki, Dopromond, Faunee Rise, Gadra Uplands, Hadaf Highlands, Imomena, Jenth Ridges, Kabela Downs, Kakapela, Kamarela Mounds, Katagas Rise, Keenoa Tors, Masau, Menamo, Napalago, Nazguk, Neebau Cliffs, Norga Tors, Odril, Parnor, P'Sapas, P'Tikor, Sanakir, Shada, Shashyf, Shyf, Shynako, Sliv Elenon Rise, Sotai Gagalia Headlands, Ubikokeli Highlands, Vry Naasu Headlands, Welpremond Downs, Whisvomi, Zhano Headlands

Hirsutism: A manifestation of excessive hairiness in humans and other homonids

i.e.: Abbreviation for the Latin phrase "id est", translating as "which means" or "in other words" or sometimes "in this case," depending on the context. Often confused with *e.g.*

Idiomatic: characteristic

Ingurgitate: To swallow up greedily or in large amounts.

Insular: isolated

Invertebrate: A creature without a backbone.

Islands: Asiotuxoo; Bosinela; Hoinain; Kaotoon; Mezh-Vowmi Isle; Rokalel; Svimohzish Isle; Ucea; Ulendar, Isle of; Voritti

Irontop: Dwarven fortress in the Ka'Asa Mountains.

Jhurijany: Dejy term for servitor mummies.

Kalamar: The largest and most populous nation on Tellene, Kalamar is the central kingdom of the Vast Kalamaran Empire. Its current lands include Kalamar, Basir, Dodera, O'Par, Pekal, Tarisato and Tokis. The cities of Doulathanorian and Karasta also lie within this empire's boundaries.

Karasta: Dwarven kingdom in the Ka'Asa Mountains; it is considered a 'protectorate' of the Kalamaran Empire.

Lathlanian: Elven city located within the Lendelwood.

Lingua franca: A language so pervasive that most people can comprehend it (though often as a second tongue). It often serves as a bridge language in situations where two parties cannot understand each other's native speech. French served this role in centuries past but English is today's *lingua franca*. It should be stressed that no such language exists in the Kingdoms of Kalamar as there is no universally dominant culture.

Littoral: The part of a body of water that is close to the shore.

Malignity: Intense ill will or hatred; an act or a feeling of great malice.

Mar'Klem: A grevan term roughly translating as "touched by madness by the hand of the gods."

Merchant's Tongue: This language is often misinterpreted as a lingua franca permitting easy communication between merchants and travelers regardless of their geographical background. In fact, it is shorthand for any number of distinct regional pidgin tongues that have developed to facilitate trade or other simple interactions where the parties cannot comprehend each other's speech. Common 'Merchant's Tongue' pidgins are Svimozish-Renaarian and Kalamaran-Renaarian. Kalamaran-Hobgoblin is also a frequently encountered pidgin.

These abbreviated languages are constructed from words and sounds borrowed from either tongue and easy to pronounce by both parties. Pidgin languages have no written component and are considered to limiting and disreputable forms of communication .

Mesoglea: A translucent, jelly-like substance that serves as structural support for water creatures that lack bones, cartilage or similar means of support.

Missionem: Latin for "mission"

Moniker: nickname or pseudonym

Morphology: The study of the form and structure of organisms without consideration of function or, specifically, the form and structure of an organism or one of its parts.

Motley-Minded: Lacking good sense or judgment; foolish, unwise.

Mountains: Byth, Counai Heights, Dashahn, Deshada, Elenon, Jorakk, Ka'Asa, Kakidela, Krimppatu, Krond Heights, Legasa Peaks, Lopoliri, Lozhen, P'Rorul Peaks, Sliv Elenon, Tanezh, Vrykarr, Yan Elenon

Musth: A recurring condition affecting bull elephants in which they demonstrate highly aggressive behavior

Netherdeep: A vast network of underground tunnels and caverns beneath the surface of Tellene.

Neuropathy: A disease or injury affecting the nervous system; brain-eating zombies suffer memory loss and raging madness as a result of the pain.

Nictitating: A transparent or translucent third eyelid that can be drawn across the eye for protection and moisture while maintaining visibility.

Nocturnal: Term used to describe creatures that are primarily active at nighttime.

Nom de guerre: A French phrase meaning "names of war" or "war names."

Objet d'art: A French phrase meaning "work of art" or "object of artistic merit."

Olfaction: sense of smell

Omnivorous: Feeding on both flesh and plant matter; a combination of herbivorous and carnivorous.

Ovoviviparity: producing eggs that remain inside the mother's body until hatching

Paroxysm: sudden outburst of emotion

Parthenogenesis: Asexual reproduction in females, where embryos grow and develop without fertilization by a male.

Peevish: irritable

Pelselond: One of Tellene's three moons.

Per se: A Latin phrase commonly translating as "in itself" (without referring to anything else, intrinsically, taken without qualifications, etc.).

Phagosome: A cellular compartment in which organisms can be killed and digested; an internal section of a giant amoeba.

Phenotype: Any observable characteristic or trait of an organism, such as its morphology, development, physical properties, bevavior and products of that behavior (such as a gorilla's arranged nest of vegetation).

Pheromones: chemicals excreted by certain creatures that elicit responses from other individuals creatures

Physiognomy: appearance

Plasmasol: The fluid state of cytoplasm, such as in a giant amoeba.

Plasmashell: The more solid state of cytoplasm, such as in a giant amoeba.

Pneumostome: A breathing pore in the right side of an air-breathing land slug, snail or tentaslug.

Predation: The act of a predator eating its prey.

Predilections: partialities

Prehensile: useful for seizing or grasping objects

Pseudopodia/Pseudopod: temporary armlike protrusion used by cells for locomotion and food gathering

Quadrennial: Something that recurs every four years; lasting for or relating to a period of four years.

Ramataj Rock: Massive red sandstone formation in the Khydoban Desert.

Reanaaria Bay: A large, deep bay in eastern Tellene. Major cities and city-states along the bay include Aasaer, Baethel, Dynaj, Geanavue, Giilia, Saaniema, Thygasha, Xaarum and Zoa.

Reticulum: part of the stomach of some cud-chewing animals

Rivers: Agateli, Badato, Banader, Brolador, Crondor, Dalmond, Deshada, Doreba, Durbattum, E'Korug, E'Liral, Ek'Ridar, El'Korek, Falikelopi, Ivelo, Izhoven, Jendasha, Jenshyta, Jorakk, Kylban, Lendel, Lower Byth, Omdal, P'Lider, P'Lobas, P'Lokur, Renador, Ridara, Shyf, Upper Byth, Zhano

Roynish: Depending on context, this word can mean mangy, paltry, troublesome, scabby or indicate inferior quality.

Rumen: paunch, part of the stomach of some cud-chewing animals

Rupicaprine: Having upright horns with backward-hooked tips,

Sanguivorous: Feeding on blood.

Sapient: An organism that can judge a situation and act according to experience and thought rather than instinct. Often confused with sentient.

Saurian: belonging to, resembling, or pertaining to lizards; also a species of lizard man. Sometimes known as sauroid.

Sauroid: belonging to, resembling, or pertaining to lizards; also a species of lizard man. Sometimes known as saurian.

Scintillant: sparkling

Seas: Brandobian Ocean; Kalamaran Sea; Svimohzia, Sea of; Xaaboemio Sea (Sea of the Dead)

Sentient: An organism with consciousness and the ability to feel and perceive. Often confused with sapient.

Serpentine: resembling or characteristic of a serpent; also a species of lizard man.

Shijarinjany: The Dejy term for royal mummies.

Simble-Skamble: Rambling or disjointed.

Simulacrum: Any image or representation of something (often having only a slight, unreal, superficial or vague semblance).

Sovereign Lands: A commonly used term referring to the civilized lands on Tellene.

Straits of Svimohzia: Straits separating the Svimohzish Isle from the main continent.

Svimohzia: Name for the massive island dominating the southwestern portion of the continent of Tellene. Its kingdoms include Ahznomahn, Meznamish, Ozhvinmish and Zazahni. The Brandobian colonies of Bronish and Vrandol, as well as the hobgoblin kingdom of Ul-Karg, are also herein. The Vohven Jungle covers much of southern Svimohzia.

Taxonomy: The classification (usually finding, describing and naming) of species, organisms, things or concepts.

Tellene: A continent, though its inhabitants believe it encompasses the entirety of the world. Thus, they consider all lands to be part of "Tellene." Tellene has an overall mild climate, with the southernmost tip lying at roughly 20 degrees latitude and the northernmost explored areas resting at about 54 degrees latitutude. The known lands include the kingdoms of Brandobia, the Kalamaran Empire, the cities and city-states of Reanaaria Bay, the Wild Lands, the Young Kingdoms and the Svimohzish Isle.

Terraverse: The material universe (sometimes called the prime material plane)

Thermocline: A thin but distinct layer in a large body of air or fluid, where temperature changes more rapidly with depth than it does in adjacent layers.

Thinchejany: A Dejy term for the rattlebone mummy.

Thrasonical: Boastful or bragging.

Trichome: Outgrowth or appendage

Turtle: May refer to testudine reptiles (*e.g.*, terrapin, tortoise) or to a species of lizard man.

Ursine: Bear-like

Ungulates: Animals with hooves

Veshemo: The largest of the three moons of Tellene.

Vexsome: Something causing or likely to cause harassment or aggravation.

Viviparity: Retention and growth of a fertilized egg in the body of the mother until the offspring is able to survive on its own

Wetlands: Alubelok Swamp, Avdoron Mires, DuKem'p Swamp, Ehniven Marsh, Ep'Sarab Swampland, Erasar'Kol Marsh, Ivez Estuary, Kannej Swamp, Legesep Lowlands, Mewhi Marshes, Otekapu Fens, Pel Brolenon Marsh, Tharakka Morass, Udo Bog, Whiven Marsh

Wild Lands: Northern Fhokki, Dejy and mixed Fhokki-Dejy nations, including the Lands of Drhokker, Shynnabyth, the Lands of Skarrna, Slen, Tharggy, Thybaj and the Lands of Torakk. Draska is rumored to lie in the mountains of the Wild Lands.

Xenophobic: Fear of outsiders

Young Kingdoms: These independent cities, kingdoms and duchies, many of whom were once subjects of the Kalamaran Empire, include Cilorealon (elven), Ek'Gakel, Ek'Kasel, Korak, Norga-Krangrel (hobgoblin), Shyta-na-Dobyo, and the cities of the Elos Desert. The latter includes Alnarma, Dijishy, Ehzhimahn, Miclenon, Prompeldia and Shrogga-pravaaz (humanoid).

Zenith: Culminating point

Also Known As...

Aarnz Hound: Ape Wolf, Gorund, Shadow Hound, Stalking Hound

Amoeba, Giant: Gelatinous Slime, The Blob

Anaxar: Anax, Giant Mantis, Gint'mur

Animating Spirit: Blesdar, Fabric Phantom

Ant, Giant: Ankur, Sulum

Ape: Angry Man of the Jungle

Arakian: Barakan, Burrower, Death Beetle, Krumur, Tunnel Terror

Barrow-Wight: Cairn Creature, Witch-corpse, Vostarr

Basilisk: Great Mar'un, Stone Kregalus

Beetle, Giant: Armored Crawler, Kravan

Boar: Hogzilla, Razorback, Tusker, Warthog

Brownie: Browney, Forest Folk, Kafla, Wee'un

Bugbear: Bogeyman, Giant Goblin, Goblibear, Great Goblin

Camel: Baktaar, Grint, Sand Mule

Catoblepas: Gru, Katopa

Centaur: Horse Men, Kentauroi

Centipede, Giant: Slaas, Slink

Changeling: Doppleganger, Kamaloi

Cheetah, Wooly: Hurjara, Miracinonyx, Morgg

Chimera: Chimaera, Rabela's Spawn

Cockatrice: Vohven Terror, Zazahni Cock

Cyclops: Chycosh, Great Eye, Skarran Giant

Devil: Azagon, Horned Fiend, Scrann

Dinosaur, Megalosaurus: Harnzai, Sugok

Dinosaur, Pterosaur: Warshandii, Yardran

Dinosaur, Tyrannosaurus Rex: Ghanozhi, King Lizard

Drake: Kanfrum, Mynraax

Dryad: Tree Sprite, Vila

Dwarf: Deep Folk, Draskan, Karastan

Eagle, Giant: Akurr, Eshji, Ogatala

Elemental, Air: Marut, Pavan, Sylphid

Elemental, Earth: Bhümi, Kshiti

Elemental, Fire: Agni, Fire Spirit, Tejas

Elemental, Water: Jala, Undine

Elephant: Loxodon, Oliphant

Elf: Aralarai, Doulathan, Kyndri, Lathlani

Ent: Treant, Tree Giant, Tree Shepherd

Ettin, Lesser: Gronk

Fantom Dog: Adjule, Devil Dog, Moor Hound

Gargoyle: Goji, Stone Demon

Ghast: Crypt Lurker

Ghoul: Apse Horror, Dead Riser

Giant, Hill: Hill Lumberer, Hurler, Narumph

Giant, Hoar Frost: Death's Ally

Gnole: Raagh'gum (Orcish), Noll

Gnome: Dalgul, Fulmaran, Mythar

Goat, Giant: Cabra, Capara

Goblin: Ashugg, Ga'uk (Orcish), Goter

Golem, Clay: Ajja-Vonan, Brinu

Golem, Flesh: [Creator name]'s Monster

Gorgon: Burakog, Khalkotaur

Gouger: Bloody Biter, Marabok, Vipago

Grel: Grunge Elf

Grevan: Gretan, Har'Korri, Sar-Grevan

Griffyn: Akelone, Galausor

Hag: Black Annis, Crone, Yaga

Halfling: Amberhair, Harfoot, Longfellow

Harpy: Aellopos

Haunt: Farada, Restless Spirit

Hippogriff: Wylamouranna (Low Elven)

Hobgoblin: Kargi, Krangi

Human: Brandobian, Dejy, Fhokki, Kalamaran, Reanaarian, Svimohz

Human, Brigand: Bandit, Cutthroat, Highwayman, Thug

Hydra: Lernaea

Hydra, Aquatic: Borgakk, Ladon, Rockworm

Imp: Katatra, Mangato

Kobold: Dovurin

Leech Man: Blood Thief, Shepherd's Bane

Leprechaun: Jakobie, Tur'nylan

Lindwyrm: Coeruuk, Draaxin

Lion: Jungle King, Razhvar

Lizard Man: Kregur, Slazeen, Zekiran

Medusa: Lornae, Myrzix

Merman: Neaesquatilian

Minotaur: Homatori

Mountain Lion: Catamount, Cougar, Deercat, King Cat, Mountain Screamer, Panther, Red Tiger, Silver Lion, Sneak Cat

Mummy: The Damned

Ogre: Aanaagrugr (Orcish)

Ooze, Corrosive: Peragic, Vorkkus

Orc: Ork, Ukak

Orkin Wardawg: Goraz, Pig-Dog, Shronhund

Owlbeast: Alucrel, Feranoc, Strovia, Thelkk

Pegasus: Neeloor

Pixie-Fairy: Faeriefolk, Paelifa

Rakshasa: Rakkosh, Srinpo

Rat, Giant: Sumatran

Roc: Rukh

Rusalka: Swamp Witch

Satyr: Byrein, Tovine

Scorpion, Giant: Agaroshy, Vezano

Screecher: Akana

Shadow: Shadowman, Darkling

Siren: Mariners' Bane, Sea Maiden, Sea Nymph, Sirine

Skeleton: Creth, Trondak

Skitter-Rat: Cave Squirrel, Shadow Scurry, Skuridar

Slime, Flesh-Eating: Nik'Lo, Vuulaan

Smilodon: Dythnar, Sabre-Toothed Tiger, Shindri

Spectre: Ciguld, Karigon

Sphinx, Crio-: Relonak, Tamdin, Thrayk

Sphinx, Hieraco-: Elgord, Falcon Cat, Vashji

Strix: Bloodbeak, Maulsquito, Strzyga

Sturm-Wolf: Thalnarkk

Swamp Death: Bolog, Living Bog, Shazvim

Tarantubat: Tel-tulmeramika (Low Elven)

Tentaslug: Killer Snail, Vrazz

Tetzylwyrm: Dratzen

Tick, Giant: Blood Gorger, Grypt

Tiger: Tigris, Vigral

Toad, Giant: Great Paddock, Rizhor

Troglodyte: Sleestack

Troll: Jotunn

Vampire: Upyr, Vampir, Vampyr

Warg: Vargr, Wearg, Wyrg

Wasp, Giant: Dolicho, Vespula

Weasel: Ermelin

Wererat: Rat-man

Werewolf: Man-Wolf, Wolfman

Will-O-The-Wisp: Corpse Candle, Fool's Fire, Will-O-Wisp

Wolf: Lukos

Worm, Titanic: Grandfather Worm, Shahul

Wraith: Eternal Wrath

Wyrm: Drakon, Drakus, Harkoon

Wyvern: Sky Viper, Wyvere

Yeti: The Abominable

Zombie: Walking Dead, Zuvembie

Zombie, Brain-Eating: Infected, Living Dead, Zombi

Monster	HP	Init	Spd	Rch	Atk	Special Atk	Dmg	Def	Special Def	DR	ToP	SZ	MV/s (jog)	Saves P/M/D	Tenacity	FF	AL	EPV
Aarnz Hound	26+2d8	-1	4	short	6		2@2d4p+2/2d8p	4		3	8	M	15	7/5/6	Steady	-2	NE	300
Amoeba, Giant	35+4d8	0	6	medium	7	VF 11 or incap	4d4p	0	hiding mastery	10c/8p/2h	n/a	H	5	9/na/4	Steady	n/a	non	250
Anaxar	36+5d8	1	10	long	12	grab and bite	4d4p+2/6d6p	5	PC shield	8 (4 underbelly)	n/a	H	15	9/na/4	Brave	n/a	non	925
Animating Spirit	20+4d8	-4	3	short	8	constrict	2d4p or 3d4p/s constrict	6	victim suffers damage	9	n/a	n/a	5	8/immune/8	Fearless	n/a	NE	492
Ant, Giant Soldier	10+3d8	0	5	short	5	VF 10 poison	2d8p	2		4	n/a	T	5	3/4/3	Brave	n/a	non	100
Ant, Giant Worker	5+2d8	0	8	short	3		2d6p	2		3	n/a	T	5	3/3/3	Brave	n/a	non	40
Ape, Gorilla	30+4d8	-1	4	medium	8		2d4p+6/2d3p	3		6	8	L	15	10/7/8	Steady	-2	non	450
Ape, Killer	30+5d10	-2	3	medium	12	club Spd 5 for 2d6p+7	2d4p+7/2d3p+3	6		8	8	L	15	13/8/8	Steady	-2	NE	925
Arakian Brood Watcher	30+5d8	-1	7	medium	9	enzyme poison	2d12+2	5		9	n/a	L	15	10/8/9	Fearless	n/a	non	700
Arakian Queen	40+12d8	0	n/a	short	n/a	mind control	0	2		8	n/a	E	0	10/16/4	Cowardly	n/a	non	1000
Arakian Warrior	25+3d8	0	8	short	7	enzyme poison	2d10p	4	shoot webs	6	n/a	M	15	8/5/6	Brave	n/a	non	300
Arakian Worker	18+2d8	5	10	short	4		2d6p	0		6	n/a	M	10	4/0/2	Cowardly/Fearless	n/a	non	10/48
Barrow-wight	27+4d8	-1	10	medium	11	CON drain	2d4p	3		19 (10 silver)	n/a	M	10	11/immune/11	Brave	n/a	NE	792
Basilisk	24+5d8	4	10	short	9	salt gaze, VF 9 poison	2d10p	3	blood paralyzes	5	8	M	5	9/7/8	Steady	3	non	850
Bear, Black	29+4d8	-1	4	short	8		2d6p+4	-1		9	11	L	20	9/8/7	Steady	-4	non	417
Bear, Brown	36+6d8	0	4	medium	12	hug	2d6p+7	3		11	12	L	20	14/10/11	Steady	-3	non	792
Bear, Grizzly	41+8d8	0	4	medium	16	hug	2d8+p9	6		13	12	H	20	18/13/15	Brave	-2	non	1425
Bear, Cave	42+9d8	-2	3	long	18	hug	3d6p+10	9		12	13	H	20	20/14/15	Fearless	-2	non	1842
Beetle, Giant	10+d8	0	10	short	1		2d4p	-1		3	n/a	S	5	1/0/1	Cowardly	n/a	non	11
Beetle, Giant Bombadier	14+d8	1	11	short	2	VF 8 poison	2d4p	-1		2	n/a	S	5	2/0/2	Cowardly	n/a	non	40
Beetle, Giant Boring	12+d8	2	10	short	0	chew shield	2d4p	-1		3	n/a	S	5	1/0/1	Cowardly	n/a	non	11
Beetle, Giant Fire	17+d8	2	12	short	1		4d4p	-2		3	n/a	S	5	2/0/1	Cowardly	n/a	non	25
Boar	25+3d8	2	10	short	6		4d4p+4	0		4	12	M	15	6/6/6	Steady	1	non	242
Boar, Giant	34+5d8	2	9	short	8		6d4p+7	0		5	14	L	20	12/12/12	Fearless	4	non	500
Brownie	8+d8	-2	4	short	3	curse, magic	d4p	11	invisibility	0/1	n/a	T	10	17/19/20	Nervous	-2	NG	100
Bugbear	32+3d8	-1	10	bw+1	7		bw+5	0/6	shields	3/6	8	L	10	7/7/7	Steady	-5/-4	CE	175
Camel	22+5d8	0	10	short	2	spit	d6p-2	3		2	7	L	30	2/2/2	Nervous	-7	non	30
Catoblepas	18+3d8	0	10	short	1	death glance, VF 7 poison	d6p-4 bite or 4d4p hooves	1		4	n/a	L	5	1/1/1	Nervous	2	non	388
Centaur	28+4d8	-1	10	bw+1	8		bw+3 or 4d4p hooves	5/11		7 (or 9 or 12)	7	L	30	8/8/8	Brave	-5/-4	CG	325
Centipede, Giant	d4	-1	5	short	1	VF 5 poison	0	1		0	n/a	T	5	0/0/0	Cowardly	n/a	non	14
Centipede, Massive	13-3d8	-2	8	short	4	VF 8 poison	d6p	1		3	n/a	S	10	4/4/4	Nervous	n/a	non	200
Changeling	25+4d8	-4	6	medium	10		bw+6 or d12+6	4	shapechange, mind reading	8	7	M	10	20/immune/20	Nervous	0	NE	1000
Cheetah, Wooly	20+3d8	-3	5	short	7		2@2d6p+1/4d4p	5		4	6	M	35	4/4/10	Steady	3	non	375
Chimera	40+7d8	0	2	medium	12	fire breath, VF 8 poison	2@2d4p+4 claw; various bites	4		11	6	L	20	12/12/12	Brave	2	non	1100
Cockatrice	10+2d8	2	10	short	5	stone touch, VF 7 poison	4d4p+4	7	weasel urine kills	0	3	S	5	5/5/5	Nervous	-1	non	500
Crocodile, lesser	30+5d8	-1	7	short	9		4d4p+4	4		5 (3 underbelly)	7	H	10	9/9/9	Steady	3	non	400
Crocodile, greater	40+10d8	-1	6	short	14		4d4p+10	4		8 (4 underbelly)	n/a	H	10	14/14/14	Brave	3	non	1150
Cyclops	52+14d8	5	11	long	22	-6 ranged/hurled	4d10p+16	8		8	12	G	20	28/16/19	Brave	-4	CE	2300
Devil	27+7d8	-3	5	medium	13	magic, VF 13 poison	bw+6 or 5d4p+7 fork or 2d4p tail	8	regeneration, immune to fire/poison	18 (10 silver)	n/a	M	10	14/18/12	Fearless	n/a	LE	1313
Dinosaur, Megalosaurus	30+12d8	2	10	medium	12	pin size ≥M underfoot	6d6p	6		6	9	G	25	15/9/12	Brave	-4	non	1067
Dinosaur, Pterosaur	m:12+3d8 f:10+1d8	1	10	short	4		3d4p	3		2	5	M	fly 30	4/2/6	Cowardly	0	non	100

Monster	HP	Init	Spd	Rch	Atk	Special Atk	Dmg	Def	Special Def	DR	ToP	SZ	MV/s (jog)	Saves P/M/D	Tenacity	FF	AL	EPV
Dinosaur, T-Rex	35+18d8	-2	5	long	18	tail swipe	10d8p or 4d6p	5		9	13	G	20	10/6/9	Fearless	-4	non	2000
Dog, wild/hntng/wrking	16+d8	-2	10	short	2		1d4p+1	4		2	7	M	20	2/2/3	Nervous	-1	non	22
Dog, guard/sentry	21+2d8	-2	10	short	3		2d4p+2	3		2	3	M	15	4/2/2	Steady	0	non	84
Dog, war	26+2d8	-2	9	short	4	pack mauling	3d4p+2	4		3	0	M	15	5/2/2	Brave	0	non	100
Drake	36+11d8	2	3	long	25	tail swipe, breathe fire	2@2d12p/4d12p or 3d10p	9	immune to fire	13	4	E	15	24/16/18	Brave	-5	CE	3300
Dryad	19+3d8	-2	7	short	8	magic	bw-2	3	teleportation	0	4	M	10	17/23/19	Nervous	1	N	250
Dwarf	33+d10	5	13	bw-1	4		bw+1	-3/3	+6 vs giants, trolls/ogres; shields	0/5	7	M	5	10/9/8	Brave	-3/-4	LG	84
Eagle, Giant	30+3d8	-2	5	short	9		2d12p/2d8p	5	flight	3	7	L	fly 60	9/8/10	Steady	1	non	400
Elemental, Air	25+10d8	-5	n/a	n/a	5	hurl victims	2d12p within 10 ft	special	only cold/slow does damage	0	n/a	H	fly 75	see text	Brave	n/a	non	1500
Elemental, Earth	35+13d8	6	7	medium	24		6d8p	8	size G for knock-backs, spell immunity	18	n/a	H	5	24/na/24	Brave	n/a	non	1900
Elemental, Fire	30+11d8	-2	7	medium	21	ignite	4d8p	special	only water/cold does damage	0	n/a	H	15	21/na/21	Brave	n/a	non	1750
Elemental, Water	32+12d8	-1	7	long	12	drown	special	special	only fire/cold does damage	0	n/a	M to H	15	see text	Brave	n/a	non	1425
Elephant	40+10d8	0	6	medium	8	initial head-butt	4d8p+4 or 3d6p or 5d6p	0		8	n/a	E	20	11/8/6	Steady	-8	non	1000
Elf	21+2d10	1	9	bw	5		bw	4/10	Init die 1 better; shields	6 (10h)	4	M	10	3/6/5	Brave	-3/-4	CG	100
Ent	35+10d8	-3	4	long	20	animate trees	3d6p+8	9		6	n/a	G	15	20/20/20	Fearless	2	NG	1800
Ettin, Lesser	36+6d8	0	6	long	10		6d6p+5/3d8p+5	2	Init die 3 better, no rear Def penalty	6	11	H	15	12/7/9	Steady	-7	CE	1242
Fantom Dog	25+3d8	-2	9	short	7	Con drain, howl panics	1d4p	5	run on air	18 (9 silver)	n/a	M	20	6/immune/8	Fearless	n/a	NE	350
Gargoyle	24+4d8	-2	2	short	8		2d4p+4	1	resistant to fire	12 (5 silver)	n/a	M	10	10/6/9	Steady	n/a	CE	417
Ghast	25+4d8	-1	3	short	7	stench	2@2d4p+2/2d8p	1	immune to fear/sleep	3	n/a	M	15	9/immune/9	Brave	n/a	NE	425
Ghoul	24+2d8	-1	3	short	6	fear	2@2d4p/2d6p	1	immune to fear/sleep	3	n/a	M	15	6/immune/6	Steady	n/a	NE	290
Giant, Hill	47+8d8	3	10	long	16	hurl rocks	4d6p+8 or 2d4p+6	7		6	10	G	10	20/12/14	Fearless	-6	CE	1425
Giant, Hoar Frost	47+10d8	2	12	long	18	hurl rocks	4d8p+10	8		9 (20 cold magic)	11	G	15	18/18/18	Brave	-7	NE	1750
Gnole	30+2d8	4	11	bw+1	5		bw+3	-4	Init die 1 better	6	7	L	15	6/2/5	Brave	-2/-1	CE	122
Gnome	20+d8	4	8	bw-1	3		bw-1	4/8		3	5	S	5	1/2/3	Steady	-3/-2	NG CG N CN	42
Goat, Giant	29+4d8	2	8	short	6	double knock-back	5d4p or 1d6p	3		5	12	L	20	7/4/7	Nervous	0	non	175
Goblin	17+d6	3	8	bw-1	3		bw-1	2/6	shields	0/2	6	S	5	3/2/4	Nervous	-2/-1	LE	22
Golem, Clay	80	6	10	short	21		5d10p	6	immune to most magic	30h/30p'12c	n/a	G	5	21/21/21	n/a	n/a	non	3000
Golem, Flesh	70	3	5	medium	13		3d12p	2	immune to most magic	18	n/a	H	15	13/13/13	Brave	n/a	non	1425
Gorgon	30+8d8	-2	10	med	9	petrifying breath	4d6p+8/4d6p or 3d12p	6		9	10	L	15	10/8/8	Brave (bulls)	-5	CE	1400
Gouger	24+2d8	4	10 (6 gnaw)	long	6 (12)	grab victim & holdf fast; victim has reduced Def	4d6p/2d6p	4	Hiding 90%	2		M	5	4/3/6	Steady	-7	NE	240
Grel	30+2d8	2	8	bw	6		bw+2	2/6	+65% Sneaking & Hiding; shields	0/3	6	L	10	5/3/5	Fearless	-2/-1	CE	140
Grevan	35+4d8	-1	7	medium	8		bw+6	3/9		2/7	8	H	15	9/8/10	Fearless	-7/-6	NE	500
Griffyn	25+7d8	-2	3	short	14		2@2d4p+4/4d8p	6		7	6	L	fly 35	12/12/13	Brave	0	non	1075
Hag	18+6d8	-1	7	M	4		2d4p+4	2		0	4	M	10	10/12/7	Cowardly	4	NE	675
Halfling	17+d8	1	8	bw-1	1	+3 w/ bows & slings	bw-2	4/8	-1 Init die; Hiding & Sneaking 50%; shields	2	6	S	5	1/2/3	Steady	-3/-2	LG	20

Monster	HP	Init	Spd	Rch	Atk	Special Atk	Dmg	Def	Special Def	DR	ToP	SZ	MV/s (jog)	Saves P/M/D	Tenacity	FF	AL	EPV
Harpy	18+3d8	-2	5	medium	8	charm song	2d6p/(d6+d4)+4	3	flight	2	4	M	5/25f	7/9/9	Nervous	2	CE	575
Haunt	20+3d8	-1	10	short	5	possession	1d3p	7	blessed silver weapons required to hit	5	n/a	M	15	5/na/5	Brave	n/a	any	275
Hippogriff	30+3d8	-1	3	short	9		2d6x2/2d10	2	flight	3	7	L	10/40f	9/8/11	Brave	-2	non	492
Hobgoblin	22+d10	2	10	bw	5		bw+1	-2/4		4	6	M	10	5/5/5	Brave	-1/-2	LE	67
Human: Berserker	25+1d10	5	11	bw	2		bw+2	0/+6	shields	0/3	9	M	10	2/1/2	Brave	-3/-4	chaotic	67
Human: Brigand	21+1d6	2	8	bw	2		bw	1	shields	2	5	M	10	0/1/1	Nervous	-1/0	C(E)	34
Hydra	45+4d8 per head	8 - 1 /head	10/# heads	long	2 /head		2d8+X/head	2 body, 10 heads	heads immune to ToP	body 10, heads 5	8 (b), n/a(h)	E	10	2x#heads for all	Brave	-1 x #heads	non	varies
Hydra, Aquatic	40+3d8 per head	8 - 1 /head	10/# heads	long	2/head	varies	2d8+X/head	7 body, 12 heads	heads immune to ToP	body 7, heads 4	8 (b), n/a(h)	G	10	2x#heads for all	Brave	-1 x #heads	non	varies
Imp	8+2d4	-4	2	short	5	poison stinger	d4p/2d3p-3 or 1	6	immune to fire, toxins, disease; regeneration	13 (4 silver)	n/a	T	5/20	10/16/14	Nervous	n/a	LE	242
Kobold	13+d4	3	6	bw-1	2		bw-3	4/8	shields	2	4	S	5	2/1/2	Nervous	-1/0	LE	17
Leech Man	10+d4	-1	6	short	4	anesthetic bite	2d4p	7		0	2	S	10	3/3/6	Cowardly	-3	non	50
Leprechaun	6+d8	-3	10	bw-1	3	Enfeeble	2d4p-4	11	magic	0	2	T	5	27/30/31	Nervous	-3	CN	100
Lindwyrm	33+7d8	0	3	medium	14	toxic bite	3d8p/2d8p x2	8		9	11	H	15/25sf	14/9/10	Brave	-4	non	1200
Lion	25+4d8	-3	5	medium	9	grab prey, bite	2@2d4p+4, bite 2d6p+6	4		4	6	L	20	9/7/8	Steady	2	non	492
Lizard, Giant Subterranean	30+6d8	-2	7	short	10		4d6p	6	immune to tail damage, immune to webbing, poison resistant	6	8	L	15	10/7/9	Steady	-2	non	450
Lizard Man	21+2d8	0	9	bw	3		bw+2	0	shields	2	6	M	10	3/2/3	Nervous	-3/-2	N (CE)	45
Medusa	18+6d8	-1	7	short	9	petrification, poison	2d4p/1	0	no flanking or back-stabs; 1 Init die better	0	2	M	10	10/14/12	Nervous	2	NE	1200
Mermen	23+d8	0	10	M	4		2d6p+3 spear	0/4	shields	2	6	M	1/20 swim	4/4/4	Steady	-5	N	67
Minotaur	32+6d8	-1	7	bw+1	11		bw+6 or gore for 4d4p	3		6	9	L	15	13/9/11	Brave	-7	CE	675
Mountain Lion	20+2d8	-3	5	short	7	grab prey, bite	2@2d4p+2, bite 2d6p+4	4		3	5	M	25	7/6/7	Nervous	2	non	350
Mummy	28+6d8	5	7	short	16	mummy rot	2d8p+9	7		24	n/a	M	5	16/na/12	Brave	n/a	NE	1425
Mummy, blood	25+5d8	2	7	short	14	mummy rot	2d6p+5	6		9	n/a	M	5	13/na/10	Brave	n/a	NE	825
Mummy, noble	32+8d8	2	7	short	18	mummy rot, magic	2d12p+6	7		26	n/a	M	5	18/na/15	Brave	n/a	LE	1850
Mummy, rattlebone	16+3d8	3	5	short	6		2d4p+4	4		12	n/a	M	7.5	5/na/4	Fearless	n/a	NE	200
Mummy, royal	30+10d8	0	6	medium	20	Domination, mummy rot	2d12+10	12		28	n/a	M	5	21/na/17	Fearless	n/a	LE	2300
Mummy, servitor	28+5d8	4	7	short	12	spells	2d4p+6	5		19	n/a	M	5	12/na/9	Steady	n/a	NE	975
Ogre	34+4d8	4	8	long	5		2d10+6	-1/5		9	9	H	15	8/2/4	Steady	-2/-1	CE	242
Ooze, corrosive	30+4d8	-2	10	short	8	corrosion	4d6p	0	immune to fire & cold	12c/8p/2h	n/a	L	1	10/na/2	Brave	n/a	non	325
Orc	23+d8	5	9	bw	3		bw+2	-4/2	shields	3	6	M	10	4/1/3	Steady	-1/0	NE	34
Orkin Wardawg, greater	38+4d8	1	7	short	9		4d4+5	5		5	9	L	20	9/7/9	Steady	2	non	350
Orkin Wardawg, lesser	30+3d8	0	9	short	7		4d4+1	3		4	8	M	20	7/5/7	Steady	2	non	122
Owlbeast	34+6d8	0	3	short	12	hug	2d8+7x2/2d4+7	2		11	13	H	15	14/8/11	Brave	-5	non	810
Owlbeast, Great Horned	39+8d8	1	3	medium	14		2d10+8/2d8+8 x2	3		12	14	G	15	16/8/11	Fearless	-5	non	925
Pegasus	27+6d8	-2	5	medium	9		4d4+2	5	flight	6	7	H	20/40f	9/1/12	Steady	-6	LG	675
Pixie-Fairy	7+d4	-2	5	short	4		1d4p	11	invisibility, flight	0	2	T	2.5/30	0/4/6	Nervous	2	CG	20

Monster	HP	Init	Spd	Rch	Atk	Special Atk	Dmg	Def	Special Def	DR	ToP	SZ	MV/s (jog)	Saves P/M/D	Tenacity	FF	AL	EPV
Rakshasa	22+7d8	-4	5	medium	12	spells	2@2d4p+5, bite grabbed prey for d6p+5 (no DR), use weapons	9	illusions	25, (on >6 with +6 weapon)	8	M	20	27/33/30	Steady	1	NE	1425
Rat, Giant	6+d4	0	10	short	0	may carry disease	d4p+1	-1		1	7	S	5	0/0/3	Cowardly	-3	non	12
Roc	40+18d8	-2	3 (peck)	long	25		12d6 (twin claw grab), 7d6p (peck)	10	flight	3	12	E	15/50f	31/19/27	Brave	-1	non	2500
Rusalka	19+4d8	-1	5	medium	8	charm	strangle & drown	6		3	n/a	M	10/20swim	7/na/8	Steady	n/a	NE	575
Satyr	13+2d8	0	10	bw	3	charm music	bw -1	0	charm music	2	3	S	10	2/5/3	Nervous	3	CN	242
Scorpion, Giant	14+d8	0	10	medium	5	grab, poison	2d4p+3/1	0	Hiding 90%	2	nil	S	5	5/5/5	Steady	n/a	non	242
Screecher	10+3d8	0	0	none	0		0	0	noise	4	nil	S	0	4/na/-6	n/a	n/a	non	5
Shadow	26+3d8	-4	10	medium	7	Strength drain	d4p+1	0	2 (-4 in brt light) Sneaking & Hiding 100% in dim light	16 (8 silver)	n/a	M	30	7/immune/7	Brave	n/a	NE	417
Siren	16+d8	-2	10	bw	-1	Charm song, Mage Spells	bw -4	-2		3	2	M	10	-1/6/4	n/a	2	Chaotic	575
Skeleton	27+d8	0	9	bw	1		bw -1	1/7		3c/9r/13p	n/a	M	10	1/immune/1	Fearless	n/a	non	67
Skeleton, animal	15+d8	0	10	short	2		3d4p	1		0c/6r/10p	n/a	S	15	0/immune/0	Fearless	n/a	non	100
Skeleton, monster	30+3d8	-1	8	bw+1	5		bw +3	5/11		4c/1Ch/14p	n/a	L	15	5/immune/5	Fearless	n/a	non	230
Skitter-Rat	8+d4	-1	10	short	0	rearward strike	d6p+1	4	hiding 80, sneaking 75, climbing, listening 70	1	8	T	15	0/0/3	Steady	-2	non	30
Slime, flesh-eating	50	n/a	n/a	n/a	3	turn to slime	special	n/a	turn to slime	0	n/a	M	0	3/immune/na	n/a	n/a	non	200
Smilodon	32+8d8	-1	4	medium	16	grab prey, bite	2@2d6p+5, bite 2d10p+8	9		5	8	H	20	16/14/15	Brave	1	non	1100
Snake, constrictor	19+2d8	3	10	short	4		2d4p+3	-4	trapped prey may be hit	1	4	M	5	4/2/3	Cowardly	2	non	100
Snake, poisonous (asp)	2+d4	-2	10	short	6	poison, spit venom	1	4		3	4	T	5	1/1/6	Nervous	2	non	133
Snake, rattler	2+d4	-2	10	short	3	poison	1	2		3	4	T	5	1/1/5	Cowardly	2	non	84
Snake, xullith	27+4d8	-1	7	medium	12		3d4p	5		4	7	L	10	7/5/9	Brave	3	non	725
Spectre	25+5d8	-4	10	medium	13	CON/DEX drain	d6p	6	may be spellcaster	21 (1? silver)	n/a	M	10	13/immune/13	Nervous	n/a	LE	1075
Sphinx, Andro-	38+12d8	-2	5	medium	22	roar	3d12p+3	13	spells, flight	4	12	G	15/30f	24/22/21	Fearless	-6	CG	1850
Sphinx, Crio-	32+10d8	-2	3	medium	19		2@5d4p,6d6p butt	12	flight	3	11	H	15/25f	21/17/18	Brave	-7	N	1425
Sphinx, Gyno-	30+8d8	-3	5	medium	16	18+ MU	5d4p	14	flight	1	11	H	15/25f	16/25/20	Steady	-2	N	1500
Sphinx, Hieraco-	35+9d8	-3	3	medium	17		2@6d4p, 4d8 bite	11	flight	2	11	H	10/40f	17/13/17	Brave	-3	CE	1425
Spider, Big	d3+1	-4	10	short	-2	poison	0	4	-1 Init die	1	n/a	T	5	-2/-2/-2	Nervous	n/a	non	25
Spider, Gargantuan	40+10d8	-4	6	short	19	poison	2d6p+10	body 10/legs 2	-1 Init die	body 2/legs 8	n/a	H	20	19/19/19	Brave	n/a	CE	2075
Spider, Gigantic	25+4d8	-4	8	short	8	poison	2d6p	body 4/legs 2	-1 Init die	body 2/legs 6	n/a	M	15	8/8/8	Steady	n/a	non	417
Spider, Huge	15+3d8	-4	9	short	4	poison	2d4p	2	-1 Init die	2	n/a	S	10	4/4/4	Steady	n/a	non	200
Spider, Large	5+d6	-4	10	short	1	poison	1	3	-1 Init die	2	n/a	T	5	-1/-1/-1	Nervous	n/a	non	45
Spider, Massive	30+6d8	-4	7	short	13	poison	2d6p+7	body 6/legs 2	-1 Init die	body 2/legs 8	n/a	L	15	13/13/13	Brave	n/a	non	925
Spider, Very Large	10+d8	-4	10	short	1	poison	d3p	2	-1 Init die	2	n/a	S	5	1/1/1	Steady	n/a	non	100
Strix	10+d8	-1	10	short	7	blood drain	d4p+4 + (d4p/10s)	1	flight	0	5	T	20	2/0/4	Cowardly	0	non	67
Sturm-Wolf	43+5d8	-1	4	short	13		4d4p+8	9		16&a	12	H	20	15/12/13	Brave	-2	CE	925
Swamp Death	35+9d8	-1	4	medium	16	suffocation	4d8p	8	fire/cold resistance, spell immunities	16d4, 7h	n/a	L	5	16/immune/16	Fearless	n/a	non	1500
Tarantubat	d6	0	10	short	-1	poison	1	8	flight	0	2	T	1.25/25f	-2/-1/3	Steady	2	non	20

Monster	HP	Init	Spd	Rch	Atk	Special Atk	Dmg	Def	Special Def	DR	ToP	SZ	MV/s (jog)	Saves P/M/D	Tenacity	FF	AL	EPV
Tentaslug	30+6d8	-1	6 (12 ea tncl)	long	8	grasp prey	2@4d4p+5 (6d6p)	-1		16c/12p/9h	n/a	L	5	13/6/7	Fearless	n/a	non	533
Tetzelwyrm	35+6d8	-4	10 (or 3)	long	12		2d12p+4 (+2@4d4p+2)	8		10	n/a	H	15	10/8/11	Brave	-4	non	815
Tick, Giant	12+3d8	3	16	short	5	blood drain	2d4p + (d4p/10s)	0	victim may be mistakenly targeted	4	n/a	T	5	5/3/4	Nervous	n/a	non	67
Tiger	30+6d8	-2		medium	13	grab prey, bite	2@2d4p+5, bite 2d8p+7	8		3	6	H	20	14/11/14	Brave	1	non	925
Toad, Giant	20+4d8	-2	8	short	6		2d4p+4	0		4	4	M	5 (hop 10)	6/4/6	Nervous	2	non	275
Toad, Giant Poisonous	25+6d8	-1	5	short	10	poison	2d8p+6	6	poison	8	7	L	5 (hop 10)	9/6/12	Steady	2	non	800
Troglodyte	20+2d8	0	10	bw	3	musk	bw +2	0/6		2	6	M	10	4/1/3	Steady	0/1	NE	60
Troll	36+6d8	-2	3	long	13		2@2d4p+8/4d6p	5	regeneration	6	n/a	L	15	16/8/14	Fearless	n/a	CE	925
Vampire	26+8d8	-6	5	short	19	CON drain, charm	2@d4p+4/d6p+4	10	summon animals, transmogrify, regeneration	25 (13 silver)	n/a	M	10/25	19/immune/19	Fearless	n/a	LE	2275
Warg	35+4d8	-1	6	short	7		4d4p+4	7		4	10	L	20	8/6/7	Brave	-3	NE	350
Wasp, Giant	8+d4	0	10	short	4	poison	d4p	4	flight	1	n/a	T	5 (30 f)	1/2/7	Fearless	n/a	non	20
Weasel, Common	6+d4	-2	10	short	1		d3p	0		1	5	S	5	1/1/2	Nervous	1	non	10
Weasel, Giant	21+2d8	-2	7	short	3		2d4p+2	3		2	7	M	15	3/3/5	Steady	1	non	84
Wererat	21+3d8	-2	7	medium	7	cause lycanthropy	bw or 2d6p	2/6	high DR vs. steel	13 (3 silver)	8	M	15	5/7/10	Nervous	0	NE	350
Werewolf	26+5d8	-2	5	short	10	cause lycanthropy	4d4p+6	7	high DR vs. steel	14 (4 silver)	10	M	20	12/9/10	Steady	-4	CE	575
Will-o´-the-Wisp	10+7d8	-1	5	short	9	ignore DR	2d8p	26	flight	7	n/a	T	15	9/immune/26	Cowardly	n/a	NE	625
Wolf	21+2d8	-2	10	short	3		2d4p+2	3		2	10	M	20	5/2/4	Nervous	-2	non	84
Wolf, Dire	27+3d8	-2	8	short	5		4d4p	5		3	10	M	20	7/2/5	Steady	-2	non	122
Worm, Titanic	40+15d8	3	5	medium	20	swallow	4d12p, 4d4p (stinger)	6		16	n/a	C	5	31/8/11	Steady	n/a	non	2000
Wraith	27+9d8	-4	10	medium	17	CON drain	d8p	8		25 (13 silver)	n/a	M		17/immune/17	Fearless	n/a	LE	1842
Wyrm	35+10d8	3	3	long	17		2@2d10p/4d10p	7		11	12	E	15/30f	23/15/18	Brave	-5	CE	1700
Wyvern	35+7d8	-2	5	medium	13	poison	4d6p/1d6p+3	6	flight	9	12	G	15/30f	14/10/13	Brave	-3	NE	925
Yeti	30+5d8	0	5	medium	8	hug	2@2d4p+5	6	cold resistance	10	9	L	10	11/5/7	Brave	-2	N	417
Zombie	24+2d8	6	4	short	4		d4p	0		8	n/a	M	5	4/immune/0	Fearless	n/a	non	100
Zombie, monster	30+4d8	6	10	short	8	overbear	2d4p	0		12	n/a	L	5	8/immune/0	Fearless	n/a	non	266
Zombie, brain-eating	20+3d8	3	10	short	6	overbear	d6p	2		7	n/a	M	10	7/immune/2	Fearless	n/a	non	180